To mari

"And the light shineth in the darkness
and the darkness comprehended it not."
— JOHN 1-5,

I hope you enjoy the read.

John C. Spooles

HAPPY 50TH ANNIVERSARY!

We at Trafford believe that it is the responsibility of us all, as both individuals and corporations, to make choices that are environmentally and socially sound. You, in turn, are supporting this responsible conduct each time you purchase a Trafford book, or make use of our publishing services. To find out how you are helping, please visit www.trafford.com/responsiblepublishing.html

Our mission is to efficiently provide the world's finest, most comprehensive book publishing service, enabling every author to experience success. To find out how to publish your book, your way, and have it available worldwide, visit us online at www.trafford.com/10510

www.trafford.com

North America & international
toll-free: 1 888 232 4444 (USA & Canada)
phone: 250 383 6864 ♦ fax: 250 383 6804
email: info@trafford.com

The United Kingdom & Europe
phone: +44 (0)1865 722 113 ♦ local rate: 0845 230 9601
facsimile: +44 (0)1865 722 868 ♦ email: info.uk@trafford.com

10 9 8 7 6 5 4 3

PART ONE

~~~

FAMILY ABANDONS ANCESTRAL HOME

CHAPTER 1

Dogs barking in the distance announced the return of the village trader from across the Prusso-Polish border. Iachob Litvak, hunched on his seat at the front of a heavily laden wagon, coaxed a weary team of horses along the winding clay and gravel road that led into the village of Lubicz. He had been gone since early morning and now the slowly sinking sun stretched his shadow to the far side of the ditch where it flitted playfully among the trees.

Today Litvak was anxious to return to the village because, in addition to his cargo of merchandise, he had some important and encouraging news for his old friend, Axel Berglund, the village furniture maker. From here it was only about one kilometer to his own home on the other side of the village where his wife would have supper waiting for him, but tonight he would be late.

He straightened himself up and pulled a well-worn gold watch from his breast pocket, then glanced at the setting sun which was now a large bronze sphere perched above the horizon. He slid the timepiece back into his pocket and urged the horses to pick up their pace. As he approached the village his mind drifted to thoughts of the character and destiny of the community and its inhabitants.

Lubicz was at the junction of the roads leading to Brodnica and Olsztyn, in the northwest sector of Poland, which had been occupied by Russia for almost a hundred years. None of the area's inhabitants was old enough to have been there that day back in 1815 when the Congress of Vienna sliced the country into three parts for the third time in its history, dividing it irreverently among its age-old adversaries, Prussia, Austria and Russia. Neither had anyone in the village experienced the days when their country was a proud and independent nation which for several centuries had been one of Europe's great powers.

To Litvak, it had always been apparent that in spite of the many years of occupation the villagers had lost little of their Polish character and pride. Stories of greatness and better days had been passed along diligently from generation to generation and the inhabitants of Lubicz, like those of hundreds of other villages, towns and cities in the divided country, still considered themselves Poles. Their fierce nationalism defied all attempts to change them over to the ways of their conquerors. The oppression resulting from the many years of occupation had not obscured the hope in their hearts and, for many, each day brought their beloved country one step closer to its long-awaited return to its former position as a nation of rich heritage and influence.

Litvak had crossed the border early that morning and spent the day trading in the Prussian zone, only eight kilometers to the northwest of Lubicz, in the city known as Torun in the Polish language and Thorn in German. Because his forays to the towns on the Prussian side were so frequent, Litvak was well known to the officials on both sides of the border and they allowed him to cross almost freely into both sectors.

But Litvak knew that there was more to this lenient arrangement than simple familiarity. The officials understood that he was providing a useful service to the people on both sides of the border. To the Prussians, traders like him provided access to a receptive market for the products produced by the emerging manufacturing enterprises in their zone. To the Russians, who were anxious to attract much needed German marks to their treasury, it was sensible to encourage traders to export products from the villages on their side of the border. To the landless Jews, dispersed along the borders, the trading activity provided a means of survival.

Consequently the inspections of the contents of Litvak's wagon were often casual and nearly always irregular, depending upon the mood of the officers and the proximity of the supervising inspectors occasionally sent from Warsaw or Berlin. From past experience, the officers on the Prussian side knew that Litvak's incoming cargo usually consisted of grain, potatoes, vegetables, dressed poultry, pork, knitted woolens and handmade wooden furniture. On the return trips, the Russian officials had become accustomed to Litvak's cargo of the usual variety of manufactured items such as tools, cloth, dishes, tobacco and spirits. But Litvak also knew that familiarity is not always sufficient and had been careful to maintain the favor of the officials and expedite his passage by occasionally placing a bottle of spirits conveniently near the customs house door where the officers would be sure to see it.

Litvak took a deep breath and gazed thoughtfully at the slowly approaching village. Over the years it had become his home and its inhabitants had come to value and respect him. To most of the villagers of Polish descent he was a partisan like themselves who could be trusted as a friend and confidante. They also appreciated that, as a merchant, Litvak supplied them with access to the more prosperous communities on the Prussian side and, because of his frequent trips to the Prussian zone, considered him to be a much sought after source of news and information. Some of the locals even proudly claimed that Litvak's store and warehouse added stature to the village and, together with the marketplace and the ancient church, made Lubicz "almost a town".

The rim of the sun was still visible when Litvak entered the village. He drew hard on the right rein and the horses reluctantly entered a rutted lane that led to a small furniture shop.

The wagon creaked its way along the hard-packed dirt road, its wheels picking up brown dust and dropping it in billowing clouds which floated gently behind the slow-moving vehicle. Little children, their eyes wide with curiosity, ran alongside the wagon hoping to catch a glimpse of the wonders that it contained. Older people interrupted their conversations and waved to the trader from inside their picket fences then resumed their discussions.

Axel Berglund was standing at the entrance of his small shop as Litvak approached, his lanky body framed by the doorway. His rough hands and broad shoulders bore evidence of many years of hard physical labor. A narrow forehead, sharp chiseled nose and fair complexion revealed his Nordic origin, although in his dress and manner he was no different than the other villagers. Berglund had been doing business with Litvak for several years and over this time they had become good friends. The hand-made furniture which he produced was eagerly sought after by the wealthy Prussians on the other side of the border where Litvak had arranged numerous sales for him over the years.

With a slight tug on the black leather reins Litvak brought the team to a halt at the hitching rail near the front of the shop. The horses, frothing at the mouth and covered with patches of shiny sweat, welcomed the reprieve and snorted repeatedly to clear the dust from their noses.

"You had a long day, Pan Litvak," observed Axel as he approached his visitor.

"Yes, Pan Berglund," replied Litvak, dismounting stiffly from the wagon. "The Prussians are becoming more and more skilled at bargaining and I, you might say, also looked around a bit." Axel detected a factitious tone in his voice.

"And what are our friends over there doing these days?" he inquired.

"I suspect that, as always, they are doing much more than they would have us believe," Litvak replied. Then, as he tied the horses to the hitching rail, he lowered his voice. "But perhaps we should go inside and talk for a moment while the horses catch their breath. I have something important to tell you and I would not want a soul to hear it beside yourself. As you know, sound carries too well on these still fall evenings."

"Come in. Come in," implored Berglund, convinced by Litvak's discreet actions that this time the trader might have more than the usual stock of rumors from the other side.

They entered the house and he produced a bottle of vodka from an old wooden cupboard, filled two glasses, and proposed a toast. "Our compatriots in the Russian zone have learned one useful thing from their oppressors and that is how to make good vodka. To your health, Pan Litvak."

Litvak threw his head back, downed the vodka, then eased himself into an ancient wooden chair. With a deep breath he leaned forward, pressing his torso into the edge of the table and stretching almost across its worn surface. His eyes pierced the narrow space between them.

"My friend, I think that I have found your son!" he blurted out excitedly. Litvak had rehearsed the announcement in his mind during the entire trip back from Torun until he felt that he could no longer contain it. Now that it was said, he slid back into his chair and waited for Axel's reaction.

For several moments Berglund remained motionless, his stare fixed on Litvak. He stood up and straightened his bony frame, then waved his hand in front of his face as if to dismiss the whole idea. "You are a good man, Pan Litvak, but you know that you should not expect me to believe that. I have heard so many idle rumors since they took our son away that I cannot believe any of them anymore.

"And why should I? Here it is 1910. Nine years since that unfortunate and ill-conceived happening. Nine years of hoping and listening. First he is in this town or village and then in another, but no one has ever talked to him.

Nine years since we and the other parents have seen or heard anything to give us hope. If our children are alive and well, why have we not heard from them? If our son and the others are out there, why has he not contacted us?"

"Be patient, Pan Berglund and let me finish," chided Litvak. "You, yourself have always told me that you would never give up hope as long as you live. Now that we may have found your son, you scoff."

"You misunderstand me. I did not say that I have given up hope, or criticize what you are telling me, my friend. What I am saying is that I have given up listening to rumors. I have gotten up my hopes too many times only to have them broken again. How do I know that this is not just idle gossip or a scheme designed to demoralize us all? If he is out there, why does he not write or send a message?" Berglund pulled up a chair and sat down. He placed his clasped hands on the table and buried his face in them.

"My friend, how is he to know where you are unless somebody tells him? Remember that you moved here after the uprising," Litvak reminded him. "In any case, I am giving you my word. I am convinced that we are on the right track now. My informant swears that he saw your son in Torun. He says that your son and eleven other boys were taken from a Prussian trade school and placed into apprenticeship at the Torun Works foundry several months ago. They are now lodged in a men's dormitory in the factory compound. It is near there that your son was seen. I have no reason to doubt the story."

Berglund looked up, his face drawn, and eyes focused on Litvak. "Even if I am to believe all this and he is there as you say, how are we to get to him? He is probably being watched very closely."

"That should not be too difficult," explained Litvak, relieved that his friend was becoming more receptive. "As far as my informer can tell, there is only one watchman patrolling the dormitory area at any one time. The one that works the evening shift is Polish and apparently knows the background of the new apprentices. It appears that because of this, he is fairly lenient with them; I suppose as lenient as he dares to be. He allows them to have some visitors in their quarters and they can come and go pretty much as they please as long as they are in by ten o'clock at night."

Axel Berglund remained silent, deep in thought. The sun had gone down and the room was dark. He reached for the oil lamp and lit it.

"Your son did not have a chance to write because, even if he had known where you were, he and other boys were kept in isolation at a boarding school in Prussia," continued Litvak. "They were not allowed to communicate with anyone on the outside, including their parents.

"Now that your son's formal academic training is over, he has much more freedom, but as far as we can tell, he cannot leave Torun without permission. But we understand that he is allowed to receive certain types of callers, including peddlers, and that is how I propose to get to him. I will arrange for one of my associates to observe his habits and then happen to be there one day when the boy is outside the compound by himself. I understand that he takes walks alone in the evening before supper."

Axel stared at the flame of the oil lamp glowing through its smoke-stained glass chimney. He shook his head in apparent disbelief. "You are so sincere, my friend, that I cannot help but believe you. But if what you say is true, what can I do to help?"

"Nothing just yet," replied Litvak. "Once we have established that he really is your son, we will determine if he can get away for a few hours. If he can, I could meet him somewhere on this side of the border and take him here. It is only eight kilometers, and without a load and with fresh horses I can make it there and back in about an hour."

Axel remained deep in thought for a moment, staring at the flickering yellow flame, and sprang to his feet. The look of hopeless despair suddenly left his face. He leapt off the chair took Litvak's hand in both of his and shook it vigorously.

"My good friend, if I could see my son just one more time before I die, I would be forever indebted to you. All these years of waiting will not have been in vain. Forgive me for doubting your story. It is the way of a disillusioned man. I would be the last one to question your good intentions. You seem to have thought everything out so carefully, and rather than hinder you in the task I will leave the next step to your good judgment. Even though I may appear somewhat skeptical, I will not stand in your way."

Litvak stood up and headed for the door. "Good. I hope you will not regret it. I must be leaving now. The night has many eyes and a man does not leave his horses tied to a hitching rail too long unless he has urgent business or is imbibing, both of which arouse idle curiosity. You will hear from me as soon as I have some news. Good night, Pan Berglund."

He untied his horses and pulled himself up into the seat at the front of the wagon. The tired horses reluctantly started up for the short trip to the other side of the village where Litvak's warehouse and stable were located. As the wagon headed toward the road, he glanced back at Berglund who was gazing out the window into the dark night. A contented smile lit up Litvak's bearded face.

~~~

The leaves on the ancient oaks, bronzed by the late afternoon sun, shimmered and rustled restlessly in the soft breeze. Below their branches a well-worn path stretched out to a gravel covered road which only hours before had borne the burden of the day's traffic. Now the road was empty except for a tall, lanky youth who entered it from the footpath. The young man walked briskly along and then turned into a narrow tree-lined lane which skirted the east side of the Torun Works complex.

Walking more slowly now, he casually glanced around from beneath a black peaked cap. After several steps he paused and crouched down to do up his boot strap. A moment later he heard footsteps and looked up to see a man carrying a valise entering the lane behind him. As he stood up the man hurried toward him, assessing him with a quick focused glance.

"Is your name Berglund?" he asked in a quiet voice.

"Yes," replied the young man cautiously. "Yes, I am Erik Berglund.

How did you know me?" He started to walk again toward the complex.

"I have a message for you from your parents," the man announced in an earnest tone.

"Who are you anyway and how did you find me?" Erik stopped and eyed the man suspiciously. "And if what you say is true, how do my parents know where I am?"

"I am just a peddler who works in this area, and it may be better if we walk toward your quarters and talk along the way. I understand that you are allowed to talk to peddlers." The young man hesitated but did not answer. "When we get to your billet, I will go through the motions of showing you my merchandise and in that way if anyone comes in they will not suspect that I am anything other than a peddler. Let us start out for your dormitory now. Before we turn around, you will make a motion for me to come with you. All right, let's go now."

Erik was taken aback by the peddler's authoritative manner, but he waved his hand in an exaggerated sign for the man to follow him. They started back toward the path, Erik walking briskly ahead of the peddler but constantly glancing backwards to observe his every move.

"You say that you have a message from my parents. Are they well? How did they hear about me? You still have not told me, how did they know where I am?" The questions gushed out of Erik's mouth now.

"Slow down, slow down," admonished the peddler. He spoke German with a Polish accent. "They are well and living in Lubicz, a village on the Russian side not far from here, where they fled after the uprising. I understand that the Russians have not bothered them much, no doubt because they have many other things to occupy them these days. Your father is still making furniture and much of it is being sold on this side by Litvak, the village trader. Your mother is also well and so is your brother Stanislaw."

"Oh thank God for that." Erik heaved a sigh of relief. He was becoming convinced that the man knew something about the family when he correctly mentioned the brother's name. "And who are you? How did you know where I was?"

"It is better that you do not know my name at this time. But you must trust me. As to knowing who you are, there are ways of finding out these things."

They entered the dormitory and walked quietly through the hall into Erik's quarters.

"May I continue?" asked the peddler, his eyes scanning the room around him.

"Yes. My roommate is not here and there does not appear to be anyone else around," replied Erik.

"Now listen carefully." The peddler spoke in a near whisper. "If you want to see your family, we can arrange for a vehicle to pick you up on the south-east side of the city and take you to Lubicz whenever you can get away. If necessary, you will be returned here the same night. If you agree, I will get the message back to my contact so that he will be expecting you."

Erik removed his cap and ran his fingers through his thick auburn hair. He pondered momentarily, then sat on the edge of his bed, his eyes fixed on the stranger, mentally assessing his sincerity.

"I'll do it," he said, jumping to his feet. "In fact, you could not have come at a better time. Today my foreman told me that all the boys in our unit will receive their first extended leave at the end of this week. If we do, I will be able to stay away two whole days. And if what you say is true, then I could spend them at Lubicz with my family."

He paused momentarily, deep in thought, contemplating the timing of the proposed event. "Tell your man to meet me on the road near the junction of the Drweca and the Vistula Friday just before dusk. I will be at the south end of the old bridge that crosses the Drweca near there."

"It is as good as done," the peddler assured him. "Look for a thin man with a short black beard, driving a wagon. His name is Litvak. Iachob Litvak."

Erik stuck out his hand. "Thank you, whoever you are. Thank you for the wonderful news." He selected a belt and a pair of leather shoe laces from the open case and handed the man some money. The peddler closed his bag and walked out of the building into the street. Erik watched him disappear into the twilight then fell back on his bed and covered his eyes with his arm, deep in thought.

CHAPTER 2

In the austere, but spotless, mess hall which served the occupants of the adjoining men's dormitory, Hilda the cook scurried around the long roughly hewn wooden table at which twelve talkative youths were seated for the evening meal. Her bulky form moved gracefully behind the young men like a mother hen fretting over her brood, her presence lending warmth to the stark surroundings. She was aware that for the new boarders who had only recently arrived from the trade school in Prussia this type of attention was unfamiliar, but this only enhanced her motherly instincts.

The astonished young men still relished their new-found luxury. For their previous nine years as wards of the state they had become accustomed to routinely approaching the serving table with their white porcelain-coated metal plates and cups to receive equal portions of bland fare meted out by poker-faced servers. In their new environment, with all the food they wanted being served to them by a solicitous handmaid, they suddenly felt grown-up and important.

But to Erik not even this comparative affluence was sufficient to soothe the excitement or erase the anxiety that he was experiencing this evening. Lost in thought, he observed the room with a distant gaze. In two days, if what the peddler had told him was true and if all went well, he would be reunited with his parents and brother.

He wondered if the peddler was genuine or if it was some kind of a trick. Questions bounced around in his head. Why would the peddler not give his name? How did they find out where he was? But the stranger did seem sincere. He had decided he would take a chance and give it a try.

"Eat up, Erik," prodded Hilda. "You eat like a bird. One would think that you are in love or something."

Erik smiled but did not respond.

"Don't think that I did not see you and Roman scheming something with that baker's daughter when she delivered the bread yesterday," teased Hilda.

A roll of laughter rose around the table as Erik fidgeted uneasily at Hilda's joshing. The howls stopped suddenly as the sound of footsteps echoed through the corridor and approached the dining hall. Hans Schindel, the director of apprentices, appeared at the door and walked briskly to the front of the table where he stopped and stood at attention. His square torso was packed into a tight fitting tunic which was fastened snugly under his chin where his neck should have been. Without a word of greeting Schindel surveyed the startled youths now sitting in silence.

"Boys, over the past several weeks you have shown me and your employer that you are dependable men who can be trusted and who can accept responsibility." Schindel's voice exuded authority. "To show our appreciation, I have recommended to your employer that you be given a two-day furlough beginning after work this Friday. You may go anywhere you wish except across the border into the Russian zone. Anyone caught doing this will be dealt with severely. You will all be back at these barracks Sunday evening and at your workstations Monday at 0700 hours sharp."

"Thank you, Herr Director," intoned the young men. The director turned, military-like and marched out of the room into the hall.

The youths rose from the table chatting excitedly as they returned to their quarters. Erik entered his billet and kicked off his boots before stretching out on the bed. His roommate eyed him curiously. The two of them had been together since the uprising nine years earlier when they were taken away from their parents in reprisal. Although different in many ways, they seemed to complement each other and this helped them through the lonely years when they were separated from their families.

Unlike Erik who was serious, methodical and temperamental, Roman was careless, easy-going and fun-loving. His large mouth and straight white teeth seemed to be fixed in a perpetual smile and his eyes shone mischievously from under a mat of tousled brown hair.

Roman lifted his head off the pillow and observed his roommate. "Is something bothering you, Erik?" he asked.

"No. No. Everything is fine."

"You can't fool me, Erik. I know you too well. We are both friends and can trust each other. You don't have to be afraid of me. You know that we have always shared our secrets."

Erik stared silently at the ceiling, then threw his feet unto the floor and sat up. "Very well, Roman. I know that I can trust you and that is not why I have kept my secret." He lowered his voice to a whisper. "You see, late this afternoon when I was out walking, a stranger approached me and told me that my parents are living not far from here in the Russian zone. He said that he has a contact who could take me to see them this Friday and then bring me back again. You know how much I have missed my family and how I was afraid that I would never see them again"

"What wonderful news, Erik! I would think that you would be jumping for joy instead of worrying yourself sick. Tell me, what is the problem that is troubling you?" asked Roman.

"There are really two things that concern me. One is that I am not quite sure that I trust the person who brought me the news. He would not tell me his name or anything else about himself, except that he works with a Jewish trader who is a friend of my father. The second worry is how I would explain my absence of two days if anyone should check up on me. I felt that I had no one to go to for advice and direction, therefore, I worried."

"Ah, you should have told me all this earlier and you would have saved yourself a lot of worrying. That's what good friends are for, are they not? I just happen to have answers to both of your problems right now," confided Roman.

"So what do you know that I don't know?" snapped Erik.

"This is no time to be touchy. Cool heads work better than hot ones." Roman remained calm. He lowered his voice and moved closer to Erik.

"You heard Hilda's remark about Lydia, the baker's daughter. Well, it so happens that I have been meeting her some evenings in the past while and she has invited me to spend my time off at her parents' place in the country. So if anyone asks, I can say that you were with us."

"And you talk about me keeping secrets from you! But what if someone should ask her?" pondered Erik.

"Lydia will say anything that I ask her to say," boasted Roman.

Erik observed his friend's confidence with amusement and heaved a sigh a relief. "I never would have suspected you of being a tom-cat," he said, shaking his head in disbelief.

"Just goes to show you how well I cover my tracks," laughed Roman. "And as for your other problem, if it makes you feel any better, I could go with you and if you still feel uneasy after you see the man who the stranger said will take you to your parents, we can both turn around and come back."

"Very well," said Erik in a relieved tone. "I like your plan and I feel so much better about the whole thing already. Now here is my plan. I will be meeting my father's friend Friday at dusk. He will pick me up at the end of the old bridge at the south-east side of the city and will take me across the border and then on to Lubicz. The man said that I would be taken back whenever I wish, so I will probably stay with my family until Sunday afternoon and come back in the evening. If you can tell me at what time you will be back here Sunday evening, I could arrange to meet you in the lane outside the compound and we could come in together."

Roman stared at the window deep in thought. "I have an even better idea," he announced. "You can be on this side of the old bridge at six o'clock Sunday evening and I will meet you there, then we can come back together. We can also leave at the same time on Friday evening and in that way no one will suspect a thing."

A broad smile pushed a frown off Erik's face. He jumped to his feet and slapped his arm around Roman. "You are a great friend, Roman, and so full of brilliant ideas. I am sorry that I did not confide in you earlier. I felt that I wanted to sort it all out in my head first. And, by the way, why did you keep your close friendship with Lydia a secret from me?"

"We have always done things together and I could not bear to see that you were no longer a part of something that I was doing," explained Roman. "Now, Lydia and I have a plan which will soon involve you. But why don't we save that until after you return from Lubicz?"

~~~

The ancient wood and steel bridge framed and dissected the top half the huge September sun as it sank slowly below a low ridge of hills in the distance. As the gray shadows lengthened and spilled over the landscape, the two young men strolled casually to the foot of the bridge. They stopped and listened. Behind them the muffled sounds of the city provided the acoustical background for the spirited chirping of sparrows protecting their territorial rights in the trees along the river. The evening air was warm and still and the sounds cut through it effortlessly, fanning out in all directions. They threw some pebbles at an old tree stump and then listened again. Suddenly the clunking of wagon wheels sounded in the distance. The muted sound grew louder and then stopped. Sounds of horses snorting drifted across the river.

"That is he," said Erik, leaping toward the bridge. "If I am not back in five minutes, I'll see you Sunday evening at six."

"Good journey," called Roman as Erik disappeared into the shadows.

A wagon and its driver stood silhouetted against the fading glow of the evening sky. The horses pranced nervously as Erik approached.

"Berglund?" asked the man in the wagon.

"Yes," replied Erik. "I am Erik Berglund."

"Climb up," ordered the driver.

Erik stepped on the spoke of a wheel and lifted himself up into the seat. He peered at the driver through the dim twilight. The man put out his hand.

"My name is Litvak, Iachob Litvak," he said as the wagon began to move. "I know your father well. He has arranged for me to meet you here."

"What about the border guards?" asked Erik, peering into the distance.

"Just leave them to me," replied Litvak. "Don't say a word. I will handle them."

The two remained silent as the wagon, heading east, approached the Prussian port of entry. A dim yellow light shone through the window of the sentry house as they drew near. The lone border guard approached the window and looked out. Litvak called on the horses to stop.

"Who is it?" called the guard as he appeared at the door.

"It is I. Litvak."

"You are late today. Did you have to do some extra haggling or could you not get rid of those inferior Polish products?"

Litvak listened closely and sensed that the guard was in a good mood. He recognized him as a younger officer who often worked the more unpopular late shifts.

"No. I could not decide which of those fine Prussian products I should take back," he quipped as he leaned back into the wagon to pick up a bottle wrapped in a brown paper bag.

"All right, get going before I change my mind and make you unload everything," taunted the border guard. He started back toward the sentry house, then paused and stared through the darkness directly at Erik.

"No. Hold it! Who is that with you?" His voice assumed a new authority.

"Oh, him? He is my helper. My back was not feeling too good today and I needed someone to help me unload the bags of potatoes, so I brought him along," explained Litvak as he descended from the wagon and placed the bottle of schnapps near of the door of the guard house.

"You are getting slothful and rich at the expense of the poor Polish peasants," said the young border guard only half in jest. "Where is your helper from?"

"Lubicz," answered Litvak.

"All right. Move along." The border guard waved them on. The horses strained at the harness and the wagon creaked under the heavy load. The two riders heaved a sigh of relief and remained silent as they approached the port of entry on the Russian side. Livak brought the horses to a stop, but finding that the port was unmanned, he steered the horses and wagon into the dark night on the road to Lubicz.

"Now that, my boy, is the difference between the Russians and the Prussians," said Litvak, looking back at the empty border post.

"I think that tonight I like the Russians' way best," said Erik, "especially tonight."

~~~

The rim of the full moon peered over the east horizon then began its gradual incline into the starry sky, providing welcome illumination for the horses and riders. In the fields beside the road the early grains and vegetables had already been harvested and only a few stands of ripened corn and some root crops and pumpkins stood in isolated patches among the stubble and plowed plots. The combined scents of drying straw, corn stalks and yellowing pumpkins filled the cool evening air with the pleasant aroma of harvest. In the grass and bushes, great armadas of crickets chirping their choruses in full voice stopped abruptly as the wagon passed by, then resumed again as it disappeared into the silvery darkness.

Litvak broke into a Yiddish song which Erik did not understand. He stopped suddenly. "Well Erik, you could not have asked for a more perfect evening on which to return to your parents, especially since I decided that we would surprise them."

"The opportunity to see my family would make any evening perfect," said Erik. "But you are right. The country does appear especially peaceful tonight."

"Yes, indeed. This is a wonderful time of the year. Nature has worked hard all summer and is now getting ready for a rest." Litvak paused and his eyes swept the horizon. "But then, the land is always peaceful. It is the people who create disharmony," he remarked sadly.

They rode along without speaking for a while longer, each lost in his own thoughts. Litvak broke the silence. "For example, just think seriously about this very road that we are on now," he began. "In Roman times it used to be known as the Amber Trail and since then some of Europe's most bloody and crucial battles were fought along its length. If nature had not provided so amply for their disintegration, the bones of the war dead would be a meter deep in places."

"And for what?" asked Erik. "The land is as divided now as it ever was."

"You are right, Erik. And nowhere is this more evident now than in

Poland. But you mark my word that before this century is very far advanced, Poland shall once again be reunited."

"It is nice to hear you say that, but what will that achieve for most of the Polish people?" asked Erik. "If they remain as they are now, or return to the impoverished conditions of the past, what is the difference? I think the Prussians have the right idea. They derive their strength from their resources and their people, not from some emotional attachment to history as the Poles do. And the part of Poland that is under their control is all the better for it. Maybe it is time that the Polish people realized that material progress is more important than political sentiments."

"I see that you have been well schooled, Erik, and have developed a critical mind," remarked Litvak, impressed by Erik's maturity. "This will stand you well in life. But allow me to tell you something that I have learned over the years.

"The relentless search for wealth is the act of a desperate man. It is better that a man find himself first; who he is and what he is doing here. That is what keeps alive man's awareness of his own uniqueness. Otherwise he gets tossed around like a feather in the wind. If he does not know where he is going, he will not get there. That is why history and philosophy are so important. History tells mankind where it has been and philosophy encourages man to ask himself where he is going and why. Once these questions are answered, then goodness and prosperity follow naturally."

"You may be right, Pan Litvak, but I plan to devote my life to building, not destroying. That also takes creativity and I enjoy being creative," said Erik.

"I can see where your parents will be very proud of you, my boy, but enough of this serious philosophizing. We are getting close to Lubicz and you want to be in a happy mood when we arrive," suggested Litvak.

CHAPTER 3

The horses, sensing that their destination was near, quickened their pace. As they approached the village, the lights in the windows shone dimly on the horizon. Coated in the silvery white light of the moon, groups of buildings began to appear on both sides of the road, their dark forms huddled together like animals in a storm. At Litvak's urging the horses turned into a narrow lane that stretched eerily into the shadows. The light from a window appeared through the trees on their left.

"This is where your parents live," announced Litvak as he guided the team and wagon into a grassy driveway, skillfully squeezing the rig between a picket fence and a row of trees.

Erik peered into the dark shadows cast by the trees in the moonlight. He felt his heart beating inside his chest. The dull orange light of an oil lamp shone faintly through a window of the small cottage. A door opened and the lamplight spilled out over the small wooden platform in front of the house. A tall, gangly man emerged and stopped to listen. Litvak called on the horses to stop.

"Is that you, Pan Berglund?" Litvak called to the man standing on the platform. "Come and see what I have brought you."

Axel Berglund approached cautiously. His strained his eyes to see through the darkness. "Oh, it is you, Pan Litvak. What are you doing here so late?" Then observing the young man up on the seat beside his friend, Berglund suddenly realized that Litvak had kept his promise. With his eyes fixed on the dark figure in the wagon, he approached the vehicle slowly and then stopped. Litvak pointed to the young man and nodded his head. "There he is."

Axel clasped his hands together and raised his eyes skyward. "Good Lord, you have brought back our son. I thank you for this great blessing." Then with a dash of youthful agility he ran back to the house and shouted through the door, "Mama, come quick! Come and see who is here."

The woman stood in the doorway, her ample body casting a shadow over the wooden platform. She started walking toward the wagon speculating audibly to herself. She came to where her husband was standing and hesitated. Erik leaped out of the wagon and ran to her. He reached down and embraced her tenderly. Her tears flowed over his hands as she kissed them.

"My baby, my baby," she cried as Erik leaned over and kissed her. "Where have you been all these years?" She backed up and surveyed her son. "How you have grown. Have they been feeding you well? And look at this. You are not wearing a coat on a chilly night like this." She glanced at Axel who was standing by and watching. "Don't just stand there. Welcome him home," she scolded.

Berglund was amused by his wife's excitement. "I will, as soon as you give me a chance," he said. He put his hands on his son's shoulders and they embraced silently. Then realizing that they had forgotten about Litvak sitting up on the wagon, Axel feigned a command. "What are you waiting for? Get down and unhitch your horses. This is no time for formalities. It is a night for celebration!"

Litvak climbed down from the wagon as a figure appeared out of the darkness, coming down the garden path, and approached the spirited group. Erik's brother Stanislaw had observed all the activity from his house nearby and came by to investigate.

"He has arrived. Erik is here. Litvak was telling the truth," an elated Axel announced to Stanislaw. "Do you recognize your brother, Erik?" Stanislaw greeted his brother with a long embrace and left to tend to the horses as the others entered the house, Litvak tenderly cradling a bottle of German schnapps, wrapped in fancy glossy paper.

"Here you are, Pan Berglund, this is help you celebrate this happy occasion," said Litvak as he handed the package to Axel.

Berglund removed the wrapping from the bottle and peered at the label, squinting in the dim light. "What is this, Pan Litvak," he roared. "I take you for an honest man and you present with this foreign made poison to celebrate our son's return."

"Do not be too hasty in your condemnation," pleaded Litvak. "This is not the slop that they usually sell us. It is a brand that they make for themselves. Bourgeois stuff."

"You should not look a gift horse in the mouth," chided Mrs. Berglund as she set out the glasses. "The man is being kind and thoughtful and you complain, especially when he has just brought us our greatest gift."

"I know him too well to be offended by his remarks," Litvak assured her.

~~~

At his mother's urging, Erik sat at the front of the table and fidgeted nervously as the others assumed their positions on either side. Axel and Litvak, both in a jovial mood, drank toasts to Erik, to each other and to peace. A bowl of jellied cold chicken and a plate of poppy seed rolls appeared miraculously from her ice box and pantry only moments after Mrs. Berglund had fretted about not being prepared for the occasion. Tea from a large earthenware pot filled their cups and soon the emotional atmosphere which had prevailed earlier turned into one of joyful celebration.

"So tell us about yourself, Erik. What have you been doing for all those years?" said Axel observing his son. "They could not have been too hard on you, judging by your size." The schnapps had already altered his mood.

"Well father, I think that the size comes from you," responded Erik. "But the whole experience was not all that bad. That is not to say that I did not miss you all greatly, especially for the first while when I was still so young. After that unfortunate day in Wrzesnia nine years ago we were all taken to Posen by the Prussian authorities. All sixty boys from our parish were placed in a residential school where we were taught the German language and history, as well as mathematics and science. At the age of fourteen I was transferred to a vocational school with all the others, also in Posen. There we were each assigned to a trade. Because I was good at mathematics and drafting, I was enrolled in the mechanical technology course."

"Did they feed you well, my son?" interrupted his mother.

"The food at the residence was plain – not as good as I remembered yours to be, mama – but we usually had enough. We were required to wash our own plates, cups and cutlery and make our own beds every day. But that was not the difficult part. What most of us found the hardest to endure in the first year or two was being away from our families. But we eventually got used to it and lived in the hope that one day we would all be reunited and that some time in the future we would be able to move about more freely. For me that day appears to have arrived, thanks to you all, and especially to Pan Litvak."

"Praise the Lord for his great mercy," said his mother, casting her gaze upward.

"But as we all know now, the freedom that we all wanted so badly was not to come about until after we had completed our technical training. One day about five months ago, the headmaster ordered all of us into the school auditorium for a special assembly. When he entered the room he was accompanied by some of the senior teaching staff and some strangers whom we later learned were German and Prussian industrialists. Some military personnel were also present.

"The headmaster called us forward one by one and members of the visiting team interrogated each of us. When my turn came one of them asked me if I was Jewish. I replied that I was Polish. Then why did I not have a Polish name, he asked. I explained that one of my ancestors had fought in the Swedish-Polish war and decided to remain in Poland after the war, where later he and his descendants all took Polish wives, but kept their Swedish name. They could not understand why my father, the descendant of an enemy soldier would have sympathized with the Polish in the insurrection at Wrzesnia. I explained that my mother came from a long line of Polish stock whose lineage could be traced all the way back to the Radziwell family and that the passion which she had for her people may have infected my father. This seemed to satisfy them."

"We taught you well," interrupted his mother, "and you did well to remember all that at such an early age."

"They then asked me what type of work my father did. I replied that he was a furniture maker. This immediately seemed to attract the attention of one of the industrialists present. Did my father build his furniture by hand or machine, he asked. I replied that he did it mostly by hand. Did I ever help with the work in the shop? Oh yes, I said, I worked there after school every day until I was ten. The industrialist and the headmaster then had a short consultation and I was dismissed.

"The next day I was summoned to the headmaster's office. He advised me that the management of Torun Works was interested in me and would like me to apprentice there. In addition to the training which I would receive at the employer's expense, the company would provide me with free room and board and pay me a modest wage. The headmaster said that he was proud of me since my friend Roman and I were the only ones from our group selected by this company to work in their drafting department and I was the only one who was chosen to be groomed for product design work. In about a week we were transferred to the Torun Works and I began my apprenticeship.

"After we arrived at Torun things began to change for us. We were assigned to the single men's dormitory where we each share a room with another boy. My roommate's name is Roman Potoski. He is also from Wrzesnia and we were together during our whole stay in Posen. Our cook Hilda is a jolly frau and we often help her with the kitchen chores. In return she allows us to help ourselves to food from the kitchen almost anytime that we are hungry and she is still around to keep an eye on us.

"At the foundry we are now receiving further training and are also becoming more involved in production work. Our employer provides us with work clothes and pays us what I am told is a fair wage. So, except for the control that they have over our freedom to move about, we are treated quite decently. But just this week they introduced a new arrangement which allows us time off from work and we can now leave the compound and our quarters. We are free to move about anywhere except in the Russian zone. So here I am," concluded Erik with a broad grin.

"But son, this is the Russian zone." His mother had a puzzled and worried look on her face.

"Ah yes," said Erik, "but no one there except Roman knows where I am."

"God protect us. Turn down the lamp, father, before someone sees that he is here," fretted Mrs. Berglund.

"Don't worry so much, mama," counseled her husband. "The people in this village are our friends and furthermore no one saw him arrive. It was too dark."

"Just the same," advised Litvak, "we can't be too careful. These are ominous times and you never know whom you can really trust."

"But why would anyone want to harm us? May we not celebrate the return of our son in peace? We have not harmed anyone," Mrs. Berglund protested.

"The truth is that by being here, Erik is breaking the rules," explained Litvak. "Also, because Erik has lived on the other side for several years he knows what is going on there, as also do I to some extent. The big difference is that I see only those things that are meant to be seen. Erik has probably seen much more. But for me, it is not what I see that worries me so much, but what I hear from my friends in the Prussian zone. And if some of what I hear is true, then I can understand why the authorities there would want to remain discreet."

"You have aroused my curiosity, Pan Litvak," remarked Axel who had been listening attentively to Erik's story and the conversation between his wife and Litvak. "You mentioned a few days ago that there is more going on in the Prussian zone than meets the eye. What kind of stories do you hear? What are they scheming this time?"

"It is not so much a matter of scheming as one of preparation," explained Litvak. "As we all know, there is much posturing and political intrigue going on these days both within and among the countries of Europe. Everywhere the forces of national pride and past grievances are pulling away at the seams and one of these days the whole thing is bound to come apart. And if it does, Germany and her territories want to be ready, and they are doing just that, except that they do not want anyone on the outside to know about it."

"I can understand their logic, but what has this got to do with us?" asked Axel. "We are already a conquered and divided nation."

"It is not so much the question of who we are as where we are that will involve us in what is likely to occur in Europe," explained Litvak. "The resumption of hostilities in Europe, when it comes, will immediately involve the existing alliances and their territories."

"But we are not even a country. So why should we worry?" asked Axel.

"Because for many years Germany has maintained that the territory between the Vistula and the Dnieper is rightfully and historically hers. Any new conflict will provide her with the opportunity to again claim that territory?"

"May the good Lord protect us again," sighed Mrs. Berglund. "Must we never escape the wretched violence? The soil of this land is already soaked in the blood of my people. There is no country in Europe as cursed as this one and no people as unjustly condemned."

"No one except the Jews," corrected Litvak. "You Poles have at least clung to some of your land, even though at this time you are not masters of your own house. As for us, we have nothing. For centuries we have been scattered around like so much dust."

"Ah, yes," remarked Axel, "but when dust comes together it forms soil and soil forms land, and land is the basis of a nation."

"You are kind, Pan Berglund, "but I am afraid that neither you nor I will live to see that happen. But we must not abandon hope. Let me propose a toast to the new Poland to come."

Axel filled their glasses. Litvak lifted up his glass. "To Poland."

"To Israel," responded Axel.

They downed their glasses and stared in silence at the flame of the burning candle in the middle of the table, each engrossed in his own thoughts. Litvak stood up slowly.

"It is getting late. I must be on my way. My wife will think that I am lost."

"You are too clever to get lost," scoffed Axel. "Stanislaw, give the man a hand with his horses. Erik, you stay inside out of the reach of prying eyes," he ordered.

Axel and his wife followed Litvak to the door, showering him with thanks for finding returning their son. As they walked toward the wagon Litvak explained that he would return Sunday afternoon and take Erik back to the border crossing near Torun.

"When you come, would it be possible for you to arrive a little earlier. I have something important to think about and I need your learned advice."

The serious tone of Axel's voice convinced Litvak that the problem which his friend wanted to discuss was a weighty one. He agreed to arrive early. Stanislaw had already hitched the horses to the wagon and he handed the reins to Litvak who pulled himself up into the vehicle and drove off into the darkness. The three Berglunds returned to the house.

"It's nice to be back together again," said Erik with a contented sigh. "I had almost forgotten what it feels like to be part of a family."

"God is great," said his mother. "You have had a long day Erik. I have a bed all fixed up for you in the spare room. I have kept it ready for you since the day we came here. Let us all retire so we will be all rested up tomorrow."

"Yes," mused Erik, "it has been an eventful day. It feels like a whole year has gone by since this morning."

CHAPTER 4

Shafts of brilliant sunlight were already streaming through the tiny polished window panes of the room when Erik awoke next morning. He looked around at the unfamiliar surroundings – the clean soft bed with its feather quilt and pillows and the crucifix and tapestry on the wall. Suddenly he remembered where he was. In the kitchen the hissing sound of water boiling in the kettle on the wood stove announced that his mother was already up and preparing breakfast. He leaned back against the pillows and surveyed the scene. He wondered if this is the way things had been during his long absence. Memories of his boyhood days swirled through his head – his friends, the games they played together, the chores which he so grudgingly did for his parents.

Then there was the day of the dreadful uprising which he barely understood at the time, except that it had something to do with freedom to use the Polish language in their school. He remembered his father throwing half a dozen Prussian officials across the school room before the Prussian constables overpowered him and took him away. It was the last time that he saw his father until last night, because a few days later the children of the parents involved in the uprising were taken away to the state school in Posen. The men who participated in the insurrection were all hauled away in a police wagon and locked up in the local jail awaiting trial. He remembered his mother hanging on to the wagon. When the horses lurched forward she fell to the ground wailing. That was the last time that he saw her.

His mother, passing by the door, looked in. "You are up so early. Why don't you sleep some more?"

"I can't," answered Erik. "My wake-up time over the past nine years has been six o'clock and the timepiece in my head does not let me sleep any longer than that. So I have just been lying here enjoying the nice soft bed."

"Well then, get dressed and come for breakfast," said his mother affectionately. "Your father will join us as soon as I call him." She looked out the window. "No need to do that. Here he comes now."

When Erik entered the kitchen his father was already sitting at the table. "Hey Erik, you are up already." He was surprised, but delighted to see him. "Maybe after breakfast you can come and help me in the shop like you used to do."

"Now wait a minute, father," admonished Mrs. Berglund. "He did not come here to work."

"But I would still like to see what you are making, father," said Erik. "I have many fond memories of your shop in Wrzesnia. Remember how my job used to be to carry the wood ends into the house for firewood? That was one job that I really enjoyed."

After breakfast Erik and his father walked through the vegetable garden and past the stable on their way to the workshop to avoid using the lane and arousing the neighbors' curiosity. Inside the shop small piles of newly finished furniture parts were stacked neatly on the workbench waiting to be assembled. Erik ran his fingers over a newly planed piece of hardwood, admiring its grain and texture. On the floor a heap of fresh shavings exuded a tangy fragrance.

"It's so peaceful here, father," said Erik.

"Yes, son. I spend many happy hours here. A man is fortunate if he enjoys his work. Many people do not and they are to be pitied."

Axel placed a piece of wood into the vise and ran the plane over its length. The shavings fell to the floor in curly loops. He ran his hand over the wood, caressing its grain.

"This shop has helped me to keep my mind off many things while you were away and I surely would miss it if something..." He stopped suddenly as if he had said something which he had not intended to do.

Erik's curiosity was aroused. "If what, father?"

"Nothing, son, nothing." He struggled to regain his composure.

Erik gazed squarely into his father's eyes. "I am not a child anymore, father. You don't need to keep secrets hidden from me."

Axel placed the plane carefully onto the workbench in front of him and sat down on a rough wooden stool.

"All right, Erik. Forgive me for holding back like this. Tomorrow I would have discussed this matter with you anyway, but since my tongue slipped and, as you say, you are a big boy now, I will share my secret with you. Only Stanislaw and I know about it at this time, so I would like you to refrain from mentioning it to your mother just yet."

"Go on, father. Go on. You don't need to worry about me telling mama anything." The suspense was taxing his patience.

"Well son, you heard what Litvak said last night about what he suspects is going on in Europe right now. It is not like him to become serious about something unless he is assured that it has some substance. I am convinced that he knows something, perhaps more than he cares to admit. You see, son, that man has contacts in many places and he also has access to much information that we do not have. His comments last night certainly strengthened my own suspicions."

"What suspicions, father? What are you talking about?" Erik pleaded.

"My suspicions that we are on the eve of another conflict, a war like the world has never seen before. And Poland – this very ground on which we are standing now – will be right in the middle of it."

"That is one man's opinion, father," argued Erik. "Litvak may be exaggerating or misconstruing things. You know how those Jews are. They are always so suspicious. They don't trust anybody it seems."

"I am getting to be an old man, son, and I have observed many things in my lifetime." Axel spoke slowly, choosing his words carefully. "I am no longer influenced by rumors and idle talk. I think that I also know whom I can trust. Trust is a product of one's own experiences as well as one's knowledge of the individual upon whom the trust is placed and what that individual represents. On that basis Litvak's word is good enough for me. But just to convince you that I am not a complete fool, I must tell you that I have that same information from other sources, not just Litvak."

"Like whom?" asked Erik

"Like your mother's relatives in Warsaw," answered Axel. "You may wonder why I act this way about things that concern Poland, since I am not truly Polish. But as you know, your mother comes from a long line of noble and distinguished families. Granted that many of them are now living obscure and anonymous lives in the Russian, Austrian and Prussian zones, but a few have attained important positions with the present governments in all three sectors of Poland. One of these is her cousin Wladimar Bashinski who has an important position with the government in Warsaw. He has contacts in high places all over Europe and should know better than I do what is going on, and what he tells us agrees with Litvak's observations."

"But father, I live in one of those places and should know something about these things, too, and yet I have not seen anything in Torun or anywhere else to support what you say. Sure, they are educating their young people and teaching them trades and professions. They are building new factories and improving their farm production. They are improving their transportation facilities. If the Polish people had done the same a hundred or so years ago they would not be in the predicament in which they find themselves today. You have to give the Prussian and German people credit for managing their resources well. But to accuse them of secretly preparing for war, I feel that is unwarranted."

"Very well, son. As you say, you should know, and perhaps some of us are overreacting. So let us not waste our precious time arguing about things that we do not understand or have any control over. Let us talk about ourselves. Why don't we start with you? I hardly know what you are doing over there."

Erik was relieved by his father's suggestion that they change the subject. He sat on a wooden box across from his father and stirred the wood shavings with a stick. "Well, as I said last night, I am an apprentice at the Torun Works foundry," he explained. "I am being trained in mechanical drafting and design. At the foundry we make all sorts of metal parts for other manufacturers all over Germany and other countries in Europe. I find the work very satisfying. I am also fascinated by metallurgy and hope to get a chance to become involved in that sometime."

"That sounds most interesting, son. What kind of parts do you make? What are they used for?" asked his father.

"For production machinery mainly – the kind they use in other factories. But we also make parts for engines and motors, bicycles, wagons, trains, guns..."

"What kind of guns?" interrupted Axel.

"You know the kind. Small bore rifles mainly. We make the barrels and the small metal parts for them. They are sent to another manufacturer for assembly," explained Erik. "We make thousands of them." Erik hesitated and observed his father. "My foreman tells me that most of the rifles are exported to America and Australia."

"I wonder what the Americans and Australians do with all those rifles," pondered Axel.

"My foreman tells me that the settlers in America and Australia need rifles to hunt animals especially bison," explained Erik innocently.

"Is that so, son? Did he not also tell you that the American bison has been nearly extinct for more than fifty years?"

Erik gazed upon his father, then noticing the smug look on his face he realized that he had made his point. They joined together in a hearty laugh that rang through the rafters of the old building.

"Let's go to the house and talk to mother," suggested Erik. "I am beginning to see now what you mean, even though I am not completely convinced myself. But you still have not finished telling me what you started to say before we got involved in our argument about international politics."

"Perhaps we should go into the house and tell mama about it at the same time," said Axel.

The smells of cooking cabbage, meat, potatoes and apples blended together with the aroma of spices and herbs and drifted through the open door into the still, warm autumn air. Mrs. Berglund rushed around the kitchen performing a dozen tasks simultaneously with precise movements.

"That sure does smell good," said Erik, stepping through the doorway and startling his mother.

"You must be hungry, Erik. I prepared something special for you; something that you used to love when you were at home."

"Oh, I do hope that it is your famous cabbage rolls," guessed Erik.

"You smelled them. That's why you knew. You smelled them," she laughed.

"I could eat a dozen of these, mother," said Erik, lifting the cover off the large pot on the stove and blissfully breathing in the steamy aroma. "Oh look at those! I haven't had anything like that since I was home."

Mrs. Berglund filled their plates and the two men sat down and ate in silence. She studied their apparent preoccupation with their thoughts. Her curiosity finally triumphed.

"I did not think that my cooking was so good that it would stop you two from talking," she commented.

Axel looked up from his plate and absent-mindedly wiped his chin with his shirt sleeve.

"Your food is always the best in the world, mama, but that is only part of the reason for our silence."

"Then what is it?" she demanded.

Axel remained silent for a moment contemplating his next move. Suddenly his eyes lit up and he laid down his fork and knife.

"Don't you think it would be nice to have lots of land where we could raise a big garden and maybe some chickens and a few cows?" he asked enthusiastically.

Mrs. Berglund stopped in the middle of drying her hands on her apron when her husband spoke. She walked to his end of the table and fixed her eyes upon him.

"What are you getting at, father? Say what you have to say. Don't talk nonsense," she scolded.

Axel fidgeted nervously. "I have been thinking, mama, that if what Litvak said last night is true, and if what your cousin Bashinski told Stanislaw is really about to happen, maybe it would be better if old people like us were not here to see it." He spoke in a gentle voice while observing the reaction in her face.

She placed her hand on Axel's wide, bony shoulder. "So that is what you have been keeping bottled up inside of you all this time. You should not have because I also have been thinking about those things. I kept telling myself that it can't be true, while deep inside I know that it is. When I was younger and had the energy it did not bother me so much, but at my age and with two sons of military age, it would be too much to bear." She cast tender glances at Erik. He had stopped eating, captivated by the exchange taking place between his parents.

"You are right, father," she continued. "I don't think that at my age I can stand to see my sons slaughtered and my grandchildren taken away."

Axel's face brightened. He had not expected this type of a response from his wife. The surprise was delightful and his face broke into a broad smile.

"But what can we do?" she fretted. "You know that in time of war there are not many places in which to hide in Poland. They come at us from every direction; the Prussians and Germans from the north and west, the Russians from the east and the Austrians and Hungarians from the south. The only ones that we don't need to worry about anymore are the Turks, and that is only after a thousand years of harassment. Then there are the Italians. You never know about them. One day they are your friends and the next day they are your enemies. The only real friends that we have are the British and the French, and sometime I am not so sure about the French. But how can they help us when we are surrounded by enemies?"

Axel realized that his success so far had been better than he had anticipated, but he also knew that his wife's love for Europe and Poland might defy reason and upset his plans, so he would have to choose his words carefully.

"I had another idea. I thought that we could move away from Poland completely," he said as he observed her reaction.

"What? Move away from Poland? How can I do that!" she pleaded. "You know that the bones of my ancestors from a hundred generations back are buried in this soil and you want me to violate their memory by running away from my own home? The banks of the Vistula River are the graveyard of many of my ancestors who died to protect this land from her enemies.

May God have mercy on their souls. How can I abandon my beloved country after all that they had to endure and sacrifice in order to defend this land so that we may enjoy it?"

"You forget, my dear, that Poland does not belong to the Polish people anymore. It belongs to the conquerors and in a few more years it may be only a memory of a state that once was, like the Kingdom of Bohemia; so there really is not much left to enjoy," said Axel.

Mrs. Berglund glared at Axel in defiance, the color mounting in her face and contrasting sharply with her graying hair which was pulled over her head into a bun at the back of her head.

"I will never abandon hope. As long as Polish blood runs through my veins, I will continue to live and hope for the liberation of my country." She paused and observed the puzzled look on Erik's face. "And anyway, at our age where would we go?" she pleaded in a helpless tone.

"Canada," answered Axel, relieved at her partial surrender. He thought he saw his son cringe.

"Canada?" she reared back in disbelief. "Incredible! Why that's on the other side of the world! The wild animals there are probably more dangerous than the Russians and Prussians are here. And the cold! I hear that it is always winter there. Of all the places in the world, why Canada?"

Axel leaned back in his chair. "Well, first of all, those things that you say about the country are not entirely true. Canada is a huge country. In area it is bigger than all of Europe put together. And sure, some parts of it are wild and some are cold, but other parts are no colder, and in fact maybe less cold, than Poland. The land there is new and anyone can own land who wants to work it. And now this land is free. But the best part is that there are no wars. People from all parts of the world leave their old hostilities behind and live peacefully side by side," explained Axel.

He was about to continue when Stanislaw entered the room. "I am glad you're here, son. Now you can tell your mother and Erik what Wladimar Bashinski told you in Warsaw about Canada."

"Has Erik persuaded you so quickly to give away our secret?" he asked his father.

"It is hard to keep secrets from your own kin. It's like keeping them from yourself," apologized Axel. "I know that we would have liked to gather more information from Litvak and the others before we arrived at a decision, but I couldn't hold myself back and I let the horse out of the barn."

"Well then it is too late to close the barn door." Stanislaw's broad smile revealed that he, too, was relieved that now there were four to share their secret.

"Good. Now that we all know what we are talking about, why don't you explain with your own mouth what Bashinski explained to you in Warsaw."

"That would please me very much," said Stanislaw, "but first I would like to get some food into the mouth that you speak about."

They laughed as Stanislaw filled his plate from the pots on the kitchen stove. He sat down at the table with slow deliberate motions. He was tall and lean and the contours of the muscles in his arms and chest showed through his shirt. Because he was older than Erik, he had escaped being taken into custody by the Prussians following the aborted uprising in 1901. During Erik's absence he had married and moved into a small cottage a short distance from his parents' house. The yard was large enough to enable him to keep a cow and some chickens. His wife tended a large garden while he helped his father in the furniture shop. But Stanislaw loved the land and land in Russian-occupied Poland was scarce and not readily available to Poles. He had listened to stories about the homesteads available in Canada and went to Warsaw to investigate. Upon his return he convinced his father that they should emigrate from Poland and seek a new life in Canada.

"So you two were hatching a plan to steal away and leave me here by myself. Now, is that a nice thing to do to your son and brother?" quipped Erik in apparent jest.

"Oh no, Erik," his father corrected him. "We did not start to form our plan seriously until after we heard that you were in Torun. Stanislaw, go ahead tell him what you heard and saw in Warsaw."

"I had a long discussion with Bashinski there last week," began Stanislaw. "He told me how a large number of Polish people were emigrating to Canada and America. They say that it is easier to get to Canada than to America because Canada is concentrating on getting its central plains settled with farmers. Many of those who have gone there have written back and described the conditions which they have experienced. They describe a magnificent country with enough of everything for everybody. There it does not matter which country you come from. Everyone is treated equally and fairly. Polish people work and live side by side with Germans, Russians, Jews, English, Scots, French and many other nationalities to build a new country where there will be freedom and opportunity for all. Old grudges which have existed for centuries here are forgotten as people go about building their new homes. At school the children are taught English, but at home and in the community the families are allowed to use their own languages and continue their old traditional ways if they choose."

"What about the weather and the loneliness?" asked Mrs. Berglund. "Who does one talk to in the wilderness?"

"Oh, it's not that bad, mother," explained Stanislaw. "The weather is not much different than that to which we are accustomed in northeastern Europe. As far as loneliness is concerned, there is really not much time for that. They have more than enough happening to keep themselves occupied, and besides, people from a certain country tend to settle in close communities. That way they can help each other as well as preserve some of their old ways. They build their own churches and converse in their own languages. Some of Bashinski's relatives are already there. In their letters they speak glowingly of rich virgin land that requires little tilling and is free from weeds. They describe how the forests abound in firewood and logs which are free for the taking, as well as in wild fruits, nuts and mushrooms. The rivers and lakes are teeming with fish, and wild chickens and rabbits come right up into the farmyards."

Stanislaw's excitement was penetrating his mother's recalcitrance. "How could you two keep all this from me for so long? Sometime you treat me like a child, father," she said staring at Axel.

"Oh no, mama," explained Axel. "We just did not want to worry you with all this until we were certain that Erik was safe. As soon as we saw him here we agreed that we should have a family discussion. However, I should say that we had originally intended to have this discussion tomorrow after you and Erik had a chance to get over the excitement of his return. But he pried it out of me." Axel glanced at Erik and winked.

"Are you sure that all these things that you hear about Canada are not just propaganda and land promotion schemes?" asked Erik.

"I checked into that aspect of it, too," replied Stanislaw. "Uncle Bashinski and I went to the Canadian Immigration Office in Warsaw and talked to an officer there. And do you know what? He spoke Polish. He had been in Canada only ten years when he got this important government job. He told us which city he came from. I believe it was Lodz. Among the photos that he showed us were some of other Polish families who have already settled there. The pictures show the type of homes that they have built on their farms. Many of them are quite similar to the cottages one sees around here. They dress differently there, but for special occasions they sometime wear traditional Polish attire. You should have seen the size that wheat grows to out there. I saw a picture of a man standing in a field of wheat and you could barely see his hat."

Axel and Erik laughed at Stanislaw's enthusiasm and apparent exaggeration. "Maybe he was a short man," quipped Axel.

"They told us at the immigration office that any family that is willing to settle on the land can get one hundred and sixty acres of land free. This is about sixty-five hectares. There are many large areas that are still available for settlement," continued Stanislaw.

Axel whistled in disbelief. "That is a lot of land for free."

"If you should decide to go," remarked Erik, "will you have enough money to take care of everything? I imagine that you would need quite a lot of it."

"Stanislaw says that the only thing that we need to worry about is to have enough money for the passage there and some to live on until we start growing our own crops. As far as the cost of obtaining the land is concerned, that is almost nothing. All that one has to pay is ten dollars for a homestead registration fee. That comes to about twenty-five rubles. We can take some of our things with us from here because the Canadian railway company has a special transportation arrangement for settlers."

Axel hesitated momentarily in the manner of a lawyer concluding his argument. He turned to his wife. "Well mama, what do you think?"

She paused for a moment, gazing serenely out the window into the distance. She turned around slowly and answered in a soft voice. "Only if my cousin Wladimar tells me himself that what you two have said is true, and then only if Erik comes with us, too."

As his mother spoke, Erik sat in his chair deep in thought. All eyes in the room focused on him. With his elbows resting on the table, he covered his face with his hands to steal a moment of privacy. Only the crackling of the wood fire broke the silence. The decision seemed to take an eternity.

"I do not think that it will be such a simple matter for me to decide to go with you, since I still do not enjoy that degree of freedom," he finally stated. "But do not let that hold you back. You proceed with your plans." He closed his eyes and continued to examine his thoughts, then revealed his decision. "I will consider carefully my situation in Torun and perhaps I may be able to join you later."

"That is good, my son," said his mother, as though she alone understood the gravity of the situation. "But let us put our trust in the hands of the Lord. He alone will decide our fate and lead us in the way that is best for us. May His will be served." She turned to the crucifix and crossed herself.

"What you say is true, mama, but we still need to point ourselves in the right direction if we want Him to lead us," quipped Axel.

Stanislaw sat with his arms folded as he followed the course of the discussion among his parents and brother, arranging in his mind the parts that their decisions would play in the plan that he had already set for himself. To him, their decisions were important, but not crucial, since he had already decided that he would leave Poland with or without them. If they came also, it would make his own departure that much easier because fewer ties would have to be severed. Now that his mother and brother had spoken, his weathered face beamed in approval. He stood up slowly, stretching his lean body toward the low ceiling.

"I will go and tell my wife," he announced. "She will be pleased to hear that we will not be alone in a new country." At the door he stopped and looked outside. Anna and her two children had just entered the yard.

"I see them heading this way now," he noted.

Stanislaw opened the door wide and two small children, a four-year-old girl and a younger boy, entered reluctantly, followed by their mother. They peeked at Erik from behind their mother's skirt.

"Don't be shy," said their father. "This is your uncle Erik. He doesn't bite."

"These two will make a couple of fine Canadians. What do you think?" thundered Axel gleefully.

The two youngsters, recognizing that they were the centre of attraction timidly approached Erik, observing his facial expression. "Go sit on your uncle's knee," ordered Axel. Encouraged by their grandfather, the two children approached Erik and he lifted them up to his knees. His face broke into a broad smile as he glanced around the room to observe the expressions of the others.

"Do you know that this is the closest that I have been to children since I went away," Erik explained.

"You look very natural with them and the children really take to you. That means that you will make a good father," said Anna observing Erik.

~~~

The bells of the village church pealed their melancholy cadence as they had done every Sunday morning for more than three hundred years. When Erik awoke his mother had already left for the early morning mass. In the kitchen his father laid out the dishes for the breakfast that his wife had prepared before she left for church.

"Good morning, son. You are just in time for breakfast," said Axel when Erik entered the kitchen. "This is going to be another eventful day, so we should face it with a full stomach."

They helped themselves to sliced cold pork, hard boiled eggs and hot cornmeal cake which Axel had placed on the table.

"I asked Litvak to come early," said Axel after they had finished their meal. "I thought that we could use his advice on some of the things that we discussed yesterday." Axel recognized the skeptical look in Erik's face. "You do not appear to be convinced of Litvak's wisdom in some of these things. But I am, because I have no reason to think otherwise. Over the years he has given me good advice in many different things and I have come to trust him like a brother."

"Yes, I think I know what you mean, father," said Erik. "On our way down here the other night we had a long talk. He sounds like an honorable and intelligent man. I am sure that any advice that he can give you will be very useful."

"If you believe that then why do you not appear to respect him?" Axel looked at Erik inquisitively. "Could it be something that you learned at school during those years that you were away?"

"I have been asking myself some similar questions since I first saw him, and that could be one of them. There just seems to be something inside of me telling me that I should not trust him. I do not want to feel that way but I do," said Erik.

They looked out the kitchen window and watched Mrs. Berglund walking down the footpath toward the house, her face rosy from the cool morning air. She shuffled through the leaves that had fallen and formed a golden carpet which gleamed in the bright morning sun. A flood of brilliant sunlight rushed into the kitchen when she opened the door. She handed Erik a small package wrapped in crumpled brown paper. He eyed the package curiously.

She took it back from him. "I will open it for you," she said, removing the paper wrapping to reveal a small wooden crucifix. She put the crucifix in Erik's hand. "Take this back with you. It has been blessed by the priest. Meditate on it in times of trouble or despair. Let it remind you that the source of all strength and hope is God."

Erik fingered the crucifix awkwardly then took it to the bedroom and placed it gently beside his backpack.

"On this side we are very fortunate," said his mother when he returned to the kitchen. "The Russians have not interfered with our church. May the good Lord protect the Czar for showing this good judgment and guide him into the way of peace."

"The czar has too many other problems. He has no time left to fight the Pope, too," remarked Axel with a twinkle in his eyes.

CHAPTER 5

The fading September sun had already commenced its descent when Litvak drove into the yard in a one-horse cart. Only Axel heard him arrive. The others were in the house where Anna and her mother-in-law scurried about the kitchen preparing the dinner, and Erik and Stanislaw were deep in conversation. Litvak's entrance reminded them that time was fleeting and soon Erik would have to leave. Erik tried unsuccessfully to hide his dismay.

"Is it almost time to leave?" he asked.

"No. We still have some time left," replied Litvak with a note of levity in his voice. "You still have time to spend with your family, but we should leave here at around five o'clock if we are to arrive at your rendezvous by six."

Axel looked around the room and detected that a melancholy mood was replacing the happy atmosphere which had prevailed earlier. He clapped his huge hands together in front of his face and roared, "What are all these sour faces doing here? The world is not about to end. Stanislaw, fetch that bottle of fine Polish vodka from the cupboard and let us drink a toast to our future and to our good fortune in the new world."

Litvak cast an inquisitive glance at Axel. His dark beard could not hide the bewildered look on his face. "I do not care to drink a toast to a mystery. Please, what is this new world business all about?"

With an air of exaggerated exuberance, Axel broke the news to Litvak. "My good friend, Stanislaw and I have been discussing now for some time what we can do to change our lives and those of our children and grandchildren. More recently we have been thinking about what you told us Friday night, as well as what we have been hearing from others. This weekend we all agreed that since the clouds of war are once again on the horizon all around us, and since mama and I are too old to run and our sons are too young to die, we chose the only other alternative and that is to leave."

Litvak observed Axel momentarily in apparent disbelief. "You make it sound like it was a quick and easy decision, but I am sure that it was more than that. I am shocked and cannot think of the appropriate words for the occasion. Nevertheless, you are fortunate to have a family that thinks clearly, Pan Berglund. Don't think that I have not thought about the lure of America myself. I would make the same decision tomorrow if my dear wife had the good sense to agree to it. As it is, I am afraid that it will not happen and we will remain here and hope for the best. But that is enough about my sorrowful state. You, no doubt know where you are going and can share the secret with me."

"We are still looking for good advice. That is why I asked you to come early thinking that perhaps you could give us some information and counsel. We have heard about the free land that is available to settlers in Canada and thought that maybe we could try to get some of it. They say that it is some of the best crop and grazing land in the world," Axel explained.

Litvak sat down slowly, with a faraway look in his face. He shook his head in disbelief. "How quickly things can change in a person's life," he mused. "I too have heard about the free land available in Canada and I understand that what you say is true. But if you would tell me about these things and not keep it all a secret, I might be able to help you." Litvak feigned exasperation. "Through my contacts in Warsaw I have already made it possible for several families to get their visas and passages arranged. It can be a difficult task, but one which can be made much simpler if you know how."

"One of the Canadian immigration officers in Warsaw whom Stanislaw contacted speaks Polish well. He can explain to us what is required," said Axel.

Litvak looked at the others plaintively, his outstretched palms in front of him. "So here I am trying to help the man and he scorns me. Has pride got no bounds?"

"It is not as simple as it sounds, father," explained Stanislaw. "In addition to the visas there will be birth certificates to secure, health warrants to acquire, ocean passage to arrange, decisions to make with regard to our specific destination, and many other details. We will need all the help that we can get. It will take several months to complete all of this. Even if we start now, it will be spring before we are ready to leave."

"Oh, how fortunate you are," said Litvak. "How I would love to have a piece of that land, just a small plot that I could call my own. But for me that is impossible."

"You?" Axel appeared surprised. "I thought that your people were merchants, not farmers."

"We are merchants out of necessity, not choice," explained Litvak quietly. "We were the original farmers, remember? Long before anyone else got the idea to till the soil, except maybe the Mesopotamians, we were farmers. But our land had been taken away from us so often that we have had to give up our claim to it and seek shelter in commercial enterprises. But why are we wasting time talking about me when it is your lives that will be changing. And what about Erik? How do you propose to get him out of the Prussian zone?" Litvak aimed his question at Axel.

"If he can make his way across the border, he could join us on the day that we leave," Axel assured him.

"Of course. And the rooster will lay an egg. How far do you think that you will get with a fugitive at your side, especially since most of the emigrants bound for Canada embark at Hamburg?"

"All right, all right, I see your point. It's just that you have done so much for us already. I do not feel right asking you for any more help," he explained.

"So who is asking? No one is asking for help. I am offering it," corrected Litvak.

"Since you are so willing, anything that you can do for us will be appreciated," said Axel humbly.

"Now you are talking sense," said Litvak.

"We shall begin immediately."

Axel filled their glasses and raised his. "To the future."

"To the future, Pan Berglund," toasted Litvak. "And to the future of all of your beautiful family gathered here today. May you have many more reunions like this one."

The farewells were as cheerless as the arrival had been joyful. His mother's weeping made it difficult for Erik and the others to remain composed. Axel wiped the imaginary sweat off his forehead with the sleeve of his shirt, propitiously running it across his eyes at the same time. "Control yourself, mama," he admonished his wife. There is not much to cry about now. Our son has been found and he will soon be back. We have much to be thankful for."

"Yes, mother," added Erik. "I will send word with Pan Litvak's man as soon as I can. And it should not be too long before I see you again now that I have more freedom to move about."

"No need to worry about anything," Litvak reassured them. "All that Erik has to do is send us his message and we will be there promptly." He moved closer to Erik and spoke in a lowered voice. "Let us review our plan for today. This is what I propose that we do. When we get close to the border I will take a little-used trail which leads to a farmhouse facing the boundary line. There is no sentry at that point. The farmer who lives there is named Dashevski and he will be expecting you. At the appropriate time you will enter the main road which runs in front of the house and follow it to the bridge. Once on the road, no one will notice you as the road is well traveled and many people from Torun take it. It will take you to the Drweca and the bridge. How do you feel about that idea?"

"I am afraid that I cannot improve upon that plan. It sounds good to me," answered Erik.

The final handshakes and kisses were showered upon Erik inside the house in order to escape the attention of the neighbors. Once outside, Erik leaped into the cart and joined Litvak on the seat. As they turned into the lane, Erik looked back and acknowledged the waves of the small group left behind. The vehicle and passengers disappeared around the corner and the others returned to the house in silence.

~~~

Litvak held the reins taut as the horse arched its graceful neck and trotted effortlessly onto the open highway. Compared to the mode of travel of two nights earlier, when they moved slowly through the night in a heavily laden wagon drawn by two draft horses, their new mode of travel was the ultimate in speed and comfort. The sound of the narrow wheels moving over the road surface had a hypnotizing effect on them. Litvak broke the long silence.

"What do you think of the idea that your father and brother have?" he asked.

"It will not be easy for my parents," answered Erik. "I am concerned about them traveling that distance at their age. But once they get to their destination, Stanislaw and Anna will be there to help them out. It will be difficult for mother to abandon her beloved Poland, but the separation might do her good. She has suffered too much and deserves to spend her remaining years in peace."

"I have never seen your father so intent on doing something since he arrived in Lubicz. Between your arrival and his new plan, he seems to have taken on a new life. But I will dearly miss them. They are decent folks. And how about you Erik, what are your plans?" asked Litvak.

Erik stared at the road stretching out ahead of them. "I think I will remain here," he said slowly, and then added, "for a few months anyway. After I get some more experience at the foundry it should be easier for me to get work over there. You see, I don't think that I want to be a farmer."

"That is your choice, of course," observed Litvak. "But don't forget, when you make up your mind and are ready, let me know. I will be there to help you if you need me."

~~~

An opening in the overhanging branches of a thick willow hedge, shaped like a mushroom by browsing animals, marked the spot where the little-used wagon trail accessed the main road. The green leaves of the willows had not yet changed color and shone in stark contrast to the brown grass on either side. Dense hazel bushes cut off the view from the road like a curtain. Litvak steered the horse through the opening and followed the grass-covered trail.

"This is a good route with which to become familiar," he advised Erik. "It is mainly used by the local farmers driving their hay wagons and it crosses the border at a most inconspicuous and unguarded spot. If you should want to travel unnoticed this is a good road to take."

The small vehicle bounced violently on its springs as they followed the rutted trail. After what seemed like two or three kilometers they came to the bottom of a small knoll at the top of which stood a small whitewashed cottage surrounded by lattice fence and shaded by four large trees.

"That is Dashevski's place. I must turn around and go back," said Litvak. He brought the horse to a stop behind a large oak. "You will go directly to the house. Knock and tell them your name. They are expecting you, so do not be afraid." He held out his hand. "It has been an eventful time for all of us. Bless you, my boy, and may good fortune shine upon you."

Erik shook Litvak's hand and jumped out of the cart. "Thank you, Pan Litvak. Your kindness shall always be remembered."

He cautiously approached the tidy cottage following a path that cut through a colorful flower garden. He knocked on the door. Someone stirred inside.

"Who is it?" asked a man's voice in German.

"It is I, Berglund."

"Oh yes. Come in."

The man and his wife asked him no questions, but they seemed to be aware of who he was and where he was going. From the front yard of the Dashevski home the smoking chimneys and roof tops of the houses in Torun were clearly visible. It was only a twenty minute walk to the bridge, they told him. The road was well traveled and used mainly by the local farmers so he should be able to walk along it relatively unobserved.

The brilliant orange rays of the descending sun spilled across the landscape when Erik stepped out of Dashevski's gate and headed for the road at twenty-five minutes to six. Because he was unfamiliar with the road he thought that he would take a few extra minutes to reach his destination. The Dashevskis had assured him that because it was Sunday evening there would not be many travelers on the road except for the local people. Indeed, the area was almost deserted as Erik walked toward the town, except for groups of children out playing in their yards or watching over small herds of cows. But in spite of this Erik felt that he was at centre stage and a thousand eyes were focused upon him. He walked briskly, his eyes concentrating on the outline of the city ahead of him. Barking dogs emerged from the yards and snapped at his heels, increasing his feeling of conspicuousness. He did not turn his head, but out of the corners of his eyes he imagined that he saw faces in the windows of the houses that he passed, watching him suspiciously. The descending dusk and unfamiliar landscape added to his alienation. The familiar outline of the bridge in the distance stilled his anxiety and he felt a warm comfortable feeling coming over him. He accelerated his step.

Aware that he was a few minutes early for his rendezvous with Roman, he leaned over the rusty railing and stared at the swiftly swirling current of the Drweca. The water, brown with mud which had been washed from the upstream fields during a recent rainstorm, flowed lazily toward its destiny with the mighty Vistula. Relaxed after his anxious moments only minutes before, Erik stared at the water, hypnotized by its soothing movement and sound. Suddenly remembering his appointment with Roman, he straightened up and walked to the other side of the bridge.

Everything was quiet. There was no one there. Had Roman forgotten their arrangement? He listened intently for a few seconds. The sound of water trickling over a stony obstruction nearby floated through the still air, punctuated only by the ebb and flow of the muted sounds from the nearby city. Suddenly there was a crash in a nearby hazel bush and a dark form darted out in front of him. Erik froze.

"You are right on time," laughed Roman, brushing the stems and leaves off his clothes. Erik stood transfixed, pale and terrified. He recognized Roman.

"Are you trying to kill me? My heart nearly stopped," he gasped.

"I was just testing to see if you were alert," explained Roman. "On the contrary, it is good for your heart. It conditions you for the real thing should it ever occur."

Erik regained his composure and wiped his brow with the back of his hand. "You just wait, my friend, I'll get even with you." They walked toward Torun still laughing at Roman's caper.

The low barrack-style single men's dormitory stood sentinel-like in the gathering darkness. Hilda stood in the open kitchen door silhouetted in the yellow lamplight. When she recognized the young men her round face broke out into a broad smile.

"Well, if it isn't my two favorite boys," she called. "Welcome home. You must be tired and hungry. I have saved some delicious food for you – something that will stick to your ribs. Come in and sit down."

Hilda shuffled into the kitchen and quickly emerged with two plates covered with cold meats, cheeses and dark bread.

"Tea will be ready in a minute," she announced. "It was lonely around here without you two boys. Did you enjoy yourselves?"

The two young men looked at each other blankly waiting for the other to answer.

"No. You do not have to explain. I know that you young roosters have secrets that you would rather not share with an old lady." Her massive bosom shook as she laughed. She watched with obvious delight as the young men devoured huge slices of bread piled high with sliced meats and cheese, and grunted contentedly. They helped Hilda to clean up and returned to the dormitory.

Their billet seemed far removed from the world of which Erik had been a part only a few hours ago. He lay on his back staring at the ceiling. The familiar surroundings offered a haven of security and escape from the unsettled reality of the outside world. In some ways he felt glad to be back and away from the fears and suspicions of the other world which he had just visited.

"My head is spinning from all that has happened during the past two days," he sighed.

"I can't wait to hear it all." Roman tried to hide his curiosity and anticipation. "But you can tell me later. We will have lots of time to talk."

"Oh, no. I want to share it with you promptly. It's just that I do not know where to begin."

Erik's mind consciously began to organize the events of the past forty-eight hours as his eyes focused on a fly preening its wings on the ceiling. Scenes from the past two days marched through his mind and he arranged them in the proper order. He sat up in bed to begin.

A loud knock at the door startled the young men and they jumped to their feet. Roman opened the door cautiously. Outlined against the dim light in the hallway stood Rudolf Doering, Erik's foreman at the foundry. The puzzled looks on the young men's faces betrayed their bewilderment as they tried to appear composed. Doering appeared not to notice. His flushed face always suggested that he had just run a kilometer or climbed a hundred stairs, but reflected no other expression.

"Ha. That is what I like to see, punctuality," announced Doering. "I am glad to see that you two boys are back on time. Erik, I have a message for you."

His voice assumed a more official tone as he reached into his pocket and handed Erik a folded piece of paper. "On this paper is the name of the head of our division. He wants to see you an hour before our regular starting time tomorrow."

Erik opened the paper. The name on it appeared blurred. "Thank you, Herr Doering. I will be there," he blurted.

The two young men stood motionless as the foreman's footsteps faded down the hallway. Erik slumped in his chair, a note of desperation in his voice

"Oh Lord. You don't think that they are on to me, Roman?" He closed his eyes in deep thought. "But how could they be? Only you knew where I was. Nobody else saw me." He paused. "Unless..."

"Unless what?" Roman jumped to his feet, his face flushed. "You do not think that I betrayed you?"

"You are being very foolish, Roman. That thought never entered my mind. I was thinking that maybe what my father's friend, the Jewish trader, said is true. He warned me Friday night to stay out of sight as much as possible and not trust anybody, not even my parents' neighbors. In these days of uncertainty one can never become too overconfident, he said."

"Ah, let us come to our senses," pleaded Roman. "The whole thing probably has nothing at all to do with your trip to the other side. Anyway, I told everyone I could that you are going to be with me all the time. We will make up a foolproof story that no one can question or expose."

The task of inventing a plausible story describing their activities for the past two days occupied them for the next few hours. Speaking in hushed tones they pieced together imaginary events and places which occupied them during the fictitious weekend. When they were satisfied that the story sounded convincing, they retired for the night and Roman was soon fast asleep.

But Erik was denied the reprieve that sleep alone could bring. In the deep crevices of his brain, numerous fantasies were being contrived. One by one they catapulted to the center stage of his mind, swelled to a crescendo then faded into space only to be succeeded by other more forceful images. He concentrated on thoughts which would relax him – his father's shop, Saturday morning in his mother's kitchen, the rippling waters of the Drweca – but these scenes were quickly erased by the assault of the other more powerful images surging through his brain. In the light of the moon flowing through the window, he looked at the clock on the wall. It was two-thirty.

"Dear Lord," he prayed silently, "I know that I am often a skeptic and some time I don't believe in your divine presence, but if you are out there, help me through this night."

He reached for the crucifix which his mother had given him and clutched it. By three o'clock he dozed off into a fitful sleep. He dreamed that Monday morning had arrived. Just as he finished his breakfast a squad of soldiers marched into the mess hall and took him to the general's office.

Behind the huge desk was Hilda, dressed in a general's uniform, her huge bosom covered with medals and ribbons. On her left eye was a wire-framed monocle through which she observed him. Her gaze pierced him to the core.

"Is this the prisoner? Bring him to me." she ordered. She stood up and walked around him, scrutinizing him carefully. Removing her monocle she proclaimed in a thundering official voice, "Berglund, you are charged with impersonating a Prussian. We have been watching you carefully and have concluded that you are really a Jew. As punishment you are sentenced to be banished to Canada for the rest of your natural life. However, to make the sentence more fitting to the crime, you shall be required to swim the distance between Hamburg and Halifax. That is all. Take him away."

The soldiers marched Erik to the beach and the squad leader pointed across the water to the west. He looked at the water stretching endlessly into the horizon. Small ripples covered the surface as far as he could see. Erik removed his jacket and boots and walked slowly into the murky water. It was warm and clingy, like oil. He swam for a long time until he came to a ship moored in the ocean.

His eyes followed the tall rust-encrusted hull to the top of the vessel where he observed Litvak standing on the deck looking down over the railing. He wore the uniform of a British admiral. Litvak motioned for him to come on board. As Erik reached for the ladder lowered down for him, he missed the rung and the vessel pulled away. He awoke with a start, his flesh cold and his skin covered with goose pimples.

In the dim light of the moon, he noticed that the hands on the clock were on twelve and five. His temples throbbed as he sat up in bed. If he got up now, he reasoned, he would have ample time to finish breakfast and arrive promptly for his appointment with the division head as Doering had ordered the night before. Roman was still fast asleep. Erik dressed quietly and tip-toed out to the washroom in the hall.

In the kitchen Hilda was surrounded by boiling kettles, steaming pots of porridge, hot frying pans, loaves of bread and jugs of milk.

"My, aren't you up early today," she observed when Erik entered the dining hall.

"Yes, I am," replied Erik. "I have an early appointment with the division head."

Hilda whistled to indicate her astonishment. Erik remembered his dream and observed her strangely. "Don't you ever sleep?" he asked.

"Oh yes, I do. But when I do, I sleep. I don't sneak around the bushes the way some tomcats around here do." She gave Erik a perceptive sideways glance and broke into a hearty laugh.

CHAPTER 6

The pewter-gray dawn crept in slowly and nudged out the darkness, making room for the reluctant morning light. Erik left the dining hall and walked toward the foundry administration and research wing. Each step forward seemed to drain the small remnants of energy within him. The guard observed him curiously when he presented his pass at the gate. Erik wondered if this is what it would feel like to be walking toward the gallows.

At the front office in the administration building the two night watchmen had just been relieved by the day crew. One of them checked Erik's pass, then returned it to him. He did not appear to be concerned about Erik's unusual arrival time. The second watchman sat behind a desk. He motioned to Erik to come to closer.

"I have an appointment with Herr Schmidt," said Erik, handing the watchman the piece of paper with the appointment time and place which he had received from Doering the night before. The watchman referred to the appointment book on the desk.

"Follow me, Berglund," he instructed.

They walked past several empty executive offices whose occupants had not yet arrived. In some of the larger ones the well-stocked bookcases and fine furniture testified to the lofty positions held by their occupants. They stopped in front of Number 12. The door was closed but a bar of yellow light spilled out from under it. The guard knocked and a deep raspy voice inside answered.

"Who is it?"

"Berglund to see you, sir," announced the watchman.

"Oh, yes. Come right in Berglund."

Erik stood in front of the large wooden desk. Its polished surface reflected the light of the two desk lamps perched at each end. A tall man with graying mustache and neatly-cropped sideburns sat in a large chair, framed by its huge back which was upholstered in shiny black leather and trimmed with polished wood. His piercing blue eyes surveyed Erik quickly. He motioned him to sit down.

"My name is Schmidt," he said. "I have been hearing a lot about you, Berglund."

Erik thought that he felt his heart sinking into his stomach and he swallowed hard. He tried to speak but no sounds emerged from his dry throat.

"Yes, you are a most unusual one," continued Schmidt. He opened a file and perused it. He closed it and laid it on the desk while observing Erik.

"Berglund, you show a lot of promise. Your foreman reports that you are intelligent, conscientious, ambitious, a good draftsman and designer and a potential metallurgist. Nowadays there are not many young men who exhibit all these qualities and we consider ourselves fortunate that you have been chosen to work here." He paused and lit a cigarette, removed it from his mouth and blew the smoke at the burning end.

"We are about to embark on the development of some important new products here." He spoke slowly, his eyes fixed on Erik. "This will demand a lot of talent and ingenuity, as well as hard work, dedication and trust." He drew out and emphasized the latter. "We think that you have all these qualities, Berglund, and we feel that you will fit in well with the team that we are building. Starting next Monday you will begin to spend half of your time in the research and development center here and the other half at your old work station. Since you speak both German and Polish well, I have advised your foreman to also assign you the responsibility of helping to observe some of the new technicians that are assigned to your present department and help to choose those that are above average for this project. To compensate you for your added responsibilities, I am putting through an order today for a raise in pay for you starting immediately."

"Thank you, sir. I am flattered that you have so much faith in me. I will do my best." He strained to get the words out.

"I should mention again, Berglund, that there is a lot of trust that goes with this assignment and there will be some confidential information involved which must remain here at all times," admonished Schmidt in a stern voice.

"I understand, sir," said Erik.

"All right now. If you have no questions you may get back to your own department. Herr Doering has been advised about this arrangement and will help you to make the transition. Good luck, Berglund. Keep up the good work."

Erik started toward the door when he heard Schmidt's voice behind him. He turned around.

"By the way, Berglund, do you have a lady friend?" asked Schmidt.

"No sir," he answered.

"That is too bad," said Schmidt. "A bright young man like you should be thinking about settling down. There are lots of nice young German girls around."

"But I am only twenty, sir," explained Erik.

"Yes. Maybe that is a bit young, but it may be time to start looking," remarked Herr Schmidt. Erik thought he detected a smile on the man's face. "By the way, Berglund, I understand that you have a family."

"Yes sir. They live in Lubicz, in the Russian zone."

"Yes. I know the place. Do you ever see them?" he asked.

"I would very much like to, sir." Erik dodged the question skillfully.

"Well maybe that could be arranged," said Schmidt. "We will let you know."

"You are very kind, sir. Thank you again."

Erik pulled the heavy door shut. As he stepped outside, the dark ominous cloud of fear which he had carried into the room lifted abruptly, leaving him exhilarated and relieved. He seemed to float though the corridors and across the courtyard. His feet, which earlier had felt like lead, turned into gossamer, flying buoyantly over the hard-packed ground. The day shift workers were arriving, and as he made his way through them, he felt a sensation of swimming through a sea of faces. He realized that he would have to tell somebody quickly or he would not be able to contain the good news. Doering was at his office when Erik arrived. But before Erik had an opportunity to announce the news, Doering stuck out his hand.

"Congratulations, Erik." He pumped Erik's hand. "I am sure that we can put together a competent and efficient team."

This was the first time that Doering had called him by his first name. His heart pounded inside his chest. A strange and delectable feeling consumed him.

~~~

Roman was leaning against the door frame of their billet with an apprehensive look on his face when Erik returned from the foundry. It was obvious that he had been waiting anxiously for his roommate's return.

"Well...?" His voice trailed, revealing that he did not know what to expect.

"Sit down, sit down," exhorted Erik with new-found bravado. He was having difficulty controlling his enthusiasm and Roman, recognizing that the earlier anticipated tragedy seemed to have been averted, sat down, relieved.

"You were right!" blurted out Erik. "We did let our imaginations run away with us unnecessarily. Herr Schmidt only wanted to inform me that I was being transferred to the research and development department on a part-time basis. He also wants me to help to mentor some of the new Polish speaking apprentices when they come in."

"So you fall into the pig trough and come out smelling of flowers. Congratulations. But I must be careful what I say. You are an upper crust now and I am just a lowly junior apprentice." Roman sounded almost serious.

"Don't be silly," scolded Erik. "We are friends, and our friendship transcends our positions. I will hear no more of that seniority stuff. And beside that we are both Polish and, therefore, are in the same shoes regardless of our occupational titles."

"I am glad that you are not one of those whose head is subject to fits of swelling," remarked Roman, "so please accept my sincere congratulations. I tell you what. Remember that comment I made about including you in some of my future plans before you left for Lubicz? Why don't we celebrate your promotion by following up on those plans? Lydia has a friend named Angela. She is a Polish girl from the Austrian zone who works in the textile factory here as a pattern designer. According to Lydia she is very anxious to meet you. Maybe the four of us could get together this Sunday and you can get to meet her."

"That sounds good," said Erik, "but as you know, I have not had many occasions to meet girls, so I am a bit awkward in that department."

"I am sure that you will get along just fine," Roman assured him.

"How can all these wonderful and exciting things happen to a person all at one time?" asked Erik as he flopped down into his bed.

"Maybe it's because of your virtuous living," quipped Roman with a mischievous twinkle in his eyes.

~~~

Even though it was still early in the afternoon, the weak autumn sun and low hanging clouds made the hour appear later than the clock on the wall indicated. It was two-thirty on Friday and Erik was gathering his drafting equipment in preparation for the move to the research and development department. Foreman Doering emerged from his office followed by a tall, lean man in a white smock. They walked to the edge of Erik's drafting table and the red-haired, clean shaven man held out is hand.

"My name is Herman Richter. I am from the research and development department," he said.

"I am honored to meet you, sir." Erik immediately felt comfortable and relaxed in the man's presence.

"Herr Richter is the director of the special research project with which you will be involved, Erik," said Doering. "He is one of the country's best engineers. So don't try to outsmart him."

"Don't let Rudolf frighten you." Richter's forehead wrinkled when he smiled. "I am sure that we will make a good team. Are you ready to come with me now? Perhaps we can go to the other building and I could show you your new workplace."

"If Herr Doering is agreeable, I am ready," answered Erik.

"Herr Richter and his project take precedence over what we are doing here," counseled Doering. "As of now you will report to him except when you are working or doing training or assessments in my department. Good luck, Erik. Don't forget who taught you all that you know about drafting and mixing alloys." Erik thought that for the first time since he had known him, he detected the trace of a smile on Doering's face.

The research and development department was housed in a large one-storey building consisting of two wings. Erik had often walked by it and speculated on what its mysterious white-smocked inhabitants might be doing there. Now he and Richter were inside the long hallway leading to the smaller wing of the building which was divided into a number of offices, drafting rooms and laboratories. Near the main drafting room, a large blue-print library accommodated what appeared to be thousands of drawings. Across the hall from it was the reference library where scores of books, magazines and papers were stacked neatly on ceiling high shelves.

They walked through the other wing of the building past an army of machines, ranging from punch presses, brakes, shears and lathes to power saws, grinding equipment and drills, which stood sentinel-like in orderly formation. In two of the larger rooms several small blast furnaces were surrounded by neatly arranged bags of molding sand and assorted cast iron dippers with long handles. Groups of men stood around the machines and equipment preparing them for the day's operations, but the orderliness and cleanliness of the area reminded Erik more of a hospital than a foundry.

As he followed Richter, Erik was wide-eyed with wonder at all the elaborate equipment and the apparent efficient organization of the facility. They walked through a door with a small window at eye level. Behind it was a large office with a desk in one corner and a number of drafting tables and stools located around the room. Metal moldings of many shapes and sizes, some elaborately machined and highly polished hung on the walls, neatly attached with fine wire to labeled cardboard backings. On a long table in the middle of the room were spread several blueprints and drawings of numerous projects all looking complex and alien even to Erik's trained eye. In some of the cupboards and on the stands, technical books were stacked in neat piles. On the wall, wood cases with glass doors held bottles containing substances of various colors, interspersed with samples of various alloys.

"This is my place," explained Richter. "Yours is next door. You can get to it from my office or from the hallway. Come, I will take you there."

The bare office was considerably smaller than Richter's. Its previous occupant had removed everything, leaving the office desolately empty except for a small desk and a chair, a drafting table and stool and a bookcase. But to Erik it represented the ultimate in accommodation because it was to be his first private workplace. He carefully arranged his drafting equipment on the table and looked up to see Richter observing him.

"This is beautiful. It is just great. I know that I am going to like it." Erik could not contain his excitement.

"That is good. A man works better in satisfactory surroundings." Richter looked pleased. "Now if you would come back to my office I will give you a key to the place and sign your pass card. No one can get in here without an identification card. It is the rule."

Richter printed Erik's name on the official looking card and signed it. Then he gave it to Erik for his signature. He handed it back to Erik after checking to see if it was in order.

"There. You are now a privileged member of this organization. But you should really have something to put it in." He reached into his desk drawer and brought out a new brown leather wallet with a card-sized window and handed it to his astounded new assistant. "Now that you are duly installed, you may go back to Herr Doering's department and come back at three-thirty this afternoon and we will talk about our work plans for next week."

At three-thirty sharp Erik was back at his new office. Several minutes later Richter returned to his desk and motioned for Erik to come into his office. "Look Erik, it is getting too late in the day for us to start anything new, so there is really no need for you to stay around here especially on a

Friday. Why don't you go back to the residence and I will see you Monday morning."

"Thank you, Herr Richter," said Erik as he turned to leave.

"You may call me Herman. Yes, I think that we will get along just fine."

CHAPTER 7

In stark contrast to the bustling activity during the week, the grounds of the Torun Works complex were quiet and uninhabited on Sunday morning. It was a lonely place to spend a Sunday and Erik was delighted that he had been invited to join Roman and his friends. After Hilda's breakfast of sausages, eggs, brown bread and coffee, Erik and Roman changed into their best clothes and boarded a tram that would take them to the west side of the city. By the time they arrived at Lydia's house she had already returned from church. When she opened the door her beaming face and sparkling eyes revealed her excitement.

"Well, I see that your shy young friend has assembled sufficient courage to accompany us on our devious mission," she laughed.

"Be careful about how you talk about my roommate here." Roman feigned a dour look. "There was a new development this week which I did not have an opportunity to tell you about. He is now one of the chosen few – a pivot in the organization."

"Stop being mysterious, Roman. Tell me the news," she pleaded.

"Our friend here got promoted this week. He is now a vital part of the establishment, a mogul in the research and development department," announced Roman with exaggerated homage.

Erik blushed at the antics displayed by his friend. "Please Roman, don't overdo it. After all, I haven't even started yet, and it is only a job," he pleaded.

"Oh Erik, that is wonderful," said Lydia enthusiastically. "Angela will really be pleased. She is such a lovely person and a good friend. And she is Polish, too. I know that you will like her. She does not live far from here. Shall we start walking to her place now?" Lydia skipped down the wooden stairs followed by the two young men.

Angela lived across from a small park shaded by great oaks and beechnuts. These magnificent trees provided the local townspeople of Polish descent with one of their few remaining connections with the past, as many of them had been planted prior to the partitioning of the country. Well worn benches stood under each of them. In the summer time the old timers sat on the benches reflecting on old glories and speculating about the future. Near the center of the park stood a fountain, another reminder of Poland's happier days which had not yet fallen prey to the Prussian influence in the city.

The gilded sunlight caught the brightly colored leaves and enhanced their brilliance as they broke away from the trees and floated gently toward the ground. The three young people shuffled through the thick natural carpet playfully as they crossed the park, pausing motionless from time to time to catch a tumbling leaf before it fell to the ground. Roman fixed his eyes on a gently falling leaf and followed its erratic descent. During his intense concentration, Lydia sneaked in behind him and pushed a handful of leaves inside his collar. Feigning exasperation, he chased her to the other side of the park, Erik following close behind.

The trio, chatting and laughing loudly leaped onto the front steps of the weathered old stone house where Lydia's friend Angela lived with a relative. Lydia knocked gently. There was no answer. Roman delivered a loud rap and an impatient grunting sound came through the door. An old man with a thick white moustache and an embroidered shirt cracked open the door and peeked out, then opened it the rest of the way. Lydia greeted him in Polish.

"Good morning, grandpa. Is Angela at home?"

The old man squinted at the girl, his white eyebrows almost touching his eye lashes. "Oh, it is you Lydia," he wheezed. "Sure, sure. She has been waiting impatiently since she got home from mass." He shuffled to the end of the staircase and called up. "Here is someone to see you, Angela."

A slim, wide-eyed young woman appeared at the head of the stairs and stopped briefly to survey her visitors. Upon seeing who it was, she descended eagerly, a big smile covering her small round face. Erik noticed that her silky brown hair was done up into two wide braids which were wrapped around her head, crowning her brow. Her soft pink complexion was enhanced by the scarlet rosette embroidered on her white blouse. He thought that she seemed out of place in the dark somber surroundings of the old house.

Erik fidgeted awkwardly as Lydia and Roman made the introductions and announced that they had planned a picnic at a pleasant secluded place on the west side of the Vistula. It was somewhat more than a kilometer away and would be an enjoyable walk before lunch, Roman explained. They agreed that it was a good idea and returned to Lydia's house to pick up the picnic basket which she had prepared earlier. The house was located near the edge of the city and only several more city blocks and a grassy field stood between them and the river bank. Their walk took them to a knoll overlooking the river and they gazed in silence at the magnificent panorama ahead of them.

Below the embankment stood the Vistula, one of Poland's great waterways, flowing peacefully northward toward the Baltic. At school they had been taught that along these banks and others like them along the river's course were fought some of the greatest battles in the history of Europe. For centuries the river had formed a natural barrier for invading armies from both the east and the west. Since earliest times the river had also played a major role in the northward expansion of Poland toward the Baltic Sea. As a result of some geological freak, most of the east side of the river was flanked by powerful moraine banks, while its west bank was swampy and dotted with sandy ridges which were covered with thick grass and shrubs – a treacherous landscape for advancing armies.

But on this quiet Sunday morning in 1910 it was peaceful. There had been no wars for many years. The river made its way slowly, peacefully and relentlessly northward as it had done for thousands of years before. The four young people found a comfortable spot overlooking the majestic river and sat down on the grass for their picnic.

Roman and Lydia chatted jovially as they served the food which Lydia had prepared earlier. They noticed Erik and Angela casting fleeting glances at each other. After enjoying their picnic of cold meats, cheese, bread and sweet rolls, Roman winked at Lydia tacitly and asked if she was interested in walking down to the bank of the river to look for shells. She quickly agreed and Erik and Angela were left alone.

Erik glanced apprehensively at Angela and gathered up his courage. "What part of Poland do you come from?" he asked shyly.

"Krakow. As you know, it is in the Austrian zone."

"What are you doing in the Prussian zone then?" he asked.

She seemed pleased that he appeared to be genuinely interested in her. "It is a long but familiar story," she said. "I had to come to the Prussian zone to get work. My mother is a widow and cannot work to support herself because of a crippled leg. So it fell upon me to support us both, and the only opportunity available to me was in the Prussian zone. I save every mark that I can and send it to her." She paused and gazed upon the river below them. "The poor thing worked so hard and suffered so much to allow me to get a decent education. I just regret deeply that I cannot be with her, but the way things are in Austrian Poland, jobs are a real luxury, especially for women."

"But I understood that conditions on the Austrian side are much better than on the Russian side and at last as good as they are here in some respects," remarked Erik.

"Oh yes, there are many conditions over there which are to be preferred, such as the freedom to use the Polish language in both elementary and secondary schools. And to some extent a degree of self government is exercised by the Polish people through the Provincial Diet. Perhaps one of the most remarkable achievements of our people in the Austrian zone has been their contribution to the spectacular growth of Polish language schools both in number and quality. Unfortunately though, the region has advanced much farther intellectually than economically, and work is scarce unless one wishes to pursue a teaching or bureaucratic career. For a woman this is almost impossible. So here I am."

"I am so glad that you are." Erik immediately realized what he was saying and blushed.

"Do you really mean that?" asked Angela, her face lighting up.

Erik fidgeted nervously and muttered an awkward remark in an attempt to change the subject.

"What happened to your mother's leg?" he asked.

Angela paused before answering trying not to show her disappointment at the sudden change of subject. "She was shot in the leg during the insurrection of 1863," she explained.

"I am sorry to hear that. Can you tell me some more about it?" said Erik.

Angela gazed at the ground as she recalled the story of the tragedy which her mother had related to her many times.

"Mama was only twelve when she was wounded. When she was young it did not bother her much, but now in her old age she has some trouble getting around."

"You said that she was shot. How did that happen?" asked Erik.

"She was living with her parents in a small village in the Russian zone when the uprising occurred. One day some Russian soldiers swooped down upon the village destroying everything that got in their way and shooting at the women and children. Mama was hit while running across a field to hide in the forest. She was carried to safety by some young boys and nursed back to health by an old woman in the village. Later she fled to the Austrian zone with her parents where she got married and I was born. But that's enough talking about me. Tell me something about yourself now."

Erik squirmed and threw small pebbles at an imaginary target in front of him. "There is not much to tell. My parents and I were also affected in the aftermath of an unfortunate counteraction back in 1901. We were living in Wrzesnia at the time.

"The incident occurred when the parents of the children living in that town resisted the teaching of religion in the German language in our schools. When one of the Prussian teachers severely beat up a number of children for speaking Polish in his religion class the parents went to the school and turned on him and other teachers in the school. Some of the teachers were badly beaten. My parents were among those involved.

"When the Prussian soldiers arrived, the school-age children of the parents who participated in the altercation were removed from them and taken to state institutions. I was taken to a German language school in Posen when I was ten. At fourteen I was placed in a trade school and just a few months ago I became an apprentice at the foundry at the Torun Works. Since then I and the others have been given more independence than we had at any time during the nine year period. And I will share a secret with you. Last week I went to Lubicz to see my parents for the first time, even though it was against the rules." Erik was getting brave. "And do you want to know another secret? You and Lydia are the first girls that I have spoken to in all those years."

"Yes, I sensed that you felt somewhat uneasy around us. But I hope that you will get used to me in time," said Angela.

"You mean that I can see you again," blurted out Erik.

"I would love that very much," she replied placing her hand on Erik's arm.

Lydia appeared suddenly over the top of the knoll screaming wildly as Roman followed close behind holding a crayfish in his outstretched hand.

"Get that thing away from me, Roman," she yelled.

"Oh, he is such a cute little creature," he said, stopping to tickle the crayfish's belly. "Look it likes you."

The crustacean, its red eyes bulging, curled its tail and clamped its claw on Roman's finger.

"Aha, I see that it is on my side," laughed Lydia as Roman struggled to shake off the crayfish.

As the sun began its descent toward the horizon, they gathered their things and started out toward the city chatting and laughing as they walked away from the river.

CHAPTER 8

The cold gray dawn had not yet lifted and lights still shone through some of the windows of the sprawling industrial complex. Erik was on his way to his first day on the new job. He did not know what to expect. The events of the past few weeks had unfolded like a series of acts in a drama, with him at center stage. His excitement mounted as he approached the research and development wing of the complex. The guard at the entrance of the research center gave him a quizzical look, but asked no questions when Erik confidently showed his pass. Inside the building, engineers, technicians and laboratory personnel were arriving and others were already emerging from their offices attired in white smocks and carrying the tools of their trade.

Erik entered his office through the hallway door. The door to the adjoining office was open and he observed that Richter was already at his desk. Richter looked up from his papers and acknowledged Erik's arrival. He stood up and strode casually across the room and greeted his new assistant. "It is good to have you here, Erik," he said. "I am going to need all the help that I can get. We have to get going immediately on our new project. The Imperial War Office has designated our project as one of top priority. Originally I had hoped to be able to give you some orientation in our total research program, but the message from Berlin has changed all that. I realize that with your limited exposure to metallurgy in particular we are expecting a lot from you. But we are also aware of your natural abilities and your innate skills. That is why you are here. Come into my office and I will introduce you to the project."

Richter unlocked a wall cabinet located behind his desk and removed a shiny new firearm from it. Erik recognized it as a bolt action rifle assembled from the castings which he and the others had been producing in Doering's department. Richter passed the weapon to him and Erik fingered it tenderly. The parts were exquisitely machined and the stock and grip were formed from prime pieces of hardwood whose grain was enhanced by a smooth, shiny finish. Erik was momentarily awe-struck by the magnificence of the firearm. Richter smiled proudly.

"Do you recognize some of the parts in this beauty," he asked.

Erik could not hide his astonishment. "Yes, we made the barrel and the other castings in the foundry. It really is a beautiful object when all the parts come together."

"I am glad that you feel that way," said Richter, "because our job is to make it even better. Your particular task will be to redesign the barrel to enable the rifle to withstand an increase in its firing capacity from one to three rounds per second without overheating. In other words, our task will be to design and produce a semi-automatic rifle. My job will be to redesign the firing and ammo-feed mechanisms. You will be responsible for the barrel. I understand that you have performed some experiments with various combinations of metals for the barrel of this rifle. The barrel which you see on this model is made from the alloy which you helped to formulate and is largely responsible for your presence in this department."

"I am happy to have had a part in producing such a magnificent product. What will the new improved model be used for?" asked Erik innocently remembering his conversation with his father in Lubicz.

"Our function here is to research and create new products. The question of their eventual use is left to the marketing department," answered Richter. "As researchers and developers we must satisfy our creative needs through invention, not ethics. Marketing and politics are better left to those best suited for it."

"I am sorry, sir," apologized Erik. He recognized that his exuberance had carried him outside of his domain.

"Your interest is quite understandable. It reminds me of myself when I was your age," said Richter. He rearranged some of the drawing on his desk. "We will begin immediately. You will have a free hand in redesigning the barrel and you may start as soon as you are ready. But before you begin, I would like to take you around to meet the people in the metallurgy department. These people will cooperate with you as required. In addition, I have arranged for someone to work with you; somebody whose skills will complement yours. His name is August Hepner and he will be here tomorrow. If in the future you should need any more help, let me know and I will arrange to get it for you."

Erik returned to his office and put away his drafting equipment, then opened his book on metallurgy. He leaned back in his chair in deep thought. So far, the world, it seemed, was applauding his every act, but as he had just discovered, he must be careful not to question the plot.

~~~

Absorbed completely by the challenge given him, Erik became thoroughly immersed in the project's development. His co-worker, August Hepner, turned out to be a German technician from Dresden several years his senior. He was good at computations, but his lack of imagination left him somewhat barren of innovative ideas. This responsibility fell to Erik, an area which he relished and in which he excelled. Because their skills complemented each other, they worked well together. Hepner's command of mathematics enabled him to calculate formulas as fast as Erik could perceive them. Erik, on the other hand, found calculations a nuisance that interfered with his sense of invention.

Richter lived up to his promise and gave them complete control of their project. On those rare occasions that he came around to see them, it was usually to ask if they required anything. By early November the specifications for the new design were completed and they were ready to begin experimenting with the alloys. Erik took the drawings and calculations to Richter and explained the design to him. He followed Erik's explanations with a profound interest.

"Look Erik, you and August have been working very hard on this project and I would like to give your plans the attention that they deserve," he said without taking his eyes off the drawings. "Why don't you both take the balance of the week to rest up. That will give me an opportunity to study your plans carefully. If they look good, then you may begin your experimentation with the alloys early next week."

"Thank you, sir," said Erik. "I hope that the design pleases you. We are anxious to begin the castings for the prototypes." He could not bring himself to call Richter by his first name as his manager had suggested when they first met.

Erik locked his copies of the plans in his desk and walked slowly back to his quarters. He reflected upon the events of the past weeks and his thoughts turned to Angela. What a wonderful opportunity this was to see her again, he thought. For the past few weeks his time and effort had been almost completely devoted to his product development work and even though he had often thought about Angela, he had made no attempt to contact her or even mention her to his roommate, who had also remained silent on the subject.

When Roman returned to the dormitory after work that day he could no longer hide his disenchantment with Erik's apparent clumsiness in dealing with Angela and was surprised by his roommate's renewed interest in her.

"It is about time that you tore yourself away from that cold iron to which you are so dedicated and thought about a real live and warm human being. Lydia told me yesterday that the poor girl is distraught at your total lack of respect for her feelings," he admonished his friend.

"I am sorry to hear that, Roman. I did not realize that she was that interested in me and I did not want to appear to be a nuisance. Why did you not tell me about this earlier?"

"Because the poor girl kept her feelings to herself. She did not even reveal them to Lydia until this week. But anyway it is not too late to undo the damage. We can follow up on your plan and I can ask Lydia to get word to her that you can see her this Saturday after she gets home from work. From there on you are on your own," said Roman with exaggerated chagrin.

Saturday morning dawned bleak and blustery. Gusts of wind picked up dust and cinders and formed small eddies on the street and empty lots. After Roman returned from the foundry and they had eaten their midday meal, the two young men boarded the tram for their cross-town journey. When they arrived at their destination, Erik reluctantly left Roman at Lydia's door and proceeded to Angela's house. He knocked and shifted nervously from foot to foot as he waited for the door to open. Angela appeared at the door and observed her visitor, trying to appear indifferent. Her delight at seeing Erik could not completely hide the evidence of annoyance in her face. She stepped aside as a sign for Erik to enter.

Inside the house, Erik fingered the buttons on his jacket uneasily as he attempted to make conversation. Angela appeared to be occupied with other thoughts as she busied herself arranging things around the room. Erik quickly realized the message that Angela was attempting to convey and he surprised them both when he stammered, "I am sorry that I neglected to keep in touch with you. This does not mean that I did not think about you every day and every hour, but my involvement with the challenge of my new job and the demands that it placed upon me made it almost impossible to come and see you any sooner."

Angela interrupted her task and stared at him defiantly. "Yes. Roman has been keeping us informed of your progress and told us that you are involved in something very important," she said coldly. "But he did not want to say exactly what it is that you are doing. What is so important about it that you do not have time for anything else?" She cocked her head in a taunting motion. "What is so crucial about what you're doing there anyway?"

"Oh, I am just helping to develop a new product," he replied, trying to appear casual.

"So you are helping to design a new product? Well then, what is all this secrecy about it? What kind of a product is it that is so important?" There was a note of cynicism in her voice.

"It is just a firearm – one that will be an improvement over an older model." He wished that she would drop the subject, but she seemed determined to pursue it.

"Just a firearm you say? What kind of a firearm? You mean a weapon, don't you?"

"It is just an ordinary semi-automatic rifle." He paused and noted that she was waiting to hear more. "It is a beautiful piece of work. I think it is one of the finest in the world."

Angela's mouth fell open. She did not attempt to hide her disgust at Erik's feigned casualness. She paced up and down in front of him, her hands on her hips.

"I think that I detect something now about your wonderful product and the part that you are playing in its development. Oh Erik, what have they done to you?" she remarked sadly. "Are you not aware of what you are doing? Are you not aware of the perilous times in which we are living? Don't you realize that the future of Europe may be partly in your hands and the hands of other arms designers working obliviously in their drafting rooms and laboratories. And you call yourself a Pole! Do you know what this could mean to what is left of the Polish people as well as to the other peaceful nations of Europe? Well, if you don't, you should think about it. If I didn't know you better, I would say that your values are disgusting."

Shattered by the barrage of criticism, Erik pondered momentarily. He was shocked and deflated. His project and Richter's confidence in him now seemed far removed from reality, and insignificant. He wanted desperately to forget the whole thing and win back her respect.

"Do not get the impression that I have not considered some of the consequences which you mention. But what am I to do? I must continue, since I have nowhere else to go," he pleaded hoping she would show some sympathy.

"But Erik, you cannot continue doing what you are doing. You must think of something." Without taking her eyes off him, she eased herself into a cushioned arm chair.

"Don't pretend that you do not enjoy it," she scolded. "If you didn't, you would do something about it. I can not believe you when you say that you have no choice. You told me that your parents live in Lubicz on the Russian side. Why do you not go and live with them?"

"Do you honestly believe that that I would be allowed to go into the Russian zone and live with my parents after what I have been through and what I know? No Angela, I do not think that is a reasonable alternative," he replied.

"But Erik, you can not continue doing what you are doing now. You must think of something."

He shook his head in despair. "That is not easy to do under the circumstances, unless I…" He paused as if to examine the thought before he spoke it, reminding him of his father's earlier embarrassment in a similar situation.

"Unless what?" she asked.

He hesitated momentarily and with a note of desperation in his voice, he said in a near whisper. "Unless I take the advice of my family and their friend and do what they suggest."

"And what is that, Erik?" she asked calmly.

"Leave Europe, completely. Move to America."

Her hands fell away from her hips. The tenseness in her face disappeared and Erik was relieved to catch a faint hint of a smile on her face.

"I am sorry that I underestimated your sensitivity, Erik," she apologized. "You are fortunate to have such wise parents to counsel you in these things. But in spite of all the things that I have said to you today, I will still miss you and hate to see you go so far away. I will miss you if that happens. I only wish that I had such an opportunity."

"Maybe some day you will. Who knows?" predicted Erik, pleased that he had managed to allay her wrath. In spite of her criticism, he admired her conviction and looked at her affectionately. She smiled back. "Angela, do you realize that I do not even know your last name?" he said.

She let her arms hang loosely over the sides of the old arm chair. "Klaczek. My mother says that we are direct descendents of the old noble class," she laughed out loud for the first time. "But even if we were, nowadays that does not make any difference. We have all been reduced to a peasant class. History has seen to that."

Erik's eyes opened wide in disbelief. "My mother also comes from a noble family. She is the cousin of the Bashinskis in Warsaw. You may have heard of them. She will be thrilled to hear about you and your family. Do you know what I am thinking? You and I may be cousins sixteen times removed. Who knows?"

They both laughed at Erik's conclusion. He felt a closeness developing between them. Erik realized that he had vindicated himself and felt good about it. He became aware of a warm glow inside of him and vowed in his mind that he would cultivate her friendship.

"I wish that you were able to come with me the next time that I visit my family," he said.

"Do you really mean that, Erik? I think that would be wonderful. You know, there is really nothing to stop me if you really want me to go. So you had better not mention it unless you mean it. I have permission to visit my mother in the Austrian zone and to get there I am allowed to travel through the Russian sector if necessary. So my passport is good in all three zones. All that I need is an invitation and some time off from work."

"You are lucky. For me it is not quite that simple," explained Erik. "You see, those of us who were taken from our families have not yet completely regained our freedom to visit our parents. We have to wait until we get permission to leave Torun, and so far I have only gone there once – without permission. I took a chance and nothing happened. But I am hoping that the situation will improve soon and if it does I would like you to go with me."

She glanced at him with a look of acquiescent approval. A quivering jolt ran through his body, leaving him with a pleasant feeling inside. He remembered Herr Schmidt's remark that morning several weeks ago about a young man needing a girl, as well as the interviewer's question regarding his family. Things seemed to be falling into place.

"Maybe I can do something to make it happen," he said quietly.

"Sure you can, Erik." She gave him a peck on the cheek and he blushed crimson.

"Are you hungry? I'll go and find us something to eat," she said.

CHAPTER 9

In the small fields surrounding Lubicz only a few cabbages, turnips and sunflowers remained to be harvested. Inside the village, garlands of dried corn, onions and garlic hung from beams under eaves and ceilings, and bags of potatoes, turnips and beets huddled together in earthen cellars. Stacks of firewood were piled neatly behind the cozy cottages and the now completed harvest exuded an air of comfortable readiness for the coming winter.

A drizzly fog had moved in from the Baltic and coated the leafless tree branches that waved in the breeze, making them look like long silvery minnows. Tiny droplets settled on shingles throughout the village and they shimmered gently in the gray light like patches of gossamer. Smoke from the weathered clay brick chimneys defied the laws of nature and drifted downwards instead of up. Axel Berglund and his wife sat near the kitchen stove absorbing the warmth of the crackling fire.

"I see by the way the smoke is dropping to the ground that we may be in for a long spell of rain," observed Axel.

"Yes, that always happens around the time of the Jewish holy days. I do hope that Stanislaw gets back from Warsaw before dark," she fretted.

"Oh, he should have no trouble at all if the train is on time. If it is, he should be back any time now," said Axel, checking his pocket watch.

"Do you think that we will be able to sell this place?" she asked, busying herself with the pots boiling on the stove.

"Litvak said he would have no trouble selling it – for a good price, too. There are a few young men around the village who would like to get married but have no place to which to take their brides. I am not worried. That old horse trader can sell anything." He paused and stooped down to look out of the window. "He should be coming around one of these days. I have some pieces of furniture for him, ready to go."

The sound of hob nails rubbing against the iron boot scraper outside the door announced Stanislaw's return. He entered, still carrying his brown leather satchel, and shook the moisture off his cap.

"I have good news, so I came straight here," he announced excitedly. "Our application for immigration to Canada has been accepted. The passports will be ready before Christmas and all that we have left to do now is to get a doctor's certificate and arrange our travel. Canadian immigration officials in Warsaw were very helpful. They asked what kind of countryside we would be interested in. I said some place where there is good soil, lots of trees and maybe some small lakes nearby. They told that they were just opening up such a place for homesteading in a province called Manitoba. It sounded so good, I said we would go there."

"That is wonderful news, son," beamed Axel. "You have done so much in so short a time. Now you even have me all excited about the whole thing.

Did you find out if they need any furniture makers out there?"

"The country is new, father. They need craftsmen of every kind. I am sure that you will have no trouble making use of your skills, but you will also be eligible for your own homestead."

Mrs. Berglund paused in the middle of stirring a pot on the stove and remained motionless throughout the conversation between Axel and Stanislaw, not wanting to miss a word. Her face lit up as she observed their excitement. She, too, was becoming infected by their enthusiasm.

"So when do you think that we will be going?" she asked.

Stanislaw was surprised by her sudden interest. "The immigration people said that if we leave here early in March we should arrive there in time to erect a log cabin as a temporary shelter and put in a garden. You see, the springs there are later than ours, so if we arrive there by the first of May we will still have time to do all this," he explained. "They told me that there are lumber mills nearby and I will be able to cut down trees and take the logs to the mill during the winter. Later we can use the lumber to build a better house, perhaps even a cottage like this one. Until we get our own land cleared I can work for the established farmers in the area to earn some money."

"It all sounds so good that even I am getting anxious about going," confessed his mother, her admiring dark eyes fixed on Stanislaw.

"There is one small problem though," explained Stainslaw. "Cousin Bashinski suggested that since Erik may be following us later, we should try to move as inconspicuously as possible. He says that he can arrange comfortable passage for us on a freighter between England and Halifax. That way our names will not appear on the list of passengers embarking at Hamburg and it will be more difficult for anyone to trace our destination in the new world, should anyone want to do so. I don't understand why they would, but Bashinski said it would be better that way. He says that Erik knows too much about what is happening on the other side."

"Bashinski knows more about those things than we do, so we should take his advice. But our poor Erik," sighed Mrs. Berglund. "I just hate to leave him alone with all those wolves. He is as innocent and naïve as a lamb and they are liable to tear him apart."

"He is old enough to take care of himself," explained Axel. "Don't forget that he is twenty years old now – not a child as we remember him. And beside that, Litvak promised to arrange to get him out safely when the time is right, if he wants to leave."

"I do wish that we could get a message to the boy and ask him to come home again. We should tell him about our plans soon so that he can start making his own," she fretted.

"That is a good idea," he agreed. "Litvak should be around soon, maybe tomorrow. I will ask him to try to get a message to Erik in Torun."

~~~

Richter was at his desk, hunched over a set of drawings studying their detail when Erik arrived at his office early Monday morning. Immediately upon seeing him, Richter jumped to his feet and rushed into Erik's office.

"Erik, those drawings are excellent. I also went through your calculations and your proposed formula for the alloy and they all appear to be sound. You may begin experimentation with the new alloy this morning if you wish." Richter was exuberant. "I have asked Herr Doering to release you from your duties in his shop so that you can concentrate only on this project. We may be onto something big here."

"I am pleased to hear that you are satisfied with my work, Herr Richter. I will start to work on the trial formulas for the new alloy immediately." He was getting caught up in Richter's enthusiasm.

"That is good," said Richter smiling broadly. "I have always admired people with dedication to their work, especially young men like you." He got up to leave and paused when he reached the door. "By the way, Erik, Herr Schmidt tells me that your family lives on the Russian side of the border. Is that true?"

"Yes," replied Erik cautiously. "My parents and one brother live in Lubicz, only a few kilometers from here."

"I suppose that you would like to see them sometime," suggested Richter.

"That would make me very happy. As you may know, I have not seen them for a very long time." Erik was testing Richter's knowledge of his family circumstances.

"Yes. That is what I understand." Richter looked concerned. Erik was relieved. "Anyway, you will be pleased to hear that Herr Schmidt has arranged for a special clearance which will permit you to go across the border whenever you wish. If you wish to visit your parents, you will now free to do so. Your papers will be ready this afternoon. They will identify you to the Prussian authorities and also help you to pass through the Russian ports of entry without any problem."

·   "You and Herr Schmidt are very kind," exclaimed Erik. "Thank you both."

"You have earned it, Erik, and this organization always rewards achievers." Richter placed his thumbs in his vest pockets and looked directly at Erik. "I know that you will understand that this is a special privilege which is to be respected."

"Oh, I do, sir, and I appreciate it," answered Erik convincingly.

"And by the way, my name, as I said earlier, is Herman," said Richter as he disappeared through the door.

~~~

The narrow road skirting the east side of the foundry complex was deserted when Erik entered it to take his daily walk before supper. With the late autumn days getting shorter, the sun was already low on the horizon and the opaque shadows of dusk were creeping in. A dry, blustery southeast wind blew in from the steppes of southern Russia. Whirling eddies picked up the dry leaves and deposited them in heaps along the chain link fence. The air was filled with the pungent smell of burning vegetation in the surrounding fields where farmers had spent the day cleaning up the land for next year's crops. The leaden sky and chill in the air served notice that winter was not far away. Recent heavy frosts had already transformed the grassy ditches to a swaying mass of lifeless brown. Nature had completed another cycle of life and death and was ready for a rest.

The gloomy scene put Erik in a retrospective mood. As he walked he reflected on how events had changed his whole life in recent weeks – his promotion, the enthusiastic acceptance of his development work by Richter, his freedom to visit his family and, of course, Angela. He recalled the time only four days ago when she chastised him for unwittingly contributing to the potential future destruction of his own and other innocent people.

Maybe she is right, he thought. She is a sensitive and intelligent person. Perhaps there is something to those war rumors about which she, and even his own parents, are deeply concerned. But it can't be true. Those people at the plant, they are just ordinary men like us, doing their jobs. Foreign countries are always anxious to buy arms from Germany, so what is wrong with improving their design? Germany is well known throughout the world for the quality and precision of its machinery and metals products. The people are resourceful, inventive and disciplined. Perhaps if Poland had concentrated more on these traits it would not be in the circumstances that it finds itself today. But then again, why was Richter so upset when asked for whom these arms were being produced? He wished that Angela was there so he could discuss his thoughts with her. He looked up abruptly and observed a man carrying a case emerging from the shadows and heading toward him. As the man came closer Erik recognized him as the same peddler who had first brought him news of his family.

"Good evening, Berglund," said the man curtly. "Shall we walk back to your quarters and talk?"

Erik was taken aback by the man's incursive manner, but on such a depressing evening even this unusual visitor from the outside was welcome sight. His brusque approach was almost amusing and Erik smiled at him.

"I am glad to see you again," he said. "Let's go in. My roommate is out for a while and if you have something to tell me, we will be alone."

"I do have something to tell you, otherwise why would I be here?" said the peddler, appearing impatient.

They entered the billet and Erik closed the door. The peddler opened his case and arranged the contents methodically as he spoke quietly in Polish.

"Your parents are completing their arrangements to move to Canada. They will be leaving from Southhampton, England in late March."

"Why Southhampton? Why England? Why not Hamburg from where everyone else embarks for America?" asked Erik.

"Because of you," answered the peddler. "We know that the Germans keep passenger lists for all the ships leaving their ports for North America. It may not be easy for you to get away when the time comes if they discover that your family has left Europe for Canada."

"There must be dozens of Berglunds sailing out of Hamburg. Why would they be so concerned about me?" Erik was bewildered at the unusual arrangements that were being undertaken on his account.

"Because your uncle Bashinski in Warsaw, through his intelligence network, knows what is going on here in Torun and the project in which you are involved. He feels that you should arouse as little suspicion as possible, and after your parents have left you can slip away quietly and join them. That way no one will know where either you or they are. But then you can do whatever you wish. I am only the messenger."

Erik whistled softly to indicate his amazement. "You people seem to know more about me than I do. But in spite of what you say, I know that they don't really care about where I go or what I do as long as I do my job here properly. Why, just yesterday I received permission to cross the border freely. I am free to go anywhere, even to the Russian zone."

"That development is good, even though your analysis of the whole situation is not," observed the peddler. "It will make the situation simpler for you to go and see your parents and they are very anxious to see you again. Now what should we tell them?"

Erik stood up and paced the floor in front of the peddler his eyes focused on the floor. He stopped and straightened out his body. "Tell them that I will come this Saturday," he announced with exaggerated bravado. "There will be no need for your Litvak to pick me up this time. I will either come by coach or walk." He hesitated for a moment. "And also tell them that I will bring a friend with me."

The peddler closed his case as he cast a curious glance at Erik, then walked out of the building into the darkness.

~~~

Erik ran up the stairs of the small wooden veranda attached to the old stone house and knocked. He waited. There was no answer and there were no sounds behind the door. He knocked again, this time louder. After what seemed like a generous portion of eternity the door opened a crack and the bushy white moustache of the old man appeared in the dim light coming from inside.

"Good evening, uncle," he said in Polish. "It is me, Erik. Is Angela home?"

The creamy while light from the solitary lamp in the room penetrated the darkness and illumed Erik The old man put his face close to Erik's and grunted his recognition. He opened the door wider and stood in the opening.

"She did not say that you were coming."

"I know," said Erik. "She is not expecting me, but I must see her. I have something very important to ask her."

"I will call her," said the old man. "You stay here." He closed the door and left Erik standing outside in the dark. Muffled voices penetrated the closed door. Suddenly the door flew open and Angela appeared in the entrance.

"Erik, what are doing here at this time of the night?" She was surprised and excited.

"I am sorry to disturb you," he apologized, "but I just had to see you tonight."

"You don't need to apologize, Erik," she said tenderly. "I am happy to see you at any time. Do come in. Is something wrong?"

He sat down on the edge of the wooden bench in the entranceway as the old man eyed him suspiciously.

"I cannot stay long because it is getting late," he said, looking directly at the old man standing at the bottom of the stairs. "No, nothing is wrong, Angela. But just today I received permission to go and visit my family in Lubicz. I could not wait any longer to tell you. I am planning to go there this Saturday and I want you to go with me. I know that my family would very much like to meet you."

"Oh, what a wonderful idea, Erik," Angela exclaimed. She stopped and put her hand up to her forehead and closed her eyes. "But it may not be possible because I have to work until noon on Saturday and you may want leave before that."

"Yes, that could be a problem because the coach will have left by then." He thought for a moment. "But since Lubicz is only eight kilometers from here, perhaps we can walk that far," he suggested, eyeing her reaction. "Or we may be lucky and get picked up by a farmer or a merchant in their vehicle."

"That sounds like fun, Erik," said Angela. "Did you hear that, uncle?" Erik has invited me to visit his parents."

The old man cleared his throat. "Young girls should not travel alone with strange men."

"Erik is not a stranger, uncle. We have known each other for several weeks now. And beside that we may even be cousins – sixteenth cousins," she said, laughing. The old man frowned.

"Then it is all set. But instead of you coming all the way here, why don't I meet you somewhere on the other side of town," she suggested.

"How about at the end of the tram line? That is near the bridge where the highway going east begins," said Erik.

"Yes, that is a good place for me. I can be there at two," said Angela.

"Don't forget your passport," said Erik as he prepared to leave.

The old man eased himself into a well-worn leather armchair and lit his pipe. "Young people these days no longer have any respect for old values and authority," he huffed.

"Ah, hush uncle," said Angela, "I am sure that you were no different at our age."

CHAPTER 10

The trolley screeched to a stop at the terminal and Angela emerged into the crowd. She was bundled up in a long woolen coat and a fur hat, and carried a multicolored knitted shoulder bag. She stood with her back to the cold breeze from the north and hoped that Erik would recognize her. She turned around and noticed Erik standing on the wooden platform in front of the station, his canvas backpack at his feet. He took his eyes off the passengers emerging from the trolley and noticed Angela standing on the platform. He picked up his backpack and ran toward her.

"I must have missed you coming off the trolley. You look so different all swaddled up like that," blurted out Erik.

"I can understand why you would. You have never seen me dressed like this before. But since we are walking all the way to Lubicz I thought I should dress warmly," explained Angela. "But isn't this exciting Erik? I am actually going to meet your family."

"Yes. It is very exciting for me, too. So let us get going. We have a long way to go."

They walked hand in hand toward the old iron bridge. Halfway across the bridge they stopped and looked over the railing at the boats plying the waterway in both directions. Below them the reddish brown water flowed swiftly as if in a hurry to keep its appointment with the Baltic Sea. Logs, pieces of timber and other debris scurried along the surface. At the end of the bridge the Russian official manning the port asked for their passports and enquired where they were going. He examined Erik's special visa and then wished them a good journey.

The November sun competed valiantly with the cold northwest breeze but came out second best, its weak rays providing only brief spells of radiant warmth as fleeting dark clouds crossed its path. They walked along the edge of the road, their faces glowing pink in the chilly autumn air. Carts, wagons and rigs of various descriptions wound their way along the road. After they had covered about a kilometer a delivery van approached them from behind. When it came alongside of them the driver called on his horses to stop. The driver was dressed in a sheepskin coat and a fur hat which was tied under his chin. The cap framed his ruddy face and black moustache.

"Good day, my fellow travelers. How far are you going?" he asked in Polish.

"To Lubicz," answered Erik.

"That is a long way to walk," said the man. "Climb up here and keep me company. I am going past Lubicz."

Erik helped Angela to the seat at the front of the van beside the driver and he sat on the outside. The horses started up.

"My name is Erik Berglund," he said as they shook hands. "This is my friend Angela. We are going to visit my parents in Lubicz."

"I am Sosnowski," said the man. "Jan Sosnowski. My brother and I are in the florist business. We operate a greenhouse in Plozk and take turn delivering plants and wreaths to Torun. I also have a small shop in Krakow, but business was so bad that I had to join my brother in Plozk. Business is so much better in Torun than in the Russian or Austrian zones. You have to give those Prussians credit. They are very enterprising and prosperous people."

"You are a long way from Plozk," observed Erik.

"Oh yes, that I am. Normally I would have started back yesterday or early this morning, but there was a big funeral in Torun today, so I am a day late. Now I will not get to Plozk until tomorrow. I will take the horses and rig back to Plozk and then take the train to Krakow for a few days," he explained.

They looked at him inquisitively.

"My family is still in Krakow and I try to get there to be with them as often as I can," he continued. "My wife tries to run the florist shop to the best of her ability during my absence."

"I am from Krakow, too," Angela blurted out, revealing her excitement.

"Oh, isn't that a coincidence," said the surprised man. "I thought you were from Lubicz."

"Not me. Erik's family lives there," she explained.

"What is your last name?" asked Sosnowski. "Maybe I know your family."

"Klaczek," replied Angela. "But it is not likely that you will have heard of us. You see, my mother is a widow and she does not get around much anymore because of a crippled leg."

"I am sorry to hear that," said Sosnowski. "What are doing away up here then, " he asked.

"Working in Torun," she replied. "I am working here to support my mother because there is no work for me in Krakow."

"That is unfortunate," he said, shaking his head. "These are not good times in the Austrian zone, especially if you are Polish. That also explains why my family is there and I am here."

They stopped talking and gazed at the shimmering waters of the Vistula visible from the road through the leafless tree branches. The road followed the steep bank of the river and then gradually steered into the open countryside. The muted clanking of the wagon wheels provided a resonant background to the long conversation which followed. They talked about conditions in the Russian zone and about Erik's family and his father's business. Erik told Sosnowski about the insurrection and how he was taken from his parents at the age of ten and only recently received permission for the first time to visit his parents. The man expressed his sorrow but was happy that things were finally working out so well for them. Lubicz came into sight as they talked.

"Please come to my parents' house and meet my family," suggested Erik. "You can rest your horses and have something to eat yourself. My father has a stable and a well, and my mother always has something on the table."

"I really should not because it is getting late and I still have a long way to go," said Sosnowski, "but you two young people are so pleasant and happy that you have made me happy, too. I am sure that your parents are wonderful people and I would very much like to meet them. Thank you. I will accept your invitation, but I will not stay long."

Erik guided Sosnowski to his parents' street and into the yard. Angela observed everything around her with wide-eyed wonderment.

"This is a lovely and peaceful village," she whispered to Erik. "I love it already."

Axel Berglund stood beside the small wooden gate at the front of the house and observed the approaching trio in the strange vehicle. When he recognized Erik he ran toward them, his gangly body swaying in awkward movements.

"You are full of surprises, Erik," he called. "What is this, a private coach?"

"No, father. We were walking along the highway and this kind man – Pan Sosnowski – gave us a ride in his delivery wagon."

"Us? What do you mean us?" asked Axel.

"Oh, I mean Angela and me," explained Erik alighting from the wagon. "Did you not get my message? This is my good friend Angela," he said, helping her down from the vehicle. "She will be staying with us until tomorrow."

"This is too complicated for me to understand," said his father throwing up his hands. He turned to Sosnowski. "Let us unhitch your horses, my good man; and come into the house for a while."

"I cannot stay long as I still have a long way to go. But I accept your invitation with gratitude," said Sosnowski as he prepared to unhitch the horses from the wagon.

Inside the house introductions were made quickly and Axel returned from the front room with the bottle of schnapps that Litvak had given him earlier. He toasted Sosnowski and Angela ceremoniously and welcomed them to his home. The room soon buzzed as they all talked at the same time. Mrs. Berglund darted sprightly between her son and his companion, throwing questions at each of them without waiting for them to complete their responses. She declared that the Lord had answered her prayers by softening the hearts of the Prussian masters sufficiently to allow her son to come home freely. Her attraction to Angela was immediate and they were soon tracing their ancestry to determine if they had a common line.

"There have been many generations since the Radziwill family ruled, and so many changes. But I would not be surprised if we came from the same limb," she confided in Angela. "Our great and noble families may have been scattered about and reduced in circumstances, but we have kept one thing, our dignity and pride, and I see that you still have yours, Angela. Why don't you tell me more about yourself?"

Mrs. Berglund listened attentively, clicking her tongue desolately, as Angela related her story. She described the uprising of 1863, her father's death and her mother's wound, their poverty and the necessity of her having to work in the Prussian sector in order to support them both. Mrs. Berglund expressed her deep concern over Angela's situation and assured her that the Lord would help her to cope.

"It is not too hard on me," explained Angela. "I enjoy my work in Torun. I have made a few friends and now I know Erik. But my poor mother, I feel so bad about her. She finds it harder and harder to get around by herself, but she has no other choice. If I could only be with her, everything would be so much better."

The florist and Axel interrupted their conversation and stopped to listen to Angela's story. Sosnowski stroked his chin, in deep thought.

"Angela, maybe I can help you solve your problem," he proffered while still deep in thought. "Like I said, we have this small shop in Krakow which my wife still tries to operate. But she is getting older and her rheumatism is getting worse all the time. Why don't you come and work for us? Your training will come in handy as we sometime cater to some wealthy Austrian families who seek advice from us on many things to do with arranging and decorating. I am sure that your talents will at least be partially put to use. I will try to pay you as much as you are earning now so that your income will not be reduced."

"Oh, Pan Sosnowski, I cannot believe what I am hearing," exclaimed Angela. "This has been a most fateful day."

"God works in many wonderful and mysterious ways," Mrs. Berglund reminded her.

"Of course, I will come and work for you and your wife," said Angela. "When may I start?"

"As soon as you can terminate your employment in Torun," replied Sosnowski.

"My employer would probably want me to stay until they find a replacement for me. This may take two or three weeks, I think. But give me two weeks. In two weeks I should be able to know more definitely. My uncle can get another one of his nieces to live with him. But what about my poor Erik? He will be all alone again." She gazed with sad eyes at Erik.

"Oh, don't worry about me," said Erik. "I will be very busy on my project for a while. And after that, who knows? We may decide to follow my parents to America."

"We? You mean that I can come with you?" Angela asked, her eyes wide with excitement.

"That could probably be arranged," replied Erik, trying to appear nonchalant.

"Oh, my God. I don't know if I can take all this excitement in one day," sobbed Angela.

"Just take it easy, my dear," advised Mrs. Berglund, putting her arms around Angela. "Place everything in the hands of the one above and He will guide you one step at the time."

Sosnowski rose and thanked his hosts for their hospitality. "I must be leaving now. I can travel a few more kilometers before nightfall." He turned to Angela. "Would you like me to contact you in two weeks when I am in Torun?"

"Please do, Pan Sosnowski. I hope that everything would be ready by then. Here, I will write down my address in Torun." She handed the slip of paper to Sosnowski.

"And here is the location of our shop in Krakow," said the florist writing the address on a card. "You may come to work as soon as you arrive."

Erik and his father helped Sosnowski with the horses and drew water from the well for the animals. When they were hooked up to the wagon, Sosnowski lifted himself into the seat and drove out of the gate, waving as he turned into the lane.

Erik and Axel returned to the house and found Angela and Mrs. Berglund sitting at the table, deep in conversation. They stopped talking when the men entered.

"One does not want to leave two women alone too long," laughed Axel. "You never know what kind of a scheme they will come up with."

"Women rarely get the world into trouble," Mrs. Berglund reminded her husband. "It is always the men who do. But anyway, let us not argue about things like that. Let us get the most of the short time that the children will be with us."

CHAPTER 11

The days and nights seemed to flow by as in a dream. Erik could feel the excitement building in the Research and Development Department. All those in the department who were involved with the project focused on deadlines that they were assigned, each reporting to their own project director who, in turn, kept Richter informed on the progress being achieved. Erik had not yet been told what the official name of the unit was, but he noticed a reference to the Arms Design Department in some of Richter's memos. During the past few weeks he and August had worked on the new alloy all day and into the night, experimenting with various blends of ingredients and additives until they achieved what they calculated would be a perfect combination of strength, hardness and heat resistance. Now they were ready to pour a batch and test it under working conditions.

If everything went well, this would also be Angela's last week in Torun. Because he and August had worked late every night of the previous ten days, Erik did not get to see her. Roman, who visited Lydia regularly, brought news of Angela to Erik and from this he knew that everything was going according to plan. He sent word back with Roman that he would see her as soon as this phase of the project was completed. Roman said that Angela understood.

It was Tuesday of the third week and Erik and August arrived at the research department early. The sun was just rising, turning the eastern sky blood-red as its rim appeared over the horizon. Erik glanced at the spectacle for a moment then turned his face away. His mind was on the task that would occupy them that morning. They had selected this day as the one on which they would fire a sample of the new alloy and pour the first batch. Using the drawings which Erik had completed earlier, they had designed and assembled the mold and calculated the machining operations which would be required. When Richter and the other technicians arrived, the small furnace had already been fired and the mold carefully set out. They watched as the gray mixture turned red and then slowly liquidized.

The orange-red molten metal flowed like a glowing icicle from the crust-covered ladle into the mold. The molten metal eagerly occupied the empty form in the sand mold and then stopped, slowly changing its color like a chameleon from white to orange-gray to black.

Erik waited a few minutes, then struck it gently with a small hammer to assure himself that it was hardening well, then left it to cool. Confident that this part of the project was completed satisfactorily and on time, Richter and the other technicians returned to their own tasks.

The next morning Erik and August lifted the rough, scaled casting from the mold and took it to the machine shop. They watched as the skilled machinists turned the rough piece of metal into a straight and smoothly polished rod. Erik left the specifications for the boring operation with the machinists and he and August returned to their workplace.

In another machine shop, Richter and his assistants were working frantically on fabricating and assembling the firing mechanism. He had set Friday morning as the time that the new weapon would be tested. It was to be a private testing, involving only those who had been involved first-hand in the development.

By Thursday morning, the new barrel was ready for its initial testing. Erik and August emerged from the machine shop carefully cradling their creation in a flannel-lined wooden box. They took it to their office and meticulously checked its dimensions. Erik held the barrel toward the light and peered through its delicate bore. "Those boys in the machine shop really know their business," he declared.

Late that afternoon Richter asked them to bring the barrel to the machine shop where he had been working on improving the firing mechanism. They left the barrel with Richter and returned to their office. He told them that the weapon would be assembled by morning and that they should go home and enjoy a good rest. It was all over except for the final trial. This would be Erik's first evening away from the research department, but he was too tired to enjoy it. He filled up on Hilda's cooking and then collapsed in his bed.

~~~

By late Friday afternoon, the freshly assembled firearm, complete with a newly designed firing mechanism and cartridge magazine was ready for the initial trial. The development team assembled in the indoor firing range where Richter reverently lifted the weapon from its wooden box and mounted it on a tripod.

They watched as a technician placed six cartridges in the magazine and one in the chamber. Richter set the mechanism on single shot manual, aimed and pulled the trigger. A clean, resounding explosion crackled and echoed from the rafters of the building and was followed by the immediate ejection of the spent cartridge. It fell to the floor with a dull tinkle. Guarded sounds of satisfaction immediately replaced the tension which was so evident among the group before the firing.

"That was beautiful," said Richter, his eyes gleaming with excitement. "Let us try a single shot on target. Here August, you're a good marksman. Try it."

August placed a shell in the chamber and assumed the firing position. He trained the weapon on the target across the range and pulled the trigger. The crack of the explosion and the zap of the bullet hitting the target were almost simultaneous. August completed the safety precautions on the weapon and Richter ran to the target.

"Nearly a bull's eye," he called back. "Right inside the circle. Good shot, August!" He returned to the group, a contented smile on his face. "Now comes the crucial part; a six shot rapid fire test to determine the heat resistance of the new barrel."

On Richter's signal, a technician recorded the pre-firing temperature of the barrel, and then the weapon was secured in the firing position. Richter checked the firing mechanism and placed a shell in the chamber. He installed the loaded magazine and set the weapon on automatic fire. He motioned to August to take over. August placed his right shoulder solidly against the richly polished wooden stock, aimed and pulled the trigger.

The short purr of six shots condensed into two seconds reminded them of a wooden shingle pulled rapidly across a picket fence. A quick check by the technician on the temperature of the barrel confirmed that it remained well within the established safety limits. One minute later two more magazines of six shots were fired, then three more, then four. The barrel temperature remained within safe limits and the accuracy of the weapon was well within acceptable targets.

They glanced approvingly at each other and then broke into jubilant laughter. Richter shook Erik's and August's hands and slapped them on the back. They dashed around shaking hands congratulating each other. When the exuberance died down, Richter asked for their attention and solemnly addressed the group.

"This is a great day in the history of this establishment and this country. Gentlemen, I think that we may have just tested the world's most advanced small bore weapon, all achieved in a record amount of time. This, gentlemen, is not merely a gun, it is a precision instrument. It is a machine of superior design and quality. I congratulate you all, but particularly I would like to single out Erik Berglund and August Hepner for their special contribution to this achievement. The barrel which they have designed and developed is what will set this weapon above any other in the world. But all of us here can be proud to know that we have advanced Prussian excellence and technology an important step forward."

Richter carefully lifted the weapon off its tripod and carried it into his office, followed by Erik and August. He wrapped it in a large piece of brown flannel cloth and placed it inside a cupboard, then carefully locked the door and put the key in his vest pocket. He patted his pocket smugly and flashed an approving grin at Erik and August.

"I think that we can all go home now," he said, smiling.

~~~

Delicate spikes of white hoarfrost laced the trees and sparkled on the rooftops. The air was still and filled with the muffled sounds of the city. Erik walked into the street and hailed a cab to take him to Angela's place. The horses pulling the cab pranced nervously as Erik mounted the vehicle. Billows of steam puffed out from their nostrils as their hot breath mixed with the cold morning air. A cold Arctic air mass had moved in overnight. Puddles of water which filled the depressions in the street the day before were now frozen ice and made cracking sounds when the wheels of the cab rolled over them. Even though the sun was still two weeks from its winter solstice, the murky gray, slushy season had surrendered to the onset of the forthcoming winter on schedule.

Erik leaned back into the seat of the cab deep in thought. Much was due to happen in the next few weeks. Angela would begin her new job in Krakow and his parents and brother would commence in earnest the preparations for their move to Canada. And what about him? What kind of work would Richter give him now that the prototype of the semi-automatic rifle was completed? Would Angela disappear from his life forever? It has been an eventful period, thought Erik as he gazed into the distance. He wondered what lay ahead for all of them.

Angela was waiting inside the narrow hallway of her uncle's house when Erik arrived. Her red eyes bore witness to the sadness of the farewells which had taken place in the cottage minutes earlier. All her belongings were packed in two large traveling bags. Erik picked them up and carried them out to the cab as Angela followed, waving to the old man who had been her landlord and guardian for over a year.

"Good bye, uncle," she called. "Don't neglect your sore back. Erik will come and see you whenever he can."

"God bless you, little one. Don't worry about me. I will be all right. Take care of yourself." He leaned on the door frame for support and waved slowly as the cab drove away. Angela slumped back in her seat, wiped the tears from her eyes and heaved a deep sigh. She sat gazing into the distance as if waiting for the next scene in her life to unfold. The cab entered a main thoroughfare and picked up speed. Angela leaned forward in her seat and dabbed her eyes.

"Poor mama. She must be counting the minutes now. I wrote and told her that I would be there tomorrow, but she has not had time to reply. She sat up straight and glanced over at Erik. "I also told her about your wonderful parents and their plans for the future."

"Did you tell her about our future?" asked Erik innocently.

"No. Of course, not. What could I tell her?" she asked. "I know that you have hinted at something from time to time, but so far it is all just a puzzle to me. How do I know that you are not just teasing me?" She sat closer to him and he blushed crimson. "Anyway, Erik, I think that you are more interested in your work than you are in me and you know how I feel about that." She placed her head on his shoulder. "And beside that, do you believe for one moment that I would cross the ocean with a single man and without my mother?"

Erik fixed his eyes on an imaginary object outside the cab window and fidgeted. "I did not say that you would be traveling with a single man or that your mother cannot come with us," he said.

Angela tossed head back in surprise. It was her turn to blush. "Why Erik, I do believe that you are serious. Is this a proposal?"

"It would probably be better described as a pre-proposal; sort of an advance notice," he stammered.

"No doubt it is one of the first of its kind in history. But I love it." She leaned over and kissed him on the cheek.

The cab stopped in front of the railway station and they stepped out, gazing into each other's eyes.

~~~

Stanislaw was waiting near the station platform at Kujawski in his one-horse cart. They threw their bags in the back of the vehicle and squeezed tightly into the narrow seat beside Stanislaw and headed for Lubicz. "This is the Lubicz coach service," Erik jokingly explained to Angela. Their laughter rang out through the still air as they headed toward the parents' cottage.

"I was in Warsaw again this week," said Stanislaw as they turned the corner. "Uncle Bashinski says that he hopes to see you sometime soon." He waited for a response. There was none. Erik was deep in thought. "You know that he is one of the leading proponents of Polish independence as well as a senior official in the Provincial Diet."

"Now that is a dangerous combination. How can he be both?" asked Erik.

"The first one he practices privately," answered Stanislaw.

"Why does he want to see me? He doesn't even know me," said Erik, trying to sound indifferent.

"But he knows about you, particularly about what you are involved in at Torun Works," said Stanislaw. "And that is what he wants to see you about."

"Oh, good lord," exclaimed Erik, "you would almost think that walls have eyes and ears these days. Other people seem to know more about me than I know about myself."

"Walls don't have eyes and ears but people do," responded Stanislaw as he guided the horse and cart into the driveway of their parents' home.

The smells of food cooking, the crisply ironed table cloth and cleanly swept floor all testified to the preparations which had taken place at the parents' home in anticipation of Angela's and Erik's arrival. Compared to the emotional drama which unfolded during their previous visit, this one resembled a more relaxed homecoming. The welcomes were shorter and a congenial family atmosphere quickly emerged. After only a few minutes Angela joined Mrs. Berglund in the kitchen and followed her around the room, engaged in a steady conversation.

"Why have you decided to move to Canada?" Angela asked.

"It was not my decision. My husband and son are adventurous. They want to be pioneers in a new land. As for me I am only going along to look after them. My heart is here and will remain here forever."

Mrs. Berglund perched her short rotund figure on the edge of a chair and sighed. "I am tired Angela. I carry in my heart a hundred years of suppression. And now they say that we are about to be annihilated again. This time maybe forever. We are like ants scurrying away from the approaching wagon wheel. Do you think that I am doing the right thing, Angela? Leaving my home and running?"

"If what you say about the future is true, yes," replied Angela.

"True? How could it be otherwise? For centuries Europe has been a cauldron of violence. Nowhere else has man's inhumanity to his weaker brothers been more evident than here. If they detect a sign of weakness, they pounce upon you like a bunch of vultures. This continent has been cursed by

God." She leaned back and paused, staring at the window. "But Poland has suffered the greatest injustice of all. Our once proud heritage has been battered until there is nothing left but anger, sorrow and pain. Soon there will be no life left in us; and no hope.

"But what else could we expect? We were warned many times but no one would listen. More than three hundred years ago Grabowski wrote that the enemies' roads into Poland were always open and free. In those days the Turkish cavalry could come and go as it wished, looting and destroying everything in its path. Poland did nothing to stop them. Now we have the Prussians, Austrians and the Russians, all partaking of the carrion. But the Prussians are the worst. They feel that this whole country rightfully belongs to them. Their presence today is the price that we have to pay for the generosity of our mediaeval kings who allowed the Teutonic Knights to fool them with their religious pretensions. For how did Prussia establish its presence on Polish ground if not in the guise of the Knights of the Cross?"

Angela was absorbed in Mrs. Berglund's story. "How do you know all this?" she asked.

"Next to my Bible, I love my history books best," confided Mrs. Berglund. "If we don't study our history and learn from it, Angela, we will make the same mistakes over and over again and will never progress. History is one of our greatest teachers."

"And do you think that Poland has learned anything from its history?" asked Angela.

"Yes, I believe we have. We have learned to be wary of our old enemies and to choose our friends carefully. And we have also learned to be patient and ready. My relatives in Warsaw tell me that the Prussians are preparing to unleash their ultimate vengeance against us. But his time we will be ready. The spirit of Poland is wounded but not dead, even though its borders are no more. I sorrow for my countrymen who will lay down their lives one more time for the cause. My heart is especially heavy when I think that my own son may be helping the enemy and I pray that he will come to his senses. But I am too old now. I will only get in the way. So I will leave and spend the rest of my days in peace."

"I think that Erik is ready to take your advice and leave also. And he says that he might take me with him," said Angela.

Mrs. Berglund placed her hand on Angela's arm. "May the good lord give him the presence of mind to do so," she said. "You will be a blessing to us all."

Jan Sosnowski, the florist from Krakow, arrived Sunday at noon. He carried a large bouquet of carnations and ivy and presented it to Mrs. Berglund.

"I captured a little bit of summer in my brother's greenhouse and wanted to share it with you good folks," he said.

"You are a very kind man," said Mrs. Berglund. "Green has a certain mystery about it at this time of the year. It haunts us with memories of the past and reminds us of the future."

"Indeed it does, and the future bodes well. I went to see your mother," Sosnowski spoke to Angela. "She was so happy when she heard the news. I thought that she would throw her cane away and dance for joy. I felt like dancing myself when I saw her happiness."

"The poor dear, said Angela. "I hope that everything will be better for her now."

"It will. It will," the florist assured her. "There is nothing like the presence of one's own flesh and blood to restore a person's will to live."

Axel Berglund pushed two of his best wooden tables together to accommodate everyone at the homecoming meal Stanislaw and his wife Anna arrived with their children and she and Angela chatted away happily as they helped Mrs. Berglund prepare the table.

The meal completed, they gravitated into intimate groups for small talk, except for Stanislaw and Sosnowski who pondered the logistics of having everyone at the right place later that day. They agreed that Sosnowski would take Angela to the railway station where she would board the train to Krakow, while Stanislaw would drive Erik to the Prussian border where he would cross over on foot. Too quickly, it seemed, the time came to leave. Amid the sad farewells which followed, promises were made to meet again soon. After the two vehicles disappeared out of sight, Axel and his wife returned silently to the house.

"The place seems empty now that they are all gone," said Mrs. Berglund sadly as they entered the house.

"Yes. It takes people to make a home," said her husband, "and one does not realize this until they are gone."

~~~

For more than two decades the winters in central and Eastern Europe had been severe. The old-timers who remembered the dry, mild seasons of 1858 to 1868 and the almost snow-free winters of that decade blamed the change on the huge explosion of the Krakatoa volcano in August of 1883. They explained that the dust and smoke which had enveloped the northern hemisphere after the blast had kept the sun from warming up the land and there had been widespread fear that a new ice age was about to begin. But in the winter of 1911 the gradual moderation which began early in the century continued and the cold weather arrived late enough to remind the inhabitants of the more normal years which preceded the volcanic eruption. Perhaps they had returned.

By mid-December the moist air from the Baltic began to mix with the cold Arctic currents sweeping in from Siberia and produced snow which covered most of the region. In Torun, the slush season had come and gone as predicted. (Slush season is the name that the local people had given to the late autumn period which preceded by about three weeks the actual setting in of winter.) It was a wet, gray mini-season, which seemed to agonize between the well defined fall and winter seasons and depressed much of the population.

Erik had not traveled to Lubicz or Krakow since Angela had left, but he promised himself that he would visit her the day after Christmas. He would spend Christmas with his family. Angela wrote every week. She had settled into her new job and was enjoying it. Sosnowski and his wife treated her like a daughter. Her mother seemed to revive as soon as she arrived home and was now able to get around without a cane.

At Torun Works a well ordered routine occupied Erik fully during the period. He, August and Richter worked steadily perfecting the new semi-automatic weapon in preparation for its mass production. They estimated that early in the new year its manufacture would begin and their research and development group would assume work on a new project. Richter had already dropped subtle hints about the prominence and priority that had already been assigned to their next development but refrained from discussing it further. They would be introduced to it after the holidays, he said. For now they must devote all their energies to the task at hand.

Erik realized that his first Christmas with his family in Lubicz would also be their last one together there. According to their letters, the plans to migrate to Canada were proceeding well. With Bashinski's help, Stanislaw had obtained the passports for his parents and for his own family. Canadian immigration officials in Warsaw had already prepared the way for both Stanislaw and his father to qualify for 160-acre homesteads in western Manitoba. The community which they had all agreed upon was called Ralston. Settlement in the village and surrounding countryside had only been in progress for about twenty-five years and some good land was still available to the north and east. This is where the Berglunds would settle. They would be surrounded by newcomers from many parts of Europe. The village itself and the land south of it were already occupied by settlers from England and the older parts of Canada. To the west there were Scottish and German immigrants and to the north and east Polish, Ukrainian and Romanian. They would be part of a veritable international community, explained Stanislaw.

Erik was impressed with his brother's thoroughness, efficiency and determination. He recalled that Stanislaw had always been the organizer when they played together as children and wondered what he had been like while growing up during Erik's long absence. He was also surprised at how his mother had resigned herself to the idea of moving, at first largely in despair, but now with some degree of anticipation. He wondered if Angela had anything to do with it. He felt slightly guilty for not becoming more involved in their plans and vowed that before he returned to Torun after the holidays he would do something about it.

Two days before Christmas Richter announced to Erik and August that they should not worry about returning to the department until the day after New Year. Since they had completed their project and were not beginning the next one until after the holidays it would be pointless to do so, he said.

"Are you going to Lubicz to see your family," he asked Erik.

"Yes," replied Erik without hesitation.

"I suppose that it is not necessary for me to tell you that what we do in this department is secret information and is not to be discussed with anybody, not even your closest friends and relatives," remarked Richter.

"No sir. We know the rules," they both assured him.

"Good. You are free to go now. Merry Christmas and thank you both." He shook their hands and returned to his office.

On the day before Christmas Erik took the local passenger train to Kujawski, which was the closest village to Lubicz with train service. Because no one knew when he was arriving, Stanislaw did not meet him at the station and so Erik walked the short distance to Lubicz. The clean, tidy room and the smell of cooking which greeted him when he entered the house testified to the preparation work that had occupied his mother over the past several days. On this day of his arrival she was fasting, as had been her custom for many years. She embraced her son and prevailed upon him to sit down, relax and enjoy his homecoming.

"This is our last Christmas here" she said. "Let us rejoice in our good fortune. The Lord has been good to us. He has brought us all back together. What else can we ask for?"

Memories of previous Christmases flooded his head as Erik savored the joys of spending this special day with his parents and his brother and his family. The sounds of the church bells ringing during the Christmas mass, the greetings from friends and neighbors, the carolers and the food brought back recollections of the Christmases of his early childhood days – those happy but sometime troubled times in Wrzesnia. They talked about this and other things late into the night.

CHAPTER 12

The next day Stanislaw drove Erik to Kujawski where he boarded the train to Krakow. Angela was waiting on the platform when the train pulled into the Krakow station. A fur hat covered her head and most of her face. Her slim body was clad in the same heavy woolen outfit that she wore on her first visit to Lubicz. A broad smile covered most of that part of her face that was still visible between the fur hat and her scarf.

"You must feel like a rag doll with all that heavy clothing on," laughed Erik as he sprang from the steps of the coach and squeezed her in his arms.

"It is my mother. The poor dear fusses over me as though I am still a child," explained Angela. "She will not let me out of the house unless I am dressed like this."

"She must be a very considerate person to be so concerned about you all the time," surmised Erik.

"You will soon see for yourself," said Angela.

The city of Krakow was further inland than Torun and less influenced by the mild maritime air masses. Hard packed snow covered the streets and the steel runners of the sleigh emitted a strange euphony of groans and squeaks as they slid over the porcelain-like surface. The cab driver, still in a festive mood, treated them to a disjointed medley of Christmas carols and old Polish folk songs as they left the city centre and turned into the residential part of the city. The jovial driver's singing was interspersed by numerous hearty laughs, the cause of which escaped the two amused passengers. The performance, though unusual, broke the monotony of the gloomy day caused by the low-hanging gray clouds and the nearly deserted streets. They laughed along with him and joined in a song when the words were familiar to them.

A short, slightly built woman with graying hair and a woolen shawl over her shoulders met them at the door when they entered the small wooden house. She hobbled away to make room for them in the narrow entranceway, holding on to the wooden railing.

"So this is Erik," she said to Angela. She gazed at him intently and said, "The way she spoke of you, I thought that you surely would have wings."

"Oh mother, your sense of humor might embarrass poor Erik. Please go easy on him. He is not yet used to being around women," she pleaded.

They removed their heavy clothing and entered the kitchen where Angela checked the covered pots simmering on the stove.

"Angela has told me so much about you," said Erik to her mother, "that I feel that I have known you for years."

"That's my dear Angela. She is always saying good things about everybody. I missed her so much that I thought that I would die. Now that she is back again, I am convinced that I could never go on living without her for long," confided Mrs. Klaczek.

"Don't worry, mother, I will not leave you alone anymore. If I do leave I will take you with me wherever I go," Angela reassured her. "Erik, why don't you go and sit in the front room for a few minutes while mother and I get things organized in the kitchen."

The small cottage occupied by the mother and daughter teemed with evidence of Angela's presence. Imaginative placement of ancient furniture and discreet use of inexpensive decorations lent warmth and color to the modest home. Erik was shown a large old sofa in the front room which would be his bed for the night while the two women would sleep in the only bedroom. He insisted that he should go to the nearby inn, but Angela's mother would not hear of it. Angela announced that she would prepare the dinner while Erik and Mrs. Klaczek would entertain each other away from the kitchen.

Soon the aroma of food cooking filled the house and Angela dashed between the kitchen and the small dining area, setting dishes and silverware on the table and carrying steaming bowlfuls of food from the stove.

"She wants to impress you," confided Mrs. Klaczek.

"She already has," said Erik.

Angela lit a candle in the center of the table and announced that dinner was ready. As they ate, Erik told Mrs. Klaczek about his parents and about their plans to emigrate.

"You mother must be a very brave woman to face the demands of a long voyage and starting a new home in a strange land," she noted.

"She is doing it for my father and for my brother Stanislaw. She loves them both very much and would not go against their wishes even though it breaks her heart to leave."

"She loves you, too," Angela reminded him.

After dinner Erik helped Angela with the clean-up while her mother rested her ailing hip.

"That was a dinner fit for a king," said Erik patting his stomach.

"I am glad that your majesty enjoyed it," she said. "I enjoy cooking for you, Erik. You appreciate my efforts." .

"In that case the future should bring forth much joy for you because I plan to give you a chance to do a lot more cooking for me."

"Don't just plan, Erik. Do something about it," Angela pleaded.

"Would you do it? I mean, would you really marry me if I asked you?" he sputtered.

"I thought that you would never ask," she said, her eyes shining with excitement.

She placed the dishes that she was carrying on the corner of the old cast iron stove and threw her arms around Erik's neck. The dish cloth which she had been using hung limply on her arm as they embraced.

"What's all the excitement here?" asked Mrs. Klaczek as she came hobbling out of the bedroom. They broke their embrace and turned toward her.

"Erik has asked me to marry him, mother," announced an ecstatic Angela. "At least I think he did. Isn't that wonderful?"

"I have never in my life heard of anyone asking a girl to marry him while doing the dishes," said her mother. "But since he did, may the good Lord pour his blessings upon you both and guide you through this happy period of your lives." She paused and sighed deeply. "Oh, that your father was here for this happy occasion, Angela."

"Maybe he is mother. Who knows?" said Angela, glancing upward.

They sat around the kitchen table late into the night planning for the forthcoming marriage. They agreed that the wedding should be held in Krakow in late February or early March before Erik's parents and brother left for Canada. Since they did not know many people in Krakow it would not be necessary to hold the wedding ceremony in the church. The chapel would be large enough. The advice of Father Swiederski of the local parish would be sought on this matter. Angela agreed with Erik that it would be better if no one at Torun Works knew about the marriage. He would keep it a secret until after his parents left for Canada and after his own decision about whether he would follow them. Because of this, only the closest friends and relatives would be invited – the bride's and groom's parents, Stanislaw and his family, the Bashinskis from Warsaw and, of course, the Sosnowskis.

"We must let Pan Sosnowski know right away," said Angela. "He will be delighted to hear the news."

"Why don't we do that first thing tomorrow morning?" suggested Erik. "We can walk over to the inn and take a cab from there."

"That is a good idea," agreed Angela. "He insisted that you come and see them as soon as you arrived. Now they will be doubly pleased."

As Angela had predicted the night before, the Sosnowskis were delighted to hear the news. But the florist also knew this meant that he would soon lose Angela.

"I knew that this was too good to last, having someone as dependable as Angela around the shop," lamented Sosnowski. "But anyway, Mama has had a chance to rest up and is feeling better, so I will have to ask her nicely to come back to the shop."

"We are thinking of following my parents to Canada," said Erik, "But because of the nature of my work I will not be able to leave with them. Angela will remain here until we are ready to leave, maybe sometime later in the summer."

"That is good news, Erik. Of course Angela is welcome to remain with us as long as she pleases." He leaned against a counter stroking his chin pensively. "I was just thinking Angela. Your mother's house is rather small. Why don't you and Erik have your wedding at our place?"

"Oh Pan Sosnowski, you are like a father to me," exclaimed Angela. "Thank you for your thoughtfulness. Just for that you can give me away in marriage, if you don't mind."

"It will be an honor, my child," said Sosnowski, "It will be a great honor."

Buoyed by Sosnowski's support, they returned to Angela's house and dove energetically into their wedding plans. They chose the second Saturday in March as the most appropriate date for the occasion. They all agreed that with some luck most of the snow would be gone and the spring rains will not yet have begun. Erik would ask Stanislaw to contact Bashinski in Warsaw and invite him and his family to come. When consulted later in the day, Father Swiederski agreed that the ceremony could be conducted in the chapel. They concurred that the reception would take place at Sosnowski's house and the food would be prepared by Angela and Mrs. Sosnowski.

When Sunday arrived, the plans were complete. Erik boarded the train in late morning and disembarked at Kujawski. Stanislaw was not aware of Erik's arrival and Erik walked the short distance into Lubicz. Erik broke the news to his family even before he had removed his coat and boots. They were delighted and relieved to hear of their son's decision to ask for Angela's hand.

"I will feel much better now, knowing that you will not be left alone when we are gone," said his mother.

"And I know that Angela will not allow him to remain where he is once she understands what is going on there," Axel assured her. "She is a determined young lady, that one, and she will keep her eye on him."

"She already does know what I do at Torun Works," said Erik, "and she is just as concerned as you are, or maybe more so, about the consequences of what I am involved in."

"Just goes to show you that I am a good judge of people," said Axel smugly.

Roman was stretched across his bed dozing when his roommate returned late Monday night. Erik excitedly broke the news of his engagement even before he had removed his hat and coat. Roman got out of bed and drowsily pulled his lanky body up to its full height. He squared his shoulders and blinked. Still somewhat dazed, he repeated the words that Erik had just uttered and then his face broke into a broad smile.

"So you asked Angela to marry you. It just goes to show you that you cannot trust these quiet types!'" pronounced Roman. "While others are talking, they are busy thinking."

"And acting," corrected Erik, throwing his traveling bag into the closet and slumping down into a chair.

"But not a word to anybody here," he cautioned. "There are still many things that I have to work out and it is better that no one is aware of my plans at this time."

"My lips are sealed," promised Roman, placing a make-believe tape over his mouth, "but remind me again in the morning in case I am still asleep and this is all a dream."

~~~

Early Tuesday morning Richter summoned Erik and August to his office. He appeared excited and somewhat apprehensive. "The time has come to reveal the next project," he announced, trying to contain his enthusiasm. He appeared shrewdly profound as he leaned back in his chair and observed the two men. His expression turned more serious when he stood up and moved to sit on the edge of his desk.

"Gentlemen, this is a great occasion in our careers. We have been honored by none other than the great Kaiser Wilhelm himself. The Imperial Army Weapons Department has heard of our good work here and as a result the Kaiser's government had commissioned us to undertake another project. This one is of great significance to Germany itself and indeed to all of Europe." He paused and focused his attention on Erik. "Your contribution has been especially noted and appreciated, Erik."

Without waiting for a response he stood up and paced around the room gazing at the ceiling, his hands clasped behind his back.

"As you may have already concluded in your own minds, this firm is becoming increasingly involved in the armament business." He was starting out slowly, choosing his words carefully. "I say business because that is what it is. Manufacturing armaments is a business like any other, except that it is nourished by political tensions and the ambitions of world leaders and governments. While the fortunes of this organization are largely tied to the political and economic conditions at home, its strength also lies in developing exports abroad.

"I will understand it if you may have some misgivings about being involved in making products that could be used for destructive purposes, but as I said before, we, the employees of this organization, must not concern ourselves with the politics of the business. We must leave that to the politicians who are better equipped for it. Our job is to produce to the best of our ability whatever products our bosses tell us to produce and forget about the rest."

Richter paused briefly as if expecting a reaction. Both Erik and August remained silent, Erik deep in thought.

"If you are concerned about the consequences of this policy," Richter continued, "then let me assure you that if we don't supply these countries with arms, England, France, Belgium and a host of other arms producing countries surely will. It is a fact of life in this business. Did you know that in the Chinese-Japanese War of 1894 both sides had the privilege of using arms made in this country and neither of them complained that we were supplying the enemy? War is a game played by rulers and politicians for their own aggrandizement. We simply supply them with their toys."

Erik shifted his weight nervously from side to side. "But that can't be true when an innocent country is attacked by a stronger and more ambitious neighbor," he uttered.

"There is no innocent participant in war. The one who is attacked may be guilty of sins of omission," Richter explained.

Erik looked around him in apparent disbelief. August seemed to be engrossed in Richter's speech. Erik wondered why Richter was telling them these things. Was he unsure of their dedication to the project? Was to trying to stir up national pride? Erik recalled Angela's apparent disgust when she heard about what he did at the foundry and her admonishment to him to reconsider the consequences of his involvement. Then he remembered his father's astute reaction to his story of the American bison. How did he know about what was going on here? Suddenly his father appeared wiser. Abruptly he realized that many things which in the past had seemed insignificant and of consequence only to someone else, now intimately involved him. The weight of responsibility which he had until now shrugged off was bearing down on his own shoulders. As Richter continued, his voice seemed to ebb and flow as if coming from another reality; an illusion, unrelated to Erik's picture of a more simple and perfect world.

"There are indications that the next war will be fought largely from barricades and on the seas. The era of hand to hand combat is over," Richter continued. "It will be more a war of machines. The Imperial Army Weapons Department would, therefore, like to see us develop a light quick-fire gun capable of being used as a portable artillery weapon on land and as a cannon at sea. Our strategic planning engineers believe that the barrel size would have to be somewhere in the range of ten to fifteen centimeters."

He walked over to his desk, unlocked a drawer and brought out some photos and sheets of drafting paper. "I have here a number of pictures and drawings of most of the guns in that class which are now being produced. They are all of old and inferior design. If you wish to examine first hand some of these existing models, we could arrange to have them brought here. To begin with, however, I suggest that you examine these pictures and choose the models which you feel that we should attempt to improve upon. Do not concern yourselves with the firing mechanisms or the ammunition. I will take care of those things. Your job will be to design and machine the all-important barrel. It must withstand the heat generated by rapid fire and must ensure distance and accuracy. It is matter of tolerance – tolerance in terms of temperature and thrust. The whole plant is at your disposal. When you need anything, ask for it. I will provide you with a privilege card which will be recognized in all our departments. You may start immediately. Good luck in this new venture."

They stood up slowly and returned to their own desks, each engrossed in his own thoughts.

Richter's voice reverberated through Erik's head that evening as he sat down to dinner with the other apprentices. Although he saw the movement of their lips and knew that conversation was taking place around the table, his mind could not tune in to it. Portions of Richter's lecture that afternoon boomed in his head like a bell tolling in a belfry. "Our job is to design and produce armaments." "War is a game." "We must not concern ourselves with the politics of this business." He remembered his mother's initial revulsion followed by her astute analysis of the events that were insidiously overtaking Europe. He thought about Angela and her genuine concerns for the innocent victims of these political and economic adventures. How could he have been so naive as to ignore and even ridicule the views of all these people who were close to him and loved him so dearly?

Hilda's rotund figure moved silently from one end of the table to the other, returning periodically to the kitchen for refills or a new course. She stopped beside Erik, moved back a step and surveyed his demure visage.

"Now, boys, here is a real life picture of a man in love," she announced with a playful chuckle.

"This time you may be right," answered Erik in a serious tone.

"If I didn't know any better, I would say that you are lying. Don't forget to invite us all to your wedding," teased Hilda.

"I think that I might just surprise you all," prophesied Erik.

"You probably will too," said Hilda as she shuffled into the kitchen for the dessert.

~~~

The short dreary days of January passed quickly. Torn between his moral principles and the challenge provided by his new project, Erik's love for creativity won out. Glued to his desk and drafting table he sketched and calculated for hours, completely oblivious to his surroundings. His mind was too occupied to return to the questions which had plagued him before he began the project. He countered any fleeting doubts with Richter's advice, "There is no innocent participant in war. The one who is attacked may be guilty of sins of omission."

After studying several alternatives, he and Richter's team agreed that they would concentrate on the development of a thirteen centimeter caliber long range gun, one which they hoped would combine the accuracy of the ten centimeter model with the power and distance of the fifteen centimeter design. Specimens of each of these models were brought into the research center and dismantled. Long hours at the drafting table produced numerous variations of the two existing weapons. By late February the new design began to take shape on paper and Richter was pleased with their efforts. He calculated that by late spring or early summer they should have all the parts cast and machined and a prototype ready for testing as early as September.

Angela's letters arrived faithfully and regularly. She described in detail the arrangements that were being made for their wedding. Everyone she knew in Krakow was supportive and helpful. Mrs. Sosnowski was as excited as if her own daughter was to be married and was having her whole house scrubbed and decorated for the joyful occasion. She would make her own wedding dress, Angela wrote, since money for hiring a seamstress was scarce. She hoped that Erik would not be too frightened to show up. As for herself, she was very excited and was counting the days until the event.

The letters from Lubicz were more businesslike. The Berglunds were busy winding down their affairs, the most recent letter said. Their passage to Canada had been arranged and the tickets would be picked up by Stanislaw in Warsaw some time before they are ready to leave. Litvak had agreed to handle the sale of both the parents' and Stanislaw's homes and surplus belongings. After paying for their passage and train fares they calculated they would have sufficient money left to purchase horses, implements, tools and some building materials in Canada.

Litvak had been a good counsel and agent, the letter said, and they would very much like to invite him to the wedding to show their appreciation. The Bashinskis in Warsaw had written saying that they were looking forward to meeting Erik and his bride. They also said that their research had revealed that Angela and her mother were indeed distant relatives of Mrs. Berglund's side of the family, albeit many generations removed. Angela would be elated to hear this, Erik thought, but he also wondered why an important man like Bashinski would go to all the trouble to confirm it.

With Angela gone, Erik had no one left with whom to share his private thoughts except his roommate Roman. Together they agreed that it would be best to keep the news of his forthcoming marriage a secret around the plant. But Erik did not discuss the conflict that had occupied his mind since he returned from Krakow, between the concerns of Angela and his family and his dedication to his work.

In the privacy of his own mind, he was coming to the conclusion that his best strategy would be to devote his total energies to his work until the project was completed and then listen to Bashinski's reasoning about why he should leave Europe with his family. He enjoyed the success that he was experiencing at Torun Works and with his reputation growing he could see a bright future for himself in the organization. But what if there were to be a war as his family and Angela believed? What would happen to her and her mother? These thoughts were too personal for him to share with Roman.

His decision to defer the solutions to his problems until after he had talked to Bashinski provided some mental release. Perhaps Bashinski, who appears to be such a worldly and dominant person, could use his influence to prepare the way for his and Angela's emigration when the time came. Bashinski may even have contacts in North America which would help him to obtain suitable employment there, maybe somewhere near where his family will be living. Everything was falling nicely into place except the problem of what to do about Angela's mother. Angela had already indicated that she would not leave without her mother. Erik decided to throw this in with the other concerns on which he would seek Bashinski's counsel. Suddenly he became very much aware that lurking somewhere behind the scenes there was this mysterious personality named Bashinski whom it was becoming increasingly impossible to ignore.

Roman recognized the strain that had been brought upon his roommate by his work and approaching marriage. He drew generously upon his wit and humor in an attempt to divert Erik's attention from the multitude of problems which occupied him. Dubbing himself the matchmaker, he jokingly heaped approval upon his roommate's romantic prowess and predicted that ample matrimonial rewards would befall him after the wedding. Erik appreciated Roman's antics and his conspicuous attempts to ease his tension.

"I think that I will need to have you along to remind me about those fantastic predictions in case I get second thoughts," suggested Erik. "Do you think that you could come?"

"I thought that you would never ask," replied Roman with obvious delight. "Now everything will surely be right," he said proudly. "After all who ever heard of a wedding without the matchmaker present? Now all that we have to do is to figure out how to get away from here Friday afternoon so that we can be there all ready for Saturday morning."

The logistics of arriving in Krakow on time for his own wedding had somehow escaped Erik's mind until now. He realized that to be there for Saturday morning they would have to take the afternoon train on Friday. But neither of them had obtained permission to take this time off from work.

"Why don't you just ask your old friend Richter to arrange for us to leave work at noon Friday? I am sure that he has some influence with Herr Schmidt who could release me a few hours early. Anyway, he owes you more than you owe him," suggested Roman.

"I'll try it, but what if it doesn't work?" fretted Erik.

"Then you will be no worse off than you are now. At least you will have tried."

"I'll try it, but if I am not there for my wedding, the curse will be on your head," warned Erik.

"Why mine? Why not Richter's?" countered Roman.

Richter wasted no time in arranging for Erik's and Roman's absence from their workplaces Friday afternoon and Saturday morning. "Do not be shy to ask for these small favors," he told Erik.

"Where else would two young apprentices like us get that kind of consideration?" Erik asked Roman as they settled down in their seats on the afternoon train to Krakow.

"I told you that they need you more than you need them," said Roman.

<center>~~~</center>

That night, every corner of the small cottage vibrated with the sounds of intimate greetings and joyful reunions. The old mantle clock had long ago chimed midnight by the time the weary celebrants finally succumbed to exhaustion on the sofa, benches and even on blankets on the floor.

At sunrise the next morning Erik, Roman and Stanislaw left for the Sosnowski house to help with the final preparations. Back at the Klaczek house the others were still sitting around the breakfast table when a loud knock on the door startled them. When the door was opened, a tall, erect and well dressed man stood in the doorway holding an armful of packages and carrying a leather travel bag. The man's wide shoulders, already made wider by the heavy woolen coat he was wearing, almost filled the doorway. His well-groomed white moustache crowned a wide grin. They were taken aback by his imposing presence.

"Well, aren't you going to ask me in? My name is Bashinski." He observed them with a twinkle in his eye.

Angela was the first to recover from the surprise arrival of the early morning visitor. "Oh, Uncle Bashinski! You surprised us. We did not expect you until a little later. Do come in," she blurted.

"I thought I would come early and see the bride before she left," said Bashinski as he removed his coat. "Here, Angela. Here are some gifts from my mother. She could not come because of her poor health. When one is over eighty years old they do not want to risk breaking their fragile bones on Poland's neglected railroads and streets."

He handed Angela the packages. "Open them. Let's see what she sent," he suggested.

Angela wrung her hands with excitement. She fumbled nervously with the string and wrapping before getting the first box open. A lacy white wedding gown sprang over the edges of the box.

"Is this for me," she sobbed, beholding Bashinski's smugness.

Bashinski nodded in the affirmative.

"You are so kind and thoughtful. You are all so kind. I love you all," she exclaimed, holding the garment in front of her.

"Why don't you try it on?" suggested Bashinski.

"Oh, I will. I will. Here Anna," said Angela to Stanislaw's wife, "you pick up the skirt and I will carry the front."

They disappeared into the bedroom, holding the dress between them. A few minutes later they appeared in the doorway. Angela stepped gracefully in front of Bashinski and bowed.

"You look perfectly angelic, just like your name suggests," pronounced Bashinski.

"It is beautiful," gasped Angela, "and it fits. How did you know my size?"

"Oh, we have spies," answered Bashinski. "Here. See what is in this box," he said, thrusting the package at her.

With trembling fingers Angela slowly opened the package, exposing a delicate bridal headpiece. She picked it up gently as the headpiece sprang into the shape of a tiara, exposing the delicate white material which resembled hoarfrost on a spider's web.

"I just can't believe my eyes," she whimpered.

She threw her arms around Bashinski's broad shoulders and kissed him on the cheek.

"You are a wonderful family and I shall be proud to be a part of it," she cried.

"And we shall be very proud of you, Angela," said Bashinski. "Now before we proceed with our preparations, I have a short announcement to make. For reasons which will become known to you later, the wedding ceremony will not be held in the chapel as planned. Instead, it will be held at Pan Sosnowski's house. I have discussed this with Father Swiderski and Pan Sosnowski and they have agreed to the new arrangements. I see that Erik is not here, but perhaps we can get the message to him quickly."

"He probably already knows," said Angela. "He was on his way to the Sosnowskis when you arrived."

CHAPTER 13

The clock on the wall of the parlor of the Sosnowski house announced that it was one o'clock as the guests began to assemble. Flowers and greenery brought in fresh from the greenhouse earlier that morning filled the room with color and aroma. A white cloth with lace borders covered a table at the front of the room on which lay a small wooden crucifix.

Father Swiderski entered, followed by Erik and his best man, Stanislaw. The room was hushed. On the wall the clock ticked away the seconds as they awaited the arrival of the bride. There was a rustle of silk as Angela appeared at the head of the staircase and made her way down elegantly, followed by Anna, her bridesmaid. Suppressed sounds of admiration emerged from the small group as they observed the new bride descending the stairs.

Jan Sosnowski, in a crisp white shirt and dark suit was waiting at the bottom of the stairs. Angela took his arm and walked to the front of the table where Erik and Stanislaw were standing, their hands clasped behind their backs. Father Swiederski picked up the prayer book and solemnly began the marriage ceremony. His voice broke the anxious silence which had preceded Angela's appearance. The guests soon became involved in the ceremony with their responses and then witnessing the vows of the young couple to each other and to God. The demure but joyful ceremony climaxed with the announcement by the priest that Erik and Angela were now man and wife. After delivering the blessings to the couple, Father Swiederski turned to the assembled group and began his homily.

"As man is conceived and born in love, so he must live and die in love if his purpose in this world is to be fulfilled. Only in love do we find God. He is not present in power or possessions. In marriage we see the ultimate expression of man's faith in love, not only as it is demonstrated in terms of the relationship between man and woman, but also as the expression of the divine law in worldly terms. For what person would enter into a contract to procreate himself if he or she did not have faith in themselves, and hope in their future and the future of the world? This is the process through which humans strive to achieve the perfection of which their being is capable and for which they were sent here to do. For even though it may take many generations to achieve that perfect state, we all continue to have faith that humans will not give up their quest for the kind of world that will usher in the New Jerusalem. We all await the day when man's inhumanity and selfishness will be extinguished forever. Only then will love prevail in its purest form.

"Today we are witnessing an example of our faith in the God of love. For as the dark clouds of uncertainty continue to gather on our horizon, we see a young couple who through faith in the future are joining together to surmount the cruel realities of this world. Even thought the dismal past has given them little cause for hope and the future forebodes even more troubles, they are not discouraged. For, as did their parents and grandparents before them, they know that together they can bring that new day closer when man will have won the war against himself, and reached the Promised Land.

"Friends, there is joy in heaven today," proclaimed the priest, raising his hands upward. "Let us extend this joy into this earthly realm by declaring our love for this man and this woman newly joined in the eyes of God. Let us also proclaim our peace and love toward each other and all the world. May God have mercy upon us and bless us all."

Kisses and handshakes accompanied the congratulations and good wishes as the newly-weds moved through the small crowd. Sober faces and eyes which only minutes earlier had been moist with tears were quickly transformed into beaming and joyous expressions.

In the dining room, the long, brightly polished wooden table stood adorned with flower arrangements and the host's best china and silverware. At the urging of Sosnowski, the wedding party and guests took their places around it and Stanislaw proposed the toast to the new married couple. The room was filled with the sounds of many voices, tinkling glass and laughter.

"What is a wedding without music?" demanded Axel Berglund after the dinner was over and the guests congregated in small groups to converse.

"Can anyone here play the violin or the balalaika?" asked Sosnowski. "We have both of these instruments here," he added, reaching into a closet for the musical instruments.

Litvak stepped out of the crowd and checked the violin briefly then slowly removed it from its case. He caressed it fondly, then grasping the instrument between his shoulder and his bearded chin, he tuned it and coaxed a polyphony of sounds from it before breaking into a familiar Jewish wedding song.

"Whenever I play, I always start with that song," he explained after playing several bars, accompanied by the clapping of hands. "It is like a theme which gets me in the mood to play on. Now if we can find someone who knows the balalaika we will try to play something more appropriate for this occasion so that the bride and the groom may dance at their own wedding."

Everyone was quiet, their expectant looks gradually turning to disappointment. For a moment it appeared that Litvak would have to play alone, until Bashinski picked up the instrument and began to strum it. Then, apparently satisfied with its sound, he launched into a familiar old Polish wedding dance. Recognizing it, Litvak joined in on the violin as the assembled group watched and listened, surprised at the melodic rendering of the hastily assembled duet.

The music filled the room with alternating refrains of joy and sorrow; memories of the tragic history of Eastern Europe recorded in song. Like most of its music, the song reflected that unique blend of struggle and persecution which had been part of life in that region throughout history, interspersed with interludes of happiness and celebration. Even the music created for the happiest occasion such as weddings, seemed to have this haunting quality. They listened, captivated by every note played by Litvak and Bashinski. Their music spoke of those brief interludes of joy that each generation had experienced amid the raging seas of sorrow and suffering, bringing memories and tears to the eyes of the older people who had experienced the times. The duo swung into a more festive melody and soon the celebrators' mood for dancing mounted. After much urging, Erik agreed to try to dance while protesting strongly that he had never done it before.

"Don't be shy, Erik," urged Angela. "I will show you how." The group moved aside to make room for the bride and groom. Erik stepped reluctantly into the middle of the circle with Angela. After a series of missteps and considerable vocal encouragement from the group, Erik appeared to grasp the basic movements and soon the others joined in.

The festivities continued while outside on the western horizon the dying rays of the sunset cut off the last remnants of light streaming through the windows. The lamps were lit when Litvak and Bashinski laid down the instruments and called for an intermission. They both agreed that the impromptu musical performance had stimulated their thirst and the guests clapped their approval.

The exaggerated quietness brought on by the absence of music soon seemed out of place and an injustice to the happy occasion and the reluctant musicians were persuaded to again pick up their instruments. Repeated cajolery also persuaded the newly wedded couple to once more lead the dancing. Refreshed by the short interlude and refreshments, Litvak and Bashinski poured out their musical renditions as Erik and Angela stepped onto the dance floor. After several steps into a dance, Angela glanced at the window at the north side of the room. She stopped suddenly and cast a quick glance at the face of a man attentively observing the scene from outside the window. Angela looked again to ensure that she was not imagining it all. Her initial impression was correct. The face was still there, but upon detecting Angela's stare, it moved away quickly. Angela screamed and the music stopped.

"There is someone at the window," she gasped, pointing toward the north wall. Stanislaw ran to the window and looked out. He observed a man turning the corner and disappearing behind a hedge.

"Yes, there was an intruder. I saw him running away," he announced. "There is no point in following him. He is probably a long way from here by now."

Their festive mood quelled by the peeping incident, the party gathered into several small groups and engaged in serious conversation. Glancing around the room, Erik noticed Bashinski and Litvak in an animated discussion in a corner of the parlor. Bashinski caught Erik's eye and motioned to him to come over. Leaving Angela with Anna and Roman, he joined the two men. "I hate to introduce a serious note into this happy occasion," apologized Bashinski, "but since the intrusion has already changed the mood of the celebration and because our time together is limited, I would like your permission to discuss some important matters with you."

"I am at your mercy," said Erik, hoping to allay some of the tenseness he detected in their faces. He lifted his eyebrows quizzically when he noticed that Litvak did not leave them alone.

"That is all right," Bashinski assured him. "I know Pan Litvak well. We have worked together on many occasions and anyway, he will be part of the arrangement that I want to propose to you."

"It is a small world," quipped Erik.

"Yes, in many ways it is," agreed Bashinski, "and you might be surprised to hear how much we know about it, including your own private world."

"Yes, I have already been alerted to this fact. Exactly how much do you know?" asked Erik.

Bashinski paused and observed Erik. "Well, for starters we know that you are engaged in arms design and development at the Torun Works and that you are considered to be one of the brightest young designers in Prussia today."

Erik was taken aback by Bashinski's intimate knowledge of his activities and flattered at the man's description of his technical abilities.

"I am just another technician doing my job," he said, trying to appear modest. "The accounts that you may have been hearing about me may be greatly exaggerated."

"We have no reason to doubt our sources of information," Bashinski assured him. "And you yourself may not be aware of your value to them. But we are. For instance, we know that you just recently perfected a small caliber weapon and that you are now involved in the development of a medium bore rapid fire cannon. And we also know that the success of this whole project depends heavily upon you."

The shock of hearing the candid and accurate revelation by Bashinski about his knowledge of Erik's involvements temporarily stunned him. His mouth opened to express his disbelief but no words emerged.

"We also know of the Kaiser's plan to pursue his territorial ambitions and that the preparations are even now proceeding on his plans to pursue them," continued Bashinski. "But what we do not know or understand is why one of our own people would help him to do it."

Erik blushed deeply. "Are you talking about me?" he blurted out.

"None other," replied Bashinski. "And I propose to stop you. Since we are both Polish and I am your relative, I hope that you will not object to my intrusion."

Erik quickly realized that Bashinski was serious and he suddenly feared that the man's concern would soon turn his own comfortable world upside down. Sure, he had planned to leave Torun sometime after his project was complete, but he wanted to leave on good terms with his employers, especially Richter whom he admired.

"Those people have been very good and fair to me and I cannot do anything to make them think that I do not appreciate it. What has Poland done for me and what will my future be if I hitch my horse to the Polish wagon? Poland could learn a lot from the Prussians. If the Polish had concentrated more on advancing their production capability and efficiencies in the past, instead of on their politics and bureaucracies, they would not be in the predicament in which they find themselves today.   No sir. The Prussians have done nothing to hurt me," explained Erik.

"You are right about that if you consider that taking you away from your parents was fine, but your parents may not agree," said Bashinski.

Erik glanced across the room and saw his parents in conversation with Angela. He sat down, his forehead resting on his hand.

"Please forgive my insolence. I was already planning to leave Torun for America," he apologized.

"Yes, I was pleased to hear that from your brother," said Bashinski, "but it will not be as easy as you think it will be because, you see, you know too much. They will never simply just let you go. However, Pan Litvak and I have a plan, but we will need your full cooperation. We will determine when it is the right time for you to leave and how you will go about it. But before we discuss that further, I have one request to make of you."

"And what is that?" asked Erik. "I am prepared to do whatever I can, but the plan will have to involve Angela and her mother, otherwise I will remain in Torun."

"That is good," replied Bashinski, "because what I want you to do may not be easy or safe and it will take a lot of courage. But you will never be left on your own. There will be a lot of people helping you. I want you to make duplicate drawings of the project on which you are now working and take these plus your formula for the alloy for the new model gun barrel out of Prussian Poland to us or to one of our allies. We want you to keep secret the amounts of one of the ingredients in the alloy to ensure that what you leave behind will never be used against our people."

"But what will happen if they catch me doing this?" For the first time Erik looked seriously disturbed.

"If you work things right, there will be a minimum of risk involved. As for us, we will work to make things as easy as possible for you. The whole Polish underground and our friends elsewhere will be at your service when you need them. We will be in constant touch with you, monitoring your progress and delivering instructions. We will determine the best time for you to leave Torun and advise you of this well in advance. All your documents will be ready for you, as well as Angela's and her mother's.   Your transportation will be arranged and your escape route carefully plotted."

"And when will all this happen?" asked Erik.

"It will depend upon when the prototype of the project on which you are now working will be ready for testing."

"They have scheduled it for late summer or early fall," answered Erik, his voice fading to a near whisper.

"Your removal will be arranged for the week after the prototype is tested," concluded Bashinski. "Meanwhile we will keep in constant touch with you as necessary." He paused for a moment in deep thought. "I almost forgot. There is something else. We will need a code word to introduce our agents to you and you to them. Would you like to suggest something?"

Erik looked around and saw his father and Sosnowski engaged in conversation beside a vase of white carnations.

"How about 'White Carnation' or something like that?" suggested Erik innocently. "Something that will remind us of when our accord began."

"White Carnation? That sounds good. Harmless enough and not so common that anyone would use it in the normal course of conversation, so we will use it," said Bashinski. "From now on, the key words will be White Carnation. When anyone speaks them in your presence, you will know that he or she is one of us. The same goes for you. It will identify you to anyone that you feel may be carrying a message from us." Bashinski paused. "And by the way, if that face in the window tonight should belong to whom Pan Litvak and I think it might, don't be surprised if they start watching you more closely from here on. But do not worry. You are too valuable to them. They will not do anything foolish. And we will not give them any reason to be suspicious. Also, we will ensure that your parents get away safely and that Angela and her mother are properly cared for until your departure is arranged. You have my word."

"Thank you, sir," said Erik in a barely audible voice.

Angela observed her husband's ashen face when he returned to her. "Oh, Erik, you look like you have just seen a vampire. You must be tired. Why don't we sit down for a while and rest."

Erik sat down and observed the wedding guests gathered together in small groups preparing to leave. He knew that soon they would all come around to wish him and his new wife a happy and prosperous future, a future in which fate had intervened only moments earlier.

"Let us enjoy this evening, Angela," he suggested. "This may be the last that we will have together for a long while."

"You are being elusive again Erik." warned Angela. "Don't try to keep anything from me now. Have you forgotten our wedding vows already?"

"As soon as we are alone I will tell you everything," he promised. "Remember that day in October when you accused me of being insensitive toward my family and our own people? Well, I am about to prove to you all that I am not and that I am prepared to do something about our own destiny and maybe even that of our people."

"Oh my dear, dear husband, I am so proud of you. I will stand beside you whenever you need me, and even if we are separated for a while, I will understand."

Slowly the guests departed, leaving only the Sosnowskis and the immediate family behind. Their voices seemed to echo through the empty room which only a little while earlier had been filled to the beams with the din of conversation, laughter and music. The Sosnowskis offered their guest bedroom to the bride and groom, Bashinski and Litvak retired to a nearby inn and Erik's parents and brother returned to the home of Angela's mother for the night. Darkness entombed the quiet street in front of the Sosnowski residence. The clock in the parlor struck twelve and the memorable day was over.

The new day, drenched clean by an early morning shower, glistened in the brilliant March sun. The day had barely dawned when the last of the family and guests prepared to leave for home. Erik's parents with Stanislaw and his family and Litvak boarded the early morning train, as did Bashinski, each party going their separate directions. Later in the afternoon Erik and Roman stood on the platform waiting for the train to Torun. Standing between them, Angela clung to Erik's arm in silence, oblivious of her surroundings. The train roared into the station raising clouds of dust and cinders along the platform. Erik and Angela lingered in an emotional embrace until the last boarding call. He and Roman climbed into the coach and took a seat beside the window where Angela could see them. Passengers carrying bags, packages and children in their arms scurried around to pick the best seats. The shrill whistle sounded twice and the train eased out of the station. Angela, her eyes red with tears, waved slowly until the rear of the train disappeared into the horizon.

~~~

At the Torun Works, the world did not seem at all affected by the previous Saturday's events in Krakow. The two young men each resumed their routines where they left off the previous week. Erik saw no evidence of anyone regarding him in any unusual manner. He worked silently and pondered some of the events of the past few days. Bashinski's proposition, in retrospect, seemed somewhat extreme to him now. There was nothing to indicate that Richter or any of the other senior people at the research and development department had any sinister motives. They were busy doing their jobs the same as always. Erik wondered if all that Bashinski had said was anything more than exaggeration by a passionate Polish nationalist. But then again, did not Richter say that their job was to produce and not to question?

Erik was painfully aware that some of the people closest to him were taking Bashinski's dire predictions seriously, so much so that his parents were even now making final plans to leave Europe. He realized that in two weeks he would see them for the last time as they would be leaving the following Monday. It must take a lot of conviction to leave one's home for a strange land thousands of kilometers away. Anticipating an emotional final visit with his family, Erik invited Roman to accompany him to Lubicz.

They arrived in Lubicz late Saturday afternoon. At the Berglund house a gloomy pall hung over the scene like a gray shroud as Erik's parents moved around silently, making final preparations for their departure. The kitchen which on their last visit had radiated warmth and hominess now seemed lonely and barren. The rest of the house and Axel's workshop, now devoid of most of their contents, stood estranged and aloof as if to disown the former owners for their callous abandonment. Everyone moved around mechanically hoping to complete the unpleasant task as quickly as possible and escape from the grip of the present.

"I really do appreciate your coming with me this time," said Erik to Roman when they were alone. "It would be difficult for me to return to Torun by myself after today."

"That is what friends are for," Roman assured him. "You would do the same for me, I am sure."

Each of them went about their tasks silently, speaking only in subdued tones. In the larger front room, Mrs. Berglund worked in silence, placing as many valuable items as would fit in a large steamer trunk and arranging the rest neatly to make the taking of inventory easier for Litvak. She sat down wearily when Erik and Roman walked into the room.

"This is the supreme humiliation." She tried to hold back her tears. "Forced out of my own home by persecutors and tyrant pigs, probably never to see it again!" She raised her eyes upward. "May we be the last of the generations to be thus humiliated and may God grant that your children will live in peace wherever they may be."

"You are sad to be leaving your beloved Poland, mama," said Erik, "but sometime it is for the best. People have been moving about for thousands of years, even before there were countries and borders. It is man's nature to seek new horizons." She returned to her task, tears falling down her cheeks.

Stanislaw entered the room and moved around, checking on the preparations. His excitement at beginning a new life in a new country seemed to affect the others. "Cheer up, mama. This is not the end. It is the beginning," he chided. She wiped away her tears and returned to her task. Axel, buoyed by his son's good humor, continued the preparations with renewed cheerful energy.

"Don't forget the vegetable seeds, mama," he reminded his wife. "We will have great garden in Canada this year. Make sure to take the broad beans. They may not have heard of this delightful delicacy there."

Outside the sun warmed up the soil and the birds in the trees filled the air with song, oblivious to the drama that was unfolding inside the house. By Sunday afternoon the trunks were all packed and ready for strapping. The rooms were now bare and cold. Earlier in the day Litvak had removed much of the furnishings and taken them to his warehouse. Soon Erik's parents would leave for Litvak's house where they would spend the night. The next day Litvak would drive them to the railway station where they would take the train for Amsterdam. Heeding Bashinski's advice, Stanislaw had arranged for them to board a ship at Liverpool which would take them to Montreal. This would mean that they would travel by boat from Amsterdam to London and then by train to Liverpool.

"In that way, you will leave no trail," chided Litvak.

"It is easy for you to make light of the situation," protested Mrs. Berglund. "You are staying in your home. But it will not be that easy for an old lady like me to jump from train to boat and then from boat to train and back a dozen times."

"Maybe not," agreed Litvak, "but once you get on board that ship in Liverpool, they will treat you like a queen. Bashinski has seen to that."

The moment which Erik had dreaded all weekend finally arrived. It was time for him and Roman to leave for Torun. Tears swelled up in everyone's eyes as his mother clutched him in her arms, refusing to release him.

"Don't worry, mama," Axel comforted her. "Erik will be following us soon. It is not as if you will not see him again."

"God be with you my son. Take care of yourself," she said as she kissed him again and again before releasing him.

Erik returned her kisses, embraced his father and his brother and then turned and walked toward the gate with Roman following close behind. At the gate he wiped the tears off his face with his sleeve and then turned around and waved. As he entered the road he noticed that his father had his arm around his mother who was weeping hysterically.

In the coach back to Torun, Erik and Roman remained silent for most of the trip.

"It's a cruel world out there," said Erik as they neared their destination.

"So I am beginning to see," answered Roman.

"Do you realize that I may never see them again?" said Erik.

Roman nodded, trying to suppress the sadness in his own heart.

~~~

The April sun blazed brilliantly in the clear blue sky, bathing the earth in its warmth. Across the street from the compound the soft green hedges, covered with fat, newly opened buds stood in contrast to the snowy pink cherry blossoms. In the trees the birds poured out their spirited songs and performed their annual mating rites among the branches. It was not a day to be inside any walls. Erik and Roman left their billet early to escape the Sunday morning throngs around town and made their way to the banks of the Vistula River. They stopped near the spot where the two had picnicked with Lydia and Angela the previous September and watched the swollen waterway wend its way to the Baltic Sea. From their vantage point they could see across the river to where the soft green meadows stood fenced in by black cliffs of spruce and pine.

· Erik remarked about how it seemed like years since he and Angela had their first conversation only a few paces from where they stood. He shared his feelings with Roman about how much he missed Angela, especially when his mind was not totally occupied with his work. Roman listened silently. They sat down and Erik reminisced about all the events that had taken place in his life since that delightful day – the reunion with his family, his promotion to the Research and Development Department, his parents' departure from Europe and his marriage to Angela. He confided to Roman that he felt that too much had been crammed into his life in this short time and he was afraid that the future might be threatening to crowd him even more, as if impatient to speed up the unfolding of time. Roman who had listened in silence felt the heaviness in his friend's soul.

"Why don't you share some of those good fortunes with me," he grinned.

"I wish I could, dear friend. I wish I could," replied Erik smiling at Roman's attempt to relieve the anxiety.

Hypnotized by the flowing water, the young men stopped talking and gazed at the panorama until the sun nudged the midday point in the sky. They opened the basket of food that Hilda had prepared for them and hungrily devoured the cold meats, cheese and bread which she had packed. After a brief nap they stood up and took one more look at the panorama before beginning their walk back toward the city.

At the edge of town where the houses boldly encroached on the countryside, the storks had returned and were busily engaged in building their chimney-top nests. They persisted in their task undaunted by the occasional puff of smoke from the chimney or the curses of the irate burghers on the ground below. In the distance the call of the cuckoo to its mate rose above the gentle roar of the river on one side and the sounds of the city on the other. Erik and Roman walked across the grassy knoll between the houses where the early spring flowers waved their heads gracefully in the soft breeze, providing a kaleidoscope of green, yellow, purple and red. The density of the buildings increased until they were at the edge of the city where the tram line began its course into town. They boarded the trolley and rode into the city, each absorbed in his own thoughts.

CHAPTER 14

In the Research and Development Department work was proceeding feverishly on the production of the prototype of the new field gun. A precise analysis of the specifications of the two models whose designs were being scrutinized revealed to Erik and August where modifications would result in improvements. The basic design of field guns had not changed since the weapons were first produced and most of the world's existing models went back to 1896. Richter explained that most generals felt that since no improvements were made to the weapons in all that time, they were now becoming obsolete for use in modern warfare. This was the need that the new model which they were developing would fill.

Erik's and August's calculations indicated that there did indeed appear to be considerable scope for refinement in a number of areas. They felt that the new model could achieve greater distance by increasing the length of the barrel, by improving the quality of its machining, and by increasing the thickness and changing the composition of the barrel wall. The question of firing frequency heat resistance was left to Erik for resolution.

He knew that it would not be difficult to improve on the existing models, but he wanted to produce a barrel that would be the best in existence. This could be achieved, he thought, by varying the amount of certain critical components in the alloy that he was developing. By incorporating the changes in its design, plus a new alloy for the barrel, the prospect of completely revolutionizing the field gun industry was virtually assured. For Erik this prospect was both exciting and unnerving.

He stared approvingly at the drawings, and then closed his eyes in deep thought. He knew that in order to remain on schedule he would soon have to begin concentrating almost exclusively on the composition of the alloy for the barrel. This would pose a problem for him since he would also have to continue preparing the specifications for the experimental designs and he could not rely on August who was neither an innovative designer nor a metallurgist. Earlier in the day Richter had suggested that perhaps it was time to transfer another technician to the project.

Because he wanted to keep the formula secret, Erik did not want an experienced metallurgist working on the project. But now the idea came to him that he would ask Richter for an assistant apprentice, and furthermore, he would ask for his roommate Roman. He and Roman had discussed metallurgy for several months since Erik himself had become more involved in the science and since then Roman had read everything on the subject that he could find. Recognizing his interest in the subject, Roman's supervisor had already recommended that he be given the opportunity to work with metallurgical formulas whenever possible. His emerging skill and unusual fascination with the science was gradually becoming recognized by his superiors and lately Roman was spending more time in the metallurgy department.

Elated at the idea, Erik rushed into Richter's office and proposed that Roman be assigned to the project. Richter did not respond enthusiastically at first because, he said, he wanted the best qualified person to assist Erik. When Erik explained that the two of them were very compatible and worked well together, Richter noted that this may be a way to make the most efficient use of the time remaining for completion of the project. He would speak to Roman's supervisor, he said.

Roman's supervisor told Richter that his apprentice had exhibited unusual talent in working with metallurgical formulas and because of his fascination with the subject should probably be steered into that vocation and be given the opportunity to work on formulations whenever possible. For these reasons he had loaned Roman to the metallurgy department on several occasions. Roman's file also showed that the apprentice had been training as a machinist but had recently been combining the two disciplines and should become a more valuable worker as a result.

When told by Erik that he had recommended to Richter that he should come to work in their department, Roman was ecstatic. Not only was he grateful to have an opportunity to spend all his time in metallurgy, but also for the chance to work next to Erik, whom he respected.

Richter moved quickly on Erik's recommendation. By Wednesday Roman had been rushed through security clearance and provided with identification which would allow him to enter and leave the Research and Development Department. True to his commitment to secrecy, Erik had not revealed to his roommate the exact nature of his activities in the department. Roman had known that they were of a confidential nature and had not pressed Erik for more information. But now that he was to become a part of the team his curiosity heightened.

He did not have to wait long to satisfy it. At midmorning Roman's supervisor brought him to Richter's office. The engineer welcomed him warmly and he and Erik took him to his new workplace. He was assigned to a workplace next to Erik, identical in size and configuration. A door between the two offices would give them easy access to each other, explained Richter.

"Erik here will explain to you what we are doing here and the secrecy attached to our project," said Richter. "You will, of course, not divulge any information about our activities to anyone." He paused and added with a twinkle in his eye. "This includes your friend Lydia."

Roman looked astonished at the mention of Lydia's name. "How did you...?"

Richter laughed. "I see that you too are surprised at how much we know about you. But it is our business to check carefully on everyone who comes to work in this place. And in case you are wondering, no, we did not get any of our information from Erik."

Surprised by Richter's casual manner and comforted by Erik's presence and support, Roman quickly adjusted to his new surroundings. The two of them moved freely between their adjoining offices as Erik prepared to familiarize Roman with the work that had gone on before he arrived and what remained to be done. He unfolded some large drawings and laid them out on his drafting table.

"This is our project," he said, trying to remain casual and pointing to a sketch of a field gun. "I will take you around and show you the two models which we are using as the basis for some revolutionary design changes. If it works, this will be the only 13 centimeter gun in the world."

Roman lifted his eyes away from the drawing and observed Erik's casual attitude.

"But this is a weapon. For killing people," he said in a barely audible voice.

"We don't concern ourselves with those things here," Erik tried to assure him. "We are researchers and developers. That is our job." He was starting to sound like Richter.

Roman nodded in reluctant agreement and returned to his office where he pored in silence over the drawings and specifications for the rest of the day.

The dormitory was silent except for the spasmodic fits of laughter from the rooms down the hall. Hilda had prepared and served a generous and delicious evening meal. They lay on their bunks, their bodies satisfied, but their heads swimming in turmoil. Roman had not spoken to Erik about his new job since they arrived back from the Research and Development Department. Roman stood on the edge of his bed and looked at Erik.

"Erik, do you realize what you are doing in that place?" he asked. "Have you considered what may be the end result of your actions? Have you given any thought to the potential victims of your brilliant inventions? They could be your own parents, or brother, or your wife. My own parents are now in the Prussian zone and probably safer than the people that you love and yet I would not be able to bring myself to do what you are doing. Your total lack of sensitivity really surprises me. No wonder you did not have the courage to tell me what was going on there," said Roman with obvious disgust.

Erik jumped to his feet in defiance. "Just a minute Roman, give me a chance to defend myself. Just because I don't talk much does not mean that I don't think." He collapsed on his bed and motioned to Roman to sit down in a nearby chair.

"I was not going to reveal this to you so soon," he said in a low voice, "but since you have shamed me into it, I have no choice."

Roman cast curious glances at his friend and sat down. "You see, Roman, when you think it over carefully, I have no other alternative but to continue doing what I am doing now," explained Erik. "And I am not going to blame anyone except myself for what happened. I must admit that I got caught up in the excitement of being involved in such important work and I appreciated the encouragement that they gave me. I was flattered by the praise which I received. Before I knew what was happening to me it was too late. Knowing what I know now, do you think that they would let me go somewhere freely, on my own accord? Of course not. So what is the alternative? I feel that the only thing left for me to do is to do as I am told – at least for the time being. If and when the opportunity presents itself, I will leave this place and go somewhere else. And I plan to do just that, as soon as the prototype is finished. Until then, for me, it is business as usual."

"Then why did you drag me into this thing? I was perfectly happy where I was," demanded Roman, obviously perplexed.

"Because you are part of my plan," answered Erik.

"I am part of your plan? That is just great," hissed Roman. "Does that mean that in your mind I am not capable of making my own plans?"

"I would like to say that you are," said Erik. "But you see Roman, my friend, because you and I are friends and live together, they probably suspected that you knew what was going on in that department. If there was any suspicion, it was put to rest when you became part of the Research and Development Department. You are now right up there where they can watch you. And if you keep your nose clean, you will not be considered to be part of my plan when it comes to pass. You see, Roman, now we are each in charge of our own destinies."

"And you, my friend, never cease to amaze me," said Roman. "Although I liked you much better the way you were when we first arrived here."

"You might say that we are victims of our own talents," said Erik.

~~~

A letter leaned against the side of one of the cubby holes which served as a mailbox and message center inside the entrance to the dormitory. The handwriting was free-flowing and graceful. There was no need for Erik to open the letter to find out who sent it. He knew immediately that it was from Angela. He opened it eagerly.

It felt strange to be a married woman and not have a husband around to remind her of it, she wrote. The Sosnowskis and everyone else were kind and helpful, but she still felt alone and empty. The early days of May were fresh and filled with the smells of spring. It would be so nice if he was there and they could walk together in the still, cool evening and just listen to the birds praising the season in song.

She was lonely, he thought, as he folded the letter and placed it back in its envelope. He pictured her walking through the park alone, stopping to look at the spring flowers and the newly emerged soft green leaves. The gloomy shadow of loneliness crept into his mind and then settled in his soul. Suddenly his work and everything that had occupied his mind in recent weeks became ambiguous and unimportant. He needed to see her and nothing else mattered. He resolved to ask Richter for several days of leave.

Richter agreed that Erik had been working hard and needed a break, but he would have to clear it with his superiors before he could grant him the leave Erik requested. Next morning Erik entered his workplace listlessly and with heaviness in his heart sat down on his drafting stool. Richter strode into the room looking pleased.

"Well Erik, I got it! I got permission for you to take a few days away from work. You don't have to be back until Wednesday. But it was only granted on the condition that it will not affect the completion date of our project."

"Thank you, Herr Richter," blurted Erik in excitement. "I promise to make up every minute of lost time."

"That is very thoughtful of you, Erik, but you don't really owe anybody here anything. The organization gets good value from your efforts," said Richter. A troubled look came over his face and he lowered his voice. "But if I were you, Erik, I would be very careful about where I am seen. I know that it is none of my business, but take my advice. I give it to you in good faith and as a mentor."

Richter acknowledged Erik's silent concern and returned to his office without further explanation. Erik thought back to what Bashinski had told him the day of his wedding. Now he was receiving the same advice from another different and unexpected source.

The train wheezed and puffed and spewed out acrid smoke as it raced into the endless horizon. Erik sat staring blankly at the landscape as it glided past the dingy square window. The hours seemed like days as the train loitered at the station stops along the way. Passengers embarked and disembarked into endless seas of faces. His thoughts could focus only on his destination and the smiling face that would greet him there. How surprised she would be when he suddenly appeared at her door!

The late afternoon sun turned into a fiery orb as it descended slowly toward the undulating skyline. Suddenly a second set of railway tracks appeared, then two more fanned out from the main one and Erik knew that Krakow was only a few more minutes away. Finally the locomotive whistled and the wheels groaned in protest as the brakes were applied and the buildings of Krakow slid by, very quickly at first and then slower and slower.

Inside the coach the passengers discoursed excitedly, straightened out their clothes and gathered up their belongings. The conductor weaved through the aisle shouting "Krakow" and the train ground to a stop.

The dark green shadows of the spring evening crept over the city as Erik boarded a cab and rode toward the street where Angela lived. He knocked softly at the door and waited. The street was still and empty except for another cab which had just arrived and stopped on the other side of the street. The door opened slowly at first and then flew wide against the banister. She fell into his arms and showered him with kisses.

"Why did you not let me know that you were coming?" she asked, her eyes filling up with tears.

"Because I could not wait for my letter to get here," he replied. "I had to see you right away or I would have lost my mind."

"Oh, you poor sweetheart," she said. "You must be awful lonely." She took his face in her hands and gazed lovingly at him. "But let us not stand here. Let us go in."

As he walked through the open door he turned and observed the cab still parked on the other side of the street. A man in the passenger's seat looked away as Erik stared at him through the fading light.

"What is the matter, Erik?" she asked with a concerned look.

"That man in the cab. He looked familiar. I know that I have seen him somewhere before. But where?" He took one step into the house then turned around and looked across the street. The cab was gone.

"I remember now," said Erik. "That man sat across the aisle from me on the train. It is very strange that he should be coming to the same part of the city as I am, and also the same street."

"It is probably just an unusual coincidence that only happens once in a lifetime," said Angela softly. "Come on in a little farther so I can show you to my mother again. She has forgotten what you look like, she says. But you talk about coincidences. I just received a letter from your parents today, the same day that you arrive. Now that's a coincidence!"

"Lord protect us! Who have we here?" asked Mrs. Klazcek, peering across the dimly lit room.

"Don't worry, mama. It is only Erik," announced a gleeful Angela. "He has come back to see us."

"Thank God for that. I thought we were being robbed," said Mrs. Klazcek as she hobbled across the room. "It is a good thing that he has arrived. Now we can show him to the neighbors to prove that he really exists."

"Now, mother," scolded Angela. "You know that the neighbors are not worried about things like that." She took Erik's arm. "Come and sit down and we can read the letter that came from your parents today."

She lit the lamp above the kitchen table and put the letter in front of Erik. He recognized his mother's handwriting below a string of postmarks and stamps bearing the bust of England's King George V. His mother's handwriting and the foreign king's bearded face presented a strange juxtaposition. Only then did he truly realize that his mother and family were indeed in a strange and distant land. He could not conceive of his mother being anywhere except in her beloved Poland. He continued to gaze at the envelope containing the letter.

"Come on. Pull it out it and read it," urged Angela. "It is a most interesting letter and paints a beautiful picture of their new life."

He withdrew the letter from the envelope and opened up the pages.

After many days on the ship and trains we arrived safely. We are staying with a Polish family while Stanislaw works on getting the homestead arrangements completed. We visited the place that would be our home. Right now it looks like a wilderness, heavily treed on the lower ground and covered with shrubs and prairie grass at the higher elevations. A neighbor had already plowed up a patch of grassland for us – enough for a garden and to grow some oats for the horses. Horses? Yes. Stanislaw has already purchased two with some of the money that they brought with them from home.

This is like another world. Everyone welcomes you. They are so glad to see someone from the old country. Help is all around us. People everywhere are building homes and barns, clearing land and constructing roads. Stanislaw is a fountain of boundless energy. He stops only long enough to eat and sleep. There is no time for suspicions or animosity here. Everyone is too busy. War is not even mentioned, except in conversations about the old country.

This is a huge country and often lonely. Would you believe that it took us four days to get to our destination by train? And they say that it takes another three or four days to get to the west coast of this country.

The weather has been surprisingly pleasant. There was still some snow on the ground among the trees and in shaded areas when we arrived, but it disappeared soon after. Stanislaw and his father are like a couple of school boys, not knowing which task to tackle first.

They have chosen a spot on which to build our temporary home and maybe by the time you and Erik arrive we will have our permanent house ready for you. After our cabin is ready, Stanislaw and his father plan to build one for him and his family. Perhaps, when you arrive, you and Erik will prefer to stay in the closest town which is twelve kilometers away.

"Twelve kilometers!" gasped Erik.

"In a country that size, it probably feels like next door," said Angela, laughing at Erik's disbelief. "You go ahead and finish reading the letter while I fix something for you to eat. You must be starved. We have so much to talk about. What a wonderful evening this is going to be for us. Thank you for coming, Erik. This is just the most beautiful surprise that you could have given me."

A shaft of morning sunlight streamed through the window as they got out of bed and stole quietly into the kitchen, careful not to awaken Mrs. Klazcek while they had their breakfast. Outside the street was quiet and nearly deserted. They walked slowly across the small park toward the main thoroughfare, hand in hand. Erik was sure that the world had never behaved quite like this before. The mid-morning sun was warmer and more radiant then it he could ever remember it. The air was filled with pleasant smells and in the trees the birds sang in clear and melodious tones as they flew from tree to tree establishing their territorial rights and performing their mating rituals. Angela looked up into his face and smiled.

"The world is celebrating our love," she whispered.

"And respecting our privacy," he added.

They made their way back to the little cottage. Inside the front door they found a note from Angela's mother saying that Sosnowski had dropped in and decided to take her to his place so that Erik and Angela could have the day to themselves. "How very thoughtful of them," said Angela. "Let's go and sit in the back yard where no one can see us." They sat on a small bench and leaned back against the wall.

"This married life is delightful," remarked Erik contentedly.

"You haven't tasted half of it yet," said Angela with a mischievous look in her eyes. "Just wait until I get you into the house all alone."

"Show me right here. It's so beautiful outside so why go in," said Erik.

"Fine. But you have to catch me first," she said, amused by his innocence. She ran into the house with Erik in pursuit. He chased her around the living room and she bolted into the bedroom. He followed her close behind and caught her in his arms. They fell onto the bed and Erik kicked the door closed with his stocking-clad foot.

~~~

Angela was standing beside the cast iron kitchen stove cooking their dinner. He sat at the kitchen table watching her.

"Wouldn't it be wonderful when we start living together, just you and I?" she said.

"It should not be too long now," responded Erik. "I am sure that Uncle Bashinski is working on the arrangements right now."

"Uncle Bashinski? I thought that you were suspicious of him. But now you call him uncle. Did something happen to change your mind about him?"

"The way that things are going, I suddenly feel that we are fortunate to have someone like him in the family. I feel more secure now knowing that we have someone like that out there working for us," explained Erik. "At first I thought that he was nothing more than a meddling old bureaucrat, but the more I hear of him, the more respect I have for him. He certainly seems to be well informed. How he knew what I was doing at Torun Works is still a mystery to me. But he knew. Almost better than I did."

"Don't forget that he knows Litvak, and Litvak knows everything that is going on around there," Angela reminded him.

"Now there is another individual whom I don't quite understand," said Erik. "Why do we need to have a complete stranger like him concerned with the intimate affairs of the family? Why is it that we have to be involved with all these mysterious people? Why can't we be like Roman and Lydia? They go about their lives and nobody pays any attention to them."

"Maybe it is because you are different, Erik. Have you ever thought of that?" she explained. "But why don't we just forget about all those things for now? We have only one more day together, so let us enjoy it. We may not see each other again for another month or more," she added sadly.

Erik stood up and kissed her on the cheek. "I am so lucky to have found you," he said.

It seems that nothing arrives more slowly than a long-awaited day or more quickly than a dreaded hour. The day of Erik's departure dawned gray and rainy. They waited for the train on the station platform, Angela clinging to Erik's arm. The imminent departure of the train was soon announced and the passengers surged forward to board the coaches. Erik thought he noticed a familiar face in the crowd. He looked again. It was the same person who had been on the train the previous Friday and who he had seen in the cab when he had arrived at Angela's home. Erik pretended not to notice him as he bade Angela good-bye. He held back his tears as he looked back and saw her on the station platform waving.

Erik entered the coach and noticed that the now familiar face took a seat several seats up and across the aisle. They did not look at each other. Erik tried to convince himself that it was all a coincidence, but an uneasy feeling overcame him even as he tried to deal with the sadness of once again having to leave his beloved wife behind. The mystery man remained on the train until they arrived in Torun and then disappeared into the crowd at the station.

~~~

Richter welcomed Erik and seemed delighted to have him back. Erik found his workplace exactly as he had left it and they immediately resumed work on the highly classified project. Richter did not ask his charge where he had spent his four days of vacation and there was no evidence of suspicion in his voice or manner. Erik felt relieved and dove into his task with a new determination. Roman, who was now part of the research and development team, returned to his highly spirited ways and refrained from discussing the morality of their occupations with his roommate.

The problems of the world and the events taking place around them seemed insignificant and removed from the busy atmosphere of the Research and Development Department. Erik was happy except for the loneliness in his heart for his beloved Angela. He wondered if it would not be better if they forgot about going to America and stayed in Torun where he could continue working in the job that he loved. In his next letter to Angela he mentioned this idea and that he wanted her to come and join him in Torun. In a tersely worded response she begged him not to make any decisions until after they had talked about it.

That opportunity came late in June. In the sweltering midday heat he boarded the train for Krakow and leaned back casually in his seat. As the train pulled out away from the station he glanced across the aisle at his fellow passengers and noticed a familiar face. It was the same man whom he had seen on his last trip to Krakow. He looked away and the warm perspiration on his body turned to a cold sweat. He shivered. Perhaps he is just a regular traveler who happens to be assigned to this coach, he reasoned in his mind. But why would he appear in front of Angela's house just as he too was arriving? Was that also a coincidence or was Bashinski right when he said that Erik was being watched? And who was it that they had seen at the window on their wedding night? But if he was being watched, why did Richter, who had warned him to be prudent, not show any signs of suspicion, or even concern, upon his return from the last trip to Krakow? And above all, why would anyone be interested in following him? He was just a technician doing his job. He leaned back and fell into a fitful sleep.

There had been a change in their plans to leave Europe, Angela explained in hushed tones as they rode in the cab after leaving the railroad station in Krakow. Bashinski wrote saying that there may have to be an adjustment in the proposed arrangements, but to leave everything to him and the new instructions will follow later.

"Sometime I feel that I am a prisoner of this man Bashinski," complained Erik.

"Oh, you are a prisoner alright, but not of Bashinski," Angela corrected him. He gave her a puzzled look as the cab pulled up in front of the house.

"We may not be going to the same place as your parents," Angela broke the news after they entered the house. "Bashinski hinted that when everything is settled, we may be going somewhere where your talents would be better utilized."

"This whole thing is getting too complicated for me," sighed Erik. "Like I said in my letter, I would just like to stay where I am and continue doing the work that I enjoy. Why can't they just leave us alone – all of them? I think I will put the whole thing out of my mind and just live one day at a time from now on."

"Yes, Erik. Sometime I feel just like you do and perhaps even going to stay with you in Torun," she agreed. "But then again, it may not be that simple. So for now, let's just forget everything and enjoy our short time together."

"This time we only have one full day to ourselves, so let's make the most of it," said Erik, taking Angela into his arms.

~~~

Back in Torun the next day, Erik woke up shortly after daybreak. It was still too early for breakfast so he went for a walk on the familiar footpath skirting the foundry compound. It was a golden morning, with the warm rays of the sun chasing away the few wisps of fog that were left behind by the cool darkness. As he walked beside the wall of the building, he felt the stored heat from the bricks and concrete warming the cool morning air. In the trees the birds flitted about busily, feeding their young then flying away in search of more food.

Soon the air would be filled with the sounds of commercial activity but for now the stillness soothed his troubled mind. He returned to the dormitory refreshed and invigorated. The other residents were already seated around the table having their breakfast.

Hilda brought his plate and clicked her tongue. "Why don't you just marry the girl and save yourself all this misery?" she chuckled.

Erik attempted a feeble smile and Roman winked at him across the table.

Richter entered Erik's office as soon as he and Roman arrived. His shoulders were uncharacteristically stooped and his face was drawn. There was a meeting of the project team in the conference room, he announced.

Richter's voice was apologetic. "Men," he said in a genial tone, "I am most pleased with the progress that you are making on this project and wish to compliment you all on your efforts. So what I have to say is in no way a reflection on the standard of your work.

"Late last Friday we received orders from Berlin that we must curtail all the travel of our research workers both inside and outside our borders until after the completion of this project. To ensure that this will happen, I have been instructed to retrieve your passports and travel documents immediately and hold them here until further notice. You will deliver these to me before the end of the day. I hope that you will understand that this is all in the interest of security and I trust that it will not cause you any hardship," he said, looking directly at Erik.

They nodded their acknowledgement and Richter returned to his office.

"Well, what do you think of all that?" asked Roman when they returned to their billet that evening.

"I think that we should go about our business in a normal way and see what happens," suggested Erik. "After all, there is not much else that we can do," he added as he picked up a pen and sheet of paper.

"Who are you writing to?" asked Roman.

"Angela," Erik replied.

"I wonder how she will take it," said Roman.

"Probably better than I am right now," remarked Erik.

The letter was short and the message terse. He apologized for his inability to visit her as soon as he had planned and promised that the moment that the project was completed and his passport and visa returned he would be on the train to Krakow. Send my regards to Bashinski, he added.

He and Roman went for a long walk toward the city center and he dropped the letter in a mailbox several blocks away from the Torun Works compound.

Angela's letter arrived two weeks later. Erik studied the envelope curiously. It seemed to be more soiled than usual and the flap opened easily. She wrote that she felt sad about Erik's inability to come out to see her but she understood. Perhaps one day soon they would be together for good. His uncle had paid them a visit and said that he really loved the flowers that she and Erik had planted on his last trip to Krakow in May. He knew how much Erik loved carnations and if he wanted to buy some nice ones there was a flower stand in the marketplace in Torun where they sold some of the best ones in the city.

Erik placed the letter back in the envelope with a puzzled look on his face. It was a strange letter, he thought, not at all like any other that he had received from her. They had never talked about carnations. He wondered what she meant, and then he recalled Bashinski's instruction in connection with the word "carnation." At that time he found it strange that Bashinski would agree to a password as simple as carnation, so he put it out of his mind. Now another piece of the complicated puzzle was falling into place as predicted. He shook his head in disbelief and tore up the letter into tiny pieces.

~~~

The hot, humid days seemed to follow each other endlessly as they worked tenaciously on their project. To escape the suffocating heat inside their dormitory, Erik and Roman would spend much of their spare time outdoors. Since the decree forbidding travel outside the immediate area had come out, the two had spent more time exploring the city and the surrounding area looking for points of interest or observing the downtown crowds and mingling with them on Saturday afternoons.

They discovered and explored the old city which still harbored many of the buildings constructed during the twelfth and thirteenth centuries, including the ruins of the castle built by the Teutonic Knights, who had governed the city and region during that period. The next Saturday, they climbed the leaning tower and walked along the old city walls which skirted the river, then gazed in awe at the centuries-old Town Hall and the Dominican Monastery. This was once Mikolay Kopernik's town, who later became Nicolas Copernicus when the foreigners could not pronounce his name. This was a town oozing history. Except for his longing for Angela, Erik found his new-found lifestyle most enjoyable.

In the midst of their explorations they discovered a secluded fishing hole near the confluence of the Drewca and Vistula Rivers. A large tree leaning out over the water provided a good spot from which to drop their lines into a deep, shaded depression that the fish seemed to prefer during the simmering heat of the summer. This isolated site provided them with a number of relaxing reprieves from the hectic work atmosphere at the Research and Development Department and rewarded them regularly with the excitement of enticing the more venturesome inhabitants of the water hole to take the bait dangled before them. Hilda would react vociferously when they arrived with their catch but always agreed to prepare them for the residents of the dormitory if someone offered to do the scaling and cleaning.

Roman also had obligations to Lydia and Erik was at times left to do things by himself. On the last Saturday in July, he left his friend with Lydia and made his way toward the marketplace. He stood around and watched the animated transactions taking place around him. The activity and atmosphere was a welcome respite for him after another intense week of constant preoccupation with formulas, calculations and drawings. He was fascinated by the curious interactions of the people engaged in the market's activities – the sellers, the buyers and the shifty pickpockets and beggars, all responding loyally to their survival instincts.

As he wandered around the marketplace Erik remembered Angela's letter that had stated that Bashinski had directed him to a certain flower stand which sold carnations. He walked around until he came to a flower stand and stopped to look at the flowers. The flower merchant went about his business and paid no attention to Erik. He started walk away then stopped at an adjoining stall and looked around. Only a few meters away an old man sat on a bench slouched over his cane observing his surroundings. As Erik walked toward him, the man observed him intently through his bushy eyebrows.

"Do you have a pfennig for a poor man?" he wheezed as Erik walked by him.

Erik stopped and reached into his pocket to find a coin. The old man's eyes remained fixed on Erik's face.

"They have some beautiful flowers here, especially carnations. Is that what you were looking for?" he asked.

"Yes. Maybe I was," replied Erik absentmindedly.

"The man at the first stall that you stopped at has the best ones. I know him. If you tell me your name I could ask him to make a special bouquet for you to give to your sweetheart."

"Oh, I don't have a sweetheart. The flowers are for me. My uncle told me about this place."

"And what might your uncle's name be?" he asked.

"Bashinski," answered Erik.

"Then your name must be Berglund," hissed the old man.

"How did you know that?" asked Erik, his voice reflecting both his surprise and suspicion.

"I have been waiting for you for the past two weeks or more," replied the beggar. "It is about time that you showed up here. I have been carrying a message for you from Bashinski for I don't know how long now. You young people have no respect for promptness these days."

"And what did my good uncle have to tell me?" asked Erik in a polite voice, trying to appease the old man.

The man's eyes swept the surroundings. He lowered his voice. "Your uncle has everything arranged except the date of departure. That part is up to you. What message do you want to send him?"

"Tell him that the idea is still fine with me, but that the project may not be completed for a month or more," said Erik in a low voice.

"And you will bring the drawings? Colonel Bashinski says not to leave without them," the old man cautioned him.

"Yes. I am working on a duplicate set right now. They will be ready as soon as the final tests on the product are completed." Erik stopped talking abruptly, hoping that he had not already revealed too much.

"Good. Two weeks from today, your peddler friend will meet you at the usual spot at three in the afternoon. You will provide him with whatever new information you have at that time. If you should need to send a message to Bashinski in a hurry, you will find me here any day of the week. Do you have anything else to say to the colonel?"

"No," responded Erik, as he turned to walk away. He stopped suddenly and returned to the beggar. "Tell him that there may be another person needing his help later. His name is Potoski; Roman Potoski."

"Potoski, you say. I'll see that he gets the message."

Erik walked past several vegetable stands then turned around to see if the old man had moved from his spot. He was still seated on the bench, scanning the milling crowd with his squinty eyes. Erik suddenly realized that he had spoken freely to a person who may not have been whom he said he was and that this could lead to serious problems for himself and Roman. But then, the old man did know the password that he and Bashinski had agreed to and he also knew Bashinski's name, although he referred to him as Colonel. He would have to be more discreet in the future, thought Erik. He pushed his way through the milling throng of people and made his way into the street and back to the dormitory.

~~~

During the week Erik and Roman agreed to go to the fishing hole that Saturday as soon as they got away from work. Since Roman would not be seeing Lydia until Sunday they could spend most of the afternoon at the river if the weather was favorable. Planning for this diversion helped the week pass quickly and early Saturday afternoon the two friends boarded the tram, carrying their fishing rods and tackle baskets. No one had yet discovered their spot so again they had it to themselves as they baited their hooks and leaned back against the tree's large branches that reached out over the water. A soft breeze picked up the cool, moist air from the surface of the water and lifted it upwards, cooling their faces as it moved. In the distance the muted noises of the city broke the silence but where they sat there were no other sounds, except those of the birds darting among the trees and the trickling of water as it passed through submerged branches and danced around exposed rocks along the bank.

"I wonder how deep the water is here," mused Erik.

"Probably deep enough to drown," said Roman. "I wouldn't want to fall in here unless I was a good swimmer. If you fell in there they probably wouldn't find your body until it got to the Baltic."

"And why would they find it then?" asked Erik.

"Because the salt water would lift it up to the surface," explained Roman.

"And that would be only if there was something left of it to come to the surface," added Erik. He sat up quickly and looked at Roman. "You know Roman, you just gave me a excellent idea. For some time now I have been thinking about how I could make a clean disappearance and not implicate anyone left behind and I think that you may have just solved my problem."

"You mean that you are going to fall into the Drewca? Now that would be a clean disappearance alright," snickered Roman.

"Oh no, I don't mean to fall in, but I could make it look like I did. You see, I could leave my fishing gear, boots and other items of clothing on the bank to be easily discovered. They would conclude that I fell in and was washed into the Vistula and out to sea."

Roman eyed his friend with amusement. "You would probably do it, too, and no one would be the wiser."

Erik's line went taut and he leaned over to retrieve his catch.

"Better be careful," warned Roman. "We don't want to see a preview of the great escape."

CHAPTER 15

Early Monday morning Erik and Roman announced to Richter that they would be ready to pour the first batch of the new alloy for the barrel later in the week. Richter was delighted and apologized that they would have to wait for the final assembly to take place, as his team had not yet perfected the firing mechanism.

However, they could proceed with their work in the foundry, as the machining of the barrel would take some time. That is good, thought Erik. While Richter was concentrating on the firing mechanism, he would have time to complete the duplicate set of drawings for Bashinski without having to worry about being discovered.

On Wednesday the mold stood ready to receive the pour. In the small experimental foundry, Roman prepared the furnace and Erik carefully measured the required ingredients for their newly developed alloy. On the recorded formula Erik had showed the content of carbon, silicon and a secret ingredient at a fraction different than the amount that they would actually use. Only the two of them knew the actual proportions of these elements and they had sworn each other to secrecy.

The newly poured molten metal flowed into the large mold and slowly cooled from a fiery red to dingy gray. After a few minutes the two technicians, with careful and precise movements of their picks and tongues, coaxed the still-smoking casting away from its mold. It looked warty and discolored. Erik cocked his eye and examined it from a distance with one eye closed and the other observing the straightness of the casting. He tapped it with a small hammer and listened to the sound. They both nodded approvingly and left it to cool under the watchful eye of the security guard. Smiling contentedly they returned to their offices.

The machine shop buzzed with excitement next day as Erik and Roman, assisted by August, wheeled the huge casting into the room and hoisted it carefully onto the lathe. For two days the lathe whirred laboriously, spewing delicate shavings and slivers of metal onto the shop floor. The two young men watched proudly as the cylinder, like a caterpillar growing into a butterfly, changed slowly from a scaly gray metal pole to a shiny cylinder. One week later it stood on its own special stand, machined and polished. Roman applied a thin oily finish to it and they stood back proudly and admired its perfection. Leaving Roman in charge, Erik left the shop and soon returned with Richter.

The engineer ran his fingers tenderly over the smooth finish and whistled in amazement. He leaned over and examined the inside of the barrel. With a pair of calipers he measured the thickness of the wall, then with a gauge he checked the inside and outside diameters of the openings at each end of the cylinder. Richter observed the barrel from a number of angles. He ran his fingers through his thinning hair, then stood back and shook his head in disbelief.

"This is a beautiful piece of work, boys. I am deeply pleased," he said with sincerity. "If the alloy you used is the right one to withstand overheating, then we may be on to a major technical breakthrough."

"No reason why it shouldn't be," said Erik. Roman detected a hint of smugness in his face. "Roman and I spent most of the summer experimenting with it."

"Yes, but only a test under field conditions will tell. Nevertheless, I am proud of your team and I will personally see that you are all properly rewarded," promised Richter.

~~~

The still, humid air hung heavily over the compound. Inside the building only the sounds of doors closing for the weekend broke the silence as the few remaining workers tidied up after another week of production. On the hard-packed gravel path outside the compound, Erik walked slowly, deep in thought, occasionally kicking a loose pebble into the ditch. A man carrying a leather case entered the path as he neared the intersection. He put down his case and wiped his forehead with a red handkerchief. Erik approached and recognized the man as the peddler who had brought him the first message from his parents. The two men greeted each other curtly and the peddler followed Erik into the dormitory. They entered Erik's and Roman's billet and sat down on the beds opposite each other.

"I was told that you would have a message for me to take back," said the peddler.

"What sort of message are you looking for?" Erik, prodded, observing the man's reaction.

The peddler's impatience was showing. "Let us not waste time. What message do you want me to take back to Bashinski?"

The mention of Bashinski's name revealed clearly that the Colonel was seriously following up on the plan that had been laid out for him. Though he had spent many sleepless hours challenging the idea of leaving the security of his job and abandoning Richter who had displayed an enduring confidence in him, Erik felt that it may already be too late to change the course set before him. Now he must make his final decision. Bashinski was waiting for his directions in Warsaw and in front of him was the peddler nervously shifting from one foot to the other waiting for the message. He wondered what Angela would want him to do. She had already expressed her opinion on the matter on several occasions. He remembered again her shock at hearing of his involvement in the armaments business and how patiently she had accepted his difficult situation. Would she continue to accept it if he were to bring her to Torun and to continue working at Torun Works? She probably would, just the two to be together, but would she be happy? Would they let him bring her back now that he was so deeply involved in such a sensitive project? A few weeks ago he would have had no doubts that they would, but since Richter asked him to return his passport and visa, he wondered about how much freedom he really had left. He could see that the peddler was getting impatient. Erik stood up and faced him.

"All right," he said with an air of finality in his voice," Get this message back to Bashinski. "We will be testing the prototype sometime between September tenth and fifteenth. I am hoping that it will be a success. But even if it is not, I should be ready to leave shortly after that; perhaps in five days or less."

"Bashinski has arranged for a small commercial fishing boat belonging to the provincial government in Warsaw to pick you up near the junction of the Vistula with the Drewca," said the peddler. "Your wife and her mother will both be on board the vessel when it picks you up. Once you are on board you should be quite safe, as the Vistula is considered to be a neutral waterway between the Prussian and Russian zones. There is an old dock about one kilometer from the mouth of the Drewca. Bashinski's boat will be there on the minute. All that he needs to know is the exact day of your departure."

Erik closed his eyes in concentration. His face reflected his agony and the gravity of the decision.

"It may be better if I disappear at midweek when everyone is totally occupied with their work," he said slowly. "Maybe I can say that I am sick. Let me think about it. Perhaps I can send a message with you later when I have decided."

"This is the last time that you will see me," said the peddler. "From this day on you will send your messages through the old man at the market." The peddler closed his case and prepared to leave. Erik lifted a corner of his mattress and removed a folded set of blueprints.

"Guard these with your life," he whispered. "Make sure that they get to Bashinski as soon as possible. Tell him that there are more to come."

"Do not worry. He will have them the day after tomorrow," said the peddler. He put the drawings into his case and stepped out into the hallway.

The stillness of the hot, oppressive air inside the dormitory closed in around him. He knew that now there was no turning back. He felt trapped, alone and vulnerable and wished that Roman was there so he could confide in him. But Roman had already left to visit Lydia. He walked slowly away from the dormitory and sat down under an ancient beech tree, staring at the cloudless sky.

~~~

A cold front moved in from the Baltic, gently at first, like a huge gray fleece stretching across the horizon. As it raced inland and collided with the sun-drenched hot air, it reared upward. It rumbled and cracked and sent flashing bolts of lightning back to the ground. Large drops of rain pelted the dry ground, hardened by weeks of drought, forming reddish brown puddles. The storm passed noisily into the distance and the soothing cool breeze poured in through the open doors and windows and flowed into the streets and fields. The clean, soft air caressed the bright green grass washed clean by the rain. Nature had once again revealed both its fury and its benevolence to man and his environment.

Erik and Roman watched the spectacle through the window of the machine shop. The barrel of the newly developed gun stood silhouetted against the dripping window panes and reflected the flashes of the receding storm. They glanced at it uneasily, each of them privately imagining the fury that their creation might one day unleash.

When they returned to their offices on the other side of the wing, Richter arrived and announced that he had completed the design work for the improved feeding and firing mechanism and that the parts were being cast. As soon as the parts were machined, they would start assembling the prototype, probably early in the following week, he said.

Richter examined the gun base that Erik and August had improved and cast while he worked on the feed and firing mechanism, and grunted approvingly. Barring any unforeseen delays and allowing themselves two weeks for assembling the components, Richter speculated that the prototype could be ready for testing by the first of September and for field trials ten days later. This would put the final test at around September eleventh, he said.

Assembly of the prototype began the following Monday in a heavily guarded room across the hall from the Research and Development office. Upon entering and leaving everyone submitted to a thorough search by security personnel. Nothing was taken out of the room except with Richter's permission. Erik and Roman were overwhelmed with the respect which their presence seemed to induce in the assistants and junior technicians on the project. Pride swelled within their chests and pushed the last remnants of guilt out of their hearts.

Pinned on the wall of the assembling room was a large blueprint of the weapon. As the days passed, the numerous parts came together in an intricate arrangement, each one complementing the other and becoming a part of the whole. The weapon began to take shape, its long exquisitely machined barrel imparting an image of elegance and awesome authority to the machine.

"Some people paint in oils, others compose music, but we – we are artists in metal," said Richter proudly as the weapon neared completion.

On the last Friday in August the prototype was completely assembled and mounted on its base. Richter announced that they would transport it to the indoor range and run it through its initial firing test first thing Monday morning.

~~~

Intense feelings of fear and guilt returned to haunt Erik as he sat by himself after Roman had gone to see Lydia that Saturday afternoon. Loneliness filled his heart and he longed desperately for Angela. After he had realized that her letters to him were being intercepted, he wrote and told her what he suspected; then there were no more letters. He wondered what she was doing that afternoon and whether she was thinking of him. Did she know how he was doing and how things were progressing in his work, he wondered. Of course she would, because Bashinski would keep her informed on what was going on here, he reasoned. Maybe there was a message from Bashinski waiting for him. He left the dormitory and headed toward the marketplace.

Erik found the old man beside an empty stall leaning on his cane. The beggar saw Erik approaching and walked slowly toward him. They met and the old man stopped.

"Good afternoon, Berglund," he said.

Instinctively Erik slowed down then continued to walk past the beggar.

"If you are looking for carnations, there are some nice ones over this way," snorted the old man, with an amused look on his face.

Erik stopped and reached in his pocket for some coins.

"I am too old to play games. Why did you not stop?" scolded the old man.

"I wanted to make sure that it was you. Also, in case I am being watched I did not want to make it appear as though I know you," explained Erik.

"You have learned well. But do you really think that there could be another person that looks like me?" he chortled.

"I will remember that next time," said Erik. "Do you have any messages for me today?"

"Yes. Everything is in readiness. They are waiting for you to name the day."

"It looks like it will be around the twentieth of September. But I am not yet sure," said Erik.

"Bashinski understands. He will wait for your word," said the beggar. "He also says that your friend Roman should follow you in two or three months. This will allow some time for things to cool down after you leave. But if things get too hot for him, the arrangements can be sped up. As for you, as soon as possible after the field trials you are to go and see Dr. Weinburger on Kasprowy Street. Use the password. He will provide you with a medical certificate saying that you should take a week away from work to recover from nervous exhaustion or something like that. That is all for today. And, oh yes, Bashinski compliments you on your drawings."

"That is good. I am glad he likes them. I will look for you again one week from today," said Erik as he headed into the crowd.

~~~

A small entourage consisting of Richter, Herr Schmidt the plant manager, Erik, Roman, August, several technicians and two ballistics experts from the Imperial Army Weapons Department in Berlin accompanied the new field gun as it was wheeled out of the assembly shop, looking ominous under a canvas shroud. The small procession wound its way through the corridors of the Research and Development Department and out into the adjoining indoor firing range. Except for the absence of spectator stands, the former railroad roundhouse resembled an ancient arena. It had no windows, but several skylights in the roof allowed shafts of sunlight to penetrate the emptiness of the enormous room. As they entered, Erik noticed that, near the point almost opposite the entrance, sandbags were piled about five meters high and several meters thick. Two targets stood in front of the sandbag wall.

The gun was wheeled onto a concrete pad and the canvas cover removed. Two of Richter's assistants entered the building pushing a small cart with two rounds of ammunition on it.

"Do you realize that I had to have these shells custom made?" said Richter. "Not much else that one can do when this is the only gun of its size in the world, is there?"

The shells were carefully unloaded and placed on a stand near the new weapon.

"These rounds are not fully charged," explained Richter. "We did not want to blow the building apart."

They emitted nervous laughs as they envisaged this possibility.

Under Richter's instructions the gun's carrier was lined up with the first target and the stabilizers adjusted. With a precise routine, the various parts of the weapon were given a final check by the engineers and technicians. Richter declared the gun ready and a shell was inserted in the breech by a ballistics expert. He motioned to the bystanders to take their places behind a sandbag barricade and closed the breech. With an eye on the target, the expert made the final adjustments in the gun's aiming device. Then with his open palm held up above his head, he indicated that all was in readiness. He tripped the firing mechanism, and then released it.

The massive building shuddered from the resounding blast and the sandbag wall quivered then settled around a gaping hole near its middle. Through the billowing dust they saw the target knocked off its stand and lying in front of the hole in the sandbag wall. The gun had remained solid on its stand. Richter emerged nimbly from behind the barricade and checked the firing mechanism, and then the gun was pointed at the second target. The last shell was inserted and the firing mechanism tripped. Another explosion shook the building and the second target fell over. At Richter's signal they all jumped out from behind the barricade and each conducted their assigned tasks on the weapon's parts. Everything was intact. The first firing test was a success. Herr Schmidt looked pleased. He motioned to the group to gather around him.

"This has the makings of a fine machine," he said approvingly. "On the basis of today's demonstration, I have so much confidence in its field performance that I propose to invite Colonel Weiss from the Imperial Army Weapons Department in Berlin to be present for the field trial next week. I know that I can count on all of you to perform as professionally as you have done here today."

"We will make sure that the Colonel goes away favorably impressed, Herr Schmidt," said Richter as he placed the canvas cover reverently over the gun.

~~~

The bounty of the fields and orchards was stacked high in the stalls in the marketplace and pleasant aromas filled the air. Erik watched the noisy Saturday afternoon crowd milling about and listened to the drone of voices that was interspersed by bursts of laughter and the shouts of the vendors. Oh, Innocence, how fortunate is he who harbors you in his bosom, Erik reflected poetically. Only a short distance away the monstrous tool of death lay hidden, waiting for the signal from the political masters to unleash its fury, and then for the victims to be identified by their presidents and generals. But then perhaps these were the lucky ones, he thought. At least by not knowing about tomorrow, they could enjoy today. For him the day was already a burden. The knowledge that he carried screamed inside his head until he thought that he could no longer contain the secret.

He walked slowly to where a small crowd of people were engaged in a discussion, determined to warn them about the looming apocalypse. He drew a deep breath and opened his mouth to speak. The group turned and waited to hear what he had to say. Suddenly he noticed the beggar observing him intently a short distance away. Erik exhaled deeply and walked toward the old man. The beggar went through his begging routine and Erik reached into his pocket and brought out a coin.

"Do not do anything foolish, young man," the beggar admonished him. He took two furtive glances sideways and lowered his voice. "In only ten days you will be gone from this place. It is all set for one week from Wednesday. The time is at five minutes past twelve noon. Have you got that?" Erik nodded. "There is an old dock near the junction of the Drewca and Vistula. They will be there at that time. Do not show yourself until the boat docks and the captain appears on the deck, then get on board as fast as you can. Be sure to bring the rest of the drawings."

Erik's face had a strained and expectant look as though waiting for further instructions.

"That is all the instructions I have for you," said the beggar. "As for your friend, Roman, give him our password on the day you leave and I will be here with his instructions after you are gone."

"After you are gone!" The words had an ominous and final ring to them. Erik stood motionless and watched the old man shuffle out into the crowd. He knew that there was no turning back now. The form for his future was cast and he had not had a hand in shaping the mold. He turned away slowly and walked away from the crowd.

~~~

The morning was bleak and cheerless with intermittent periods of fine drizzle. Erik and Roman arrived at the door of the Research and Development Department to find Richter waiting for them. A company cab arrived only minutes later and the three men boarded it silently. Richter appeared to be relaxed, but introspective. They waited for him to speak.

Richter looked out of the window at the sky. "They say that there is a fog bank moving in from the north. Conditions should be perfect for testing. People in the area will hear the noise but they won't know from where it is coming."

The cab turned into a bumpy side road, tossing the passengers roughly from side to side. They had left the suburbs and farms behind and were entering a scrubby wasteland. Richter explained that the test range was located several kilometers away from Torun and spanned about five hundred hectares of desolate sandy dunes covered with stunted shrubbery and interspersed with marshland.

The armed guard at the gate checked their identifications, and then waved them through. They walked the last short distance to the firing range, stumbling along a rock-strewn footpath. The area did not show any signs of recent use. When they arrived at the firing range they noticed that the gun had already been positioned and was ready for loading. It stood starkly outlined against the desolate sky. Erik gazed at the barrel which had so intimately occupied him for many weeks. It looked strange and defiant, seemingly denying their former close relationship.

They heard the sound of a moving vehicle and voices coming from behind them and saw Herr Schmidt and an army colonel and his aides disembarking from an Imperial Army vehicle. Richter walked to the clearing and escorted the men down the footpath. He introduced Colonel Weiss to Erik and Roman and the other technicians. The colonel shook hands stiffly and gave Erik a curious and stony look. Richter explained that they would test the weapon for distance, accuracy and heat resistance. The colonel walked around the gun, followed by Herr Schmidt, and inspected the firing mechanism and barrel. He made approving sounds and seemed impressed.

Colonel Weiss stepped back and asked that preparations be made for firing the weapon. Richter gathered the small group around him and explained that a sandbag bunker had been set up nearby for their safety and that the armaments specialist would load and fire the gun. The colonel agreed with the routine and they stepped back behind the sandbags and watched as the first shell was placed in the breech. Richter gave the signal to fire. A flash of flame burst out from the end of the barrel, the ground shuddered and the shell screamed through the still, misty air. An uneasy silence followed the noisy blast as they stood transfixed in their positions. The field telephone rang. It was the spotters. Richter covered the mouthpiece and announced that the shell landed approximately one thousand meters away as planned, almost on target. He asked the spotter for placement directions.

"Stand by for close fire, two degrees to the left," Richter shouted into the telephone.

He returned to the rear of the gun and positioned himself beside a shell stand on which ten rounds were stacked. He handed the first shell to the specialist who inserted it into the breech. The firing mechanism was cocked and released. The explosion shook the ground and the flash of fire pierced the heavy curtain of fog. With precise movements, the two men repeated the maneuver six more times, the shots crashing through the air every thirty seconds. Richter motioned to Erik and he and Roman ran to the barrel and recorded the temperature of the barrel.

"Three hundred and five degrees Centigrade," shouted Roman.

Herr Schmidt turned to the colonel with a smug look on his face. "Normal steel would be red hot after something like that," he said.

Colonel Weiss shook his head in disbelief. The telephone rang. Richter picked it up and repeated its message to the others.

"Beautiful placement. Every shell landed within a five meter area."

Colonel Weiss strutted excitedly between the gun and the bystanders. He shook the hand of every member of the team and congratulated them individually and as a group.

"This is a beautiful weapon," he said. "I will certainly see that the Kaiser hears about your good work here. Our great Imperial Army has taken a great step forward today, thanks to all of you."

"We will continue to refine the weapon," Herr Schultz announced proudly. "We think that we can increase its maximum range and also work toward a muzzle velocity of 1500 feet per second. We hope that in less than a year it should be ready for full production."

"I hope that there is no need to remind you, Herr Schmidt, that this work must proceed with the highest level of security in mind," warned the stern colonel.

"I have already taken steps to ensure that, Colonel Weiss," said Herr Schmidt. "I have complete trust in everyone that is involved in this project."

"Nevertheless, one can never be too careful," the colonel reminded him.

CHAPTER 16

Erik's face was drawn and his body stooped. He walked slowly into his workplace, pressing his forearm against his abdomen. He hoped that Richter would see him arriving. He sat down slowly and placed his head down on his folded arms. When he heard the sound of footsteps behind him, Erik looked up and saw Richter standing beside him with a concerned look on his face.

"Is something wrong, Erik?" he asked.

"I am sorry, Herr Richter," Erik apologized. "It is really nothing. I should be fine in a few minutes."

"I have never seen you like this before," said Richter. "I am sure that something is wrong. If you don't feel well, say so. We cannot all feel well all the time, you know."

"It's nothing serious. I just have not been sleeping and eating well lately and my stomach feels like there is a stone in it," said Erik.

"You have been working too hard, Erik," said Richter. "Why don't you go back to your dormitory and rest up for a while. If you do not feel better by the afternoon, I suggest that you go and see a doctor. I'll explain to Herr Schmidt that you are not well."

"Thank you, sir. You are so kind and I really appreciate your concern," said Erik. "I think I will take your advice and go and lie down for a while."

"Don't rush back," said Richter.

"I won't," answered Erik. "Thank you for everything, Herr Richter."

"I told you before that my name is Herman," said Richter.

Later that afternoon Erik located Dr. Weinberger's office on the second floor of a commercial building on one of the city's main thoroughfares. He entered the office and looked around apprehensively. Several patients sat in a waiting room and a woman in white uniform sat behind a desk checking an appointment book. Erik walked up to the desk, his eyes fixed on the woman's face.

"My name is Berglund. I would like to see Dr. Weinburger," he said, feigning confidence.

"Do you have an appointment?" asked the woman.

"Yes, I do," responded Erik.

The woman looked at the names in the appointment book. She shook her head.

"Did you say your name was Berglund? I do not see you name here," she said. "Are you sure you made an appointment?"

"Yes, I was talking to the doctor myself," Erik replied.

"Wait a minute," said the woman. "I will ask the doctor."

She entered a room behind a closed door and returned with the doctor.

"Yes?" said the doctor. "The nurse tells me that you have an appointment. I do seem to recall seeing you before."

"You must have forgotten," said Erik. "I am the person who sold you the white carnations at the market last Saturday."

"Why, of course," said the doctor. "Now I remember. I will see Mr. Berglund right now, nurse."

They entered an examination room and Dr. Weinburger closed the door. He sat on a chair and observed Erik.

"So you are Erik Berglund. I have been expecting you. Colonel Bashinski says that you are a very important person."

"I am just a machinist apprentice," explained Erik trying to sound humble. "I think that the colonel is making a big thing out of nothing."

The doctor shook his head. "Colonel Bashinski is not one to overstate things. So I believe him. Anyway, my name is Dr. Adam Weinburger and I have been asked to help you. How many days do you need?"

"Eight days, starting tomorrow," said Erik.

"Dr. Weinburger took a medical report form from a drawer and completed it.

"I am saying here that this patient is suffering from physical and mental fatigue, complicated by a digestive disorder, and that he should rest for nine days and then report back to me. A tonic, light exercise and fresh air are recommended during this period." He signed the report and gave it to Erik.

"With a medical report like this, you can do many things," he suggested. "See me if things do not work out as expected or if you need an extension. Good luck, Erik. Give my regards to Colonel Bashinski."

He opened the door and Erik walked through the waiting room oblivious to the stares of the waiting patents. He made his way down the stairs and out into the street then proceeded directly to the Research and Development Department. Richter saw him coming and met him as he entered the office. He had a pained expression on his face. He looked at Erik's medical report and shook his head with a concerned look.

"We have come through a very difficult period which has drained your energies," he said. "I am sorry that I drove you so hard. But now that the project is nearly complete we can slow down our pace. Are you sure that you will be all right at the dormitory?"

"Oh, yes. I will be quite comfortable there. Roman and Hilda will see to that. Dr. Weinburger said that I should get lots of sun and fresh air and I plan to do some fishing when I am feeling a bit better," said Erik.

"Thank you very much for your help and everything that that you have done for me." Erik was beginning to realize that this may be the last time that he would see his mentor. "Now, if you don't mind, I will go and put my drawings and equipment away before I leave."

"Please do," said Richter. "And don't worry about rushing back. As I said, we don't have a new project and the old one is well in hand."

"I will not," promised Erik.

"Before you leave, Erik, I have something to give you," said Richter. "Something came from Berlin for all of us this morning. He reached into a drawer in desk and brought out a leather-bound case. He opened it and passed it to Erik. Inside was a bronze medal with the bust of the Kaiser on the front and the Imperial Army coat of arms on the back. "Each member of our team received one of these in appreciation of our achievement, but you deserve it above all. And here is a commendation from the Kaiser himself. He handed a certificate to Erik. His name was embossed on it in gold letters.

"This is a great honor. I shall take these with me wherever I go," said Erik.

"You were going to receive it from Herr Schmidt later, but I got his permission to give it to you earlier. Maybe it will help to speed up you recovery."

"I am sure it will," replied Erik, trying to sound innocent. "I am proud to receive this honor."

He returned to his office and looked around, dejected that he would not see it again. He folded a drawing of the plans for the new field gun, checked to see if Richter was watching, and put it inside his shirt, then he placed his drafting equipment in a cabinet for the last time.

~~~

At the dinner table that evening the other residents cast sympathetic glances at Erik who had arrived late and sat down quietly. Conveniently arriving at the table ahead of Erik, Roman ensured that the news of his roommate's illness was effectively disseminated before supper began. Hilda displayed her compassion by showering him with attention.

"Eat," she insisted. "You don't expect to regain your strength if you don't eat well."

"Hilda, you should get married and have some children of your own to look after," Erik suggested. "You would make a good mother."

"Maybe. But tell me, who would have me?" she feigned desperation. "The men nowadays all want sweet young ladies. But just look at me! No. It is too late for me. But never mind, I still have all you boys to look after. So eat! Don't sit around gawking."

A chorus of snickers arose around the table and the young men returned their attention to their plates. After supper Erik and Roman walked slowly through the hallway on their way back to their billet. As they entered the room, Roman cast a long concerned look at Erik.

"You do not look too well. I suggest that you go to bed right away."

"I am not really sick, Roman," said Erik softly.

"And I am not really Roman Potoski. I am really a prince; the son of the King of Lithuania," said Roman in a mocking voice. "You do not look like a person who is going to jump over a fence either."

"Maybe not. But the truth is that I am scared. You see Roman, the plan is set. I am leaving this place next week and the thought frightens me." He heaved a sigh of relief and slumped down into a chair, relieved at having shared the secret with someone for the first time.

"You deserve to be scared. Keeping all that stuff bottled up inside of you when you could have shared it with me, your friend. Who do you think you are? God?" scolded Roman. "And what about me? Did you not say that I would somehow be involved in this whole scheme?"

Erik stood up slowly and closed the door. "The first stage of the bigger plan only came together today when I received a fake medical report from the doctor. You see, Roman, feigning sickness is part of the whole scheme. By being sick, I don't have to be as visible as I would be if I were at work. That also gives me time to devote to the next stage of my plan, which is to set up the background for my disappearance. After I have left, the organization in Warsaw..." Erik paused. It was the first time that he had referred to Bashinski and his network as The Organization. "...Bashinski's people will start working on a plan for you," Erik continued. "He says that you should follow in about two months. By that time every one here should have recovered from my disappearance. The possibility of suspicion will be much less if we go one at a time."

"Now hold on a minute! Assuming that I am part of Bashinski's grand plan, what assurance do I have that he will get me out of here safely?" asked Roman, his voice dripping skepticism.

"Only his word. The same as I have. And so far he has come through in every respect," replied Erik. "In fact, he has already set up your channels of communication. For starters, you will use the same contact as I am now using and also the same password. If at any time anyone comes up to you and mentions that particular word in any way, you will know that the person is part of Bashinski's organization. These people will deliver messages to you and carry messages back to Bashinski. If it makes you feel more comfortable, I could arrange for you to meet one of these contacts this Saturday."

"And indeed you should," declared Roman. "You have kept me out of this long enough."

"And so we shall," agreed Erik. He sat close to Roman and spoke in a low voice. "My own plan is to feign a drowning accident, at the spot where we discussed this possibility earlier under more casual circumstances. My doctor's report recommends rest and fresh air. What better place to combine these two than at our old fishing hole? I will go there late Wednesday morning and at five minutes after twelve a boat will pick me up and take me north. On Monday morning you will inform Richter that I am coming along fine – regaining my strength and stamina. On Wednesday morning you will tell him that I felt good enough that morning to go fishing. Late that evening you will report my absence. You will be distraught and concerned. It will, of course, be too late for them to go searching for me, assuming that they will be so inclined. In the morning, if they do look for me, they will find my belongings on the river bank. The conclusion will be simple. I fell off the tree into the river, drowned and was swept out into the Vistula. By the time they decide what to do next, I will be halfway across the Atlantic."

Roman's face reflected his disbelief of Erik's plan. He paced around the room, his hands clasped behind his back.

"Is it really necessary to go through all that?" he finally asked. "Why don't you just take the train and go to Hamburg or some other port and board a ship for America, the way that other people do?"

"Because Bashinski thinks that we know too much, and because of that we would no be allowed to leave freely. He also mentioned something about not leaving a trail and because of that we cannot go the same way that everyone else does," explained Erik.

"How did we get mixed up in this complex situation?" asked Roman. "Here I will be left all alone, my best friend is a fugitive, and I am not even so sure that I really want to leave this place. Suddenly I feel very helpless."

"You are not really alone, Roman. You have Lydia. And they could arrange for you to take her with you if you wish. And when you discover how many people are out there working on your behalf, you will no longer feel helpless. You will be surprised, the same as I was," Erik assured him. "And as for your thought about not leaving, you seem to have forgotten that several months ago you accused me of being more concerned about working with that cold iron, as you called it, than about the lives of our fellow countrymen."

"Yes, and then you proved me wrong by marrying one of them," laughed Roman.

~~~

Assorted sounds floated through the air as the crowds milled about the marketplace, punctuated by the occasional shouts of hawkers selling their wares. The two young men stopped and admired the displays of produce stacked high in the sellers' stalls. The colors and smells of new corn, carrots, beets, cabbage and other vegetables, fruits, fresh-baked breads, smoked sausages and cheeses tempted their senses and taste buds. At the stalls, well-dressed socialites were unceremoniously jostled aside by weather-beaten peasant women in kerchiefs as they fought for the small available spaces. Early morning imbibers, leaning against the walls and posts and fortified by the bloom of alcohol, discarded their inhibitions and taunted the passers-by.

"You know, I am going to miss this place," remarked Erik. "These are real people here, as real as they come. This is society in its most authentic form."

"When left alone, people are the same everywhere," observed Roman. "I am sure that wherever you go, you will find them just as real and just as interesting."

"But maybe not as colorful," said Erik. "Let us see if we can find that old friend of mine."

They found the beggar bent over this cane, observing the crowd. He seemed surprised to see Erik and ignored them when the two of them approached.

"It is all right," said Erik. "This is Roman Potoski, the person I told you about last week. He will be your next customer."

The old man surveyed Roman critically as Erik reached into his pocket for a coin. He strained to straighten his back to get a better look at Roman's face.

"Potoski?" he wheezed. "Yes, Potoski, I will be on this street whenever you need me...if you say the right word," he ended with a chuckle.

Roman was taken aback by the old man's shabby appearance and strange manner. He looked at Erik expecting an explanation.

"This is one of the messengers that I spoke about," explained Erik. "He will get your message to Bashinski quickly if you ever need him."

"What brings you here today, Berglund?" asked the old man. "Have your plans changed, or did you bring the papers?"

"No," replied Erik. "Nothing has changed. I just wanted Roman to meet you. The plans are the same and I will have the papers with me when I leave. Have you received any new instructions?"

"Nothing has changed," said the beggar.

"Thank you for your help," said Erik. "I hope you serve Roman just as well."

"I will. May Almighty God watch over you, son," the old man said to Erik as he shuffled away.

"You mean that he is one on Bashinski's agents?" asked Roman in disbelief.

"One of many, I believe," replied Erik.

"One never knows whom he passes on the street these days," remarked Roman.

"Your surprises are just beginning," Erik predicted.

~~~

In the trees outside of the foundry compound under which Erik had walked so many times, flocks of chattering sparrows announced the arrival of morning. It was a welcome sound as he had slept but little and the silent night had seemed too long. Through the window he saw the fiery orange rim of the rising sun which promised another clear day and a glorious finale to the waning summer. Erik moved silently about the billet, not wanting to wake his roommate. But Roman had not slept well either and he too, welcomed the morning. They washed and went to breakfast early. Hilda reminded Erik that he needed the rest and should not be up so early. He told her he was feeling better and was going fishing and that he wanted to get there while the fish were still hungry. She wrapped up some cheese, sausage and bread and pushed the package at him as he was leaving.

It was a tense and hushed farewell. Erik and Roman promised each other that they would meet again at another time and another place. After receiving the password, Roman departed for his workplace and Erik began his preparations to leave.

He put on a pair of light pants and carefully concealed a copy of the blueprints in the side pocket. He placed his money and identification papers in another pocket and then pulled on another pair of pants over the first, smoothing them out carefully so that there was no evidence of the first pair. He stuffed his backpack with a few of his valuables and placed the package of food that Hilda had given him on top of all these. As he checked his closet for the last time he noticed the citation and medal which he had received from the Imperial War Department. He opened the leather case and admired the bronze medal then placed the two items in his backpack. He didn't think for a moment that he might be making a mistake.

Erik walked away from the dormitory and the compound without looking back, his fishing rod over his shoulder and the backpack on his shoulder. Everyone was now inside the plant working. It was still several hours before his rendezvous with the fishing boat, so he decided to walk all the way to the river.

The air warmed up quickly as the late summer sun beat down through the cloudless sky. It would be a good day for river travel, he told himself, but the visibility would also be excellent. He would have to be extra careful. On a day like this there would be no room for error. But he was ready. He had rehearsed his act diligently the day before by walking through the thick underbrush along the river's edge to the abandoned dock. It would take him eleven minutes to get there from the fishing spot.

There was no one at the river when he arrived. He hid his backpack under a bush and climbed into the overhanging tree to pick a safe and comfortable limb on which to sit. Without baiting his hook he dropped the line into the water and leaned back against the entangled branches. Everything had gone well so far and he was pleased and almost relaxed. He still had a lot of time left before his next move so he leaned back and rehearsed it in his mind. He would leave the spot at exactly fourteen minutes to twelve and follow the same route that he had taken the day before. This would give him a few minutes to spare. He still had some time to pass and he did not want to fall asleep. He swung his legs, moved the rod and line from side to side and whistled his favorite tunes. As he adjusted the branches behind his back, his eyes caught sight of a man walking along the river bank. The man carried a fishing pole and dropped the line in the water at different places from time to time. He shielded his eyes from the sun with his hand as he gazed directly at where Erik was perched. When he spotted Erik, he approached slowly.

"Ah, good morning," he spoke in German. "I thought I heard someone whistling. Are the fish biting here today?"

"I have caught some here in the past, but none today so far," answered Erik.

"Do you mind if I join you?" asked the stranger. "I will fish off the shore."

"Glad to have your company," lied Erik.

Things had suddenly taken a new turn and Erik hoped desperately that the appearance of the stranger would not interfere with his well-laid-out plan. He checked his watch. It was only ten minutes after ten. There was still a lot of time left, but if the man should decide to stay until noon he would have to figure out a new strategy. The man baited his hook and expertly cast it into the river. He repeated this several times and in a few minutes had a bite. He pulled the fish in and baited his hook.

"Say, this is a good spot for fishing." He sounded pleased. "You must know this part of the country well. Do you live in Torun?"

"Yes, I do," replied Erik.

"So do I," said the man. "Where do you work?"

"At the Torun Works," answered Erik. "But I am not going to work today. I am recuperating from an illness and I come here to relax."

"That is a good idea," said the stranger, "and this is a good place to do that. There is nothing like fishing to relax a person. I am sorry to hear about your illness. I did not go to work today either. I am waiting to meet a friend and then we plan to go further down the river."

Erik was relieved to hear this. The man turned around to see if this friend was arriving and as he did his line went taut and the pole bent into a jerking loop. He had another bite.

"Hey, this is indeed a good place to fish," said the stranger as he removed the fish from the hook. "I wonder why you are not catching anything. What kind of bait are you using?"

"I have a minnow on there," answered Erik uneasily.

He checked his watch, trying to appear casual. It was nearly a quarter after eleven and the man just had another bite. Damn him, thought Erik. I hope he does not stay all morning.

"You should check your hook," advised the stranger. "Maybe the fingerlings have eaten your bait."

Erik reluctantly pulled in his line. The man noticed that the hook was not baited.

"See. Just as I thought. Your bait is gone. Do you have anymore?"

"No, I don't'" said Erik as he fidgeted with his hook.

"Here, have one of mine," said the stranger.

"You are very kind," said Erik. He walked along the overhanging tree trunk and took the minnow from the man. He baited his hook slowly and threw it into the water, silently praying that the fish would not take it.

The sun was approaching the high noon point in the sky, the time when Erik knew the fish would normally cease to bite. It must be getting close to twelve, he thought, and the man was still there. In his mind he frantically began to devise an alternative plan. Perhaps he could say that he was going up the river to look for a better place and he could get to the old dock before the fishing boat arrived. He could then leave his shirt, boots and one pair of pants on the bank and it would appear that he disappeared while swimming.

He would wait until ten minutes to twelve and then depart.

Several more minutes passed torturously. Mercifully, the fish had not begun to bite again. Erik's heart pounded in is chest. Trying to appear casual, he checked his watch again. It was twenty minutes before twelve.

"Are you going back to town to eat?" asked the man.

"No," replied Erik. "I brought some lunch with me."

"I hope my friend arrives soon," said the stranger. "I am beginning to get hungry myself."

Erik cast anxious glances over his shoulder. After what seemed like a generous portion of eternity, he noticed a neatly dressed man walking down the path along the river bank. He could not be the person for whom his new found friend was waiting. He was not dressed for fishing, thought Erik.

"Ah, there he is now," said the stranger. "Thank you for your company. Maybe we will meet here again some time."

"It was a pleasure," responded Erik trying to hide his anxiety.

The stranger picked up his fishing equipment and string of fish as his friend approached and made his way along the embankment. Erik cast a quick look at the new arrival. He busied himself with his rod and line while observing the men out of the corner of his eye. They walked down the footpath and disappeared around a bend. Erik dug out his watch frantically. It was nine minutes to twelve. He hung the fishing pole and line securely over the branch. Leaving his lunch and jacket on the bank, he picked up his backpack and walked briskly through the undergrowth in the direction of the old dock.

CHAPTER 17

The crumbling old dock was located at the crown of a secluded loop in the river. Heavy timbers which had been driven into the river bed many years ago showed the scars left by boats, logs, ice floes and flotsam. Small boats now used the battered structure only occasionally for unscheduled stops. Erik approached the dock cautiously, stopping periodically to peer through the thick shrubbery. All was clear. There was no sign of anyone anywhere. Startled crickets leaped out around his feet as he ran down the unused trail, staying close to the overhanging bushes. Suddenly he came to a small clearing among the trees and bushes, at the end of which stood an old dock with a boat tied to it.

He picked up his step and moved quickly toward the vessel. As he approached he noticed that it was a somewhat neglected and weather-beaten fishing boat about twenty-five meters long. On its bow was the name *Mazovia* in peeling black paint on a white background. A tall, stocky bearded man wearing a captain's hat walked nervously on the deck, shading his eyes and scanning the river bank. Erik leaped out into the open and came into the man's view. The captain waved to him to come on board and a deckhand began to untie the rope. Erik jumped onto the deck, the boat's engine coughed and the vessel veered away from the battered pier.

"You are four minutes late," said the captain. "We thought something may have gone wrong."

"Nothing serious," said Erik, trying to catch his breath. "Just a small unexpected holdup."

"My name is Huta," said the captain. "Come on down below. Someone is waiting for you."

They walked down several wooden steps and he pushed open a narrow door. The captain bowed his head to avoid striking the transom. Erik followed close behind and they entered a small room. His eyes still accustomed to the bright sunshine, Erik squinted around the small unlighted area. The small cabin seemed to be filled with people, some sitting on rough-hewn furniture and others standing against the walls. As his eyes got used to the darkness, Erik glanced around the room and noticed several faces which he recognized. They were all smiling and appeared to be relieved at his arrival. His eyes picked out Bashinski and Litvak standing at the back of the room, while sitting at a small table were Angela and her mother. The whole scene seemed surreal. The group joined in a restrained and muted cheer of approval as Angela ran to Erik and embraced him.

"Oh, my poor beloved husband," she blurted out through her tears. "I thought that I would never see you again."

When the long embrace was broken, Bashinski approached Erik with a tall, slender, fair-haired young man in tow. He was dressed as a deck hand. Bashinski held out his hand.

"Welcome home, Erik. I am pleased that everything worked out well for you and all of us," he said. "Before you get too involved, I would like to introduce you to Major Sliworski of the Polish National Army."

"Polish National Army?" Erik sounded surprised.

"Underground," explained Bashinski matter-of-factly. "Major Sliworski is very interested to know if you were able to bring the rest of the drawings."

"Yes. I had no problem doing that," said Erik. He dug his hand into the pocket of the second pair of pants and produced the blueprints. He hand them to Bashinski.

"If the gun is as good as they say it is, you have just done your country a great favor," said Bashinski.

"The people from Berlin were very pleased with it," said Erik.

"Did you debase the formula as you were instructed?" asked Bashinski.

"Yes. I changed the ratio of some of the ingredients that went into the alloy," explained Erik.

"Good work, Erik," said Bashinski. "I am very proud of you. We can talk later. Now I'll leave you two alone. You, no doubt, have much to talk about."

The vessel veered right and the passengers below deck knew that they were leaving the Drewca River and entering the Vistula. The engine groaned loudly and the boat picked up speed. Captain Huta climbed down the narrow wooden stairway and entered the small cabin. He announced that the boat had entered the Vistula River and was now passing Torun.

"Hug the east bank and try not to attract any undue attention," advised Bashinski. "If the Prussian River Patrol intercepts you, cooperate with them as we discussed earlier. Our papers are all in order. We should have no problem."

Colonel Bashinski motioned to the others in the room to come closer. "We have taken every precaution to prevent any confrontation with the Prussian authorities," he said. "We are in an international waterway and should not be bothered by anyone. But should we be intercepted for some reason and should the river patrol come on board, it will be necessary for everyone here except Angela, her mother, Major Sliworski and myself to conceal themselves to prevent suspicion.

"In the forward hold there are several narrow compartments used for storing fishing nets. There is just enough room in each of these for one person to stand up and not much more. In the event of a boarding inspection, Erik and Litvak will enter these compartments. The women will remain here and I and Major Sliworski will join the captain on deck.

"However, unless Erik's absence is discovered early and they become suspicious in Torun, I do not expect any problems. We should be in Danzig sometime after nightfall. Bornholm Island is our destination and we should be there by noon tomorrow. Captain Huta knows this river and the Baltic coast like his own backyard, so we have nothing to worry about in that regard. So, for the time being, relax and make our newest passenger feel welcome."

~~~

The sea-bound current carried the *Mazovia* smoothly and swiftly through the wide channel of the Vistula. Below deck Angela and Erik were engrossed in each others' accounts of the events that had taken place since their last meeting in Krakow.

So far their departure from Torun had gone well. Above deck, Bashinski and Sliworski observed the variety of vessels that plodded the waterway. Much to their relief, each of them seemed to be intent on its own missions and oblivious of the others. The yellow rays of the sun bounced off the waves and the boat's wake with brilliant flashes. Behind them the buildings of Torun became absorbed into the purple horizon and blended in with the treed and grassy landscape on the far side of the broadening waterway.

Captain Huta and a deckhand walked down the narrow stairs and motioned to Bashinski and Sliworski to follow. The deckhand entered the small galley adjacent to the cabin and took some cold meats, cheese and bread from the boat's pantry. He began to cut these up into small slices and placed them on a large plate. The plate was placed on the table and everyone was asked to help themselves. As they ate, Bashinski stood up and spoke to the group.

"I would like to thank you all for enabling us to carry off this operation so smoothly," he began. "As the details of the remainder of this mission are unknown to some of you, and especially to Erik, Angela and Mrs. Klaczek, who will be the most intimately affected, I would like to explain them to you now.

" We will stay on this vessel until tomorrow. As we pass Danzig tonight, the boat will probably be boarded by Prussian customs officers. I am confident that the official papers which I carry from the Ministry in Warsaw will satisfy them and that there will be no inspections below deck. If they board the boat, I will reveal my identity – namely an official of the provincial government in Warsaw. The rest of the men will be identified as part of the crew or officers from my office at the Ministry of Fisheries. Major Sliworski and Litvak will be part of my staff and Erik will be part of the crew. Angela and Mrs. Klaczek will be identified as Captain Huta's mother-in-law and niece on their way to visit relatives in Gdynia in the Prussian zone. I will provide you all with your new names and the names of the relatives that the women are on their way to visit. You will commit this information to heart before we reach Danzig. Once we pass Danzig and reach the international waters of the Baltic, we should be free from any further inspection. That should happen later tonight.

"Late tomorrow morning we will dock at the port of Ronne on Bornholm Island. There Erik, Angela and her mother will board another boat for Southhampton, England. At Southhampton they will board a Serbian freighter sailing out of Trieste called the *Drina* and leave for Halifax, Canada Saturday. From Halifax, the three of you will take the train to Windsor and then cross into the United States at Detroit."

"What is this about us crossing into the United States? I thought that we were going to join my family in Canada?" asked Erik, surprised.

"Yes, that was the original plan," explained Bashinski. "But when we discovered how much you know we thought that your talents would be more effectively used in America. You see, Erik, you have a special gift. You have a good head for analyzing and developing things. You should not let all this go to waste. Canada's economy is very young and her manufacturing industry has just started to develop. For example, they have no arms industry there, whereas in the United States they are very interested in building up that business."

"But I can do other things beside design armaments," argued Erik. "I can design components for agricultural machinery or transportation equipment, or whatever else a growing country needs."

"Just about anybody can do that, Erik," explained Bashinski, "but very few engineers or technicians can do what you can with weapons, so it is better that you put your talent to its best possible use – the pursuit of peace."

"Peace?" exclaimed Erik indignantly. "How do you translate guns into peace?"

"Very simply," explained Bashinski. "It is called balance of power. And when it comes to determining where the balance of power should reside, I personally want to see it stay in the hands of the friends of Poland."

"Poland? There has not been a Poland for over a hundred years," exclaimed Erik bitterly.

"Maybe not on the political map," said Bashinski, "but in the hearts of millions of our countrymen and women, Poland is alive. There are no people in Europe who love their country more than the Poles and that love shall one day resurrect their beloved country."

"Yes, I know all that," fretted Erik. "My mother is a good example of such a person. But what has all this got to do with the United States of America and with me?"

"Plenty," said Bashinski. "You see, more and more the final battles of a war are fought around the international negotiating table. We learned our lessons when the Treaty of Vienna was signed and all those at the table forgot us. We will not make that mistake again. This time we will cultivate and strengthen those friends who hold no old unreasonable grudges against us, who will understand that our ambitions are honorable and deserved and that we stand in no one's way except those who would desecrate our land.

"The time will come again to sit around the table and I expect that it will come soon, but before it does we will fight until we faint from exhaustion. Then, when the negotiators sit around the table the next time, they will remember that we died fighting and declare that our determination should be rewarded. In order to do this, we must prepare now.

"But because we are surrounded by enemies, we must go out and cultivate new friends and we must say to them that we want to work with them to see that the divine rights of Poland are restored, as well as the rights of all the other suppressed nations on the European continent. Only then will there be peace. So that is what I meant when I said that you will be making an important contribution to the cause of peace."

"Perhaps what you say about Poland and all those other countries is true," said Erik, "but I do not want to become involved in these things. I am sure that there must be technicians and engineers in America who are as good or even better than me. I just want to be left alone to build a home for Angela and me."

"And so you shall," Bashinski assured him. "There is nothing in our plan that will deny you this wish. It has all been arranged and is waiting for you even now as we speak. Do you realize how lucky you are to have all this done on your behalf? When you arrive in Halifax, Mr. Earl Dixon of the United States Immigration Department will meet you there. He will have a Polish speaking interpreter with him who will identify himself with the password which we have been using. They will have the necessary documents ready for all of you. You will be accompanied by them to Windsor and then to Toledo."

"And what do I do when we arrive at this place you call Toledo? Do I go around telling people that I am good at designing guns and cannons, so please hire me and I will make some for you, too?"

"There will be no need for that sort of thing," explained Bashinski, trying to remain patient. "In Toledo a position will be waiting for you at the Research and Development Department of Burlington Industries Incorporated. There will be a company-owned house waiting for you, located next door to a Polish speaking employee from the same plant. They will make your adjustment to American life as simple as possible."

"And what about my parents and brother?" asked Erik despondently. "When will I be able to see them?"

"They will be living a long way from where you will be, that is true – about two thousand kilometers by rail," agreed Bashinski. "But there will be nothing stopping you from visiting them after you are settled in America and have worked a while. The people of America and Canada can cross each other's borders freely and you will have time to do this because your employer will provide you with a fully paid vacation each year."

"All this sounds very good," conceded Erik, "but somehow I feel that I have lost control of my own life."

"And I understand why you might feel this way," agreed Bashinski. "But when you think of it, were you really in control of your own destiny in the place that you left behind? I do not think that you were. You made the decision to leave and we are trying hard to help you make the transition easy for you. So, in that respect you are fortunate. You see, if you were just an ordinary immigrant, you would be left to your own devices. And in a strange country with a different language and culture this could be a traumatic experience."

Erik threw up his hands in resignation. Angela, who had been listening to the conversation, took his hand in hers.

"Colonel Bashinski is right, Erik," she said, consoling her distraught husband. "It will make things a lot easier for us in America. If we do not like it, we can always try something different. We are young and our whole lives are still ahead of us. We can afford to make some mistakes along the way." She looked at Bashinski and he nodded in agreement. "Is it all right if we go up on deck now?" she asked. "We need to be alone for a while."

"We should be passing Grudziadz soon," answered Bashinski. "I asked Captain Huta to give a signal when we passed the city. After that you may go up as there will not be as much traffic on the river. While we are waiting, perhaps you could tell us about how your departure from Torun went, Erik."

"Yes," agreed Angela. "In all the excitement, we have not had time to talk about that."

"Except for one incident, which I will explain when I come to it, everything went pretty well as planned." Erik shifted his weight on the rough wooden chair, then settled back and described the events which preceded his boarding of the *Mazovia*.

~~~

Appearing satisfied that the instructions were understood by all, Captain Huta placed his weather-beaten captain's hat on his head and walked up the narrow stairs to the deck. He entered the bridge and took over the wheel from the deckhand. Below deck, Colonel Bashinski, now appearing solemn and earnest explained that the boat would soon be arriving at the forks in the Vistula. A turn to the left would take them past Danzig, the ancient Polish port that was once known as Gdansk. The boat would then head into the Gulf of Danzig and the Baltic. Once they were past the port, there would be no more possibility of an inspection party boarding the vessel. Meanwhile, they should be ready if an inspection should occur. They pored over the pieces of paper that they had received from the colonel describing their new identities. They devised a game of calling each other by their assumed names. Bashinski then collected the papers and he and Erik went up on deck.

In the last light of the late afternoon sun the hazy skyline of the city of Grudziadz was barely visible behind them. Only minutes after the rim of the sun disappeared below the horizon, the river darkened and the waterline blended into the solid shadows of the landscape. As the *Mazovia* plodded ahead steadily under the watchful eye of Captain Huta, the river traffic became heavier. Lights began to flicker all around them, marking the location of the many vessels that plied the waterway. Ahead, the hazy glow of yellow light marked the spot where the city was located.

As the vessel drew closer to the port of Danzig, a single beam emerged from among the others and headed toward them. As it approached, Captain Huta cut the engine and the *Mazovia* glided to a standstill. The approaching boat pulled up alongside and stopped. Three uniformed men stood on the deck of the boat, their figures silhouetted against the pale light emerging from the small cabin.

"Prussian Customs, Port of Danzig Authority," called one of the uniformed men in German. "State your identity and business."

"*Mazovia*, fishing vessel from Warsaw, commanded by Captain Huta and owned by the provincial government," shouted Captain Huta. "We are headed for the Baltic to check up on some of the boats in our fishing fleet. Our holds are empty."

"May we come on board and check your registration?" shouted one of the officers.

"Certainly. You are welcome," answered Captain Huta.

The pilot maneuvered the boat against the port side of the fishing vessel and the two officers clamored aboard. They entered the bridge and silently examined the boat's log and registration.

"Do you have anyone else on board beside your crew?" one of the officers asked the captain.

"Yes. I have two ladies, both relatives of mine from Warsaw, whom I will drop off at Gdynia where they will stay with some members of their family. And we also have on board Wladimar Bashinski, an official of the provincial government in Warsaw and two of his officers who will be conducting the inspection of the Russo-Polish fishing vessels in the Baltic."

"May we speak to Herr Bashinski, please?" asked the officer.

Captain Huta sent the deckhand down to ask Bashinski to come up to the bridge. Colonel Bashinski arrived and greeted the officials courteously.

"May we please see your identification papers, Herr Bashinski."

The older of the two officers examined the documents, peering at them through the dim light inside the bridge. He seemed satisfied and returned them to Bashinski.

"What is the nature of your business on this trip, sir?" asked the junior officer.

"I was commissioned by the Minister in the Provincial Diet in Warsaw to conduct an inspection of the Russian-Polish fishing fleet in the Baltic."

"Very well, sir. You may proceed."

They turned to Captain Huta. "Do you have the passports for your two female passengers?" one of the officers asked.

"Yes. They are right here." The captain opened a leather pouch and took out the documents. The two officers checked the passports, made some notes a in a log book, them stamped them.

"Thank you, captain. You may proceed to your destination."

The custom officers jumped off the *Mazovia* into their own boat. The engine roared and the boat disappeared into the darkness in the direction of the port. The *Mazovia's* engines accelerated and the boat's bow pointed north toward the Baltic. In the west the last faint glow of the late summer day was swallowed by the inky darkness. Captain Huta knew that the moon would not rise for another hour. By that time the vessel would have left behind the familiar coastal landmarks and be headed out into the open sea.

CHAPTER 18

Roman ate his meal in silence. He hoped that no one would ask him about Erik's absence. Because he had missed several meals during his alleged illness, no one seemed to be unduly concerned about Erik's absence on this particular evening and no questions were asked. Roman returned to the dormitory and sat down on the edge of his bed. His eyes wandered across to Erik's empty bunk and he felt empty inside. A haunting loneliness pounced on him from every corner of the desolate room. He leaned back on his pillow and closed his eyes.

When he awoke the room was dark. He stood up and lit the lamp. It was a quarter to ten on the clock. He sat down and wondered where Erik would be at that moment. Anyway, he reasoned, Erik had asked to report him missing after it got dark and it would not get much darker than it was right now. Roman stood up and stepped out of the room. He made his way through the darkness to the nearby residence of Herr Schindel, the dormitory director. He paused briefly at the door, and then knocked. After a long silence he heard the muffled sounds of movements inside the house. The door opened a small crack and the director peeked out through it.

"Yes. Who is it?" he asked.

"It is I. Roman Potoski, from Unit B."

"Yes, Potoski. What do you want at this hour of the night?" asked Schindel impatiently.

"It is my roommate, Erik Berglund, Herr Schindel. He went fishing today and had not returned," replied Roman, feigning distress.

"Ach! He probably stopped at the inn to drink some beer," said Schindel opening the door wider.

"But he said that he would be back for supper, sir. And it's not like Erik to stay out late," said Roman.

"Don't worry, Potoski," advised Schindel. "If Berglund does not return by morning, report it to Herr Richter at the center. He is the one who should be worried. Good night, Potoski."

Schindel closed the door and Roman returned to the dormitory. Roman's encounter with the dormitory director had turned out better than he had expected. He wondered if there was someone else around to whom he could speak about Erik's absence. There was light in the kitchen and when he looked in he saw Hilda making preparations for breakfast. Hilda let him in when he knocked and Roman, appearing distraught, told her about Erik's failure to return.

"Do not worry too much. He is probably out there somewhere being nursed by that lady friend of his," said Hilda with an all-knowing twinkle in her eye.

~~~

The evening was calm, and the sky black and teeming with stars. Behind the *Mazovia* the blinking lights of Danzig became dimmer and dimmer until they disappeared and only a pale yellow haze remained where the lights had been. The two small lamps on the outside of the bridge struggled to light up the deck of the boat but seemed insignificant when seen against the impregnable blackness and the enormous canopy of stars overhead. Her engines purring rhythmically, the bow of the *Mazovia* cut through the inky water blindly and almost effortlessly. On the left, the point of the Hel Peninsula loomed ominously out of the water. This was the last familiar landmark that the captain would see before the boat headed out to sea. Soon he would have nothing but the stars to guide him and he would set the course of the small fishing boat to the northwest.

In the cramped cabin below deck, the atmosphere was becoming more buoyant and cheerful. Earlier tensions appeared to have eased and the subdued conversation of the past ten hours became more unrestrained. On the bridge Captain Huta, whistling contentedly, set the boat on a full rhumb line and turned the watch over to his deckhand-mate while he went down below. The conversation stopped abruptly when the captain entered the cabin. They stood up and clapped in appreciation of the captain's capable handling of the day's events.

"Thank you everyone. It has been a good day. Everything went as planned," said the captain, beaming. "I will ask the steward to bring some food and the best drink that we have. We will celebrate our success."

Still dazed by the fast-moving events of the day, Erik and Angela stayed close to each other and as they moved about the small cabin she clutched his arm timidly. The captain and the steward-deckhand passed the glasses around and they drank to the couple's future in the new world.

"Thank you my friends," said Erik, summoning his waning energies. "Angela and I are indeed grateful for the effort that you have all put into this exercise and the risk that some of you must have taken. I hope that we will be able to live up to the expectations that have been created for us." He stopped and looked over at Angela inquisitively and she nodded in the affirmative. "My dear Angela and I want you to be the first to know that after we get to America there will be three of us – four counting Angela's mother. Our child, who was conceived in Poland, will be born in America next February."

They all stood up and applauded and cheered the announcement.

"What better way to carry the memory of your beloved country into your new life in America?" remarked a delighted Bashinski.

Erik glanced around the room to where Litvak was standing beside Major Sliworski.

"With you permission, I would like to say one more thing," Erik said. "Over the past several months we have all been too occupied for me to express my appreciation to the man who made all these things possible by reuniting me with my family in Lubicz several months ago. I want to use this occasion to thank Pan Litvak for everything that he has done for all of us and would like to propose a toast to his health and happiness."

For most of the afternoon and evening, Litvak had stayed close to Major Sliworski. They had engaged in serious discussion and from time to time had consulted with Bashinski and Captain Huta. The four of them seemed to guide the events from behind the scenes and, like theater directors, watched approvingly as the scenes played themselves out. Litvak now seemed touched by Erik's speech and walked humbly to the center of the room and glanced around the group of people.

"Erik and Angela; may luck, good health and good fortune be with you wherever you may go," he began. "Thank you for expressing your appreciation for something in which I played only a small part. To all my friends here, I would like to say how happy I am to have been asked to be a part of this operation. For those of you who may be wondering why I have been involved in these events, I would like to say that there are many reasons for this. First and foremost I did it for my dear friends from Lubicz, the Berglunds, who among all people have accepted me as an equal. Then I did it because of my love for families everywhere and my belief that they should live together in freedom and dignity. And finally, I did it in order to repay the Polish people in a small way, for the kindness which they have bestowed upon my wife and me over the years.

"For although they remain crushed between three powerful and suppressive adversaries, these people have continued to exhibit those human qualities that have stood them so well over the centuries – love for their country and for suppressed people everywhere, pride in the past and hope for the future. Because of this, I know that the Polish people will survive and Poland will one day soon rise again and return to its former glory. So, I too, would like to propose a toast, this one to Poland and to men like Colonel Bashinski and Major Sliworski, to Erik and Angela and to their families and to all of you who will one day soon cause Poland to rise from the ruins of humiliation and defeat."

Around the room the dim light of the small oil lamp hanging from the ceiling revealed the sober looking faces of Litvak's audience. Angela and her mother wiped their eyes with their handkerchiefs and the men cleared their throats and stared at the floor. Litvak's sincerity appeared to have struck a chord of nationalism in Major Sliworski who moved to the center of the room. He stretched his body to its full height as though to emphasize what he was about to say.

"My friends, I am deeply touched by the respect and love which Pan Litvak has expressed for our people. Although he had helped us in many ways in the past, this is the first time that he has expressed his sentiments so eloquently and sincerely. Now, I think that it is up to us to live up to the expectations which Pan Litvak has set for us.

"This year marks the one hundred and nineteenth anniversary of Poland's complete domination by foreign masters. Now, as we face the most impending peril of our own time, we must ask ourselves in whose hands the fate of our nation rests. As Pan Litvak said only a few moments ago, it can only rest in our own hands. This is not the first time that we have been faced with such an enormous task. Over the centuries the soil of Poland has been packed hard by the marching feet of foreign armies. Desired by the Russians, bled by the Turks, humiliated by the Prussians and wooed by its other neighbors, our country was never at rest. Our people had little chance to learn. So it is not surprising that they made many grievous mistakes.

"But the most tragic blunder of our own making occurred when our ancestors tolerated the establishment of a new Prussian state on the shores of the Baltic, whose ancient capital we have just passed. The tragic consequences of that great mistake have largely been responsible for our misfortunes over the past century. Now, three hundred years after that concession, the Germans claim that they have a right to all the land of western Poland, and in particular the provinces of Pomorze and Poznam, not to mention Silesia in the south. They forget that this was Polish territory for almost a thousand years before they arrived.

"German imperialism is even now moving the centers of its military and industrial structures toward the basin of the Vistula, through its handmaiden East Prussia. Yet these Prussians have nothing in common with Germany, historically, geographically or politically. Even their language is different. But they are being used by Germany as an excuse to take over territory which is rightfully ours. So unless we and our friends can recognize this and ensure that Poland, when it is restored, has a territory which corresponds to its historical and demographical boundaries, the threat of German imperialism in Europe will never be removed. Neither shall the continent experience permanent peace.

"That is our task, my friends. The course of Europe is largely in our own hands. How we use this opportunity will determine the fate of all of us and perhaps even the whole world."

Throughout Sliworski's impassioned speech, Bashinski sat shaking his head approvingly. When Major Sliworski had finished, Bashinski shook his hand vigorously

"What you say is very true, Major," he said. "I only wish that more Poles had heard your speech and learned why we, as a nation, face extinction. You are correct when you say that the piece of tranquil country which we traversed today as we sailed down the Vistula is probably the most strategic militarily of any geography in Europe. And the city of Danzig, which we just passed this evening, like a thief in the night, is where it all began. But enough of this seriousness. Let us celebrate our first victory. Captain Huta, where are you hiding that bottle of superior Polish vodka?"

The captain refilled their glasses and after explaining apologetically that they would have to take turns sleeping on the cots, he returned to the bridge. The men agreed that they would let the women use the cots and that they would either sleep on the floor or stay up all night. Erik helped Angela's mother into one of the cots then went up on deck. He joined Litvak who was sitting on a wooden chest gazing at the sky. A radiant moon had risen and was flirting playfully with the fleeting white clouds. They watched the spectacle in silence.

Erik broke the silence. "You know, Pan Litvak, that moon reminds me of the night that you and I rode on the road from Torun to Lubicz about a year ago. I find it hard to believe that it is the same moon. It seems so long ago and so many things have changed. Except the moon, that is. It is still up there, somehow taunting us, it seems."

"You are right, Erik. It is one year ago, almost to the day, that we first met," reflected Litvak. "That was quite an eventful day for you, just as this day has been. I could feel your excitement that night, as well as your anxiety."

"Yes, I really didn't know what to expect," said Erik. "I felt quite a lot like I do tonight in that regard, except that so much has happened since then that I feel that I am a different person than I was a year ago."

"You are quite right." said Litvak, "The appearance of the moon hardly ever reflects the mood of the beholder. It never changes. Maybe that is the creator's way of saying that we may change often, but He always remains the same. A hundred, even a thousand years from now, our descendents will look at the same moon and reflect that it is the same heavenly body upon which men gazed in the twentieth century. But I wonder if they would have changed by then."

"You know Pan Litvak," said Erik, "my father told me that you were a wise man, but not until today did I realize the depth of your wisdom and sincerity."

They remained silent, their eyes fixed on the boat's wake which reflected the moonlight in brilliant flashes then settled into a long silvery white line.

~~~

Several long blasts from the boat's horn startled the dozing passengers below deck. They had talked late into the night, but fatigue, induced by the previous day's activities and excitement, eventually triumphed and they fell asleep in various uncomfortable positions in the small cabin.

Awakened suddenly by the blaring sound of the horn, Erik jumped to his feet and ran up the stairs to the spray-covered deck. Bashinski and Litvak followed him. Dawn had already pushed out the last shadows of the night and with it came the cool breezes off the land mass to the north. The cold flow mixed with the warm air above the water's surface and the humidity in it had condensed into a thick fog.

Off the starboard side, a rocky hulk appeared momentarily and was quickly swallowed by the advancing fog bank. On the bridge, Captain Huta, his eyes peering intently through the dense fog patches, continued to guide the *Mazovia* northwestward as he had done most of the night.

After sailing all night they had reached Bornholm Island and were skirting its south shore. Captain Huta knew the waters around Bornholm Island well, having served there with the fishing fleet on several occasions. At just over one hundred kilometers from Danzig, the island was situated closer to Germany and Sweden than to Denmark, to whom it belonged. Because of its strategic location amid these three countries, the island had become known as the sentinel of the central Baltic. The island's unique granite formations, particularly on its north shore, made it an important source of granite blocks for mainland Denmark as well as its neighbors. Its coastal waters teemed with herring and supported a flourishing fishing industry on the island upon which several prosperous fishing villages, such as Sandvig, Gudhjem, Allinge and Svaneke thrived.

The captain followed the coast line of the rugged island on his way to the small port city of Ronne on its west coast, where Erik, Angela and Mrs. Klazcek would board another boat for England. Gusts of wind swept in off the land, cut through the dense fog and pushed billows of the white mist out to sea. Up on the deck, the four male passengers caught sporadic glimpses of the irregular coast line of the island. From behind the hillocks and dunes occasional images of fishermen's cottages poked through the fog and were followed by fleeting scenes of meadows and pines.

The enticing aroma of frying fish wafted through the stairway from the galley below. The boat's steward-deckhand, who was now also doubling as a cook, was frying freshly caught herring for breakfast.

"That smell is enticing," said Bashinski to the others. "Shall we go and see from where it is coming and check to see if the ladies are awake yet?"

In the cabin, Angela and her mother appeared refreshed after several hours of sleep and a change of clothes. They sat on a small cot, swaying with the motions of the boat.

"Did you sleep well? Are you hungry?" Erik rattled out in a concerned voice.

"After all the excitement that we had yesterday, falling asleep was no problem," said Angela. "Where are we?"

"We are sailing along the south coast of Bornholm Island," Bashinski answered. "In a short while we will be swing over to the northwest and should be in Ronne before noon."

"This must be the route that your ancestors followed when they invaded Poland more than two hundred years ago," Angela said to Erik.

"When I was a child my father used to tell me that the Swedish army walked across the Baltic Sea to get to Poland," said Erik, grinning mischievously.

"All the more reason why they would have stopped here. They were probably tired from all that walking on the water and needed the rest."

"That's a good girl, Angela," said Bashinski, amused by her clever wit. "Don't let him get the best of you, although he may be interested to know that this island was once called Bergunland and may be the origin of his father's ancestors."

His eyes red and squinty from the long hours of strain, Captain Huta entered the cabin and greeted his passengers. He sat down heavily on a bench. "Well, we have been fortunate so far," he said. "The sea has behaved well and we have not had to deviate from our course. But it is likely that there will be some rough water when we get to the west side of the island because the wind is picking up from the north. In one way this has been a blessing because it is blowing the fog away and had improved our visibility. So let us all have a good breakfast and get ready to disembark in about three hours."

A pan filled with steaming herring was thrust through the narrow doorway between the cabin and the galley by a grinning deckhand turned cook. The tempting aroma from the small fish, breaded and fried to a golden brown, filled the small cabin. Plates were removed from a storage chest and the hungry passengers eagerly laid claim to a spot along the narrow table. The deckhand-steward, turned cook, returned with a heaping bowlful of sliced bread and a pot of steaming coffee and served his captain and the appreciative passengers.

The wind, sweeping in from the northeast and aided by the ascending sun, dissipated the fog curtain and brought Bornholm Island into full view, exposing its most westerly tip. Captain Huta steered the bow of the *Mazovia* into the swelling waves coming down from the open sea. As the captain had predicted earlier, the strong northeast winds off the Swedish mainland was stirring the water into angry whitecaps. The small vessel tossed about unceremoniously as the captain struggled to steer the boat close to the coast line.

Clusters of small buildings along the waterfront announced that the port city of Ronne was not far away. The density of the buildings increased as the vessel struggled toward the northwest and the captain adjusted its direction and headed for the port. In the distance the outline of one of Bornholm's famous historic round churches appeared.

A flotilla of fishing and other types of vessels, of assorted sizes, design and vintage, were moored at Ronne's sheltered wharf and hemmed in by a wall of sprawling wood-frame warehouses and fish packing plants. Near the end of the pier was a sleek white cruiser, its Union Jack flag taut on the flagstaff. It stood high above the small fishing boats, its graceful lines and curves exuding dignity and confidence. As Captain Huta guided the *Mazovia* alongside the elegant cruiser, Erik noticed the name below its bow. It was the *HMCS Dover*.

"There she is, Erik," announced Bashinski proudly, "all set to take you to England. You can always count on the British to be there right on schedule."

CHAPTER 19

The sound of numerous footsteps in the hallways and muffled voices in the adjoining billets signaled the start of another day at the single men's dormitory at the Torun Works. Roman awoke from a restless sleep. Long periods of subliminal, anxiety-induced dreams, punctuated by short intervals of disturbed slumber, had left him with throbbing temples and gritty eyes. He welcomed the dawn and the opportunity to escape from the confines of his room.

After sitting silently through breakfast, he hurried to the Research and Development Department. Richter arrived early and listened attentively to Roman's description of the events of the past twenty-four hours. As Roman spoke, he noticed the expression on Richter's face change from one of surprise to concern and then alarm. After instructing Roman not to leave his office, Richter hurried out the door and half ran toward the office of Herr Schmidt.

The oppressive silence which followed Richter's departure from the office convinced Roman that a storm was brewing somewhere and it would soon engulf him. He reminded himself that he must not make any slips or he would arouse suspicions that may implicate him later if Erik's plot was to be discovered. He knew that Erik would soon be safely out of reach, so he had to think only of himself. It was a sobering experience which he had not anticipated.

The silence was abruptly broken by the sound of a number of excited voices in the hallway and hurried footsteps moving toward Richter's door. Richter and Schmidt arrived first, followed closely behind by several other men who appeared to be plant officials.

"Why did you not report this earlier, Potoski?" demanded Herr Schmidt.

"I told Herr Schindel about it last night, sir," answered Roman, "but he advised me not to worry about it until morning. He thought that perhaps Erik was staying out late somewhere."

"I thought that he had some kind of a curfew here," growled Herr Schmidt. "But we will take care of that later. Right now I want you to take the rest of us to the exact spot where you think that Berglund went yesterday."

They found the scene exactly as Erik had intended that they should. Because of its seclusion, few people frequented the spot and nothing had been disturbed. Erik's fishing pole was still anchored between the branches of the leaning tree and the line dangled lazily in the gentle current of the river. Under a small bush on the bank they found his bait pail, scaling knife, lunch and jacket. One of Herr Schmidt's men climbed the leaning tree trunk and examined the pole and line. He looked down into the water and shook his head dejectedly.

"Does it look like the poor bastard fell into the water and drowned?"

groaned Herr Schmidt.

The official nodded his head in the affirmative.

"Well, what should we do now?" asked Herr Schmidt. The scowl on his face indicated his impatience with the official. "You are the director of safety and plant security. Think of something."

"We will report this to the Torun Police Department and they will probably drag the river for the body," said the director. He climbed down the tree and instructed his assistant to go back to town and alert the police.

In about an hour a small boat with several police officers in it arrived on the river. Several more police officers appeared and followed the footpath to the spot where the others waited. Three officers operated the boat with a series of rake-like hooks attached to the back of the vessel and moved downstream toward the junction of the Drewca with the Vistula. The boat later returned to Erik's fishing spot and repeated the process in another part of the river.

Roman watched the operation from the bank with Richter, Herr Schmidt and the other plant officials. He was alternatively overcome by fright and amusement. When Richter spoke, Roman feigned distress and expressed hope that if Erik had indeed drowned, his body would be recovered. Richter comforted him occasional with a faint smile and small talk, but Roman recognized signs of uneasiness in his voice. He wondered what Richter was thinking and whether the man's thoughts involved him. Nearby, Herr Schmidt paced up and down impatiently and Roman thought he detected one or two suspicious glances coming from the senior official. He reminded himself to remain calm and act out the part in the way that would be expected of him. Roman longed for the day to end, but the sun was still at its high point in the sky and he knew that they would be there for a long time to come.

The police guided the boat slowly up and down the river, the dragging apparatus recovering numerous pieces of waterlogged timber, submerged tree branches and other debris, but no body. After a short discussion with Richter, Herr Schmidt returned to the city. The sun dipped slowly toward the horizon as signs of frustration and impatience appeared among the police officers and the plant safety and security officials.

"The body must have been washed out into the Vistula. We will never find it out there," said one of the police officers.

"You may as well call off the dragging operation. They must have covered the whole area at least twice," suggested the director of safety and security.

The police officer agreed and he waved the boat back to shore. They returned to town and Roman arrived at the dormitory in time for the evening meal. The other residents cast sympathetic looks at Roman as he nibbled listlessly at his food. It was obvious that the news had gotten around the residence. Hilda served the meal in silence. Her eyes bore witness to the grief which she had experienced upon hearing the news. She spoke softly and consoled Roman.

"How foolish it was of me to talk so silly when you came here last night. But who would have thought that such a thing could happen?" she said to Roman.

How well everything had worked out, thought Roman to himself as he concentrated upon his act. He knew that Erik would be proud of him and he wondered where his friend and roommate was at this time.

~~~

A tall, slender man in a naval uniform stood on the forward deck of the *Dover*. He motioned to Captain Huta to come on board and the captain climbed up the gangplank, followed by Bashinski and Major Sliworski. The officer greeted them all and took them below deck. In a few minutes, Captain Huta emerged from below and returned to his boat.

"Captain Roberts is ready to receive you on board the *Dover*," he announced to Erik, Angela and Mrs. Klazcek. "My crew will help Mrs. Klazcek on board and transfer your belongings. You may proceed on board as soon as you are ready."

The clean, painted deck of the British cruiser shone brightly in the midday sun as Erik and Angela stepped off the gangplank. They stopped and stared at the neat, almost antiseptic appearance of the boat. Several deckhands moved about the deck, engaged in what appeared to be preparations for departure.

"What a beautiful boat," Angela whispered to Erik as she clung timidly to his arm. He nodded in sincere agreement.

Captain Huta's deckhand assisted Mrs. Klazcek on board the *Dover* and the three newly embarked passengers followed one of the ship's junior officers below. At the bottom of the companionway, Captain Roberts held out his hand and welcomed them on board his ship. Beside him stood a young man in a white uniform whom Captain Roberts introduced as Antos, their Polish speaking steward.

· "Show our passengers to their quarters and see that they get whatever they need during our voyage," Captain Roberts instructed Antos.

"Aye, aye, sir," Antos responded.

"What luxury!" exclaimed Angela as she surveyed the compact cabin with its upholstered chairs and bedspread-covered berth.

"I will be at your service throughout this trip," said Antos in Polish. "If Mrs. Klazcek wishes, I will help her to her quarters now. After you have washed up and rested a while I will take you to the captain's quarters. He will explain your schedule to you."

The young steward patiently assisted Mrs. Klazcek into the adjoining cabin, Angela following close behind.

"Will you be all right now, grandma?" asked Antos.

"Yes, son. Bless you. Angela will be close by if I need her. You speak Polish well," observed Mrs. Klazcek.

"My parents are from Warsaw. They live in Liverpool now," Antos explained. "I understand that you are from Krakow. I love Krakow. I visited there several times."

"Yes. It is the heart of Poland. Warsaw is its head," jibed Mrs. Klazcek.

"I will be back in about an hour," said Antos. "We will talk some more then."

"Bless you, young man," said Mrs. Klazcek as Antos stepped out of the cabin. She turned to Angela. "Where are they taking us?" she asked.

"We are on our way to Southampton, England. Colonel Bashinski said that we will board a big ship there that will take us to Canada," explained Angela. "But do not worry, mother. We are among friends. They will take good care of us."

"May the good Lord protect us all. We will be safe in His hands, but these people can help Him if they wish," said Mrs. Klazcek, raising her eyes upward. "I am very tired, Angela. I would like to rest for a while." Angela placed a pillow under her mother's head and covered her with a soft woolen blanket. She returned to her cabin and washed and changed her clothes.

Some time later Antos returned and accompanied Erik and Angela to the captain's quarters. They found Captain Huta, Colonel Bashinski, Major Sliworski and Litvak all sitting at a table with Captain Roberts. A bottle of spirits and some glasses stood on a silver tray. The men all stood up when Angela and Erik entered. They were discussing the balance of Erik's and Angela's voyage, Bashinski explained. Erik and Angela listened to the conversation taking place in English and were surprised at Bashinski's and Sliworski's command of the language. They also concluded that Captain Huta and Litvak spoke no English, as from time to time Sliworski interpreted for them what was being discussed.

"Well, now that our guests of honor are here, shall we explain our plan to them?" asked Captain Roberts.

"Yes. If you agree, I will explain the first leg of the journey," said Bashinski.

"Please do," said Captain Roberts.

Colonel Bashinski cleared his throat and began speaking in Polish. "Pan Litvak and I will be accompanying Captain Huta back to Warsaw. Major Sliworski will remain on board this boat and escort you all the way to Southampton. There he will see you safely on board the Serbian freighter, the *Drina*, and then he too will return to Warsaw. You will board the *Drina* Sunday and if all goes well, you should be in Halifax two weeks from Wednesday and in Toledo by Saturday of the same week. Major Sliworski will brief you on the North American part of your journey while you are sailing to Southampton."

Angela squeezed Erik's hand as they listened attentively to Bashinski's instructions.

"Do not be afraid, children," said Bashinski in a tender voice. "You are in good hands and among friends. I will leave you now with Major Sliworski and Captain Roberts. Good luck in your new home in America. May we all meet again some day."

Bashinski kissed Angela's cheek and embraced Erik. They all ascended to the deck where the three men left the ship to board the *Mazovia*. On the deck of the *Dover*, Erik and Angela waved as they watched the small fishing vessel leave the harbor and head out into the Baltic.

~~~

Antos quickly proved that he was a dedicated steward. As soon as Erik and Angela returned to their cabin, he appeared with a tray loaded with bowls of soup, cold beef slices, cheese, raw carrots, buns and a pot of tea. He informed them that the cruiser would soon be departing for England but they could begin having their lunch if they wished. The vessel shuddered slightly when the engines accelerated and the propeller engaged. The hoarse sound of the ship's horn was barely audible below deck, but the gentle swaying motion of the vessel told them that they were moving out of the harbor. After they had eaten, Antos removed the dishes and tray and told them that they would be having a visitor later that afternoon.

As expected, a knock sounded on the door some time later, and Erik opened it. It took him a moment to recognize the man who stood before him. Sliworski, now scrubbed and clean shaven, stood at the door, dressed in an English sports coat and slacks and wearing a shirt open at the neck. The transformation from his earlier grubby appearance, unshaven and dressed in a deckhand's garb, was so remarkable that Erik was momentarily taken aback. Sliworski recognized Erik's surprise and smiled. Erik suddenly realized that their visitor was young man, perhaps only a few years older than himself. He invited him in.

"I am sorry, I did not recognize you for a moment," apologized Erik.

"That is understandable," said Sliworski. "I almost did not recognize myself when I looked in the mirror. I thought we should spend some time together today. Yesterday's schedule was hardly conducive to socializing, so we still barely know each other."

"I will go and see if my mother would like to join us," said Angela. "The poor dear is frightened after all the things that have happened in the past day or so."

"Yes, I can understand her feeling that way. It has not exactly been a normal stream of events. Do bring her in if she wishes to come. We can all have a pleasant visit."

Angela returned pushing her mother in a wheelchair that Antos had left in the woman's cabin. Sliworski settled back into one of the chairs and Erik sat on the edge of the bed.

"Well, here you are, America bound," said Sliworski cheerfully. "So much has happened since I first met all of you that you probably have not had an opportunity to wonder how I fit into this arrangement, so if it is all right with you I will try to explain.

"As Colonel Bashinski told you yesterday, I am a member of the Polish underground army, so I am keenly interested in what is going on. In case you are wondering about this army that has no country, I will explain that there is indeed such an organization, with headquarters in Warsaw. We are an army-in-waiting and my task is to help cultivate friends all over the world so that when the right time arrives, we will be recognized by those in power who can help us in our cause.

"The fact that you are on this boat at this very moment, and I am with you, is evidence that this strategy is working. At home, the number of our active members is not great, but we are ready to mobilize all loyal Poles within hours, and since many of them have already received training from our enemies, we will not have to spend much time on that."

"But are you not afraid that you will be discovered?" asked Erik.

"Of course there is always that risk, but that is part of the job. It is largely for that reason that we operate out of the Russian zone. It is a lot safer than in the Prussian or Austrian zones."

"Yes. That is what my husband used to say, too," sighed Mrs. Klazcek, "and look at where he is now. May God have mercy on his soul."

"The reason I say that," explained Sliworski, "is because we are convinced that the Russians are not anxious to consider any imperialistic adventures at this time. They have been badly beaten by the Japanese and the rumblings of a revolution in their own backyard keep getting louder. Any action that might cause a Polish uprising at this time could be both costly and embarrassing for them. So they close their eyes to some of the things that they suspect are happening and hope that when they open them again, these things will have passed.

"But the Prussians, or perhaps more appropriately the Germans, now that is a different story. They are rich, resourceful and clever and in addition to that they are ambitious. We know that it is simply a matter of time before they embark on their next military adventure. They admit that this is necessary if they are to achieve the national goal in which they strongly believe. The Germans have historically considered the Poles as their natural enemies. And that is because throughout the centuries we have stood in the way of their ambitions and their perceived destiny. It was back in the eighteenth century that their man Herder proclaimed that, in all of Europe, only Germany possesses the rights to an ordained destiny. He boasted, with a great deal of conviction, that everything in the history of mankind points to the necessity of German rule for the whole world. Many Germans continue to foster these ideas even to this day. But am I boring you with my ranting?"

"No. Please go on," said Erik. "This is a part of history that I have never heard."

"Then there was another German by the name of Shiller who predicted that some day the whole world will be German," Sliworski continued. "He claimed that the German spirit has been chosen by providence itself to work for the development of all mankind and only the German mind was able to comprehend these sacred matters. And while their intelligentsia was thus praising and uplifting the German spirit and confidence, do you know what was happening in Poland? Its nobility was selling it piece by piece to its enemies. And finally, when all its parts were severed, the enemies moved in and struck at its heart.

"So now Poland is no longer a thorn in Germany's side and they can concentrate on the next step in their grand plan. Who will be next, I am not sure. But some of us think it will be Russia. If this is true and comes to pass, then we propose to turn this to our advantage. While Germany and Russia are bleeding each other to death, we and our friends will be driving nails in both their coffins. And when that is all over, a new Poland will emerge from the ashes."

"Yes, but at what cost?" asked Erik. "I once heard Litvak say that the part of Europe between the Vistula and the Nieman Rivers will be the target in Germany's next war and anything standing between them and this goal will become fodder for their cannon."

"It is true that Prussia has always maintained that the part of Europe between the Oder and the Nieman rightfully belongs to the German Empire. Of course, we all remember that most of this land was once Polish soil. But since we will not be there to defend it this time, the Russians will feel obliged to do so. So while those two giants are engaged in combat, our army will be waiting and watching from the outside. When they are both so weak that they can no longer fight, we will move in and claim what is rightfully ours."

"Do you really believe that it will be that easy?" asked Erik. "After all Poland is not even a country at this time, nor does it have a recognized government. And when they had a chance to do these things in the past, their politicians and bureaucrats squandered it."

"Of course not. We will not be able to do it alone this time. We will need the help of our friends. We will have to convince these friends that they, too, will benefit from our proposed strategy. If a war should start, we will put a part of our underground army at their disposal. In times of peace we will strive to keep the cause of the Polish people before the great legislatures of the world. We will keep reminding them of the great sacrifices that Poland has made to maintain the balance of power in Europe and that the Polish state must be restored so that it can continue to assume that role.

"We have learned our lessons of survival well. When you have no power, you have to be shrewd. We must work on their sympathies. We must continually fan those issues which politicians like. Why, at this very moment I am nurturing a friend in the British House of Commons who will push his parliament to pressure Germany, through diplomatic channels, to release the Polish children who were taken away from their parents, at the same time as you were, following the minor uprisings of 1901 and 1904. Who can disagree with that? As you might expect, the Germans say that these youth are free to return to their parents at anytime they please, but that they do not want to do so. But you know and I know that they are still veritable prisoners in the Prussian zone. Some have even been taken to Germany proper."

"That is not entirely true," said Erik, "at least not as far as Roman and I were concerned, because for a while we were free to go anywhere. But that is not the case for all of them. When we left Posen to come to Torun, some of the others were sent to Breslau. We have been exchanging letters with some of them and they told us that they are not allowed to leave the Prussian zone at any time. A few of them say that they have no desire to do so, so the Prussians are correct to some extent on that point. Perhaps we were more fortunate in Torun, but I think that it was mainly on account of our supervisor, Herr Richter. He used that as a reward for our hard work and we appreciated it. However, I also know of several Polish boys at Torun who worked in other departments and still had not received their freedom to cross into the other zones as we did."

"That is just the kind of ammunition that I will need to convince Clayton Beatty, my friend in the British parliament," said Sliworski. "If you could give me the names of some of those young men who are still confined to Torun and Breslau, he would have some concrete evidence in support of his claim, and I would be most grateful to you."

"Certainly, I can provide you with the names, but I would want to be sure that this will present no danger to them. They are still my friends. I am not concerned about myself because I will soon be far removed from those things and no longer a part of it."

"I will certainly ensure that their safety is not compromised. But do not feel that you can wash your hands clean of this thing. Once you are involved in this game, it is difficult to escape it."

"When I get to America I plan to forget all these politics and petty jealousies and just go about living my own life. I understand that America is a place of the future, so I plan to leave the past behind and start a new life for myself and Angela."

"And don't forget about this one," said Angela, patting her abdomen.

~~~

The bow of the *Dover* cut steadily and swiftly through the Baltic, and headed out into the Kattegat and around the northern tip of Denmark into the North Sea. After obtaining a signed statement from Erik describing the status of the Polish youth in the Prussian zone, Sliworski spent much of his time on the bridge with Captain Roberts. On his short visits to their cabin, Sliworski refrained from further talk about politics or war. He spoke of America and of Erik's family whom he had gotten to know during their last few weeks in Europe. When he spoke of Warsaw and the future, his eyes became fierce and very sad. Sometime they would see him on the deck, his arms folded, gazing serenely at the sea.

Since there was no one on board except them and the crew, Antos spent much time in the passengers' cabins. He fussed over Mrs. Klazcek and jokingly promised her that he would come and see her in America. She responded that he was a good boy and would be greatly blessed, but he should not make promises that he couldn't keep.

The calm sea and the luxurious surroundings provided a pleasant interlude for all of them after the stressful situation of the previous few days. Erik and Angela never left each other's side. They walked hand in hand on the deck, talking steadily and stopping from time to time to gaze into each other's eyes. The hours were pleasant and flew by quickly. All too soon, it seemed, Antos came down and announced that they would be arriving in Southampton.

The *Dover* slid almost effortlessly into the berth. They came up from below deck following Antos who carried their few belongings. Unlike the serenity below, on the deck everything seemed to be noisy and in motion. On the wharf, motor and horse-drawn vehicles jostled each other along the narrow lanes and gaping warehouses, their drivers hurling torrents of abuses at each other. Captain Roberts came down from the wheelhouse and shook their hands and wished them a pleasant journey. Sliworski conferred briefly with the captain then followed the three departing passengers down the gangplank. He hailed a cab and asked to be taken to another part of the dock.

They found the *Drina* moored among a fleet of merchant vessels flying strange flags and bearing exotic names. Sliworski spoke to a sailor at the bottom of the ship's gangplank while the driver unloaded their bags and Angela's trunk. Three sailors came down and one of them asked Sliworski to follow him up the narrow gangway with the rest of the passengers, while the other two sailors remained with the baggage. When they reached the deck, the ship's captain appeared from the bridge and walked toward them. He smiled broadly through his graying beard as he approached. He held out his hand and spoke to them in Polish.

"Welcome aboard the Queen of Trieste, which we call the *Drina*," said the captain jovially. "I am Captain Mikovic. My men will help you to your cabins. You should not be lonely on this voyage because there will be quite a number of other passengers on board." He waited for a reaction from them, but they waited for him to continue. "Pan Sliworski may have misled you and told you that this was freighter. Well, he is only half right. There are so many people wanting to get out of Europe these days that our company wanted to help out, so we are carrying both freight and passengers. I will come down to see if you are settled in well after I have welcomed the other passengers and had a few words with Major Sliworski."

Compared with the luxury they had enjoyed aboard the *Dover*, the cabins to which they were taken by a steward were simple, almost spartan. The bunks and the few pieces of furniture were made of unfinished wood and the gray paint which once covered the walls was either worn off or peeling. All the furniture except the chairs was attached to the wall or the floor. Mrs. Klazcek was given an adjoining cabin, with a narrow door between them. After making her mother comfortable, Angela joined Erik in exploring the small confines of their cabin and unpacking some of their belongings. After agreeing that their accommodation was indeed superior to what they had experienced on the *Mazovia*, they sat down on their berth. There was a knock on the door and Sliworski was shown in by the steward.

"It is not the Queen of Trieste, but it will get you there," said Sliworski apologetically. "As I told you earlier, we thought that taking a freighter from here would make it almost impossible for anyone to follow your trail. So if anyone does foolishly decide to look for you, it will appear that you have disappeared completely."

"I do not think that I have left any reason behind for anyone to consider looking for me. As far as they know, I am at the bottom of the Vistula," said Erik. "In any event, this accommodation is good enough for us and we appreciate all that you have done for us. If I may have offended you during our talk aboard the *Dover*, I would like to apologize. I was tired and still a bit confused and maybe even frightened. In fact, I understand your concerns about the things you spoke about and I will not go against the plans that you and Colonel Bashinski have arranged for me."

"You do not need to apologize," said Sliworski. "Just by leaving what you were doing at Torun you have indicated your conviction and made a sufficient contribution to the plan that we talked about. But you will, no doubt, have a chance to do more once you get to America. That will be up to you. My task is to ensure that you get to your destination safely and to this end Colonel Bashinski and I have arranged for someone to meet you on this ship once you get into Halifax harbor to provide you with the necessary papers and instructions for the last part of your journey. Captain Mikovic is aware of the arrangements and will instruct you if there are any changes."

He stood up and held out his hand. "This is the end of our present meeting. Maybe one day we will meet again. That will depend upon how history unfolds. But even if we do not, I will hold good memories of you all. Good luck in your new life." He entered Mrs. Klazcek's cabin, bade her farewell, then left by her door.

"That is a very dedicated and serious young man. One day he will share in shaping the history of the world," she predicted when they entered her cabin.

The sounds of voices and footsteps outside the cabins signaled that preparations were being made for leaving the port. Erik and Angela were headed for the door to see what was happening when a knock sounded. When they opened it, Captain Mikovic stood outside with a steward at his side. He appeared to be in a jovial mood and asked to come in.

"As you may have guessed from the ruckus outside, we are getting ready to sail," he said. "We are scheduled to leave the dock at 1700 hours, which is five o'clock in your language. Like me, this boat is old, so it will take us from twelve to fourteen days to reach Halifax, the first port in North America at which we will dock. But we have plenty of everything we need on board so we can all take it easy and enjoy the trip. There are several Polish speaking families on board in case you should want to visit. You will be taking your meals in the crew's dining area so I have set up a schedule which the steward will explain to you. I see that you are old hands at this business, judging by the way in which you have settled in so quickly."

"This is the third boat that we have been on so far and we haven't even gotten out of Europe yet," explained Erik.

"Well, maybe we can change that, if we can get this old tub started," said Captain Mikovic with a loud laugh. "I must go now and get ready to leave so make yourselves comfortable. I would like you all to join me for dinner one night during the voyage."

"We would be honored," said an excited Angela.

"No. The honor will be mine. I will send word with the steward," he said as he stepped into the passageway.

About half an hour later the engines groaned loudly and the ship shuddered and rolled gently. Their long voyage to North America had begun.

CHAPTER 20

Burdened by her age and the cargo which she had picked up in Southampton, the old freighter lumbered into the English Channel and out into the Atlantic. On the lower deck the doors to the cabins were opened cautiously, first by curious children and later by the adult passengers who met in the passageway to exchange greetings and small talk. They spoke Serbian, Greek, Hungarian, Polish, German and various Slovakian dialects. Their communication barriers faded quickly as they discovered common languages and experiences. Encouraged by the crew, the passengers found their way to the upper deck, the men first – leaving their wives and children below deck – and later the whole family.

They accepted Erik and Angela readily, referring to them as 'the young couple from Krakow.' As the ship moved farther into the Atlantic, the talk among the passengers gradually moved away from nostalgic reminiscences of their old homes to expectations in the new. The sad and frightened faces which had been evident earlier gradually changed to guarded smiles and beaming eyes as the trauma of leaving behind the familiar old environment was overtaken by the excitement of the new adventures ahead. The anticipation grew as they related their hopes and dreams for their futures in a new country. Stories about relatives and friends in the new world increased in exaggeration and extravagance with each telling.

Attention to the shortcomings in the accommodations aboard the *Drina* was deflected by Captain Mikovic's determined efforts to involve his crew in the daily activities of the passengers. The crew took turns sharing their own dining area with the passengers. In the evenings the mess hall was transformed into an entertainment room where music, dance and song from the home countries were performed by the crew and the passengers.

The stewards assigned to attend to the needs of the passengers spoke the language of the group in their charge. After only two days at sea, the crew and passengers developed a close kinship, exchanging greetings and recalling places and experiences familiar to both. Members of the crew who had visited American and Canadian ports related their observations to the wide-eyed individuals who gathered to listen to the stories in awe and amazement. To Erik and Angela the ordeals of only a few days ago seemed far away and unrelated to the present. Mrs. Klazcek, caught up in the communal atmosphere, hobbled among the cabins making friends and exchanging stories from both happier and sadder times. The world outside Europe was already beginning to look better than they had anticipated.

Erik, Angela, and Mrs. Klazcek were in their cabin on the morning of the third day at sea when the steward delivered a note from Captain Mikovic inviting them to join him at the Captain's table for dinner that evening. Angela was elated and excited and her mother said that she was honored. They sent their immediate acceptance back with the steward.

At the appointed hour they arrived at the mess and were shown to the captain's table by a Polish speaking steward. Captain Mikovic had already arrived and was seated. His dark blue uniform was neatly pressed and he wore a white shirt and dark tie. When his guests arrived at the table he stood up and shook their hands. He helped Mrs. Klazcek and Angela into their chair and sat down himself.

Captain Mikovic was a portly man with broad shoulders which swayed slightly as he walked. His beard was neatly trimmed to the shape of his face. He surveyed them all quickly with his inquisitive eyes and smiled.

"I have been somewhat remiss in not having you join me here sooner." He spoke good Polish. "I know that you are someone important, judging by the concern that Colonel Bashinski had for your welfare when he arranged for your passage aboard my ship."

"Oh no, please don't feel that way," remarked Erik. "We are just ordinary people moving to a new country to seek a new life."

"You are also very modest," said Captain Mikovic with a hearty laugh. He leaned across the table and spoke softly. "Since when are ordinary immigrants met by a boarding party of American officials at a Canadian port?"

"They will be in Halifax to take me to my new job in America." Erik tried to appear casual while glancing uneasily at the steward who had been standing nearby during the conversation. The captain waved the steward away and leaned back in his chair.

"Do not worry, folks. You are safe and in good hands here. Colonel Bashinski and I have known each other for many years and he told me who you are and where you are going. But as far as the crew and the rest of the passengers are concerned, you are regular passengers. That is why I waited three days before asking you to join me for dinner. I hope that your voyage has been pleasant so far. Shall we begin our dinner?"

They nodded in agreement and the captain beckoned the steward to begin serving the food and drink.

Captain Mikovic was in a talkative mood during the seven course meal in which the main dish was roast lamb. He proudly explained that he was the second generation of Mikovics to command the ship. He had served as a seaman under his father and moved up through the ranks to the captaincy. The talk then turned to the affairs of his guests and the captain declared his happiness at hearing that Angela was with child and related that he, too, had a family back home. Over her objections, the captain insisted that Mrs. Klazcek would receive special attention from the ship's doctor during the balance of the journey. The doctor would call on her every day until they arrived at their destination. As they rose to return to their cabins, everyone agreed that it had been an enjoyable evening. The captain wished them well for the remainder of their journey.

"Send word with the steward if there is anything that I may be able to do for you," he insisted as they left his table and headed for the door of the mess hall.

Life aboard the *Drina* was assuming a routine pattern as the ship plied its course steadily westward. Then on morning of the fifth day at sea Erik was on the deck and overheard a watchman report that the vessel was approaching a cloud bank. The cloud was barely visible in the horizon and looked like a black wall in the distance. As the vessel moved closer, it became more apparent that they were approaching a weather front which could be a North Atlantic storm. There was a buzz of excitement among the crew when the word got around that the ship was sailing toward an approaching weather front. Upon the orders of the ship's officers the crew checked the boat deck on the windward side and tied down anything that was loose.

Captain Mikovic came down from the bridge and moved about quickly, conferring with his officers and briefing the crew on the mid-deck. When he was satisfied that the preparations were proceeding well he headed for the companionway. A few moments later he was at the door of Erik and Angela's cabin.

"We are expecting to run into a small storm in a short while and because of Mrs. Klazcek's condition, it is probably best that she remain in the cabin for the duration of the storm. Since this is the windward side of the ship, it is a good idea to ask her to stay in her berth where the bunkboard will ensure that the roll of the ship will not cause her to fall."

"Thank you for you concern, Captain," responded Angela. "We will do as you say."

The lights inside the ship assumed an accentuated brightness when some time later the ship entered the dark low-lying cloud. Although it was still midmorning it was dark and gloomy outside. Suddenly a blast of wind hit the ship, catching the suspended lifeboats and swaying them violently. The bridge creaked on its wooden moorings and the smoke from the stack swirled about the deck. The waves grew larger. A wall of water, almost as high as the hull itself, struck the old vessel broadside with a muffled thud. The vessel shuddered and rolled listlessly from side to side before regaining its balance. Long blasts from the ship's foghorn, sounding like the roar of a wild animal cornered by its stalker, penetrated the sheets of rain which now enveloped the vessel.

On the bridge, Captain Mikovic grasped the wheel firmly in his powerful hands and kept the ship on a steady westward course. He had ridden out many Atlantic storms and knew that this one would last several hours. And he was correct. It was not until six hours later that the wind subsided and the sky began to clear. On the western horizon the sun hung suspended like a flaming disk in the rain scoured sky. The bright orange sunlight pushed long shadows across the deck and gilded the tips of the ebbing waves. The old ship steadied herself and continued forward defiantly, once again a victor in the battle against the relentless energy of the angry sea.

One by one the passengers climbed up the companionway on unsteady legs. Most of them had not eaten since breakfast and knew that they would not be able to face food again until next morning. They watched the sun sink into the horizon in line with the ship's bow as the vessel cut through the now docile sea. The captain handed the wheel to his first officer and returned to his quarters, where he had not been since early that morning, and the ship continued undeterred on its westerly course.

The morning dawned clear and calm. In every direction the horizon stretched out into apparent infinity. On the deck many of the passengers strolled about or sat quietly enjoying the warmth of the ascending autumn sun. Below deck, Erik and Angela sat at a small table poring over a Polish-English dictionary that Bashinski had given then. They selected some of the more common words that they thought they would need to know and laughed at each other's attempts at pronouncing some of the longer ones. While Angela's mother slept, they speculated about what things would be like in their new home in America. They wondered if the house that Bashinski said was waiting for them would have a special room for the new baby. They agreed that if their baby turned out to be a boy, they would call him Wladimar, after Colonel Bashinski. They wondered if Bashinski and Litvak had got back safely to Warsaw and Lubicz.

"You know, it is now ten days since I fell into the Drewca. I wonder if they have found my body yet," snickered Erik.

~~~

Acting on Herr Schmidt's orders, a complete curfew was placed on the single men's dormitory at the Torun Works complex. None of the residents that lived in the same wing as Erik and Roman was allowed out of the building except to go to their workplaces. A meek and dejected Herr Schindel, somewhat deflated by the events of the past few days, explained to the residents that the temporary inconvenience would allow the plant security and police to complete their investigation into Erik's disappearance more quickly. When this was over, things would get back to normal. By the end of the week of Erik's disappearance, each of the residents in the wing had been interviewed, as police tried to fit the puzzle together. Hilda, whom the investigators had questioned longer than any of the others except Roman, was indignant.

"The poor boy is lost, maybe dead, and they come around here every few hours asking silly questions. They should be out there looking for him, the whole lot of them," she fumed as she served the evening meal. "Look at Roman here. Do you think that if he knew what happened to his best friend he wouldn't tell them? Of course, he would and so would we all. But what can we tell them when we know nothing."

By this time Roman had repeated his story so often that he was beginning to believe it himself. That Saturday he returned to the dormitory tense and exhausted. He sat alone in his billet, wishing that the whole incident would soon be forgotten so he could begin to plan his own departure. Since Erik's disappearance, he had not had an opportunity to contact either Lydia or the old beggar at the market square. He suddenly felt cut off from the outside world. This is really strange, he thought to himself. He had not felt like this for a long, long time. Was it because of Erik's absence or was he beginning to feel imprisoned, he pondered.

He was about to doze off when footsteps in the hallway aroused him. As he sat up on his bed a heavy knock rattled the door. It sounded official and he rushed to the door and opened it, expecting yet another interrogation. He knew he was right when he saw Richter, a uniformed policeman and another man in civilian clothing.

"We are sorry to disturb you again, Roman," apologized Richter, "but these police officers would like to check Erik's belongings."

Roman watched as the uniformed policeman and his partner in plain clothes systematically removed each piece of clothing which had belonged to Erik from a closet and laboriously checked every pocket and seam in each garment. The uniformed policeman replaced them in the closet and made some notes in his notebook. The three men then engaged in a short hushed discussion outside the door.

"Are these all of Erik's belongings?" asked Richter when they returned.

"Yes, except what he wore on the day that he disappeared," answered Roman.

"Roman, did Erik ever show you the medal and citation which I presented to him on behalf of Colonel Weiss?"

"Yes, he did," answered Roman.

"And do you know where he kept them?"

"In the top drawer of that chest over there," responded Roman.

Richter and the police officers searched the drawer carefully, but the medal and citation were not there.

"They are not here." Richter seemed disappointed.

Roman shrugged his shoulders and Richter looked at the police officers submissively.

"I think we had better report this to Herr Schmidt," he said.

Richter's pronouncement convinced Roman that the whole affair was becoming more serious and complicated than either he or Erik had imagined it would. He wondered what Richter meant when he said that the matter should be reported to Herr Schmidt. It seemed like a long time between his latest interrogation and Monday morning. The long torturous hours seemed endless, in a prison that was once comfortably familiar but now had an illusory quality about it.

Roman arrived at his workplace early Monday morning eager to involve himself in his work in order to take his mind off the events that had been impinging on his otherwise carefree life. But this was not to be. Richter was already there waiting for him with his hat and coat on.

"We have to go to police headquarters this morning to talk to Captain Bauer from Berlin," Richter announced.

"From Berlin?" Roman was taken aback.

"Yes. From Army Intelligence in Berlin," replied Richter.

"But what does he want with me?" asked Roman. "I have already explained everything that I know several times over."

"This should be the last time." Richter tried to reassure him as he sighed deeply.

A constable of the local police met them as they entered the police headquarters. Richter accompanied them to a small scantily furnished chamber which he referred to as a special interrogation room. When the constable left to announce their arrival, Richter sat down heavily and propped his face inside his cupped hands. In the silence which followed, Roman surveyed the room. Metal tobacco can tops which served as ashtrays were scattered around the old wooden table which was covered with scratches and cigarette burns. Four heavy wooden chairs were placed one at each side of the table. There was only one other piece of furniture in the room, a pew-like bench upon which they were sitting. The walls which were once white were yellowing with age and smoke. The room struck Roman as being completely out of the character with the rest of the building, which seemed clean and well maintained.

In the silence that followed Roman felt his own heart beating heavily. He tried to calm his anxiety by diverting his thoughts to other less turbulent times but Erik's face kept appearing in his mind. He looked at Richter who was also deep in thought. Although it appeared that it was Richter's decision which indirectly led to this latest investigation, Roman still felt his presence reassuring. Richter was a dedicated technocrat, but he was fair and only tolerated bureaucracy when it positively affected matters close to his domain. Otherwise he secretly despised bureaucrats who he said were a hindrance to progress. Roman recognized these qualities in his boss and admired him for his convictions.

The constable returned, followed by a uniformed army captain carrying an official looking leather briefcase. The captain sat at the end of the table and Erik and Richter sat across from each other. No one spoke as the captain flipped through several reports in the file. He proceeded to ask Roman the same questions that he had answered several times before. Only when he came to the record prepared by the local police investigators did he ask for clarification of several details. The interview with the captain was turning out to be less rigorous than Roman had expected and he was beginning to relax. Finally the officer closed the file and looked directly at Roman.

"Did Berglund ever mention anything to you about a fishing boat based in Warsaw?'

"No sir. As far as I know, he knew no one in Warsaw who had anything to do with the fishing business," replied Roman.

"Did you know that your roommate was married?" asked the captain.

"We did not discuss our personal lives." Roman tried desperately to avoid telling a direct lie. In any event, his answers did not seem to concern the captain who turned his attention to Richter.

"I am afraid that your prodigy has fled the continent, Herr Richter," he said with finality.

"How can you be so certain?" asked Richter.

"Our informant saw him on the river bank at fifteen minutes to twelve on the day of his disappearance. He seemed to be quite distraught and looked at his watch several times in the period between eleven and a quarter to twelve. We also know that a vessel of the provincial government in Warsaw tied up briefly at the old dock on the Drewca a few minutes later. The Harbor Patrol at Danzig boarded the boat that same evening but did not check its passengers. The captain of the boat said that he had two women on board bound for Gdynia. On the return trip through Danzig the two women were not on board. The captain told us that they were still in Gdynia but our check later revealed that they had not been dropped off at that port. In fact the boat did not even dock there. The failure of the local police to locate the body made us suspicious, but when you reported that the citation and medal were missing we were convinced. Our investigations have proven, almost conclusively, that Berglund left the country aboard a Polish fishing vessel for an unknown destination."

"I am indeed sorry to hear that." said Richter. "He was one hell of a talented young man."

"I only hope for our own sake and his that he did not take anything more sensitive with him than the citation and medal," said Captain Bauer as he replaced the file in his brief case.

"I am sure that he didn't," said Richter. "All the blueprints and formula calculations were left in his office."

"We will see," said Captain Bauer.

~~~

The buzz of excited voices outside their cabin door told Erik and Angela that something unusual was happening. It was Wednesday afternoon, the day that the ship was scheduled to reach Halifax. Erik stuck his head outside the door and looked down the alleyway. A group of passengers were milling about, engaged in animated conversation.

"We can see land. We can see Canada!" an excited father informed Erik, almost in tears. The man ran up the companionway, followed by his wife and children. Erik stepped back inside the cabin and closed the door.

"We are nearly there. We have arrived," he broke the news to Angela. "They say the coast is in sight. Hurry. Let us go and see for ourselves."

The hazy silhouette of the distant coastline stood like a giant purple sea serpent on the horizon. Although the sun shone brightly, no features were visible from the deck of the ship because of the distance and the light distortion caused by the vapor filled air. But this did not reduce their elation at the sight of the new land.

"Our new home," announced Erik. "Isn't it beautiful?"

Angela squeezed his hand and smiled in agreement.

The *Drina* plodded through the choppy waves with determination as her passengers stood against the railing gazing at the approaching land. Prominent features on the landscape were becoming more distinct as the coast came into closer view. One of the crew members explained to the passengers that the hump of land which stood higher on the horizon than the rest of the landscape was called Citadel Hill. It overlooked the city of

Halifax and from its summit one could see the ships as they would enter the harbor from the open sea. From the foot of the hill, the sailor explained, the city reaches out in all directions until it approaches the sea or converges with the rim of the forest, which is itself girded by the sea.

As the ship drew steadily closer to the land, certain features on the landscape came into view. Against the dark green backdrop of the forest, church spires and other buildings emerged as white or brightly colored specks.

As the sun dipped into the horizon, the ship left the open sea and entered the stream-like narrows. In the late afternoon shadows, the banks and cliffs on both sides of the channel seemed to provide just enough room for the vessel to squeeze through and no more. Erik heard the same sailor as before explaining that the narrows which the vessel was traversing was called "The Stream". It was a deep channel formed between the mainland and George's Island, which lies close to the shore. Beyond the narrows was a deep open area of water, a perfect harbor called "Bedford Basin", or more affectionately, "The Basin". It was there that the *Drina* would cast her anchor before proceeding to her berth the following morning.

The ship nosed her way slowly into the sheltered basin and groaned to a reluctant halt. A rattling sound in the ship's bow announced that the anchor was being dropped. As she lay motionless in the still waters of the harbor, the excited and anxious passengers stood at the railing gazing timidly at the city where they would disembark next morning. As soon as the *Drina* dropped her anchor, a launch left a small dock which extended out from a gray stone building at the water's edge and headed toward the ship. As it came closer, three men dressed in topcoats and hats were observed standing near the stern. The pilot maneuvered the launch alongside the *Drina* and the deck hands let down the ship's ladder. The three men climbed up onto the deck and a crew member escorted them to the bridge and Captain Mikovic.

Erik and Angela had not yet emerged from their cabin as many of the other passengers had done. They recalled Sliworski's instructions that someone would be coming on board to meet them and explain the rest of their journey to them, so they waited. It was quiet in the alleyway as most of the passengers were either on the top deck or in their cabins. A knock on their door broke the silence. When Erik opened it, Captain Mikovic entered, followed by three men in business attire.

"Well, I have come to deliver your welcoming committee as I promised I would," said the captain in Polish. "First, I would like to present Mr. Earl Dixon of the United States Immigration Service. Then here we have Mr. Ronald Cook of Canadian Immigration and Mr. Michael Pankiw from Burlington Industries in Toledo.

"Welcome to Canada and America," said Dixon in English, removing his hat and shaking hands with Erik and Angela. "Mr. Pankiw here will explain your schedule for tomorrow and will also escort you to Toledo. We have your papers in order for entry into the United States of America and Mr. Cook will clear you through Canadian customs and immigration as soon as you disembark. Would you like to take over now, Mike?"

"Glad to," said Pankiw in English. Switching to Polish, he repeated to

Erik and Angela what Dixon had just said. He urged them to leave all the arrangements to him, have a good rest and be ready to leave next day. There was much to talk about, but they would have enough time to do this on the long train ride to Toledo and beside that, they would be neighbors in that city. He was taken to Mrs. Klazcek's cabin and was introduced to her by Angela, while Erik stayed with the others. Captain Mikovic, the two immigration officials and Pankiw prepared to leave.

"I will be at the foot of the gangway tomorrow morning when you disembark," said Pankiw. "I will take you to Mr. Cook who will clear your travel through Canada. We will leave you all now. Have a good sleep because we will be on that train in about twenty-six hours."

Captain Mikovic stepped into the next cabin and said farewell to Mrs. Klazcek. He returned and held out his hand to Erik and Angela.

"I will not be able to see you off the ship tomorrow, so I will say good-bye now. I think I can say to Colonel Bashinski that I have delivered you safely to your first destination and that I left you in good hands. I hope that you enjoyed your time with us and I wish you good luck in your new home."

"This ship has been like a home to us," said Angela. "We will always remember this voyage and your kindness toward us."

Captain Mikovic and the others exited the cabin and they were left alone. "Let us go up and take another look at our new world, then we can come back and get our things ready for tomorrow morning," suggested Erik.

~~~

They were awakened abruptly by a loud knock on the door of their cabin. When Erik opened it, a steward was standing outside in the alleyway. "Breakfast will be served in half an hour," he announced. "After that you will have another hour and a half before all passengers disembark. By that time it will be 0800 hours and the immigration hall will be open. Make sure that you have all your belongings packed and ready to take with you. I'll see you all at the breakfast table."

The ascending sun was peeking over the nearby hills when Erik, Angela and Mrs. Klazcek arrived on the main deck with their bags and belongings. Flocks of gulls squawked loudly as they flew over the deck looking for food. Reflections of orange sunlight flashed off their shiny feathers as they milled about overhead ready to swoop down at the sight of any morsel tossed onto the deck by passengers or crew.

A low rumble inside the bowels of the ship and the grating creak of chains on pulleys announced that the anchor was being raised and the ship would soon be in motion. As the ship moved slowly toward the dock, the deck hands and officers scurried around the deck in preparation for docking, while dispensing good wishes to the disembarking passengers. After saying farewell to the friends they had made on the ocean journey, the passengers huddled together in family units surrounded by bags and boxes containing what would soon be their only remaining tangible memories of their old world.

CHAPTER 21

Intermittent blares of the *Drina's* horn penetrated the still morning air and kept her course clear of traffic. She moved slowly, as though cautiously feeling her way toward the waiting spot at the pier. Sitting high on the bridge, the pilot skillfully guided the vessel into her berth and brought the massive hulk to a stop. Dock workers waited on the pier as the deckhands lowered the creaking gangplank and the landing began.

The passengers moved cautiously down the gangplank, children clinging to their mothers' skirts and men struggling under the weight of bags, bundles and boxes which they carried down the steep incline. On the dock, immigration officers directed them to the nearby Immigration House in several languages.

A steward pushed Mrs. Klazcek's wheelchair down the gangplank, with Erik and Angela following close behind. As he had promised, Pankiw was at the dock waiting for them. His smiling face was a welcome sight in the unfamiliar surroundings. They entered the immigration office where Immigration Officer Cook stamped their passports routinely and cleared them for travel through Canada to Detroit. At the other wickets and counters, immigration officers and immigrants struggled desperately to communicate with the help of interpreters. Erik viewed the ensuing frustration and remembered what Bashinski had said about the privilege of having all the arrangements made for them in advance. It was difficult for him to comprehend how the colonel's influence could reach all the way to this immigration hall thousands of kilometers away, but apparently it did.

When they emerged from the immigration office, Pankiw looked at his watch and announced that they still had about three hours before their train would depart. He thought it would be a good opportunity for them to buy some North American clothes and perhaps even do some sight seeing. After leaving their baggage with a porter at the railway station, Pankiw hailed a cab. They rode to the waterfront business center only several blocks away and entered a department store.

Stands of merchandise of many descriptions, from food to clothing to hardware, filled the well stocked emporium. Aromas of fruit, vegetables and ground spices mingled with the tangy scent of recently tanned leather and the clean smell of cotton and linens, the mix of smells changing as they moved through the different departments. They walked past the kitchenware and linen counters to the clothing department. Erik and Angela stared wide-eyed at the variety of merchandise on display. Blue denim work pants and coveralls with shiny studs and colorful labels were stacked according to size and style. Jackets, mackinaw coats and sweaters hung in long rows along the wall. On the next table were the work shirts in grays, browns and dark greens, then the gray socks with white heels and toes, and beside them the big red and blue handkerchiefs with small white dots.

The creaky floor, which was oiled black, changed to varnished hardwood when they entered the business and dress clothing section. A slight, short bespectacled man with gray hair and groomed moustache approached them, smiling broadly. He had a tape measure hanging around his neck and several pens and pencils in his shirt pocket.

"Are you folks looking for something special?" he asked.

"My friends here just arrived from Europe," said Pankiw. "I would like them to look at something nice to wear; not too fancy."

Brandishing his measuring tape with flair, the clerk took their measurements and selected several garments in their sizes from the racks and counters. Rubbing the material between his thumb and forefinger, he urged them to feel the superior quality of the garments. Pankiw, appearing to be wise in North American ways, quickly examined the selection and waved off most of the items as being unsuitable for his friends. The clerk obliged with a bigger selection.

After more than half an hour of haggling between Pankiw and the persistent clerk, they emerged arrayed in their new attire: Angela in a modest woolen skirt, white blouse and light brown jacket; Erik in a tweed jacket, dark pants and a brown-striped white shirt, and Mrs. Klazcek in a skirt, long-sleeved white blouse and knitted woolen sweater. Outside, Pankiw stepped back and surveyed the trio.

"If they had kings and queens here, some people would surely say that I am in the company of royalty."

"Royalty? Let us not put the curse of Europe upon this decent place," sneered Mrs. Klazcek.

The waterfront street was already crowded with shoppers, sailors, fishermen and immigrants as they walked slowly beside the limping Mrs. Klazcek. The train was not scheduled to leave for about two hours and Pankiw suggested that they engage a cab and do some sightseeing. The soft salty air was warming up in the bright sunshine and they agreed that this would be an attractive alternative to sitting in a crowded railway station waiting room. The driver of a calash at the end of the street was quick to oblige and helped Mrs. Klazcek into the open vehicle while the others climbed in. Pankiw advised the driver that they had about an hour to spare and preferred to spend it viewing the inner city and its people.

The tour began along the waterfront amid the bustle of the dockside traffic, punctuated by the sounds of blaring ships' horns, dockworkers' shouts and waves lapping up against the pier. Carts and wagons rattled along the cobblestone street, carrying their passengers and merchandise to and from the ships and warehouses. The morning air was rife with the smells of fish, tar, bilge water, rotting wood and manure. They turned toward the opposite end of the docks where trains shunted and coupled noisily, the smoke funnels of the steam locomotives belching acrid black smoke and cinders into the air.

Like many other eastern seaboard cities of North America, the Halifax of 1912, which was a previously slumbering port city, had suddenly been called into service to channel the thousands of European immigrants who poured through it on their way west and to handle the commercial shipping which followed them. Except for the original old stone structures near the waterfront, many of the commercial buildings were drab and characterless, as if constructed for emergency use today only to be abandoned later. The houses, especially the earlier Victorian models, exuded a certain charm in spite of being covered with the every shade of paint imaginable.

Many of the people who saw the city only briefly wondered why, with all the beautiful natural rock around the city, almost every dwelling was constructed of wood. The earliest of these wooden structures were already displaying the ravages of the salt air and high humidity, with their walls showing signs of decay and their paint peeling away from the wood. But the large stone buildings were a welcome contrast. These were fashioned in early Georgian style and constructed from native stone, obviously quarried nearby, since the city seemed to be built upon a rock covered by only a thin layer of topsoil. Their well proportioned lines, impressive doorways and high sloping roofs stood out as sheer architectural delights in a sea of monotonous warehouses and commercial buildings.

"This is one of the oldest cities in Canada," the driver volunteered when he noticed their surprise at seeing the aging stone edifices. "The next building on the right will be the city hall." The driver stopped the horses in front of the building. Above the arcade the coat of arms stood above the words *E mari mercus*. "Wealth from the sea," interpreted the driver. "This place lives by the sea."

As they moved farther away from the waterfront, the streets strained steadily upward as if conspiring to escape the pull of the sea. They reached a plateau where they were greeted by the smells of the nearby forests of balsam and spruce, of the autumn flowers, of late breakfasts cooking in the houses along the street and of laundry hanging out to dry.

Pankiw pointed at his watch and the driver turned the vehicle around for the return trip. The calash rolled effortlessly down the steep decline, past cozy little parks where old men sat on benches smoking their pipes and contemplating the sea below. Young mothers pushed their prams and fussed over their babies as they enjoyed the fading warmth of the autumn sun. Coy young ladies, eyed by the noisy sailors on shore leave from their ships, tried unsuccessfully to hide their delight at being noticed.

Cabs and people were arriving from every direction when they reached the railway station entrance. In the large open waiting room Dixon was seated on a long wooden bench peering anxiously at the crowd of people. When he saw them he jumped to his feet and pushed his way through the crowd to meet them.

"Hey! What happened to you folks? I thought maybe you had all gotten lost," he fretted.

"We decided to do some sightseeing while we waited for the train," explained Pankiw. "After twelve days at sea, I thought it might be a nice change for them to get a close-up look at some trees and grass."

"Good idea. But next time take me along," suggested Dixon. "This is not the most pleasant place in which to spend a couple of hours."

Dixon explained that while they were gone, he had arranged for their trunks and bags to be checked at the baggage counter for passage to Windsor, except for the ones that they would carry aboard the train. The baggage handler was waiting for them to show him which bags they would be taking. They rushed to the baggage counter and shortly after the train's departure time was announced they made their way to the gate. Around them, throngs of people milled about then sorted themselves out into groups at the various gates, like bees swarming together to choose a hive. At each gate, the sheepskin vests and embroidered shirts worn by clusters of men, women and children revealed their origins but not their destinations. The waiting individuals gazed timidly at the strange surroundings, finding occasional comfort in words of assurance in familiar tongues from each other or from immigration or railway employees.

The gates opened one by one and the crowd emptied onto the loading platform outside the station. On board the train Erik and Angela discovered that Pankiw had already reserved their seats in a sleeping car that morning. He explained how the seats would be made into beds for the night by the porters and the women could use the lower berths and the men the uppers.

The buildings, sea and landscape began moving past their windows shortly after they had settled into their seats, slowly at first, then rapidly picking up speed. Wafts of dark smoke swirled angrily past the window, telling them that their coach was not far from the locomotive. Their tickets were punched by a red-faced conductor with small gold-rimmed glasses and a prominent paunch. He advised them that their first major stop would be Montreal in about seventeen hours. They would arrive there at five o'clock in the morning, stop for an hour and then continue to Toronto. There they would transfer to another train for a shorter ride to Windsor.

"We should be in Toledo early Sunday morning," said Pankiw.

"Toledo. That sounds like such a long way from Torun," said Erik.

"And even farther away from Krakow," added Angela.

~~~

The train roared relentlessly westward, spouting smoke and steam, with its whistle blaring authoritatively as it sped noisily past villages and through crossings. The passengers watched the landscape flowing endlessly past their windows – meadows, rock outcroppings, sparkling lakes, rivers and streams and millions of trees. Towns and villages with strange names followed each other with monotonous irregularity. They talked about the scenery, Europe, America and their families. Their eyes and bodies were weary when the train stopped in Montreal and they welcomed the opportunity to try out their unsteady legs on solid ground before resuming their westward journey.

"This country seems to be endless," remarked Erik after the train had pulled out of the station and was once again heading westward. "Here we have been traveling for more than a day and you still say that we have a long way to go."

"Yes," replied Pankiw, "and even then we will have covered less than a third of the distance across this land. This country is so massive that for a long time no one wanted it. To those who saw it for the first time, it appeared awesome, almost untamable. So they left, saying that it was worthless wasteland, of no use to anybody."

"You know, that is really amazing when one considers that in Europe thousands of lives have been sacrificed at times fighting over less land than a person can walk across in one day. And all that time this beautiful land was sitting here almost uninhabited."

"I wonder if land was really what they were fighting for or whether it was not mere vanity – the quest for power and the settling of old accounts," remarked Pankiw. "It seems to me that people somehow get along with each other when they leave behind them those old environments with all the age-old hatreds and prejudices. Man seems to become a new and more noble creature when he escapes those bonds and strives to be his own person. But let us wait for you discover this for yourselves when you settle into your new home. I know I have."

"I could never become too involved in those things," remarked Erik. "You know, in spite of what happened to me in my childhood I still felt no hatred for the Prussians. In fact, I guess I admired them in some ways. They are an industrious people who take pride in hard work, orderliness and discipline. Maybe every nation, including Poland, could learn something from them."

"Maybe the reason you feel the way you do is because you are still young, but had you stayed there longer you may have felt the same as your parents did at one time," said Pankiw.

"My mother, yes. But not my father. He was too independent of mind to get caught up in such things."

"I did not know your parents so I cannot say for sure. But I did hear about your father getting quite involved in something very controversial in Wrzesnia some years ago, so he must have had some opinions on the matter," said Pankiw.

"I suppose you are right. Maybe he just became too disillusioned and cynical after that experience to care anymore," reflected Erik as he stared out the window.

The towns and villages were now closer together and the conductor informed the passengers that they would be arriving in Toronto in about two hours. Those travelers who were making connections to Windsor would have to wait about three hours before their train departed. This was sufficient time for their baggage to be transferred from one train to the other and for the passengers to stretch their legs around the station. The conductor wished them well in their new home in America.

The shadows of nightfall were already lengthening and lights were flashing by the windows when the grinding of the wheels braking against the rails announced that the group was finally arriving at its initial destination and that they were getting close to the end of their journey. The train ground slowly to a stop and Erik and Angela followed Pankiw excitedly down the steps to the station platform, with Mrs. Klazcek between them.

At the front of the train the locomotive chugged contentedly as though enjoying the respite after the long journey from Halifax. Inside the station, the thunder of trains moving on overhead tracks and the clamor of milling crowds of passengers and railway workers filled the cavernous building with a steady roaring sound.

"This seems like a nice place," said Angela to Erik when they stepped outside of the station and were walking along the street. "Why don't we just stay here?"

"Because you heard what Sliworski and the others said. They need us at the other place," he replied.

"Sliworski and the others seem so far away now that they are nearly out of my mind," said Angela, "so why don't we just say that we changed our minds?"

"Because we do not have the proper documents to stay here and also because we did make a promise to Bashinski that we would go to Toledo. But maybe some day we can come back here to visit. We will not be very far away," suggested Erik.

It was almost midnight when they boarded the other train for the next leg of their journey. Pankiw assured them that the trip to Windsor would be a short one compared with the distance they had just traveled. At Windsor they would cross the bridge into Detroit and then take another short train ride to Toledo. They would be in Toledo early Sunday morning where Pankiw's wife, Christina, would be anxiously waiting for them. The thought of a home-cooked meal and a bed appealed to the weary travelers.

Because of the short distance involved, the train had no sleeping cars and they rode in a day coach. They sat across from each other, too tired to talk, their heads bobbing from side to side in erratic interludes of sleep.

A pink haze stretched dimly across the eastern horizon when they detrained at Windsor. Fatigue from the many days of travel and excitement had extracted its toll and the three travelers moved about mechanically following Pankiw silently as he retrieved their baggage and ordered a cab for the trip across the river. There they were joined by Dixon who spoke briefly to the officials at the U.S. immigration post. He took an envelope out of his pocket and spread a document before the immigration officer. The officer read the document and stamped the passports which Dixon then presented to the three travelers. The officer observed Erik curiously.

"Welcome to the United States of America," he said warmly.

Pankiw shook their hands enthusiastically. "My friends, we are almost home now. Welcome to my wonderful adopted country. May your time here be long and as happy as mine has been."

The final leg of the voyage that had begun for Erik eighteen days ago at the abandoned dock on the Drewca River now consisted of only a short train ride between Detroit and Toledo. The group sat robot-like as the blurry landscape sped past their window. When the conductor announced that the next stop would be Toledo they were aware that it was now daylight outside, but otherwise time and place had lost their meaning.

~~~

The cab driver sported a large red moustache and sunken piggish eyes. He drove silently, almost consciously ignoring his passengers.

"Third house from the corner," Pankiw directed.

The cab driver pulled his rig over to the curb and proceeded to unload their trunk and bags.

"You people come from Europe?" he asked in heavily accented English.

"My three friends here have just arrived in America from Poland," Pankiw answered.

"I did not know that there is such as place as Poland anymore," the cab driver said cynically. "Me, I come from Munich. That is in Germany, you know. Not long here."

They were too tired to engage in conversation with the driver so they left him and walked single file up the narrow concrete walk leading to the house, loaded down with their belongings. A tiny face pressed against the screen of the front veranda then dashed into the house.

"They're here, mama. They're here!" the young boy shouted excitedly.

"Now remember what I told you, Joey. Our new neighbors will be very tired, so be nice to them," advised his mother. "They will not be able to speak English yet, so speak to them in Polish."

She opened the screen door and the weary travelers stepped into the veranda.

"This is my wife Christina. We call her Teena," announced Pankiw proudly as they crowded into the small vestibule inside the house.

The three women observed each other and then embraced emotionally, their eyes sparkling with tears of joy.

"You must be almost dead after your long journey," fretted Teena. "Your beds are ready. As soon as you have had something to eat, you will want to go to bed for a while and rest up."

No one objected to Teena's suggestion and the table which had been previously set in anticipation of their arrival was soon laden with a variety of traditional dishes.

"What a feast," commented Mrs. Klazcek as she observed the table. "I heard that this was a land of plenty, but even so, I did not imagine I would see all this."

"Oh, it is not much," said Teena blushing. "I thought that you would be hungry for some old fashioned Polish food, so I made a little of everything." She glanced shyly at Angela's abdomen. "I see that you have to eat for two. When is the happy day?"

"February," responded Angela. "If it is a boy we will call him Wladimar, after Erik's relative in Warsaw."

"That is nice Polish name. In English they will probably call him Walter," said Teena.

"Wal-ter," Angela repeated the name. "That sounds just as nice as Wladimar."

The excitement of arriving at their new location overcame the group's weariness and revived them temporarily. The table which Teena had prepared for them seemed to represent a fitting celebration of the end of a demanding and sometime risky ordeal and the beginning of an unknown future. As they dined and talked about the things back home that were familiar to them all, the occasion seemed to Erik to represent a meeting of the old familiar ways with the new unfamiliar ways still to be experienced.

Their hosts explained that they had come to Toledo from Katowice twelve years ago with their parents. Michael Pankiw, whose father had been a coal miner in the old country, began by working as a laborer, but after learning English had trained to become a machine operator at Burlington Industries. Michael explained that he would be working with Erik in the product research department. Pankiw assured them that they would soon learn to speak English but meanwhile there were many other Polish speaking people nearby with whom they could speak in that language. People were waiting to welcome them and soon they would become a part of the community. Pankiw suggested that if they were up to it, right after dinner they would be able to see the house next door which the company had made available for them.

"Who could be tired at a time like this?" Angela declared, and Erik agreed.

The house was located next door to the Pankiws. Except for the color, the two houses were almost identical two-storey structures with gambrel roof, screened verandas and large front windows. Inside, the living room was at the front, the small dining room and kitchen at the back, and three bedrooms upstairs. An area between the back steps and the lane provided sufficient space for a garden and several trees.

"This is beautiful," exclaimed Angela happily as they examined the vacant upstairs rooms. "This one can be our bedroom and the one next to this can be Wladimar's and the one at the back can be mother's. Oh, this is just wonderful."

Erik smiled contentedly at his wife's exuberant approval.

"On Monday we can all go and pick out some furniture," suggested Pankiw. "The store will deliver Tuesday and by Wednesday you can move into your own house. By Thursday you might even be ready to go to the factory with me and meet some of the people there."

"This is more than anyone can ever hope for, Michael," remarked Erik. "I will never be able to repay everyone involved for all this. I don't even know where to start."

"You may start by calling me Mike. Everyone here calls me that," said Pankiw cheerfully.

"Mike," Angela repeated the name. "That sounds almost as nice as Walter."

~~~

With the dollars which Sliworski had received in exchange for their marks and rubles at the money exchange in Southampton, Erik and Angela excitedly embarked on a furniture shopping junket first thing Monday morning. Mike and Teena accompanied them while Mrs. Klazcek stayed home with Joey. Her excitement fanned by the task of setting up a new home, Angela flitted happily among the crowded displays of furniture in the shops, sitting, feeling their texture and chatting constantly with Erik and Teena. Erik was amused and delighted as he admired her cheery dedication to the task. He had not seen her so overflowing with enthusiasm since the day they had set out from Torun to Lubicz almost a year ago. He felt good inside and smiled approvingly at Mike and Teena.

Michael Pankiw, now well versed in the ways of his adopted country, was anxious to share his knowledge with Erik and Angela. By drawing heavily on his stock of experience and advice the Berglunds were able to stretch their resources to acquire sufficient items to furnish their kitchen, living room and the two bedrooms and still have a small amount of money left over. Angela admired the baby furniture, but agreed to postpone the purchase until after Erik commenced working.

"It is better anyway that you should wait until you know what color you will need," Teena advised her.

"What do you mean by that?" asked Angela.

"In America the color blue is for baby boys and pink is for girls," responded Teena.

"That is no problem for me," beamed Angela. "I already know that we will need blue."

Her innocent frankness amused Erik as he cast bashful glances at the small protrusion now showing on her abdomen. She reached for his hand. The four happy shoppers left the store all chatting at once and boarded a street car for home.

The furniture delivery van arrived late Tuesday afternoon and the movers carried each piece of furniture to its designated location. By the time dusk had fallen, Erik had arranged the furniture to Angela's satisfaction and the two new householders sat down to admire the result. They slumped in their chairs pleasantly exhausted and discussed what they would have for their first meal in their new home in America.

They heard a tap on the front door. Before Erik could answer the door, it flew open and Mike and Teena squeezed in, their arms loaded with pots and pans. "Good evening, my good neighbors, roll out the new table and let us see if it works well," announced Mike.

The smell of steaming hot food filled the room. Angela spread a table cloth on the new table.

"Oh, you wonderful people! You should not have done this. Erik and I were just wondering what we should prepare for our first meal here, but we forgot that we have not bought any food yet. And now all this!" gasped

Angela.

"You have many years of cooking ahead of you," remarked Teena. "There is no need to rush into that long career tonight when you are both so tired. Tomorrow we can go to the grocery store and you can buy whatever you will need."

Mike disappeared out the front door and returned a few minutes later with a bottle of wine and four glasses. He filled the glasses and raised his in a toast.

"To many happy and prosperous years, my dear friends. May your lives be blessed and fulfilled in every way. God bless us all, but especially Angela and Erik, whom He has seen fit to send to live among us."

"This is one of the happiest days of my life," said Angela, wiping tears from her eyes.

"This is no time for tears," admonished Mike. "It is time for joy and laughter. Your new life has now truly begun."

~~~

The street car creaked and rattled along the route to the city's industrial section. Erik sat silently watching the shops, houses and parks slide by. Beside him Mike talked steadily, trying to relieve the tension. The gate keeper at Burlington Industries greeted Mike and asked who his companion was.

"This is Erik Berglund. He will be our product development technician in the new products division."

"Didn't know there was such a department," said the gate keeper.

"Well, you know now," said Mike.

Inside the building the scene was strangely familiar. Except for the different faces and language, Burlington Industries was not unlike Torun Works. In one wing of the building, rows of metal cutting, shaping, drilling and grinding machinery clattered noisily under the watchful eyes of their operators. In another wing was the foundry where castings of various shapes and sizes were being produced. In the end wing was the shipping, receiving and warehouse department. They walked across a paved yard to a brick building which housed the research and development section. Erik was surprised at the absence of security personnel as they entered the unguarded entryway. He glanced at Mike inquisitively.

"It's a small department," Mike explained. "Everyone knows everyone else, so a stranger would soon be detected."

This soon became obvious to Erik as they entered the building. Inside were six spacious work places facing a wide open area, three on each side. Mike explained that each of these accommodated workers on separate projects. At the end of the building, several metalworking machines were arranged for use by the project workers. Although there were men working in each of the glassed-in offices facing the work area, no one was at the work stations or operating the machines.

"You will be working in the last room over there," Mike pointed out. "Let's go and see if Ed Brooke is in. He will be your supervisor."

Through the eye-level windows surrounding the room they noticed a man poring over a set of drawings on the drafting table. Mike rapped on the door. The man rose and sauntered toward them. A fringe of gray hair surrounded his bald crown which ended abruptly at his bushy eyebrows. He wore a striped shirt with the sleeves rolled up and a narrow leather belt which strained to hold his wide girth.

"Oh, it's you, Mike. Come in," he remarked. "When did you get back?"

"Saturday," replied Mike. "I brought Erik Berglund around to get a view of your great domain."

"Welcome aboard." Ed pumped Erik's hand enthusiastically. "I am Ed Brooke. Have you learned English yet?"

"He's only been in America four days," Mike reminded him. "What do you expect?"

"That you are not a very good teacher. That is what I expect," teased Ed. "Anyway," he continued, looking at both Erik and Mike, "this here is the Burlington Industries' brain bank." He circumscribed the area occupied by the research and development department with his outstretched arm. "Here great things are about to happen which will establish this company as one of the most progressive in America in our new line of business. We will be surpassed by no one."

"Stop exaggerating," warned Mike. "Erik might think that he is back in Prussia."

"Maybe I am exaggerating, but I understand that the front office has some pretty big plans," Ed confided. "Fred Sutton couldn't wait for Erik to arrive."

"Tell Sutton that Erik will be in tomorrow morning," said Mike.

"I'll catch him before the end of the day." He turned to Erik. "As of tomorrow, you will be one of us. See you in the morning."

Mike interpreted and Erik smiled at Ed as they turned to leave.

"Well, what do you think of it?" asked Mike as they stepped out of the building.

"It seems so friendly and easygoing. I can't wait to learn English so I can understand the discussion as well as catch the mood."

"Oh, you will, soon enough," said Mike.

~~~

"Old Sutton", as he was known to almost everyone in the product research and development department, was a short stocky man in his early fifties, with a perpetually smiling face and threads of silver running through his straw-blond hair. They said that he had gotten the job as head of the department because of his ability to relate to people at all levels in the organization, from the president to the maintenance crews. He saw his role as being a buffer between the company's hard-nosed, profit-oriented management and the small group of visionary inventors and researchers that the company had attracted. It was for this reason, rather than his inventiveness, that he had remained in this unit since it was formed a long time ago.

As was his habit, Sutton had arrived early Wednesday morning and was leaning over a table covered with drawings and sketches when Mike and Erik entered his office. He looked up and when he recognized Mike he strode across the shiny hardwood floor with an outstretched hand to greet them.

"So this must be Erik. Welcome aboard the Burlington express." He grinned as he gripped Erik's hand and shook it.

Mike interpreted the welcoming words and made the introductions. Erik felt immediately at ease in the man's presence. Sutton turned to Mike and teased him about making a vacation out of his assignment to meet Erik and accompany him to Toledo. Mike countered that had he not been there, Erik would probably not have gotten past Toronto.

"Well Erik," said Sutton enthusiastically, "I am glad that you chose to come to Toledo and to Burlington Industries in particular. I hope that you will never have occasion to regret that decision. Come in and sit down for a minute and we will talk about our work here and where you will fit into the organization."

In addition to the drafting table, covered with specifications and drawings, and his long cluttered desk, Sutton's office contained several chairs and a round conference table. They sat around the table and Sutton leaned back in his chair.

"Well, I hear that there are some interesting things going on in Europe these days, Erik, and we would like to get in on some of the action." Mike interpreted and Erik nodded. "We can only manufacture and get rid of so many gears, pulleys, pinions, shafts and valves. Is that not right?"

Mike agreed. "Yes sir. What this company needs to do is get cracking on some new products. Something that is in demand all over the world all the time."

Erik listened carefully as Mike interpreted Sutton's remarks.

"Like what?" he asked, perhaps knowing how Sutton would reply.

"Like arms for example," said Sutton. "We are told that there is a war going on somewhere in the world almost every day of the year. There is no better consumer of products than war. Its appetite is insatiable. What other occupation is there in which its participants receive payment for destroying? Why shouldn't America get in on this bonanza? And what's to say that we can't get started right here in this shop?"

Sutton observed Erik as Mike explained what he had just said.

"I have had some experience in that business," said Erik. "In fact I was told that this was the reason why I was coming here. It was explained to me the day that I fled Torun."

"Yes, we know that you have had some experience," remarked Sutton.

"In fact we have some samples of your work right here." He leaned over and unlocked a cabinet drawer and removed a set of drawings. "Do you recognize these?" he asked as he spread them out on the table.

"These are my drawings," gasped Erik. "Where did you get them?"

"Washington," replied Sutton.

"But I gave them to Bashinski."

"I guess it's all in the family, as they say," grinned Sutton. "There is nothing sinister about this whole thing. America's friends over there want us to develop our own arms production capacity so that when they need them we can supply them. In a way that is a good thing for the United States, too. Today's technology is making it more difficult for a nation to remain neutral and isolated as America has tried to do. The world is getting smaller and we can no longer ignore what is going on in Europe or anywhere else. And we also have to start thinking about our own defenses, as well as those of our friends elsewhere." Sutton paused as Mike interpreted.

"Do you know what America's greatest achievement in the arms development business has been so far?" He asked. "The Lewis machine gun. A fancy air-cooled design which fires 47 rounds of 303 shells. The only trouble is that it does not like to get dirty. If the enemy should decide to attack us on a rainy day, God help us, we're in big trouble. The damn thing will jam every time."

Sutton opened the drawing showing the detail of the 13cm prototype designed by Erik and the others at Torun Works.

"Now here is something that even I can get excited about. This type of a gun can be used for anything – as an artillery weapon, for coastal defenses, on ships, on vehicles, perhaps even on trains and tractors. Who knows what else? All that remains to be done is for me to convince management that the company can make a profit producing these things and we're in business."

Erik ran his hand across the drawing as if to convince himself that it was really his. The work was obviously his own. He recognized his lines and his lettering, but it all seemed like a relic from another lifetime. He felt the excitement building up inside of him as Mike explained what Sutton was saying.

"Tell Mr. Sutton that I can't wait to get started," gushed Erik.

~~~

Saint Joseph's was a new parish and the church which was built just over twenty years earlier was already too small for the fast expanding Polish community. The church had quickly become the focal point where mass was served regularly and numerous social and cultural activities were held in its basement. Michael and Teena had already advised Father Wozny that they would be bringing the new arrivals to church this Sunday. Erik had not attended mass since before he had been taken away from his parents in 1901, but Angela had gone to mass regularly.

"Just do as I do," counseled Angela when Erik worried about having forgotten the order of the service.

The music and voices filled the nave of the church and flowed out through the open windows into the street as they arrived. Mrs. Klazcek wiped her eyes with her handkerchief and nodded approvingly at Angela when they had seated themselves in the pew.

"The Lord is good. May His name be praised. He is everywhere; even here," she whispered.

After the benediction, Father Wozny publicly welcomed the new arrivals and asked his congregation to do likewise. "Today we have a new family in our midst. They are Erik Berglund and his wife Angela from Torun, and her mother Mrs. Klazcek from Krakow. Please make them feel at home as you yourselves were made welcome here on your own arrival."

Outside of the church, waves of parishioners greeted them, shaking their hands and embracing them fondly. They had come here from all over the former Polish territory and from other countries to which their parents and grandparents had fled. Now they were all Americans, but they were hungry for news from the old country. It was only after the newcomers had agreed to visit some of them over the next few months that the Pankiws were able to pull Erik and Angela away from the crowd.

That afternoon they were surprised by a visit from Father Wozny who remembered that the formerly vacant house would need to be blessed before Erik and Angela settled in and this was a good opportunity to do it. Erik watched with curiosity as the priest moved reverently through the rooms reciting prayers and sprinkling holy water on the naked walls. Angela, her head covered with a shawl borrowed from Teena, followed the priest with Michael and Teena, softly repeating the required responses. Because he did not wish to offend his wife and good friends, Erik did not voice his acquired skepticism regarding the usefulness of the ceremony, but when the ritual was over, he thought the house felt cleaner and his own spirit was uplifted. The ceremony over, they returned next door for the Sunday dinner. For now, it seemed that their lives were perfect and that nothing could change that.

CHAPTER 22

Erik's first few weeks at Burlington Industries were in some way strangely similar to his days in Torun. The work he was performing resembled what he had done in Torun when he first arrived there. There were of course some subtle differences. Instead of German, the language was English. Instead of Roman, his workmate was Michael and instead of Lydia there was Teena. But there was one major difference in his life and he was reminded of it every evening when he entered the door of his new home. She was there waiting for him with small talk about Teena, Joey, the neighbors, and her mother who was her companion all day. In spite of her increasing bulkiness, Angela had arranged and decorated their home simply and tastefully, drawing on Teena's experience in America but retaining reminders of the old traditions. It seemed to Erik that she had always been with him.

There were also a few differences in the style of operation at Burlington Industries. Sutton explained that there was some hesitancy on the part of senior management to decide on what line of products the R and D department should concentrate on developing next, so the staff was kept busy improving the company's existing product lines. There seemed to be no rush to get into the new product line as there had been in Torun. This was a welcome change for Erik who remembered well the tensions which often gripped the research and development department in Torun. Privately, on some especially uneventful days, he missed the excitement and intrigue of the last months in his old job, but kept it to himself. However, these nostalgic flashbacks became fewer and fewer and he soon succumbed to the security and comfort of his current situation.

It was now a few days before Christmas and the first snowfall of the season came down wet and clingy, slowing down the traffic and making Erik and Mike late for work. Erik was removing his water-soaked boots when Sutton stuck his head inside the door of his small office. Looking forward to his comfortable routine, he had no idea that this day's events would be much more unexpected than the others.

"We are going to have a surprise for you today, Erik," he announced.

Erik, whose now limited command of English permitted him to understand what Sutton said but was not sufficient to piece together a suitable response before Sutton disappeared, sat up and speculated what the surprise might be. Perhaps Mike might have some explanation, but he too disappeared shortly after they arrived and did not return. Erik hoped that Sutton had news about starting work on the new product line, but at this time of the year it probably had something to do with the American custom of giving employees a gift just before Christmas, reasoned Erik as he went about his work.

It was early in the afternoon and still neither Mike nor Sutton had returned. Erik was at his drafting table concentrating on a drawing when he heard the door of his office opening quietly. He swung around on his swivel stool to see who it was and blinked in disbelief. He slipped off the stool and stopped in his tracks.

"Roman? Is it really you, Roman? How did you get here?" The words gushed out erratically, reflecting his surprise and disbelief at the sight of his former roommate. Roman was standing beside Mike inside the doorway, both of them grinning broadly. Erik ran toward him, clasped his hand and then held him in a tight embrace.

"Roman! My dear old friend. I can't believe this. Surely I must be dreaming. How did you get here and how did you know where I was?" The words rushed out staccato-like. Erik was almost in tears.

"My departure was not as dramatic as yours, and of course, Bashinski knew where you were," explained Roman in his usual light-hearted manner. "Bashinski fixed us up with some fake passports and assumed names and we traveled as regular immigrants. Well almost. I understand that our immigration clearance process and reception here was somewhat more complicated than yours was, I must say."

"Our? What do you mean our?" blurted out Erik.

"Ours. I mean ours: Lydia's and mine."

"Lydia? But she is one of them. How did you get away with that?"

"No longer one of them," corrected Roman. "You see, I married her in Warsaw shortly before we left and now she is one of us."

"Roman, that's fantastic! But you make it sound like it was so simple for you. Why did they make such a big thing out of my departure then?" asked Erik.

"Because Bashinski learned from your experience and, of course, your case was a lot more sensitive than mine. You know more than I do and you were more valuable to them. So Bashinski thought that there should be a better way. One Monday morning I just did not return to work. We took the train to Hamburg under assumed names and were on the ship before they even missed us. Of course, Lydia's parents knew about what was happening but they agreed to pretend that she ran away with me without their permission."

"And Bashinski's agents – the beggar and the others – were they involved?"

"They certainly were. That old beggar in the market square; he was a sly one. He delivered all the instructions and carried back my messages. I don't think that anyone suspected a thing, even though they were still burning from your bizarre departure. You should have seen old Schindel sweating when he had to explain why he did not report your disappearance sooner. And poor Herr Richter. He was convinced until the last minute that you had really drowned and he was filled with remorse."

"What do you mean, until the last minute?" asked Erik.

"I mean until they discovered that you had not really drowned, but took off right under their noses."

"But who would give them that information? I thought that only you and Bashinski's people knew about the plot," fretted Erik.

"You did," said Roman.

"I did?" Erik flinched at the suggestion. "What do you mean, I did? I didn't tell a soul about it except you."

"It's not what you said. It's what you did that gave the plot away," explained Roman. "As soon as they found that your medal and citation from the Imperial Army Department were missing, they were convinced that you had run away. Also, one of their private eyes visiting from Berlin saw you fishing in the Drewca just before a mysterious Polish fishing vessel made its way up north."

"You know, I kind of wondered what that well-dressed man was doing on the river bank that morning. Someone suspected me all the time. I am really sorry that I caused everyone so much trouble," fretted Erik. "It is too bad that I didn't just leave the way you did."

"Maybe it was just an accident that you were observed that morning. One can never be sure about those things. In any event, it may not have worked out as well for you as it did for me if you had gone about it differently," said Roman. "But anyway, we are all here, safe and well, so it doesn't really matter anymore how we did it."

"Indeed not. Forgive me for being so self-centered," Erik apologized. "I still can't believe it, but if you are really here, you must come out and visit us immediately. Angela will be overjoyed to see you and Lydia. You may stay at our place as long as you wish. We have a spare room and it's yours for as long as you want it," offered Erik.

"We were hoping you would say that," interjected Mike. "Roman's house will not be ready for at least another week and it would be much nicer for them to stay with you than in a hotel. But let us go to the hotel now and get Lydia. Old Sutton said that we could take the rest of the day off."

Erik gathered his equipment and pushed it into a drawer. He kept his eyes focused on Roman as though he was not yet convinced that his friend was really there.

"I have so much to ask you, I don't know where to start," he said to Roman as they walked toward the door.

"If you think you have a lot to ask me, just wait until I start with you," said Roman.

"You two will have enough time for all that," said Mike. "You see, Roman will be working here with us."

"It will be as though nothing has changed except the time and place. This whole thing still feels like a dream," mused Erik as they entered the hallway.

~~~

The house reverberated with the sounds of excited voices and laughter. They all spoke at once, eager to explain all the events that they had experienced during their months of separation and anxious to hear about the experiences of the others. While Erik and Roman sat at the table engaged in intense discussion, Angela and Lydia told one another the stories of their own experiences in Krakow and Torun. Lydia had visited Angela's uncle in Torun shortly before they left and had brought a letter from him. He was lonely and missed having her around the house, but his other nieces and nephews visited him regularly. Lydia described her separation from her own family and her sadness at maybe not seeing them again. They agreed that it was difficult to leave people that one has loved behind, but the trauma of leaving old friends and familiar places behind was soon replaced by the excitement of the present and their plans for the future. The house that Roman and Lydia would be moving into was only a few doors down the street, a happy and convenient arrangement made possible by Burlington Industries.

As the days passed, Roman and Erik greeted their renewed friendship like a pair of adventurous schoolboys. Inseparable, they explored the city, pushing the familiar frontiers back daily and excitedly describing to their wives the wonders of their new discoveries. On Saturday afternoons all four of them would scurry, wide-eyed and exuberant, through the commercial sections of the district, Angela waddling behind the others, unperturbed by her fullness.

Soon the excitement of Christmas filled the air, fanned by the sounds of ringing bell, carols and cordial exchange of greetings. Stores along the avenue were stocked with an abundance of special holiday merchandise – toys, decorations, fruits, nuts, dressed poultry, hams, breads, cakes and candies – all eye-catching and sometimes exuding pleasant and inviting smells.

After one afternoon of last-minute shopping, their arms clutching bags and parcels in a variety of shapes and sizes, the group clambered aboard the streetcar and headed for home, agreeing that this was a great place to be young and free. Soon, large flakes of fluffy snow began to fall and the shopkeepers and clerks closed the shop doors and boarded the crowded streetcars to join their families for Christmas Eve. The streets, which only hours earlier had been crammed with people were now nearly deserted. An almost eerie calm replaced the spirited activity which had filled the streets and shops only hours earlier.

The newcomers from Europe had not been forgotten by their newfound friends and fellow countrymen in the community. Early that evening, groups of carolers and well wishers included the two new couples in their rounds. It was early morning by the time the tired foursome returned from the midnight mass and retired to prepare for another active day on the morrow.

Over the past several days, Teena had been busy preparing a traditional Christmas feast and they were invited. Except for his last Christmas at his parents' home in Lubicz, Erik had not experienced the traditional holiday since he was taken from his parents, and Roman had not seen anything like it in ten years. As they sat around the food-laden table they recounted their early childhood Christmases and enjoyed their reintroduction to the old traditions. Memories of their previous Christmases in a more alien environment flashed through Erik's mind, but he refrained from talking about it for fear of spoiling the happy mood of the moment.

The post-holiday weeks appeared somewhat anticlimatic to Erik and Roman as they settled into a routine at Burlington Industries. When fits of loneliness overtook one of them, he would find solace and lightheartedness in the other. The cold, dreary days of January grudgingly gave way to the wet, snowy days of February and they anxiously awaited the fulfillment of Angela's term. Teena, the eldest and most experienced of the three young women, helped Mrs. Klazcek maintain a vigil over Angela while Erik was at work and also insisted that she be called the moment the arrival of the baby appeared imminent. Angela drew strength and comfort from the knowledge that Teena would be present. She noted Erik's increasing anxiety and chided him about being more worried than she was.

~~~

A cold front drifted in from the north, picking up moisture as it crossed the lakes. During the night the city was covered with a heavy layer of new snow which continued to fall unabated throughout the night. Angela had been unable to sleep and in the still-dark hour of early morning she awakened Erik.

"Erik, I've had these pains in my abdomen since around midnight and they are getting stronger. I think the time has come."

"I'll go and get Teena. Why did you not wake me up sooner?" Erik jumped out of bed and dressed quickly.

Plodding through the deep snow, Erik broke a trail to the Pankiws' house. Mike answered the door after several knocks.

"Erik, is something wrong?"

"No, Mike, but I think that Angela's time has come. Do you think Teena could come now?"

"Of course. I will get her up right now. You go back and stay with Angela," said Mike as he ran up the stairs.

The spare room which Teena and Lydia had prepared earlier was to become a maternity ward and when Teena arrived a few minutes later, they tucked Angela into bed and made her feel comfortable. Teena took charge of the preparations and they soon had towels, blankets and basins in readiness. When dawn began to break, the intervals between Angela's labor pains became shorter and her face was beginning to show signs of strain. In the early morning light, Erik looked out of the window at the deep snow which covered the street as far as he could see. He noted that no one had yet broken a trail through it.

"You should go and get Dr. Stern. I think the baby will be born this morning," advised Teena. "Better take Mike with you," she added after glancing out the window.

As he ventured out into the street again, Erik wondered how anyone would be able to traverse it except by foot.

"Do not worry about that," said Mike when Erik informed him of his concern. "The doctor's house is only a few blocks from here. We can walk there and then he can decide how he chooses to get back to the house."

The two men ploughed their way through the deep snow leaving a crooked trail down the street. Puffing and wheezing, they climbed up the stairs of Dr. Stern's front door and knocked. Dr. Stern was already dressed in his suit when he answered the door of his combined office and residence.

"What brings you here so early?" he asked. "I hope it is nothing serious."

"It's Angela," they both blurted out excitedly. "She thinks her time has come."

"Relax, boys. These things happen every day," counseled the doctor. "I'll come down there in a few minutes. Is somebody with her?"

"Oh yes. Her mother is there and Teena has been with her for a while now. She has everything all set up for you."

"Then Angela is in good hands. How close together are the pains?"

"The last few were about fifteen minutes apart," replied Erik.

"It will be a little while yet." The doctor opened the door and looked out. "One is not likely to get a cab on a day like this. So I guess I'll hoof it along with you. But let's have a cup of coffee first."

When the trek back to Erik and Angela's house began, some early morning delivery vehicles had recently gone down the street leaving tracks which they followed single file. All three of them took turns carrying the doctor's bag, stopping occasionally to rest and change their position in line until they arrived at Mike's house.

"I think I will leave you now and get myself down to the plant," said Mike when they stopped at his front gate. "I'll tell Old Sutton that you will not be in today, Erik. Hope everything turns out well. See you tonight."

Erik and Dr. Stern thanked Mike for his assistance and continued on next door. Teena was in the kitchen preparing breakfast and Mrs. Klazcek was upstairs with Angela. The doctor removed his coat and overshoes and walked up the stairs to Angela's room, followed by Erik and Teena.

"How close are they now, Angela?" asked Dr. Stern.

"About ten minutes. So glad you could come," said Angela softly.

"Glad to be here. You just relax and don't worry everything will be fine."

The doctor checked Angela's pulse and took her temperature.

"Everything seems fine. The baby should arrive in about half an hour. Take it nice and easy and let me know when the pains are less than five minutes apart. Now let's take a look at your stomach."

Teena interpreted what the doctor had said and pulled the covers down below Angela's thighs. Dr. Stern felt her abdomen.

"Uh, huh. Everything looks normal," he observed. Then turning to Erik he suggested, "Well, no need for us men to hang around. Let us go down and see if we can scare up some breakfast. Smells like it is ready." He sniffed the air in apparent delight.

After setting before them a breakfast of smoked bacon, fried eggs and potato slices, toast and a steaming pot of coffee, Teena returned to Angela. In only a few minutes she came down and reported that the pains were now less than five minutes apart. Dr. Stern finished his coffee and after putting on his white smock he entered the bathroom and scrubbed his hands. He started up the stairs then turned around and said to Erik, "I will call you in as soon as the baby is born."

The pains were now only moments apart. Angela's face was tense and sweat covered her brow. Teena rolled the covers down, except for a light sheet. She held Angela's hand tightly while Dr. Stern held his hand flatly against Angela's stomach.

"All right, Angela. Take it easy. Put your knees up. That's a good girl. Now spread your legs apart. When you feel the contractions, push hard," the doctor instructed as Teena interpreted.

On the third push the head began to appear.

"It looks like a normal delivery. Relax, Angela, and push hard when the contractions begin again." Angela followed the doctor's directions, confident that he was in control and drawing on his experience with many such situations. In the next series of contractions, the baby's shoulders emerged and the rest of the body slid out almost effortlessly. Dr. Stern slapped the new arrival on its behind and when the baby responded with a loud wail he cut the umbilical cord and tied it up close to the baby's abdomen.

"Fine looking boy you have here, Angela," said the doctor.

Angela was crying for joy. The doctor handed the baby to Teena who was holding a blanket ready to receive him.

"Here you are. Clean him up for his company. He looks a bit too slippery to handle as he is."

Teena put the baby on a small table which had been prepared for this purpose and after wiping him with a warm wet cloth and gently rubbing some oil over his body she wrapped him in a soft new blanket and handed him to Angela, her face covered in a broad smile.

"My dear little Wladimar," she said lovingly. "You are just like I imagined you would be. Look Erik, he looks like you," she exclaimed as Erik entered the room.

"Yes, Angela. He is beautiful. But he looks like you, too," replied the elated father.

"You have had a hard morning, Angela," said Dr. Stern. "Try to get some sleep now and Teena will look after your son while you rest."

~~~

The flurry of excitement and activity following the birth and baptism of Wladimar was beginning to subside. On his birth certificate, the baby's name was recorded as Walter. It would be a simpler, more American name, explained Mike. At home he could be called by whatever name they wished, but when he got to school, a strange European name which is hard to pronounce may not serve him well. In America it was better if you did not try to be too different, said Mike. This was the great melting pot of the world into which hordes of ethnics were deposited and mixed together and then emerged as a smooth homogeneous whole.

"But look at all the people in our parish church," exclaimed Erik. "They speak their own tongues and worship in their own language just as they did in Europe."

"Sure. What we do at home and around our homes is our own business. But in public and at work, we are all Americans," explained Mike. "It is a good arrangement. Everyone is free to do as they wish, as long as they do it privately."

"It is a very peculiar arrangement," mused Erik, "but I think that I am going to like it. I notice that at work no one seems to be too concerned about who you are or where you came from."

Both Erik and Roman were still somewhat overwhelmed by the casual atmosphere at Burlington Industries. In the research and development department they busied themselves by improving the design of machinery parts and by formulating new alloys for use in gears, bushings and shafts. They walked in and out of the building unimpeded and at will. At first they missed the order which had existed at Torun Works, somehow feeling that their work no longer deserved the security and importance that it once did. But the freedom associated with the new arrangement was humbling and comfortable at the same time. Getting accustomed to it was easy.

Sutton complimented Erik and Roman on their work but made no further reference to the development and production of arms about which he had appeared so excited when Erik arrived. Maybe it was just a passing notion that was forgotten. Here, Europe and its wars seemed so far away that they wondered if all that preoccupation with war among the people there was nothing more than idle talk resulting from frustration and boredom. After all, it was 1912, well into the twentieth century, and the world was becoming far too sophisticated to ever become involved in that kind of senseless devastation and carnage again.

In the research and development department, the gears and bushings and other machinery parts emerged from the moulds in all shapes and sizes. They were measured and machined and sent to the lab for testing. In the foundry, their clones were dumped into barrels and then shipped to different parts of the country to take their place in the machines of the nation.

CHAPTER 23

Winter unleashed its last display of fury early in March by emptying the last of its snow-laden clouds over the city. The late snowstorm broke the monotony of the numerous dull, gray days which had preceded it but did little to release the inhabitants of Toledo from their feelings of confinement. Erik and Angela, weary from the excitement of the past few months, had languished in the eventless days which had set in following the birth of their son. They had used this period to rediscover each other and to joyfully speculate on their future. They lavished attention on Walter and rejoiced at his every new achievement.

The mailman trudged through the fresh snow, stomped heavily up the front steps and clanked the metal mailbox lid. Erik, hoping for news from elsewhere in the world, opened the front door wide enough to reach into the mailbox. It was a letter from his family in Canada.

Stanislaw described how their first winter in Canada was going. His colorful description made it sound like an adventure story. So far they had only had enough time and money to complete three rooms of their log house and so each room served a number of functions, he wrote. But the temporary congestion rewarded his family with a new feeling of closeness as they all huddled together around the wood-burning stoves on cold winter nights. The wood for the stoves had to be cut and hauled out of the forest. It was so cold that at night the stillness was sometimes shattered by the loud twang of tree trunks splitting from the frigid air. And stars! There were millions of them, their twinkling rays reaching down and embracing them from all sides. The family felt that the universe was really out there vying for their attention, he wrote.

On moonlit nights, if they watched closely, they would see rabbits playfully dashing around the snowbanks and under the trees. In the evening, just before dusk, partridge would come around in flocks, settling in nearby trees and curiously observing the activities below. With a small bore rifle Stanislaw could easily pick out the fattest one for the roaster.

But all was not sweetness and light, he explained. As the winter snow accumulated the roads sometimes became blocked for days at a time, making it increasingly difficult to travel the six miles to town. The horses would become exhausted from drawing the sleigh through the deep drifts and then the family might go without tea, coffee, sugar, flour and kerosene for days, until they or the neighbors could break the trail into town. If the winter turned out to be unusually long, Stanislaw wrote, they could run out of feed for their horses and cattle. Some of the neighbors were luckier, as they could already haul hay and straw from the older established farms several miles away. In spite of these hardships, they were looking forward to summer when they planned to clear some bush and break the land for planting crops. They also hoped to get an early start on building a new barn.

Their parents were adjusting well to the pioneer conditions, Stanislaw continued. They were delighted to hear about Walter's birth and were looking forward to seeing him before their days ended. Would it be possible for Erik and Angela to come out to visit them this summer? Stanislaw asked. He said it was a beautiful place in the summer where nature was not yet spoiled by man. And furthermore his parents would be overjoyed. In Canada he went by the name of Stanley, added Stanislaw. It was easier for people speaking other languages to say Stanley.

"Isn't that a beautiful letter," remarked Angela. "Stanislaw is ever the optimist, planning for the future while enjoying the present even when times are difficult." She paused and observed Erik. "Do you think we will go and see them?" she asked.

He put his hands in his pockets and straightened out his lanky body in his chair. "It would be nice if we could do it. Stanislaw says that it would be good for our parents to see their grandson. You never know how much longer they will be around at their age. I'll ask Sutton. The worst that he can do is say no. If he says yes, we will save some money and take the trip in July or August."

Sutton had no objection to Erik's request. In fact this summer would be a good time for Erik to take the trip because they might be starting work on a very important new product line early in the fall, he said. Until that time the plant will be operating routinely so Erik would not be missed for the three-week period he would need for the trip.

~~~

Sutton's agreement to an extended vacation would enable Erik to spend several days with his parents and still leave enough time for travel. He and Angela planned to start their trip around July 20 and return on or about August 10. Walter would be old enough to sit up during the train trip and this would make it easier for Angela. Mrs. Klazcek, with memories of the trans-Atlantic trip still fresh in her mind, insisted that she would stay at home and look after the house. Roman and Lydia would come and see her every day to ensure that she was managing well on her own. With all their plans in place, their excitement mounted each day as they anticipated seeing Erik's family again.

On the day of their departure they had already had their bags packed for several hours when the cab arrived to take them to the station. Once on the train they retraced the route that they had taken from Toledo to Toronto almost a year earlier, except that this time they were rested, relaxed and more familiar with their adopted environment.

In Toronto, Erik and Angela were excited about beginning the next leg of the journey and seeing a part of the country they had never seen before. They looked around in delight as the transcontinental train chugged its way out of the station crammed with yet another load of immigrants on their way to the Canadian west. Bewildered men and women with droves of children clinging to them sat pensively in their third class coaches watching the countryside fly past. Older people in strange garb gazed at their surroundings and spoke to each other in hushed tones. It was the same scene that Erik and Angela had witnessed on their trip from Halifax almost a year earlier, but now it seemed somehow foreign to them. They settled back in their tourist class coach, played with Walter and and shared stories with a few Polish-speaking immigrants sitting near them.

The vastness of the rugged landscape appeared even more awesome as they traveled across the Pre-Cambrian shield of northwestern Ontario. Flanked by majestic rock outcropping and millions of trees, the crystal-clear lakes sparkled emerald-like in the summer sun. Small creeks and rivers rushed feverishly alongside the railway and under the numerous steel bridges as if racing the train to the sea.

"I wonder how they ever built a railway here," mused Erik. Walter was asleep and Angela was leaning toward the window viewing the changing panorama with intense interest. She straightened out and concentrated on her response.

"You see, Erik, this is an example of what can be done if man channels his energies into constructive pursuits, rather than the destructive occupation of war. Can you imagine what Europe would be like today if all the fighting that has been going on there for about eighteen centuries or more had not taken place? What could man have achieved if he had used that energy to build instead of destroy? And all those lives that were sacrificed. I wonder how many potential poets, artists, musicians, scientists and engineers were struck down before their flower could bloom. And how many philosophers and teachers who could have shown us the way?"

Erik picked up her hands in his. "Yes, Angela, we have really messed things up. But maybe they will get better in this century. Here we see a good start in that direction."

The landscape changed suddenly when the train left the rocky shield and entered the plains of Manitoba. The difference was so immediate that it seemed as though a stage director had changed the play and a new stage was set up which bore no resemblance to the previous act. The rocks were now gone and the rushing rivers became lazy winding creeks. The trees were still there but they were fewer and broad-leafed instead of evergreens, surrounded by fields of jet-black soil and waving grain. Evidence of man's struggle to win over the land was everywhere. Farmers stood beside their plows, wiped the sweat off their brows and watched the train go by. Herds of cattle grazed where buffalo had once roamed.

Then suddenly there was prairie! No more trees, except those marking the location of marshes and meandering creeks and rivers. To the west, as far as the eye could see, a green sea of grain and grasses waved in the breeze. Puffing greasy black smoke and belching steam, the locomotive veered right when the tracks came to a wide river of muddy red water and began to slow down. The conductor walked through the coaches, swaying from side to side, announcing that the next stop was Winnipeg. A buzzing sound of excited voices arose as the passengers stood up and moved about preparing to disembark. Some had been on the train for several days and nights and longed to walk on solid ground again. Among those were Erik, Angela and their young son, Walter.

The train slowly ground to a stop and hissed lazily while yardmen opened little doors on the locomotive's undercarriage and checked the bearings and hubs for heating and wear after the long journey from the east. On the station platform, the immigrants poured out of the coaches in family groups, admonishing each other to remain together while they received their instructions. Immigration officers, speaking through interpreters, dispensed directions and advised the new arrivals to pick up their baggage and report to the Immigration House where they would remain until the trains taking them to their final destinations departed.

Erik and Angela watched as the immigrants, many still dressed in the clothes they brought from the old country, wound their way to the Immigration House. The immigrants looked bewildered and frightened.

"This is where my parents and Stanley and his family spent a few days," remarked Erik.

"Yes," replied Angela, "when I read about the Immigration House in their letter, it sounded so strange and far away. I never thought that we would be standing in front of it so soon."

~~~

They picked up their luggage, entered the huge rotunda inside the station and checked the schedule board for the departure time of the last leg of their trip. There at the end of a long list of place names it stood: Ralston – CP No168 – LV 1120 ARR 1945. Erik and Angela had just enough time to present their tickets at the wicket and board the train once again. Baggage handlers were busy placing valises, trunks and boxes inside a car marked EXPRESS, near the engine, and several cars down a conductor stood at the door helping people up a small stool and into the coach. He checked their tickets for their destination.

"Ralston? You will be with us to the end of the line. Take the last coach, please," he instructed. "We will be there at about a quarter to eight if all goes well."

As the train sped over the flat terrain, a flat and treeless valley stretched for miles in all directions until it dissolved into the blue horizon. It seemed as though they were sailing through a green sea of still water.

"This used to be the bottom of the great inland lake called Lake Agassiz," remarked the conductor when he observed their fascination with the landscape. "They say that the depth of the water here where we are now was six hundred feet. Not too long ago either. Only ten thousand years."

"It's big," remarked Erik in his newly acquired language, shaking his head. "And so flat. Hard to believe."

"Good land, though," said the conductor. "You know what? The topsoil here is two to three feet deep, close to a meter in your terms. It is easy to farm. There are not many places in the world like it. But we will soon be crossing a series of ancient beaches. You will recognize them by the sand and gravel knolls which are still just barely visible. After that we will be getting into the parkland area. Beautiful country, but takes a lot more backbone and sweat to farm there." He carried on down the aisle, swaying from side to side with the movement of the coach.

The changing landscape did indeed bear witness to the challenge which it posed to the new settlers. There were more trees. The land was rolling and the soil shallower with an abundance of stones near the surface. But the country was beautiful and the fruits of the settlers' toil were already evident. Handsome farm houses, either recently completed or under construction, rose alongside the log and sod covered cabins which had served to protect the settlers from the brutal elements during the first few years. In the pastures and fields, grazing cattle looked up to observe the noisy train dash by and farmers waved from their farm machinery or wagons and from the tops of great stacks of hay.

In the numerous small villages along the route, freshly painted commercial buildings whose false fronts faced the packed dirt main streets revealed the haste with which the communities had been constructed. Everywhere the building rush was on, as if a race to catch up with time had begun. The rapping sound of hammers resonated through the air when the train stopped briefly at the stations to unload freight and discharge passengers.

Lengthening shadows marked the end of a long summer day and the blazing sun poured out its last remnants of radiance as the train slowly ground to a stop alongside a wooden station building painted dark red. The name, neatly inscribed in black letters on a white background, announced that this was Ralston. Along the street outside the station, several teams of horses hitched to various types of vehicles pranced and snorted at the sight of the noisy, smoke-belching black monster on the tracks. On the platform in front of the building, people waited expectantly to see who had arrived on the train.

Erik and Angela looked out of the coach window and their hearts leaped with excitement when they noticed a group of familiar faces. There on the platform, thousands of miles from Lubicz and Torun were Stanley, his wife Anne and their boys. They rushed through the aisle and climbed out of the coach. They fell into each others' arms.

"Well, what do you think of it? Isn't it as big and beautiful as I told you it was?" asked Stanislaw as they broke their embraces and clung to each other's hands. His hands were rough and calloused and a great smile covered a weathered brown face from which his eyes shone like those of a school boy.

"It is huge. And so new," agreed Erik.

"And they say that there is almost as much of it again west of here. This is it, Erik. This is the promised land," boasted Stanislaw as he circumscribed the horizon with his outstretched arm.

With the baggage loaded they climbed up into an open topless carriage with two seats facing the front. "For some reason they call this rig a democrat around here," explained Stanislaw. "We borrowed it from a neighbor for this special occasion. The horses are ours though. How do you like them?"

"The horses are beautiful, but the vehicle does not look anything like the

Democrats we have around Toledo." Stanislaw did not get the joke.

The large draught horses headed out of the village, drawing the heavily laden vehicle easily as its passengers all talked at once. On his mother's knee, Baby Walter sucked on a tea biscuit which Stanislaw's wife Anne had brought and watched the landscape slowly slide by.

~~~

It was already dark, but a nearly full moon lit up the rough trail into which they had turned to reach the Berglund homestead. When they reached the clearing on which the yard was located they were greeted by pale orange shafts of light shining from two small windows ahead of them. A dog barked excitedly at the approaching vehicle and stopped when it realized that it was Stanislaw returning. In the moonlight, the outline of another building and two stacks of hay loomed silently at the edge of the clearing. Stanislaw stopped the horses in front of the log building with the lights. The door opened and a man and a woman peered out into the night.

"We're home," shouted Stanislaw joyously. "Come out and see who we brought back."

The scene reignited Erik's memories of the night only two years earlier when he and Litvak arrived at his parents' home in Lubicz. They helped each other down and Stanislaw's oldest son unloaded the bags and the groceries which Anne had bought in town while the other held the reins and then drove the horses toward the barn. The hushed stillness of the night was stirred by the emotional scene which played itself out as they greeted Erik and Angela. Tears flowed onto ground which until several months ago had not felt the footsteps of man.

They all moved indoors into the rustic surroundings of the pioneer home which still smelled of newly hewn wood and fresh earth. In the light of two kerosene lamps Erik and Angela noticed the unpainted but smoothly planed furniture which they knew had been shaped and assembled by Axel. On the huge cast-iron kitchen stove, steaming pots exuded familiar smells and teased their appetites.

"Well, son. This is it," announced Axel. "It is a little different than our home in Lubicz, but it keeps us warm in the winter and dry in the summer. We have been busy and have done a lot, but there is still much to do. Do you like it?"

"It is nice, father, but it is so quiet. Don't you ever get lonely here?"

"Lonely? Who has time to be lonely?" huffed Axel. "There is so much to do and see and experience that by the end of the day you are too tired to be lonely. Even mama here who we thought would miss our old home has been too busy to think about it."

"Oh, I think about it all right," remarked Mrs. Berglund. "But it all seems so far away, almost as if in a dream. So I try to forget about it, especially when cousin Bashinski writes and tells us that things in the old country remain the same. Old grievances and suspicions continue, as does the talk of imminent war. They don't seem to be happy in Europe unless they are fighting or preparing for a war. We are, at last, safe here, but my heart bleeds for those who have remained behind. But what can we do? We are so few and so far away. I only hope that one day man will come to his senses and peace will prevail. But that is not likely to happen in my lifetime."

With Walter fed and tucked into a small wooden bed given up by one of the couple's sons, they dined and talked into the night. When they prepared to retire, exhausted and happy, the sky just above the trees was turning to a soft magenta, announcing that while they were talking the sun had made its trip below the horizon and was now preparing to return and bring in a new day.

The apparent isolation of the homestead was misleading. During the next few days, visitors appeared seemingly out of nowhere when word got out that the Berglunds' son and family had arrived for a visit from the States. Recent arrivals from many parts of the Polish territory and other European countries maintained a steady trek to the homestead, looking for news from the old country. Upon his father's advice, Erik told them that he had arrived as a regular immigrant but chose to work in the United States for a while. Perhaps that was just as well, they suggested, since he did not look much like a pioneer farmer anyway.

They were surprised at how much there was to see and do in what initially appeared to be an isolated and lifeless environment. Stanley introduced Erik to the wonders of the frontier country – forests unexplored by white man that teemed with wild life and flora, creeks and small lakes with schools of fish flashing in the sunlight, bushes laden with ripened berries and expansive prairie land waiting for the plow.

The second-hand plow which Stanislaw had acquired the previous summer stood at the end of a partly tilled field, its shares and moldboard shining except for a few blotches of rust which showed where droplets of moisture had settled since it was last used. Stanislaw hitched a four-horse team to the implement and got one of his sons to drive the horses while he held on to the control handles. Erik watched with fascination as the centuries-old sod turned over slowly, black and spongy, in long narrow strips along the newborn field. At each end of the field Stanislaw stopped the horses to give them a chance to rest. He broke off pieces of the furrow and crumbled them lovingly with his fingers.

"Just think, Erik. After all the thousands of years that it has taken to create this soil that it should be me who would change its form. This is a privilege and a responsibility that only a few people will ever have. I am changing the face of God's earth."

Erik was amused and touched by his brother's exuberant innocence. "I wonder what this country will look like a hundred years from now, Stanislaw," he mused.

"Unspoiled and improved. We will look after it and make sure that it does not go the way of Europe. We will make it a haven for peace-loving people," vowed Stanislaw, gazing over the top of the trees at the end of the virgin field.

Erik studied his brother's face. "You know, Stanislaw, you really are a man of deep convictions."

~~~

The Berglunds' fascination with pioneer life and the people involved in it occupied their days to the fullest. Axel basked in the company of both of his sons and together they explored the surrounding countryside, discovering new sources of wild fruits, mushrooms and firewood. Drawing on her experience, Anne provided Angela with motherly advice on child rearing and Mrs. Berglund passed along secret family recipes. Visitors dropped in daily and friendships were forged.

Before they realized it, the time for them to leave had arrived. Since the whole family wanted to accompany Erik, Angela, and Walter to the railway station, a neighbor provided them with an extra team of horses and a buggy to accommodate a part of the group. The sun had not yet peeked over the treetops when the two vehicles rolled out of the yard and out onto the trail leading to the main road.

"I feel like I am part of a procession," laughed Erik.

"That's because we are being treated like royalty," said Angela happily.

"They are all so wonderful. I almost hate to leave," said Erik.

"We will come back some day. And then we might even stay," she consoled him.

The train had already backed into the station from the Y-track where it had spent the night. Crew members were rushing about in preparation for the trip back to the city. Farm wagons arrived, carrying cream cans, egg crates and produce for shipment to the processing plants down the line. The iron tires on the wagons made a crunching sound when they passed over the gravel coating on the road. On the station platform, farewells were being said to the departing friends and relatives, including the Berglunds. Erik was embraced by his mother.

"It seems like I am always saying good-bye to you, son. Even when you were a little boy, you were always sneaking away from me. You always wanted to be alone and free. I feel like I will never see you again."

"Don't fret, mama. The next time we will meet here we will be together for good, I promise." Erik choked back the tears.

"The Lord willing, son. The Lord willing. Only He knows these things."

The locomotive chugged contentedly inside its bowels as the conductor took his place beside the coach entrance and called, "All Aboard." Erik and Angela wiped their tear-streaked cheeks as they settled into their seats beside the window. Up front, the engineer slowly opened up the throttle and the train chugged slowly out of the station and into the early morning sun. The groups of people on the platform, waving their farewells, disappeared behind the black smoke pouring out of the accelerating locomotive.

The long return trip was almost anticlimactic. The journey itself had lost some of its fascination and excitement. Erik and Angela spoke quietly about the action-filled days they had just spent with the family. They recounted the many interesting incidents and discussed the people they had met. The end of the excitement seemed to have had a calming effect on Walter as well and he sat quietly on his mother's lap looking out the window or sleeping. As they drew closer to their destination they speculated about how they would find things at home and what would be the first things that they would do when they arrived.

Roman and Lydia met them at the Toledo station when they disembarked, exhausted but relieved to be at the end of the long journey. In the cab on the way home Erik and Angela described their journey and visit, while Roman and Lydia explained how things had gone during their absence.

"Old Sutton is anxious to have you back," said Roman. "He says that we will be starting something new next week."

"That will be a nice change," replied Erik. "I was getting a bit bored with designing and improving all those gears and stuff. Sometime I miss the excitement of our days in Torun."

"Do not talk like that," scolded Angela. "Have you forgotten so soon the tensions and restrictions with which you lived there? You should count your blessings."

"Oh, I do, Angela. But at the same time I feel that I am getting rusty, just like those gears and bushings that we make, after they have been lying around for a while."

Lydia and Teena had cleaned the house in preparation for their return and, with their husbands, had weeded and watered the garden. Everything around the place was neat and orderly. Mrs. Klazcek had enjoyed the solitude. The rest and the long sunny days had been good for her leg and she was again walking around sprightly with the aid of a cane.

"Oh, thank you all so much," exclaimed an appreciative Angela. "You are all so wonderful. I don't know what to say."

"What are friends for," asked Lydia, "if they don't help out by doing little things like this for you?"

~~~

Sutton strode into Erik's office and announced that there would be a meeting of the research and development staff that morning at ten.

"We held it back until your return because of the important part that you will be playing in the project that we will be discussing. How are things in the north woods? Must be nice to be back in civilization." The skin on his face folded like a leather pouch when he smiled.

"Yes. It is nice to be back, but it is nice up there, too," said Erik. "Maybe the people don't have everything that we have here, but they are very happy just the same."

"I guess you can't miss what you have never had. Like they say, 'what you don't know won't hurt you.'" Erik shrugged off Sutton's philosophy and pondered what he had said about the changes that were about to take place at

Burlington Industries.

This was the first time that Sutton had summoned all the R and D staff together since Erik's arrival at Burlington and some of those present were only casually known to him. Beside Mike and Roman, there were several engineers, technicians, draftsmen and machinists present, some of them from the production department. They sat around a long wooden table in an area that served as a boardroom as well as a quiet space for reading and studying.

Sutton arrived with a sheaf of papers and drawings which he dropped on the table.

"Are we all here?" He checked to see who was present. "OK let us get started. As you may know, management is looking around for a new range of products that we could start making here, something more profitable and without the keen competition that our existing lines must face. Almost anyone can make the things that we have been making and almost everybody is. The company wants to go into something more sophisticated, more specialized; and so they sent our marketing people over to Europe to find a hot selling item and they believe they found one."

He unfolded a large drawing and stuck it up on the wall.

"This is it. Several countries in Europe are looking for an improved new military rifle and we think we can make one here. This drawing is of a new model now being produced in Prussia, but not yet sold outside of that country. Some people here will recognize it because they helped to design it. I am speaking of Erik and Roman, but especially Erik because he worked with it from its very beginning. To our knowledge it is the best firearm of its kind that is available now. But I think that we can improve on it and sell the improved model to the countries that may be looking for their firearms in places other than Prussia and Germany.

"So we will begin working on this project immediately. Erik and Roman will experiment with the design and the constitution of the barrel and breech. Some of you will be working on the design of the hammer, lock, magazine, and so on. I think that we can improve on the barrel design because we have access to information on how the Prussian model was constructed. Our big challenge will be to design the firing mechanism as we do not have the specifications or know the composition of the individual parts."

"Because the Prussian model has not been released for sale in Europe, we have been unable to obtain a model of it as yet. And the way that things are going in Europe these days, it does not appear likely that we will be able to do so very soon. But if they can do it, there is no reason why we can't do likewise. Bert Taylor here will assume responsibility for this aspect of product development. He and his men will work closely with Erik and Roman and others directly involved to ensure that all the component parts are compatible. The other division heads will ensure that their experience and facilities are available to Bert and Erik and their crews. Our target is to have a working model in six months. That will make it around February 15, 1913. I will be meeting with you individually and together to gauge our progress from time to time. Any questions?" A young draftsman raised his hand.

"Yes, Webster."

"Mr. Sutton, if you say that the Prussian model has not been obtainable, how come we have official drawings of the firearm from what appears to be a company in Prussia?"

"You are very observant, Webster," responded Sutton. "This is an exact duplicate of an original official drawing which Washington acquired through some friends in Europe. You will note that the specifications for the breech and other parts of the firing mechanism are not shown on the drawing. But the drawings do show us what they look like and that is valuable information. And, of course, we think that we can improve on their design, anyway. So that is what I meant when I said that we have a real challenge ahead of us. Any more questions?" He paused. There was none. "All right, then.. We will begin planning the project this afternoon. I will be around with instructions and the individual work plans. Good luck, men!"

Erik and Roman ambled back to their office.

"Well, you should be happy now," remarked Roman.

"You have to admit that it is a lot more exciting than making gears and bushings for steam engines and farm machinery," answered Erik.

"Do I hear you saying that you have no sensitivity at all about what we will be producing?"

"Oh yes, but I feel better because this time we will be making weapons for the good side," said Erik.

"But is still a weapon – designed for killing – nothing else. Does that not bother you at all?" asked Roman in apparent disbelief.

"Of course it does. But what can we do about it? I remember Richter telling us one day that if we didn't make weapons, someone else would. It is not weapons that kill people. It is people who kill people. Guns are not the cause of the killing, it is the people, usually speaking through their governments and helped along by ambitious generals and politicians. I feel that I have no control over these things. But if you feel so strongly about it, maybe you should consider disassociating yourself from the project. I am sure that everyone will understand. And they probably need someone to continue doing work on gears and bushing and things like that."

Roman appeared to be taken aback by Erik's abruptness. He paused momentarily, his face drawn, deep in thought. "You said it well, Erik. There is nothing that we can do about it   At least this time we are on the good side, as you say."

CHAPTER 24

At first the new project appeared to be going well. While Bert Taylor experimented with various firing mechanism designs, Erik and Roman varied the size and composition of the barrel, made sketches and drew up specifications for a proposed breech for the new firearm under development. By Christmas, a row of gun barrels was displayed in Erik's office, all machined and finished to various specifications and ready to be chosen for the new weapon.

However Taylor, who had tried to adapt the Mauser turn-belt system used in the Springfield rifle to a European styled chamber and barrel, had not yet produced a practical design. It soon became apparent that the project was falling behind schedule and Sutton summoned all those involved to an emergency meeting early in January. The concern that Sutton had about the lack of progress was reflected in his face as he called the meeting to order.

"Gentlemen, needless to say, management is somewhat bothered about the slow progress being made in the development of our new product. It appears obvious now that our target date of February 15 will not be met and our prospective customers in Europe are getting impatient. I have called you together to advise you of some changes in management responsibilities. As of now Carl Steiner here will take over the task of designing the firing mechanism and will also help me coordinate the whole project. Bert Taylor will become more closely involved in developing the ammo feed device and Erik Berglund will continue to work on the barrel design.

"We have acquired existing models from nine countries in Europe: Italy, Germany, Belgium, Turkey, Britain, Austria, France, Romania and Russia, and also Japan. We will examine each of these models to determine which has the best features for incorporation into our model. None of these is perfect. There is considerable room for improvement in each of them. But that is not our problem. What we want to do is check to see if any of these models have any features that we should consider incorporating into an American model which will be the best damn rifle in the world. Management wants the decision on its design to be made by March 1, a prototype by July 1 and production to start no later than one year from now. So let us put our minds and talents to the task. I know that we can do it."

At first Carl Steiner favored the Austrian Mannlichen Carbine M90, but abandoned it in favor of the French Manlichen-Berthier because it featured a more modern Lebel turn-bolt with front locking lugs. For his initial design he chose to combine this system with a 30 inch .303 barrel designed by Erik.

By March 1, the design work was finished and the drawings completed. Sutton was elated and approved the development and assembly of the prototype, but insisted that further subtle changes be made in the design in order to set it apart from the European models. Steiner agreed.

Erik and Roman used the alloy that Erik had developed at Torun Works for the prototype barrel. Steiner asked to see the formula before the pour for the prototype barrel took place. He studied it assiduously.

"Where did you get this formula, Berglund?" he asked.

"This is the formula that I developed at the Torun Works when we worked there," replied Erik.

"How did you get it here?" asked Steiner. He sounded agitated.

"I brought it with me when I came to America," explained Erik.

"Did you have permission to do so?"

"No, I didn't. But I figured that since I developed the formula, it belonged to me as much as it did to Torun Works," replied Erik.

This explanation appeared to unnerve Steiner. His voice sputtered as he pulled nervously on his thick blond hair.

"Berglund, I too worked in arms production in Germany, but I had the decency to leave what belonged to Germany in Germany. We will not use that formula. I must ask you to vary one or more components, but whatever we use must not be the same."

"You are in charge. I will do as you suggest, but I still think that we have a good formula right now."

Steiner swung his broad shoulders around abruptly and stomped out of the room. Erik looked at Roman quizzically.

"Well, what do you think of all that?"

"It does not add up, but I guess we will have to go along with it," suggested Roman.

~~~

The assembly of the prototype had to be delayed for a month because the machining department had difficulty finishing the parts for the firing mechanism to the required degree of precision.

"This never would have happened in Germany," complained a harassed Steiner. "In this country, the machinists seem incapable of machining anything finer than a railway car axle."

Erik and Roman had produced several barrels using a range of alloys around the formula which they had developed in Torun, but stayed away from the original mixture. When Steiner called for the assembly of the prototype in mid-April they were ready. The assembly team completed the prototype in five days and Steiner invited the development team to be present at the firing range on April 25 to view the weapon's first firing test.

A makeshift firing range was set up in an abandoned gravel pit outside of the city. The rifle was already positioned on a tripod as a safety precaution when Erik and Roman arrived. Steiner and Sutton were checking the ammunition and reviewing the procedure. When everyone had arrived, Steiner placed a cartridge in the chamber of the prototype firearm. Sutton asked everyone to step in behind the nearby sandbags while Steiner took up a position beside the weapon and cocked it. He spread his legs apart and planted his feet firmly on the ground.

"All set," he called.

"Let her go," directed Sutton.

Steiner pulled the trigger. A loud crack sounded and the target shook from the impact. Sutton jumped out from behind the sandbags.

"That sounded good, Carl, just great!" he exclaimed. "Fellows, we have just heard the first shot ever fired by a Burlington-made firearm."

The two men examined the firing mechanism and the barrel.

"Looks fine," declared Sutton. "Let's try another one. Try for the bulls-eye this time to see how accurate it is."

Steiner placed another round in the chamber and lined the sights up with the target. He squeezed the trigger. Another crack and the target shook on its legs. A technician checked the target.

"Third ring from the center at two o'clock," he shouted.

"Not bad. Not bad at all for the first trial," said Sutton. "Put on the magazine and let's try some repeaters."

They returned to their viewing positions behind the sand bags as Steiner attached the magazine filled with six rounds of ammunition. He lifted his right hand to indicate that all was ready.

"Go ahead, Carl," shouted Sutton.

Six shot in rapid succession indicated that the weapon was functioning properly.

"Check the barrel temperature," ordered Sutton and two technicians quickly attached thermometers to the barrel.

"Just a bit hotter than we had expected," said one of them, "maybe by 40 or 50 degrees."

"Good enough," said Sutton. "We can work on improving that. Let's pack it up, boys. We've had a good day."

"Well, what did you think of that?" asked Roman after they had returned to the plant.

"Not quite as exciting as similar events in Torun, but I am satisfied just the same. You know, I think that we can reduce the heat factor if that barrel considerably if Steiner would let us."

"I know," replied Roman. "But if they are not interested, why should we be?"

"That is right," said Erik. "Let's go home. It's quitting time."

~~~

The production line for the Burlington .303 Mark 1 was slowly taking shape in an unused brick building adjacent to the main Burlington Industries foundry. Machines of various types were set up in neat rows, positioned to complement each other's operation. In the other half of the building, assembly line areas were installed where the workers would receive and assemble the machined parts from the other side of the plant. Production was scheduled to begin on January 15, 1914.

Erik and Roman were asked to transfer to the foundry where they would oversee the production of the barrel until the system was operating smoothly. Sutton was satisfied with the formula and design used in the prototype and they had ceased to experiment with new alloys and designs.

Personnel brought in from several other areas of the plant, plus a crew of newly hired workers, commenced limited production of the Mark 1 rifle on schedule. Burlington Industries salesmen took the first production models and anxiously embarked for Europe. After several weeks they cabled saying that some customers were interested enough to order sufficient numbers of the firearm to conduct field trials. These orders would keep the production line busy until June or July, Sutton estimated. The salesmen returned to America and production began.

By late spring, reports began to arrive at Burlington Industries saying that the Mark 1 was not performing up to expectations in field trials. The firing mechanism tended to jam under muddy conditions or when sand got into it; also the barrel got too hot under rapid fire. Unless these weaknesses were corrected, there would be no more orders, they reported.

Sutton called a meeting of the development group and explained the dilemma. Erik and Roman were ordered to resume experimentation with new alloys and Steiner was asked to refine the firing and ammo feed mechanisms. On July 10, development on a new Mark 2 model began in earnest.

~~~

The joys of motherhood were reflected in Angela's face as she watched Baby Walter progress through his various stages of development, from learning to crawl to taking his first wobbly steps. She was excited when he suddenly vocalized what she was sure were words. Each day she greeted Erik with accounts of Walter's latest accomplishments as the object of their attention proudly demonstrated his newly acquired skills.

"He looks more like you every day, don't you think so?" Angela would proclaim.

"I don't know, Angela," Erik would answer. "As you know, I cannot see myself, so how can I tell?"

Angela's mother agreed that Walter did, indeed, remind her of Erik, especially when he was mischievous. At other times he resembled his mother more.

Mrs. Klazcek was undaunted in her attempt to live with her disability, but the demands that this placed upon her often left her drained of energy. In recent months she had seemed content to sit in her wheelchair and observe her daughter and grandson from whom she seemed to draw the will to live.

Around the middle of the month a letter dated June 25 arrived from Bashinski in Warsaw. It was the first time that he had written since their arrival in America. Bashinski related that he had heard about Erik and Angela's circumstances in America from Stanislaw in Canada and he congratulated them on the birth of their son. He felt he had to write because the political situation in Europe was very unstable and that a breaking point could be reached any day. If this did happen, and it now appeared inevitable, he said, this may be the last chance that he would have to write. He was also pleased that Erik's work was going well and suggested that he should try to avoid staying too close to the hot temperature of the blast furnace and should try to maintain a low profile as much as possible in order to keep his work secure and useful.

"I see that my good uncle is still talking in riddles," sighed Erik. "Sometime I think that he is becoming senile."

"You should not talk like that about your great uncle," scolded Angela. "He is a very intelligent man, and furthermore he is older and wiser than us."

Near the end of the letter Bashinski noted that he had been reading that America had historically been free of rats but now, he understood, they were coming over on ships from Europe. If Erik had any rats in his shop, he should try and avoid them or they may take over, the way they had in Europe.

"Poor old Europe," mocked Erik. "Now it is blaming its problems on rats."

"I think that your uncle is trying to tell you something, Erik," said Angela. "Maybe you should read that part of the letter more closely."

~~~

News of the June 28, 1914 assassination of the Archduke Francis Ferdinand of Austria-Hungary was received with almost total indifference in Main Street America. It was nothing more than Old World jealousies – a settling of accounts – according to the popular press. But in Europe the event was leading to a crisis between Austria-Hungary and Serbia. The Austro-Hungarian government accused Serbia of being responsible for the assassination because of its tolerance of the Greater Serbian movement within its borders. The dual monarchy insisted that this nationalistic movement posed a threat to the Austro-Hungarian Empire and had to be suppressed. An ultimatum was sent to Serbia on July 23, submitting ten specific demands, most of which involved the suppression of anti-Austrian propaganda in Serbia.

After persuasion from both Great Britain and Russia, the Serbians accepted all but two of the demands, but on July 25 Austria deemed the reply unacceptable. A modification of the terms was sought by Russia, who warned that if Austria declared war on Serbia, Russia would march against Austria. Animosities which had their beginnings tens or even hundreds of years earlier festered and were threatening to erupt into bloody violence. Great Britain, watching from the sidelines, realized the dangers which the developments posed for all of Europe and attempted to mediate the dispute. A British proposal was advanced on July 26, asking for a conference of the four great European powers – France, Germany, Italy and Great Britain – to settle the dispute but it was rejected by Austria.

In an attempt to stifle the Greater Serbian movement, Austria declared war on Serbia on July 28. Feeling compelled to live up to its commitment, Russia partially mobilized its army against Austria. Germany immediately warned Russia that if it continued its belligerent stance against Austria it would face the threat of German retaliation. Russia's refusal to heed the warning led to a declaration of war by Germany on Russia on August 1, 1914.

Trouble was also developing in Western Europe. On August 2, German troops crossed Luxemburg and next day Germany declared war on France. Belgium, declaring itself neutral, in accordance with the Treaty of 1839, called upon the signatories to the treaty to observe their guarantee. On August 4, Great Britain sent an ultimatum to Germany demanding that Belgian neutrality be respected. Germany refused and Great Britain immediately declared war on that country.

World War I had begun.

Battles were now raging on two fronts and the tentacles of the European conflict threatened to engulf the whole world. In America, the press of August 5, 1914 chronicled the events of the fast moving drama on front pages around the country. Weary commuters riding trolleys home after a hard day's work read the headlines then turned indifferently to other parts of the paper.

~~~

Columns of smoke arising from the encampment of the Second Russian Army were clearly visible from the yards and porches of Lubicz on the morning of August 6, 1914. Service Corps officers who drove their wagons into the village seeking to purchase food supplies and wood were directed by the villagers to the Jewish merchant Litvak. Food supplies which previously would have been taken to Torun for sale were gathered in the village square and sold to the Russian army.

Two days later the whole Russian regiment marched through Lubicz to camp on a knoll overlooking Torun. For several hours the boisterous infantrymen poured through the village, their peaked caps perched cockily on their heads and dark patches of gleaming sweat showing through their tunics. They grinned broadly through their beards at the groups of villagers gathered to stare in awe at the spectacle.

The Russians had quickly assumed the offensive following the declaration of war and the full scale outbreak of hostilities. The regiment camped near Lubicz was dispatched to form the left and rear flank of the main army fighting inside East Prussia. News reaching Lubicz from the front indicated that early victories had allowed the First Russian Army to advance into East Prussia as far as Tannenberg and the Masurian Lakes region. But two weeks later the tide had turned and the Russians were soundly defeated in the Battle of Tannenberg. The victory provided General Hindenburg with sweet revenge for the humiliation that the Teutonic Knights had suffered from the Poles on that very same battle field in the 15th century. When the battle was over, the stench of the dead soldiers and horses filled the countryside.

Three days later, the regiment that was camped outside of Torun was ousted by the Germans and began its eastward retreat. The remnants of the regiment dashed through Lubicz like weary foxes being chased by pursuing hounds. The Germans arrived in the village looking confident and efficient in their pointed helmets, leather leggings and silver-buttoned tunics.

By September 1, the eastern front was moving toward Warsaw and Litvak's military customers were paying in marks instead of rubles for the produce of the local farmers. Bashinski and Sliworski had fled Warsaw and were already mobilizing the new Polish army, with Sliworski's underground army forming its nucleus.

CHAPTER 25

Sutton and the quality control inspectors examined the first production run of the new Mark 2 Burlington .303 waiting on the packing floor. As they walked along, Sutton slapped the wooden stocks of the rifles with his palm to indicate his approval of the batch. The lot was ready for shipment. Steiner had modified the ammo feed and firing mechanism and replaced the top feeding Mannlichen-type box with the bottom feeding Lee-Enfield type. For the barrel, Erik returned to the formula he had developed at Torun Works, a change which no longer seemed to concern Steiner. Range tests were completed satisfactorily and the company's sales team once again returned to Europe.

Because war was raging on both sides of the European continent, Burlington officials decided to establish a new sales base in London. Several days after the arrival of the Burlington salesmen in London, two officers from the Free Polish Army accompanied by a British army officer, arrived at the small warehouse and asked to examine one of the Mark 2 rifles. The officers handled the weapon expertly, feeling its weight and balance while discussing their conclusions in Polish. The older of the two Polish officers requested ten of the rifles for a field test. Before they left, he signed the purchase order – Wladimar Bashinski, General.

Three days later, Bashinski returned to the Burlington warehouse in London and ordered 5,000 Mark 2s and promised to purchase another 20,000 if these performed well in battle. In addition, France, whose soldiers were dissatisfied with firearms of its own design, was desperate for new and superior weapons. The Burlington Industries salesmen returned to Toledo with good news for the production department.

~~~

In spite of the warnings issued by the Polish banker and economist Bloch in 1887, who had forecasted the end of hand to hand combat, generals on both sides of the new war were still obsessed with Napoleon and Waterloo. They entered the war convinced that the secret of success in battle was the offensive action of aimed fire, supported by the superior force of bayonet carrying troops who would charge, overrunning all that was before them. The British, on the other hand, believed that the well-bred horse still occupied a distinguished place in battle as an adjunct to the gun-toting infantry. The result of years of brainwashing in military colleges forged visions of consecutive units of soldiers attacking in straight lines, rendering the aimed fire of the enemy incapable of stopping their advance.

It did not take the belligerents long to discover that the superior fire power now available found these orderly straight lines perfect targets for rifles and machine guns firing into the formation from the flanks. Hundreds of thousands of officers and men on both sides were lost before the fallacy of prewar military theory was proven. Attacking troops suffered casualties as high as 75 per cent. With the onset of winter, both sides realized that they could not afford any more losses of manpower and they dug themselves in. The age of trench warfare had begun.

Since the German army was solidly entrenched on French and Belgian soil, the stalemate of the winter of 1914-15 could only be broken by the Allies resorting to new modes of warfare. The attention turned to heavy artillery and other as yet undiscovered vehicles to penetrate the barbed wire and to traverse the terrain that was riddled with trenches. But the equipment to fight such a war was scarce or even non-existent.

~~~

New orders for the Burlington Mark 2 failed to materialize. Preparations for the spring offensive of 1915 were based on artillery fire and the scramble for heavier but easily transportable guns began. Rifle production in other parts of the arms producing world was sufficient to satisfy the reduced demand for the weapons.

A meeting of the research and development group was called by Sutton early in January. He announced the production of the Mark 2 rifle would be confined to North American demand. Sutton announced that the research and development unit would turn its attention to the development of a light field gun and a tracked combat vehicle called a tank. The first priority would be the field gun.

Sutton unfolded a drawing and tacked it on the wall. Erik immediately recognized it as the one that he had taken with him from Torun Works. He glanced over at Steiner who sat with his arms folded staring at the drawing.

"This is a drawing of a few major component parts of a 13 cm gun currently being developed in Europe. It promises to be one of the most versatile medium-sized weapons ever produced, far superior to the 1896 models now being used. It is not yet in common use on any of the fronts, but we know that when it is perfected it will be one of the best in Europe," explained Sutton. "Our job is to come up with something as good or better. All the components will be designed and manufactured right here, so we will have complete control over its design and production. Carl Steiner will be in charge of the whole project. Erik Berglund will again be responsible for designing the barrel and stand and producing these for the prototype. He will be assisted by Roman Potoski. Since the war in Europe may not last too much longer after the spring offensive is launched, we have set July 1 as the target date for completion of the prototype with field testing shortly thereafter. Because of the critical timing involved, management is not likely to accept any excuses for failure to meet these deadlines. I know we can do it, men. Now let's get started."

Sutton put his pointer down and clapped his hands together in a grand finale. The men gathered around in small groups, absorbed in discussions concerning the announcement. After several minutes they dispersed to their work stations. Erik and Roman returned to their office where Erik slumped into his chair, his arms dangling over the sides.

"Well, here we go again, Roman. Somehow it seems that I have been through all this before."

"That's good, Erik," said Roman "It should get easier each time. When do we start?"

Erik unlocked a desk drawer open and removed a brown envelope. He opened it slowly and pulled out a half sheet of white paper with some figures on it.

"We'll start right here, Roman, with our old formula from Torun," said Erik smugly.

They laughed at the irony of the situation and pulled their chairs together to study the formula.

~~~

Except for occasional clashes between the two sides in the no-man's area between the trenches, the Western Front remained almost stationary throughout the spring and summer of 1915. The British, who were experiencing a shell shortage, advocated a 'hold the line' policy until the ammunition factories in the United Kingdom and the United States could gear up their production. At the insistence of France, the Allies made several dismal offensive moves against the German lines only to discover that the enemy had already established a second line of defense, well out of range of any bombardment that the Allies may mount. The well-drained, weather-proofed German trenches crisscrossed each other for a distance of six miles and provided a formidable defense system. The day of the New Armies had arrived but military technology was caught napping and the soldiers still found themselves without military hardware suitable for the occasion.

Only on the Eastern Front did the operations conform to the prewar theory of mobile warfare. There the vast distances had combined with the featureless terrain to give both sides relatively easy see-saw victories early in the war. Four Russian armies advanced through Galicia, taking both Przemysl and Bucovina, and by March 15, 1915 were ready to move into Hungary. In April, however, a counteroffensive by the German and Austrian armies began to drive the Russians back and by late summer had driven them out of the original Polish territory. Here, too, the acute shortage of munitions and the general incompetence of the Russian commanders caused them to lose so many men and supplies that they were unable to play any further decisive roles in the war.

In early June, Erik was met at the door by Angela holding a letter in her hand. It was postmarked London and the return address was simply W. Bashinski and a street address in London.

Bashinski's letter this time was unrestrained and lucid. "Our enemies are strangling each other to death and we must be ready to jump in, when they are gasping for breath, to deliver the final blow. My comrades and I are standing by, waiting for this fateful day, but we will need new and better tools to finish the war. We are counting on you and our American friends to create and produce these tools. Please don't let us down. Long live Poland, strong and free!" He hoped that they were well and that their new son was thriving.

~~~

By mid-June six small cannon-sized gun barrels stood in a row on top of a heavy wooden platform in the research and development laboratory at Burlington Industries, exquisitely machined and polished. Erik and Roman had varied the Torun Works formula slightly in each one of them to determine which would be the best combination when the field tests were done. Sutton gazed admiringly at the barrels and tapped hem with a small hammer to hear the resonance of the steel, then covered them with a sheet to keep out the dust.

In another laboratory, Erik and Roman were putting finishing touches to a steel stand for the new weapon. It was designed to enable the gun to be attached to a vehicle or to the solid floor of a ship or railway car.

The July 1 deadline arrived and the barrels and platform still remained in store. That afternoon Sutton called a meeting of the R and D staff involved in the project. When everyone had assembled, he entered the room with a somber look on his face.

"Men, I regret to have to announce that some parts of this project have failed to meet the deadline and we have asked management for an extension and they reluctantly granted it. Fortunately for us, events in Europe indicate that the war there will not be over as soon as previously anticipated, so the pressure upon us is not as great as it once was. However, if we are to come up with a good product and take advantage of the markets out there, we cannot waste any more time than necessary. Since our present delay is due to the slow development of only one part of the product, I will not mention any deadline for those of you who have completed your part of the project. You may continue to refine the designs that you have already developed. Any questions?"

"Where did the delay occur?" asked Roman.

"In the design of the firing mechanism," answered Sutton curtly.

In the front row, Steiner was sitting sphinx-like, his eyes focused on Sutton. He remained in his seat until all the others had left.

The hot humid breeze blew in through the window from the outside and mixed slowly with the stale air inside the room, but did little to overcome the oppressiveness of the mid-summer heat. Erik wiped the sweat from his brow and gazed intently at a set of drawings in his office. Roman leaned his lanky body against the door frame, undecided whether to stay or return to his equally uncomfortable work area.

"Things are different here," he drawled.

"Why do you say that?" asked Erik.

"Well, here we are in the middle of August and no one seems overly concerned about our project. If this was Torun, can you imagine what Richter would have done?"

"Yeah, I see what you mean. He probably would have reported us to the Kaiser by now," laughed Erik. "Anyway, America seems to be more preoccupied with peaceful pursuits and that is just fine with me."

"Yes, but what will happen if we do not succeed in this project?" pondered Roman.

"We will just go back to making gears and hubs, and bushings and pulleys, and more gears...and...," droned Erik.

"Does that not bother you anymore?"

"No, Roman. I am becoming Americanized."

By early September boredom was setting in and Erik and Roman asked Sutton for a project that would occupy them while they waited for further progress in the new product. Sutton leafed casually through a trade magazine and called them over to his desk. The magazine was open at a sketch of an awkward-looking vehicle which appeared to ride on a continuous track. They looked at it curiously.

"This is a crawler tractor," explained Sutton. "This is a very early design, but an exciting idea just the same. Now if we can just place some guns on it, can you just see those German infantrymen in Europe jumping out of trenches when they see it coming?"

They looked at each other, amused at the idea, wondering if Sutton was serious.

"Here," said Sutton closing the magazine and handing it to Erik. "Study that machine and see if you get any ideas. If you do, put them down on paper. Maybe some day we can use some of them."

Like school boys whose creativity was challenged, Erik and Roman produced scores of drawings over the next few weeks showing various contrived uses for the unusual vehicle on tracks. In their imagination they saw it as a draught machine, a building demolisher, an all terrain vehicle and a mobile fort. They discussed how the continuous track could be improved and how the vehicle could be steered. All these ideas were recorded on paper and they awaited Sutton's reaction.

Early in October, Sutton was waiting in Erik's work area when he arrived. He looked nervous and distraught and it was obvious that he had not come to discuss the crawler tractor.

"Bad news, Erik," he announced as Erik entered. "Our project continues to be in trouble. We need some new approaches so I have taken Steiner off the project and I want you to take over his function."

"But I know nothing about firing mechanisms and things like that. I am just a draftsman with some knowledge of metallurgy," protested Erik.

"Take it for a while, Erik. Work with the other fellows. See what you can do with the drawings that Steiner has produced," pleaded Sutton. "A lot of this work is just common sense and I know that you have plenty of that. Look at all those successes that you had in Torun. If you could do it there, why can't you do it here?"

"I will try," conceded Erik. "But it may take longer than the company can afford."

"We'll take a chance on that," said Sutton. "Take Roman with you. The two of you make a good team."

~~~

Although the drawings prepared by Steiner exhibited the principles upon which a firing mechanism for field gun worked, there were no specifications to show the dimensions of the parts or how they would fit together and operate in relation to each other. This discovery indicated to them that they would have to start again from the beginning in their task of designing the apparatus.

"If we only had Richter's drawings here, we would have the answer immediately," mused Roman.

"Yes," replied Erik absent-mindedly. He appeared to be deep in thought. Several seconds later he jumped to his feet. "That's it, Roman. You have just hit on a great idea," exclaimed Erik. "We will get Richter's plans."

"What do you mean? How can we possibly get Richter's drawings?" asked Roman.

"Maybe we can't get the original thing, but I think I know someone who may be able to get us the next best thing – a description and a set of specifications of the 13cm gun."

"Like who?" Roman was astonished by Erik's conviction.

"Uncle Bashinski. That is who."

"Well, if he can get you out of Torun, I am sure that he should not have too much trouble getting a few figures for us," agreed Roman. "But first of all, how do we find him?"

"I have an address for him in London," said Erik. "I will write to him tonight."

It gradually became painfully evident to them that there would be even less than they had expected in the work that Steiner had done that would help to move the project along. Erik and Roman realized that they were on their own. Steiner, who had returned to routine design duties, was unable to explain the basis for his design and they no longer sought his input. Partly out of necessity and partly as a ploy to put in time until they heard from Bashinski, Erik asked for and received permission to completely redesign the mechanism. He and Romaan assumed the task half-heartedly at first, knowing that much of what they were doing would have to be discarded if and when Bashinski delivered the real thing. But as the weeks passed and no response came from Bashinski they began to fear that they were irrevocably on their own,

"Too many things could have gone wrong," reasoned Erik. "Bashinski may no longer be in London and even if he is and did get my letter, he may have thought that it would be too risky to go after the information. But why doesn't he at least respond to my letter?"

Several days later his question was answered. On March 24 a letter arrived with a London postmark. Noting the small size of the envelope, Erik fingered it cautiously, fearful that it would not contain the information that they needed. He slit the envelope with a knife and discreetly removed the contents. The letter contained three onion-skin pages and a snapshot. On the front page was a note signed by Bashinski.

"I am sorry for the delay," he wrote. "It has been a snowy winter in northern Europe and the only access we had to the information you requested was by going through the original Eastern Front between Warsaw and Tannenberg which is still difficult to penetrate. It took some time, but a mutual friend of ours from Lubicz eventually located an abandoned unit which was a casualty of the earlier retreat. He was able to retrieve the enclosed information. I hope that it will be useful. Please hurry. We need all the help that we can get."

Erik unfolded the sheets of thin paper. The specifications were there, carefully drawn in miniature, but complete in every detail. Someone had taken the pains to patiently record and label all the dimensions of the mechanism and show how each part related to the others and to the complete unit. A close-up snapshot of passable quality rounded out the information package.

Erik hurried over to Roman's house and showed him the material from Bashinski. They looked at each other in disbelief.

"Litvak! Of course, it was Litvak. He is the only one who is still there. He is as cunning as a raven and as stealthy as a fox. It had to be Litvak," remarked Erik.

"But how could he have pulled off a stunt like this right under the noses of the occupational forces?" pondered Roman.

"With his phantom brigade. That's how," explained Erik. "Don't you remember them?"

"Yes. How could I forget? Most of them are so inconspicuous that they blend in with the landscape, like our old friend at the market place."

~~~

Over the next four weeks the reduced scale figures provided by Bashinski were meticulously transformed into full scale drawings on regulation sized drafting paper in Erik's drafting area. Neither he nor Roman had apprised Sutton of the source of their information and the manager watched their progress with an assumed detachment. The exuberance with which the two young technicians were attacking the project made him feel confident that that some important results were imminent. And he was not to be disappointed.

On the last Friday in April, Erik telephoned Sutton and advised him that the preliminary designs were ready. Sutton arrived at the door within minutes. He hesitated briefly as if to prepare himself for the unexpected, then headed straight for the drafting table. His eyes quickly scanned the whole drawing then began to focus on the details, one by one, nodding his approval after examining each of them. After several minutes he backed up and looked at Erik and Roman in apparent amazement.

"This looks very good to me, fellows. I would like our chief industrial engineer to take a close look at the design to determine its accuracy." He rolled up the drawing and put it under his arm. "Why don't you two take the rest of the day off and I will see you on Monday. You have been working hard over the past few weeks and probably need a short break."

Early Monday afternoon Sutton arrived at Erik's office with the drawings, a broad smile sending wrinkles to the edge of his receding hairline. He spread the paper on the drafting table and secured it.

"I think that you have something here, boys. Our engineering people say that the design is theoretically sound. We will start to put a prototype together immediately. Erik, I want you and Roman to act as consultants in the production of the components since both of you had some experience with this product in Europe. Both of you will come to my office tomorrow morning and I will introduce you to the rest of the crew and the work area."

As scheduled, next morning Sutton briefed the hand-picked product development staff. There were two engineers, a machinist, a metallurgist and two mold makers. Erik quickly recognized that Steiner was not among them.

"Gentlemen, the war in Europe is forcing this country to become increasingly concerned about our capacity to defend ourselves. No country can consider itself completely isolated from the rest of the world anymore. New technology in warfare can now bring destruction to anyone who is not prepared. The days of the infantry and cavalry in face-to-face combat are over. New weapons are necessary if we are to secure our defenses. You will all soon have an opportunity to contribute something to this end. Something that we hope will be a very important part of our defense system, as well as a means of support to our friends who are currently involved in the war."

He tacked Erik and Roman's drawings to the wall beside the blackboard and asked everyone to gather close enough to see them.

"This is a design for a medium heavy, but versatile, gun with a diameter of 13 centimeters. We hope that it will have a muzzle velocity of more than two thousand feet per second and a range between twelve and fifteen thousand yards. We also hope that it will be superior to anything of a similar size now being produced in Europe."

Sutton pointed to the drawing showing the complete weapon. "The design for the barrel was completed several months ago. There are six barrels in storage which will be tested on the prototype models which we will build. They are waiting for the rest of the unit, specifically the firing mechanism. The design for this part of the gun is now complete and over the next few weeks we will fabricate the parts and then put everything together into a prototype.

"Because of security concerns, I will be the only one who will have access to the complete drawings except for Erik Berglund whom I have chosen as project consultant. A special area of the plant has been set aside for this project and you will be the only ones allowed to enter. We are set to start organizing ourselves for the project this afternoon."

Sutton led the crew to the area of the plant which was to be the nerve center of the development. A series of small offices lined the outside wall of the large room. There were no windows except for the skylight from where shafts of sunlight fell onto a clean concrete floor.

"OK, fellows. This is it. You will find an office with your name on the door. Here is a key for each of you which will let you into the room. No one else has one except me. So if anything is missing or goes wrong, this group here will be responsible, no one else. But I am sure that will not happen. So get yourselves organized and we will get things rolling tomorrow morning. Good luck!"

Sutton left the large room and the door lock clicked behind him. The new improved field gun project was finally getting back on track, ten months behind schedule. The development team looked at each other silently then dispersed to their former work stations.

CHAPTER 26

Bees, their thighs laden with yellow pollen, buzzed lazily among the sun-drenched lilac blossoms and dandelions in the back yard. Erik and Angela proudly watched Walter romp through the tender green grass, stopping periodically to pluck a dandelion bloom and pull out its small golden petals. The warm June sun and the still air seemed to isolate the garden from the rest of the world. Only a few subdued Sunday morning sounds from the street and the laughter of the neighbors' children broke the silence.

"Ah. This is the way to live," grunted Erik as he stretched out on the grass.

"Yes," responded Angela. "It is too bad that we don't get a chance to relax like this more often. It seems that you are always so busy with your work that we don't have the time to spend together anymore."

"I agree," said Erik, "and I have been thinking about that lately. But things are getting more organized around the plant now so I will be able to think more about us. Anyway, we will just have to make time from now on. There is no end of work for any of us, so let us not try to finish it all at once. But look who is talking. I'll tell you what. How about if you and I went on a picnic next Sunday, just the two of us, like we did in Torun? We can leave Walter with Lydia and Roman and just spend some time by ourselves. We can leave early in the morning and spend a full day together."

"That sounds exciting, Erik. Let's go and ask them right now."

Roman waved casually from the front porch where he and Lydia sat watching the activity out on the street as Erik and Angela entered the gate.

"Hey. Where have you two been?" he asked. "We have not seen you for a whole day. Come up and introduce yourselves."

"We would like to ask you a favor." Erik stood on the front step looking in the door.

"Don't be shy. Come on up," pleaded Roman. "Whatever the favor is, consider it done. Don't ask, just say what it is."

"Angela and I thought that it would be nice if we could be alone for a few hours. So we thought that, perhaps, next Sunday we would go for a walk and a picnic down beside the river," explained Erik.

"If you could take Walter until we got back we would not have to worry about mother having to get out of bed to look after him," added Angela.

"Why not? You can start planning your retreat as soon as you are ready," said Roman. "Lydia and I are alone too much of the time anyway. We need somebody else around once in a while. Is that not right?" asked Roman as he pinched his wife.

"What I need is some time alone, away from you," laughed Lydia, pushing him away.

~~~

The mold makers on Erik's development team had produced a number of patterns and forms which were neatly lined up on a long table at the far end of the room. Several of the component parts had already been formed and were being machined to specifications. The crew worked well together and the project showed promise of being in the prototype stage in six weeks or less.

By mid-week, Erik and Roman were satisfied that the project was on schedule and left the special area at the normal quitting time. Partway across the compound they encountered Carl Steiner. They were about to turn away, hoping that he had not seen them when Steiner called out.

"Hey, you two experts, where have you been?"

"Hello Steiner," responded Erik as the man approached them. "Nowhere. Just around the research and development area."

"Aha. I hear that there are some big things going on there," said Steiner in a friendly tone.

Erik and Roman were taken aback by Steiner's congeniality, but reasoned in their minds that perhaps this was his normal personality away from the workplace.

"We are continuing the struggle from where you left off," said Roman.

"Yes. It is not an easy task, as you know," confided Erik.

"Well anyway, I am sure that you are doing fine," said Steiner. "But you look kind of tired Erik. Looks like you could use a rest."

"I just need a day or two to relax," agreed Erik. "In fact my wife and I are planning to do just that this Sunday. We are going to that park beside the river at the end of the streetcar line. We will take a picnic basket and just sit around on the grass all day."

"That is a good idea. Maybe I can talk my wife into doing the same," said Steiner. "At what time are you going?"

"Real early. Probably around eight o'clock, so we can miss the crowds and also have a full day out there."

"Enjoy yourself. I might see you there," said Steiner as he turned to leave.

"Say. That fellow is not so bad after all," remarked Erik.

"I still don't trust him," said Roman.

~~~

The cloud cover which had converged on the city overnight rolled out into the southeast and stretched across the horizon like a low mountain range. As the sun came up over the roof tops, Erik and Angela had their willow sapling basket packed and were dressing the sleepy and dazed Walter. They rushed around excitedly, talking in hushed tones to avoid waking up Angela's mother. After a last minute inspection, they closed the door gently and dashed happily down the street to their friends' house. Roman and Lydia were already dressed and having breakfast at the kitchen table.

"Looks like you will have a good day for your outing," said Lydia.

"Yes. We didn't think we would when we went to bed last night with all that cloud around, but luck is with us," replied Erik. "If you are ready for Walter, we will be on our way so we can miss the crowds."

"We have been ready and waiting for an hour, so away you go. Do not worry about a thing," said Lydia.

Erik hugged his son and handed him over to Angela. She held him close to her chest and kissed his cheek.

"Be a good boy, Wladimar, sweetheart. Mommy and papa love you."

Angela said it felt strange to be away from their son for the first time. As the streetcar whined its way toward the outskirts of the city, its passengers gradually disembarked until Erik and Angela, sitting at the back of the car, were the only ones left.

"Do you know what this reminds me of, Erik?" asked Angela. "It reminds me of that Christmas when you first came to Krakow and we took that cab to my mother's house. It was only you and I and the driver."

"Yes it does, except that the driver was quite an entertaining character. He turned a dreary day into a happy one. It was the beginning of a new life for us," reminisced Erik.

"If this is another beginning, Erik, I am happy with the way it has started out," said Angela happily. She moved closer to Erik and took his hand in hers.

The streetcar leaned sharply to the right and then straightened out to traverse a small concrete bridge crossing a creek.

"Last stop coming up," shouted the conductor.

Suddenly a muted boom broke the stillness of the morning air and lifted the trolley up into the overhead cables, sending flashes of light through the clouds of dust. The broken vehicle fell heavily into the chasm created by the explosion and crumbled into a scrambled heap. An eerie quiet settled on the scene.

The resulting short circuit in the overhead cables alerted the street railway operators that something unusual had occurred up the line and an inspector was dispatched to check up on the trouble. He gazed incredulously at the twisted wreckage at the creek's edge and rushed to call the police.

Urging the gathered curious onlookers to stand back, the police officers cautiously descended to the edge of the creek and peered into the wreckage.

"There are two people in the back part of the car," shouted one of the officers.

They moved in closer, pushing aside pieces of the demolished vehicle.

"They both appear to be dead. Mangled all to hell," said the police officer.

"Now, what crazy son-of-a-bitch would do a thing like this? I wonder where the conductor is," asked the other policeman.

"Probably in the creek where the front of the streetcar landed. There does not appear to have been anyone else on board. We will try and find the conductor and determine for sure if anyone else was on board. These two appear so young. Look, their picnic basket is still beside them. What the hell is this world coming to?" observed the distraught police officer.

A plain-clothes detective arrived and conferred briefly with the police.

"Get an ambulance," he ordered. "I will see if I can find something that might identify them."

~~~

Roman and Lydia had just arrived at the Berglund house to see how Angela's mother was faring and were preparing her breakfast when a knock sounded on the door. A tall, slender man, dressed in a two-piece suit and wearing a hat stood at the door with a uniformed policeman.

"Is this the home of Erik Berglund?" asked the man in the civilian clothes.

"Yes," replied Roman reluctantly.

"I am Detective Perry of the Toledo Police Department and this is Constable Roark. Do you live here?"

"No, we are neighbors and good friends of the Berglunds. My name is Roman Potoski. Why do you ask? Is something wrong?"

"There was a bad accident this morning involving a streetcar and I regret to advise you that both Mr. and Mrs. Berglund were killed," said detective Perry grimly. "Did they have any close relatives living in this house or somewhere else in town?"

Roman's face turned ashen gray. He blinked and focused again on the detective's face, hoping that it was all a dream and the whole scene would disappear. But it was not a dream. Detective Perry produced a notebook and was preparing to write. "Yes," said Roman in a barely audible voice. "They have a young son and Mrs. Berglund's mother lives here."

Lydia came to the door to see who was there. She looked inquisitively at Roman's ashen face and at the two men standing at the door.

"Is something wrong?" she asked with a concerned look on her face.

"They came to tell us that Erik and Angela have been killed in a streetcar accident," answered Roman.

"It can't be true! We just saw them this morning! It must have been someone else," she exclaimed, her voice breaking into a whimper.

"I am sorry, but we believe that it was Erik Berglund," said the detective. "We found this on his person and his identification papers were in it."

"Yes. That is Erik's wallet," said Roman submissively. "I recognize it. It is the one he got from Richter."

"After all that those two have gone through," sobbed Lydia. "How can something like this happen to them? They were just starting to enjoy life."

"That very often happens," said Detective Perry. "May we come in and get some information for our investigation?"

"Yes, please do," said Roman. "But what should we do about Angela's mother? She is not a well woman. The news could be very hard on her."

"She will have to hear about it sooner or later," said Detective Perry. "We may as well tell her now."

They entered the house and sat down in the living room. Roman and Lydia went to get Mrs. Klazcek and pushed her wheelchair into the room.

"These are two policemen, Mrs. Klazcek," said Roman in Polish. "They have brought us some sad news and you must be strong. They say that Erik and Angela were both killed in a street car accident this morning."

Mrs. Klazcek sat silently in her wheelchair, and tears began to roll down her wrinkled face.

"It was just not to be," she sobbed loudly. "The curse of Poland has followed us even here. Now my baby is gone. The only thing I had left. The Lord may as well take me too. I have nothing left to live for."

Lydia wiped the old woman's eyes with a handkerchief and held her trembling hand. "These gentlemen would like to ask us a few questions," said Roman.

Angela's mother stared blankly at the two policemen. She was silent and did not move. Then she blinked her eyes. "What can I tell them?" she asked.

"I am going to ask Michael Pankiw to go and tell Father Wozny about what happened so he can start preparing for the funeral," said Roman to Lydia after the police officers left. When Michael and Teena were told the news and they immediately offered to do whatever they could to help Roman and Lydia with the arrangements that would need to be made.

Late Sunday afternoon Roman prepared a terse but simply worded telegram and sent it to Axel Berglund in Canada. It said simply that Erik and Angela were killed in a street car accident Sunday. The funeral would be Wednesday. Would they be able to attend? If yes, please send a telegram, he wrote.

As neighbors, co-workers and friends from the parish streamed through the house late Sunday and through Monday to offer their condolences, Mrs. Klazcek sat expressionless in her wheelchair. Attempts by Lydia and others to coax her to take food and rest failed and a doctor was called to examine her. He advised that the woman should be taken to hospital immediately after the funeral as she seemed to be losing her will to live. Mrs. Klazcek received the suggestion indifferently.

Local newspapers announced the tragedy in bold headlines next day. In the days preceding the funeral the whole city shared the shock of the mindless act which had snuffed out the lives of two young people and an elderly streetcar conductor who was soon to retire. The police department continued its investigation, but could discover no motive for the act. Newspaper writers and concerned citizens speculated about why anyone would want to destroy the lives of a young immigrant draftsman and his wife. There appeared to be no reason at all why this should have happened and they concluded that the two were innocent victims of mistaken identity in an act of sabotage or an assassination attempt that went wrong.

~~~

During the night a violent early summer thunderstorm inundated the countryside around Ralston. Rushing water had carried away some small bridges and culverts, cutting the road links to the surrounding hamlets and farmsteads. The dirt roads stood soaked and shiny in the morning sun, some of them traversable only by foot or on horseback.

When Jim Banning, the railway station agent at Ralston entered his office Monday morning, the telegraph keys were already clicking. He sat down and acknowledged that the line was open. As the message came through, he transcribed it with two fingers on the keys of the rickety typewriter. He signed out and looked at the message, then ran for the telephone. Several sharp turns of the small handle on the side of the telephone box elicited a response from the operator.

"Put me through to the general store in Middleton, please," he said tersely.

The switches clicked and buzzed erratically. "Hello. Hello. Operator." shouted Banning.

"I am sorry Mr. Banning. I cannot seem to get through. The lines seem to be down or out of order," apologized the operator.

"Oh no. Please keep trying. This is very urgent. Ring me when you can get through."

Farmers arriving in town later in the morning from the surrounding farms stood in groups on the sidewalks along the main street discussing the damage that each had experienced from the heavy rainfall. The area east of town seemed to have been hit the hardest, they said.

The operator did not call back. Jim Banning closed the wicket facing the waiting room in the railway station and walked briskly the three blocks to Main Street. He entered the Bradley Bros. general store and went straight to a small office at the rear. His friend Bob Bradley was at his desk.

"Bob, you know that Berglund family that lives three or four miles on the other side of Middleton?"

"Sure. I know them well – the old man Axel and his son Stanley. Good people. They have only been here two or three years. Why?" asked Bradley.

"I have to get an urgent message to them, but the phone line to Middleton is out. Something very serious has happened. There has been a death in the family; two in fact," said Banning gravely. "Their son and daughter-in-law."

"Oh dear, what an unfortunate time for this to happen," fretted Bradley. "They say that the small wooden bridge east of town has been washed out. The only way to get there is probably on horseback."

"I wish there was someone in town who could take this message to them. They may want to go to the funeral," said Bradley.

"When is it?" asked the merchant.

"Wednesday in Toledo, Ohio."

"It's about a two day trip, Jim. They'll never make it. This is Monday."

"I know, Bob, but at least I would have tried."

"Tell you what," said Bradley after a pause. "I'll get one of my boys to take the message out to them. There is not much doing here after that storm anyway."

"Are you sure you want to, Bob? I didn't really come here to ask you to do it. I just wanted someone to share my concern with," said the agent.

"No problem, Jim. They are nice people and good customers. It is the least that I can do for them at a time like this."

~~~

Axel Berglund leaned on the fence and gazed at the puddles in the yard and garden.

"Nice rain, but a bit too much," he said to Stanley.

"Yes, we needed it badly, but not this much," agreed Stanley. "I hear that some of the bridges are out." He looked down the long stretch of muddy road.

"Hey, there is someone coming this way on horseback. I wonder who it could be in all this mud."

They watched the rider approaching, straining their eyes to see who it was.

"Looks like that young fellow that works in Bradley's store. I wonder what he is doing away out here," pondered Stanley as the rider drew closer.

The young man guided his horse into the farmyard and dismounted. As he approached the two men, he dug into his pocket and took out an envelope.

"Good morning. Mr. Banning at the station had a telegram for you but the line is down and he couldn't phone the store down the road. He and the boss thought you should have it right away and sent me to deliver it," said the boy.

"That's odd," said Stanley. "We were not expecting any telegrams."

Stanley opened the envelope and read the message. He stared blankly into the distance, then read it again.

"What is it, Stanley? Is something wrong?" asked Axel.

"This is terrible, father! There has been an accident and both Erik and Angela were killed," said Stanley.

"Oh my good God!" exclaimed Axel. "How did it happen?"

"Streetcar accident. That's all it says. The telegram is from his friend Roman," responded a subdued Stanley. "How can we tell mother? It will be too much for her to bear."

"I am sorry," said the messenger. He jumped up on his horse and rode away. Axel and Stanley walked slowly toward the house. They entered and looked silently at each other and at Mrs. Berglund. She observed them curiously.

"I saw the boy on horseback. Is something wrong?" she asked.

"There has been an awful accident, mother, and Erik and Angela were both killed," whispered Stanley.

Mrs. Berglund sat down beside the table and covered her eyes with her hands.

"You did not need to tell me. I saw it in your faces when you came in," she sobbed. "It seems that the poor boy was not meant to live peacefully like other men. He was pursued until the end. I had a feeling the last time that I said good-bye to him that I would not see him again. May God have mercy on their souls!"

The stillness in the room was disturbed only by the chirping of birds outside and the soft footsteps of the family cat as it moved from one part of the room to another. Talk would have seemed an unwelcome intrusion into the sacred privacy of their thoughts. After a while, Stanley moved in his chair and Axel cleared his throat.

"The funeral is Wednesday. We could never make it there in time even if we could afford it," he said.

"We will soon be with them anyway, father. So why go all that way just to see their lifeless bodies," she sobbed.

"Stanley," said his father, "write a telegram to Roman at Erik's address and tell them that we cannot attend the funeral. It is too late for you to take it to Ralston today, but the first thing in the morning you can take a horse and go. Ask Roman what is to happen to the young boy and tell him that if they want to send him here to live with us, we will find someone to go there and bring him back."

Stanley stood up slowly and walked toward the door. "I'll do that, father. But now I must go and break the news to Anna and the children."

~~~

The new telegram was delivered to the Berglund house in Toledo by a wispy youth in an ill-fitting uniform on the afternoon before the day of the funeral. Sutton had arrived at the house and he and Roman were discussing Erik's affairs.

"It may be better for the boy to go and live with his relatives, especially since his grandmother may not be here very long herself," suggested Sutton after hearing what the telegram said. "I could arrange for the company to pay for the boy's train fare and for sending his belongings up there. That is part of the great tragedy when things like this happen, when there are children involved. We have to think about the child. The parents are gone. I wish that I could let you go with the child Roman, but we must get going on our project as it is now several months behind schedule and I will need you to take Erik's place on the team."

Lydia joined them in the discussion and they agreed that a telegram should be sent to the Berglunds suggesting that someone from there should come and take Walter back to Canada.

"I will ask them who will be coming and when, so we can have everything ready," said Roman. "I will do that right after the funeral."

"Meanwhile we will have to do everything we can to reduce the shock for the poor child when he finally realizes what has happened and that he will never see them again. But now we have our hands full with the funeral."

Curious onlookers, whose interest was aroused by the press reports, mingled with friends and co-workers as the two caskets were lowered into the grave. Father Wozny completed his prayers and sprinkled holy water on the caskets. Angela's mother sat quietly in her wheelchair and whimpered softly. As the crowd dispersed she pulled on Lydia's sleeve. Lydia put her ear close to the old woman's face.

"I think my time has come," she whispered. "I feel like there is a big rock on my chest and my arm is going numb."

"Hurry, Roman," shouted Lydia. "We have to get Mrs. Klazcek to the hospital."

The young intern on duty entered the hospital waiting room where Roman and Lydia waited after delivering Mrs. Klazcek to the emergency room.

"Are you folks her family?" he asked.

"No. We are her friends. Her son and daughter-in-law were the ones killed in the streetcar accident last Sunday and who were buried today."

"She is in very grave condition. Seems to have given up her desire to live and that explains why. If you know who her doctor is, I will call him. Also, it would be a good time for the last rites to be administered if she is a religious person."

Mrs. Klazcek passed away that night and her body was laid to rest beside the fresh mound of earth which covered the bodies of her daughter and son-in-law.

"Why are they putting everyone in the ground?" asked Walter. "Will we be going down there, too?"

"Yes we will," answered Lydia, "but not for a long time yet, the Lord willing."

"Who will I live with in our house now?" asked Walter, clinging to Roman's finger.

Roman and Lydia looked at each other. They both shook their heads sadly, observing the look of innocence on the face of the small boy.

"Wally, sweetheart," said Lydia, "you will soon be going to stay with your uncle and grandparents in Canada."

"Can-da? Is that where they make candy?" asked Walter innocently.

"No, no, Walter," laughed Lydia. "That's the name of the country. Your grandpa and your other grandma live there on a farm. They have horses and cows and all kinds of things that we do not have here in the city."

"Will papa, mommy and grandma be there to see all those nice things with me?" asked the boy.

"No, Wally, but your other grandma and your grandpa and uncle and aunt and cousins will be. You will all be together."

"Will I get to ride a horse like the policeman?"

"When you are older. Right now the horses are too big for a small boy like you," explained Roman.

A delivery vehicle was parked in front of the house when they returned from the funeral and the driver was standing at the front door.

"Is this the home of Roman Potski?" he asked when he saw them coming up the walk.

"Yes, that is I," said Roman.

"Parcel from Merritt's Department Store. "Sign here, please."

"I wonder what it is," pondered Roman when they entered the house. "We did not order anything, did we?"

"No," answered Lydia. "Let's open the carton and see."

The polished wooden head of a rocking horse peered at them when they removed the paper and opened the carton. Roman lifted it carefully out of the box.

"Must be a mistake," he remarked, with a puzzled look on his face.

"There is a small packet attached to the saddle," observed Lydia. "See what it is."

Roman opened he brown wrapper and a smaller white envelope fell out. He picked up the envelope and opened it.

"It's a card. It says 'From the management and friends at Burlington Industries.' It must be a present for Walter."

"Yes. I remember Mr. Sutton saying the other day that we should all try to make things as easy as we can for Walter. That is very nice of him to think of this."

"See Walter," said Lydia. "This is your horse. It is not alive like the big ones at the farm, but you will be able to ride it in the house until you are big enough to ride the real horses." Walter approached the wooden horse shyly, feeling its ears and mouth. Roman lifted him carefully into the flannel-covered wooden saddle and placed his feet in the stirrups. The boy sat quietly for a moment then reached over and held on to the two round handles attached to the horse's head.

"That is it, Walter. Just lean forward and back and pretend that this is a real horse," said Roman approvingly. He took a long slender package out of the box and opened it. It was a pop gun and a holster.

"Oh boy," laughed Lydia. "You are all set for life on the farm, Wally."

~~~

Walter had spent several days with Roman and Lydia when the telegram arrived from Canada saying that Stanley's wife, Anna, would becoming to take the boy to the grandparents. Since Anna did not have her documents to travel into the U.S., it would be appreciated if some one could take him as far as Windsor where Anna could meet them at the railway station. Please advise when Anna should arrive in Windsor and allow three days for travel time, the telegram said.

The events of the past two weeks had made it necessary for Roman to be away from his work for several days. Because of the emergency caused by Erik's death, the target date for the completion of the project at Burlington Industries was postponed for another two weeks. As Sutton had suggested, it would now be difficult for Roman to be away from the project for even the shortest time. If he and Lydia could take Walter to Windsor on the Sunday morning train and return to Toledo on the evening train, Roman could accomplish this without taking any more time away from work. A telegram to Stanley suggested this arrangement. The response arrived the next day. They would arrange for Anna to meet them in Windsor the following Sunday. Roman confirmed the arrangement. Sutton was at the door when Roman answered the knock Thursday evening.

"I have the boy's ticket," said Sutton.

"Come in, please," said Roman. "I want you to see something."

Walter, still dressed in night clothes, was perched on the wooden rocking horse, swaying nonchalantly in the small wooden saddle, the pop gun in one hand and the reins in the other.

"Boy! That kid is going to need a real horse when he gets bigger," said Sutton. "I wonder if there is anything that we can do to ensure that he gets one."

"His relatives up there are poor homesteaders," said Roman. "I knew them in the old country and I know that if they can afford it, they will do it for him."

"Maybe the company can help to make it happen." Sutton removed a billfold from his breast pocket and took out a bill.

"Here, Roman. Here is a hundred dollar bill. Put this somewhere safe where it will stay for a few years so that when Walter is ready for a horse, it will be there for him."

The boy's belongings were gathered and being packed into the steamer trunk that Angela had brought with her from Krakow. Lydia was in the process of filling in the remaining empty spots with items that she knew Angela and Erik would have wanted their son to keep. She went upstairs and came down with a small framed photograph of Erik and Angela. Roman removed the backing from the frame and placed the bill between the photo and the matting, then put it together again.

"Here. Walter." Lydia handed the photo to the boy. "This will always remind you of your dear parents. Keep it as long as you live and that will keep their memory alive."

"Yes, son," added Roman. "And when you are older and need a real horse, open the back of this picture, like this, and there will be something inside to help you get it. He showed Walter where the hundred dollar bill was placed and how to remove it from inside the frame.

"I want to show it to grandma Klazcek," said Walter.

"Remember what we told you, sweetheart," explained Lydia. "She is not here anymore."

"She is in the ground with mama and papa, isn't she?" Walter's lips curled and his eyes glistened with tears.

"Yes, she is Walter. But she is happy there," said Lydia, mopping her eyes.

~~~

The train for Detroit was in the station, its engine chugging contentedly and belching acrid smoke when Roman and Lydia arrived with Walter early Sunday morning. The sun had just begun its ascent and the coolness of the night still lingered in the air. Harried passengers were moving about, straining to see the car numbers and asking the conductor and trainmen at each entrance for directions. They entered the coaches and the train began to slowly ease out of the station.

The customs and immigration officer on the Canadian side, who had read about the tragedy in Toledo two weeks earlier, expressed his regrets and welcomed Walter to the country. He told Walter that he would not have to worry about streetcars where he was going, only horses.

"I have a horse," said Walter.

A concerned agent at the railway station ticket window informed Roman and Lydia that the train from Toronto was delayed and would not be arriving until 1800 hours and the one leaving for Toronto was scheduled for 1850 hours. Roman knew that the last train to Toledo from Detroit was at 1700 hours.

"What can we do?" fretted Roman. "If we stay until the train from Toronto arrives, we will not be able to get back to Toledo tonight."

The agent recognized Roman's dilemma. "You can leave the boy with us," he suggested. "It will be quiet here until later in the day so we can keep an eye on him. There is a cot at the back here in case he wants to sleep. As soon as the passengers from Toronto disembark, we will page the lady that's picking him up and bring them together."

Roman glanced at Lydia and explained in Polish what the agent had said. They agreed that they would take the agent up on his offer.

"There is not much else that we can do if we want to leave today," he said to the agent. "We appreciate your offer. Thank you. I am sure the boy will be fine with you."

They left the names of Walter and Anna and their own with the agent, embraced Walter and left the station for Detroit in a cab.

Walter excitedly explored the many wonders of the railway station under the watchful eyes of the agent and his colleagues. With several hours before the next train, the station was nearly empty and Walter sat down on the floor at the end of a long bench. Tired from the excitement and drowsy from the stale air in the building, he quickly fell asleep. A small door leading outside to the side street had been left open to let the fresh air into the building. A big yellow, long-haired dog walked in through the door, smelled the boy and lifting up his hind leg urinated on him. The agent looked up and noticed what was happening. He poured out a torrent of curses at the dog and ran out and picked up the whimpering boy.

The agent carried the boy into the ticket office and explained to the others what had just occurred. They opened the small bag that contained Walter's personal items for the trip and took out a clean suit of clothes, shirt, socks and underwear. At one end of the building was the train crews' waiting area with a tub and laundry facilities. The agent carried Walter into the room where they removed the soiled clothing, washed him and put on a clean set of clothes.

The Sunday Express from Toronto thundered into the station, shaking the wood and concrete platform and stirring the hot afternoon air. With shirts open at the collar and fanning their faces the passengers emerged and entered the waiting room through the doors leading from the platform. A plain young woman, dressed in a skirt and colored blouse stood in the middle of the waiting room and looked around. She watched as the other passengers picked up their bags and left the station. A look of fear came over her face.

"Anna Berglund, please report to ticket agent at wicket number four." The message was repeated several times.

The woman moved toward the wickets and checked the numbers from a distance. She picked out number four and walked timidly toward it. She stopped in front of the wicket and looked in apprehensively. The agent looked up and smiled.

"Are you Anna Berglund?" he asked.

"Yes," she replied in a barley audible whisper.

"I am sorry," said the agent. "The people from Toledo had to leave in order to get home today. They left Walter with us. Are you here to meet him?"

"Oh yah," she stammered excitedly. "I thought he lost. I'm not speak English good. My husband he speak English better, but he no can come. Too busy. Haying time. His grandfather too old. I his auntie."

"Don't worry Anna. You are doing just fine. I am sure that you and the boy will get back with no problems. Bring Walter over," he called to one of the clerks.

Walter appeared from an inside office clutching a candy bar and a bulging paper bag. The agent took him to Anna.

"This is Aunt Anna. She will take you away to your grandma and grandpa."

Walter regarded the woman shyly while slowly munching on his candy bar. She approached him and crouched down.

"Hello, Walter. I Anna. You a nice boy," she said. He placed his bag on the floor and put his arms around her neck.

"My mommy and papa and grandma are gone into the ground," he told her. "Are you going to be my new mommy?" The boy embraced her and she held him close to her. Her eyes glistened as she smiled. "Yes, I be you mama now."

"The nice man gave me something," said Walter as he displayed the contents of the paper bag

"Look," said Anna. "Peanuts, chocolate bars and oranges. That is nice, Walter."

"I have the boy's ticket made right to his destination," explained the agent. "Let's see. Ralston, Manitoba. Is that right?"

"Yes," responded Anna. "Ralston is right. We go there."

"Walter's clothes are in a bag in the office. Bill, the porter will get it. His trunk is checked right through to Ralston. You will have to change trains in Toronto and again in Winnipeg. Do you understand?"

"Yes, yes. I understand. I do that when I come from old country not long ago."

"The train to Toronto is loading in about fifteen minutes. The porter will see that you get on it safely. You will be in Toronto in time to catch the train to Winnipeg at eleven thirty. Have a good trip."

"Thank you, mister," said Anna. "You a very nice man."

She took the boy's hand and walked toward the sign saying "To Trains" with Bill the porter showing the way.

PART TWO

~~~

THE FOUL TASTE OF REVENGE

CHAPTER 27

The small log and clapboard cottage at the edge of the clearing stood gray and weathered against the thick motionless forest, its square windows keeping watch over the open farmyard, sloping gently to the south. Across the clearing, where just twelve years earlier, tall majestic aspen, burr oak, birch and poplar had stood, an unpainted barn and a cluster of smaller buildings huddled together. The yard narrowed to a channel-like opening in the trees through which a well worn trail ran into the open field beyond. A twisty rail fence followed the contours of the clearing, marking the boundaries which separated those on the inside from the off-limits territory on the other side. Within its confines, farm animals of various species grazed or pecked contentedly.

Behind the cottage, a narrow wooden gate opened into a well-beaten path that cut through the grove of trees and meandered to the back door of a two-storey dormered house. This was now Stanley and Anna's home. Its newness was reflected in the clean unpainted clapboard siding and cedar roof, not yet showing signs of weathering. The new building stood naked against the open field in front of it. Its only protection from the elements on the west side were a number of straight rows of newly planted spruce, box elder and elm saplings, still struggling to become established and be ready to perform their shelterbelt function in the years to come. Beyond the plantation, and in line with the outbuildings in the adjoining yard, a convoy of farm machinery and wagons stood in a row as if ready for combat. In the distance were the undulating outline of a meadow and the green cliffs of still undisturbed aspen, poplar and willow groves.

This was the domain of Axel Berglund and his son Stanley, settlers and pioneers in a new land. Every square foot of the farmyard bore witness to the time and labor that the two pioneers had invested in it, and the green fields stood as monuments to their toil and perseverance. The time had come for the elder of the two to sit back and enjoy the fruits of their labor.

The old man and the boy sat beside a thicket of wild cherry trees, protected from the hot noon-day sun by an overhanging birch. They tossed pieces of sticks at an imaginary target. A pollen-laden bumble bee droned lazily as it flew through the air in search of late summer blossoms. On the clothes line, attached to the corner of the small cottage and stretching out to a tree at the end of the clearing, patient barn swallows lectured noisily to their offspring on the soon to be acquired art of flying. The boy looked up and watched the two draft horses standing against the rail fence, their tails swishing sporadically from side to side to fend off the flies.

"Do you think that we could train old Prince for horseback riding, grandpa?" asked the boy, intently observing the bay gelding.

"I don't know, Walter," replied Axel. "Work horses are not hard to train, but they are not the best riders in the world either. They are too slow. Why do you ask?"

"I would like to help around the farm and I thought that if we had a horse, I could ride out to the far pasture and round up the milk cows after school," said Walter.

"You already are good help to us in a lot of ways, son," said the old man, " and I don't mind going to the pasture for the cows, although I must say that these old legs are starting to complain a bit these days."

"Grandpa, do you remember that old wooden horse that I brought with me from Toledo and how I rode it until I was about five years old?" laughed Walter.

"That horse gave you a lot of pleasure. I remember saying to Stanley that you were a natural horseman." Axel glanced at the old work horse and shook his head. "Instead of training old Prince, maybe we should think of getting a pony for you and Stanley's boys – maybe after harvest, if we get a good crop. There are some nice ones over at the Garwood Ranch that are for sale. I'll talk to old Jim Garwood about it the next time I see him. Maybe I can strike up some kind of a deal," mused Axel.

The boy gazed at the ground, deep in thought. Suddenly he jumped to his feet.

"Grandpa, I just remembered something," he said excitedly. "You know that picture of my real mother and father that I brought with me? I remember Roman saying to me that if I really wanted something badly sometime, to look inside the picture and there would be something there to help me to get what I wanted."

"I wonder what he meant by that'" pondered Axel. "Let's go and see if there is anything to it."

Inside the living room of the tranquil cottage, Mrs. Berglund sat on a wooden bench fanning her face with a rhubarb leaf.

"To what no good are you two up to on a hot day like this?" she asked.

"We want to look at that picture of Erik and Angela," said Axel.

"Look at what?" inquired Mrs. Berglund suspiciously. "Sometime I wonder who is the child here, you or Wladimar. Why do you want to look at this all of a sudden?" She took the picture off a shelf in a cupboard and handed it to Axel.

"Well, here it is, son," said Axel checking the back of the frame. "I don't see anything different about it."

Walter took the picture and examined it in silence. He put it on his lap and gazed across the room, deep in thought.

"Oh, I remember now what Roman said," he remarked jumping up with excitement. "He said that whenever I need something really badly to open the back of it…right here."

Axel reached into a side pocket of his overalls and brought out a set of pliers. He cautiously removed the small pins holding the cardboard backing and removed it. A United States hundred dollar bill lay flat between the backing and the matting of the picture. Axel recoiled in astonishment.

"This is hard to believe, son," he marveled. "How could you have remembered this after more than seven years?" You were only three and a half years old at the time."

"There area few things that I remember real well from back then," explained Walter, "and this is one of them. The others are when they put my parents into the ground and when that mean dog piddled on me."

"Well, the money is yours, Walter," said Mrs. Berglund. "Don't let your grandpa talk you into anything foolish. Put it in the bank the next time that you go to Ralston."

"Oh no, grandma," said Walter. "We are going to buy a pony from the Garwood Ranch; one that I can use to go after the cows."

"And maybe even to ride to school in the fall," added Axel.

Mrs. Berglund shook her head in feigned disbelief. "It's no use my saying anything intelligent. You two seem to have made up your minds."

Walter dashed out the back door and through the garden gate to Stanley's house, shouting the good news to his older cousins.

"He is so much like his father was at his age, before they took him away," said Mrs. Berglund wiping away the tears with her apron.

"I'll go and see old Jim Garwood next Sunday after church, "said Axel. "We'll see what he has for sale in cow ponies."

On the shady side of the house, Laura and Jon, the two youngest children of Stanley and Anna were preparing and washing vegetables for the noon-day meal. Inside, Anna was setting the table for Stanley and the two older boys who would soon be arriving from the fields. The garden gate clanged and Walter ran excitedly down the path toward the house. He saw Laura and Jon and rushed toward them.

"Guess what?" he announced ecstatically, "Grandpa and I are buying a pony."

"Oh yeah," remarked Laura without looking up from her work. "And where is the money coming from?"

"From inside the frame of my parents' picture," answered Walter.

Laura and Jon looked at each other and smirked. "Yeah," continued Walter. "When grandpa and I started to talk about horses, I mentioned that wooden horse that I used to have and that made me remember the money that my father's boss put away for me to use when I got older. It was inside the picture frame; a hundred dollars in American money, just like I remembered."

"Oh boy," gushed Jon. "Will I be able to ride it?"

"It will be Walter's pony if grandpa is going to use that money to buy it," counseled Laura who was the older of the two.

"Sure, you will be able to ride it," said Walter, but first we will have to buy it. Grandpa will be going to the Garwood Ranch to see if they have one."

~~~

Its neck bent in a graceful arch, the pacer, drawing a buggy, turned off the main road into Berglund's lane, leaving a cloud of dust lingering in the air. Jim Garwood drove up in front of the new house and stopped beside a hitching post. He took off his hat and blew the dust off it. Stanley appeared from the direction of the barn.

"Howdy, Stan," said the rancher. "Nice place you folks are building up here."

"Thank you, Mr. Garwood," responded Stanley. "It has been a lot of hard work, but we are happy with the way things are going."

"Your father and I talked about a riding pony for the young ones the other day. Did he tell you about it?" asked Garwood.

"Yes, we talked about it. We felt that it would be a good idea, especially since we will be grazing cattle on that crown land east of here next year. It will be nice to be able to send one of the boys down there on horseback to check up on them from time to time. But I don't think we will have enough money to do that until after harvest. Ah, here comes my father now."

Axel appeared on the path connecting the two houses. He gave the pacer an admiring look.

"Good day, Jim," he said. "That is a beautiful animal."

"My best," said Garwood. "I plan to take her into the trotters' race at the fair next summer. But that is not what I came to talk about. I found a young filly out in the pasture. A nice quiet one. Should be good with children. Her mother was real lady. I'll sell her to you if you are interested."

"That sounds great, Jim," said Axel. "I'll send Stanley down there with the boy sometime when it is fine with you. I am getting too old for those things now. I plan to spend the rest of my life puttering around the yard and garden."

"Aw, come on, Axel. Don't let them put us out to pasture just yet," laughed Garwood. "There are a lot of miles left on both of us yet. Anyway, think about it. I think you'll like this filly when you see her."

"I'll be around this Saturday morning or as soon as it rains, if that's fine with you," said Stanley. "I have a few more loads of hay to bring in while the weather stays dry."

"That will be just fine," said Garwood. "I've got my men going hard at the haying now, too. I will be looking for you."

An overnight shower had left the dirt road slippery on the top, but still hard underneath the surface, and the mud gushed out from beneath the wheels of the buggy carrying Stanley, Jon and Walter to the ranch. The Garwood property was located in the older settled area to the south. Jim Garwood had arrived from England as a young man almost thirty years earlier and had established a thriving cattle business. Some neighbors hinted that he had been a remittance man, living off the money that arrived regularly from his family in England. "How else could he have come this far so fast?" they asked. Others, however, said that the secret to his success was hard work and good management. He was tough as nails, but if anyone was trying to make a success of their homestead and was working hard, he would be there to help when needed.

A small herd of horses ran snorting around a corral at the ranch when they arrived. Jim Garwood ordered one of the farmhands to catch the filly called May and bring her out.

"She's from good stock, Stanley," he explained. "Her mother was one of the most dependable riders we ever had. In fact, I've had my grandchildren riding May since I last talked to you and they love her. We called her May because she was born in that month"

Walter walked slowly toward the filly and touched her gently on the nose. The filly reached out and brushed his cheek. The boy put his arms around the filly's neck.

"I've never seen her go for anyone quite like this before," exclaimed Garwood. "She seems to like the boy. Let's help him up and have one of the men lead her around a bit."

Walter's eyes gleamed with excitement as he was helped up onto the bare back of the filly. He held on tightly to the animal's mane. His body followed the movements of the animal as it walked in a circle.

"That boy is a real natural," said Garwood when they sat down in a room inside the bunkhouse that served as an office. "That filly could bring me a hundred and fifty dollars on the market easily. But I like that boy and I can see that he will make a good rider and look after her well. So, I'll give her to you for a hundred, Stanley."

"What do you boys think?" asked Stanley.

"She seems so gentle and smart," offered Jon.

"I love her," gushed Walter. "And I'll take good care of her, Mr. Garwood."

"I guess there is not much else to say," said Stanley. He dug into his pocket and brought out the one hundred dollar bill. Garwood looked at it curiously.

"This is American money, Stan. Where did you get it?"

"Walter brought it from Toledo when he came to live here. It was given to him by my brother's employer.

"You mean that he's had the money for all that time?" asked the rancher.

"Yes. He was saving it for something that he really wanted and he decided that a pony is what he wants more than anything else."

Garwood shook his head in disbelief. He put the bill inside a cash box inside his desk and stood up.

"The boys will need a saddle," he said. "I have one in the tack room that no one is using. I'll have one of the men bring it out."

"But we can't pay you for it, Mr. Garwood," explained Stanly. "We will not have any cash until after harvest."

"Who said you have to pay?" asked Garwood. "Tell you what. I'll strike up a deal with the boys. If they check up on my fences around our pasture out your way once in a while, they can have the saddle. And you know,

Stanley, riding a horse without a saddle is like sitting in a buggy without a seat."

"I'll sure do that for you, Mr. Garwood," beamed Walter. "I'll check your fences for you every day."

"Once every two weeks or so will be fine, boy" said Garwood. "Just let me know if you see places that could use some mending."

Stanley drove the team home and Jon sat beside him. Walter sat with his legs hanging over the open tailgate of the buggy. He held on tightly to the filly's reins as she followed them home. He checked her markings and noticed that she was a solid bay except for a small star on her forehead.

"May is a good name." he called to Stanley. "She has a star on her forehead, but we'll still call her May, the same as Mr. Garwood did."

~~~

The winter's first snowfall covered the trail and the brown stalks of dead grass marked the edges of where the beaten path had been. May followed the snowed-over trail that wound its way toward the one-roomed school house a mile away. In the trees on each side of the trail, curious partridges cocked their heads as Walter rode by. Rabbits dashed from behind the snow covered bushes and watched him from behind the trees. From atop the filly, Walter observed the variety of animal tracks in the fresh snow and recognized them as those of rabbits, weasels, grouse and squirrels. He noticed two sets of larger tracks and got off the pony to take a closer look. They were either dog or coyote tracks, he thought, probably coyote because dog tracks usually differed from each other. Stanley had told him that no two dogs made the same kind of tracks, unless they were identical to each other. The tracks led to the willow bluff in the center of the field.

Walter arrived at the school yard, tied the reins around May's neck and released the filly. She turned around and walked back over the same trail toward the farmstead. Since September, Walter had trained the pony to take him to school and return to the farmhouse where Axel would take off the saddle and halter and then let her go into the pasture or into the barn. As long as the weather remained mild, Walter and his cousins would walk the mile back to the homestead after school was over.

The harvest had not been good and in order to help pay the bills and taxes Stanley and his father had found it necessary to sell the two pigs and one steer that would have provided meat for the two families during the winter. A small field which escaped the early frost yielded enough grain to be saved for seed the following spring and a few bagfuls to be milled into flour. Axel and Stanley sat around the hot wood stove to plan how they would feed themselves and the livestock through the winter. The frost damaged grain crop had been cut for forage and there was enough hay and straw to feed the cattle and horses and some left over for sale. But there would not be enough grain left over for the brood sows and for the horses during the spring work. Old Jim Garwood said that he would trade some of the grain he had left over from the previous year for hay, if they needed it. Axel agreed that he would go down and talk to him about it.

"If we can solve that problem then all that we will have left to worry about is meat for the table'" said Stanley. "We have enough potatoes, turnips, onions and other root crops in the cellar to take us to spring and Anna has a barrelful of sauerkraut, another one of dill pickles and lots of dried mushrooms, beans and peas."

Walter and Jon sat at the kitchen table helping Laura with an arithmetic problem for school next day. They recognized the seriousness of the discussion between Stanley and Axel and tried to follow the conversation between the two men. Walter suddenly left the table and walked confidently toward them.

"I'll get you some meat," he said. "There are dozens of fat partridges along the trail to school. When I come home after school they sit in the trees watching May and me go by. I can almost hit them with a stick. And rabbits. I've never seen so many rabbits as there are this year. Those willow bluffs by the meadow are full of them. Just give me permission to use that small 22 rifle and I'll get all the meat we need."

Axel listened to the boy, his face at first reflecting his surprise and then his approval. He waited for Stanley to respond.

"All right, son," said Stanley. "You seem to have figured this thing out carefully and I am willing to let you give it a try if your grandfather agrees. But first I'll have to teach you how to use the rifle safely. And we'll have to get May used to the sound of rifle shot or you'll end up head first in the snow bank. We'll go out after the chores Saturday morning. I'll pick up some short shells when I am in town tomorrow."

~~~

"When you shoot partridge with a small rifle, aim for the head not the body," Stanley advised Walter after he had fired at a tin can set on a fence post. "There are two good reasons for this rule," he said. "One is that the body feathers on the bird will often deflect the bullet and the other is that, even if the bullet should penetrate the feathers, it will spoil much of the meat. The same goes for shooting rabbits. Shooting a rabbit in the body will contaminate the meat and spoil the skin so you will not get a good price for it. Aim for the head. If you miss, it is better than making an unclean hit."

Walter was shaking with excitement after hitting the tin can with his first two shots, but he listened carefully and wondered how anyone could be as wise as Stanley was in these things.

"Don't let the small size of this firearm fool you, Walter," counseled Stanley. "It is a dangerous weapon in the hands of a careless person. In the hands of a responsible person, it could be meat on the table."

"How about coyotes, Uncle Stanley?" asked Walter, his eyes wide with excitement. "Where do I aim if I see a coyote?"

"This rifle is too small for that size of animal," warned Stanley. "Better stay with small game for a while. But if you should go for bigger game later, you will use a long shell and aim just below the ear. A nice clean shot there will kill him dead and the skin will be perfect. You have a nice steady hand."

You have hit the can both times. With some practice you will be able to place your shot exactly where you want it. Monday I will build a holster for you to hang on to the saddle, one that that you will be able to reach easily, and you will be able to start carrying the rifle around with you starting Tuesday. But remember never to take it off the saddle until you need it."

The first shadows of the early winter dusk crept across the landscape quickly as the last rays of sun sank below the horizon. Distant sounds penetrated the still air; dogs barking, cattle mooing, children laughing and shouting. They stopped and Walter was alone with May on the trail. They both stood very still and Walter slid out of the saddle onto the snow covered trail. A small flock of partridge flew across the clearing and settled on an aspen tree a short distance inside the bluff. They were open and visible from the trail. Walter put a cartridge in the chamber and patted May's neck.

"Nice girl. Keep still. Don't be afraid."

He cocked the firing mechanism. Ping! The bird dove, head first, into the snow below the tree. May stamped her front legs nervously, and settled down. On another branch the other birds observed Walter and the pony. Walter stepped back, took aim and fired. Another bird fell. The remaining birds were beginning to get restless and preparing to fly away. Walter raised the rifle and fired. A third bird fell into the snow. He ejected the shell and led May to the spot under the tree where the birds had fallen. The three dead birds were partially buried in the snow. Two were shot through the head and the other through the neck. Walter tied their legs together with a piece of binder twine, mounted the pony and galloped home.

"Son, you have learned well," said Stanley, proudly surveying the birds. "They are nice and fat. The shots were clean. How many cartridges did you use?"

"Three," responded Walter.

"Three?" Stanley was astonished.

"There is really nothing to it, Uncle Stanley. They just sit up there in the branches real still and I aim for the head, just like you said. Ping; and down they come. Tomorrow, I am going after rabbits," announced Walter.

The local settlers discovered that most animals in the area followed a seven-year cycle during which their numbers increased steadily until they reached a peak. Nature then stepped in and unleashed a disease of epidemic proportions or reduced the food supply until only enough of the species were left to begin the cycle anew. This winter the rabbit cycle was near its peak. At sundown they appeared in small groups, playing beneath the snow-laden hazel and red dogwood bushes. Nature had not yet begun its extermination process.

At sunset of the first day after bagging the partridge, Walter stopped May at the spot where he had observed the rabbits the previous evening. He peered intently into the distance, watching for movements under the bushes. In the lengthening shadows, the movements of the all-white rabbits against the snow, was only discernable to the sharpest eye. Walter had watched the animals and studied their habits every day as he rode past their favorite haunts. He called on May to stop. The boy and the pony stood still at the edge of the hollow. A movement inside the bushes revealed two rabbits feeding on the green twigs. Walter raised the rifle and fired. The first animal fell over and kicked its hind legs twice then remained still.

The second rabbit went right on feeding. Another shot rang out and the rabbit slumped into the snow. Walter left May on the trail and walked through the snow into the hollow. The shots were both clean, just below the ear. He tied the rabbits to the saddle and rode over to the stand of young aspens on the rise where he had shot the partridge the day before. Without getting out of the saddle he fired three consecutive shots and three birds fell into the snow. He picked them up and turned the pony's head toward home. A good hunter only takes what he needs for food, Stanley had told him, and he had bagged enough meat for several days.

Nature continued to provide the Berglund households with the meat that their farm labor had denied them, and as the winter wore on, Walter became a seasoned hunter. Soon the bright sun and the mild southwesterly winds of late March softened the snow until it became difficult to maintain a footing on the snow-packed trail. Patches of black and brown appeared on the knolls and small pools of water collected in the ruts and ditches. The rabbits' fur was becoming tainted with the new summer coats of brown pushing up through the white and their skins no longer had any commercial value. Also, their breeding season had begun and it was time to stop hunting them. Stanley was going to town next day and asked Walter if he wanted to send his furs to Bradley's General Store for grading and sale.

Carrying a glowing barn lantern up the wooden ladder, Walter pushed up the trap door and stepped into the attic of his grandfather's cottage where the skins were stored. He passed the pelts to Stanley, then descended the ladder and lined them up along two long wooden benches. They counted them. There were eighty-nine rabbit skins and fifteen squirrels. They tied the bullet-shaped skins into bundles and put them into a burlap sack ready for Stanley to take to town next day.

Dave Bell, Bradley's fur buyer checked the skins carefully, placing his hand inside the flat tube-like hides. He stroked the fur, and checked the skins for damage.

"I'll pay top grade prices for these," he said. "They have no holes in them and the fur is of good quality. Thirty cents a piece for the rabbits and fifty cents for the squirrels. Let's see. That comes to thirty-four dollars and twenty cents. And I'll throw in five boxes of shells as a premium."

"Those are good prices, Dave," said Stanley. "I am sure that Walter will be pleased with them."

That evening when Stanley returned, an excited Walter ran to his uncle's house to see how the fur sale had gone. Stanley pulled out a bundle of bills and two coins and placed them in front of the boy.

"There you are, son. The fur buyer at Bradley's liked your furs very much and gave you a good price for them. Thirty-four dollars and twenty cents. That is a lot of money these days. What are you going to do with it?"

Walter flipped slowly through the paper money and thought for a while. "I was thinking that it would be nice to go and see Mr. Garwood race his horse at the track this summer, so I would like to use some of the money to go to the fair. And the rest of it, I think I would like to save it for a bigger rifle so that maybe next year I can go after bigger game."

"Both of those sound like good ideas to me," said Stanley. He reached into his pocket. "And I almost forgot. Dave Bell who works at Bradley's also gave you five boxes of ammunition, so you are all set for next winter's hunting season."

~~~

A late fall followed one of those rare growing seasons when all the elements of nature complimented each other perfectly and the land brought forth a harvest high in both quantity and quality. When the first snow flakes began to fall on the frozen ground, the bins, lofts and cellars were filled with a bounty of well ripened and preserved crops. The lean days of the previous year were soon only a memory which would provide grist for the discussion mill around the hot stove during the winter months.

Old Jim Garwood took advantage of the unusually warm late fall weather to graze a herd of yearling steers in the pasture near the Berglund's homestead. Walter fulfilled his obligation to the old rancher and occasionally rode May along the fence line to ensure that the livestock were securely confined. On the day of the first snowfall, he rode over the light layer of snow, following the fence line watching for wildlife in the trees and bushes. True to the predictions of the local homesteaders, the rabbit population had declined drastically, but other furbearing species such as muskrats and weasels seemed to be plentiful.

At the edge of a clump of gnarled willows he noticed a pair of larger tracks coming from a small clearing and following the fence line. He recalled the time a year earlier when the same kind of tracks crossed the trail to the school house. He got down off the saddle with the small rifle under his arm and studied the tracks. They were almost identical and only freshly made, perhaps only minutes earlier. He mounted the pony and was riding along slowly when his eyes detected a movement under some bushes on an overgrown trail. He called softly to May to stop and they remained perfectly still, blending in with the dense hazel bushes. Two coyotes appeared slowly from the unused trail and froze in their tracks. They stared at the motionless boy and pony. Walter, moving slowly, placed a shell in the chamber of the small rifle, the two coyotes watching his moves. He gently patted May on the neck, lifted the rifle to his shoulder and aimed. He pulled the trigger and one of the animals slumped to the ground. The other animal glared defiantly at the boy. He ejected the empty shell and quickly placed a cartridge in the chamber. The coyote was starting to turn when a shot rang out. The animal stumbled and turned toward the boy. He replaced the spent shell and fired. The animal's legs folded and it fell into a heap beside the other coyote. Walter left the pony and approached the two animals cautiously. He poked one of them with the rifle butt. They were both motionless and dead. He tied their hind legs together, hooked the animals on the saddle and headed out toward home.

The kerosene lamp had already been lit and its light streamed through the kitchen window of Stanley's house when Walter returned. He unsaddled and watered May then picked up the coyotes and half dragged them across the yard toward the house. Stanley met him at the door.

"Look, Uncle Stanley. Look at what I got this time," Walter blurted out excitedly, pulling the carcasses onto the doorstep.

"Why, those are coyotes, son," said Stanley. "Where in heaven's name did you get them? And what did you use for a gun?"

"I got them down by Garwood's pasture with your small 22 rifle and three short shells," beamed Walter.

"You are some hunter, son," said Stanley. "No one will believe me when we tell them that you got two coyotes with a four dollar rifle and short shells."

Anna heard the conversation outside the front door and was overcome with curiosity. She looked at the dead animals on the door step and gasped.

"Walter! What are you doing here with those wolves? Get them out of here before you frighten the children with them."

"That's all right, auntie," laughed Walter. "They have been dead now for almost an hour. In fact they are already stiff. And they aren't wolves. They're coyotes."

"I don't care what you call them. Get them out of here. They look so fierce."

"They are probably the ones that were stealing your chickens last summer," said Stanley. "You should thank Walter for putting an end to that."

"Look Uncle Stanley," said Walter, "I got the first one right in the center of the forehead. The bullet must still be in his head. For the other one I had to use two shots because the first one went through its neck. The second shot went in just under its ear, like you taught me to do."

"Good work, Walter. We will skin them tomorrow and when they are dry we will take the furs to Bradley's. You should get a good price for them."

The fur buyer at Bradley's General Store stroked the hair on the coyote pelts tenderly and observed Walter.

"These are a couple of real beauties. Not too many like these left. Most of the animals have moved away into the park since the settlers moved in. Where did you get them, Walter?"

"Beside Garwood's pasture, near our place. They've been around there for quite a while. I remember seeing their tracks in the snow a year ago," replied Walter.

"Hey, boss," the buyer called to Major Bradley. "Come and see these. They're really something."

Major Bradley came out of his office and greeted Stanley and Walter. He picked up one of the pelts and examined it. His eyes caught the bullet hole in the forehead area of one of the skins.

"Now, the guy who got this one is a real hunter," he remarked.

"It was Walter," said Stanley proudly, "with our four dollar 22-calibre rifle. He's a great shot. He can shoot a partridge right through its head every time."

"You're some shot, Walter," said the Major eyeing him closely. "I can't believe that this is the same tyke that got off the train what only seems like the other day."

"More than eight years now," said Stanley.

"Is it that long? Where did all that time go?" remarked Bradley. "Give Walter the top price for these two, Dave," he advised the buyer, then turned to Stanley. "When you are finished with Dave here, come into my office, Stanley. I would like to see you for a minute."

On the wall behind Major Bradley's desk hung a picture of King George V of Great Britain, bearded and wearing a red tunic generously decorated with medals and yellow braids and ribbons. The picture's caption read "His Majesty King George V, King of Great Britain, Canada, Australia and all the Dominions Overseas and Emperor of India." A bookcase beside the desk was filled with books displaying historic and military titles. On the top shelf a small Union Jack flag hung limply on a short staff fixed into a polished brass base. A photograph of the major in his World War I uniform leaned against the wall. Stanley and Walter sat in leather covered chairs with ornately carved wooden arms.

"You know, Stanley," said the major. "I am a military man and I like to encourage young people who are responsible and well disciplined. I always thought that Walter here would grow up into a responsible boy and it looks like I was right. I think that he will be something different some day. I also like the way he shoots – straight and clean, so I would like to help him to develop that skill."

He reached down into a box on the bottom shelf of the book case and brought up a shiny new rifle. "Just the other day I received a small shipment of 22-calibre rifles from the States. It is the first time that I have carried this make, so I would like to have someone test it for us. Right now I think that there is no one better to do this than Walter." He handed the firearm to Walter. "Here, get a feel for this one. It's a ten-shot repeater. Takes either short or long shells. What do you think?"

"It's a lot heavier than ours," said Walter, "but it sure feels good."

"Take it home and try it out on some game. Tell me how it works for you. Is it accurate? Is it too heavy to hold steady? And whatever else you find out about it," advised Bradley. "Then if you like it and decide to keep it, I will let you have it for half price – $25.00."

"I sure would like to do that for you, Mr. Bradley," said Walter, "if my uncle agrees." Stanley shook his head in the affirmative.

Bradley stuck his head out the door and called to his man. "Dave, give Walter a few boxes of shells, two of each size at no charge and mark down one of those new rifles out to Stanley on trial."

"Oh, thank you, Mr. Bradley," beamed Walter. "I will keep a good record of how it works and give you a good report."

"I know you will. That is why I am picking you to do this," said Bradley.

The orange sun dipped slowly toward the horizon behind them as Stanley and Walter drove on the country road toward the homestead. Stanley sat on a wooden crate at the front of the sleigh box directing the horses and Walter leaned against the tail gate watching the countryside slowly sliding by. In the snow-covered field on the other side of the barbwire fence he suddenly noticed the black ear tips of a jack rabbit.

"Look, Uncle Walter," he said quietly, pointing to the animal.

Stanley pulled back on the reins, bringing the horses to a slow gait.

"Try you new rifle," whispered Stanley. "See how it works. I'll keep on driving slowly so as not to frighten the rabbit. Use a long shell. It has more distance."

Walter reached into his pocket and took out three shells. He placed one in the chamber and two in the ammunition clip. The jack rabbit stood up on his hind legs, observing them curiously. Walter placed the stock of the rifle against his shoulder, leaned against the sleigh box and aimed. A crack rang out and the horses lunged forward, and stopped when Stanley pulled hard on the reins. The rabbit went down on the snow-covered stubble, kicking up its legs.

"You got him with the first shot, Walter," said Stanley proudly. "Unload the rifle and go out there and get him."

Walter climbed through the two strands of barbwire fence and picked up the dead rabbit by its hind legs. The animal's ears touched the ground as he carried it through the snow back to the sleigh."

"Say, that is a nice animal," said Stanley. "It should give you a nice pelt and all of us a fine dinner. You know, jack rabbits are really hares and they taste almost like chicken."

He took the rabbit from Walter and examined the carcass. Walter held the reins as the horses pranced nervously. He watched Stanley and wondered how anyone could be so knowledgeable about so many things.

"I see that you got this one in the head, too," said Stanley. "I guess there is not doubt about the accuracy of that rifle. Major Bradley will be pleased to hear that."

"I want to try it on some partridge. I'll watch for them in the trees along the road," said Walter.

"Change to short shells for partridges. It's fairly easy to get close to them," advised Stanley.

Stanley was right. For some reason, partridges and grouse choose dusk as their favorite time to sit on tree branches and observe the action around them and soon Walter had bagged several partridges and two grouse. The lingering twilight gave way to darkness and the large silvery moon lit up the clean white snow as the two travelers drove into the farmyard. Stanley and Walter unhooked the traces from the sleigh and led the horses into the barn.

Stanley removed the harnesses. The livestock in the barn were munching contentedly when they closed the barn door for the night. They returned to the sleigh with smug grins on their faces, removed the jack rabbit, six partridges and two grouse and carried them to Stanley's house.

"We had ourselves a great day," said Stanley to his wife. "It's almost too good to be true. First Walter got a good price for his pelts, and Mr. Bradley gave him a brand new rifle to try out, and look at what we gathered on our way home."

"I am proud of you two," said Anna, "but you had better help me with the skinning, plucking and cleaning of these creatures or I will serve them to you with their feathers and fur on. Take one of the grouse and a couple of partridges to your grandparents, Walter. They will enjoy a change from the tame meat. You go with him, Stanley. It's is kind of dark outside."

Weary, but still flushed with the excitement of the day, Walter related the events of the trip to the elder Berglunds. His grandmother checked the birds and felt their meaty breasts. She paused and looked at Stanley.

"This truly is a land of plenty," she said. "I remember you telling me about these things back in Lubicz, but I did not really believe everything you said. Now I do. You and Walter make a good pair."

"Yes, we sure do," said Walter proudly. "Uncle Stanley teaches me so many good things." He paused and looked at Stanley. "Do you think it would be OK if I called you dad?"

"Why sure, son. You know I have always treated you as my own son. So I would be proud to have you call me dad."

Stanley looked at his parents. Mrs. Berglund wiped a tear from her face.

CHAPTER 28

The news of Walter's coyote shooting incident and the acquisition of the latest model rifle swept through the one-roomed school house quickly and he became somewhat of a celebrity. It also gave rise to feelings of resentment among some of the older boys. During the lunch hour the boys gathered around Walter who explained the events leading up to the shooting of the animals and Major Bradley's surprise at his success.

"That is not so great," said one of the boys authoritatively. "I know someone who can shoot coyotes while holding the rifle in one hand and riding at full gallop."

"I could probably do that, too," countered Walter, "but my dad taught me to treat rifles with care and respect the animals. He told me that it is very important to kill cleanly and only take those animals that you can use."

"Ha! Listen to this big shot telling us what his father taught him. I didn't even know that you have a father. I heard that you are really one of those kind that people call bastards."

Walter put his sandwich back into a brown paper bag. His face turned white, then red.

"Now look here," he blurted out angrily, "maybe the man I call my dad is not my real one. But I am no bastard. I remember my parents and the day that they were killed. We have a picture of them. I could bring it to school and show it to you all."

"Anyone can get a picture," taunted the boy. "That does not prove anything. I still say that you are one of those you-know-whats."

Walter jumped to his feet and made a lunge for the bigger boy. The group opened up into a small circle. The adversaries clenched their fists and approached each other. Just then, the teacher, back from lunch at the teacher's residence, walked in the front door and the crowd dispersed.

"Is it wrong for me to call you dad and mom?" asked Walter at the supper table that night.

Stanley and Anna were startled by the boy's question. They looked at each other inquisitively.

"I told you the other day that it is fine for you to call me dad," said Stanley. "We have treated you like a son and your cousins have treated you like a brother. Why would you think that it is not right to call us mom and dad?"

"Someone at school today told me that I was one of those bastard children," answered Walter.

"Now look here, son," said Stanley. "I knew your father when he was living and so did your aunt Anna here. Your parents were wonderful people who came to an early death because of the madness of some crazy person to whom they never did any harm. Your father's friend Roman and his wife Lydia were there when you were born. We still have the letter that your real parents wrote when you were born and how happy they were when you arrived. They came here and visited us when you were just a baby. So don't let anybody tell you that no one knows who your parents are. And if they ask what your father looked like, you can tell them that he looked just like you."

"What really happened to them?" asked Walter.

"They were killed in a street car accident, as we explained to you before. But why? No one really knows because there was no proof of exactly what happened. We think it had something to do with the kind of work that your father was doing at the factory where he worked. It was during the war and many crazy things were going on in the world. Many of us think that your parents were the victims of some sort of international politics."

"What does international politics mean?" asked Walter.

"Over in Europe many of the countries are mad at each other because of things that happened a long time ago," explained Stanley. "So they try to get even by going to war against each other and doing all kinds of crazy things that we don't see in this part of the world. Sometimes innocent people like your parents get caught up in this craziness. But we are safe here, so there is no reason to worry about things like that here."

"Just remember that your parents were two beautiful people who really loved you while they were here," explained Anna. "Maybe you were too young to remember them well, but we knew them and we can tell you that you can be very proud of them both. But since they are gone, your uncle Stanley and I would like you to continue being our son as long as you wish. We love you as if you were our own."

"Thank you, mother and dad," said Walter softly. "Some day I will find out who took my real parents away from me and if I do, they will pay for it."

"It is not good to fight evil with evil, son" counseled Stanley. "We are here, away from it all. Maybe we should just forget it all and try to enjoy our new life here."

"How can any one forget a thing like that?" asked Walter with disbelief.

"Maybe you will when you get older. Pray to God that He will help you," said Anna.

In his prayers that night, Walter asked God to help him resolve the questions that filled his mind and to guide him in seeking the revenge which he wanted. The excitement of the day kept him awake after all the others in the house had fallen asleep. It was after midnight when he finally fell asleep and slid into the mysterious world of dreams.

In the front yard of his grandparents' cottage he saw a young man in the uniform of an army major, similar to the one he had seen in the photo of Mr. Bradley in the major's office. It was a bright, warm sunny day and many people milled about the yard. It was a special occasion. He realized that the young man in the uniform was himself. He stood in the middle of the group of people, preparing to leave. Out of the crowd certain people whom he recognized came toward him one at a time. The first one was an old lady with a limp.

"Do you remember me, Wladimar? I am your grandmother Klazcek. They killed my husband and crippled me. Don't ever forget that." She shook his hand and walked past him.

An older man with thinning hair and glasses came toward him. "They murdered your mother and your father," he said. Walter recognized Mr. Sutton from Toledo.

"Go and get them. You're a good shot," said Mr. Garwood as he shook Walter's hand.

The crowd parted and Walter's parents walked through the opening hand in hand. They came up to their son and stopped. "You are doing this for us and we are proud of you," said Erik. His mother embraced him and kissed him on the cheek.

Major Bradley rode up on a white horse. He was dressed in his uniform and held a riding stick. Walter mounted May and he and Major Bradley rode toward the gate.

"I'll stop them. I'll stop them," he looked back and shouted as they turned into the road and galloped away.

"Walter. Are you all right?" Anna was standing beside his bedstead, holding a lamp. "You were talking in your sleep so loudly that I was awakened."

"Yes. I am all right." He turned over and went to sleep.

All around him the colors were exceptionally bright and the sounds unusually clear as Walter walked toward the barn next morning. Stanley was examining a manger that needed repairs.

"Good morning, Walter. Do you know where the hammer might be?"

Walter walked to a spot under the trap door leading to the loft. He kicked over a covering of hay and exposed the hammer.

"How did you know where it was? Did you leave it there?" asked Stanley.

"No. I didn't leave it there. I just knew," answered Walter calmly.

Stanley looked at him and shook his head in disbelief.

~~~

The hot midsummer sun cut through the leafy canopy of the tall trees, allowing only flecks of light to penetrate to the ground below. Walter and Jon walked slowly down a grassy trail toward the small crystal clear lake, with May following behind them. The settlers called it Emerald Lake because its ripples shone so brightly in the sun. They tied May to a tree and walked across the narrow sand beach to the water's edge. They looked at the wooded island standing fortress-like more then a quarter of a mile away. Walter kicked off his shoes and socks and stuck his toes in the water. The water felt cool on his hot feet.

"This water is almost lukewarm. I think I'll go in for a dip," he said.

"Come on, Jon. I'll race you to the island."

"I can't swim that far," said Jon. "And neither can you, so don't even try it."

"Oh, yeah? Well, I swam almost to the island several times when I was here alone," boasted Walter. "I've always wanted to go all the way, but I didn't think I should when I was here all by myself. But with you here, I don't need to worry."

"Don't be silly, Walter. Of course, you do," said Jon apprehensively. "What can I do if you get into trouble? I don't even know how to swim well."

"Well, you can send May in after me," laughed Walter. "She's a pretty good swimmer."

Walter removed his clothes down to his shorts and dived into the water, swimming almost effortlessly away from the shore. At about a hundred yards out, he stopped and looked back at Jon who was pacing along the shore. He grinned and waved, then slid under the water, otter-like, and swam toward the island.

As the distance between Walter and the shore lengthened, Jon strained to keep his bobbing head in view. After several minutes the shimmering water obliterated the lurching swimmer and Jon felt a stone descend to the bottom of his stomach. His eyes strained to scan the water in the vicinity of the island, but there was no sign of movement. He wondered how he would break the news to the family if Walter failed to return. Suddenly he caught sight of a figure against the dark green foliage on the island, waving his arms jubilantly. Jon's heart pounded wildly inside his chest. A minute or so later, the figure on the island moved toward the water and disappeared.

Feeling helpless and dejected, Jon slumped on a stone near the edge of the beach and gazed across the water. There was no sign of any movement. In his head, he rehearsed the news-breaking story that he would take back to his parents and imagined their reaction upon hearing it. They would probably want to know why he did not try to save his cousin. He stood up slowly and walked to the edge of the water, shading his eyes with his hand. A flock of mud hens swam across his line of vision, alternatively submerging and reappearing at different locations. Only mud hens could do a thing like that, he reasoned. Some distance behind the mud hens, a black speck appeared then disappeared again. Jon though it was another mud hen or a muskrat, but it kept getting larger as it drew closer and Jon knew that it was Walter's head that he was watching. He waved frantically and Walter lifted an arm out of the water and acknowledged the signal.

Propelling himself gracefully through the water with his arms and legs, Walter approached the water's edge, then stood up and walked the rest of the way to the beach. He observed Jon's worried look and laughed.

"What's that matter, Jon? Did you think that I couldn't do it?"

"I've never seen anyone swim like that, Walter," said Jon. "Where did you learn to swim like that and who taught you?"

"Right here in this water in front of us," explained Walter. "No one taught me. It seemed to come natural. Like walking."

"You're lucky, Walter," said Jon. "Not too many people can swim like that."

Walter pulled his clothes on over his wet shorts and untied the pony. They walked toward an opening in the trees where the trail began, May snorting contentedly as she followed the boys.

"Let's come back tomorrow and I'll show you how well May can swim," said Walter with a mischievous look in his eyes.

"You'd better teach her how to swim because you might need her sometime when you are here alone," quipped Jon.

~~~

The golden sheaves, gathered into small piles called stooks by the local farmers, formed straight lines resembling spokes from the edge of the field to the center. Heavy heads of grain leaned against each other in the stooks waiting for the threshing crews' wagons to load them up and take them to the stationary threshing machine. The 1927 growing season had been one of the best in several years and the harvest was well advanced even though September had just arrived. As they had done for the past several years, Stanley and his neighbors were part of the Garwood "outfit', hauling sheaves to Garwood's thresher as it moved from farm to farm, in exchange for getting their own fields threshed.

The "outfit" as the machine and its men and wagons were referred to in the community was now located on the farm next to the Berglunds. Stanley arrived home after dark and announced that the machine would be at the Berglund farms the day after tomorrow. This meant that supplies would have to be obtained from town to feed ten-man threshing crew. Since Stanley was part of the crew and their two older sons were hired out to other outfits, Axel was the only one left to drive into Ralston and pick up the supplies. He agreed to leave early next morning and be back in the afternoon.

Sounds of wagons rolling across the grain fields cut through the still morning air as Axel climbed into the buggy for his trip to Ralston. Only a small sprinkling of dew had covered the outside of the sheaves during the night and they would be dry enough for threshing shortly after the sun climbed over the horizon. Whistles from the smoke belching steam engines, which drove the threshing machines, working at a number of neighboring farms, penetrated the air calling the crews to the fields for another day of labor. Huge stacks of new straw, dotting the horizon like miniature golden mountains, marked the farms where the threshing was already completed. Herds of cattle which had been turned loose into the harvested fields gleaned the leftovers contentedly. The air was filled with the smells of wood smoke, steam, hot oil and new straw. Axel scanned the countryside as he drove along the road and smiled happily.

At Ralston, rows of wagons and the occasional motor truck lined up in front of the four grain elevators waiting to discharge their loads of grain into the grated chasms leading to the bowels of the huge bins. Farmers and businessmen greeted each other on the main street and hurried on their way.

As long as the weather remained clear and warm, there was little time for anything except completing the harvest.

Axel and the store clerk carried the boxes of groceries out of Bradley's General Store and placed them in the back of the buggy. The horses which had been drowsing contentedly at the hitching rail were untied and turned in the direction of the Berglund homestead. Warmed by the early afternoon sun, the team loped lazily along the narrow country road. Up in the front seat of the vehicle Axel's head bobbed as he dozed and awoke sporadically. One of the reins dropped out of his loosely clasped hand, slipped off the dashboard and hung loosely over the vehicle's double tree. Familiar with the route, the team continued unguided in a slow steady gait toward the homestead and Axel fell into a deeper slumber.

Flanked on both sides by shimmering aspen and overhanging willows, the dry dirt road meandered through the tunnel-like opening on its way to the open area up ahead. Inside the wooded bluff a large male elk selected and ate the choicest leaves off the wild raspberry bushes. He lifted his great antlered head and smelled the air. His nostrils flared as the team approached.

The animal crashed through the thick bushes and ran across the road in front of the horses. The team reared back and broke into a gallop, heading toward the clearing. Axel awoke abruptly and not realizing that he had only one rein in his hand he pulled hard to restrain the team. The tug on the horses' bits steered them off the road and across a stone-filled hollow. The right front wheel crashed against a large boulder and shattered. Axel slid out of the lopsided seat and fell to the ground, his head striking the boulder as he landed. He laid still. The horses, further frightened by the disabled vehicle, galloped uncontrolled in a large circle. They came to rest against a fence, still hitched to the three wheeled vehicle, sweating and bleeding from the barbed wire cuts.

A black Model T Ford cautiously picked its way along the narrow trail, stirring up small clouds of dust. Jim Garwood and his foreman were returning from checking up on some livestock in the far pasture. Their eyes caught sight of the two horses and the broken vehicle hard against the fence. Garwood stopped the car and they ran toward the team.

"That's the Berglunds' team," shouted Garwood. "Let's find the driver. He may be hurt."

They followed the drag marks left by the disabled vehicle and came to the small hollow. Axel lay slumped alongside the boulder, his face covered with blood from a gash in his head.

"Good God. That's Axel," said Garwood. "He seems to be badly hurt. Let's get him to the hospital in Ralston quickly. I'll get the car. You stay here with him."

Garwood ran back to the Ford and drove it close to the hollow. He laid a blanket in the back seat and they lifted the unconscious man into the car. The rancher took off his jacket, folded it and placed it under Axel's injured head.

"We have to get him there fast," he said to the foreman. "You sit in the back seat with him and I'll try to drive as smoothly as possible. We may still make it in time."

~~~

A cold front moved in suddenly from the northwest as Garwood and the foreman returned to the stranded horses. Several other passersby had already untangled the team and tied them separately to a fence post. Garwood drove back to the Berglund homestead to break the news, while another neighbor offered to lead the horses back.

The concrete steps leading up to the front door of the Grey Nuns Hospital glistened from the drizzle which had already begun. Stanley pushed open the heavy wooden door and held it open for his mother and Anna. The heady smell of disinfectant and chloroform greeted them as they entered the quiet corridor of the hospital. Because of the heavy dark cloud that had moved in, the lamps had to be lit earlier than they would have been on a clear day. The hospital sisters, clad in glistening starched white habits and wearing crucifixes moved silently through the dimly lit hallways. One of them escorted the Berglunds to the intensive care ward. She stayed as they gathered around his bed and looked gravely into Axel's ashen face.

Mrs. Berglund took her husband's hand and put her face close to his.

"This is me, your wife. Don't you recognize me?" she said softly.

Axel, his head covered with bandages, remained still and his face expressionless. They looked helplessly at the sister standing nearby.

"I think that we had better get the priest," she said in a solemn voice. "The doctor says that he may not live through the night."

Mrs. Berglund and Anna cried softly as the priest solemnly read the last rites. The doctor entered the room and checked Axel's pulse and heart beat. His face was drawn as he nodded his head.

"He is low and getting worse," he said.

"Is this what he came half ways around the world for?" sobbed an anguished Mrs. Berglund. "To die without even seeing his family for the last time."

"Be thankful mother," consoled Stanley. "He was a good man and he lived a full and honorable life, enjoying every moment of it. If he goes now, I know that he will leave without regrets."

Axel's breathing grew weaker and weaker. The doctor removed his hand from Axel's pulse at ten forty five and pronounced him dead. They filed out of the hospital room sobbing. Jim Garwood and Major Bradley sat in the waiting room as they entered.

"Is he gone?" asked Garwood.

"Yes," answered Stanley. "About ten minutes ago."

"He was a good and peaceful man," said Major Bradley.

CHAPTER 29

The Thirties descended upon the now prosperous settlements with a vengeance, bringing poor crops and low prices, and shattering the dreams that were about to be fulfilled. Through the hunting prowess which he had developed, Walter was able to keep the Berglund family in meat during the first winter of the Depression. The skins from the muskrats, weasels and rabbits which he and Jon hunted and trapped helped to provide the cash with which to buy clothing and staples for the household. Because the one-roomed school offered courses only up to Grade 8, both boys were now enrolled in correspondence courses. In the fall Walter helped with the harvest at the Garwood Ranch while Stanley and Jon worked on the threshing crew and Anna harvested and put away the vegetables from the garden which she had nurtured with pails of water from a nearby slough.

As the winter wore on, they hoped that the worst was over and the new year would bring a return to the good times of the twenties, but this was not to be. The summer of 1932 was parching dry and hot. A heavy frost in the spring had killed most of the crops and gardens. Only by reseeding and hauling water to the garden in barrels were they able to grow a few potatoes, cabbages and root crops. Stanley spent the Sunday afternoon walking through the fields and meadows. He returned to the house and sat beside the kitchen table, deep in thought.

"It doesn't look good, does it, dad?" remarked Walter.

"If things don't get any worse, we should have enough feed for the livestock, thanks to the wild hay from the low lying meadows. Money is going to be even scarcer than it was last winter. I noticed that there are much fewer muskrat houses because of the sloughs drying up. I hope the rabbit population stays up," explained Stanley. He picked up the Polish language newspaper and glanced at it. Walter watched him from across the table, then got up and walked around and stood behind Stanley.

"I'll try and get a job," he said. "Maybe I can go to one of those big cities and find work. I'll do anything. I don't care how hard or dirty the work is."

Stanley laid down the newspaper and looked up at Walter. "I know that you really mean what you are saying, son, and I hate to disappoint you, but things in the cities are worse than here. At least here we have enough to eat, even though we don't have any money." He lifted the newspaper off the table and pointed to the headline. "It says that there are thousands of unemployed people in the big cities of North America who don't know where their next meal is coming from."

Walter studied the paper over Stanley's shoulder. He had learned to read Polish as a child from his grandmother and the local priest. "Turn to the want ads, dad. You never know. There might just be something there."

Stanley ran his finger down the few advertisements under Help Wanted.

Most of them were for farm laborers to work for board and room and a "generous allowance."

"We are not that hard up yet," snapped Stanley.

He began to close the newspaper when he noticed a small display ad up in the corner of an inside page. "Now here is something interesting," he mused. "It's an ad placed by the Polish government."

"Why would the Polish government want to advertise here?" asked Walter. "What does it say?"

"It says that Poland would like former residents of that country and their families now living in other countries to offer their aid in the reconstruction of Poland's economy and in the maintenance of its security. And do you know whose name is given here as the man to contact? Jan Sliworski. Hey. I know that man. He was at your parents' wedding in Krakow and your father told me that he was on the boat that took him out of Torun."

Stanley was excited at his discovery. "Look Anna," he called to his wife. "Remember that young Major Sliworski who was at Erik's and Angela's wedding in Krakow? He has an advertisement in the Polish paper asking people to help the old country in some way."

"Sliworski? Oh, yes. He was that skinny fellow from Warsaw, a friend of Bashinski. There was something mysterious about that man. I didn't feel good when he was around," Anna recalled. "What kind of help can we give them from here? We have enough problems of our own. Anyway, the reason we came here was to get away from their problems."

"I am not saying that we should help them, Anna. It's just that I was so surprised to see Sliworski's name in a paper away out here."

Walter studied the advertisement curiously. "I wonder what they mean by maintenance of security?" he asked.

"Probably has something to do with the army," said Stanley after rereading the ad. "I have been reading a lot lately about the growing fear around Europe that some countries are preparing for another war. Maybe Poland is doing the same."

"Who would they fight against if there was a war?" asked Walter.

"I suppose it will be their age-old enemies, Germany and Russia, I guess. Who else?"

"Germany? That is where they took my father, wasn't it?" asked Walter.

"Prussia, really," corrected Stanley. "But that is almost the same thing. They were always Poland's worst enemies. They go for each other's throats every time there is a war in Europe."

Walter sat down, deep in thought. Scenes from the dream of seven summers ago flashed through his mind. He saw himself in uniform and Major Bradley mounted on a white horse. He recalled his maternal grandmother's statement that "they killed my husband," and his parents' words that he should do it for them. What was it that they wanted him to do? Then suddenly everything became very clear. This could be his opportunity to seek the revenge for his parents' deaths that he promised himself he would do. He jumped up with excitement.

"I'll go, dad. Write a letter to Sliworski for me in Polish and tell him that I am willing to help them out."

"Walter, you must be out of your mind. What do you know about that cursed part of the world?" scolded Anna. "Ask us. We can tell you many things about it and they are not good. Forget it. I will not let you go."

"She is right. Just think about it for a minute," cautioned Stanley. "What makes you think that they will take you? You are so young, with so little experience. They probably want veterans and people experienced in certain things."

"I have a lot of experience," said Walter confidently. "I can ride a horse, hunt, and swim like an otter. I consider myself a hard worker, and I am the best shot in the whole community. If you don't write the letter, dad, I will do it myself."

"You are so strong headed, Walter. You remind me of my brother – your father. He was the same. Whenever he got an idea, there was no stopping him," said Stanley.

"Yes. And look what happened to him," Anna reminded them.

"What happened to Erik really had nothing to do with his sense of determination, Anna. It was just an unfortunate accident," said Stanley.

"Sure," said Anna sarcastically. "People get blown up in street cars every day."

"I'll tell you what, Walter," suggested Stanley. "I was planning to go to town tomorrow. You can come with me and we can call on Major Bradley and show him this advertisement. He knows about things like this because he was a high ranking officer in the Great War. Maybe he can tell us what it means."

"Stanley," said Anna sternly, "if something happens to the boy, I will never let you forget it."

"He is twenty years old, Anna, and has a mind of his own," said Stanley. "He can't stay with us all his life."

~~~

One had to stretch the imagination to accept that the young officer in the photo on the shelf behind Major Bradley was the same person who now leaned back in his leather chair intently surveying Stanley and Walter. His square jaw and broad forehead still carried the marks of the younger man, but his light auburn hair was thinning and streaked with gray and the bright blue eyes in the photo shone with less brilliance in the older man. Although his grooming and posture still bore witness to the military discipline he had once acquired, his waist line attested to the more sedentary life of a businessman.

Major Bradley continued his involvement with the military throughout the post-war years. As a member of the army reserve, he spent several weeks each year at camp and at military headquarters and was the commanding officer of the district reserve units. Rumors abounded about his access to people in high places and that he and his brother were the king's own emissaries in the new settlement. But below the surface of this military-like aloofness was a sympathetic man, eager to help the struggling uneducated homesteaders with advice and even money and credit to tide them over difficult periods. Above all, he recognized initiative, hard work and self-discipline.

The major asked Stanley to read and translate the words in the advertisement and nodded sagely as he listened to the translation.

"Yes. I think I know what that means," he said. "It's better that you don't become involved in things like that, Walter."

Walter's face reflected his disappointment. He sat up straight in the heavy wooden captain's chair.

"I am going to find a way to get revenge for my parents' death even if I have to do it by myself," he said. "I don't know much about these things and I need your advice, Mr. Bradley. So tell me straight. Do you think that they can use someone like me?"

Major Bradley was somewhat taken aback. He scratched his forehead and peered into the distance. His gaze turned to Walter and he studied the young man.

"If this means what I think it does, then you do have some qualities about you that would be valuable for that type of work. You are young and strong and you speak several languages. You are also an excellent marksman with small firearms and a strong swimmer. But most important of all, you are a determined young man and this can make up for many other shortcomings."

"I want to try it," said Walter with great determination. "Can you help to get them to consider me? You know that Major Sliworski knew my parents."

Stanley's eyes shifted between Walter and the major as he followed their conversation. Major Bradley looked at him over his glasses and Stanley nodded in the affirmative.

"There is much more to this than you can ever imagine, Walter. Why don't you let me write a few letters, including one to Mr. Sliworski and find out what exactly what this is all about and how a person like you could fit into the whole thing," suggested the major. "Perhaps, if I am involved in it, things will open up a bit better for you. Give me a month or so and I will let you know what I find out."

~~~

Several light showers had saved a few fields from the extreme drought and heat and some activities were underway to salvage the lean harvest. In preparation for cutting and binding the standing grain, Stanley and Walter drove to Ralston to pick up a supply of binder twine.

"Mr. Bradley wants to see you and Walter in his office," said the clerk to Stanley when they arrived at the counter."

The major reached into his desk drawer and brought out some letters as

Stanley and Walter entered his office. He picked out an official looking envelope.

"Well, fellows, it's here and it's exactly what I thought it would be."

"Will they take me?" asked Walter, his voice exuding excitement.

Major Bradley stood up and closed the office door. He sat down and looked at the letter and at Walter.

"I don't know how to put this," he said, "but the job, if you get it, would be far from anything ordinary."

"I'll do anything. Just give me a chance," pleaded Walter.

"OK, Walter. I'll give it to you straight. What Sliworski needs is a select group of strong, young men with a good knowledge of English, Polish and German to bring information out of Germany on what is happening in that country. There is reason to believe that Germany, under pressure from that new man Adolph Hitler and his National Socialist Party, is intent upon rearming itself. They are doing this in spite of the conditions of the Treaty of Versailles which prohibits German rearmament and this is making other countries, including Poland, pretty nervous. In other words, Walter, what they need are some spies," concluded the major.

"I can speak all those languages," said Walter. "I'll do anything to get at those bastards for what they did to my parents. Please, Mr. Bradley. Would you help me get the job?" pleaded Walter.

"Walter, you cannot go around accusing people for what happened to your parents. There never was any proof of anything," said Stanley.

"That is good advice," said Major Bradley. "If you were to go, it would be better if you went with the idea of serving your own country and the Empire, than to go in to avenge something."

"I don't understand," said Walter. "I thought this job was with Sliworski. What has that got to do with serving Canada and the British Empire?"

"That is a long story which will become clearer if you are accepted," explained Bradley. He turned to Stanley. "Well Stanley, it looks like this young fellow is determined to go ahead with this. If you agree, I will write my contacts in Ottawa, Washington and London, as well as to Mr. Sliworski. This could cut a lot of corners for Walter and make it easier and faster."

"I don't think that anything that you or I can do will make him change his mind," said Stanley. "So maybe it would be better if we make things easier for him. I would appreciate any help that you can give him."

"All right fellows. Leave it to me," said Bradley. "This will take another few weeks. Keep yourself in good shape, Walter, because you are going to need it."

~~~

After two weeks of warm dry weather and twelve-hour working days, the threshing crew on the Garwood outfit nursed their aching muscles and wrists and prayed for rain. The dry summer had kept the straw short, but the heads were well filled and the sheaves heavy. It took a great many of these small sheaves too fill a wagon load and there were no rests between trips to the field and back to the threshing machine. Walter's muscles were turning hard and his skin brown and leathery. The prospect of a late morning in bed now seemed like a luxurious memory from a less demanding time. But by late Saturday afternoon a large dark cloud moved in quickly from the west and by the time the crew came into the house for supper the rain had started to fall.

The soft bed in the loft of his grandparents' house soothed his aching muscles and weary bones. It was a welcome change from the hard, thinly covered beds in the drafty bunkhouses where the crew had spent the last ten nights. The task of getting out of bed to accompany the family to the nearby country church challenged every fiber of his aching body. After the Sunday morning mass, Laura had heard a group of young people discussing that a harvest dance was being held at the school that night. They asked Laura if she and Walter were coming and she rushed to tell Walter.

"They all want you to come and call the square dances," she announced.

"Ooh," groaned Walter, "I don't know if my body will let me stay up that late."

"Aw, come on Walter," she insisted.   "As soon as you start moving about, your muscles will loosen up. Also, Jon told me he would like you to teach him how to handle May, in case you should go away soon."

After a late breakfast, the two youths led May toward the pasture near the creek. This would be the best place to get the filly used to a new master because it was part of her daily routine to be ridden across the creek to the pasture, Walter explained. Since Jon now had his own horse, he had not ridden May for several years. At the gate to the pasture, they stopped and Jon climbed into the saddle. Walter motioned to him to head for the shallow crossing through the creek. Jon brought May to a slow gallop as they approached the crossing and leaned forward when they came to the edge, anticipating the pony's jump across the water. Instead the filly stopped suddenly and Jon flew over her head into the water. He emerged wet, muddy and embarrassed, wiping his face with the sleeve of his shirt. A short distance away, Walter was bent over in laughter.

"OK if you're so smart, why don't you do it," shouted Jon.

Walter called to May and the filly walked toward him. He got into the saddle and rode toward the creek. Near the edge he patted the filly gently on the neck and she jumped over the water easily. He turned May around and jumped over the creek again.

"First lesson, Jon," said Walter sliding out of the saddle. "Always show this pony that you have confidence in her and that you trust her. Before starting the jump, pat her on the neck and tell her she can do it. If you have any doubts, the horse will feel it and live up to them. Now get up and try again."

Jon mounted May cautiously and rode around for a few seconds. He pointing the filly toward the creek, patted her neck and spoke to her quietly. May jumped easily to the other side. He turned her around and repeated the feat.

"You ride May home and wash up. I'll walk back because I need to loosen up my joints," explained Walter to his astonished cousin. "Tell Laura that I will be going to the dance tonight."

The strains of fiddle and guitar music and the stomping of many feet floated through the open window and into the still evening air as Walter and Laura approached the school house. The harvest dance had already begun. In front of the white wooden building were several automobiles and beside the small barn a number of buggies and other rigs were left where the horses were unhitched and taken into the barn.

Walter and Laura entered the school house just as the first dance was ending. The fiddle player motioned to Walter to come forward and they conferred briefly. He drew his bow across the instrument and announced that the next dance would be a square dance. Walter stood in the middle of the floor to call. Four circles quickly formed and the music began.

"Join you hands and circle right," called Walter when the dancers were ready and the music began. "Swing you partner. Allemande left." Music and laughter rang through the building as the bystanders clapped and cheered the dancers on. When the dance was over, the ladies sat down exhausted and the men filed out the front door for fresh air.

"That was a good dance," said Walter when it was all over and they walked along the trail guided by the beam of a flashlight. "I am going to miss these good times if I leave."

"Yes, Walter," said Laura, "and we will miss you too. There is no one else around here who can call a square dance quite like you can."

~~~

Jim Garwood came around Sunday evening to say that the sheaves were still wet and there would be no threshing until Tuesday morning, if the weather stayed fair and dry. Monday after breakfast, Walter followed the narrow well-beaten path through the trees to the old house. His grandmother was in the vegetable garden. She lifted her head and gazed at Walter.

"Oh my good Lord," she gasped. "It is you. As you were walking down that path I was sure that it was your father Erik who was coming toward me. You looked just like he did on that last day when I saw him in our old village of Lubicz. May God have mercy on his soul."

Walter set up a wooden crate and placed it beside where his grandmother was pulling up carrots.

"Sit down grandma. I have not talked to you for a long time. I have been thinking a lot about you folks when you were back in the old country and how hard things must have been for you at times."

His grandmother threw down a bunch of carrots, wiped her hands on her apron and sat down on the crate.

"Yes, Walter. I know what you are going to say. Your uncle had already told me and I am proud of you. It is easy to forget about one's roots when a person has lived here for a while, but I never will and I was glad to hear that you haven't either." She paused, picked up a carrot and rubbed it with her hand. "At one time our family was honored and respected in Poland," she continued. "We had friends in high places and had everything we wanted, but by and by everything was gone – position, money, honor and for a while even our country. We made many sacrifices. My final sacrifice was my son, an innocent lamb slaughtered by our enemies."

She noted the surprise in her grandson's face and stopped. Walter turned over a pail and sat on it. "Why grandma, I didn't know that you had such strong feelings about things like that," he said.

"Since you grandfather has gone, I hardly ever talk about my feelings anymore. Stanley and Anna have no interest in talking about the past. They say that those times are gone forever and that things are different here. I hope they are right. That is what Erik thought, too."

"I never told you about this, grandma," confided Walter, "but seven years ago I had a dream which I never forgot. In it, several people, including my other grandmother Klazcek urged me to go after my parents' killers. I also saw my parents in that dream and they told me the same thing. That dream has always stayed with me and made me want to do what I am going to do now. I am not doing it for Poland or anyone else, just for the memory of my parents."

"It was the Lord speaking to you, Wladimar. Do not be afraid of dreams. They are our messages from the other place. Go and do His will, even if it means smiting your enemies. You have my blessing."

"Thank you, grandma. I am sorry that I did not get to know this part of you earlier," said Walter. He took her wrinkled hand and kissed it.

"Go in peace my brave and wise Wladimar," she said. "We will talk more about it when you get back."

A period of warm, dry weather followed the weekend rain and by the middle of the following week only one day of threshing remained. Walter was pitching sheaves into the thresher when Jim Garwood drove up alongside the steam tractor. He saw Walter and walked to the back of the rack and climbed up.

"I just came back from town, Walter," he shouted above the noise of the machine. "Major Bradley says that he wants to see you."

"If you see him, tell him that I will be there the day after tomorrow. We should be all finished threshing by then."

Garwood climbed down and Walter threw the remaining sheaves into the machine then drove away for another load.

~~~

Stanley was out in the far corner of the farm plowing the newly harvested field when Walter drove the team and wagon into the yard. He unhitched the horses from the wagon, removed their harness and then turned them out into the farmyard. Relishing their new-found freedom, the horses shook themselves and rolled on the ground. Arching their necks, they ran several times around the farmyard before making their way to the trough for a drink of water. Walter carried his roll of bedding into the house and told Anna that he was going into town on horseback to see Mr. Bradley. He called May and placed the saddle on her back and rode out toward Ralston.

"Someone out there must have done some fast work for us," Bradley announced when Walter entered the office. "I received a telegram from Washington two days ago. Seems that Colonel Sliworski has arranged for you to spend some time around Washington before you go overseas."

"You mean that I am accepted?" blurted Walter.

"If you can pass the medical, I think you're in," replied Bradley. "You may be able to get that today. I'll give Dr. Hay a call now to see if he can take you."

The major rang the operator and asked for Dr. Hay's number. The doctor answered and agreed to see Walter in half an hour.

"Take this form with you and ask the doctor to fill in the information that is asked for, and bring it back to me. I will telegraph the information to Washington and you will know in a day or two if and when you will be leaving."

"You have been a real help to me, Mr. Bradley," said Walter as he was leaving to see Dr. Hay. "I don't know how to thank you."

"I am pleased to be of help. After all, there are not many people who would do this sort of thing, so I have more than a passing interest in you."

Dr. Hay grunted and uttered unintelligible monosyllables as he weighed Walter, checked his eyes and throat, thumped his chest with his curved finger, placed his stethoscope at various points and listened to his chest and back, then took his blood pressure.

"You're strong as horse and spry as a deer, young man," the doctor concluded as he completed the form which Walter had brought with him. "Take this to Major Bradley and good luck, Walter. Judging by the look of that form, you may need it. It looks mighty important." He watched Walter as he rolled down his sleeves and did up his shirt, and shook his head in disbelief. "It's hard to believe that you are the same skinny little runt that I examined when you arrived here from the States a few years ago."

"Seventeen years ago," Walter reminded him. "That was away back in 1916."

"To you young whipper-snappers that may seem like a long time ago, but for us old fellows it seems like yesterday. Take care of yourself, son. I don't want to have to mend you up when you get back."

"I will," Walter promised. The doctor signed the form and handed it to Walter.

Major Bradley examined the document and folded it carefully. He placed it in a heavy brown envelope together with a number of other papers. "Pack your things and be ready to leave, Walter. I'll send a telegram to Washington and tell them that you are all set. They'll send the instructions. Come back Friday. I should have a response by then."

"Thank you, sir. I'll be in Friday, for sure," said Walter, backing up toward the door.

"Just one more thing, Walter." Bradley adjusted his glasses down on the bridge of his nose and looked at Walter standing near the door. "I hope you have not told anyone about this."

"Only my family knows about it, and maybe Mr. Garwood," said Walter.

"Good," replied Bradley. "I think the time has come for us to watch every word that we say about this to anyone. This is for your own good and all this will be drilled into you when you begin your training. So you may as well start preparing now."

"No one will know a thing, sir," promised Walter.

The yellow and orange leaves shone brilliantly in the setting sun as Walter and May made their way along the country road. May's hoofs kicked up the soft fallen leaves as she followed the tree-lined trail on the way to the homestead. A melancholy mood overtook Walter as he rode past the familiar things that had been an intimate part of his life. He felt that they were now ignoring him in return for being abandoned. The sadness of leaving the familiar landscape behind was overcome by the excitement of beginning a new life which he pictured as full of adventure and surprises. Darkness brought a welcome end to the taunting call of the surroundings and left him free to contemplate the new life to which he was being drawn. May, possessing an instinct to which only nature's creatures have access, sensed what was about to happen and continued toward the lighted windows in the distance with her head hanging below her shoulders.

"Where can I say that you have gone when the people at the dance ask about you?" fretted Laura. "You know that there is no one else that they want to call the square dances."

"We'll just tell the neighbors that he is gone to the city to look for a job because there is nothing to do around here in the winter time." suggested her mother.

"Yes, that is a good idea," agreed Stanley. "A lot of young men from here are going to Hamilton and Toronto to try to find work in factories these days. Why don't we say that Walter has done the same?"

"Except that we want to say that he is in some city where no one else has gone to," said Anna. "It will seem odd if he goes to the same place as the others and no one can find him there. They will soon begin to talk about that around here."

"I think I have a good idea," said Stanley. "Why don't we say that he went to Windsor to work in the car factory. That's where you picked him up in the first place."

"Also where that darned dog piddled on me," laughed Walter. "But that seems like as good a place as any because I don't know of anyone from around here who has gone there"

~~~

"I hope that you are ready to leave," announced Bradley when Walter stepped into his office Friday, "because they want you to be there next Thursday. That's when the next group of volunteers begins training. You will take your basic training in the Washington area. After that, if you make the grade, you will go to a camp whose location I am not free to divulge. But anyway, we have to move fast to get you there on time. I have been giving it some thought and if you leave here on the Sunday night *Flyer* from Cathcart, you should arrive in Washington some time Wednesday. I'll drive you to the train."

"I am ready to leave anytime," said Walter. "Threshing is all over and I was just waiting for your instructions. I have enough money saved to pay my fare and for a hotel room."

"As of Sunday night, you will not need to worry about expenses, explained Bradley. "I will have your ticket to Washington and all your papers ready for you. Once you get to Washington you will be staying at the *Greenborough Hotel* where a Mr. Roberts will meet you. After that you will be in his charge."

"I'll be here Sunday. Just name the time, Mr. Bradley," said Walter excitedly.

"Not later than eight o'clock in the evening," said Bradley. He surveyed Walter from behind his large wooden desk. "Walter, do you have any good clothes for traveling in?" he asked.

"Oh yes," answered Walter. "I will wear my Sunday clothes. The same ones that I wear to church."

"That's great, Walter," said Bradley, "but you should really have a spare outfit. I'll see if we can do something about that." He looked out the door and called over a clerk from the men's clothing department.

"Choose a nice outfit for Mr. Berglund from our stock out there," he instructed the clerk. "Give him a nice suit for traveling; a shirt, shoes, socks, tie, shorts; the works. Make that two shirts and three pairs of socks. He'll need a change. Put all that on a bill and bring it to me."

Sunday after church the family and close friends sat down to a farewell dinner for Walter. His grandmother offered a prayer in Polish for good fortune and a safe return. Stanley and Mr. Garwood drank toasts to his future and wished him well in his new occupation. They tried to make light conversation, but the heaviness in their hearts surfaced in the knowledge that yet another member of the family was leaving to take on a strange task.

"This reminds me of those Sundays in Lubicz when Erik would come home and then have to return to Torun," recalled Anna.

"Yes, except that Erik was a prisoner," said Stanley. "He had no choice. He had to return. With Walter it is different. He is going of his own free will."

"It is all part of the same curse," said Mrs. Berglund in Polish. "It started with Adam and Eve and will be with us forever. It's the price we have to pay for being humans."

"Things are changing, mama," said Stanley. "People are becoming more civilized."

"Man will never become civilized. He is too evil. In the days that are coming, man's true wickedness will be revealed. He has to sink even further before he starts to climb back up again. But I am glad that I will not be here when that happens."

"Now wait, mama," said Stanley. "You are talking like we were still back in Europe before the Great War. That war taught everyone a lot of things about hate and destruction. We are now in new and better times."

"That was the first day of man's road to redemption. Our first lesson. The second day is yet to come and it is not too far away. It will decide whether a third day will be necessary. And if it is, that will be our Armageddon," prophesied his mother.

"Mother is feeling sad," Stanley explained to Mr. Garwood. "She thinks that bad things are about to happen."

A silence fell over all those around the table and they continued eating in silence.

"Well, enough of this heaviness," said Stanley with exaggerated joviality. "This is a happy occasion. It is the beginning of a new life for Walter. Let us all be happy for him. Pass the whiskey and we'll have another toast, Mr. Garwood."

"You take good care of May," said Walter to Jon while the men toasted each other. "Don't let her give you too many mud baths."

They laughed at the recollection of Jon's misadventure in trying to jump across the creek on May. The talk turned to horses and crops and the party assumed a more cheerful mood.

Walter went upstairs and changed into the clothes that Major Bradley had given him. Everyone thought that he looked like a city slicker, except for his weather beaten face and calloused hands. Soon the time arrived for Garwood to drive Walter to Ralston.

"They were sad to see me go," said Walter to Garwood as they drove along the road to Ralston. "But I am too excited to be sad."

Walter threw his cardboard suitcase into the trunk of Major Bradley's new Chevrolet. The car smelled good and he sank contentedly into the soft velour seat. The Depression must be good for merchants, thought Walter.

The *Flyer* pulled into the Cathcart station on schedule at midnight. Only two more people boarded the train with Walter. As the train pulled out of the station, Walter looked out of the window. Major Bradley was standing on the platform, smiling. Walter had not seen Bradley smile very often. Walter waved as the window beside which he was sitting passed by where Major Bradley was standing. The major snapped to attention and saluted.

CHAPTER 30

The *Greenborough Hotel* was one of those old hotels that had seen better days, but had not yet lost all its charm. The room assigned to Walter smelled of stale tobacco smoke and moth balls. On the narrow double bed two sterile looking pillows overlapped the white sheet whose ends were folded over the green blanket. A small ornate wooden table with cigarette burns around the edges had a drawer which held a Gideon Bible and hotel stationery. Above it on the faded wall was a picture of a scene from the American Civil War with drawings of the Star Spangled Banner on the left side and the Confederate flag on the right. A pole lamp with a yellowed shade stood close to the bed. Walter opened the window and sat down on the faded greenish brown upholstered chair. From the street below came the sounds of traffic and people intently going about their business. The street sounds clashed with the silence of the room and Walter felt the pangs of loneliness for the first time. He took some of the hotel stationery and sat down to write a letter home describing his trip.

His mind went back to Sunday night when Major Bradley drove him to Cathcart and wished him well. Then the train arrived on time and stopped only long enough to allow him and two other passengers to get on board. The fast train to Winnipeg sped through the sleeping towns and villages and arrived in the city in time for an early breakfast. The trans-continental for Toronto left at eight o'clock that same morning. The long trip across the seemingly endless pre-Cambrian shield with its muskeg, sparkling lakes and streams, and cascading currents swallowed up the next 24 hours. He bought ham sandwiches on white bread and coffee because he was not sure if he would be allowed to eat in the dining car. By the time he arrived in Toronto and changed trains to go to Detroit, he felt like a seasoned traveler. The papers which Major Bradley had provided him seemed to impress the American customs and immigration officers when he crossed the border and they phoned a man who came and accompanied him to the station for the last leg of his trip to Washington. He had arrived at the hotel this afternoon and was sitting in his room waiting for someone to contact him as Mr. Bradley had promised.

He put down his pen and gazed at the picture of the Civil War. A knock on the door startled him and Walter quickly put the letter into the drawer and cautiously opened the door. A short bald man in brown uniform stood in the hallway with a portable tea table.

"Room service! May I come in?" he announced.

He removed the white linen cover and exposed a stainless steel tea pot, matching cream and sugar containers, a plate of small mixed sandwiches and two tea cups. Walter reached for his billfold.

"This had all been paid for, thank you."

"But there are two tea cups. I am all alone," said Walter.

"Oh yes. I forgot to tell you. The other one is for Mr. Roberts. He will be along in a few minutes. Enjoy your stay here, Mr. Berglund."

Walter sat down and completed his letter, describing this most recent incident, and placed it in an envelope. He went to the tea table and placed the linen cloth over the tea pot when there was a knock on the door. When he opened it he saw a tall, square shouldered man with reddish hair, a prominent chin and bright blue smiling eyes. He was wearing a two-piece suit and felt hat. The man extended his hand to Walter.

"I am Roberts. Cyril Roberts from the organization that you will be joining. May I come in?"

Walter immediately felt at ease with the stranger. He opened the door wider and Roberts stepped into the room.

"I am Walter Berglund. Major Bradley told me to expect you. I am glad that you came because I did not know where to look for you if you did not show up. You see, Major Bradley did not give me any telephone numbers or addresses."

"Major Bradley was very proficient in preparing the way for you and he was right in not giving you any telephone numbers or addresses. One thing that you will soon learn about this outfit is that we are dependable and on time and that we never give out calling cards." His face carried a faint smile as he talked. He removed his hat and placed it on the end table and Walter noticed that his red hair was receding above the temples.

"Well, let's have some tea before it gets cold," suggested Roberts, sitting on the edge of the bed and pulling the tea cart in front of him. "Pull up that rickety wooden chair, Walter," he said. "Did you have anything to eat since you arrived?"

"No," replied Walter. "I did not really know where to go and beside that I did not want to miss you."

"That's too bad," said Roberts. "There are some fairly decent eating places around here. Let's have a small snack then we will go down and I'll show you around this old place. Then we can have dinner somewhere. You will be staying here until all your basic tests are completed. That may take a month. After that, if all is well, we will all go to the training school for a while, then on to England for another while before you will start working. But all these plans are between you and me. You are to reveal them to no one, not even your family. You have come an awful long way. What got you interested in this type of work anyway?"

"I had a dream when I was twelve years old and ever since then I had been waiting for this chance," explained Walter innocently. "I have been preparing myself for it ever since."

"That must have been quite a dream that persuaded you to take a step like this," said Roberts. "Would you mind telling me what the dream was about?"

"It was about my real parents who were killed in an accident in Toledo when I was three and a half years old. Some people said that the accident didn't just happen; that it was set up by someone. So as a child, I prayed that

I would receive a sign about whether I should try to get revenge for their deaths. In my dream several people, including my parents, told me to go after them."

"And how do you think that you will get at the guilty persons through this job?" asked Roberts.

"Oh, I know that I can't get at the ones who may have done it. It is the system for which they were working that I want to destroy."

"According to Major Bradley you seem to be set on doing this," observed Roberts.

"I want to do this more than anything else in the world."

~~~

Several temporary barrack-like frame buildings, backing onto a wooded knoll served as the headquarters of the operation. To the right of them were the remnants of what had once been a parade square, its potholes freshly filled with gravel and asphalt. On Monday morning, Roberts drove his 1930 Buick to the front of the first unit and pocketed the ignition keys.

"Well, I hope you didn't expect something fancy, Walter. This is it. We don't have the large budgets that some organizations have," explained Roberts. "Let's find out if there is any life in this place."

Roberts inserted his key into the lock of the dark red metal door leading into the only part of the complex that did not appear to be a part of the original structure, and entered a small lobby. Along the narrow hallway, two rows of offices ran all the way back to the end of the building. The first one had a large open window, facing the lobby. A stocky, round faced man with his graying hair combed tightly back looked through the opening at Roberts.

"Morning, Cyril."

"Morning Duke." Roberts routinely opened a small leather wallet and displayed it for the man to see, then handed some documents over to him. "This is Berglund. Walter Berglund. Those are his papers. He is my charge."

"Welcome aboard, Berglund," said the man, reaching through the open window to shake Walter's hand.

"This is Duke Holman," said Roberts, "one of a handful of remaining G2s, the most depleted unit in America."

Walter wondered what G2 was, but did not ask.

"Yeah, those of us who are left have nowhere to go except up or out," laughed Holman. "Are you going to the reception room?"

"Yeah. Has anybody arrived yet?" asked Roberts.

"A few. Not all. The thing doesn't start for another half hour," answered Holman. "See you later."

Muffled voices from the rooms on both sides of the wing echoed through the empty hallway.

All the rooms appeared to be set up as individual offices with ancient government-issue wooden desks or equally distressed tables, except for the larger room at the end which they entered. This one had a small table at the front and five larger tables arranged in the shape of a U with a number of folding metal chairs set up around them. This was the recruits' reception area and classroom. Roberts and Walter walked across the creaky plank floor to join a group of early arrivals. They were introduced to the new recruits and their chiefs. Walter's head reeled from trying to remember all the new names.

The morning was spent in introducing the recruits to their colleagues, the leaders and the building. Each of the recruits was assigned one of the small rooms along the hallway, each of which was individually equipped with a locker. One of the barrack-like buildings housed a cafeteria where soup, thick cold meat sandwiches and raw vegetables were served for lunch. During the rest of the afternoon and all the next morning, Holman sat with each recruit individually in their small rooms and asked questions regarding their age, educational background, work experience, family circumstances, church affiliation and the names and addresses of their relatives. He finger printed each recruit and obtained their signatures.

Across the parade square was a larger box-like building with wide doors, which had at one time served as a equipment depot, but more recently as a gym. The whole contingent of recruits and leaders gathered there after lunch and were introduced to the gym instructor and his assistants who conducted extensive measurements on the recruits, recording their height, weight, chest size and other body dimensions. Near the end of the day the trainer issued each recruit with new gym clothes, sweat suit, swim trunks, runners and a locker. This was the first time that Walter had ever owned any of these items and the new material smelled good as he placed them carefully in his locker. For the remaining part of the week he would have a chance to wear them for running, weight lifting and other simple exercises.

It was soon Friday, the end of the first week on his new job. "Well, what did you think of all that?" asked Roberts as drove Walter back to the Greenborough.

"It was good. But when do we start doing something?" commented Walter.

"In time. All in good time," replied Roberts. "You can't move too fast in this business."

Next Monday it was back to the gym where the recruits ran around an improvised track, climbed rope ladders and jumped over simple obstacles while the trainers watched them carefully. Before beginning their Wednesday morning program, Duke Holman arrived and presented each recruit with a temporary identification card and a black leather card holder. The leaders met the recruits for lunch and drove them to their hotels at the end of the day, but spent the rest of their time in their own offices in the main building.

"Well, Walter, what did you think of this week? Are you bored with the whole thing yet?" asked Roberts as they drove to the hotel the following Friday.

"It is not too exciting yet," answered Walter, suppressing his disappointment, "but it is interesting. On the farm I was used to always doing something."

"It will start getting a bit more interesting next week when we start horsemanship training," Roberts assured him.

~~~

On a secluded horse farm not far from the city outskirts, fifteen riding horses milled about in a corral under the watchful eyes of the trainer and their owner when Roberts and Walter drove up Monday morning. There were no thoroughbreds in the herd, but all the horses displayed good breeding and vigor. A saddle was propped against the outside rail of the corral. The trainer jumped off the corral gate and assembled the recruits.

"Today you start getting some riding instructions," he announced. "You may never have occasion to use a horse in your jobs, but riding a horse is good discipline. It also teaches you body rhythm and sharpens your reflexes. Have any of you had any experience with horses?"

Three of the recruits, including Walter, put up their hands. Two of them were farm boys who had ridden horses back home.

"Berglund, what was the nature of your experience with horses?" asked the trainer.

"I had a horse back home which I rode a lot and I have broken in a few."

"Broken in?" remarked the trainer.

"Yes. Taught them how to carry a rider without throwing him off," explained Walter.

The owner selected a horse which he saddled and led it out of the corral. The trainer walked the horse around with each of the inexperienced recruits taking turns in the saddle. The three with experience, including Walter, were allowed to ride the horse independently. Each of them rode casually around the outside of the corral, first in a walk and then in a slow gallop as the non-riders watched their techniques. Under the trainer's guidance, five of the non-riders had become novice riders by the end of the afternoon.

"Before we call it a day, would anyone like to show us some techniques that may come in handy as we become more proficient during the week?" asked the trainer.

Walter stepped on the bottom rail of the corral and surveyed the horses. "That young gelding over there. Has he ever been ridden?" he asked the owner.

"No. But he is ready to be trained," said the owner.

"Mind if I break him in for you?" asked Walter.

"Not at all," responded the owner. "But he's a pretty frisky young fellow. I wouldn't want to see you get thrown."

"I'll take a chance on that," said Walter.

The owner opened the swinging gate wide enough for Walter to carry in the saddle. He laid it in a corner of the whitewashed structure and walked slowly toward the gelding. He turned to the owner.

"What's his name?"

"Slim."

His eyes focused directly on the gelding, Walter approached him slowly and steadily with easy slow steps. The animal's head reared up and he pranced nervously but remained on the spot.

"Here, Slim," said Walter softly, reaching out with his hands. "Nice boy, Slim. Don't be afraid."

He touched the gelding lightly on the shoulder with the forefingers of his right hand, then slowly brought his hand up to the animal's neck, stroking it gently. The gelding brought his head down and smelled Walter's chest while he scratched the horse behind its ear. When the animal had lost its fear of Walter, he called for the bit and halter. He showed them to the gelding and let him smell them. Walter put the bit softly against the horse's front teeth and when they opened slightly he slipped the bit into the gelding's mouth and the halter over its ears. The horse pressed his jaws against the bit and shook his head violently.

"Nice boy, Slim," said Walter in a quiet voice. "That's all right, it won't hurt you."

He coaxed the gelding to follow him around the corral as he held on to the reins. The horse stopped and started erratically. Outside the corral, the trainer and the others watched their every move. Walter stopped and gently rubbed the gelding's nose.

"May I have the saddle now?" he asked the owner.

Walter held the reins and caressed the horse's mane as the owner showed the saddle to the horse and then placed it on the gelding's back. The horse glanced back at the saddle as the owner buckled it on. Walter led the horse around the corral again and stopped.

"All right, Slim. I am going up there," said Walter. He held on to the reins then placed his foot into the stirrup and slid into the saddle. The gelding moved sideways nervously, then neighed loudly and stood up on its hind legs.

"Nice boy, Slim," said Walter. "Get down boy. You're all right."

The horse dropped down to its four feet, kicked up its hind legs and galloped furiously around the corral with Walter hanging on to the saddle with one hand and the reins with the other.

"Open the gate," shouted the jubilant rider.

The horse galloped erratically around the farmyard for a few minutes then slowed down to a walk. Walter guided it back to the corral and slid out of the saddle. He went to the front of the horse and caressed its face.

"That was well done, Slim," he said. "See, that's wasn't so bad, was it Slim?" The horse nudged Walter with his nose. He led the animal gently by its reins then took it back to the corral. The owner removed the saddle and Walter slipped the halter and bit off the horse's head.

"You sure have a way with horses, young fellow," said the owner. "Have you broken in any like this one before?"

"A few. Only this one was a lot easier." answered Walter.

"Well, I hope you picked up a few pointers from that demonstration," said the trainer to the rest of the group. "We'll continue our horsemanship training for the rest of the week. See you all here tomorrow."

"That was quite an exhibition you put on for us, Walter," said Roberts as they drove back to the hotel.

"It's really nothing," said Walter modestly.

"I've done that lots of times before. It's just a matter of winning the horse's trust and then becoming a part of him and after that it's just a lot of practice."

"How many horses have you broken in like that before?" asked Roberts.

"Oh, I lost count. Maybe twenty five or so," replied Walter. "You see, after I was about twelve, my uncle let me train all the horses on our farm and in addition as I got older I trained a few for our neighbor, Mr. Garwood, who lives on a ranch with quite a few more horses than we had. They all thought that I was a real natural with horses and I enjoyed doing it."

"Well, it is fairly obvious that you don't need too much training in horsemanship, so maybe we can go on to something else in a few days while the other are still in that training," suggested Roberts.

"I wouldn't mind going back for another day or two to show the trainer and the rest of the fellows a few more tricks that I learned and that may be useful to them."

"Sure," said Roberts. "If it turns out to be anywhere near as good as today's show, it can't help but benefit the other trainees."

The trainer's voice rang through the still early autumn air as he shouted instructions to the novice horsemen in their saddles. By noon all the trainees had traversed the riding field several times, gaining confidence each time around. At three in the afternoon the saddles were removed, the horses put back in the corral and the trainees gathered for their briefing.

"We will quit a bit early today out of respect for your seats," said the trainer. "We want you all to be able to sit in the saddle tomorrow and that may be doubtful if we don't quit now. Tomorrow we'll test your reflexes with some exercises in timing and agility. See you all then."

Fourteen frisky horses milled about the holding compound when the group assembled next morning. The horses stopped and observed them from inside the six-foot high whitewashed plank enclosure. Outside of the compound the trainer was explaining the day's program.

"As I said yesterday, we'll do something a little different today. In your job, you will not, of course, always have access to a saddle. So if you have to use horse powered transportation, you may have to mobilize one that is not dressed for the occasion. We will practice mounting and riding a horse bareback and then later without a halter. I'll give you a demonstration and then you will all try it."

The owner led a docile bay mare from the compound and handed the reins to the trainer. He asked the trainees and leaders to form a large circle around the mare and then slipped the reins over the animal's head. He slapped the mare gently on the left rear shoulder to get her to walk around the inside of the circle. Then starting with a slow run he approached the moving mare, grabbed a hold of her lower mane and sprang onto her back. He repeated the demonstration several times then stopped to explain the technique to the trainees.

"Do not try to get on the horse's back without first getting a hold of something solid. The lower mane is the best for this. If the animal is moving, so much the better, because the forward motion will give you the momentum to get up easily. Always try to jump onto the horse's forward back, otherwise you may hurt the animal, especially if you are a heavy person. Using the horse's tail like the Cossacks and the Turks used to do is not recommended. All right now, who wants to be the first to try it?" There were no volunteers. "Walter, did you ever try this back on the farm?"

At the edge of the circle Walter smiled and nodded his head to indicate that the trainer had guessed right. He stepped out of the circle and repeated the steps performed earlier by the trainer. Buoyed by the relative ease displayed by Walter, the other trainees were soon performing the exercises with varying degrees of success. When they returned after lunch the trainer explained that the exercise which they learned during the morning was a prelude to something more difficult.

"In actual situations which you may encounter, the horse may be in the company of other horses. In such cases you will have to decide which horse is the best to choose and, once on his back, to get him to take you where you want to go without the advantage of a bit or halter. To do this, each of you will take a turn inside the holding compound where we have fourteen horses. I will demonstrate again."

The trainer entered the compound quietly. The animals watched him curiously, but did not move until he had chosen his quarry and had a hold of its mane. He shouted to get the herd moving, and jumped easily onto the horse's back. The trainer rode around the compound several times then stopped the horse and slid down off its back.

"There. That was easy enough," said the trainer when he returned to the group of trainees and leaders. "Who wants to try it?"

Two of the trainees tried unsuccessfully to perform the exercise. One was unable to grasp the mane firmly enough and lost his footing. The other was thrown by the horse after he leapt onto its back. By the time Walter's turn arrived, the horses moved restlessly about the corral, agitated and snorting. He entered the gate calmly and talked to the nearby animals. They stopped and observed him nervously, their ears stiffly upright and necks arched. Walter approached a nearby group of animals, his eyes focused on a young gelding wedged between two older animals. Talking steadily, he approached and placed his hand onto the gelding's mane. The young animal lunged forward and Walter leaped upon his back, with both hands grasping its mane. The rest of the horses were now moving together in a circle around the compound. When Walter's gelding ran in between two of them, he grabbed the mane of the closest one and jumped up on its back. A similar opportunity presented itself during the next trip around the compound and Walter changed horses again. A few minutes later he had repeated the performance several more times. The horses, snorting and puffing, stopped to rest. Walter slid down off the latest mount and made his way out of the compound. The group clapped appreciatively as he emerged from the gate.

~~~

"After today's performance I am convinced that you don't need any basic training in horsemanship at this time, Walter," said Roberts as they waited for a traffic light to change. "I understand that you are a swimmer. That will be the next program that the trainer has planned for you."

"Back home there is a lake at the edge of a park not far from our farm. On hot days I used to sneak out there with my pony and I learned to swim by myself. After a while I could swim all the way to an island which was more than a quarter mile away. If my parents had known this, they would have worried themselves sick. Maybe I was taking a chance, but I knew that my pony was there in case I got into trouble, but I never did."

"Boy, you seem to have had some interesting times out there," said Roberts. "If your swimming is anywhere as good as your riding, then I would like to have been there to see it."

"It sort of comes natural to me, like walking," said Walter.

"I enjoy swimming, too," said Roberts as he wheeled the Buick to the front door of the hotel. "Why don't we go down to the Potomac Park tomorrow and limber up a bit before the official training begins. The water should still be warm enough to swim in it. Anyway it will be more challenging for you than swimming in the indoor pool where the training is scheduled to begin next week. I'll tell the trainer that you are working on a special task."

"That would be nice," said Walter. "It will give me a chance to see more of the country around here. I am getting a bit bored with the area around the hotel and I am afraid to go too far away from it in case I get lost."

"Maybe I can find someone to show you around later," said Roberts. "I guess I should not have left you entirely on your own like this, but I thought that you would be so busy with your training that you wouldn't have time for such things. Now that you are just marking time waiting for the others, maybe I will do that. We'll pick up your swim trunks on the way out tomorrow."

Walter gazed in awe at the dazzling white Jefferson Memorial, its pillared front reflected in the mirror-like waters of the Tidal Basin. A great profusion of flowers, trees ands shrubs stretched for about two miles south to the junction of the Anacostia River and Washington Channel. The fading blossoms and brightly colored leaves spoke of the end of the summer. A few people sat on the artificial beach and some were wading in the water when Walter and Roberts emerged from the change house. There were no other swimmers around. They stuck their big toes in the water.

"It's not the Hot Springs, but it is not ice-cold either," said Roberts.

"About the same temperature as our lake back home," said Walter. "I don't mind it this cold."

"It must be around a quarter of a mile to the other side," said Roberts after they swam around the beach area for a few minutes. "Would you like to try it?"

"Sure," said Walter. "I am a bit out of practice, but you'll be around to save me."

"Let's go then," said Roberts.

They put their faces in the water and headed for the opposite side. Roberts struggled to keep up with the younger man and Walter found it necessary to stop and tread water or swim around from time to time while waiting for his older swim-mate to catch up. They reached the other side and Roberts emerged panting.

"You swim like a damned fish," he gasped. "Where in hell did you learn to swim like that?"

"I watched a mother otter teaching her kits and learned from her," laughed Walter.

"I can almost believe that," said Roberts dropping wearily to the ground.

Their goose pimples disappeared as they sat on the grass in the hot noonday sun. In about half an hour they felt ready to return to the other side. With Walter swimming slowly to remain close to Roberts, they returned to their starting point, tired, but refreshed.

"Well, I saw for myself today that we can't show you too much about swimming either, so I think I'll have to find something else to keep up your interest," said Roberts. "In any event, I'll pick you up Monday morning and we'll join the others just to see what they are doing."

Walter closed the door of the Buick and started to walk toward the hotel. He heard the car's engine accelerate and then slow down. He turned around and saw Roberts leaning out of the open window.

"My girl friend and I are going to a movie tonight. Would you like to join us?" asked Roberts.

"That would be nice," answered Walter. "I was not doing anything."

"We'll pick you up at the front door at seven. Wear your Sunday best" said Roberts. He closed the window and drove away.

Walter came down a few minutes early and watched the weekend crowd as it milled about the hotel lobby and the street outside. He felt dressed up and stiff in the suit, white shirt with starched collar and tie that Major Bradley had given him for his trip. The Buick wheeled in off the street and stopped in front of the hotel. Roberts and a young woman occupied the front seats and a younger woman sat alone in the back seat. She surveyed Walter impishly through the rear view window of the car. Roberts waved to Walter to come in and introduced the women after he sat down in the back seat.

"This here is my friend Ella," he said, glancing at the woman beside him.

He turned around to face Walter and the girl. And this is Ella's friend, Susan. I thought you might be longing for some female companionship"

Walter blushed. "I don't know what to say. This has never happened to me before," he said, casting a shy look at Susan. "The only girls that I have talked to since I got here have been the waitresses in the restaurant, and they don't seem to be too interested in talking to me."

Susan turned her face against the car window and smiled.

During the intermission, Roberts and Ella excused themselves, leaving Walter alone with Susan. He fidgeted nervously in his seat, catching glimpses of her out of the corner of his eye. He was desperate to think of something appropriate to say, but his mind was blank. She observed him with a mischievous look, amused by his discomfort.

"You're kind of shy, Walter," she said. "Don't they have girls where you come from?"

He sat up straight and cast fleeting glances at the girl. She was not beautiful, but yet attractive, with a wide mouth and round hazel eyes. When they walked into the theater earlier, he noticed that the top of her head came up to about his nose. Her reddish brown hair was curled at the ends and obscured her ears. She had removed her woolen cardigan and was holding it on her lap.

"Yes, there are girls out there, but I have never had much to do with them except at the country dances." he responded.

"What did you do at these dances?" She seemed genuinely interested.

"Oh, we always whooped it up a bit," said Walter. "I used to call the square dances and certain girls around there were great square dance fans. They liked my calling."

"That sounds like fun," she remarked. "I would like to hear more about all those fun things that you did back there. Here come Cyril and Ella. Why don't we get together on our own sometime and go to a movie or sightseeing. I don't live far from your hotel. I can show you around the city."

Roberts and Ella were approaching their seats.

"How about tomorrow?" Walter could not believe that he said it.

"I'll see you at two thirty in the hotel lobby," she whispered as the others took their seats.

Roberts passed boxes of popcorn to Walter and Susan. "How did you two get along?" he asked.

"Walter is pretty shy, but I think that I can loosen him up a bit. We are going to meet tomorrow and I will show him around."

"Good work, Susan," said Roberts.

CHAPTER 31

During the early morning the hotel cleaning staff had removed the ash trays, newspapers and debris left by the previous night's crowds. The carpets were swept clean and the furniture dusted and waiting for the day's guests to arrive. The hotel lobby smelled of stale smoke and furniture oil.

Dressed in a light blue woolen pullover, navy slacks and white shirt open at the neck, Walter leaned back into the soft cushions of the upholstered chairs in the lobby. He glanced at the clock behind the front desk. It was a few minutes after two. He picked up a magazine off the table, but the words oscillated and would not come together. He put the magazine back on the table and walked out the front door. The sidewalk was almost deserted, except for several people leaving the nearby restaurant and a man walking his Dalmatian dog.

He gazed anxiously down the sidewalk. Would she arrive as they had agreed or was she only teasing him when she said she would? He had never met a girl quite like her before. She seemed so genuine and interested in everything he said. She probably had a lot of men chasing after her and was only doing this to please her friends Ella and Roberts, thought Walter. He entered the lobby and glanced at the clock. It was 2:29. His skin turned cold and he felt goose pimples form on his arms. He sat on the edge of an easy chair and stared at the door. Several people walked by the door and he wished it would open. It did and a man and a woman walked up to the front desk. It was nearly 2:35. She probably wasn't coming. He leaned forward and put his head in the palms of his hands.

"Hello, Walter!"

He jerked his head up. She was standing at the side of the chair smiling.

"Oh, hello," he almost gasped. "I thought maybe you weren't coming. I didn't see you come in."

"I came in the side door," she explained. "It's closer that way. Well, don't just sit there in a daze. Let's go outside. It's a beautiful day." She held out her hand and pulled him up to his feet. Her hands were warm and soft. He noticed that she was also wearing blue: a navy blazer jacket over a white blouse with imitation pearl buttons down the front, and a plaid skirt. They walked out the door and stopped.

"Well, what shall we do?" asked Walter.

"Remember, I said that I would show you around the place," she said. "What would you like to see?"

"Anything you want to show me," said Walter. "The only part I have seen is the area around the hotel and a bit of Potomac Park with Roberts."

"Good. Let's go to the corner and catch a street car," she said. "We'll go down to Constitution Avenue. There is enough there to keep us going until supper time."

"Sounds great," said Walter. "Perhaps we will find a nice restaurant out there and have dinner together."

"For a farm boy, you are learning pretty fast." she laughed. "I do know a nice restaurant out there."

His eyes wide with wonder, Walter gazed at the imposing structure visible above the trees, across from the equally magnificent White House. Standing at its base they shaded their eyes and looked up at the apex of the Washington Monument.

"This is the tallest masonry structure in the world," explained Susan. "It is five hundred and fifty feet and five and one eighth inches tall."

"They must have had a long tape to measure it that closely," said Walter.

"No. It's true," said Susan seriously. "I learned that in school."

"What is that building over there?" asked Walter, pointing to a columned structure in the distance.

"Oh. That is the Lincoln Memorial. Let's walk that way and see it and then we can go somewhere and sit down on the grass and rest our aching feet."

Walter counted the columns of the Colonnade as they approached the structure.

"There are thirty-six of them," said Susan, "one for each state of the union in the year that President Lincoln died. Above the columns are the names of the present day forty-eight states. It took almost eight years to complete the building and it was dedicated just over nineteen years ago on May 30, 1914."

"You should be one of those tour guides," said Walter. "The way you have all these figures memorized, it should be snap for you."

"Maybe so," she said, "but today I am your guide. So let's sit down on the grass and look over the Tidal Basin."

"Roberts and I swam across that lake the other day," said Walter as they sat on a knoll overlooking the water.

"You're pulling my leg, Walter," said Susan. "Who would go swimming at this time of the year and who could swim all that way and back?"

"Oh, we did," said Walter matter-of-factly. "It was warm enough and I wanted to show Roberts that I could swim across it."

"Really, Walter," said Susan, "you don't need to impress me with that kind of story. And at this time of the year you would probably get arrested."

"You should ask Roberts. He'll tell you," suggested Walter.

"I will. He has already told me about your horse riding demonstration and how impressed your trainer was."

"Back home on the farm we used to do those tricks every time we got the chance and the older folks weren't watching. It was our way of having fun."

"And I'll bet you were the best of them all," said Susan.

"Yes. In certain things I was, but in others the other fellows were better."

"It sounds like you had a real nice life back there. What made you want to come here?" she asked.

"Oh, I didn't ask to come here. This is where I had to come to prepare for my job," he explained.

"And then where are you going?" she asked.

"I understand that we will be going some other place for a while, and after that, who knows."

"That is some funny business that you and Roberts are in. He just disappears for a while and then pops up again. I hope you don't intend to do that."

"I'll go wherever the job takes me," said Walter. "I have waited for this since I was twelve years old, and now that I have a chance, I'll do whatever is necessary to succeed."

"Too bad you can't stay around here, Walter," she said. "We could do a lot of things together."

Walter blinked, then regained his composure. "Well, I am not leaving just yet," he said. "We still have lots of time to do things. And who knows. Maybe some day I'll be back and we can pick up from there."

"You seem convinced that what you are doing is the right thing," said Susan.

"I have never been more certain of anything in my life," he said. "But I wish you wouldn't let that stop us from seeing each other. I enjoy being with you," he added, his voice trailing.

"So do I enjoy being with you, Walter. You are a very different person and I could enjoy seeing you every day. But if we did that you might get tired of me. So maybe twice a week would be better."

"I'll be waiting for the hour," he declared.

"You always say the right thing," she said.

"In that case why don't we look for that nice place you talked about and sit down for something to eat? My farmer's stomach is complaining," he suggested.

"There you go again; thinking about your stomach," she said. "Let's see if our aching feet will take us back to the street."

~~~

Under the keen observing eyes of the trainer, the recruits spent several days swimming lengths in the large indoor pool near the training center. Roberts advised Walter to go through the whole program and brush up on all the exercises as the ability to handle oneself in the water was a crucial part of the job. When his turn came for timing he swam the length of the pool several times, emerging at the end of the pool to take in air and resuming his underwater crossing. The trainer took notes in his record book and shook his head in apparent disbelief. Walter spent the rest of the day jumping into the water at various depths, sitting on the bottom holding his breath and floating with only his face exposed. At the end of the day he was exhausted and bored.

Back at the hotel, he leaned back on his pillow and watched the flickering reflection of the red neon sign entering the open window and bouncing off the mirror in front of him. The hypnotic effect of the tempo brought on a drowsiness and he closed his eyes. A light tap on his door awakened him. He listened to make sure that it was his door. The rap came again, louder this time. He got to his feet and flicked on the light. He expected to see Roberts in the hall when he opened the door. Instead he saw a trainee from his group standing in the hallway.

"I am sorry to disturb you. In case you forgot since we were introduced on the first day, my name is Victor Rudnicki. I've wanted to talk to you privately since I saw your demonstration with the horses. My leader told me where you stayed. He found out from Mr. Roberts, I think. So I took a chance and came down."

"Sure, Victor," said Walter. "I remember your name. We've been so busy and I've been away from the group from time to time, so we never really had a chance to talk. Come in. I had fallen asleep and am a bit groggy right now."

The young man sat in the upholstered chair and leaned forward, his hands clasped between his knees. His sun tanned face and arms bore evidence of his exposure to the outdoors prior to arriving at camp. His hair was cropped close up the sides of his head above his ears and neck. The tuft of hair at the top of his head was straight and short. His fingers were long and slender.

"I hear that you are from Canada," he said.

"Yes. But I was born in this country – in Toledo. My parents came there from Poland."

"You say that your parents were from Poland?" he asked.

"Yes. But they weren't here long. They were killed in an accident in Toledo when I was three and a half years old and I went to live with my grandparents and uncle and aunt in Manitoba. They had gone there earlier to homestead."

"My parents came to Pennsylvania from Ukraine when they were young," the young man explained. "My father was a coal miner and we live on a small farm. My grandfather was in the Czar's cavalry. When he was very old and I was younger, he would tell me about all the wonderful adventures he used to have in the cavalry. How he used to mount a horse on the dead run and things like that. When I saw you doing those things in the compound I realized that my grandfather was not stretching the truth and that it is, indeed, possible to perform like that if your are quick and well trained and if you understand horses."

"Back home we did not have too much else to do for fun, so we started out by doing tricks like picking a hat up off the ground at full gallop," explained Walter. "After a while we became pretty good at that kind of thing."

"You don't know just how good you are, Walter," said Victor. "When I saw you do some of those things, I thought that here is someone who can teach me how to be a good horseman like my grandfather was. So that's why I found out where you stay so I can talk to you personally and away from the camp. For some reason they don't seem to want us to be too close to each other, but do you think that you could do this for me?"

"Sure. Why not? The problem will be to find the horses and a place to do it."

"My leader told me that we will be going back to the farm for more training next week and he would arrange with the trainer to give us an hour or so after quitting time for you to teach me those tricks. He had talked it over with Roberts and he said it was all right."

"So we'll do it then," said Walter. "But remember that it takes more than an hour or two to pick up on these things. It takes hours and hours of practice."

"Oh, I know that I can't be as good as you are, Walter, but once I know how to do it, I will practice every chance I get. I want to be able to go home and show my parents that I take after my grandfather."

"Whatever made you get into this business?" asked Walter observing him curiously.

"It wasn't really my idea," responded Victor. "I would just as soon stay home and work in the mine, but my father says that if we don't do something soon, the Bolsheviks and Fascists will take over the world. He was shot in the leg in the last war and knows that he can't do much about it himself, so he wants me to do something, even though I can't get too excited about the idea."

"Not me," said Walter. "I can't wait to start. I decided when I was twelve years old that I would do this some day and I plan to succeed no matter what happens."

"I know you will do well, Walter," said Victor, "because you put everything you have into whatever you do. Now that I am here, I will do the same, but I'll be looking forward to getting back to Pennsylvania. Anyway, I must be going now. See you in the morning."

He stood up and shook Walter's hand then walked out into the hall.

~~~

Having gotten over his loneliness since meeting Susan, Walter found the time slipping by quickly. He wondered how much longer he would remain at the training center. Roberts answered his question the next morning.

"Well, another two weeks and we'll be all finished here," announced Roberts as they drove toward the training center.

"I sure wish I knew if I made it," said Walter quietly.

"It's still a bit early to say," said Roberts. "There will be some intensive training near the end and a few more tests. If you do well in these, you will go into phase two."

"And where will that be; here or overseas?" asked Walter.

"I am not allowed to discuss these things until the successful candidates have been chosen and even then only the successful ones will be told." They drove silently for a few blocks. Roberts broke the silence. "I understand that Victor has talked you into teaching him something about riding horses."

"Yeah. The poor guy is ready to do anything to learn some of those tricks so he can be like his grandfather."

"It's nice of you to help him. He told me how much he appreciates it," said Roberts. "By the way, have you seen Susan since last Sunday?"

"No. But I expect to see her tonight," said Walter as he stepped out of the Buick and headed for the hotel. Roberts winked mischievously and drove away.

The hotel guests were still arriving in cars and taxis, carrying bags and suitcases into the lobby when Walter returned from his evening meal in the hotel restaurant. Meanwhile some late departures were still checking out. He sat down and watched the arrivals and departures and wondered if two weeks from now it might be he who would be going through the door. Would it be to the next phase, as Roberts had described it, or back to a winter on the farm? His family would be glad to see him, but would he be able to face Major Bradley again, he pondered. Something beside him moved. He looked up and saw Susan.

"Your mind was a thousand miles away," she remarked.

"Actually, about two thousand, if you knew the truth," he answered. "It's nice of you to come. I need someone to talk to."

"Good. Shall we go for a walk? It's beautiful out this evening."

They walked slowly to a nearby park and sat down on a bench under a gnarled chestnut tree. She moved over closer to him and he felt her warm body against his.

"So what's worrying you?" she asked tenderly.

"Roberts told me tonight that in two weeks we will be through here and moving on either to another place or back home."

"It's nothing to get upset about," she said as she tweaked his cheek. "Unless, of course, you don't want to leave me."

"That is just one part of it. I am also worried about whether I will be successful and have a chance to go on," he said.

"If you don't make it, Walter, you can stay here with me. In fact, I am kind of hoping that you will not make it."

"How can you say that?" He looked at her in disbelief. "I want this more than anything else in the world."

"Even more than me?" She put her head on his shoulder and he felt her soft hair on his chin and cheek. He put his arm around her shoulder. The wind rustled the leaves in the branches above them and swirled the ones that had fallen to the ground.

"It's getting chilly. Why don't we go to a movie?" she said.

~~~

Inside the corral the groom ran in a circle, leading the horse by its bridle. In the center of the circle Walter explained to Victor the technique of mounting a moving horse. As Roberts and Victor's leader watched, Walter ran a few steps alongside the moving horse then grabbed its mane and leaped up on its back. The horse continued running at a steady gait. The groom brought the animal to a stop and Walter slid down. He walked over to Victor.

"There's nothing difficult about that maneuver," he said. "It's just a matter of both you and the horse moving forward together. The horse does not mind. Just try not to land too hard on its back. You sort of slide up and then straighten up. After you have that down pat, you can try the one where you hang on to the saddle and pick up a hat. Are you ready to try it?"

For the next three days, Victor ran, jumped and slid and by Friday afternoon he was in the compound moving from one horse to another and hanging on to the saddle with one hand while picking up a hat with the other. Walter, Roberts and Victor's leader watched the performance from outside the compound.

"I think he's got it," said Walter. "Maybe he should quit now or he may not be able to sit down for a week."

The leader waved to Victor and the young rider brought the horse to a stop. He walked out the gate holding on to his seat.

"I'll never sit down again," he moaned, "but it was worth it. Today I feel like a Cossack cavalryman. Thank you, Walter for having all that patience with me."

"You're a good learner, Victor. It was easy," said Walter.

~~~

A cold front moved in overnight and rain was pelting the window when Walter awoke Saturday morning. He dressed and went down for breakfast while the chambermaid cleaned his room. The room felt fresh and cozy in contrast to the dreariness outside his window when he returned from breakfast. He dug out a pad of paper from a drawer and sat down to write a letter to his family. In another week he would know if he would be coming back or going on, he wrote. Things were going well. He had taught Victor, one of the recruits, the art of riding like they do it back home and last week he met a nice girl who wanted him to stay in Washington.

There was a knock on the door. He opened it and saw Susan standing there, her rain coat and hat shiny from the rain. A smile covered her face and strands of wet hair covered her forehead.

"What a surprise," he blurted out. "How did you get up here?"

"By using the door and the stairs." She laughed at his surprise. "Well, aren't you going to ask me in?"

"I was just writing a letter home," explained Walter as he hung up her coat in the open closet. "In fact, I was just telling them that I had met this lovely girl who wants me to stay here in Washington."

"You're just making that up, Walter," she said. "Let's see where you say it."

He lifted the sheet off the desk and pointed to the last paragraph in the letter.

"Why, Walter, you really did say it. You're so sweet," she said as she pinched his cheek. "But how do I know that you care when you think more of this mysterious job of yours than you do of me."

"I like you very much," said Walter as he sat on the edge of the bed, "but there is nothing in the world that I want more than this job."

She sat on the bed beside him and put her arm around his neck. Her skirt pulled up off her knees as she reached up to kiss him on the cheek.

"If you knew me better, perhaps you would not leave me here all alone while you go to God knows where."

She fell slowly back on the bed, pulling him down with her.

"Why don't you try kissing me, Walter?" She brought her lips up to his.

"See. That is not so bad, is it?" she whispered, caressing his hips. "Give me your hand. Now put it up here." She took his hand in hers and placed it on her breast. He held her tightly against him and they fell over into the bed. His breathing became deep and heavy. His body trembled and he lay limp in her arms.

She lifted her head and looked into his face. "Why, Walter, you didn't do it in your pants, did you?"

He blushed and nodded.

"That will teach you for not taking them off," she laughed. "You're too innocent Walter. When you go to the bathroom to clean up just take everything off and leave it there. Don't be shy. Just make sure that the door is locked."

Outside the closed bathroom door, Walter heard shuffling movements and sounds. He emerged shyly and noticed her clothes hanging on a chair. She lay smiling on one side of the bed, her bare shoulders and arms showing above the folded sheet and blanket. He turned the lock on the door, flicked off the light and got in under the bedclothes. Her body felt soft and warm as he drew closer. Her hand went down and she pulled him over her outstretched legs.

"Just do what comes naturally," she whispered.

The room was dark and quiet except for the occasional footstep in the hallway. The rain pattered against the window. Susan stretched out leisurely and kissed him on the cheek.

"Was this you first time?" she asked.

"Yes," he admitted.

"It was delicious," she said.

"It was beautiful," he agreed.

"We can do this all the time if you stay here," she reminded him.

"It's very tempting," he said, "but let's leave that discussion for later."

They embraced again. The heavy raindrops pelting against the window panes drowned out the sounds of the traffic outside.

~~~

The basement of the large brick building which once served as camp headquarters was dark and musty. The indoor firing range showed little sign of recent use, except for eight targets at the far end, mounted behind a deep concrete pit. At the other end of the long narrow range, eight Springfield M 1903 rifles laid side by side on a rough wooden table.

A small willowy man with a hook nose and perpetual frown announced that he would teach them the fundamentals of small arms operation and maintenance. He picked up one of the rifles and held it tight against his faded army tunic, a surviving relic of the Great War. With one hand on each end of the weapon, he brought it up over his head then slowly brought it back down in front of him.

"This rifle is an adaptation of the Mauser M1898," he began. "It was a good weapon twenty or thirty years ago, but God help us if we should try to defend ourselves with it in this day and age. But it has served us well and its simplicity still makes it a good model on which to acquire basic firearms orientation."

He removed the magazine, then the bolt, explaining their function and the care required for their proper operation. The barrel and other parts were removed and placed in sequential order on a gray blanket cloth on the table. The rifle was reassembled, accompanied by step by step instructions on the proper assembly order and procedures, and then disassembled again. One by one the trainees were asked to repeat these exercises until they could perform them without having to focus their eyes on the task. As this aspect of their training progressed, the trainees noticed that their regular leaders were no longer with them.

Cyril Roberts sat across the polished hardwood table from Major Sandburn, the camp commander, in an office inside the barracks headquarters. The commander opened a file with a dark red jacket and examined some reports in it. He leaned back in his chair and his penetrating blue eyes peered at Roberts from behind the long gray eyebrows. His white, closely cropped mustache contrasted with the blushing pink skin on his clean shaven face.

"Well Roberts, what do you think of your charge, Mr. Walter Berglund?" he asked.

"He's a real wildcat, that one," replied Roberts. "Rides horses like a rodeo cowboy and swims like a bloody eel. Not too worldly, but learns fast and speaks several languages. We haven't had him on the rifle range yet, but from what Major Bradley wrote about him, that should be no problem. He practically grew up with a 22-calibre rifle in his hands."

"How about the other important trait?" asked the major.

"The guy is nuts about this job. Says that he decided when he was twelve years old that he was going to get even with somebody and he sees this as a way to do it. You know what happened to his parents. He's mad as hell at somebody about that and he wants to go after them. The problem will be how to keep the young son-of-a-gun down, not how to get him going."

Major Sandburn leafed through the file papers and grunted approvingly.

"Did you arrange for the final 'commitment to the cause' test?" he asked, smiling sheepishly at Roberts.

"Yes. And she really poured it on, too. But that didn't sway him one bit," said Roberts.

"You mean that she had to go all the way?" asked the Major, with a twinkle in his eyes.

"Yes, she actually let the young hayseed screw her. But I understand that she enjoyed it. I hate to say this, Major, but if anyone was won over, it was Susan, not Walter," said Roberts. "She says that she kind of fell for him. His innocence and roughness excites her."

"What bloody nonsense. Tell her that it is not part of her job to get involved," growled the major. He closed the file and twirled a pencil in his fingers.

"All right. The kid's in. Send him down to Fort Jay next week with the other survivors. I'll arrange for Simpson and Sliworski to pick up the Central European team as soon as they are ready," explained Major Sandburn. He looked at Roberts with an amused look on his face. "You say that the young bumpkin is wiry as a wildcat and was raised with a 22 rifle in his hands? OK. When he leaves here he'll be known as Willy 22 for as long as he is in the organization."

"Suits him just great, sir," said Roberts. "With your permission I would now like to return to the training center."

The sharp cracks of rifle fire bounced off the ceiling and were swallowed by the gray stone basement walls. One by one the recruits emptied their Springfield rifles from standing and lying positions and with one knee on the ground. In the pit, the assistant trainer tallied the score for each trainee and delivered the tally to the trainer.

"You did well in the introduction to small arms, Walter," said Roberts as they drove back to the hotel Friday. "Major Sandburn, the camp commander, has asked me to tell you that you have been successful in your first phase of training. You will be leaving for Fort Jay Tuesday morning. Please accept my congratulations also. It has been a pleasure working with you."

"You have been a great help to me, Mr. Roberts," said Walter. "With you around, I never ever had the feeling that I would fail. I felt safe and relaxed when you were around. Thank you for your help and confidence in me."

"You earned it, Walter. By the way, you will now be known in the organization as Willy 22. When you go to Fort Jay and beyond you will understand why it is necessary to have special names in this business."

"Willy 22," mused Walter. "That has a nice sound to it. I think I like it."

Roberts swung the Buick into the hotel entrance and stopped in the unloading zone. Walter placed his hand on the door handle then paused and fixed his gaze on Roberts.

"Before you leave, is it OK if I ask you one question?" said Walter.

"Sure. I hope that I can answer it," said Roberts.

"You have often spoken to us about the organization, but no one has ever explained to us what it is. In fact, when I joined, I had no idea that I would end up in Washington. I thought that I was offering myself for some service in Poland that Sliworski was advertising. What am I doing here anyway?"

"In this business we do things in what may seem like mysterious and secretive ways. Only a very few know exactly what it is all about and who is involved. I suppose that is why it is sometime referred to as the secret service. But I can give you a bit of an idea of who we are. The people who have been working with you, including myself, are the remnants of the Corps of Intelligence Police in this country. During the Great War there were several hundred of us distributed all across the nation, in Europe and elsewhere. At that time we were known as the G2s. In fact, one of our members was involved in the investigation into your parents' deaths. Now all that is left of all that is what you see here, just a handful of professionals who appreciate the importance of this business and who are striving to keep the organization alive. We also try to help out our counterparts in other friendly countries, so that is why you are here."

"When I answered the call I responded to Poland's appeal to those of Polish descent on this side of the ocean who want to help out the old country. I expected to end up in Warsaw or somewhere like that," said Walter.

"Most people would have been just as surprised as you were. But anyway, you will only be in America for a bit longer and then you will be headed for England. After a short stay there, you will, indeed, work for Poland in a way. But don't be surprised if you never get to see Warsaw," explained Roberts.

A look of surprise covered Walter's face. "In a way I am glad that it is turning out this way, because I feel a lot closer to America than I do to Poland," he said. "But Europe happens to be where my destiny is, at least according to my dream."

"You'll do a good job, Walter, wherever you go," said Roberts. "If I have any advice for you that will help you out in this business it is this: Don't become sentimental about anything related to this work and don't get emotionally involved with women while you are in the field. Anyone of these two could destroy you before you know what hit you. Above all, keep a good sense of humor. A good laugh will help you to forget many things."

"You have been a good teacher, Mr. Roberts," said Walter. "I have watched how you conduct yourself and I tried to be like you."

"I am really flattered, Walter, "said Roberts, "but I think you will enjoy working with Mr. Simpson, who will be your adviser and cohort in England. Anyway, I will be in charge of some of the training at Fort Jay. I will pick you up for the briefing Monday morning, Willy 22."

Walter stepped out of the car and turned to go into the hotel. Roberts rolled down the car window. "Don't let Sweet Susan talk you out of anything this weekend." His eyes shone mischievously. He rolled up the window and drove away.

"You're so damned innocent, Walter," said Susan when they returned to the hotel room after a movie. "Why do you want to get mixed up in a messy business like this?"

"I feel that I have to," he answered, sitting down heavily. "If we don't try to straighten out some of the things that are going on in the world, we might be next in line."

"But how can you be so sure about who is right and who is wrong," she pleaded.

"I only know one thing." His answer was blunt. "And that is that someone killed my parents, both of whom were innocent people, and that in my eyes is wrong. I have no problem accepting that."

"Yes. Walter. I knew last weekend that nothing was going to change your mind, but I couldn't help thinking about you during the week. All those things you left behind – your family, your friends, the farm, that beautiful lake you swam in. It all sounds so peaceful. I almost feel that I could go there myself to get away from it all."

"Maybe when I get back, I'll come and get you and we can go back there together and settle down."

"That will be something for me to think about while you are away," she beamed, "but meanwhile let's make the most of this weekend." She sat on the bed in front of him and squeezed his face against her bosom.

CHAPTER 32

The highly polished walnut table reflected the soft glow of the floor lamps at the front of the opulent wood-paneled room. Above the fireplace, the antique clock ticked loudly, the only audible sound in the venerable old mansion, which now served as a retired officers' club. Roberts, hands in pocket, gazed blankly at a framed print showing Confederate and Yankee forces engaged in rifle combat during the Battle of Gettysburg. He turned around and faced Walter and Victor, slumped comfortably in two large leather upholstered chairs at the rear of the room.

"They should be here pretty soon now," he said, taking a nervous glance at his watch. "You two look like you haven't a care in the world."

"Sir. You said that everything is all set and not to worry about a thing," remarked Walter. "We were just following orders."

"Yeah, you're right. I don't know why I am so jittery. Maybe it's because you two are the first team we've trained for Colonel Sliworski. Both he and Simpson have been in this business since before the Great War and are experts at it. They're masters of the game. They'll expect nothing less than the best."

"Don't worry, Mr. Roberts," said Walter with disguised bravado. "We'll make such a good impression on them that they will come back to you for more."

"You've got to hand it to these farm boys." Roberts feigned disgust. "Give them a few weeks in the big city and they become smart asses."

He peered out the window and down the street. "I was just kidding, of course. But I wonder what Sliworski will say when he sees you, Willy. He probably still remembers your father since he and Bashinski engineered that smooth departure down the Vistula River twenty years ago."

"I hope he tells me about it some time," said Walter. "I never did find out exactly what happened that day."

"Here comes a car now," said Roberts, leaning against the window frame. "It must be them."

The imposing black sedan nosed up the knoll and stopped at the entrance of the ancient mansion. A U.S. soldier in a corporal's uniform stepped out, opened the back door and snapped to attention as Major Sandburn stepped out of the car, followed by a tall willowy man wearing a tweed suit and beige shirt. His reddish mustache was neatly trimmed and his sideburns, laced with gray, protruded from beneath his dark brown felt hat. He was followed by a staid, clean shaven middle-aged man in a dark suit, white shirt and hat. The three men admired the imposing structure briefly then walked to the front door where they were met by Roberts who led them into the reception room.

"Colonel Sliworski, I'd like you to meet one of my few remaining regulars, Cyril Roberts," said Major Sandburn when they entered the room. Sliworski removed his hat and shook Robert's hand.

"And Cyril, you know this other fellow, even though you have not seen each other for a while," added the major.

"Deryk Simpson! Why it's been at least ten years and you haven't aged a day."

"You used to say that to all the girls," quipped Simpson as they pumped each other's hands.

"Yes. Those were the good old days," said Roberts. "But it seems that they are gone forever. There hasn't been much doing around here in the past few years. Not at all like those heady days we used to know during the big one. It's been almost too quiet."

"The air is the stillest just before the storm," said Sliworski, entering into the conversation. "Now where are those two prodigies you fellows have for us?" he asked, looking around the room.

"Right this way," said Roberts as he ushered the group into the library where Walter and Victor stood at attention in front of their chairs.

"Gentlemen, I give you two of our best," said Roberts as they approached the two young men. "This is Victor Rudniki, whom we now call Adam and over here is Walter Berglund, now known as Willy 22."

"This is Colonel Sliworski of the Polish Army Secret Service," said Major Sandburn. "And beside him is Captain Deryk Simpson from the British Security Service."

Simpson surveyed the young men with a broad sweep of his eyes then shook their hands warmly. Colonel Sliworski touched Walter's hand then stepped back with a bewildered look on his face.

"Excuse me," he gasped. "It is not often that one observes such an uncanny resemblance between two people. For a moment I thought I was back on the Vistula River twenty some years ago. This young man is a mirror image of his father."

"I didn't know his father, of course." said Roberts. "But this one is a real wildcat."

Colonel Sliworski observed Walter. "Wild cats are hard to tame," he explained.

"Also hard to catch," added Roberts.

Sliworski shook his head in agreement.

"Captain Simpson advises that they will be leaving for England from New York the day after tomorrow," said Major Sandburn to Roberts.

"The men are ready," said Roberts. "Everything else is in order."

"Good," said the major. "We will all go down to the mess for dinner, and then the men are yours, Captain Simpson."

"We'll be submerged for several days after we leave the day after tomorrow, so let us enjoy the next two days on land," suggested Simpson to the young men.

"Submerged?" asked Walter as he glanced at the officers with a puzzled look.

"His Majesty's submarine," said Simpson. "It was on maneuvers in the West Atlantic and we will be hitch hiking a ride back, so to speak. Have you ever been on a submarine before?"

"I've never even seen one," responded Walter innocently.

"Me neither," added Victor.

~~~

The frosted light bulbs in the overhead fixtures flooded the room with white light, a welcome contrast to the inky water outside and the dark interior of the vessel. Walter sat on his bunk, his back leaning against the wall, eyeing his caller who had just come in the door. The vessel rolled gently from side to side.

Colonel Sliworski, looking younger than his fifty-two years, sat down and leaned over in the only chair in the room, his elbows resting on his knees. He spoke in Polish.

"You really startled me the other night, Wladimar," he said standing up to prop the chair against the wall. "I thought I was seeing a spirit. That's how much you reminded me of your father."

"I didn't know what was going on when you stood back like that and just stared at me for those few seconds. Did you know my father well?" Walter asked in Polish.

"I only met him twice. Once at their wedding in Krakow and the other time on the fishing boat that took them out of the country."

"I barely remember him," said Walter. "What kind of a man was he?"

"Brilliant. I guess that would be the best description. Brilliant, but somewhat intense. He had no time for politics or the patience to become involved in such things. But it seemed that he was destined to become a part of all that, whether he liked it or not. He sort of got swept up in it because of where he was and what he was doing. I'll never forget the time that Colonel Bashinski and I told him that he was going to the United States instead of joining the rest of his family in Canada. He was very upset and accused me of plotting his destiny. In looking back now, I can't help but think that he was probably right. If we hadn't arranged for that job for him in Toledo, he might still be alive. But then, even we who are used to those types of incidents didn't think that it would happen, in the United States of all places."

"Yes. It seemed like a waste of someone's life; someone who was only trying to do his job and I understand from my uncle Stanislaw that he was real good at it," said Walter. "When I was old enough to figure out for myself what happened to them, I made up my mind to do something to put things right. I will not rest until I do."

"In a way that is what attracted us to you, Wladimar," said Sliworski. "You know that you now have three names – Wladimar, Walter and Willy.

If you don't mind, I would like to call you Wladimar because it comes easier to me."

"Sure. You can do that," said Walter. "My grandmother used to call me that most of the time."

"As I was saying," continued Sliworski, "we were most impressed by your resolve to honor your parents. But now that you are in this organization, it would be better if you were to become less passionate about that matter. In this business, patience and cool heads must prevail if you are to be effective and, indeed, to survive."

"I'll do anything I have to do in order to be a good soldier," promised Walter.

Sliworski chuckled approvingly at Walter's innocent choice of words describing his occupation.

"General Bashinski would no doubt love to have you in one of his military regiments, but we also need you in our organization. I still hope that you will have an opportunity to meet the general some day. He is a relative of yours on your mother's side, as you probably know. He was the one who engineered your father's departure from Torun more than twenty years ago. For some reason your father seemed to distrust the general at times. Maybe he was bit afraid of him, but he shouldn't have been because in some ways they were pretty much alike. Both of them liked to be left alone to do the work that they enjoyed best – your father at his formulas and designing, and General Bashinski at his soldiering. But fate changed things for both of them, bringing your father to his death and calling the general to help salvage the remnants of the Polish nation on more than one occasion when others had failed or given up. Sometime I think that your uncle Stanislaw had the right idea. Take up a quiet pastoral life and forget all of that."

Walter's eyes shone with excitement. "But look at what you people have done," he said. "You have restored your country and brought it back from the dead. My uncle does not want to talk about these things, but my grandmother told me about it. There are not many countries that can say they did this."

"True, Wladimar, true," mused Sliworski glancing at the ceiling. "But for how long? Even now the wolves are stalking us. Will we will be the first to be torn apart when the next political and military struggle occurs in Europe?"

"We'll chase them back," vowed Walter. "Back at the farm I used to stalk wolves and drill them through the head with my 22 rifle. I will do the same to them."

Sliworski laughed at Walter's ebullience. "First we'll have to find out what their plans are, Wladimar," he said. "Then we'll be in a better position to defend ourselves."

"Back in Washington I told Roberts that I would rather work for America than Poland, but now I think that I would rather work for you and your people."

"In this business it does not really matter who you are attached to," explained Sliworski. "It is how you do your job that is more important."

"You can count on me," promised Walter.

"I am convinced about that," said Sliworski. "It's been nice talking to you. I hope we get a chance to talk some more before we arrive in London."

He stood up and straightened up his lean frame as he walked slowly toward the door. As he touched the door handle he put his right hand into his breast pocket and pulled out a folded paper.

"Here is a map of western Poland and northeast Germany," he said, handing it to Walter.

"Make yourself as familiar as you can with the names of all the cities and towns. That will keep you from getting bored during our journey."

~~~

The lights inside the Royal Navy submarine took on an exaggerated whiteness as the vessel moved through the dark waters of the Atlantic. The two young men, both used to the sunny outdoors, were beginning to experience boredom and confinement. During the first four days of the voyage across the Atlantic, the submarine surfaced several times. On the latest surfacing, Sliworski invited Walter and Victor to the bridge and, from a metal platform, they gazed upon the awesome expanse of water on every side. It was a clear and calm day and the waves lapped gently against the side of the vessel. Over the horizon, in all directions, the dark sea, flashing in the bright sunlight, faded and disappeared into the distance, becoming one with the sky. Walter and Victor clung tightly to the round iron railing. Colonel Sliworski eyed them with some amusement.

"Well, how does it feel to be out here in the middle of the Atlantic with only that slippery rail to hang on to?" he asked.

"It feels like we are on some strange planet," said Victor

"Lost. I feel like I don't belong here. Everything is strange. There is nothing familiar and I feel out of place," said Walter.

"Yes, I imagine that it is quite a change from Pennsylvania or that homestead back in Manitoba. Makes one feel rather small in comparison, doesn't it? But we should be in London in about four days and you two will be able to get your feet back on solid ground."

The intermittent blare of the vessel's horn shattered the silence and announced that the deck was to be cleared and all personnel were to go below."

"Let's make our way down now. They are about to submerge," said Sliworski.

When the eagerly awaited fourth day arrived, the submarine surfaced and the faint outline of low hills appeared in the distance. In an hour or so they would be at the mouth of the Thames and would make their way slowly along the river for the last few miles toward London. Sounds of the great port greeted them as the submarine's passengers emerged from the vessel after it docked at a pier marked "For Royal Navy Use Only." The two young men clung to their bags nervously and surveyed the endless lines of vessels occupying the wharf in both directions. They walked down the ramp and stepped onto the dock on unsteady legs.

A gray Hillman Minx rolled down the ramp onto the loading area of the pier. The driver, a tall slim man of about thirty, with a thin face, deep set blue eyes and blonde eyebrows emerged from the vehicle. He walked up to Simpson and took his bags.

"Did you have a good trip, sir?" he asked, with only a hint of a Yorkshire accent.

"Yes. Thank you, Lewis. Nothing unusual except, perhaps, that we met our two new members whom we picked up in Washington and whom I would like you to meet. And you already know Colonel Sliworski, of course," said Simpson.

The driver put the bags down beside the car and held out his hand.

"This is Victor Rudnicki from America and here we have Walter Berglund from Canada. Meet Ray Lewis, boys," said Simpson.

"Say, you chaps are a long way from home. And quite a circuitous route for you, eh Walter, what with coming all the way from western Canada." He shook hands with each of them. "Welcome aboard, chaps. Hope you find London to your liking," said Lewis.

"It's so huge," said Walter in disbelief.

"I learned in school that Britain rules the waves, but I didn't realize that it took all this to do it, " added Victor, waving his hands in both directions at the numerous ships and boats of many shapes and sizes.

"Of course, these are not all ours, and these are just the smaller ones," explained Simpson. "They come from every corner of the world. You will probably see some from your own countries, if you look carefully. But you are right, Victor. It does take a lot of ships to rule the waves, and some of them are here right now."

Lewis maneuvered the Hillman Minx expertly through the stream of impatient afternoon traffic and headed down Woolwich Road. Walter and Victor stared wide-eyed out of the side windows of the small vehicle. Simpson observed them in the rear view mirror. "It would take me several hours to explain in detail the history of the area through which we are passing, but I will give you a few highlights as we drive along. It was near here that the second wife of King Henry VIII, Anne Boleyn, gave birth to a daughter who was to become Queen Elizabeth I. And it was not far from here that Anne made her last trip to the Tower of London to be separated from her head. Back there a way, is where the gallant Walter Drake threw his cloak on the muddy ground to prevent Elizabeth's dainty feet from coming in contact with the muck from the river bank."

They drove past the National Maritime Museum, part of which, Simpson explained, was once known as Queen's House. It was first occupied by Queen Henrietta Maria, whose name still appeared on the facade. Charlton Road turned into Ha Ha Road and they observed the unusual landscape of grassy mounds and hollows which is the domain of the Royal Artillery.

Ancient guns and cannons appeared spotted about the park as if ready to jump into action should the need arise. In the distance, on the right, rose the line of late eighteenth century barracks, stretching a quarter of a mile across the tightly manicured lawns along its front.

"This is it," announced Simpson as Lewis swung the Hillman Minx in front of a section of the long line of barracks. "These barracks will be your home for the next few months. Colonel Sliworski says that they make him homesick because they remind him of St. Petersburg."

Walter and Victor, each carrying large cardboard suitcases, which were dyed and pressed to look like leather, followed Simpson through the heavy door of the ancient, but well maintained building. Inside, their footsteps echoed through the empty hallways and their voices bounced around the walls and ceiling.

"There are not too many people around here anymore," said Simpson. "Everyone feels that the last war was the one that put an end to all wars, so there is not much need for a military," he added cynically. "Everyone except Winston Churchill, that is, but he is considered by most people to be a bit weird and out of touch."

In a corner office, with a large sliding window taking up much of a narrow wall, a stout, balding man sat reading a copy of *The Times*. He put the paper down when the three men approached and lit a cigarette. Simpson stopped at the door, dug into his coat pocket and pulled out two plain brown envelopes.

"Hello Bill. We are back. These are the two recruits from Canada and America, Berglund and Rudnicki. Here are their papers, all in order. They will be part of our Eastern Section."

The man checked the contents of the envelopes and returned them to Simpson.

"Welcome aboard, fellows. My name is Bill Allen." He shook their hands across the desk. "Captain Simpson will show you to your quarters. If you need anything and he is not around, call me."

"Bill is our business head around here," explained Simpson as they entered a wing with numbered doors on both sides of the hallway. "He keeps us all in line. We need someone like him these days when most people doubt our usefulness and finance us accordingly. He is a good man to know. Stay on the good side of him."

"Ah, here we are," said Simpson as they rounded the corner and entered another wing. "You will be residents of Unit M. Here are your rooms, 122 and 123. Which do you want?"

"May I have number 122, please," said Walter. "It will go well with my new name."

Simpson took the envelope out of his pocket and glanced at the papers.

"Yes, Willy, 22. Hey, that is quite a coincidence. Leave your bags in your rooms and I will show you where my office is and also the mess hall and bathrooms, showers and stuff."

The solid brick and stone structure had endured the test of time well and after serving several generations of military personnel for nearly one hundred and fifty years, showed little sign of decay. The boots of thousands of soldiers had hollowed out the stone and marble steps and stairs, but the walls and roof remained erect and solid. Outside, the massive lawns were studded with ancient chestnut and oak trees and the weapons of ages past stood in silent repose, having outlived the men who had built and fought wars with them.

Equipped with plumbing and electricity and other modern amenities, the barracks appeared to offer comfortable, if somewhat austere, accommodation. Although Simpson lived away from the barracks, he had a permanent office there and used some of the services. He accompanied the newcomers to the mess on the first day. Among the diners there, only a few were in uniform. The others spoke in various accents and some in foreign languages. Walter noticed that some of the English speaking men greeted the foreigners in their own languages.

After dinner, Simpson showed them the lounge and games room, complete with pool tables, dart boards and other games which he said were for their enjoyment. He accompanied them back to their rooms and said that he would see them in the morning and would have their schedule prepared. Meanwhile, they were to stay inside their own wing of the building.

As promised, Simpson met the newcomers in their rooms next day. He was dressed in dark trousers, a tweed jacket and a shirt open at the neck. He announced that their formal training would not commence until Monday. This would give the office a chance to get their papers in order and put them on the payroll. He handed each of them a cash advance in British pounds and told them that they would be paid a modest amount in cash and an equal amount would be credited to their accounts each month. Between now and Monday they were free to wander around the grounds, but they would not be allowed to go outside the barracks area until after their training had commenced.

~~~

As instructed by Simpson, Walter and Victor arrived at one end of a large square room in another wing of the rambling barracks. It was eight o'clock in the morning. Twenty-two chairs and desks were arranged in two lines in front of a large pockmarked wooden desk and a pitted blackboard which bore testimony to the many battle plans, both real and theoretical, that had been drawn up and analyzed on it over the years. Several other men began to arrive in pairs and threes and stood around chatting sporadically as they glanced apprehensively around the room.

At two minutes after eight, a spry man of medium stature and about 45 years of age arrived and walked to the front of the room. His black wavy hair was combed in a tight tuft back from his forehead and a short black mustache covered most of his tight upper lip. Long, black eyebrows hung like eaves over his dark eyes. He wore a sports jacket over a vest sweater and white shirt with a brown tie. He was followed by Simpson and five other men who stood along one side of the room. The man glanced quickly around the room and asked all those assembled to find a chair beside one of the desks and be seated.

"I am Major Bert Sloan, the director of your school," he announced with a faint smile. "These six gentlemen along the wall are section leaders and one of them will be your commander, mentor, guide and father confessor, during your training and if and when you are ready to commence your active service."

Major Sloan introduced each of the leaders without describing their positions in the organization or the sections which they headed. He leaned forward, with his hands propped against the top of the desk and surveyed the group of men assembled in the room.

"I want to welcome you chaps to the school. We'll get right down to business," he announced. "In case you don't already know, you are here to learn something about espionage, as this business is politely referred to in some quarters. It is nothing more than a more refined word for spying. If you survive this place until spring, we guarantee to turn you into top-notch operatives who will be able to perform your duties in your designated locations with skill and confidence. The fact that you made it this far is an indication of your ability and determination, but is not a guarantee that you will automatically succeed in this segment of your training. There is much hard work ahead for all of you.

"You were all instructed to stay in the barracks area until now. There is a good reason for this. We did not want any of you going into town and telling anyone who you are and what you are doing here. Before you will be allowed that privilege of leaving the barracks, you will need to assume what we call your 'London Identity.'

"This will be in addition to the working identity some of you already have. During the next several months we will teach you the value of espionage work, some tricks of the trade, and help you to brush up on your knowledge of the language of the target country. We will be spending a lot of time on communications and security. This matter of security is one which we will tackle immediately, since we do not want you all trotting around London in trench coats and felt hats. In fact very few people in London know that we even exist and we aim to keep it that way. And if anyone does anything to change this, he will be on the next boat to his country of origin. Your leaders will give you the basic instruction on this subject and we will have experts coming in to instruct you in the other more complicated and specialized matters."

Major Sloan wished them all well and left the room. The trainees sat silently gazing at the blackboard or at their hands on the top of the small desks. The leaders walked up one by one and announced who their charges will be, and then they all stood up and followed their assigned leaders out of the room.

Walter and Victor followed Simpson down the hall into a smaller office area equipped with a desk, two long narrow tables, a bookcase and a coat rack. A large detailed map of Europe hung on a roller on one wall and a blackboard stretched partway across the front of the room.

"You had better get used to this place," advised Simpson as they entered the room, "because we will be spending a lot of time here together over the next several months. By the way, my service name is Neal, but in London you will address me by my real name, Deryk Simpson. If anyone should ask, my occupation is teacher at a boys' school in Greenwich. Walter, you will go by your real first name in London and your last name will be Berg. Your occupation is clerk at a grain importing company whose name you will receive later. Victor, you will go under the name of Victor Redman and you are a shipper at a spice warehouse. The Berglund and Rudnicki names will stand out too much around here. I will have your identification papers and details of your working positions in a few days. As soon as you have these, and have memorized your identities to my satisfaction, you may venture into other parts of London. Meanwhile, you may write to your families back home. Tell them that you have arrived safely and are starting your jobs. I will want to see your letters before they are posted as I will be the one who will fill in the address where they may write to you."

~~~

A bank of low clouds moved in from the English Channel adding to the gloom of the dreary Sunday afternoon. Walter and Victor explored the manicured grounds of the Royal Artillery Barracks, examining the ancient guns and contemplating the age of the huge chestnut and oak trees. Overcome by loneliness, the two sat beneath a tree and contemplated their futures.

"God, this is a gloomy place," shuddered Victor. "Back home in Pennsylvania at this time of the day we would have a houseful of relatives and guests. The living room would be buzzing with conversation. In the kitchen, my mother and sisters would be preparing dinner. What would you be doing if you were at home?"

"Probably the same as you. We would all be over at Stanley's talking about the last harvest and thinking about next spring. Stanley is my real father's brother, but I call him dad because he and his wife Anna sort of adopted me when my parents were killed."

The conversation stopped and the muted sounds of the city filled the still moist air. They gazed blankly into the distance.

"Lord, those days seem so long ago and far away," continued Walter. He leaned hard against the tree trunk. "You know, if I were at home now I would be preparing for the Sunday evening dance at the school house. Tonight I would join my sisters – well, actually my cousins – and their friends and together we would get a square dance organized. Man, I really enjoyed calling those square dances. That was really fun."

"Yeah. It sure sounds like it was," said Victor. "Well, over the past few days I have been asking myself, 'What the hell are you doing here, Victor? What do you owe these people? What's in it for you?' And do you know the answer I get? Nothing. That's what I owe them. Nothing."

"Oh, I wouldn't go that far, Victor," said Walter. "We may owe them more than we think. We were lucky, you and I, because our parents and grandparents chose to leave the homes which they loved and went to America. But the peace and freedom which we take for granted did not come free. Someone had to work, fight and die for it. And furthermore, there are many people on this side of the Atlantic who are still living in fear of war and oppression. You should hear my grandmother talk about these things. You would not believe what goes on in some of these countries. Human lives means nothing if they stand in the way of someone's drive for power. But now the people want their freedom. They have been wearing the yoke too long. The days of kings and princes are over. Now everyone thinks that he has a right to be king over his own life. I think that you and I can help them to achieve this. That is my speech for today"

"You know, Walter, you sound just like my father. You should meet him some day. He has seen a lot in his day, too."

"Things will get better here when we get into it a bit more, Victor. You can't judge it by the way it seems now."

"I shouldn't tell you this," confided Victor, "but over the past few days I have been thinking about this thing and how to get out of it. I had a chance to get out in Washington. All I had to do was show that I didn't give a damn about their organization, but I decided to pretend that I was really into it, for my father's sake. I thought that he would be proud of me. But during the past few days I was beginning to change my mind again. And you have changed my mind once more, at least for now. So to hell with it. I'll stay."

~~~

The training program which was promised to them by Major Sloan and Deryk Simpson descended with a vengeance next Monday morning and continued unabated all week. For the first two hours of each day they worked with their leader, practicing their new identity and memorizing and being tested on the details of their background, place of birth, the names of their parents and brothers and sisters, level of education and where it was acquired, family circumstances, work experience, religion and the place and nature of their occupation. They also spent an hour a day acquiring and practicing the required vocabulary and accents. For another hour in the morning and two more in the afternoon, the whole group assembled in a large classroom in the rambling old barracks building. The morning session was devoted to lectures by Major Sloan on the theory and techniques of espionage. They were instructed to take notes in order that they would be able to refer to them prior to their weekly tests.

The rest of the afternoon was devoted to more practical subjects. Men with previous experience in the business taught them the skills of the trade – how to act to avoid suspicion, how to employ tricks of deception, how to avoid capture, how to observe important activities, how to enlist the services of local people, how to escape from tight situations and confinement and how to send and receive messages.

There was little camaraderie among the members of the class. They were all engrossed in their tasks, asking questions and taking copious notes. Something secretive in each of their faces spoke of the knowledge and feelings they harbored but would not share. There were no two alike. Their ages appeared to span the spectrum from twenty to fifty and they covered a wide range of sizes, shapes and appearances. A variety of skin colors, facial features and body structures indicated that they came from varied racial backgrounds.

As the weeks passed, linguists, geographers, psychologists and technologists of many types presented their lectures and demonstrations and then disappeared, to be succeeded by others.

There was no time for recreation or travel and the great city of London remained a mystery hidden behind a pall of smoke and a polyphony of sounds only a short distance away.

By late February and early March, the cold, moisture laden air masses from the North Sea began to give way to the soft, warm breezes from the south east. Simpson, who had been Walter's and Victor's mentor throughout the grueling months of training, announced that they would be leaving for the continent in a month or so. Because they were still novices in the business, their job during the coming spring and summer months would be to familiarize themselves with the locality and the habits and life-styles of the inhabitants in their sphere of operation. While they would both be starting out in the same location, later as they became more familiar with the area and their duties, they would separate and work independently. Their area of operation would be somewhere in eastern Germany, but their base would be in western Poland and they would enter Germany from that country.

"Before we let you roam around in London pretending to be Englishmen, both of you, but especially Walter, will need to polish up your accents. You both still sound like bloody immigrants. So I will ask for some special tutoring time before you go into the city."

Several days later, Simpson entered their small office carrying a black leather brief case bound by two straps with silver buckles and a clamp lock. He put it on the top of the desk and unlocked it with a key which hung on a chain around his neck. He pulled out a bundle of maps, held together by a rubber band.

"These are very detailed topographical maps of the eastern part of Germany," he explained as he removed the rubber band and stretched out the maps. "They show everything from the elevation of the land to the location of fields, forests, rivers, bridges, railroads, dams, roads, major buildings and other landmarks. There is a map for each district. I want each of you to take a map and study it carefully, memorizing all the features of the landscape. Picture the area in your minds. To help you do this, I have here a set of aerial photos taken in each of the districts, showing what the country generally looks like. Get to know the villages, towns and cities, their names and sizes, the distances from each other and from Berlin and other major centers. The next most important pieces of information are the rivers and other waterways, and the roads and railways. You will be required to know their names, exact location, routes, terminals and load limits. Starting now, you will take two hours every morning and one in the afternoon for this exercise. I will check on your progress from time to time."

"Which city or town do you think we will be working in?" asked Walter.

"We have not yet received our orders, so I cannot tell you," replied Simpson.

"Do you think that we will have a chance to see anything of London before we leave?" asked Victor.

"I think that would be a capital idea," answered Simpson. "I'll try to make some time available for you soon and we will all go and explore the old lady. But keep working on those accents."

~~~

The dry, warm spring air flowed in softly through the open window of the small barrack room. Outside the windows, birds flitted about the branches of the trees and bushes, singing, mating and building their nests. Streams of brilliant sunshine poured in, purifying the stale tobacco and musty smelling air in the building. Walter and Victor leaned on the window sill staring longingly at the greening outdoors. The door flew open and Simpson strode in, looking casual with his shirt open at the neck and minus his ever present brief case.

"Well chaps, it has been a long winter and you have been cooped up in here long enough. It is much too pleasant out there for us to be sitting around this smelly old place. What say we go out and see the world!"

Walter and Victor quickly jumped off the window sill and voiced their unanimous agreement with the suggestion.

"Good," said Simpson. "We will start out with Greenwich and work our way toward the city center. Go back to your rooms and change into something casual then come back here. Bring some money with you in case you see something that you may wish to purchase. Five pounds should be adequate; ten at the most. Bring an umbrella in case it rains."

They returned quickly, each wearing a pullover sweater over a white shirt with open collar. Simpson led the way to his Hillman. He guided it out of the barracks area into Ha Ha Road and then down Charlton. Walter and Victor stuck their heads out of the open window, devouring the fresh spring air through their flared nostrils.

"We will stop briefly at Charlton House," announced Simpson. "It and Holland House are the last Jacobean houses left in London. They were built around 1607, so that makes them over three hundred years old."

Simpson veered the vehicle into a parking stall in front of the building. The exotic Renaissance detail of the entrance captured their attention, but it was quickly diverted to the panoramic view to the west. The scene which seemed to encompass most of Greenwich and a good piece of London was awesome in its grandeur. The river wound its way like a vine among the buildings, hills and wooded parks toward the haze of the city center. On it, vessels of every description plied their way in an orderly formation in both directions. Here and there, large stone mansions presided over large expanses of grass and gardens, remnants of a more glorious past.

"All these estates once belonged to royalty and the nobility," explained Simpson. "There is one of those old houses in this area that you must see,

Walter. Being a Canadian, you will be especially interested in it. But first let us head down Trafalgar Road to the power station and try out our legs on the River Walk. It will give you a glimpse of what things are like today. They parked the Hillman and entered River Walk, following it upstream past a bustling mixture of warehouses and docks churning with activity and smelling of fish, spices, new lumber and other cargo coming off the ships. The path ran past the historic and famous Trafalgar Pub, now in an advanced state of neglect. But the beer and smoked beef on a bun which they ordered were delicious and refreshing.

Returning to the power station, Simpson pointed the Hillman in the direction of Blackheath and drove past the sweep of grass which once ran all the way to Woolwich where Henry VII massacred an army of rebels from Cornwall. It was also here that Henry VIII staged his magnificent welcome for Anne of Cleves, his ill-fated fourth wife, Simpson explained.

"The king called her the Fat Mare of Flanders," laughed Simpson as he related the story. "She only lasted about six months."

The sharp spire of the Catholic Church of Our Lady Star of the Sea presided over a park which receded into a succession of villas dating back to the seventeenth century. Simpson brought the Hillman to a quick stop in front of one of them.

"This one is called the White House; not at all like the one in Washington," he explained. "This one was once owned by a family named Lawson whose young daughter was the object of affection of one James Wolfe. He lived in that house next door. It was called McCartney House. For years the young General Wolfe visited Elizabeth and each time he returned from a military campaign he would ask her to marry him. She persistently refused and died single in 1759. By a strange coincidence, James Wolfe himself was killed that same year during the conquest of Quebec. Everyone in England celebrated his victory except the residents of this village. They saw it as a somewhat supernatural event. I thought that you might be interested in that story, Walter."

"I certainly am," said Walter, a look of amazement on his face. "We surely were not told that story in our history class."

They continued their tour around Crooms' Hill, past the Greenwich Theatre and into the vicinity of Stockwell Street and Greenwich High Street which harbored a quaint collection of old shops. At the end of these was the impressive terminal building of one of the Greenwich railway lines into London. Heading down Greenwich High Road, they came to the parish church of St. Alphege. Simpson explained that it got its name from the legend which holds that Bishop Alphege was murdered here by the marauding Danes.

"Henry VIII was baptized in the medieval church which stood on this same spot. That fellow really got around," explained Simpson.

They left the Hillman again and walked to a grassy knoll in front of Queen's House and Royal Naval College. Behind the college the outline of a group of buildings stood nestled on the Isle of Dogs, in the middle of the Thames.

"This place fairly reeks with history," commented Simpson as they sat on the grass overlooking the college. "Under this lawn, we are told, there are remains of buildings dating back to Saxon times. It would take me a week or more to show you all the historic sites here. But this is just your first tour. I am sure that you will have other occasions to see the rest of the area later. If your legs are still willing, I highly recommend the walk through the tunnel under the river to the Isle of Dogs. It is a rather eerie experience. We can come back over the bridge across the river from where we can get another view of Greenwich. We will grab something to eat on the island and then head back to the barracks. Another time we will see the sights of Old London. We will stop at the Tower Bridge and the Tower itself. We will also see Westminster Abbey, Lambeth Palace, the Houses of Parliament and the Royal Westminster where His Majesty the King resides."

"You know," remarked Walter, "just seeing this place makes me proud to be a British subject."

"Yes, Walter, this was once a great nation. Even though it was largely built on the backs of the colonies and the sweat of the peasantry, its affairs were well managed. But like so many other great nations before it, its greatness is strangling it and like all the others it will one day decline and another will take its place. I hope I am not around to witness that. But you and your children and mine will surely be there to experience it. Our job – yours and mine – is not to stop the inevitable but to give the people a chance to adjust to the new reality without losing their freedom. Nothing we can do will prevent it. It is the way of all creation. Just like in nature, every organism must be born, live and die, then be replaced by the new. Britain's flower, nourished by the talents of a vigorous and intelligent people and by the blood and sweat of many others, lasted a long time. But its time is near. It cannot last forever and its glory will soon fade and die. It is nature's way. Another will take its place, bloom, bear its fruit and die just like the others throughout history."

Simpson stood up and straightened his lanky frame. He swept the grass off the seat of his pants with his hands.

"And that will be America, Victor," he added. "Its turn has come. It cannot escape."

They strode silently toward the car and Simpson drove it down to the tunnel.

~~~

A hushed group of trainees, their faces reflecting the relief which comes with the last day of school, sat at their desks in eager anticipation. The door flew open and Major Sloan marched into the room, followed by the five section leaders. He tapped the desk with his pointer and his eyes scanned the audience in front of him.

"Congratulations, men on your successful completion of the first leg of your training here and thank you for your steadfastness and dedication. The last few months have shown us that you were well chosen and prepared for your profession and my men and I thank you for your devotion to it. It has made our own jobs a lot easier. The time has come for you to serve your apprenticeship under real working conditions and to try out some of the things that you have been taught over the past several months.

"The timing could not be better," he continued. "That man Hitler has now been in power in Germany for over a year. In his book, *Mein Kampf*, he makes no bones about what he proposes to do with Germany. His goal is to free Germany from the terms of the Treaty of Versailles and to transform her into the strongest military power in Europe. Now, there are many in this country and elsewhere who deny this, saying that Hitler simply wants to restore the economy of Germany from the dismal depths to which it had sunk under von Hindenburg. But there are a few of us here and elsewhere who not only suspect, but are convinced, that the chancellor is secretly pursuing secret military ambitions while publicly displaying restraint in everything except his program of economic recovery.

"Our job will be to determine what is actually going on in continental Europe, and particularly in Germany. Some of you have been assigned to Germany and others to her good friends, Spain and Italy. A few will go elsewhere to gauge the influence that Germany is having on other countries. We want the information that you provide to tell us and our friends whether we are being too complacent. What you do now may indeed save many lives later. Pay close attention to everything your section leaders tell you because I want to see you all safely here next winter. So, good luck to you all. I will be looking forward to seeing some good work on the part of everyone."

Major Sloan picked up his file and left the room. Walter and Victor returned to their small office and sat down silently behind their desks. Simpson arrived minutes later.

"Well boys, this is it," he said, digging into his briefcase. "Here are your papers all fixed up for you. As we said earlier, Walter will be known as Willy 22 inside the organization, but will have another identity in the area of operation. Victor will continue to be called Adam in the organization, but in Europe you too will have another identity. You will find your new names on your passports. Walter, you will be living with a farm family on the Polish side, right on the border. From there you will be able to enter Germany conveniently at any time without having to go through the official port of entry. Victor, you will be working for a florist in a nearby town. Both these families are former Prussian citizens, but their sympathies lie with the Polish people whose background they share. At first the two of you will work together, but later we will assign you each a different territory. For the first while you will just familiarize yourselves with the country, but at the same time keeping your eyes and ears open. Later, you will receive more specific orders. We will be leaving Tuesday morning, by sea."

At Simpson's request, they opened the envelopes he handed them and examined the documents. Each envelope contained a Polish and a German passport. On his, Walter was identified as Karl Teske, born in Danzig on February 27, 1912. Victor's new identity was Paul Mendyk, born in Torun on October 9, 1913. The two puzzled young men looked at each other and then at Simpson.

"Yes, sir, chaps. That is who you are as of this minute, so you had better start getting used to your new identities as of right now. The names have been chosen so that you can be equally comfortable with them in either Poland or Germany. They are neither pure German nor common Polish names." Simpson reached into his brief case and produced several pages of typewritten papers. "The names of your assumed parents, brothers, sisters and their present whereabouts; the schools you attended and the jobs you have held are all here. Each of these will be authenticated by the people named in these papers, should it be necessary, so do not be afraid to give out the information if you have to do so, but only to the authorities in the territory in which you will be working. Tomorrow you will be issued the clothing which you will wear on the continent. It is very important that you blend in as much as possible with the local people, particularly when you get to Germany. That's it for now. You will be leaving Monday morning."

"Excuse me, sir," said Walter, "but will you be going with us?"

"Yes, I will be going with you, but we will separate when we get to your destinations. While I will not be working alongside of you, I will not be too far away. Later I will instruct you on how to contact me should it be necessary."

"How will we know what to do when we get there?" asked Victor.

"Oh, you will be well instructed," said Simpson. "We will be on the boat for three days and will have lots of time to talk about those details. I will, of course, take you to the families with whom you will be living and working and introduce you to them. You will receive further instructions from them."

CHAPTER 33

The newly painted boat, tied up at the pier, gleamed in the noon-day sun. It looked like a cross between a fishing vessel and a pleasure craft. A Union Jack flew above the maze of radio wires and antennas. The name *Barrow* was prominent on its bow. Equipment for deep sea fishing was being taken on board and stored away in lockers on the upper deck. In the wheelhouse, a clean-shaven man in a blue jersey and white sailor's cap was checking the log when Simpson, Walter and Victor boarded the craft. He looked up and recognized Simpson with a broad grin.

"Good day, skipper, sir," said Simpson when the man emerged from the wheelhouse. "These are the two young men we talked about. This is Victor, who will operate under the name of Adam and this one is Walter, whom we call Willy. Boys, I'd like you to meet Duke Harrison, whose name in the organization is Teddy."

The skipper's bright blue eyes peered from beneath his wide eyebrows as he shook their hands. His snug fitting dark blue turtle-neck sweater accentuated his gently sloping shoulders. A slightly turned up nose kept his mouth in a near perpetual smile and his fair skin and light colored hair made him appear younger than his age.

"Duke is going on a fishing trip to the Baltic and offered us a lift," explained Simpson with a wink.

"Show the boys around the boat, Deryk," said Duke. "The first mate is down there somewhere getting things organized. Their bunks are all made up. They can stow their things under the bunks and in the small overhead compartments. Are we about ready to depart, Mr. Simpson?"

"Almost. Major Sloan will be dropping by with last minute instructions. He should be here any time now. With your permission, captain, we will go down below and get organized," suggested Simpson.

"Please do," said Duke.

Below deck, the stairs entered a narrow passageway which led to a small but compact galley in which a short, muscular man could be seen through the doorway. The first mate was checking the supplies for the voyage.

"Come in and meet Milford," said Simpson, "then we will settle in."

Simpson led them to a cramped cabin with two bunk beds. A wide shelf, hinged to the wall could be used as a table or desk, Simpson explained. Two folding chair leaned against the wall at the other end of the cabin. The beds had fresh white sheets and pillow cases and were covered with gray woolen blankets tucked tightly between the mattress and the spring.

"Well, here you are, chaps," said Simpson. "Hope you like it, because we will be on her for a few days."

"Looks just great, almost like our quarters on the submarine," said Victor. "It's hard to believe that they could get all this on such a small boat."

"Oh yes. She is a well designed vessel. There are two more cabins and also a small radio room in front of the galley. I will show it to you when we get moving. Let us go up now and see if the major has arrived."

Major Sloan was engaged in an animated discussion with Duke when the three emerged from below deck. He handed Simpson a large sealed brown envelope, bid them farewell and disembarked.

"Anytime you are ready, we are, sir," said Simpson to Duke.

"I will go down to the radio room and contact my family, and then we will be off," announced Duke.

The *Barrow* emitted a placid groan and pushed away from the quay under the steady hand of the skipper who invited the passengers to remain on deck during the trip down the Thames. The boat stayed near the left bank and followed the river's winding course past the West India Docks, Millwall and Greenwich Reach, then headed toward the open sea.

Duke, as he had often done on these special fishing forays into the Baltic, chose the Kiel Canal route, a 61-mile waterway extending from Brunsbuttelkoog to the city of Kiel on the Baltic coast. Sixteen hours later they stopped at the German customs office, located near the canal's coastal locks. The immigration officer checked their papers, stamped them and waved them through to the line of vessels waiting their turn to enter the locks. The officers wished Duke and his passengers a successful fishing trip, asked when they will be returning and made entries in a log.

Two days later the small boat entered the Gulf of Danzig and headed for the mouth of the Vistula River. On the miniature deck, Simpson, Walter and Victor shaded their eyes with their hands and scanned the shorelines on each side.

"Well, there she is, boys. Your parents' homeland," said Simpson.

"Gee," exclaimed Walter incredulously, "my parents left Poland through this very spot. From what I heard about that part of their lives, I would have expected to find this place filled with authorities watching our every move."

"Duke has cleared our passage over the radio with Polish authorities in the free Port of Danzig," explained Simpson. "Also, times are somewhat different now than they were in 1912 when your parents left. But things can change mighty fast around here."

"My grandmother back home will never believe this. She always spoke about the troubled times in these parts," said Walter.

"The older generation has seen many things that may seem strange to younger people such as you, especially for those of you living in North America," said Simpson.

From the bridge, Duke signaled to Simpson to come to the wheelhouse. Through the window, they were observed engaging in an animated discussion. Simpson stepped out onto the deck and joined the others.

"Walter, we have a big surprise for you. Sometime tomorrow we will go down from Torun to Lubicz and see the very place where your grandparents and the rest of your family lived."

"Oh boy," Walter shook his head in amazement. "When I decided to write that letter to Sliworski, I certainly didn't think that it would lead to this."

"This is not a dull occupation," said Simpson. "I am sure that you will discover that it has many surprises and maybe not all of them as pleasant as this one."

~~~

The Treaty of Versailles returned Torun to Poland after 103 years of occupation by Prussia and its name was changed from Thorn to Torun. Under the Prussian regime, the city had become an important manufacturing and distribution center, specializing in machinery, metal products, chemicals, lumber, furniture and beer. Many of these industries withdrew to Germany after the World War, but Torun maintained an important, though somewhat reduced, status as a key distribution and manufacturing center. Rich in history, the 700-year old city was the birthplace of Copernicus and close to the hearts of all patriotic Poles. The Prussians were equally attached to the old city, since it was their ancestors, the Teutonic Knights, who founded it in 1232, only to have it wrested away from them by the Polish Kingdom in 1411.

Vestiges of these and other historic periods were still displayed in the 14th century town hall to which Simpson took Walter and Victor during their brief stop-over in the city.

"I can see now how the Berglunds became Poles," said Walter on noting that Sweden had occupied the territory around 1703. "My grandfather did not want to talk too much about that, especially when my grandmother was around."

Back at the dockside they were met by a young Polish government officer standing beside an official looking automobile, while Duke remained on board the Barrow. The young man turned the vehicle over to Simpson and disappeared into a nearby building. Simpson drove the automobile to the east end of the city and then entered the highway leading to Lubicz. In less than half an hour they turned into a gravel road at the edge of the village and stopped in front of an aging wooden cottage.

"Well, there it is, Walter," said Simpson, "your grandparents' former home. Unfortunately your grandfather's furniture shop was torn down after the war, so you will not be able to see it."

"It looks quite a lot like the one grandfather built on his homestead, except that this one seems so lonely," said Walter. "Are there people living in it now? May I go inside and see it?"

"I would like to say yes to your going in to see it, Walter. But, yes, there are people living there and we may stir up too much interest among the local people if we went in and explained who we are, even if we made up the story. So it is better that we not do that. But I do plan to take you to see a man who knew your father very well. Why don't we that right now?"

Simpson turned the car around and headed toward the other end of the village as people in the street and in their yards stopped to stare at the rare sight of an automobile. They disembarked in front of an old wooden frame warehouse, weathered gray by many seasons of rain and sun. Simpson stopped the car beside an ancient motor truck. They emerged from the vehicle and jumped up on a narrow loading platform in front of the building. A thin man, with sharp features and a short, graying beard, emerged through a squeaky wooden door and greeted Simpson in Polish.

"Boys, I would like you to come up and meet Mr. Litvak."

Litvak shook Victor's hand, then his gaze shifted to Walter and his hand fell limply to his side. He stepped back and observed Walter more closely, speaking rapidly to Simpson. Walter understood the reason for his alarm. It was his remarkable resemblance to his father, whom Litvak remembered when he was around Walter's age. Walter laughed when he shook Litvak's hand.

"You should have seen Colonel Sliworski when he first saw me. He looked like he had just seen a ghost," recounted Walter in Polish.

"For a moment there, I though that I had gone back in time about twenty years or more. I see that you have learned the language of your people. That is good," said Litvak.

"When I went to live with my grandparents and Stanley's family in Canada, they taught me the language. I think that while I was very young, my father must have taught me some German, because it came very easy to me when I started to chum around with some German speaking friends back home. My grandmother never did learn to speak English well, so she always spoke to me in Polish," explained Walter.

"Ah, yes. How well I remember her," reflected Litvak. "She was a remarkable woman, but also very sentimental. Quite different from your grandfather who accepted things as they were and lived for the day at hand. I was sorry to hear that he had died so tragically at a time when he was enjoying life so much."

"His last few years were very happy ones," explained Walter. "He easily made the change to the new ways and had many friends. With Stanislaw in charge of the farm, he had time to do the things that he enjoyed and to spend time with his friends and family."

"This is so wonderful, hearing about my very dear old friends," mused Litvak. "But let us go inside and sit down. Then you can tell me about Stanislaw, and we must not forget about Victor here. We want to know something about him also."

They entered a cramped office in the corner of the warehouse and sat beside a sturdy unpainted wooden table. In a corner of the small room was a small cot which Litvak said is receiving more and more use as he gets older. Litvak took a bottle of red wine and four glasses from a wall cabinet.

"Let us drink to the memory of Axel Berglund," he said as he raised his glass. "This table was made by his hands nearly twenty-five years ago. It used to occupy a spot in their kitchen and we spent many happy hours around it. When they left, I bought it to keep as a reminder of my old friends. And how is Stanislaw?"

"He is a very happy man. Times are often hard, but he loves the land. When I went to live with my grandparents, he became like a father to me and I even called him that. I know that he would have liked me to stay there with him, but he did not want to interfere with my plans. In fact, he helped me to investigate this job when we saw Sliworski's notice in the Polish language newspaper."

"I am not surprised," reflected Litvak. "I remember him as a very steady man, hard working and mindful of his own business."

The afternoon sun dipped toward the horizon as Litvak recalled with amusement and nostalgia events which had involved the Berglunds. He described the plans leading up to Erik's flight from Torun in 1912 and how they were so successfully executed. The war had come soon after and for four years the region was occupied by the Germans. Litvak seemed to delight in the story about how a group of Polish partisans recovered the parts from the breech of a German field gun and had a draftsman make detailed drawings of them. These eventually reached Erik in Toledo and helped him to complete his development work on a similar weapon at Burlington Industries.

"When the gun became mired in the mud and was abandoned by the German soldiers, some local Polish partisans hitched their horses to it at night and hauled it into the woods where they covered it with branches," Litvak explained. "It stayed there until the tide of war had turned and then it was used by the Polish army to help rout the retreating enemy. The Germans never did return to get it, or perhaps they did but could not find it."

"It is hard to believe that all that happened right here," said Walter. "It seems so quiet and peaceful now."

"In this part of the world these peaceful interludes are rare. Violence is and always has been the rule throughout history. There is no sign that this will change soon, so we just become a part of it," said Litvak. "We work, laugh, sing, dance, fight, weep and die, as the seasons dictate."

"This leads us to the business at hand," Simpson interjected. "Mr. Litvak here will be one of your contacts when you begin working inside Germany. He knows the families with whom you will be living and, at times, he may arrange to pick up your messages, if necessary, and relay them back to us. The day after tomorrow we will travel to a village near the German border which will be your base for the next few months. Mr. Litvak will go with us. You will be left there until further notice. Tomorrow I will provide you with your instructions for the first month of operation. After that you will receive further directions through the network."

Walter and Victor listened attentively and Litvak nodded his agreement. They took their leave of Litvak and drove back to Torun. At the dock-side the same government official emerged from the Barrow and Simpson handed the car keys to him. He drove away without engaging in conversation.

~~~

After breakfast Simpson summoned Walter and Victor to the cramped galley below deck where they sat around a small dining table.

"This will be our headquarters for today," explained Simpson. He appeared jovial and in a good mood. "In this business you do not have fancy offices with desks and telephones." He assumed a more serious manner. "As of this moment we will all discard our normal identities and assume our new ones. I am no longer Deryk Simpson, but Neal, and Victor you are now Adam and Walter you are Willy 22. If in our future contacts you identify yourselves as Victor Rudnicki or Walter Berglund, I will not recognize you. These identities are the names by which you will be recognized inside the organization only and all your contacts with the organization will only recognize you by these names. Of course, when you are working in the field you will assume whatever identities you have been assigned as temporary fronts. We covered all this in our training sessions during the past few months and on our way down here. Now we are beginning to put all this into use. Is everything clear so far?"

The two young men responded that it was. Duke entered the galley and sat alone at another table as Simpson continued his instructions.

"Later today you will be driven to your respective families with whom you will reside in a small community near the German border. For the first month or so I will expect nothing fancy from either of you. You will be almost like tourists, taking in the sights, so to speak, but with one main difference. Your sense of observation must be honed to perfection. You will become familiar with everything in the landscape and commit all the natural and man-made features to memory. Here are some maps. Keep them out of sight when you are in your target area. Do not carry them with you. Each is marked with the areas which you will cover each week. I want you to become intimate with every road, railway, waterway, building, forest, valley, plain, gully and even trees, rocks and hedges.

"And just as important, if not more so, you must observe the people – how they live, work, act, interact with each other, how they talk and what they say and even what they wear. And you must strive to be like them. In this business you have to be so inconspicuous that no one notices you. Any questions?"

There was none and Simpson continued.

"You will not hear from me again for another month or more. Your progress will be reported through your families and our other contacts, and when I am ready to see you again, I will advise them through our network. Do not become overanxious and do not underestimate the value of what you will be doing. Always remember that it is not up to you to solve the whole puzzle, but just to provide the pieces to a small part of it."

The government official delivered the car at ten that morning. They loaded their bags into the back seat and Neal drove it through the city then westward toward the German border.

~~~

The warm spring air, freshened by the cool breezes blowing off the swollen waters of the Vistula River, carried the smells of spring through the open car windows as it sped along the road to Bydoszcz. One of the favorite cities of Frederick the Great, Bydoszcz had prospered during 147 years of Prussian rule when it was called Bromberg. It was the capital of the province of Pomorze, the much disputed territory which was claimed by both Prussia and Poland. In 1919 the Treaty of Versailles awarded the province to Poland and a program of reducing the German influence had been introduced by the Polish government. However, the population continued to be dichotomous, with loyalties considered to be well established along ethnic lines.

Across the border in Germany, a spectacular economic recovery had recently begun, engineered by the new National Socialist government. The new regime was headed by Adolf Hitler whom the aging von Hindenburg had appointed chancellor fifteen months earlier. By 1934, Hitler's National Socialist party had already acquired extraordinary powers in order to avert the national disaster which appeared to face the country as a result of political turmoil and economic crisis. Opposition to the new government was gradually abolished and the country, discouraged after its humiliating defeat in 1918 and disenchanted with the leaders who plunged it even deeper into despair, rallied behind the new party. Taking advantage of the situation, Chancellor Hitler began the introduction of a totalitarian regime called the Third Reich, or the Great German Empire.

Reports of purges carried out among the members of the opposition parties, and even among the National Socialists who were critical of Hitler's new policies, drifted across the gradually tightening border with Poland. There were rumors that the new government would seek to free itself from the restrictions imposed upon the country by the Treaty of Versailles. Depending upon their loyalties, the populace of the adjoining provinces was either elated or frightened by the developments taking place in Germany.

In Pomorze, the loyalties had already begun to crystallize along ethnic and ideological lines. Farmer Otto Radzke listened to the news from across the border. In discussions with his Polish wife, he expressed concern about the situation in Germany and was becoming increasingly convinced that the country was headed toward another military confrontation. After more than two years of living and fighting in the mud and cold of the rat infested trenches on the Western Front, Radzke saw war as a game played for the aggrandizement of politicians and generals. His vocal denouncements of things military reached Warsaw and his assistance in working for peace was solicited and obtained.

In the small villages and fields in the area between Bydoszcz and the border, farmers and peasants, oblivious to the political events to the west, were busy tilling the soil and planting their crops. Because of the depressed economic conditions, cars were a curiosity and the people stopped their work and watched as Simpson and his two passengers drove past. Walter remarked that the farms appeared to become more prosperous the farther west they traveled.

"It is largely the influence of the Germans," explained Simpson. "They have historically been more aggressive in their agricultural reforms and land management. Poland, on the other hand, had moved more slowly and consequently farming practices have not changed much over the decades, or indeed, over the centuries."

Farmer Radzke was one of the more prosperous farmers in the area. His fifty hectares of land along the border were intensely farmed with horse drawn machinery. The land was cleared and well drained. It supported forty head of milk cows and their calves, plus a number of hogs and poultry. The farm buildings were painted and well maintained and everything around the yard spoke of pride of ownership and good management.

"I hear that you are a farmer," said Radzke in Polish when he was introduced to Walter.

"Well yes, but somewhat different than the farmers around here."

"Farmers are the same all over the world," remarked Radzke, "except that some have more to work with than others. I will be looking forward to learning some things from you while you are here."

Walter's eyes scanned the farmyard and nearby fields. "I can't wait to get my hand dirty again, and I think that I can learn a lot from you," he said.

"See what I mean," said Radzke to the others. "We farmers are the same all over the world."

Simpson and Radzke excused themselves and entered the farmhouse for a conference while Walter and Victor inspected the farmyard. The two men emerged a few minutes later and Simpson held out his hand to Walter.

"So long, old chap," he said. "Mr. Radzke here will give you your instructions over the next little while. Remember what I said earlier. Don't get too impatient. You and Victor will be working together as soon as you are both ready to begin. Meanwhile I will deliver him to his family in the village. Just go easy for the first while. Enjoy yourself. I will be in touch later."

He slid his lean frame behind the steering wheel and drove away with Victor beside him.

~~~

Farm animals the world over require much the same care. They must be fed, watered, pastured, housed, bedded, cleaned and nursed when they are sick. If they happen to be dairy cows, they must also be milked every day. Walter moved into the farm routine with ease and he and Radzke soon became an efficient team, each performing his own part of the chores. Around the village, Walter became known as Karl Teske, Radzke's farmhand from the east side of the Vistula, and Victor as Paul Mendyk, the names that they were given in their personal documents. They now had two names to remember in addition to their real ones. On Simpson's instructions, they made a point of being seen together whenever possible. Privately they found it amusing that they should have received several months of intensive training in Washington and London in order to become a farmhand and a laborer in Poland.

Three pleasant weeks slipped by quickly and the farm work associated with the spring season was completed. Early summer would bring the haying season and another period of intensive labor, but for now there would be a short lull in farming activities. One evening at mid-week Frau Radzke cleared the dishes and her husband opened up a map on the kitchen table. He beckoned to Walter to come over and peruse the map.

"These were left here by Neal, with instructions to show them to you when you were ready. I think that you are now ready for the next stage of your assignment. Tomorrow you and Adam will make your first visit inside Germany. This map shows the local precincts that are close to the border. He pointed to a spot on the map.

"This is where you will enter. It is that wooded area at the southwest corner of the farm where we picked up that last load of hay. In all the years that I have lived here I have never seen a border patrol anywhere near there. You will meet Adam at this point and the two of you can wander around Germany until dark and then slip back in the same way. You will not wander too far inside the first time. Remember the instructions that Neal gave you. Act like local people and no one will notice you. Should anyone ask, you are going to Stettin to look for a job in the factories there or that you are on your way back from there. Make sure that your papers are always with you and that you have your German identity at the front of your head. After breakfast tomorrow, you will dress in your good working clothes and Adam will meet you at the border. You will proceed four or five kilometers into Germany and no further."

He handed Walter a small wad of German marks. "Use these to buy your food and, if necessary, bus fare. Also you will note what the local men of your age are wearing and you will purchase one item of similar type of clothing. To buy too much at one time may appear suspicious. I will not go with you to the border. You will be on your own. Once inside, you will forget this place, and my name will not be revealed to any German authority should you get into any difficulty there, nor to any one else that you might meet. If you do, I will not admit to knowing any of you."

~~~

The sun-drenched late May morning was filled with the sounds of birds singing in the trees and hedges, and the buzzing of bees above the clover blossoms. Occasional sounds from the nearby farms and villages cut through the still air and then faded. It reminded Walter of those glorious May mornings back home except that there were more people here. He observed them in the distance walking or driving their wagons on the roads and working in the fields. He walked casually through the stand of oaks, beeches and laurels at the end of Radzke's field and crossed the wooden rail fence into the next farm. He was in Germany! At the edge of the treed area he sat down and waited for Victor.

A few minutes later Victor emerged nonchalantly from the grove of trees and headed toward Walter. They walked together toward the road leading to the closest town which Radzke had told them was about four kilometers to the west. They remembered their instructions and surveyed the landscape for prominent features. Soon they realized that they were not alone on the straight narrow road. Children on their way to school walked along its edges or on beaten paths in the ditch. Farm wagons and an occasional motor truck rumbled along the bumpy road toward the village.

The outline of the village was already in sight when a farmer driving an empty wagon stopped and offered them a ride which they reluctantly accepted.

"Are you young men looking for work?" he asked.

"Yes, we are," answered Walter in his best German.

"Soon there will be work for everyone when Chancellor Hitler starts rebuilding the country. Just look at the condition of this road. No one can tell me that there is no work available. All that we need is someone to organize the people. There is enough work in this country to keep us all busy for a hundred years."

Walter and Victor agreed and they rode in silence for a few minutes.

"Ja," the man shouted above the noise of the wagon, "and another thing that this country needs is an army. Strong, healthy young men like you two should know something about soldiering. Every male in this country should take military training like they used to do before the days of the Wehrmacht. Don't you agree?"

Walter and Victor agreed in unison.

"Mark my word. That day is coming and not at all too soon," predicted the man.

They reached the edge of the village and the farmer turned into a narrow side street and stopped. The two young men jumped off the wagon, thanked him, and headed back to the main road.

"I'll see you on the parade square soon," laughed the farmer as the wagon rumbled along the bumpy street.

"Well, what do you think of that?" asked Walter as they walked toward the town center.

"I guess what we just witnessed was our first sample of public opinion," replied Victor. "Just like our instructor in London described it last winter."

They walked to the village business center and entered a tea house where they each ordered a piece of pastry and tea. None of the dozen or so customers paid any attention to them and they felt safe and relaxed. They listened to the conversations around them while making small talk between themselves in their best German. Most of the discussions around them concerned the planting conditions and the progress of the early seeded crops. At a nearby table a stocky old man with a well groomed handlebar moustache sat drinking coffee and smoking a well used pipe with a curved stem. He reminded Walter of pictures he had seen in his geography book. The man appeared to be a regular customer since most everyone greeted him as they entered the room. A few minutes later two neatly dressed young men came in. After what appeared to be a routine exchange with the waitress, they sat down with the old man and greeted him by his first name.

"Ja, and what is new in the post-office department?" asked the old man.

"Not much new in the post office, but things are starting to happen elsewhere," replied one of the young men.

"It is about time that things started to happen in this wretched country. What is this thing that you are so excited about?"

"We received a shipment of posters on the new employment program. The Chancellor is setting up work camps for the unemployed people and will give jobs to the laborers in public works like highway and railway construction and things that the country needs," explained one of the young men.

The old man smiled and appeared pleased. He took the pipe out of his mouth and leaned over the table to emphasize his point.

"The German race was never meant to remain idle like we have been since the war. It is not our nature. Our people are too ambitious and too industrious. We are not a bunch of sluggards like our neighbors to the east. All that we have lacked over the last few years since the war is leadership. Now that we have a new leader with many new ideas, we will surprise everyone, even ourselves, with what we can do. You just watch."

The old man was joined by other tea house regulars and the discussion returned to crops and weather. Walter and Victor finished their tea and stood up to leave, no one paying any attention to them. After walking casually around the village for more than an hour they headed north, this time determined not to accept any rides as it was still early in the afternoon. After walking about three kilometers they turned east and began their return trip to their original point of entry. Mindful of Radzke's advice to cross the boundary at dusk, they reduced their pace and stopped often to view the landscape and other landmarks as instructed by Simpson.

"You know. I just can't help but admire these people," remarked Victor as they sat under a tree away from the main road waiting for the sun to sink closer to the horizon. "They seem so anxious to start doing something. It is as if they have been held back by something and now they see new hope on the horizon and they are getting all excited about it."

"Yes, it is pretty hard for us not to like them. They are quite a bit like we are. They seem to be a very proud people with so much energy locked up inside of them that is just bursting to get out. Seems like this new leader they have is just what they need."

"So what are we going to put down in our report tonight?" asked Victor. "I didn't see anything very unusual."

"I guess we will just report what we saw and heard," answered Walter. "What we heard from the farmer who gave us a ride and from the conversation in the tea room may be of some interest to Simpson. You remember our lectures last winter? Our job is not to interpret what we see, but to report them. Someone else will do the interpretation."

"If that is all that there is to this job then I think I am going to enjoy it and maybe I will stick around for a while, "said Victor. "But from the way that Radzke talks sometime it sounded like we will be watched and harassed every step of the way."

"It is not like anything like I thought it would be either," said Walter, "but maybe things will change. Maybe he does not want us to become too bold. And this is just the first day."

~~~

They stretched out on the grass, out of sight of the people traveling along the highway, waiting for the blazing orb to dip closer to the horizon. At dusk they entered the wooded area and crossed the rail fence into Poland. That evening after supper farmer Radzke listened attentively to their description of the day's events.

"So they all seem to approve of what the Fuehrer is doing," he mused. "Be sure to put that in your reports. Also the next time, see if you can find a pamphlet or poster or some description of that new employment program you heard about today. Tomorrow you will visit another village and familiarize yourselves with another area of the region, just as Neal instructed you."

By the end of the week the two young men had visited and observed most of the villages and towns within walking distance of the border. As instructed, they had taken notice of the clothing worn by the local inhabitants and bought similar items for themselves to supplement those provided by the organization before they left England. On the pretense of purchasing postage stamps, they stopped at the post office and obtained a pamphlet describing the new employment program and gave it to Radzke. The excitement of the events which were starting to transform the sleepy countryside into a hive of activity was becoming evident everywhere and the plans emanating from Berlin seemed to be meeting with the approval of all those who came within earshot. This emerging vitality among the citizens appeared to be contagious, affecting the two outside observers also, and each day they found the energy to walk farther into the country.

Unemployed youth from the regions streamed through the villages and towns as they made their way to Stetten, Frankfurt, Berlin and other centers where large public works projects were beginning to provide jobs for anyone who wanted to work. The local inhabitants were becoming accustomed to the strange faces and took Walter and Victor to be among those job seekers bound for the larger centers. But remembering the rules drilled into them the previous winter, they did not return to the same place two days in a row. Eventually this took them farther away from the border and by the end of the second week they found it necessary, not only to spend nights in some of the local inns, but also to venture out onto the less traveled roads and trails and sometimes walking cross-country for hours at a time.

Near the end of the third week the two had spent the night at an inn located in a small village on the River Warte and were making their way back to the border through the meadows and hayfields of the surrounding farms. The warm sun and the still air filled them with a feeling of casual irresponsibility and near the end of the morning they realized that they were hungry and thirsty and that there was no town or village in sight. They walked a short distance across a meadow and came to a low hedge of bushes. Peering over the hedge they noticed a farmer cutting hay with a scythe and a short distance away a woman raking hay which appeared to have been cut the previous day. On a tree branch not far from where they were observing the couple had hung a satchel which caught their eye. Walter motioned silently to Victor indicating in sign language that the bag contained food and drink. They remained hidden behind the tall grass and bushes watching the farmer and his companion. When it appeared that they were completely absorbed in their tasks, Walter cautiously made his way to the tree, lifted the satchel, made his way to where Victor was hiding and opened it. The satchel contained a variety of sausages, cheeses and bread. A large jar of tea, still slightly warm, took up one side of the satchel and was balanced by a similar jar on the other.

"There is enough food here for six people," whispered Victor.

"Yes. There is enough for all of us. Let's take some of it for ourselves and return the rest to the branch. They will think that the spirit of the meadow took its portion before the offering was officially made," suggested Walter.

They selected and ate portions of each type of food as the farmer and his companion continued to toil in the meadow, stopping occasionally to wipe the sweat off their brow. After rearranging the leftover food neatly in the satchel Walter crouched up to take the bag back to the branch. As he straightened out he released a loud blast of gas, much to the surprise and amusement of Victor who broke into an uncontrolled giggle. The comic predicament affected Walter also. He broke into a fit of suppressed laughter. In the distance the farmer, resting on his scythe, heard the strange noises emanating from behind the hedge. He glanced toward where the lunch satchel had been and noticing its absence, he shouted to his companion that someone had taken their lunch. They dropped their implements and dashed toward the bushes where they had heard the noises. Walter and Victor still giggling fitfully leaped to their feet and ran toward the woods, followed by the cursing farmer and his companion.

"You lazy louts," shouted the red-faced farmer. "Why don't you get a job instead of stealing from poor hardworking people?" This was followed by a torrent of profanities involving the ancestry of the two retreating culprits. However, his portly stature and plus a set of suspenders which kept slipping off his shoulders, slowed down the farmer and Walter and Victor were able to quickly escape from his sight. After running for about half a kilometer they stopped, exhausted and still laughing at the experience.

"They never told us about anything like this in London," laughed Victor as he flopped onto the thick grass to rest.

"Nor in Washington," gasped Walter.

"If this is spying, then it sure beats working," said Walter.

"Yeah. Who wants to make hay when you can do this for a living?" quipped Victor.

~~~

Walter's assumption of being spared the toils of haymaking was soon to be tested. The cool, showery spring season gradually gave way to the dry, warm breezes of early summer. It was the peak of the haying season and farmer Radzke announced that Walter's help would be required over the next ten days or so for this annual chore. During this period, Victor would be occupied in tilling his employer's flower beds. The opportunity to participate in this strenuous work was not a new experience for Walter. He knew that nearly halfway around the globe Stanley was also preparing to bring in his annual hay crop, but for the first time in several years Walter would not be there to help. As they went about their tasks, he noticed that as long as they were in the fields, Radzke spoke only about farming. No mention was made about Walter's official duties in that part of the country.

"What kind of hay does your brother grow back home?" asked Radzke, as he and Walter rested on the shady side of the haystack.

"Because the land is so new, we still have a lot of wild hay," explained Walter. "Stanley calls it red-top and rye grass; but on land that once had trees on it, wild pea vines grow profusely and it makes beautiful hay. The animals go simply crazy about it in the winter time."

"Here we have to plant our hay fields," said Radzke. "The land is old and in short supply, so we have to make every square meter of it count and nurse everything along."

"Yes, I imagine that in thirty years or so we will have to do the same back home," explained Walter. "There is not much virgin land left even now."

"I hope that the situation there never reaches the point which faces the people on this side of the Atlantic. For hundreds of years now, land has been the bane of Europe. There never seems to be enough for everyone. These beautiful fields before you, which were sown and nurtured with so much love and devotion, obscure the bones and blood of many generations of Europe's youth who sacrificed their lives either to protect or conquer this land."

"Yes, my grandmother often talked about these things back home," said Walter, "but I found it hard to imagine how that could be. In fact, I find it difficult to relate to that scene even from here. It is so quiet and peaceful. Seems like it has always been like this."

"That is true, that is the way it looks now; but if only we can make it last," sighed Radzke. "If we can only make it last."

He stood up, stretched and looked at the remaining hay lying in windrows on the ground. "Looks like another day's work, then we should be all finished. On Monday, you and Paul can go about your regular business again."

~~~

Daily, the radio broadcasts coming out of Germany revealed the excitement that was building in that country. The heat of the summer paralleled the emerging political and economic temperatures in Germany. From Berlin, a steady stream of pronouncements by the National Socialist government promised that, as chancellor, Adolf Hitler had set the country upon a course which would right all the wrongs that had been bestowed upon the German people in the past. He would begin by curing the epidemic of unemployment which had gripped the nation for so many years. He and the new government would then concentrate on ensuring the security of the nation, rehabilitate the economy to bring prosperity to the people and restore the country to its former position as a major world power. One could almost hear the cheering which greeted the announcements and feel the energy which they generated among the people.

Only a few weeks earlier, on April 30, 1934, Hitler had assumed complete control over Germany's schools and appointed Dr. Bernard Rust as Reich Minister of Science, Education and Culture. The new minister immediately set about changing the curricula and promised to have modern new textbooks ready for the fall term. He publicly proclaimed that all educational agencies in the country would have two common goals, namely the formation of the National Socialist man and woman, and the nurturing of the new Reich.

In the newspapers which they brought back with them from inside Germany, official notices alerted parents that all German youth between the ages of ten and eighteen were now required to belong to the Jugend, the Hitler Youth Organization. For girls, it was mandatory to remain in the organization until the age of twenty-one. The movement had previously existed as a voluntary organization and by the summer of 1934 there were already between three and four million disciplined and uniformed youth in the Jugend. The newspapers wrote glowingly about the beneficial effects which the movement was having upon German youth by instilling in them responsibility and pride in work and achievement. If there was anyone who disagreed, that voice was not being heard anywhere.

Two days after the completion of the haying operation, Radzke informed Walter that a message had come from Simpson asking for a meeting with Walter and Victor in Bydzosycz. They left for that city next day by train and were met by Simpson at the railway station, then drove to a hotel where rooms had been reserved for them. Simpson was in a good mood when they assembled in his room for discussions.

"Well, chaps, I am pleased with the progress which you have been making and the quality of the reports that you have been providing," he said.

"Do you mean to say that this is all that there is to this job?" asked Walter with a hint of disappointment in his voice.

"For the moment, yes," replied Simpson. "But please don't underestimate the value of what you are doing. For example, your reports tell us how the local people are reacting to the new initiatives in Germany and this information is very important to our bosses."

"The mood of the people there is almost electrifying and has changed a lot even during the short time that we have been going there," explained Victor. Walter nodded in agreement.

"The government has done a good job of gathering public support and now appears to have the confidence to move forward on even bigger initiatives," agreed Simpson. "There are indications now that Hitler will soon renounce the terms of the Treaty of Versailles and embark on a massive rearmament program. In fact, he may have already begun this process under various guises. This will, in fact, be part of your new assignment."

Simpson's piercing blue eyes quickly scanned the room. He opened the door and looked up and down the hall. Satisfied that there was no one within earshot, he unrolled a map and spread it out on the table where Walter and Victor were seated. He spoke softly.

"You will have two main objectives in your next assignment," he explained. "Starting immediately you will begin to observe and report on the youth activities taking place in Germany, especially in some of the larger centers in the eastern part of the country, all the way to Stettin. To the extent that you can, observe what they are teaching these young people, what type of exercises they engage in, who their leaders are — are they civilian or military — what rules they follow, and so on. If you are able to obtain copies of their training material, these would be of great value to us. Is everything clear so far?"

They indicated that it was and Simpson continued. "Your next assignment is a bit more risky and I want to emphasize that in this segment of your work you will act as observers only until you are given instructions to do otherwise. Our contacts in Hungary tell us that the Hungarians are apparently collaborating with the Germans in the development of military aircraft. We have only scraps of information, but what appears to be happening is that the Hungarians are manufacturing and assembling the aircraft then sending them to Germany disguised as civilian air planes. In Germany they are tested and fitted with armor for military use. If this is true then it is a flagrant breach of the Treaty of Versailles. We also have information that some of these aircraft are being equipped, tested and stored somewhere in the Stettin region. You will work your way slowly into the towns and villages around the Stettin area, keeping your eyes open for aircraft movements and also on rail shipments from the south. If you see any new aircraft coming in, try to get a good look at them and report the information quickly. You will find it necessary to spend several days at a time inside of Germany now that you will be entering deeper into the territory. I will give you the name of our contact there. His code name is Horst. I will now write his real name and address on this piece of paper and you will memorize it before you leave this room and return the slip of paper to me. Is this clear?"

They shook their heads to indicate their comprehension and concentrated on the name and address written down by Simpson. It was Edgar Remke, owner of the Stargard Tailor Shop. After a minute or so they handed the scrap of paper back to Simpson.

"All right. We've got it," said Walter.

"Good. Through this contact you will receive further instructions from us. I expect that this assignment will take you through the rest of the summer and perhaps into the fall. If this is so, then I may not see you until we all return to London late in the fall. So take your time. Do not get overanxious. Remember that you are no good to us if you are in jail somewhere or dead. Now for our last piece of business."

He opened his brief case and brought out two bundles of German marks and handed one to each of them. "Remember not to carry too much of this around with you. Just enough to last you a few days. Too much money arouses suspicion. I don't know why I am telling you all this. You were supposed to have learned it all last winter. Now let's go out and have something to eat."

Early next morning they took leave of Simpson and returned to the border area. The following day they crossed into Germany and headed toward Stettin.

CHAPTER 34

The region through which they traveled to reach Stettin was settled by Slavic tribes more than ten centuries earlier and to the Poles the city was known as Szczecin. In more recent times the Germans had laid claim to the province, and from 1648 to 1720, it was ceded to Prussia. It remained a part of the German Empire following the partition of Poland in 1815. In 1933, because it was an important manufacturing and transportation center, it was chosen by the National Socialists as one of the first locations for work camps in northern Germany. Its access to the Baltic Sea via the Oder River and to Berlin by canal and rail made it one of the most strategic locations in Germany.

Walter and Victor took the train into Stettin. The spire of the Church of Saint Peter and Paul, the oldest Christian church in the Pomeranian region, was the first landmark that came into view as they approached Stettin. Inside the city they mingled with unemployed men and youth, from the eastern and northern regions of Germany and from the Prussian districts, who waited eagerly to be registered for the work camps and to be assigned to their jobs. With their German identities, Walter and Victor moved about freely in the company of either the labor camp recruits or the tourists viewing the picturesque wooded area near the city, with its imposing castle of the Pomeranian princes.

Pictures of the Fuehrer, Adolf Hitler, were now posted everywhere and the overwhelming presence of the new bureaucracy was inescapable. The playgrounds of the city's schools were filled each evening with uniformed goose-stepping Jugend members ranging in age from ten to fourteen. They marched to stirring martial music, saluted the new German flag and the large imposing posters of the Fuehrer.

During the day, the grounds of the elementary schools were utilized to provide junior youth, or Pimpfs, with what was described as "world-point-of-view" training and lessons in foreign affairs. These academic presentations were interspersed with periods of strenuous physical exercises. The leaders all appeared to be civilians wearing the uniforms of the youth organization. There were few military personnel to be seen anywhere around Stettin.

The two young men marveled at the respect and attention showered upon the youth of the city and wondered why Simpson would be so keenly interested in their programs. Impressed with all this dedication to the country's youth, the two young men mixed freely in the evenings with parents who watched proudly as their sons and daughters performed their precision drills or exhibited their athletic skills.

While watching one of these performances one evening in late July, a sudden heavy shower caused the bystanders to take refuge under the trees and in doorways of nearby buildings. As Walter and Victor rose to leave they noticed a brown envelope with some papers in it sitting on the ground. They looked at each other momentarily and with Victor blocking the view,

Walter casually picked up the envelope and slid it inside his shirt. They found shelter in a doorway across the street and when the rain stopped they made their way to the rooming house where they stayed.

Inside their room, they closed the door and the curtains, and silently examined the contents of the brown envelope. They knew immediately that it was the Pimpfs manual and some notes left there by either a trainee or a parent. Inside the first page of the manual was the slogan of the youth organization: ZAEHNE ZUSAMMEN! AUSHALTEN!

"Teeth clenched! Endure!" translated Walter.

On the next page were listed the basic tenets of the Pimpfs. These boldly stated that Adolf Hitler is the savior of the nation and stands above all, and that foreigners are not to be trusted and revenge must be taken against them. The next two principles dealt with survival, explaining that in nature the strong rightfully kill the weak and that survival of the fittest is the basic rule of life. The first chapters were devoted exclusively to a discussion of races and beliefs. Featured prominently in them was a spirited condemnation of Christianity, Judaism, Freemasonry and Marxism. The chapter ended by stating that a pure race is the only good race and that this was the German race to which the Pimpf belong. As they read the text, they looked at each other and shook their heads in disbelief.

The papers revealed that the package belonged to a ten-year-old senior member of a section. Among them was a corrected copy of a test which had been written earlier, containing both brief questions and answers, and a short essay. One question dealt with the United States of America and the answer to the question regarding the name of the president it appeared as 'Rosenfeldt – Nationality Jew.' The essay described the democracies as decadent and unnatural in that they nurtured the weak and suppressed the strong. This principle led to the Treaty of Versailles which was a masterpiece of treachery imposed on the German people. He ended by writing that only might is right and with this principle in mind, Germany will one day conquer the world. The instructor had checked the answers individually and on the edge of the paper in bold letters and red ink wrote 'HEIL HITLER'!

They slipped the packet under the mattress where it would stay until next morning when they would deliver it to Horst, the contact whose name and address they memorized earlier. The address led them to a small tailor shop on a side street a short distance from the main avenue. He was short and stocky, with a short-clipped moustache and black curly hair. He wore a vest, white shirt and blue arm bands. He looked at them through a thick pair of gold-rimmed lenses. When they mentioned the password he invited them behind the counter for a "measurement."

Horst examined the contents of the brown envelope closely. "You know, I have been trying for almost a year to find something like this, but couldn't. It seems that each member receives only one and it is not replaceable. I would not want to be the poor boy who lost these. I'll see that they get to Neal immediately."

He surveyed the two young men, peering over the top of his glasses. "Why haven't you contacted me earlier?" he asked.

"Because we had nothing to give you until today," answered Walter.

"You should have come around anyway. Neal has been asking about you. Have you got anything to tell him about the aircraft yet?"

"Nothing yet," answered Victor.

"Keep an eye on the airport, but meanwhile Neal wants you to check out a construction project taking place in the woods about fifteen kilometers from here." He wrote down the directions. "They say that it's a public works project of some kind but the security is so tight that no one can go in and out of the site except the workers, and they are carefully screened and selected for the job. I would suggest that you observe it from a distance at first, but if you should be interrogated, explain that you are looking for work and thought there might be a job for you there. Keep me informed. Do not stay away so long next time."

Following them past the counter, the contrite tailor apologized that their garments would not be ready for about a week, as the waiting customers looked on.

~~~

The growl of the powerful earth moving machines was punctuated by the clang of swinging steel tail gates on the trucks as they discharged their loads over the steep earth bank. They watched the action from the dense undergrowth in the tranquil forest nearby. Trucks and equipment entered and then disappeared behind a small hillock like ants building an anthill. A dense wire fence surrounded the area and the only access was through a gate at which a sentry was posted. Victor and Walter had taken a local bus and got off at a major intersection.

"Well, what do you make of all that?" whispered Victor.

"That is a mighty big hole that they are digging in the side of that hill. I wonder what it is," mused Walter. "Maybe it's a salt mine or something like that. Let's try and estimate how far back it goes by counting the minutes that it takes the trucks to go in, get loaded and come out again."

They chose a brightly painted vehicle which stood out from the rest and watched it entering and reappearing with its load. Their rough calculations suggested that the underground cavern was at least a thousand feet long. The location was carefully noted and they made their way back to Stettin.

"Neal will be pleased with this information," Horst assured them when they explained what they had seen that afternoon. "Apparently there are several of these things under construction throughout Germany. If you come back tomorrow I should have further instructions for you. It may be better if only one of you came and you could take turns coming here. That way it will not give rise to suspicion. Bring some sort of a garment with you; something that needs repairs or a button sewn on."

Next day the instructions from Neal were clear. "Send a report on the construction project each week. Note especially any changes in the nature of the activity and the appearance of the structure."

CHAPTER 35

As the month of July waned, so did the vibrant and enthusiastic mood that had gripped the city earlier. Repressed groups of individuals with deep concerns etched in their faces carried on conversations in subdued tones. The newspapers carried stories that the SA, or Storm Troopers of the National Socialist Party, were being reorganized under a new commander, Viktor Lutze. They said nothing to deny or confirm rumors sweeping the country that the previous SA leader, Ernst Rohm, who had been a friend of Hitler's since before the 1923 Beer Hall Pusch in Bavaria, had been deposed. Other rumors spread claiming that Rohm and a number of his lieutenants had plotted to gain control of the German army and had all been arrested somewhere near Munich and executed. Some said that, yes, Rohm had indeed been executed, but not because of insubordination, but because he was gay.

It was the first time since Walter and Victor arrived in Stettin that the prevailing optimistic mood of the city's inhabitants seemed to be interrupted. For several days, squads of Secret State Police rode through the city with machine guns mounted on open vehicles. They disappeared as quickly as they had appeared, and the city slowly began to regain its original vitality.

"Keep out of sight as much as you can and stay where you are," counseled Horst when Walter and Victor called on him. "These are tense days, with power struggles going on all around. But it is also a good time to observe things discreetly because the surveillance is largely focused on their own. Our turn at being watched will probably come later when all this has been settled."

Another trip to the excavation site revealed that construction of the underground facility was continuing at a feverish pace. A new development at the site was the appearance of a large number of cement trucks which delivered endless loads of material to the operation. They disappeared into the gaping entrance and dashed out for refills. Through the wide entrance on the other side of the construction site, earth moving equipment continued to haul and discharge their loads onto a now massive earthen shelf.

After several days, the people's vibrant mood appeared to have been rekindled. Rumors of the sordid Munich affair had passed and appeared to be forgotten or dismissed as a necessary move on the part of the Fuehrer. The summer school vacation brought hundreds of Hitler Youth into schoolyards and streets. Young girls and boys smartly arrayed in brown uniforms, marched to stirring band music or engaged in various athletic activities. On the Oder River, teams of disciplined youth participated in rowing or river crossing exercises using large inflated rafts. At the edge of the city equally determined youth maneuvered motorcycles through loose sand and obstacle courses designed to challenge their driving skills. Other groups flew hand made gliders. Everywhere their efforts were cheered by groups of admiring parents, friends and other on-lookers, who now included

Walter and Victor.

Posters appeared everywhere showing uniformed grim-faced youth beating drums and carrying swastika flags while scattering hordes of undesirable characters in every direction. "Out with the trouble-makers," proclaimed the posters, while calling for the "Unity of youth within the Hitler Youth." In Stettin, the country's young generation appeared to be rising to the challenge.

A short time later the news of the death of President Paul von Hindenburg, on August 2, saddened the faces of only the older men and women in the streets, but not of the younger generation who celebrated the death of "The last of the Junkers" or proclaimed that "Now we can get on with the job of rebuilding Germany." They cheered the assumption of the president's office by Adolf Hitler, who immediately appointed himself Fuehrer of the Third Reich. Older posters showing Hitler and von Hindenburg, entitled "The Marshall and the Corporal" soon disappeared and new ones featuring the Fuehrer alone took their place.

As the weeks passed, the population which began the summer in a sober but determined mood, now increasingly got caught up in the excitement of the events taking place all around them. Everywhere the city buzzed with activity. New factories opened almost weekly, increasing numbers of customers thronged the places of business and farmers hauled their heavy loaded carts and truckloads of produce to market squares and warehouses. In the port, ships from many nations steamed in and out daily and in the streets increasing numbers of lean, muscular young men appeared in navy, army and state police uniforms, some on leave and others making the way to their units.

Posters around the city proclaimed the coming of a giant Hitler Youth rally to mark the end of the summer vacation for students. On the scheduled Sunday afternoon, Walter and Victor joined the large crowd assembled in a field prepared for the exercise. Boys and girls in their crisp, well pressed light brown shirts, shorts or skirts and well shined boots formed into platoons and companies for the march past. Above the reviewing stand the Hitler Jugend banner flew majestically above the heads of the officials and guests. The bands struck up the stirring martial music and the platoons, preceded by flag bearers, marched proudly past giving their trade-mark outstretched arm salute as they passed the reviewing stand. The waves of marchers lasted more than an hour.

"Isn't this really something to see?" said Walter to Victor in German, his voice revealing the emotional effect that the spectacle had on him.

A mother, standing nearby, shook her head in total agreement while wiping the tears from her eyes. "I am proud to be German today. We are no longer the cesspool of Europe. Heil Hitler!"

A leader on the reviewing stand presided over the demonstrations which followed. Youth from the different groups performed feats in manual and athletic skills. At the end of the demonstrations the leader announced that a member of the Jugend would recite the new prayer for the youth movement, written by the Hitler Youth leader, Baldur von Shirach. A drum roll followed and a member from one of the platoons ascended the stage. He saluted the reviewing officials and read the prayer in a clear loud voice.

"Adolf Hitler, we believe in thee. Without thee we would be alone. Through thee we are a people. Thou hast given us the greatest experience of our youth, comradeship. Thou hast laid upon us the task, the responsibility, the duty. Thou hast given us the name (Hitler Jugend), the most beloved name that Germany ever possessed. We speak it with reverence; we bear it with faith and loyalty. Thou canst depend upon us, Adolf Hitler, Leader and Standard Bearer. The youth is thy name; thy name is youth. Thou and the young millions can never be sundered."

A great silence descended upon the large crowd as the audience contemplated the words that they had just heard for the first time. Suddenly one, then two, then several platoon leaders began to applaud. The platoons of uniformed youth joined in and the applause spread like wild-fire becoming louder and louder, consuming the whole assembled throng. The band played a few bars of familiar music and thousands of young voices broke out in the moving song Gut Nacht Kameraden. In the audience, the older men and women who had held back, impulsively joined in one by one until the still evening air rang with the sound of the band and thousands of voices. The singing stopped and while many wept, the crowd raised their outstretched arms in a salute to the new order which they had just accepted.

Walter and Victor walked silently toward the city. The crowd thinned out and the people dispersed in different directions.

"I think that we have just witnessed the beginning of something big," commented Victor as they walked alone into the night.

"The world will never be the same again," Walter prophesied.

~~~

In the sky above the city three aircraft droned lazily as they began their slow descent toward the airport at the edge of the city. From the ground they looked like flying wings with a short, narrow fuselage and rectangular tail. The droning sound was coming from the four engines on each aircraft, two of which were mounted in each of the huge wings. It was the largest airplane that they had yet seen over the city. They remembered Neal's message and quickly made their way to the airport.

A group of people were admiring the aircraft through a high wire fence facing the end of the tarmac. The shiny new machines were parked on a large concrete pad where several mechanics and maintenance people fussed over them. The silver and black planes rested on a four-wheel undercarriage and their noses had large areas of glass for the crew to see out. The lettering on the massive wings and on the tail read D-APIS.

"That is the Junkers G 38," said a man standing beside them.

"It's a beautiful plane," said Walter.

"Yes. It was designed to be an airliner," explained the man, pleased that he had an audience to which he could demonstrate his knowledge of the aircraft.

"Its wing span is forty-three meters and its length is over twenty-three meters," he continued. "It has a cruising speed of 180 kilometers an hour, but the most amazing thing about this machine is its wings. Would you believe that they can seat three persons inside the leading edge of each of those wings, in addition to the twenty-six in the fuselage and two in the nose? What a machine! There is none like it anywhere in the world."

"How do you know so much about all this?" asked Victor.

"I used to work in the factory that makes them in Dessau, but I hurt my right hand and can no longer handle the tools."

"What are the planes doing here?" asked Walter.

"I don't really know," replied the man, "but it looks as though they are being converted for hauling freight because there are no windows in them."

The two young men moved away from the group and started walking toward the city, slowly at first and then picking up their pace. "Can you believe our good fortune, Victor?" said Walter, elated. "We got all that information without even asking. I hope you remembered some of it. You are the guy with the good head."

"You are lucky that I made a point of remembering. The wing span is forty-three meters and its length is twenty-three meters. It has a speed of 180 kilometers an hour and can carry 36 people."

"Wow! You'll be in Simpson's good books now for sure," said Walter.

"Neal says not to let the planes out of your sight," warned Horst several days after he had transmitted the information about the aircraft. "He had wanted you back in London around November first, but now he says you are to stay here until you get all the information he needs on the Junkers sitting out there even if it means staying here past that date."

Recognizing that there was something unusual going on and remembering the lessons they learned about security during the winter, their vigil assumed a more subtle routine. In order not to attract too much attention they took turns observing the planes from less conspicuous positions. A nearby park bench seemed to fit the bill well as no one else seemed attracted to it. The Junkers remained on the concrete pad for about three weeks without any action taking place around them. It seemed like they were waiting for something to happen. One day near the middle of September both young men decided to visit the airport on the same day to avoid the boredom of solitude. They could not have chosen a better time to do this. As they watched, the crew entered one of the planes and started the engines. Some time later the plane taxied out to the airstrip. There the four engines revved up noisily and the aircraft sped down the runway and soon became airborne. Without gaining much altitude, it flew in a semi-circle then straightened out and headed away from the city. It soon disappeared behind the tree tops outside the city limits.

"Odd that it should fly so low," said Victor.

"Maybe it's heading for that big hole in the hill," said Walter facetiously.

"You never know," replied Victor. "There are so many weird things going on around here these days that nothing would surprise me anymore."

"Well anyway, let's head out in that direction tomorrow," suggested Walter. "I am getting anxious to get out of this place and according to that message from Simpson, we are stuck here until we find out what these planes are doing here. Maybe we can find out where that one went today"

They made changes to their original plan next morning when Victor suggested that they stroll past the airport and see if the remaining two aircraft were still on the concrete pad.

"Good idea," agreed Walter. "Maybe they are all gone by now and our surveillance job will be over."

Only one of the Junkers G 38 rested on the pad. From the distance it looked familiar, yet different than it did on the previous day.

Walter cast a puzzled look at his partner. Victor shrugged his shoulder to indicate his own quandary.

They decided to move closer to the fence surrounding the airport property. From there they noticed that the part of the fuselage that was metallic in color the previous day now had the name of an airline painted on it in red.

"I wonder why they would paint the name of a passenger airline on a plane without windows," mused Victor.

"Maybe it's a trainer for training airline pilots," suggested Walter.

"I wonder where the other plane is."

"Probably on a training flight," said Victor.

"Anyway, we'll have something new to tell Simpson this time," said Walter.

Two days later Horst delivered Simpson's instructions. "Continue your vigil, especially during the night, to see if there is any nocturnal activity," it read.

"That man is certainly going out of his way to find things for us to do," complained Walter.

"Neal does not waste any steps," commented Horst when asked to what all this may be leading. "He is one of the best in the business. Observe him and learn."

"Did you know him well?" asked Victor.

"Worked with him during the war," Horst replied proudly.

~~~

The silvery light of the full moon gilded the trees and the buildings and produced eerie shadows inside the wire fence surrounding the airport. Walter and Victor sat on a bench under a tree in the small park, hypnotized by the flashy reflections of the moonlight off the wings and fuselage of the Junkers G38. The two aircraft had remained in their former positions since the day that the third one had flown over the tree tops and disappeared. It appeared that they were parked for the night.

They rose to begin their walk toward the main road when a vehicle with only its parking lights turned on stopped beside one of the planes. The ramp was moved to the door of the aircraft and a person holding a flashlight ascended and opened the door in front of the wing. He entered the airplane and turned on a light in the cockpit. The other shadowy figures on the ground walked around the machine inspecting it and all except one of them climbed up the ramp and entered the plane. The remaining person on the ground removed the ramp and blocks in front of the wheels and returned to the motor vehicle.

In a few minutes the sound of the starter motor cut through the still evening air. One of the engines started, belching white smoke through the exhaust vent. A few seconds later another fired and soon the evening air was filled with the steady drone of the plane's four engines. The propellers made a swishing sound as they cut through the dense air. The plane began to move, cautiously at first, and then picking up speed as it taxied to the runway. At the end of the runway it stopped for a minute or so, then revved its engines and sped off into the night. The roar of the engines faded into the distance and Walter and Victor returned to the bench under the tree.

After the plane's departure the motor vehicle returned to one of the airport buildings and the two young men prepared to leave. Suddenly the parking lights of the vehicle appeared in the distance coming toward the second plane parked on the tarmac. Four figures jumped out and walked toward the plane. They walked around and inspected it then climbed on board and followed the same routine as did the first crew. Soon the second aircraft was taxiing down the runway and then flying off into the night. Now all was quiet, and Walter and Victor stood up and headed for the main road.

Early the next evening the two observers took their places near the airport fence and watched the area where the Junkers G38 aircraft were parked the previous night. They peered through the silvery white moonlight and were astonished to note that now there were six of the same wide-winged aircraft parked on the pad.

"They must have flown in a few more today," whispered Victor.

"Yes. It looks like that. Let's wait and see if they will fly any of them out tonight," Walter suggested.

At about the same time as on the previous night, the motor vehicle pulled up and delivered the four-man crew who boarded the first aircraft at the end of the line and it flew in the same direction as the others. The process was repeated until all six Junkers had roared off into the night sky.

"Neal thinks that they are operating a night flying school out there," Horst advised them next day. "He wants you to wait around tonight and see if the planes return and, if they do, how long they had stayed away."

"Did he say that after we do that we will be finished with this assignment?" asked Walter.

"There have been no new orders to the contrary," replied Horst, "except that you are to take another look at the excavation site and report on it before you leave here."

On the next night they decided to return to the airport. The moon, moving toward its last quarter now rose later in the evening and shone less brilliantly, and the activity around the aircraft started about an hour later than on the previous two nights. Each departure was a duplicate of the previous ones, smooth and synchronized as if it had been rehearsed many times prior to the maneuver.

Following the departure of the last Junker the two observers remained on the park bench, gazing across the airfield which was dark except for the lights marking the runway. The drone of the last aircraft dissolved into the distance and the night air was filled only with the sounds of the city behind them. They sat silently in the shadow of the giant beech tree, their eyes fixed on the horizon above the airport. The dark sky was punctuated only by the stars and the ascending half-moon. For more than an hour there were no signs of any aircraft in the area. They wondered if they should wait any longer when a flashing red light appeared on the northern horizon. This was followed by the sound of aircraft engines and when the craft got closer to the airport, two powerful headlights pierced the night air. The plane descended gracefully onto the runway and taxied to the concrete pad where the pilot maneuvered it to its previous spot. When the engine stopped, the crew descended and boarded the waiting vehicle which sped away toward the terminal area. They watched as the other five aircraft landed and taxied to their former positions, and the two observers returned to the street and headed toward their apartment.

Next day they returned to the excavation site and observed it from a secluded spot off the main road. Concrete trucks entered and exited on the right side of the gaping entrance while on the other side the earth moving equipment emerged, dumped their loads and re-entered the opening. The excavated material was now spread out into a large strip and leveled out to resemble a road bed. The road bed stretched out for about a kilometer on both sides of the entrance. The operation appeared to follow a routine and after watching it for almost two hours they returned to the city.

The latest instructions received by Horst from Simpson directed them to get a closer look at the crew of the aircraft leaving and returning to the airfield, taking note of their ages, dress and language spoken. When this assignment was completed they were to stand by and wait for orders to return across the border.

~~~

It was Friday evening and the two young men hoped that they would be able to get the information that Simpson requested regarding the movement of aircraft at the local airport. They remembered Simpson's decree that they would remain in Stettin until they obtained the specific intelligence sought by him. Taking their place on the park bench, they hoped that this would be the night that they would get a closer look at the nocturnal activity at the airport. The moon was in its last quarter stage and would not rise until after midnight. The area was pitch black except for one street lamp at the edge of the small park and the lights around the airport buildings. At the scheduled moment the official automobile arrived with its headlights on low beam. The two observers cautiously headed toward the chain link fence separating the airport from the park, ensuring that they did not stray into the area illuminated by the auto's headlights. They walked silently in the shadows of the trees and hedges to escape detection and stopped behind a clump of bushes near the fence and observed the crew as they emerged from the vehicle.

The crew worked swiftly, exchanging only a few words in German. In the lights of the vehicle they saw that the faces of the crew were those of young men, probably in their twenties. They were focused and coordinated, and performed their inspection of the aircraft quickly and efficiently. Except for one crew member, they were all dressed in black coveralls. The only other person in the group, who appeared to be the oldest, wore a blue tunic with an arm band carrying an insignia whose lettering was not discernable in the dark. He carried on most of the conversation, dispensing instructions and asking questions of the others, all the time making notes on a clip board which he carried. Their inspection completed, they climbed up the ramp and the door closed behind them. The driver pulled back the ramp, entered the car and drove away. As the vehicle turned sharply, its headlights swept across the fence, shining momentarily on the bushes where the two young men were hidden. They remained silent and motionless. The vehicle did not stop and they stood up and walked quickly toward the road. They were still on the sidewalk heading for the street car stop when a black automobile stopped nearby and two uniformed policemen stepped out of the car and walked toward them. When they met, the policemen stopped.

"What are you two doing here at the time of the night?" one of them asked.

"We are on our nightly five kilometer walk," Walter answered in German. "We hope to join the German army soon and want to be in good condition for our training."

The two officers stepped aside and spoke quietly. "Maybe they are a couple of fags and you know what the Fuehrer thinks of those types," they overheard one of the policemen say.

The other officer frowned. "I don't think so, but let's ask for their identification." They returned to where Walter and Victor were standing. "Are you German citizens? We would like to see you identification papers." He ordered them into the squad car and turned on the dome light. The officers both checked their papers and grunted approval. One of them opened the car door.

"All right. You may go, but if we see you around here again we will take you to the station and book you. This is a restricted area you know."

"No sir. We did not know that. There are no signs saying that anywhere," explained Walter.

"It was just declared restricted this week and the signs will be going up tomorrow. So watch your step."

The policeman slammed the door shut and the car sped away.

~~~

"Yes, we can expect things to tighten up in our business," said Horst when told about their experience with the police the previous night. "Now that the Fuehrer has overcome his internal problems, he will surely want to concentrate on national security, particularly as it may be affected from the outside. But you two do not have to worry about that for now. Neal wants you to return to Poland tomorrow and wait to be picked up early in the week."

He gave them each a brown envelope and stuck out his hand to bid them farewell. "We will not see each other again for now. Here are your transportation arrangements and some money for your trip back. You two will be good agents one day soon. You are both good observers and thorough in your work. But you will have to learn to be more cautious in your movements. As I said, up to now, things have not been too well organized on the national security side here because the Fuehrer had to clean up his own house, but I expect things to really tighten up soon. So when you are receiving further training this winter, get all that you can out of it, because if you come back to Germany you will need it. So until next spring, if I am still here, good-bye and thank you for working with me."

With Horst's ominous words still ringing in their ears they returned to their apartment, gathered up their few belongings and placed them in their backpacks. Early Saturday morning they boarded a train for the village near the border and later walked unnoticed into Radzke's farm. They parted, Victor proceeding to the village where his host family lived and Walter heading toward the Radzke farmstead.

"Well, I hear that there are all kinds of things happening in Germany these days," remarked Radzke after supper that evening.

"Yes, there certainly are," responded Walter. "Things are changing very fast there now. Even during the short time that we were there, many changes took place. The people are caught up in all the excitement and anxious to get on with rebuilding their country. They appear to have a cause now and feel that they are all part of the new system which is replacing the old one that failed them so badly."

"If Herr Hitler can continue concentrating on the rebuilding of the country and not be driven by his military ambitions, we could be seeing one of the greatest economic miracles in the world, but I do not think that he will," said Radzke.

"I did not hear any talk at all about war anywhere in the country," said Walter. "The newspapers are full of news about good things that are happening because of the Fuhrer's economic programs. There are very few soldiers around the place except for those that come out for parades at special events."

"I hope you are right, Walter," said Radzke, "but the news coming out of Germany from serious observers of the situation there indicate the Hitler will one day soon spurn the Treaty of Versailles. He is sure to receive the backing of the German people because they feel that the terms of the treaty were unfair. Also, as you just explained, they are pleased with the progress taking place there and are gaining confidence in themselves and their new system. So, if Herr Hitler decides to opt out of the treaty, I am afraid that we will be living in perilous times."

Late Monday morning Simpson drove up the narrow driveway in a black sedan with Victor at his side. He jumped out of the car and greeted Radzke and Walter.

"Well, Victor here tells me that you two had an enjoyable summer," said Simpson as he pumped Walter's hand.

"We didn't suffer much," replied Walter.

"Well, we thought that you should be introduced to the job gradually. But we'll make you earn your pay next year." Simpson feigned seriousness as he winked at Radzke. "Now get your things together and we will leave soon. Duke is waiting for us at Torun."

Simpson and Radzke entered the house and reappeared a few minutes later as Walter threw his bags into the back seat of the sedan. They all shook hands with the farmer and thanked him for his cooperation, then headed out for the public road.

In the fields, which were just being planted when they drove past them on their arrival in the spring, the farmers and peasants were now finishing up the harvest. Some were cutting corn with sickles and placing them in bunches for others to tie up into sheaves. Still other were digging up potatoes and other root crops and carrying them on their backs in jute bags. The two young men watched the strenuous activities of the farmers at their work.

"These people certainly do things the hard way," mused Walter. "I thought the German farmers were a lot more advanced. Some of them had tractors and most had horse drawn equipment. These people seem backward by comparison."

"They have been doing things this way for centuries," said Simpson. "Maybe they don't want to change."

"Is that it, or is it a case of not knowing how to change?" asked Walter. "Maybe they can learn something from the Germans."

"From what I have heard about your father, I think you are starting to sound a lot like him when he was your age," said Simpson.

Walter sat back in deep thought as Simpson drove on silently for several kilometers. Then, as if to introduce them to a whole new episode in their lives, Simpson announced, "We will be in London in about a week. The next phase of your training will begin on October 15."

~~~

The *Barrow* bobbed gently on the waves created by the wake of the boats and barges moving about the harbor. On its mast, the Union Jack hung limply, stirring only occasionally in the soft breeze. Below deck Duke greeted them with vigorous handshakes and a big smile.

"Make yourselves comfortable. We'll have lots of time to talk on our return journey. Simpson tells me we will be leaving early tomorrow."

Duke excused himself and returned to the bridge. Walter and Victor kicked off their shoes and lay back in their bunks.

"This is the life, Victor," said Walter. "You know, I have been away from home for a year already and have barely missed it, except for brief moments after reading the letters from Stanley. But the way that the depression and the weather are affecting them there, it is better for me to be where I am."

"Oh, I have missed my family on many occasions, but I must admit that this has been most interesting so far. And not too demanding," confessed Victor. "I dare not tell my father that though, or he may think that this is some kind of a wimpy outfit."

"Between you and me," said Walter, gazing at the ceiling, "Those German people were not anything like I expected them to be."

"What did you expect?" asked Victor.

"Well, from the way that my grandmother, and even some of the others in the family spoke, I expected them to be arrogant, oppressive, prejudiced..." He paused searching for the right words. "...And always scheming something. Instead I could not help but notice the endless energy which they seem to have and how disciplined and thorough they are in their work and in everything they do. Remember those kids in the Hitler Youth movement and how much pride they seemed to have in their organization? You can't tell me that something like that is bad for them."

"Yes. I felt the same way myself that day as I watched them," said Victor, "except for when we heard that young boy reciting that prayer. And when I think of it now, it sounded kind of silly. Maybe they need some of that stuff to keep the kids all fired up."

A knock sounded on the door and Simpson stuck his head in. "I have a surprise visitor here to see you two." He entered the cabin, followed by Colonel Sliworski. Walter and Victor jumped off the bunks in their stocking feet and stood at near attention.

"Well, here they are," announced Simpson. "Resting up after a long, hard summer."

"So these are the star operatives," observed Sliworski, shaking each of their hands vigorously. "Nice to see you again. You boys did some good work out there. We do know a lot more about what is going on there as a result of your work."

Walter and Victor exchanged puzzled looks.

"Yes sir," continued Sliworski, "it will be interesting to find out what use will be made of that underground cavern."

"Maybe some time we can come back and take a closer look," suggested Victor.

"I would really like to go inside of it," added Walter. "That might be something very interesting to see."

"Maybe some time you will get a chance to do that. We will watch and see when the opportunity will present itself." said Sliworski. He sat down on a folding chair brought in by Simpson. "But meanwhile, tell us what you think about our good neighbors to the west."

"Victor and I were just talking about that when you arrived," said Walter. "To tell you the truth, we couldn't help but be impressed by the progress that we saw there, and the order and discipline among the people. Quite different from what we have seen so far in Poland." They noticed Simpson shake is head in concurrence.

They were summoned to a small cabin next to the galley, where Duke's combination deckhand, steward and cook served up dishes loaded with fried, freshly caught fish, potato salad and greens. Sliworski and Simpson carried on an animated discussion before diverting their attention back to the two young men.

"So what are the people talking about over there these days?" asked Sliworski.

"Mostly about the new government and what it has done for the German economy, for their roads and railways, and what big things are in store for the future," explained Victor.

"And what do they say about the rest of the world."

"Most of them seem to be too busy to worry about the rest of the world. But they do seem to be quite upset about the Treaty of Versailles, or the Diktat of Versailles, as they call it. They think that the country was badly treated by the Allies and, of course, the Fuehrer keeps reminding them of this wrong-doing."

"Yes. Especially that part that doesn't allow Germany to arm itself," added Walter.

"Did you see much of the black-shirted SS around?" asked Sliworski.

"Not much," answered Walter, "only on special occasions such as a big political or youth rallies, or during unusual events such as the June 30 affair involving Rohm and his SA storm troopers. But even then they did not stay around for long," explained Walter.

"And how did the people react to the Rohm incident?" asked Sliworski.

"Most of the comments that we heard were in support of what Hitler did," explained Victor. "They seemed to think that the SA are a bunch of rowdy street fighters, quite out of character in the eyes of the older German people used to the disciplined and honorable Wehrmacht. They felt that the SA was threatening the tradition of the old established position of the army and defiling its reputation, so they had to be cooled off. Almost everyone seems to be in favor of a strong army, based on the old Prussian model, led by Prussian generals."

"I suppose they can't wait to try out that new army that they are so anxious to build," remarked Sliworski.

"Not really," said Victor. "They seem to be too busy rebuilding their country, and after all, did they not just sign a ten-year non-aggression pact with Poland last January?"

"Well, I see that you two are well informed and have given some thought to this whole thing, which suggests that you listened to the lectures last winter, but I am not so certain that your analysis is correct," said Sliworski solemnly. "It is true that some people, including our General Pilsudski, may have been lulled into a false sense of security as a result of the signing of the non-aggression pact. But others, like General Bashinski and myself, are more pessimistic, or maybe more realistic. Pilsudski seems to be more concerned about the Russians than the Germans. There is an old Polish saying which goes, 'With the Germans we lose our freedom, with the Russians we lose our souls.' Maybe General Pilsudski still believes in that. But I am one of those who feels that we cannot trust either of them, so we had better be prepared to fight for ourselves. But then, only time will tell and I think that the time is getting shorter by the minute. I have felt that way for a long time, but particularly since last October when Germany withdrew from the League of Nations."

Sliworski drank his tea, deep in thought, as Simpson observed the two young men's reaction to the colonel's analysis. Victor fidgeted awkwardly while gazing at the teaspoon in this hand. "Maybe what Poland should concern itself about more is modernizing its economy," he said after a long pause. "Give the people a cause other than war to think about. Look at Germany. They are rebuilding their country and, as we explained, everyone is excited about it. There are more ways to build a country than through military adventures."

"Victor, how can you be so blind, " pleaded Sliworski. "Did you not see for yourself what is going on there? Why, the reports that you yourselves sent back supported some of our wildest suspicions. The Hitler Youth movement. Those holes in the side of the hill. Are these your normal peace-time endeavors? And those aircraft you watched flying around at night. Those things are going on all over Germany not just in the areas that you and Walter saw. We have to wake up before it is too late."

CHAPTER 36

The *Barrow* plied its way leisurely through the gentle waves of the Baltic Sea. Overhead the late September sun provided a last warm interlude before the pending arrival of the gray skies and cold northern winds of early winter. Duke spent many hours during the day deep sea fishing from the stern of the Barrow and landed several good catches, the best of which were taken by the cook to the galley and fried for the hungry and appreciative passengers. The rest were cleaned and placed on ice for transport to London.

After emerging from the Kiel Canal, Duke steered the vessel toward the mouth of the Weser River and cast anchor within sight of the German coastal vessels and the town of Bremerhaven. During the next two days they moved from one spot in the area to another while Duke and Milford, the cook/steward/deckhand, cast their lines into the shallow bay. Several German coast guard vessels sailed by, their officers carefully observing the activity aboard the through their binoculars. Duke and the others smiled and waved to them. The Germans waved back and sailed away.

"We want them to get used to our ship," explained Simpson. "We may have occasion to come back here so we want them to know us. Good, steady customers, so to speak. Decadent Englishmen."

Three days later Duke guided the *Barrow* into its berth on the Thames. They took leave of the skipper and entered a cab for the trip to their place of lodging which Simpson had arranged for them.

"This year you will not have to live in the barracks," announced Simpson, "but your lodging place will be nice and close to the school, actually within walking distance. We'll go through the neighborhood where it is located so you can catch the flavor of the place. Tomorrow I'll come by and take you around the new school."

"When will we start our training?" asked Walter.

"Not for a week or two yet," answered Simpson. "But take care. Do not stray too far away from here just yet. You never know who is observing you."

"I don't know who would want to," countered Walter.

The cab stopped in front of an ancient brick house, its small lawn and flower beds displaying the same evidence of loving care and maintenance as did the rest of the property.

"It's an old place, but clean and comfortable," explained Simpson. "You can take your meals right here or in some of the eating establishments in the area. I suggest that you try the meals here and you will probably not want to change. Mrs. Jenkins is a great cook. I'll go in with you and introduce you to her. We have been using her services for some time and she will not ask any questions."

Several days after their arrival in London, Simpson dropped in at their flat and announced that the training would start the following Monday. He would meet them at the school that morning and see them get started.

The school was located in a four-storey warehouse-like building at the edge of the old residential district and near the Thames River. Its original layout had been left virtually unchanged, with the floor of the large storage areas now used for drill and calisthenics and the smaller storerooms and offices turned into classrooms. The building was of old design and style, but the floors, windows and furniture were clean and polished, and the soundproof walls newly painted. The trainees would share an office with one other person, and Victor and Walter were assigned to the same room.

There were some new faces among the trainees when they assembled for their first class, but most of them were returnees from the previous year's class. There was no initiation this time. The second phase of training began in earnest with a quick review of some of the previous year's work, but with no reference to anyone's specific experiences during the summer.

Over the next few weeks they were subjected to intensive instruction in a number of new disciplines. Dramatic coaches taught them how to act and linguists worked with them to polish up on the accents of the specific geographic areas assigned to them. Veteran agents instructed them how to calculate numbers of people in crowds, squares, parades and halls. Others instructed them on the techniques of getting people to voluntarily supply strategic military information. Each day they were taught a new trick on how to get out of dangerous situations and places. The two young men agreed that all this was demanding, but interesting.

Almost every night there were homework assignments and their free time was confined to Saturdays and Sundays. One evening late in November Simpson arrived at the flat with an evening newspaper under his arm.

"I just wanted to show you chaps something to prove that your efforts during the summer were not wasted," he said as he unfolded the newspaper. A picture of Winston Churchill stood over a story headed:

PRIVATE HOUSE MEMBER WARNS
OF GERMAN MILITARY BUILDUP

Mr. Churchill, the story read, in moving an amendment to the motion that an address be presented to the king, thanking him for his gracious speech from the throne, offered the following warning to the House:

"In the present circumstance of the world, the strength of our national defenses, and especially our air defenses, is no longer adequate to secure the safety and freedom of Your Majesty's faithful subjects."

He went on to explain why. "I do not believe that war is imminent, and I do not believe that war is inevitable. But it is very difficult to resist the conclusion that if we do not begin to put ourselves in a position of security, it will soon be beyond our power to do so. What is the great new fact which has broken upon us in the last eighteen months? Germany is rearming. That is the great new fact which rivets the attention of every country in Europe – indeed in the whole world – and which throws almost all the other issues into the background. That mighty power which only a few years ago fought almost the whole world and almost conquered it is now equipping itself once again – seventy millions of people – with the technical weapons of modern war, and at the same time is instilling into the hearts of its youth and manhood the most extreme patriotic, nationalistic, and military conceptions."

Mr. Churchill went on to warn that never in its history had England been in a position where it could be liable to be blackmailed as it was now. He warned that by the end of 1936, only two years from now, the German military air force would be fifty per cent stronger and by 1937 it would be double today's strength.

"I know the Government have been considering the matter and I understand the reasons why nothing has been done is because of frightening the population. I think it is better to be frightened now than to be killed later," Mr. Churchill concluded.

"Maybe the Treasury will see fit to give us some money with which to operate now," beamed Simpson. "They will all wonder where Mr. Churchill got the information which the War Office and the Admiralty does not have."

"Do you really mean that Mr. Churchill was using some of the information which we got during the summer?" asked Walter, his eyes wide open with curiosity.

"Why, most certainly," replied Simpson. "Plus other information which our agents send from other parts of Germany and elsewhere."

"If that is all that there is to this business then when I get back there I'll send you information that will make your eyebrows curl," declared Walter.

"I am sure you will," said Simpson, "but as you learned earlier, one cannot move too quickly in this business. You have to be content to provide one piece to the puzzle at a time, not to solve the whole puzzle by yourself, and you two did provide some important pieces to the puzzle during the summer, even though you appear to have a soft spot in your heart for what is happening there."

~~~

A deteriorating political and economic situation greeted 1935 in most of Europe. Like the rumblings of boiling lava inside a crater, events on the continent portended the pending eruption that was building up inside its bowels. In a plebiscite held in January, an overwhelming majority of the population of the Saar Basin voted in favor of the region returning to German control. On March 9, Adolf Hitler announced to the world that Germany had succeeded in creating a secret air force. Buoyed by the vote of confidence which he received from the Saar and the lukewarm reaction from other European powers to his disclosure of a secret air force, the Fuehrer announced on March 16 that Germany was discarding, by unilateral action, all the obligations which the Treaty of Versailles had imposed upon the country following the Great War.

Shortly thereafter he officially introduced compulsory military service for all men between eighteen and forty-five, and announced that in place of the 100,000 men permitted under the terms of the treaty, Germany would increase its army to 550,000 men. This army would be supplied with the same type of arms that the other European countries had already adopted. These developments brought only token protests from the signatory powers of the Treaty of Versailles and words couched in cautious diplomacy from the League of Nations. In Germany, the Fuehrer was acclaimed by the whole nation for having done what no other government before him had dared to do.

At the spy school, training proceeded at a feverish pace. Reports of the tightening up of internal security in Germany and other countries on the continent hastened the adoption of different approaches to the gathering and transmission of information. The trainees had impressed upon them the fact that more sophisticated methods of communication would be required when they returned to their assigned locations. They were introduced to the various applications of codes and ciphers and to the value and use of secret inks. In the laboratory they were shown how items of common use, like tooth paste, shampoos and even socks and underwear could be utilized for concealing these inks.

For several more days the trainees were drilled in the various ways of getting information and other forms of communication to headquarters. The use of a safe address, dead drops and couriers were thoroughly explained and demonstrated. Depending upon their theater of operation, some trainees received intense drilling in the use of radio communication. Concern about the tightening of security in Germany produced several lectures on the prescribed behavior of an agent should he be caught. The use of pills, needles, guns, knives and other ways of taking one's life were explained and recommended if silence and secrecy were threatened. In order to protect the organization and its work from being exposed, the trainees pledged themselves to silence in the event of an arrest.

"What did we get ourselves into?" asked Victor as he sprawled on his narrow bed at the end of the week. "This is getting serious. I am not so sure that I want to continue being a part of it any more."

"Yeah. And I am not so sure that you can get out of it now," suggested Walter. "I think that we are in it too deep."

"How could things have changed so much since last summer?" lamented Victor. "But you don't need to answer that. They have already explained to us about what is going on there now. Our picnic is over,"

"You know, the more I think of it, the more I realize that that fellow Sliworski knew what he was talking about," said Walter "But how did he know what was going to happen? I guess some people just have it in their bones. Like my grandmother. She never trusted anybody in Eastern Europe, not to mention the Germans. And if some of those things that she talked about should happen again, I wouldn't want to be anywhere near the place when it does."

~~~

Traffic on the Kiel Canal was almost congested with ships from many countries as the *Barrow* plied its way to the Baltic on a clear day in May.

The two young agents on board were exhausted after the months of intensive training at the spy school. They spent most of their time below deck in serious contemplation. The atmosphere above was not much happier. Warm spring breezes wafted across the canal picking up the watery smells and mixing them with the smoke and exhaust of the vessels passing by. Unlike the previous year when they sailed almost undetected, this year military police observed them at every dock and locks along the way. Official, but friendly, they checked their credentials and waved them on. As he guided the vessel confidently, Duke flashed his transfixed smile at them. Simpson spent most of his time in the radio room.

Reports from Poland confirmed that these same state police were now patrolling all the frontiers of the country. No doubt security would also be very tight at the German border. However, Walter and Victor would enter the country at the same point as a year earlier, but under the protection of night, Simpson apprised them. On their last night at sea, Simpson briefed them on their assignment. It would be a short one, perhaps a month. During that time they would continue the observations that they had started the previous summer. When this was completed, they would be recalled for reassignment. Horst would transmit their information and relay messages back from headquarters. The two young agents embarked on their assignment with some trepidation, but full of confidence.

They were surprised, upon their arrival in Stettin, to find Horst in an advanced state of tension. His stubby fingers trembled as he pointed to several newspaper clippings which announced the crackdown on subversive activities in the country.

"This fellow von Nicholai, whom they have appointed to head the secret service, has built up a stable of henchmen. They have been ordered to make this country spy proof. To help them to do this, the government has passed a decree making any act of treason punishable by death, particularly if the act involves giving any information of a strategic nature to a foreign power."

"But we were told that this is done only in time of war," said Victor, a worried look on his face.

"That is the way most countries do it, but not this one," explained Horst, with a deep frown. "In fact, they have already started to make a big thing out of it by posting the names of people who have been executed, on a board in the square."

"So what does that mean for us?" asked Walter.

"First of all you must not be seen here anymore. I have already been questioned by the SS and I am sure that they have me under some surveillance. I have had to move my radio piece by piece from this shop to my basement at home. With Simpson's permission, I have arranged a place for you to stay at the house of an old friend. She does not know who you are and what you are doing, and she will ask no questions nor mention your names to anybody. In the entrance of this old house there is a steam radiator. Behind it a loose piece of wood panel can be removed easily. Your instructions will be left there and you will likewise place your information there for me to pick up. Whenever there is anything to be picked up, the shade on the window facing the side street will be rolled all the way up.

Likewise, when you have placed anything there, you will ensure that the shade is in the up position. Is that perfectly clear?"

"Yes, it is." Their voices reflected the shock with which they received the news.

"All right. Now you must go. Here, each of you take one of these garments and carry them out with you." He wrote something on a piece of paper and handed it to them. "Here is the address. It is not far from here. Please be very careful."

As they emerged from the back room past the counter, a tall man with receding reddish blonde hair entered the shop. He had a business suit slung over his arm and a faint smile on his face as he and the two young men met beside the door. They left without looking back.

The streets of Stettin, which only a year ago were filled with job seekers and young men carrying backpacks were now inhabited by uniformed military and police personnel, women and old men. They sat beside one of them on a park bench.

"This is more like the Germany I knew," he wheezed, waving his unsteady hand toward the street. "No lazy, loitering bums living off the fat of the land. Now we can rebuild our glorious German army, just like we did under Frederick the Great."

"Yes. Things are really changing," said Walter. They stood up to leave.

"Heil Hitler," gasped the old man.

"Heil Hitler," responded Walter and Victor as they turned and walked quietly across the park to their hotel.

Next day, in order to avoid attention, they took a cab from the hotel to the address Horst had given them. The landlady, a friendly, dark haired middle-aged woman, greeted them cheerfully without asking the length of their stay or where they were from. As they passed the steam radiator, they noticed that the blind on the window was half drawn.

"We'll probably have to operate individually," said Victor after they had settled into their adjoining rooms on the second floor of the large house.

"Good idea," said Walter "That way we will be less conspicuous." He lifted the shade and looked out the window. "I can't believe how much things have changed here in just one year."

"Yes," agreed Victor. "It is hard to explain. Almost as if the whole city is now ordered – or regimented. One can almost feel a dark energy all around us. I think I can see why Horst would feel so ill at ease."

"I guess I would too if I knew that someone may be watching my every move," said Walter.

"Well, we'd better make sure that no one is watching us. It may be time for us to think about some of the things that they taught us at the school during the past two winters."

"Yes," agreed Victor. "You know, I often wondered why they bothered teaching us a lot of that stuff if we were never going to use it. Now I am beginning to think that they knew what they were doing all that time."

"Yeah. Most of those guys have probably been through all this themselves. Maybe they even knew what is happening here," said Walter.

~~~

The spot from which they had observed the aircraft through the wire mesh fence the previous summer was now posted with "Restricted" signs. Walter avoided the area and casually entered the air terminal. He went up to the counter and enquired about flights to Berlin and was handed a schedule. Several young men in flight suits with air force epaulettes on the sleeves sat in the waiting area. They engaged in a loud cheerful chatter. Walter sat on a chair behind them studying the flight schedule. From time to time, one of the young men would walk to the large window facing the runway and look out into the distance.

"That Dormier should be here any minute," one of them said.

"Unless it went down somewhere between here and Friedrickshaven," one of them said. They all laughed.

"What do you think they are flying, a Junkers?" said another flyer, feigning indignation.

This struck them all as funny and they burst into laughter. "I wish they would get here soon so we can fly it to the hanger and get home for supper," intoned one of the airmen.

"Yah. That should take all of twenty-five minutes," taunted his mate, "At that rate we should log a thousand hours in about twenty years." More laughter ensued.

Several minutes later a two-engine airplane appeared above the horizon, diving gently toward the runway. Its engines roared violently shortly after its wheel touched the ground and it headed toward the terminal. As the aircraft came into view, Walter noticed the black swastika emblazoned on the tail rudder. The plane had no passenger windows or airline name on it. It reminded him of the Junkers which they had watched the previous summer, except that it appeared larger.

Five airmen stepped out onto the concrete pad when the plane stopped and boarded it after the regular crew disembarked. As the civilian crew entered the air terminal the aircraft was already taxiing toward the runway, with the air force crew in control. In a few minutes it was aloft, flying low, toward the northwest.

The same scene was repeated three days later when Victor was taking his turn at observing the airport, and again a week to the day after Walter had first watched the maneuver. By careful observation over three weeks they determined that two planes a week were involved in the operation. This was reported to headquarters which shot a message back quickly, "Check the excavation project."

"This is the only thing that has not changed much around here," said Victor when they reached their observation point overlooking the excavation project.

"It's quieter, if that's what you mean. There are no machines going in and out of the hillside. But just look at that thing down there," exclaimed Walter in disbelief.

There was no sign of construction activity as they sat and observed for an hour or more. In the steep bank a large concrete protrusion framed two massive doors and beside them a plain concrete wall with several smaller entrances. Fronting the structure was a large concrete pad connected to a paved road or runway, stretching for what looked like a kilometer. There was no sign of activity anywhere except for the guard at the gate.

The two young men observed the structure till nearly three o'clock, estimating its size and speculating on its use. They were getting ready to leave when the roar of airplane engines directly overhead startled them. The plane veered slightly to the left and approached the runway in front of the structure. It landed some distance away from the entrance, then turned around and taxied back to the concrete pad in front of the huge doors. One of the doors rolled up slowly and two vehicles sped out. One was an enclosed passenger vehicle resembling a small bus and the other appeared to be a tractor. After positioning a ramp beside the door of the aircraft, the tractor headed directly to the front of the plane, while the bus-like vehicle stopped a short distance away. The door of the aircraft opened and the crew walked down the ramp. One of the operators of the tractor signed something handed him by a member of the crew, while two others hitched the tractor to the aircraft undercarriage. The crew entered the bus and headed for the gate as the tractor, with the aircraft in tow, entered the open door of the underground structure. The large door rolled back down and the bus sped away from the gate. The whole operation took less than ten minutes. The two observers looked at each other in stunned silence.

"Well, what do you make of that?" whispered Victor, as they stood up.

"Now I am beginning to see what Mr. Churchill was talking about last November. But boy, would I ever like to see what is in that hole, if I could only get in," said Walter.

"Yeah. But if we ever get caught around here it will be curtains for us." Victor shuddered.

"Just to be safe, maybe we should wait until dark before we start going back," suggested Walter.

They agreed and made themselves comfortable leaning against the trunk of an old oak, silent in thought. From time to time they peeked over the clump of bushes, but all activity at the mysterious structure had ceased.

The twelve kilometer trip back to the city was made all the more arduous by the darkness and by the necessity of having to remain out of sight and away from the well traveled roads. Dawn was breaking when they approached Stettin and merged into the crowds of people on their way to work. In spite of the early hour, their landlady met them in the hallway when they entered the rooming house.

"The Gestapo was around checking my guest list yesterday," she announced with a worried look on her face. "Herr Reisman said you must leave at once. There is a train for the border this morning at seven. He said to make sure that you are both on it. I will get a cab for you, if you wish."

They assured her that they will leave as instructed and she returned to her room looking worried, but relieved. The two tired and soiled young men cleaned up quickly, shaved and changed their clothes. As they passed the window, they noticed that the blind was still half drawn and knew that Horst had not left any more messages. At six o'clock a taxi picked them up and they headed for the railway station. Outside the sun was already above the horizon and the city was beginning to stir. In the trees the birds welcomed the morning in song. The world of nature was at peace and oblivious of the intrigue going on around them and the plight of the two novice agents who had suddenly become fugitives.

At the railway station the hissing of the locomotive broke the tranquility of the early morning scene. Passengers were milling about, some carrying young children still half asleep or objecting noisily to being disturbed at this early hour. Stern looking SS officers, in pairs, were already at work observing the passengers and questioning backpack carrying youths and foreigners. They stopped and glanced briefly at Walter and Victor, then moved away. The fugitives boarded the train, sat down, and heaved a sigh of relief. The train whistled its warning, and then pulled slowly out of the station. Soon it was puffing noisily and steaming through the countryside heading east toward Poland.

The two travelers disembarked at the last town before the border. Under the cover of darkness they entered Poland at the exact spot that they had used for this purpose on so many occasions in the previous summer. The familiar scene and the light in the farm house window in the distance were welcome sights. Farmer Radzke was obviously relieved but did not appear surprised to see them. They talked well into the night and after they had retired Radzke went to his radio set in the attic and sent a message to the Barrow — "They are here."

"Will pick them up the day after tomorrow," came the reply.

~~~

"I hear that things are getting a bit hot over there, true to our expectations," said Simpson when he arrived to take them back.

"The place is full of black shirts," said Victor.

"And brown shirts," added Walter. "Quite a change from a year ago."

"Yes. That fellow von Nicholai is making things tough for us," said Simpson with a worried frown. "Back in London we had to sit down and figure out some new approaches."

"Boy, would I ever like to go back and see if I can get a closer look at that hole in the ground," said Walter.

"Let's not get too adventurous just yet," counseled Simpson. "You two have given us considerable information already. We can deduce a lot from that and we have a rather good idea of what is going on there."

"I would still like to go back. I feel that we have come back with only half the information that we could have had," said Walter.

"We will see what orders come out from London and whether HQ will want more information on that particular target. They already feel that they have more than they bargained for."

They bid farewell to the Radzke family and drove down the country road. When they turned into the main road to Torun, Simpson announced that Colonel Sliworski would be on board the *Barrow* when they got there. "He asked to talk to each of you personally and we thought that this would be a good time for him to do so. He may even have news on your next assignments."

An official government automobile was parked on the dock near the *Barrow* when they arrived. Simpson parked beside it and suggested that they go down below to change and freshen up and Sliworski would be around to see them later. It felt good to be back in the now familiar cabin aboard the boat and they stretched out in their bunks waiting for the colonel to arrive.

"I wonder if Colonel Sliworski will be in uniform today," mused Walter.

"I'll bet not," said Victor. "They don't seem to be as uniform crazy here as they are in Germany."

"You know, it's really odd how one's imagination of something can be so different from what things really are like." Walter sat on the edge of the bunk and gazed at the wall across the small room.

"Please explain," said Victor.

"Well, for one thing, when my uncle, or dad as I called him, read that advertisement in the Polish paper back home, I imagined Colonel Sliworski in one of those colorful uniforms with braids and medals all over the place. I somehow pictured him at the head of great legions of soldiers, sitting on a horse like those pictures of Frederick the Great, with banners flowing in the wind, protecting the great motherland."

Victor sat up in his bunk and laughed. "Say, you have quite an imagination there, young fellow. But if he were that kind of a leader, what would he want with the likes of us?" he asked.

"I guess you're right, Victor," sighed Walter. "I guess I expected this whole business to be much more glamorous somehow. Certainly a lot more dangerous."

"Well you can thank your lucky stars that it isn't. But as you heard them talk, it is getting more that way, and you have to admit that we saw some evidence of that ourselves."

Voices and footsteps in the hallway announced the arrival of company below deck. Simpson knocked on the sill and crouched his lanky frame down as he stuck his head in the door of their cabin.

"Care to join us in the galley?" he announced.

They jumped up and arranged their clothing and hair. In the galley, Sliworski shook their hand warmly and sat down beside the small table.

"So how are our ace agents doing?" he asked.

They looked at each other wondering how and who should respond.

"Well, we are told that we are doing fine, but I think that we sometimes feel that we are not doing enough," offered Walter.

"Just listen to all that modesty," said Sliworski to Simpson. "Well, just to put your minds at ease, I for one, am well pleased with your work and I know that Captain Simpson is too."

"Have we provided you with anything useful?" asked Victor, looking serious.

"Of course, you have." Sliworski's eyed gleamed as he smiled. "You have confirmed some of our wildest suspicions. We now know that we are living next door to a huge powder keg which is going to explode sooner than later and try to blow us off the map of Europe once more, maybe for the last time."

"Pardon me, sir, " asked Victor, "but if you know that, why does Poland bother with all those non-aggression pacts with Germany and why does your President Pilsudski go around exchanging all those niceties with someone who is about to devour him?"

"Ah, ha," exclaimed Sliworski, "your quandary is well founded and your knowledge of events here impresses me. However, I am a soldier and that is a political question. But to try to answer your question, I suppose that one would call that posturing, or biding one's time while gathering support elsewhere. As a soldier, my job is to be as prepared as I can be for when the time comes, so I aim to take advantage of those niceties as you call them. But we have registered our displeasure with certain events there, the most recent being our protest against the anti-Polish demonstrations led by Goering and Goebbels in Gdansk. In addition, our so-called friendship pact with Germany has enabled our government to set up trading offices in certain major centers in that country and we can use these offices for things other than trading if necessary."

Sliworski's gaze shifted toward Simpson who nodded in agreement.

"We have one such office in Breslau," Sliworski continued, "and Mr. Simpson and I just agreed that you, Walter, will in a few weeks become a clerk in that office."

"But I don't know anything about clerking," objected Walter.

"You will learn. And you will not only be a clerk, but an expert on grains. You will be going to Warsaw for a couple of weeks where you will work in the head office of the Novy Polski Trading Company. When this orientation phase is completed, you will take up residence in Breslau, complete with a new Polish identity and papers to prove it."

"And what about me?" asked Victor, "Am I to be a clerk, too?"

"You are coming back to London with me," said Simpson. "Later we will need you to take a close look at an operation in Freiderickshaven."

"Where the heck is Freiderickshaven?" asked Victor.

"Not far from Switzerland," answered Simpson.

"How come you get all the breaks?" Walter asked Victor, feigning disappointment.

"Breslau is a nice spot, too," explained Simpson, "It is a city located on twelve islands, and not far from it is a hill in which is located one of those nice underground bunkers which you are so anxious to see. That will be your objective."

"You mean that Victor and I are going to be separated?" asked Walter.

"Yes. But for your own good," explained Simpson. "As the assignments get more focused, it also becomes more risky for operatives to work in pairs. So you may not see each other for a while now."

"Well, at least we will know what is expected of us this time," remarked Victor.

"Yes, boys," said Simpson, "Your apprenticeship is over. You are about to enter the sinister world of the undercover agent."

~~~

Colonel Sliworski leaned his elbow on the window sill of the day coach, watching the countryside rush by as the train made its way to Warsaw.

"Well, there it is," he said waving his hand across the widow, "the land of your ancestors." He fixed his gaze on the distant horizon. "Is it not a beautiful country, Wladimar? I love it very much. Too bad that your people did not stay long enough to see the rebirth of this nation after the Great War. Your grandmother, particularly, would have been happy to see our eternal adversaries driven out of this land. General Bashinski often spoke to me about your grandmother. You know that they were related to each other, and the General felt a great kinship toward your family, and great sadness after your father was taken away. The grand old man is still living. Perhaps, we will have a chance to see him while you are in Warsaw."

"My grandmother still loves this country," said Walter. "We used to say to her that her body moved to Canada, but her heart remained in Poland. Her heart was broken for a long time because she never really recovered from my father's death. She often shared her sorrow with me. One day I vowed that I would avenge my father's death and she gave me her blessing. That is one big reason why you see me here today."

"Yes, I know, Wladimar," said Sliworski. "Major Bradley explained that in a letter to me."

"Well, isn't this a small world," mused Walter. "Who would have thought that Major Bradley had contacts away out here. And if he hadn't helped me, I would probably never have gotten here. He had so much faith in me and I hope that I can live up to his expectations. But at the rate I am going, I may never get that chance."

"Do not underestimate your worth, Wladimar," counseled Sliworski. "At your age it is natural to be impatient and crave action. They told me in Washington that you are like a wildcat, anxious to stalk and claim your quarry. In our work we do not win battles single-handed. We are part of a small army, most of whom you will never see. But when all our efforts come together, they can change the course of history."

Walter gazed out the window, deep in thought. He turned his head and looked inquisitively at Sliworski. "Who is this fellow Duke that is usually with us on the *Barrow*? We hardly get to talk to him or even to see him, even though we are all on the same boat," he asked.

"I am sorry, Wladimar, but I cannot tell you that now. Maybe sometime later you will find out for yourself. Duke is a very private person and only a very few people in the organization know who he really is. He does not want to be seen too much and has a good reason for it," explained the colonel.

"Sometimes he looks so familiar, like I have seen him somewhere before. I have felt that way since I first laid eyes on him," said Walter.

"Maybe you have seen him," said Sliworski. "Who knows? Maybe you have."

A young chauffeur in Polish army uniform met them at the railway station as they stepped off the coach. He saluted Sliworski and picked up their bags, then pushed his way through the crowd to the staff car parked at the entrance.

"We will take this young man to the hotel on our way to the office," directed Sliworski as the car entered the street.

The clerk at the hotel reception desk greeted the colonel with familiar respect and welcomed Walter to Warsaw.

"Give him one of our special rooms," instructed Sliworski. He took Walter aside and briefed him. "The car will pick you up at eight tomorrow and take you to the office of the Novy Polski Trading Company. Here is a phone number if you need anything. You will stay in your room and talk to no one until your new identity has been established. But why am I telling you all this when you learned it all in London last winter?" They returned to the reception counter.

"Do not worry, Colonel Sliworski. We will look after him," said the clerk.

Sliworski thanked the clerk and shook Walter's hand.

"I hope you enjoy your stay in Warsaw, Wladimar. You will see me when all the paper work is done"

The bellhop took Walter's bags and showed him to his room.

~~~

The Novy Polski Trading Company hummed with the activities of a normal commercial enterprise. In its role as a state approved agency acting for a number of Polish exporters, it dealt directly with German importers and with state agencies. In Germany, a shortage of foreign currency made it necessary for the Nationalist Socialist government to impose severe restrictions on imports, except for food and raw materials used in the manufacture of goods approved by the state. Poland was the source of some of these much-needed foods and raw materials.

In the days which followed, Walter was exposed to the company's organization and functions and was introduced to the rudiments of document processing, filing and record keeping. His specialty was to be in the grains department, a commodity in big demand in the revitalized German economy.

His new name, Adam Nowiki, was recorded in a new passport and other official looking documents delivered by Colonel Sliworski to his hotel room on his second day in Warsaw and he was free to walk around in the streets of the city.

"Everything has been cleared for you to leave next Monday for Breslau," announced Sliworski at the end of two weeks. He appeared pleased with the progress that Walter had made. "I understand that you already knew something about the grain business and have adapted well to your new responsibility, and fit well into the business operation of Novy Polski. All this is good because a good part of your time will be spent in the company's office. Only one person in the office will know what your real involvement will be in Breslau, so you will be seen by most of the staff as just another employee. The manager of the grain department will be traveling with you Monday to ensure your smooth entry into Germany."

"You seem to have gone through a lot of trouble just to get me to Breslau. What do I have to do to earn all this?" asked Walter.

"What your main objective will be is by far the most dangerous mission that you have yet undertaken in this job. You may finally get some of the exciting action that you crave so badly. As I hinted when we discussed it briefly on board the *Barrow*, we now know that there is a large underground concrete bunker not far from Breslau, similar to the one near Stettin. We understand that it may be in a very old abandoned copper mine in the side of a nearby hill. Our other operatives were unable to determine exactly what its function is, as it has been operating under the tightest security, and activity takes place there mainly at night. Our observers have, however, come up with some interesting observations. For example, we know that the civilian gatekeeper on the midnight to eight shift is a chronic imbiber. He is also a Don Juan of sorts and sometimes secretly entertains women in the gatehouse during the late hours."

"This fellow sounds like a real pushover. All that we have to do is find a woman to drop in on him with a bottle of schnapps and occupy him while I go in and take a look around, then beat a hasty retreat," boasted Walter.

"Your plan sounds almost perfect, but its execution may not be that simple," explained Sliworski. "You see, the woman that we have in mind for this operation – the one we know we can trust – does not even know the man. So that will be your first objective; to figure out a way to bring her to the attention of the gatekeeper. And while she is cultivating his friendship, you will be in the background making sure that everything is going well and also surveying the target from a distance at every opportunity. There is one more thing that I need to tell you at this time Wladimar. As you already know, your job is one of the most dangerous there is. And this particular assignment may test the danger limits. If, for some reason the plan does not succeed and you are found inside the bunker, under no circumstances will you tell anyone who you are and what you are doing there. You will go into the target area without any identification of any kind on you, and if you should get caught and admit that you are part of the Novy Polski Company or this operation, no one in these organizations will admit knowing you. Should you get apprehended and be interrogated to the point where your resistance is depleted, you will swallow the capsule about which you learned during your training last winter and which you will always carry with you in the prescribed manner. And another thing. We are learning that a great animosity is developing there against Polish people and there are stories of people being beat up badly for speaking Polish. So, stick to German."

"I have no intention whatsoever of getting caught. But I will take nothing with me except the capsule, as you suggest," confided Walter.

"Good. Simpson told me that you are just the one to do this job. We will all be working for you and will make sure that you have everything you need to pull this thing off safely. And now, before you leave, I would like to take you to meet a fine old gentleman who has asked to see you. His name is General Wladimar Bashinski."

~~~

The old man sat in an overstuffed leather chair in the study of a large old brick house. When Sliworski and Walter entered, he peered over his glasses and rose slowly. He pulled himself erect, displaying his full military bearing of former years.

"General, this is the young man whom you asked to see," explained Sliworski after he had saluted the General. "He is Wladimar Berglund, you distant relative from Canada."

Bashiniski adjusted his glasses and peered at Walter as if measuring him carefully from head to foot, then reared back playfully.

"You know, Colonel, you caught me napping and when I awoke and saw this young man standing there I thought that I was still dreaming. Yes, dreaming of that day back before the war when I attended Erik Berglund's wedding in Krakow. This boy has an uncanny resemblance to his father, whom I remember so well."

The old man clasped Walter's outstretched hand. He pulled the young man toward him and embraced him.

"Bless you, my boy. And thank you for coming to see a burnt out old soldier. How is your dear grandmother?"

"She is well," responded Walter. "She spends most of her time gardening in the summer and reading in the winter."

"Yes. She always was a great reader that one. She could have been a great scholar or a professor under different circumstances, but as it turned out..." He paused as if to review the events of the past.

"Oh, she is quite happy where she is," Walter assured him. "She has her friends, her church and, of course, her grandchildren whom she loves very much. Although I must admit that she speaks longingly of her beloved Poland."

"Ah yes. She and millions of others who have had to leave their country's bosom out of fear and despair. But they have served us well from their adopted homes, for where would Poland be today if it had not been for the influence they and others had on Woodrow Wilson's plan for a restructured Europe after the Great War. He heeded the call of our compatriots in America and of our European friends and supported our cause at the Paris Peace Conference in 1919 which gave us our country back. May his soul rest in peace."

The general motioned to Sliworski and Walter to sit down and returned to his chair. He drew a long breath and leaned back gazing at the ceiling.

"It is now just a matter of time before our sacred soil will again be defiled by the marching feet of our age-old enemies. And, as usual, we will not be ready because we will have been too busy quarrelling among ourselves." The general focused his eyes on the two men as he leaned forward in his chair. "That, my dear friends, has been the story of Poland for most of its history. At a time when we should be wide awake and preparing for the inevitable, the country is groaning under an inept government and an overlapping and lethargic bureaucracy. I shall probably not be here when that happens, Wladimar, but Colonel Sliworski and his colleagues will soon have to lead those who still love this country into yet another struggle to defend this unfortunate land. Much as we hate war and love peace, it is not our lot to escape it. So those who are awake to these impending dangers must prepare to defend themselves and hope that our friends, wherever they may be, will see fit to help us."

"Perhaps it will not happen again, sir," said Walter. "Britain and America appear to be concerned about your safety, and with powerful friends like that, who will dare to attack your country?"

"Wladimar, Wladimar," pleaded the general, "you underestimate the deviousness of our enemies or the fickleness of our friends. Even as we sit here and talk about it, our enemies are sharpening their knives for the kill. Look at what they have done to their own countrymen who have dared to oppose them, and to the Catholic Church. There is nothing sacred anymore. But forgive me. I did not mean to fill your heart with gloom."

They sat silently, each absorbed in his own thoughts. Colonel Sliworski broke the silence. "I suppose that Wladimar can agree with you to some extent, as he has seen with his own eyes some of the things that are going on in Germany right now."

"Why, yes, I have seen some changes going on in Germany that seem to be of a military nature," said Walter. "But maybe it is nothing more than an attempt by their new chancellor to restore some confidence and pride among the people through military discipline. I must say that even as an outsider, it is difficult not to get caught up in the excitement of the changes taking place there. For example, how can anyone criticize their agricultural reforms? Who can disagree with programs designed to free the peasants from the misery that they have suffered for generations? And as for the highway and railway construction going on there; more countries should be paying attention to these things and doing the same."

The old general cast admiring looks at Walter and smiled. "Well spoken, Wladimar. Just like a true North American. You people are lucky. Because your country is new, you see things from a different perspective – one of growth and development – not from a standpoint of destruction. But unfortunately, that is not the European way. This is the cradle of greed, envy and bitter jealousies. Throughout history the system has perpetuated the myth that a nation, or individual, or country can only progress at the expense of another. That is the curse of this continent, a place which God has endowed so handsomely with everything except charity."

He placed his brow between his forefingers and thumbs of his hands and paused for a moment to review his thoughts. "As one gets older, as I have, one begins to realize that much of our activity is the work of desperate men. While some people may benefit from our actions and praise us for it, we rarely capture the joy and satisfaction which we seek and which constantly elude us. In our old age we realize that the only thing we may have gained is some wisdom. Then I ask myself, is despair the only path to wisdom? But here I go again, philosophizing when I should be listening more to what you can tell me about yourself and your beautiful family."

A valet brought tea and biscuits and the talk turned to Walter's family back in Canada and to the events leading up to their departure for the new world. It was late in the afternoon when the general rose from his chair and bid them good-bye.

CHAPTER 37

The headquarters of the Novy Polski Trading Company in Breslau was housed in a building wedged between two larger structures on a narrow street in the warehousing and light manufacturing section of the city. A set of gray granite stairs, worn deep by thousands of feet over the years and bordered on one side by a brightly polished handrail, led to the main office on the second floor. Here the company conducted its affairs with local and regional enterprises which were eager to purchase coal from the Silesian mines, wheat from the eastern plains and fish from the Baltic fishing grounds. These and other raw materials were eagerly sought to feed the rapidly growing appetite of Germany's expanding manufacturing industries. Driven by the recovery brought about by the economic policies of the new regime, increased production and consumption were demanding more raw materials from outside the country and Poland was well positioned to provide them. Business at the Novy Polski Trading Company was good.

But behind the facade of all this innocent and legitimate business activity lay the secret operation of the company; to provide a base for a small group of Polish and other secret agents. This part of the company's activities was so well camouflaged that only the manager of the company knew who the agents were, and the agents themselves were only aware of the covert activities of one other person in the organization, their leader. Walter's mentor was Karl Retzlaff, the current manager of the accounting department, with the code name Oscar. Of obvious mixed ancestry, Retzlaff looked more Italian than Polish. His black facial hair defied the closest shaves and his sharp nose accentuated his receding hairline.

In a large room at the front of the third floor level of the four-storey building were stored the business records of the company in rows of varnished wooden file cabinets. Here the company clerks pored over invoices and receipts and made entries in many volumes of ledgers. At the rear of this level were the living quarters of the temporary staff occasionally brought in from Warsaw. The living area assigned to Walter was a made-over office, with a high ceiling and a door which he speculated must have been designed to accommodate occupants eight feet tall. A window with a stark green shade half drawn looked out on the lane separating the row of buildings from those facing the next street over. A small sitting room contained two cushioned chairs, a desk with a matching stool and an empty cupboard. Behind the door was a closet with a number of empty shelves and a large metal vent in the ceiling. In a small adjoining room, a bed with a night table and chest of drawers took up most of the floor area not covered by a small oval rug, braided from coarse, brightly colored material. The bed was made with well-ironed white sheets and pillow cases. On the night table, a vase filled with a mixture of bright flowers seemed like an intrusion by nature into an alien world of brick, stone and antique wood.

~~~

After demonstrating some of the basic rudiments of making bookkeeping entries and filing invoices, Karl wasted no time in alerting Walter to the real purpose of his arrival in Breslau. There were reports of mysterious night movements of vehicles away from the motor vehicle assembly facility and from the rail lines onto the side roads leading to the hills southwest of the city. Rumors of nocturnal activity around an old abandoned copper mine had been confirmed by observation. Walter's task, as previously explained to him by Colonel Sliworski, was to enter the heavily guarded compound and observe what was actually happening in the underground cavern. He would have to complete the assignment before the first snowfall for obvious security reasons, Karl explained. This meant that he would have two to three months to observe the target from a distance, become thoroughly familiar with the landscape and roads in the area, and figure out a way to penetrate the security cordon. The operation would begin immediately.

As a means of making his presence known to the local police and SS, Karl provided Walter with an official company pouch and a bicycle. In the course of performing his regular treks to the post office, print shops, stationery suppliers and banks in the area, Walter was regularly observed pedaling his bicycle on the streets of the city. Each day he ventured farther and farther out until two weeks later he had reached the outskirts and the entrance to the main highway to the southwest. On the third weekend, equipped with binoculars and a standard reference book for birdwatchers, he crossed one of the many bridges and arrived in the hilly country several kilometers south and west on one of the main highways leading out of the city. He hid his bicycle in an overgrown hedge and set out on foot. Beside the names of the species of birds that he was purportedly observing, he made cryptic notes of compass readings, location and natural features of the landscape. Back in his apartment in the evening, he noted these features on road and topography maps of the area.

Meanwhile, the other half of the master plan was meticulously being laid out by Karl. The organization had known for some time about the existence of a peasant family of Polish ancestry who lived only about two kilometers from the underground bunker. The family had a young and vivacious daughter who, while tending a small herd of milk cows, sometimes took them out to graze near the compound in what was part of the buffer zone surrounding the bunker. So far no one had expressed any concern about this intrusion. The young girl had, for the first part of the summer, ignored the attention that she was receiving from the uniformed gatekeeper and the sentry at an alternate exit from the compound.

In the interest of cultivating the favors of the gatekeepers and in order to retain the grazing privileges which the farmer enjoyed in the area of the compound, the girl had been instructed by her family to show a friendliness toward them, especially the sentry at the main entrance. This gesture was unanimously accepted and the family's appreciation was displayed by regular gifts of milk, eggs and cheese. One day the gatekeeper asked if the family made its own beer or schnapps. The girl replied that her father made a distilled alcoholic drink mixed with fruit syrup which was highly commended by all who partook of it as being the best in the community. She would ask her father if she could bring him some. Karl's strategy was working on schedule.

~~~

The bicycle ride through the country had been exhilarating. Cool breezes from the north accompanied the descending September sun, pushing the stagnant heat of the summer to the south. When he returned to the city he laid his bicycle on its side on the grass and sat down on a wooden bench in the small park. On the streets and sidewalks the workers, clerks, businessmen, students and shoppers mingled with each other, oblivious of the uniformed SS and SA in their midst. On other park benches, older men were reading newspapers and quietly discussing their censored contents.

Meanwhile in the other countries of Europe, each struggled with its own economic, social and political problems, unaware of the events taking place in Germany which would soon affect them all. When they sat on this same park bench after work, Karl would often make this observation. He wondered what it would take for the rest of Europe to awaken to the recognition of what was happening in Germany. "Just look at all these uniforms," he challenged Walter. "Would you call this a normal situation?"

The summer of 1935 was the third one under the Nazi regime. The works of the new order were seen everywhere. It was becoming increasingly evident that no German citizen would escape its affects as Chancellor Adolf Hitler proceeded with his plans to right all the historic wrongs, eliminate unemployment, rehabilitate the nation back to prosperity and restore it to its former position as a world power. Even for an outsider it was difficult to argue with any of these goals, reasoned Walter.

Not necessarily so, argued Karl, noting that all was not as innocent as it appeared on the surface. Having effectively disposed of the organized political opposition and silenced the voice of the Catholic Church, which they labeled "political Catholicism and black-robed hypocrites," the Nazi have now turned once again to the labor front. "Honor the worker and you honor the people" shouted the Fuehrer only several months ago as millions cheered. A few weeks later the country's labor leaders were arrested and their offices seized by armed state police and secret service men. A decree announced that "the whole labor market will be consolidated under state domination." Strikes were banned, wages fixed, and all youth, male and female, required to serve in the national youth labor camps. The number of unemployed which stood at 5,800,000 in 1933, was now reduced to 400,000 and declining rapidly. "But at what cost?" implored Karl.

"They are very clever," continued Karl. "To minimize discontent among the workers, the regime has introduced a "Strength Through Joy" movement which involves them in numerous rallies, picnics and other social affairs. Workers, and indeed all citizens, are encouraged to "have a good time" while working for the glory of the state. But I know that in their homes many German families are torn apart by split allegiances. The youth who have come up through the Jugend movement offer their loyalty to the state, while the parents are nervously watching the erosion of the freedoms which they had once known and for whose return they now yearn. The state is now firmly in control and all access to change through a democratic process is blocked. The freedom to choose, which once was as real as the light of day, has now disappeared into the shadows of the Nazi night."

As he watched the people around him, Walter wondered how the citizens of Britain and America were reacting to all this. He recalled reading in the London newspapers that other countries were observing the events in Germany with awe as well as veiled admiration. How a leader could move a country out of the depths of despair to a state of feverish economic development and near full employment in less than three years was a feat to be admired. Meanwhile, most of the rest of the world was mired in a serious economic depression. Was it not just several months ago that Lord Allen of Hurtwood brought a message of good will and best wishes for success to Adolf Hitler from Britain's Prime Minister Ramsay MacDonald? And about two months later Sir John Simon, Foreign Secretary in MacDonald's cabinet announced that the government and people of Britain wanted peace above all. Herr Hitler rose to the occasion and when he named himself commander of the Wehrmacht on May 21, 1935, he gave a rousing speech on the importance of peace in Europe. In England, the London Times labeled his address "Reasonable, straightforward and comprehensive."

But peace was obviously not a part of the Fuhrer's hidden plan, argued Karl and others. By moving behind the smoke screen of disarmament negotiations at Geneva, Hitler secretly tripled the size of his 100,000-man army. And after withdrawing from the League of Nations, he instructed his adjutant to reintroduce conscription. Unknown to the rest of the world, mass production of armaments had already begun in German factories. Germany was becoming a veritable fortress, secretive and impregnable, except to the factory workers who were screened party members and sworn to secrecy. Meanwhile the rest of Europe sleeps, warned Karl.

Every factory in the country now displayed ominous looking posters warning the workers that death awaited anyone who betrayed state secrets. Other posters in public places in cities and towns listed the names of persons who had been executed in the Ploetzensee prison near Berlin after trial in the People's Court. The country's spy chief, Colonel von Nicolai, having been provided with this decree now set about cleaning up the country of foreign agents and establishing a spy service abroad. It was becoming increasingly difficult to get information out of Germany and alert the rest of the world as to what was happening there. Time was running out on Sliworski's grand plan.

~~~

Deep in thought, Karl paced around Water's small apartment and stopped before a map spread out on the table. His piercing black eyes shifted from the map to Walter and back to the map.

"Are you satisfied that you have all the preliminary information that you need for this exercise?" he asked.

"Yes. I think that we can soon embark on the next step," replied Walter.

"Good. Let us call it a day then. How about walking down to the river? We could stop at a tea house on the way down and relax before we start planning our next move. You deserve a break after all the work that you have done to now."

They locked the door to Walter's apartment and walked down the three flights of stairs into the street. They entered a tea house and sat down at a table.

"You cannot be too careful around here these days," said Karl softly in German. "I would not be surprised if those seemingly uninterested vultures are listening to everything that is going on here. After we have our tea we can go down to the park and talk more freely."

They approached the park bench and sat down. Karl leaned back and stretched out his legs casually while Walter scanned the nearby features with his trained eyes. There was no one within hearing range.

"One week from tonight at 8:45 is the appointed moment," said Karl gazing at the sky. It will be fairly dark at that hour and the girl will have delivered the daily ration to the gate keeper, appropriately treated, at 6:30, two hours before the afternoon shift ends. As you have noted, the gatekeeper is just getting used to his change to the afternoon shift and his habit is not to start drinking until a half hour before his shift is over, for fear of being discovered. He should be out cold by the time you arrive at the gate. The keys to the doors of the bunker will be attached to his belt by a metal ring which you can remove by loosening his belt. You will replace the empty bottle with another similar empty bottle which you take with you. You will then enter the bunker and make your way through as much of it as possible in twenty minutes, taking photos of anything that you think you may need to support your observations. You will then return to the gate and replace the keys on the keeper's belt and make your way back undetected, entering your apartment building by the back door and up the fire stairs. There will be no manner of conveyance for you either there or back for obvious reasons, so you may want to make your way there on foot early enough in the day, keeping out of sight. If the plan is aborted, a small broken tree branch will hang over the right side of the road, 100 meters from the gate. You will carry no identification and if you are caught alive no one will admit knowing you. Now please repeat the instructions that I have just given you."

Walter did, and Karl remarked that he had been taught well by his mentors and that things should proceed as planned. "In two days we will meet here and you will repeat these instructions to me again to ensure that all the details are still clear in your mind."

They stood up and walked casually toward the street.

~~~

The countryside was peaceful. The yellow and brown fields lay clean-shaven after harvest, dotted by shocks of corn and stacks of hay. Along the ravines and hillsides, patches of bright yellow, orange and red bushes poked out from among the dark green bluffs of evergreens and bramble bushes. The bus halted beside the roadside bus stop at the highway's intersection with the secondary road, and Walter stepped off. After the bus disappeared around the bend, he checked the contents of the bag, removed his binoculars and bird book from it and slung it over his shoulder. He walked along the hedgerows peeking through his binoculars, looking every bit the dedicated bird watcher.

After making certain that no one was watching, he disappeared into the thick bushes and sat down in a small clearing to review his plan. It was one hour and forty minutes before noon and the compass and map reading placed his location at four kilometers from his target as the crow flies and probably about five or six by following the ravine. He stood up and followed the path worn through the grass by the hoofs of cattle and sheep. Among the bushes and trees the birds flitted about playfully, observing the bird watcher who today seemed intent on some other goal.

From the shelter of a grove across the hollow, Walter observed the gate of the compound through his binoculars. In the bright afternoon sun he examined the distance between the obscured opening in the side of the hill and the gate, as he had done on many earlier occasions. The dash should take about seven seconds, ten if he followed the hedge between the concrete roadway and the galvanized chain link fence, he calculated. The light standards told him that the area would be well lit at night, but after the first one hundred meters, the road outside the compound would be dark. Trees and hedges formed a solid visual barrier along the hillside. Once outside the gate and out in the leafy undergrowth, he should be safe from observation by even torch carrying searchers.

As the sun touched the top of the trees and the shadows lengthened, a cow walked over the top of the knoll, followed by several others, and a girl. She waited until the sun had descended behind the knoll and then emerged in front of the sentry house. The gatekeeper stepped out of the building and waved to her to approach. The girl waved back, hopped onto the road and walked toward the gate. She conversed briefly with the watchman and handed him a paper wrapped package from her basket. Picking up her pace she caught up with the small herd of milk cows as they turned to head toward the farmstead.

Dusk descended quickly as the sun sank behind the hills and the lights went on in the sentry house and compound. Walter kept his binoculars trained on the gate and entrance area. The sentry sat inside the sentry house, checking his watch impatiently from time to time. After several time checks, he left the post, walked to the bunker door and inserted the key. He pushed the door part way open and then pulled it shut. The watchman then stepped onto the concrete apron. He surveyed the area around the entrance and then stared down the road outside the compound.

Apparently satisfied that all was in order, he returned to the sentry house and reached down under the table. He pulled out the bottle from its paper bag, checked the time, then put it up to his mouth and drank. Walter looked at his watch. The fluorescent hands showed eight-thirty. He returned the binoculars to their case and placed them under a flat stone. He reached for the bird guide, then decided not to leave the book behind and returned it and the binoculars to his shoulder bag. Moving quietly among the trees and bushes that he had so thoroughly examined during his many days of surveillance, he arrived within sight of the sentry house. The time was 8:34.

He peered over the top of the hedge. The watchman was seated beside the window, his head and shoulders slumped across the table.

Moving in the shadows, Walter reached the barrier between the road and the compound and crouched under it to get through. He dashed into the sentry house. The gatekeeper was out cold, as planned, a nearly empty bottle sat on the table beside his limp hand. The keys hung from a key ring on his belt. Walter opened the man's belt and pulled off the key ring. He put on the gatekeeper's hat and jacket, slipped the key ring in his pocket and walked casually toward the bunker entrance. As Karl had warned him, he would only have about twenty minutes before the watchman on the next shift would arrive.

The bolt in the lock slid easily when he tried the key. He pushed it open slowly and peeked inside. There was no one there. He checked behind him, then walked into the bunker and listened. The place was quiet except for the sound of a distant fan. Several rows of overhead lights stretched out in symmetry ahead of him as far as he could see. The only shadows were along the walls and behind the concrete pillars. In the distance the outlines of dark objects lined the open aisles. He moved quickly in the shadow of the wall toward the objects. As he got closer he could discern wheels and chassis. They were vehicles of some sort, he thought. As he got closer he suddenly realized what they were. They were armored cars, trucks and tanks, all new and shiny and all painted in brown and earth colors.

He moved quietly between the rows. There seemed to be no end to the rows of the machines. He checked his watch. It was 8:37. He paused and listened. All was quiet except for the fans in the ventilation system. He pointed the camera down the long row of vehicles and clicked; then he took several close-ups of each type of vehicle. He calculated their numbers in the hundreds. It was now 8:44. He had about ten minutes to get out of the compound. At 8:46 he arrived at the door and cautiously pushed it open and looked out. There was no one there, but the phone in the sentry house was ringing loudly. He walked quickly to the gatehouse as the ringing suddenly stopped. Dropping the keys and hat beside the sleeping gate-keeper, he looked out the window and saw two uniformed men running toward the sentry house. He recognized one as an SS officer who had apparently just arrived on a motorcycle. He picked up the empty bottle and dashed for the barrier, and squeezed under it.

"What the hell is going on here," shouted the angry SS officer as he entered the sentry house. "This son of a whore is drunk. Look! Someone is running away. Shoot. Don't stand there like a dumb ox."

Walter dashed through the hedge toward the protection of the dark shadows of the undergrowth in the distance. The purr of a machine gun cracked through the night air and a hail of bullets crashed through the slender stems of the bushes through which he just passed. He ran toward the ravine, and stopped to listen. The shooting had ceased but the voices of the angry SS man could be heard clearly in the still night air.

"Someone may have got into the bunker. We have to find out who it is. Get the dogs! We will deal with this drunken pig later." The SS officer barked the order and several voices now responded.

Dogs! Good Lord, thought Walter. He and Karl had not even considered that possibility in their plan. There was not to be an easy escape now. It may take 20 to 30 minutes for the dogs to be brought in from the barracks, but once they arrived they could outrun him quickly. He put his hand into his shirt pocket. The capsule was still there. But he had seen too much. If he could get to the river before the dogs caught up with him, they would lose his scent and he would escape. But the river was about five kilometers away. He had to distract the dogs as they followed his scent. But how?

After running hard for about half a kilometer, he tore off the gate keeper's jacket and draped it over a branch. After getting his bearings in an area that was now familiar to him, he ran hard toward the northeast. After running for several minutes he stopped and listened. He could hear no sounds except those of his heavy breathing and pounding heart.

A half moon was rising over the tree tops. There was sufficient light by which to distinguish the outline of trees and bushes. The ravine was just ahead. The higher ground skirting the hollow was now clearly distinguishable. Hard-beaten ground under his feet told Walter that he had found the path on which he had walked on many occasions while performing his surveillance. He ran hard in long strides, his feet springing off the hard earth along the path.

After running hard for several more minutes he stopped and listened. In the distance he detected the barely audible sounds of dogs barking. There was no doubt about it. The dogs had arrived and would soon be on his trail. He ran for another few minutes, then stopped and listened. The sound carried well in the still evening and he could hear the dogs snarling and barking more clearly now, as well as the shouts of their handlers. It sounded like they were just leaving the compound. From his position he calculated that he had about two kilometers head start on them.

Walter turned and ran hard for another ten minutes or more, then stopped and listened. The sounds wafting through the quiet night air was a combination of fast, excited barking mixed with yelps, and impatient orders from the trainers. He knew that they had reached the tree with the jacket on it and were deciding whether to do a thorough search of the immediate area or keep going ahead. Good, he thought, this delay would give him a chance to put some distance between him and the pursuers.

A few minutes later the dark outline of a rail fence loomed in front of him. He jumped over it and came to a narrow road used by the local farmers to get to their fields. It ran north and south. He turned left and resumed his pace. Suddenly he recognized a familiar junction in the road, one that he had used as a reference point on his map. He knew now that he was only about two kilometers from the river. The barking was getting louder as the distance between him and the dog pack was getting shorter. There were now several farm houses along the road and he knew that as the dogs got closer their barking would arouse the local inhabitants. But he also knew that he could run faster on the packed soil of the dirt road and it provided him with a straight line to the river. He picked up the pace and resumed his running.

His mouth was dry and the soles of his feet raw from the pounding of the hard ground, but he pushed on. Each step was now becoming an effort as the muscles in his legs pleaded for a respite from the torture inflicted upon them. Dark hulks of farm buildings and houses with yellow lights in their windows appeared along the roadside. To help keep his mind off his agony, he thought about his own home, thousands of miles away, and of how his folks would be gathered around the kitchen table discussing today's events and tomorrow's plans. He wondered if he would ever be part of that scene again. Sure he would. The river was now probably no more than a kilometer away and most of the going would be over flat terrain or downhill. He now had to concentrate hard to place one foot ahead of the other. His boots became heavy and his body pleaded for mercy.

He stopped and sat down on a rock. All was quiet except for the frantic pounding of his heart. The suddenly, as if they had just been let loose again, the yelping and barking resumed. It was closer now, maybe just half a kilometer. Walter put his hand in his shirt pocket and felt for the capsule. Then he listened again. During a pause in the barking he heard the familiar sounds of horses clearing their nostrils nearby. Some distance away, against dark outline of a barn, he discerned the movement of several horses inside a corral. He jumped to his feet, and taking the camera case that was still slung over his shoulder, he ripped off the shoulder strap. He quickly placed the camera in his shoulder bag and raced for a small bush beside the corral. Breaking a short length of stem from a branch he fashioned a bit by tying the camera shoulder strap to each end.

He stole quietly into the corral, talking softly to the horses as he walked toward them. In the bright moonlight his eyes quickly isolated a lively gelding and his eyes concentrated strongly on his quarry. The gelding eyed him suspiciously as Walter moved up to him and touched his shoulder, and patted him gently. He then moved closer to the animals head, scratching him behind the ears and comforting the nervous animal with gentle words. "Nice boy. Nice boy. You can help me." He let the young horse smell the improvised bit. Since the animal did not seem to be afraid of humans, Walter was certain now that the gelding was trained. The dogs were getting closer and the horses in the corral, sensing their approach began to run around nervously, the young gelding following.

There was no time left to put the bit into the horse's mouth. Walter ran alongside the gelding and grabbing a hold of his mane, jumped onto its back. Surprised by the strange intruder on his back, the gelding jumped over the corral fence and galloped onto the road with Walter hanging on desperately. Walter reached for the tuft of mane between the horse's ears and pulled his head hard to the right. The horse turned and headed in the direction of the river at full gallop. Walter glanced back over his shoulder as he hung on frantically to the horse's mane. He could see the faint shapes of the dogs coming over the small knoll and heading for the farmyard. They would follow his scent to the corral but by then he would be approaching the river. Walter stole another backward glance and noticed the lights go on in the farmhouse and flickers of numerous torches and lanterns moving erratically in the area of the corral.

The frightened young gelding was not at all appeased by the soft words of assurance uttered by its strange rider and galloped furiously along the road, Walter hanging desperately to its mane. The road began its gradual decline to the river bank and soon the shimmering outline of the waterway, reflecting the soft light of the moon, came into view. Walter glanced back again. There was no sign of dogs anymore, but in the distance the faint glow of headlights told him that the pursuers had commandeered an automobile. His problem now was not to get away from the pursuing dogs, but how to stop his nervous mount.

As the lights of the automobile came into view from the top of a knoll, the puffing gelding began to show signs of exhaustion. Its pace slackened to a slow gallop and Walter moved forward as far as he could and reached for the animal's nose. He pulled the gelding's head down and pressed the makeshift bit against its teeth. The animal opened it mouth slightly and the bit slipped into its foaming mouth. Walter slid back to the gelding's back and pulled hard on the shoulder strap reins. The horse slowed down. Over his shoulder he saw the headlights of the pursuing automobile getting closer.

The river bank was now clearly visible and the road began to turn left to meet up with the main highway and the bridge. He pulled on the reins and the horse swerved to the right, stepping cautiously down the bank. At the edge of the water he stopped and Walter slid off its back. He patted the now docile animal on its perspiring shoulder and neck and whispered his thanks. He pulled the wooden bit from the horse's mouth and after giving the animal a gentle hug and kiss on its soft nose, he gave it a gentle slap on its buttocks. The gelding disappeared into the darkness.

With the haze of the automobile lights now clearly visible near the river bank, Walter hid behind some bushes and struggled to pull the boots off his swollen feet. He tied them together and packed some stones into the toe area of the footwear and slung them over his shoulder. With the laces from one his boots and the camera strap he tied his backpack on top of his head and slid quietly into the water. He swam toward the fast flowing channel, dropping his boots into the water before he got there. He looked back. The lights of the automobile turned right and followed the road toward the bridge.

The exhausted fugitive reached the channel and floated almost effortlessly with the swift flowing water, resting his painful feet and aching body. Lights flickered and twinkled on the shore, but all that Walter had to be wary of now was the watercraft plying the river. Whenever he saw one approaching he swam noiselessly to the shore and waited in order to keep his backpack and camera from getting wet.

Walter knew that he was not yet out of danger. There was still the matter of getting back to the apartment, once inside the city. As he swam along the channel he pondered how to achieve this without drawing attention to his shoeless feet and wet clothing. His mind went back to the survival training he had received in London and he sorted out his options.

~~~

After what seemed like an eternity, the lights of Breslau came into view, a welcome sight compared to the cold, oily darkness of the river. He checked his watch. It was still only eleven o'clock. The skin on his fingers was now wrinkled from the long exposure to the water and his teeth chattered from the cold. But he had reached a decision in his plan and it called for going ashore at a specific spot, a park beside the river which he knew was the favorite haunt of young lovers in the area. The time of day was just right for what he had in mind. The landmark for which he was looking came into view and he cautiously swam toward the shore.

On shore he removed his shirt and tore it into strips of about four inches wide. He took the camera straps off the backpack, slung the pack over his shoulder and headed quickly for a clump of bushes at the edge of the park. He nestled inside the shrubbery and waited. A short distance away the voices and laughter of young people told him that his plan had a chance of success.

Several minutes later he heard the giggling of a young woman. In the weak light of a street lamp he noticed the woman and a man walking toward an isolated stretch of grass not far from his observation point. They drew nearer, fondling each other and giggling. When they reached the sand bar, the man spread out a blanket he was carrying. They embraced and fell over on the blanket. More giggling was followed by moans, and then silence. The woman, dressed in light colored clothes was more visible than the man against the dark background. She stood up first and rearranged her clothing. He remained lying on the blanket.

"Excuse me, sweetheart," she purred. "I have to go behind the bush."

"Certainly. Go ahead, dear," he answered. "I think I will stay here and watch our things. Don't get lost"

The girl headed directly for a clump of bushes and went behind them to remain out of sight. She lifted up her skirt and began to urinate on the ground. While she was concentrating on this task, Walter stole silently behind her and placed his hand over her mouth. He held her arm behind her with his other hand and pulled her down, pinning her other arm against the ground. She struggled briefly but could make no sound. Her eyes shone with fear. Walter, using his free hand formed a small ball out of a strip of cloth and pushed it into her mouth. Another one of the bandages that he had made earlier he wrapped around her head, covering her mouth. He tied her hands behind her, and using another strip of cloth, he tied up her feet, then he carried her to a nearby bush. He returned to his original position behind the shrubbery.

After lying still for a few minutes, the man stood up and folded the blanket. He stared in the direction of the bush.

"Frieda. Are you all right?" he called.

He waited for a few seconds and called again.   Walter waited. Apparently distressed by the girl's long absence, he picked up the blanket and walked quickly toward the clump of bushes, following the same route that the girl had taken earlier. He stopped in front of where Walter was hiding. When he moved closer to the bush, Walter dashed out and put a headlock hold on the man. Before the man had a chance to resist, Walter applied a move he had learned in spy school and the man's body went limp. Moving quickly before the man regained consciousness, Walter removed the man's clothes and replaced his own wet attire beside those of the unwitting donor. He used another strip of cloth to cover the man's mouth and his last one to tie up the man's hands behind his back. The strap from the camera, which had served as the horse's bit, was put to one more use, tying the man's ankles together. He carried the limp body and set it down beside the girl and covered them both with the blanket.

Walter mentally congratulated himself as he pulled the man's sweater over his wrinkled, but dry, shirt. Except for the shoes which were about two sizes too large, the clothes fit him perfectly. He swung the backpack over his shoulder and walked nonchalantly through the park and into the street. As he walked past a street light, he detected a small round hole in his backpack. He placed his elbow in front of it and picked up his step.

From about a block away, Walter noticed that there were several SS men near the Novy Polski Trading Company building. He turned into a side street and approached from the other side. They were still there. He walked around the next block and made his way down the back lane to the company building. There was a light in the window of his apartment and he made his way quickly up the fire stairs as Karl had instructed him. He pushed the door open slowly and peeked inside. The hall was clear. He tried his own door. It was unlocked. Pushing it open slightly, he peered in through the crack. Karl was sitting at the table, holding up a newspaper, a bottle of vodka and a glass in front of him. Walter flew into the room, locking the door behind him.

Karl laid down the newspaper and looked up. "Oh, you don't need to worry about this place," he said casually. "This is our oasis in the desert. We are safe here."

"Oasis? Right!" said Walter, removing his backpack. "Did you see all those black shirts out in the street?"

Karl placed his forefinger up to his mouth to signal quiet. "Oh, sure, I did," he replied softly. "But I knew that as long as they were out there you were safe."

"And how did your figure that?" asked Walter, exasperated.

"Very simple. Why would they be looking for anyone if they already had him? In fact, I don't think that gathering outside has anything to do with us. Sit down and tell me where you got those fancy clothes."

"Karl, are you not interested in how I made out at the target?" implored Walter. "And look, let me show you something. See this here hole in my backpack? That is how close I came to getting it. We have to get rid of these clothes right away"

He removed the birdwatchers' guide from the pack and opened it. A slightly flattened slug fell out of it. Karl picked it up and laughed.

"You know. With all the industrial might that this country has, they still cannot make a sub-machine gun that is much better than a fire cracker."

Karl's face became serious. He signaled Walter to move in closer and spoke in a barely audible voice. "The truth is, Willy, that I was worried sick about this whole operation. I felt somewhat ashamed at having sent a boy like you on this dangerous mission. Someone who is not even a Pole. But

Sliworski and Simpson insisted that you do it. You will never know how long each minute of this night was for me and how relieved I was to hear you at the door. I know that you did your job well, my boy. But you need to forget about the whole thing for a while and rest your body and mind. I am trying to help you get it out of your head. So relax. We will dispose of your wardrobe now and tomorrow we will go for a walk and you can tell me all about it."

"We have to protect this with our lives," said Walter, pointing to the camera.

Karl nodded in the affirmative. He removed the film from the camera and placed it in his pocket. They walked down to the furnace room with the clothes that Walter had appropriated. "No, we cannot do this. They will smell the smoke," warned Karl. They both returned to the apartment, opened the vent in the closet and pushed the clothes through the opening. Walter fell into his bed and instantly was asleep. Karl remained in the apartment all night, dozing in his chair between drinks of vodka.

~~~

The activity on the street in front of the Novy Polski Trading Company building was normal next morning when Walter painfully guided his bicycle across the bumpy cobblestone surface. His seat was raw from the bareback ride on the previous night and the bottoms of his feet seemed to be on fire, but Karl thought that he should continue his normal visible activities. After performing his regular routine, Walter returned to the office. Karl was already waiting for him. They walked out into the park and sat on the bench.

"You know what, Willy," said Karl. "Those photos are the best piece of information we have yet been able to obtain here. You are to be congratulated. How many were there?"

"Hundreds. Maybe a thousand or more," replied Walter. "I never got to the end of the bunker. I should have had more time."

"The significance of this whole exercise is not so much about how many there were, but the fact that they are there at all. That is what we were out to prove. But let us start from the beginning. Now you can tell me."

Walter was glad that he had held off telling the story until today when he was rested and less excited. "It seems like last night was a year ago, but I will start from the time I reached my observation point."

He related the string of events that resulted in his entrance into the bunker, the chase down to the river and his long swim back to the city. Karl laughed hilariously when Walter described how he had to go about obtaining dry clothes in order to escape attention once he got back into the street. "It proves that the master race is not beyond anyone else when it comes to human frailties," he chuckled as they made their way to the tea house.

His points of pain now reduced to some aching muscles and blistered toes, the next day Walter ventured farther inside the city. Brown shirted SA men and black-uniformed SS officers were everywhere he looked. The rumors in the street were that they were here in preparation for the forthcoming annual convention of the National Socialist Party in Nuremburg. But they seemed to be more involved in investigation than preparation and Walter wondered if he was the instigator of all the paramilitary presence. At the edge of the city square he stopped in front of the wall to look at the billboard. Amid the posters of the stern looking Fuehrer, extolling the virtues of the new state and calling on the citizens to do everything from working harder in the factories to growing vegetables, was an official-looking placard listing the names of persons executed for crimes against the state. He glanced through the list of names. One name jumped out at him. Edgar Remke. Was this the same Edgar Remke with whom he and Victor had worked the previous summer? "Decapitated for acts of treason at the prison of Ploetzensee, after trial in the People's Court," read the notice. Walter peddled slowly back to the office, oblivious to everything going on around him.

"I have just come back from the square. The new list is up," he told Karl when he returned.

"Then you know about Horst," said Karl solemnly.

"Yes. But how did you know about him? And, if you did, why did you not tell me about it?" asked Walter.

"Let's just say that he was an important link in the organization and that is how I knew him. As for why I did not tell you about it earlier, it is because I first heard about it the day before your penetration of the bunker, and I felt that you already had enough on your mind that day."

Walter responded with an incredulous stare. Karl gazed at the papers on his desk, running his fingers across his balding crown. He leaned back and looked at Walter.

"Things are getting more difficult here, Willy, but some of us must continue our work. As for you, your task here is completed. London wants you to return to Torun next week. Arrangements have been made for you to leave Monday. Your orders will be waiting for you there and the chauffeur will meet you at the station. They may want you to go back to London for a while, who knows?"

CHAPTER 38

Securely tethered at the dock in Torun, the *Barrow* and its crew and passengers provided Walter with a welcome link to the familiar. He stood on the deck gazing toward the west and imagining in his mind what curious events were taking place only a hundred kilometers away. Simpson was in one of the cabins, probably assessing his latest assignment and planning the next one. Duke, as always was alone in the wheelhouse. The first mate took him below deck. Back in the cabin that he and Victor had once shared, Walter reflected on where his partner was now and how he was faring. A sharp rap on the door preceded Simpson's entrance. He greeted Walter with a handshake and an approving smile in his eyes.

"Well, Willy, old boy, you pulled off another one," he said.

"Yes, but they damn near got me this time," replied Walter.

"I heard all about that. And I also heard that you have a souvenir to remind you of it," laughed Simpson. "Anyway, you deserve a holiday, so tomorrow we will start a nice leisurely trip back to London. After a week or so we will see what headquarters has for us. And, oh yes, your friend Victor will also be back in London, so you will be able to exchange yarns about your experiences."

The relaxing trip back was just as Simpson promised, but in two days boredom and loneliness set in and Walter paced restlessly between his cabin and the deck. Simpson spent most of his time with Duke, and Walter, in his lonely moments, pondered his situation and the future. He wondered whether what he was doing was of any value to anyone and whether he should continue in what was now becoming a dangerous business. Both Simpson and Karl felt that he was doing a good job, but was it worth risking his life for it. And even if he wanted to leave, would he be allowed to do so. He imagined what his family back home would be doing about this time and wondered if he would ever see them again. No doubt, there would be letters from home when he got back to London. It all seemed so different and so far away. He felt that he too, was changing and that he was no longer the innocent young boy who pleaded with Stanley to help him respond to the advertisement in the Polish weekly newspaper. As if sensing Walter's boredom and soul searching, Duke packed his fishing gear and set a steady course across the channel. They were in London that evening.

~~~

The overhead lights had just been turned on in rapid succession as the Hillman Minx entered the street leading to the flat. Simpson, deep in thought, had driven without engaging in conversation all the way from the dock. At the door, the housekeeper greeted them as though they had just returned from a shopping trip. Nothing was changed except the trees in front of the building whose leaves were surrendering their familiar green in exchange for the more temporary yellows and reds.

"Well, here you are, old chap," said Simpson as they entered the apartment. "I think you will find everything pretty much as you left it. The mail is in your desk drawer along with an envelope containing some petty cash. Methinks you are in the mood for a few days of peace and quiet, so I will leave you to yourself for a spell. Victor will be back the day after tomorrow and I will see you both then. Pity he could not have been here today so that the two of you could do the town together. Call me if you need anything."

Simpson stepped out into the hall, and then stuck his head back through the partly closed door.

"I say. I forgot to mention this earlier. Our friend Duke would like us to meet some of his friends next week, so get your best suit cleaned and pressed. They are very important people."

"OK, I will," said Walter. "That Duke fellow always did strike me as being somewhat different. I am not surprised that his friends are so special."

"All except us, that is," grinned Simpson as he closed the door.

The letters from home lamented the hot, dry weather conditions which shriveled the crops and browned the pastures. It described the giant black clouds which rolled in from the western plains and covered everything with dust. It would be another hard winter and Stanley was harvesting every blade of grass he could find to store as feed for the livestock. He did not know why he did it, because the price of the livestock barely covered the cost of shipping them to market. But they were lucky because they had enough food and fuel for the winter. Others were not as fortunate. In the cities, millions were unemployed with no idea of where their next meal would come from. So the Berglunds thanked providence for their good health and struggled on, hoping for better things to come. They considered Walter to be the most fortunate one because he had a steady job and nothing to worry about.

Slumped down in the ancient but comfortable velour cushioned chair, Walter closed his eyes to visualize the scene which Stanley described in his letter – fields parched by the unrelenting sun and scoured by the merciless winds. However, his mind could only conjure visions of the verdant meadows, luxuriant fields and shady woods that were so familiar to him. When he opened the door in response to a faint knock, Mrs. Jenkins, the landlady, wheeled in a tea cart with his dinner. He lifted the plate covers and inspected the hot roast beef, baked potatoes and green beans. Tea and chocolate cake with sauce rounded off the fare. Stanley is right, he thought, I really don't have too much to worry about here, but he wondered why they were being so good to him. Normally he would be eating down in the dining room. Was Simpson doing this to express his appreciation for what he had done in Breslau or was he being prepared for a shocking surprise?

As foretold by Simpson, Victor returned in the afternoon of the second day. Obviously delighted to be surrounded by familiar faces and a friendly atmosphere, the two young men shook hands vigorously and embraced each other as Simpson observed them with a beneficent smile.

"You two have much to relate to each other," he suggested, "but don't forget to talk about your experiences only within these four walls or when you are with me."

Walter could not contain is excitement. "Remember those riding lessons we had in Washington that everyone thought was a waste of time? Well, let me tell you Victor, if I had not taken that part of our training seriously, I probably would not be here now."

"Oh, you didn't need any lessons in that department," remarked Victor. "You showed most of us how it's done. But I can't wait to hear your story and also to tell you mine."

"I will ask Mrs. Jenkins to bring dinner for three and you two can exchange your exaggerations in the presence of a neutral eavesdropper," Simpson suggested.

They agreed that would be an excellent way in which to spend their reunion, and while Simpson consulted with the housekeeper about dinner, Victor unpacked his bags and stepped into the shower.

"I thought you would be clean enough after swimming across Lake Constance to get to your target," shouted Walter above the noise of the shower.

"Never got my feet wet once," said Victor as he emerged from the shower. "Until recently we could take a boat across the lake from Switzerland and dock right at Friedrichshafen and no one would say a word to us. The Germans are most accommodating to the Swiss, probably because they are traditionally neutral and provide them with a base from which to observe the French. But what is going on in Friedrichshafen, now that is another thing about which I will tell you later."

Victor entered his bedroom and returned a few minutes later in casual slacks, sport shirt and slippers. Simpson and Walter were slumped in their chairs, legs outstretched and arms hanging loose over the sides.

"Yes sir," continued Victor, "that place is like a damned aeronautical hutch, producing airplanes like they were baby rabbits." He glanced at Simpson inquisitively, but he lifted his hand in a gesture of approval."

"That's all right Victor, we are all one family here," he said. "You need not worry about us."

"I never did make it inside the factory where they do some of the assembly work. It is like an armed camp. But then, I never had to. I could watch from a number of vantage points and actually count the aircraft as they took off, some, no doubt, going direct to Stettin."

"I suppose things are not as simple as they used to be around Stettin either," injected Walter. "Did you hear about Horst?"

"Yes. Some of our people saw his name on the billboard in Friedrichshafen," responded Victor sadly.

"He got a bit careless," offered Simpson. "He underestimated the proficiency of the SS. Too bad. We have had a difficult time replacing him."

"Things were getting pretty tight in Friedrichshafen too in the last week or so. We could no longer go in as Swiss tourists and move around almost freely. The brown shirts followed us wherever we went, so we knew that the jig was up," added Victor.

"Old von Nicolai is really clamping down all over the place back there. No doubt he will clamp down even further after what happened in Breslau," mused Simpson, rubbing his chin pensively. "That must have been quite a harrowing experience for you, Walter."

"After that one, I will always be thankful for my farm upbringing and will hold horses and bodies of water in the highest esteem." said Walter.

"How about describing some of those hair-raising experiences that you told us about on the boat, so that Victor can hear what he missed," suggested Simpson. "But wait. There is someone at the door."

The cook and housekeeper pushed two tea carts through the door. The smell of roast chicken filled the room. Tasty and plentiful food and stimulating talk carried them well into the evening. Simpson stood up, stretched and announced that he would be leaving.

"Before I leave, I must tell you about the invitation we have received from Duke to meet with some of his friends. I mentioned this earlier to Walter. I would like you to be ready at nine Monday morning. You will be picked up at the front door. I will be there also. Wear your best clothes, with a shirt and tie. Duke moves in some pretty high class company as you will see. But enough of this. I want it to be a surprise for you."

~~~

Standing erect in their hard collars and buttoned down jackets, the two young men waited outside the front door of the flat for the Hillman Minx and its driver to arrive. The office workers, clerks and junior executives had all gone by earlier on their way to work. Now bankers and senior executives passed by in chauffeur driven automobiles, reading their papers or sitting stiffly in the back seat. Among all this activity were the lorries making deliveries, and women rushing to do their shopping early before the masses arrived. Everyone else, it seemed, was either walking by leisurely in the warm early fall morning or riding a bicycle. It was one minute to nine and no Hillman was in sight.

"He is late. That is not like him," said Walter as he watched a black Rolls Royce limousine slide up to the curb.

The majestic automobile stopped in front of the small iron gate and the chauffeur stepped out. He opened the back door and Simpson emerged. Walter and Victor looked at each other, their faces brimming with surprise. Simpson, looking awkward and uncomfortable, walked partway up the sidewalk toward them, his new shoes clumping against the cobblestone walk.

"All right, boys. There is our conveyance today," he announced, waving his hand proudly at the Rolls Royce. "Remember now. This is a very special event. I see that you are well dressed for it. Now we must all be on our best behavior."

The chauffeur stood at attention, holding the door open. They followed Simpson into the limousine and sank into the luxurious upholstery. The three passengers smiled approvingly at each other as the limousine floated with ease through the crowded streets toward the city center. In deference to the vehicle and the dignified driver, and its well-groomed passengers, other vehicles in the street kept their distance and the young men felt the stares of the pedestrians as they drove by. They sat rigidly in their seat watching the city pass by their windows.

"There's Westminister," commented Victor, remembering the sightseeing tour conducted by Simpson on their first time in London.

The chauffeur turned into Grosvenor Place and Buckingham Palace came into view, surrounded by broad expanses of lawns, gardens and pools. Slowing down gradually, the driver turned toward the palace entrance and stopped in front of the heavy iron gate. Two uniformed guards in tall fur hats marched stiffly to the double gate and opened it. They stood at attention as the limousine drove through. The two young men gawked at Simpson who sat silently, with a satisfied smirk on his face. Following the road to the right, the chauffeur drove around the end of the massive building and stopped beside an expansive lawn surrounded by trees and late blooming shrubs with a fountain in the middle. Standing beside a round, white marble table was a man in formal attire. The limousine halted and they were let out. When the man beside the table turned toward them, they knew immediately that it was Duke.

"He looks so different dressed in a striped suit and felt hat," whispered Walter.

Simpson nodded in agreement.

"Nice to see you all," said Duke, shaking their hands. "I will go and fetch the mysterious person who asked to meet you." He turned and walked toward a secluded side door of the building.

"Boy! It sounds as though it is going to be someone very important," said Victor, overcome by excitement.

"One of the most, if not the most, important person you will ever meet," promised Simpson. "Be very courteous and speak only when you feel that he wants you to speak."

With three pairs of eyes peering intently at it, the private entrance opened slowly and Duke appeared. He held the door open for a portly bearded man in a dark gray three piece suit. Two tall and expressionless men followed several steps behind him. They all walked casually toward the lawn where the guests waited, and stopped beside the round white table. The three overwhelmed visitors stood up.

"Your Majesty," announced Duke as they arrived, "I would like to present three of my sailing partners, one of whom you already know. This young man is Victor Rudniki from the United States of America, and this other gentleman is Walter Berglund from your favorite Dominion, Canada."

The king held out his hand to each of the three men. "I welcome you here as friends of our country. Both of your countries are very dear to me and I look forward to many years of brotherly relations with them. The reason that I asked to meet you is that I am exceedingly interested in the work that you are doing and wanted to tell you that I personally appreciate the value of this work. But I also want to hear what you have to say, so why don't we start with our young friend from Canada."

"Your Majesty," stammered Walter, "I never in my life thought that I would ever see you, let alone shake hands with you."

"Why not, young man?" smiled the king. "We are both members of the same Empire."

Walter stepped back nervously and observed the monarch. "When I was young child I would stand before the picture of you in our school back home and it seemed like you were there in the room always keeping an eye on things," he related.

"The queen and I are very fond of Canada," said the king. "We hope to pay your country a visit one of these years if the world remains at peace." He sat down in one of the decorative cast iron chairs and motioned to them to be seated.

"Your Majesty," said Simpson, "these two young men, who are not even citizens of Europe, have risked their lives to obtain information which indicates that the peace which you so earnestly desire is no longer secure. Even as we stand here, German factories are pouring out their tools of war. These young men have seen it with their own eyes. Unless the League of Nations does something soon, it will be too late."

"Yes, I am very concerned about the apathy in the League, Captain Simpson. But I am just as concerned about my own government." replied the king. "The apathy in the House of Commons is overwhelming. Only that brave statesman Winston Churchill appears to have any concern about the seriousness of the situation, but no one in the House pays any attention to him. And what are your impressions?" he asked, turning to Victor.

"Your Majesty," said Victor, "I came over here reluctantly and only because my father wanted me to do so. We in the United States of America do not want to become involved in the affairs of Europe. But after seeing what is going on in Germany, I can understand why people on this side of the ocean should be concerned."

"And so we are, but not maybe as concerned as we should be. Over there on the continent, war is a game and peace is but an intermission," said the king waving his hand toward the east. "It has always been thus. They speak of peace and repeat again and again that the last one was the war to end all wars. But as soon as the smoke has cleared and a new generation of young men appears, they are back at it, sacrificing yet another generation."

A secretary appeared at the edge and walked toward the king and handed him a note. The king read it and looked up at his visitors.

"I must go now. Thank you for accepting my invitation to come and listen to my sentiments. I wanted to tell you personally that what you are doing is important to my country, as well as to yours and to all our friends in Europe. As Mr. Simpson can tell you, yours is a thankless occupation.

There is no glory and no recognition in it. So that is why, when your friend Duke asked if I could spend a few minutes with you, I could not refuse. So now, as you go about your work, you will know that your efforts are appreciated. Now, good-bye and may God watch over you."

He turned and walked slowly toward the castle, followed closely by the secretary and Duke. Several paces behind, the two men with blank faces moved mechanically. The limousine appeared as the door closed behind them.

"Now I know who Duke really is and why I always felt that I had seen him somewhere before," said Walter as the Rolls turned into the street. "I saw him in a picture in Major Bradley's office back home. He really is a duke. This is too much. I'll probably wake up soon and discover that all this was a dream."

~~~

With the excitement of the previous day reluctantly receding into memory, the two young men sat in their apartment sipping coffee. When Mrs. Jenkins asked if there was anything special that she could make for them, they both said that a nice cup of coffee would provide a welcome break from the steady diet of tea, and she fulfilled their request. They drank the brew but agreed that coffee making was not one of Mrs. Jenkins' culinary strengths. By now each of them had been in London for a week or more and boredom was setting in.

"We can't say that they are not looking after us well," said Walter, sipping his coffee. "But you know what I miss the most? I miss being with other people my age. At home we were always doing things, boys and girls together. Going to church events, dances, fairs, ball games and things like that. Here we're not even allowed to be around girls when we are on the job. Maybe we might be allowed to talk to girls here in London, but where would one go to meet a girl here?"

"I have been thinking about these things myself, but Walter, have you ever wondered how long we are going to be doing this thing?" asked Victor. "I mean, to what is all this leading us? I know that we are well paid and we don't have to worry about going without anything; we have even met the king, which no one will believe anyway; but how long is this going to last and what will become of us after it is all over?"

Victor poured himself another cup of coffee, leaned back in his chair and stretched his feet across the hassock. His eyes focused on Walter who appeared to be deep in thought.

"It's a job," responded Walter, "which is more than a lot of people back home have, from what I hear."

"How true," said Victor. "My father says in his letters that things are really rough in the coal mining business and, in spite of his many years of seniority, he is next in line to be laid off."

"The situation with my folks back home is a bit different," explained Walter. "Being farmers, they will always have work. That is, as long as they can hang on to their land. Their problem is money; enough to pay the taxes and buy the things that they cannot produce. I send them some from time to time when I am back here and I think that keeps them going at times, although Uncle Stanley is too independent a person to say so. But they are used to adapting in order to survive. After all, they come from Poland and you've seen what things are like there for the peasants and most of the villagers."

"Yes. And that's another thing, now that you mention Poland," said Victor. "Do you realize that we don't even know for whom we are working? We started out in Washington, came to London, and then Poland, now back in London. If someone asks you for whom do you work, what would you say?"

"You know," laughed Walter, "no one has asked me that since I have been on this job. Everyone we associate with seems to know. But at least I know what I am working for, and that is to do what I can to remove the threat to the freedom that you and I take for granted in our countries. On this side of the ocean things are different. It's the law of the jungle. The strongest takes all, including the freedom of a person to better himself. In Europe, there are the strong and the weak, not only among individuals, but also among nations. The strong have always ridden on the backs of the weak and do their best to keep them down. For the weak there is no hope."

"But when you look at what Hitler is trying to do, don't you sometime think that he is trying to correct all those things that you describe?" asked Victor.

"You know," mused Walter, "I think I have come a full circle in the past two years or so. As I told you before, the reason that I went after this job is somehow to revenge my parents' death; that I was going to get someone for doing that to them. I was young and inexperienced and very open to the influence of others. But when I got to Germany and saw how industrious and progressive the people were, I thought that, gee, you know, these people have the right idea. What right did I have to interfere with what they had set out to do? Then after seeing what was going on behind the scenes, I realized that Hitler's plans go beyond the welfare of the German people. That he is using them to achieve his own agenda, whatever that might be. So I am back to my original motive and that is to destroy the threat to innocent people, such as my parents, before the strong destroy them also."

He paused as if to contemplate his next thought. "I think we will both agree that all those planes and tanks and armored vehicles of all kinds, and all the other things that we have not yet seen, are not out there just to fill those underground bunkers. One day soon they will roll out and all those cocky brown shirts, the Wehrmacht, the Black Shirts and Luftwaffe pilots will mount them and ride over the poor Polish peasants, over the Sliworskis and Bashinskis. And, as His Majesty King George said, if he who is king cannot get his government to recognize this threat, how can other governments across the ocean do so? How do we expect them to believe all this? If they keep on saying that these things cannot happen, what is to stop these planes and tanks from later flying and rolling over the coal mines of Pennsylvania and the grain fields of Manitoba? So I have decided that I am going to work harder than ever to look everywhere I can for new proof of what is now happening in Germany so that one day everyone everywhere will believe what we have seen, and be prepared. When I am finished doing that, I'll go back to the farm and settle down."

"Well, you seem to have given this some thought. I guess when you look at it that way, it does not really matter so much who we work for as what we are working for," said Victor. "I have never said this to anyone before, Walter, but you and I and all those other we work with, are spies and spies are supposed to do what they are told and not ask why they are doing it. You are much too philosophical for a spy."

"I hear that a true spy will work for anyone who will pay him. If that is the case, then I am not a good spy. I want to work for a cause, first and foremost. If being a spy can help me to achieve this, then so be it," explained Walter.

Their discussion was abruptly interrupted by a loud rap on the door. Walter jumped up and opened it slightly, then all the way. Simpson stood there in his well pressed tweed jacket and shirt opened at the neck.

"Come in. Come in," said Walter. "We were just sitting around talking about our job."

"Good," said Simpson enthusiastically, "because what I have to tell you involves just that."

"Would you like a cup of not so hot coffee?" asked Victor

"No thanks, Victor. I am a tea drinker myself. Coffee is for Italians, Americans and Norwegians. I remain true to the tradition."

He sat down, lit a cigarette and blew smoke at the ceiling.

"Well chaps," he began, "the season is wearing thin and it will soon be too cold and too dangerous for working in the field, but before we pack it in for the winter I have been asked by HQ for one more bit of information, which I think we can supply. It will have to be a hit and run operation, so to speak, since we will not establish a base anywhere this time. Because of the nature of the target you, Walter, will be best suited for the first operation. A similar operation on a different target will be set up for you, Victor."

Simpson paused to acknowledge their reaction. "I am ready, sir," said Walter. "And so am I," echoed Victor.

"You will need a radio receiver and transmitter for this job," continued Simpson, "so both of you will first take a four-week refresher course in radio operating. This will take us close to November and the risk of snow. But if we work fast and get our back-up intelligence work done properly, it should only be a two or three-day job. The *Barrow* will drop you off at night in the target area and pick you up after you have completed the operation and made contact by radio. After these two jobs are done we will settle in for the winter and a very interesting course in parachuting and sabotage. Your radio training will commence tomorrow at eight. See you at the school at seven-thirty."

Simpson stood up and stretched his lanky frame to its full height. "So get to bed early. You will need clear heads and steady hands for this training.

See you in the morning."

"Boy, he seems to be all business tonight," said Victor after Simpson closed the door.

"There must be something unusual about this assignment." said Walter.

"Aren't they all that way?" asked Victor.

CHAPTER 39

Four weeks of dots and ashes, radio frequencies and coded jargon were interspersed only with regular meals and periods of sleep. During these interludes their fingers continued to tap out messages on the table with forks and spoons, and on the bedstead at night.

"Your radio set must become an extension of your brain and be so much a part of you that your signal will be as uniquely yours as your signature. When this happens, the receiver will recognize you by your signal, as well as by your code name," intoned the instructor.

"So why is it so important to develop a transmitting style that is uniquely yours if you also use your code name?" asked Walter.

"It will be of no use to you at all," answered the instructor, "at least not until you get caught and someone else tries to transmit a message in your place."

A subdued burst of laughter filled the room. The instructor had won the round.

They and several other operatives graduated with a handshake from the instructor and the presentation of a personal brief case-sized transmitter and receiver set. Next day Walter carried his to the dock for his rendezvous with the *Barrow*. Simpson entered the cabin shortly after Walter had sat down on the edge of his bunk. He dropped a duffle bag on the bed beside Walter's.

"Your cold weather gear and a sleeping bag," he explained. "Light and warm. You may need them where you are going."

"And where is that?" asked Walter.

"About sixty miles from your old stamping grounds, Stettin. The place is called Swinemunde."

"That area was crawling with Gestapo when we left," said Walter.

"Stettin, yes. But Swinemunde is a smaller place, so they don't put as much emphasis on security there. But it has been established by our expeditionary team that German freighters use that port to unload strategic material, coming from a certain source, which we think could be put to military use."

"From where, exactly?" asked Walter.

"From the United States of America, we think."

"The United States?" exclaimed Walter. "But they are on our side."

"Yes. But they are also a business minded nation. Their companies do business wherever they can make a profit," explained Simpson.

"So what is the use of getting this type of information?" asked Walter.

"HQ thinks that the Nye Commission in Washington would be very interested in the details of some of these business transactions."

"Excuse me." said Walter. "I don't understand."

"Oh, I am sorry," apologized Simpson. "The Nye Commission is a committee studying the profits that American arms manufacturers make out of war. They are talking mainly about the World War, but if they can be shown that this activity is going on even now, it might make quite a difference in their recommendations."

"Sounds like we are working against great odds in this business," moaned Walter.

"At times we are," agreed Simpson. "At times we are. But our task is to continue doing our job and hope that it will do some good. So on this assignment you will try to get on board a German freighter called the *Bremerhaven*, which is due to arrive at the Swinemunde docks from New York in six days. You will board it when the crew is out on the town after their long voyage. You will go down into the hold, check the cargo, take some pictures, and then radio the *Barrow*. We will pick you up at the same point where you will be dropped off."

"It sounds simple enough," said Walter, "but I still can't get over the United States shipping war material to the Nazi."

"Oh, it is all very innocent," explained Simpson. "Their shipping documents label the cargo contents as being for civilian use, but you have seen it as well as I have that there is very little in Germany these days that is not part of their military program."

"Now I understand why you did not assign Victor to this project," said Walter.

"Yes. It would be somewhat like spying on yourself," laughed Simpson. "But don't get me wrong about Americans in general. In a pre-war period, or maybe I should say an interwar period, in any neutral country, including England, there are two sides, the optimists and the pessimists. The optimists believe that things will remain the same and they take advantage of the situation to their own benefit. The pessimists, on the other hand, tend to see things a bit different and look at the darker side of things. We belong to the latter and are, for the moment, a minority."

Walter sat on the edge of his bed and shook his head in disbelief.

"I see that you have all your stuff here," said Simpson. "We will be pushing off in about an hour. Get some rest. I'll see you later."

~~~

He was awakened by the motion of the boat as it headed into the English Channel. The cabin felt empty without his partner. He soon missed Victor and their long philosophical discussions. With Victor he felt that he could talk about his deepest feelings. There is something different about Americans, he thought. They are so practical. Everything is either white or black. If his parents had not died when he was so young, he probably would be an American now too. Would he have been like Victor, he wondered. But then, were they really so different? His thoughts were interrupted by Milford announcing lunch.

The chilly Arctic air flowed defiantly across the choppy waves and dark, billowy clouds raced across the dark blue sky. In the wheelhouse, Duke, all alone and looking stern in his blue sailor's hat and turtle neck sweater, kept the vessel on a steady course. Simpson spent most of his time in his cabin or in the radio room, his mood reflecting the somber scene outside. It was obvious that this trip was all business. Hit and run, as Simpson described it. Hit your target and then dash home before winter arrives.

The cold front had pushed its way onto the continent and over the Atlantic when the *Barrow* emerged from the Kiel Canal and headed into the Baltic. Tongues of orange reflections from the setting sun licked across the shimmering water and disappeared into the horizon. The struggling orb appeared to be winning a temporary victory over the Arctic air mass and the return flow of warmer air from the continent rushed in to take it place.

Simpson emerged from his cabin looking rested but pensive. "I think the weather is going to cooperate. It is time for some more briefing, old chap," he announced as he entered Walter's cabin, carrying a cardboard pouch.

"So far this will be the most exciting part of this whole trip," said Walter.

"Fine then. You appear to be in a good mood, so let us get down to business."

He removed a map and some picture from the pouch. "Let's take a look at the topography and terrain of the target area and some pictures of the *Bremerhaven*. First let us check the lay of the land". He unfolded the map and pointed with his pen. "Here is the dock where the ship will be anchored. Here is the town and over here is a dense wooded area, mostly evergreens – spruce and pine. Good cover. That is the general area where we propose to drop you off in three days if everything falls into place. Your landing will, of course, have to take place at night. You will take this sleeping bag and bed down comfortably and head into town in the morning."

He dug into the pouch. "Here are your identification papers, if you should need them. You will use the same name as you used in Dresden. If you move as inconspicuously as possible, you should not need them. It is better that you should not, of course. Now here are some pictures of the *Bremerhaven*, taken from different angles. It is just your average freighter." He opened and spread out a set of drawings. "And here is a sketched layout of the deck and the cargo area. Study this material and commit the details to memory, then the task should not result in too many surprises."

The door closed quietly behind Simpson and Walter gazed at the maps, pictures and drawings on the table. In his mind he translated the lines, shapes and symbols into roads, streets, docks, beaches, hills and woods. He then studied the bus routes and schedules which Simpson had obtained for him. He pictured himself making his way into town, disembarking in the busy downtown area, moving along with the crowd, then making his way to the docks. Details of the lectures of the past two winters dealing with these situations flashed into his mind like picture slides on a screen. After about three hours he gathered up the maps, drawings and pictures and returned them to the pouch. Everything should work out just fine, he thought. The gentle rocking of the boat made him drowsy and he crawled into his bunk and fell asleep.

"We picked up the *Bremerhaven's* radio signals last night," Simpson announced at breakfast. "She'll enter the Bay of Pomerania the day after tomorrow and probably lie at anchor that night and dock the following day. That makes Saturday as the likely shore leave time for the crew. We will drop you off Friday night in a nice secluded bay which I will point out to you on the map. You will be picked up at exactly the same spot as soon as we receive your radio message, unless, of course, things go awry and you need to change the plan. We will stay out of the busy shipping lanes and out of sight as much as possible. If we do not hear from you in three days – four at the most – we will assume that the mission was not a success. That makes it Wednesday night."

~~~

There was no moon. What little light there was came from the clear star studded sky. Inky waves lapped against the side of the *Barrow* as she stood silent and ghostly white in the narrow bay. Simpson and the first mate lowered the small life boat over the side. Below deck, Walter checked his gear – sleeping bag, radio, extra clothing and food rations, in case he should need to hide for a spell. Another cold Arctic air mass was building over northern Siberia and if it moved down quickly, the weather could change before the mission was complete and a warm set of clothing might come in handy. He would have to strike swiftly and return before the weather changed. Snow on the ground left too much evidence, Simpson had reminded him earlier. No signs of his short visit must be left behind as such evidence may be traced back to the *Barrow* and its crew.

They moved silently in the darkness, aware of each other's presence by their breathing and short whispered instructions and acknowledgements. Walter lowered himself into the small row boat and his packs were handed to him. Simpson let himself down over the side and steadied himself in the bobbing boat. He settled into the seat and rowed quietly straight ahead. After a few minutes of rowing, a line of white foam signaled that the beach was in front of them. Simpson jumped out and pulled the boat across the sandy beach. Walter picked up his packs and stepped out. Simpson grabbed his hand and whispered him luck, then returned to the life boat and rowed off silently.

A wall of black in the distance reminded Walter of the land features which he had committed to memory during the trip. It was the edge of a thick evergreen grove of about twenty five hectares, uninhabited and traversed by only a few hiking trails. Between him and the forest was a secondary highway which had to be crossed. He approached it cautiously, stopping every few steps to listen for sounds. The haze of approaching automobile lights and the roar of a motor on his left told him he was not alone. He ducked behind a small bush and waited. The automobile sped by, leaving a trail of dust and the aroma of combusted gasoline. He waited until it had disappeared into the night then ran across the road. His eyes were gradually getting used to the dark. He had learned that cats can see in the dark, but not humans, so he would need to move slowly and cautiously.

His search for the expected footpath was awarded when he peered through the darkness and recognized the blurred outline of an opening in the bushes at the edge of the forest. He moved toward it and his feet soon told him that he had found the hardened path. He followed it into the grove, stopping every several meters to listen for sounds. The stillness of the forest was punctuated by the occasional blast of a ship's horn and the soft distant roar of ship's engines, and vehicles moving on the streets of Swinemunde and on the highway. It was quiet and peaceful in the forest. The resin smell of the evergreens was pleasant to the senses. Inside the trees the sporadic rustle of leaves and breaking twigs told him that he was being observed by the small wild nocturnal inhabitants of the forest. He counted his steps to keep track of the distance he had walked.

Eight hundred steps. It must be close to where the path veered to the right, he thought. The map had shown a turn at approximately one-quarter kilometer inside the forest. His right foot stepped off the hard path into the grass and a spiny bough touched his face. The path had turned to the right as expected. He stopped and reviewed the plan in his mind. From here he would feel his way through the trees until he was a safe distance from the path, then he would bed down and wait for dawn. He crawled under the overhanging branches of a large spruce, put down his pack and leaned against the tree. The stars and the sky were cut off by the dense tree branches. Blackness was everywhere. After a while, the sounds in the distance ceased and the world became very small. He removed the sleeping bag from its pack and wrapped it around his legs and body. The luminous dial on his watch told him it was two-thirty. He dozed off fitfully until the phantom gray dawn seeped through the ebony black, gradually revealing the surrounding world.

Walter stood up and stretched, pushing his head and body through the overhanging branches. Some of the hardier birds, which had not yet migrated, darted silently among the boughs. The tree he had chosen in the dark was one of the largest in the grove. Its heavy branches, trained downward by the snows of many winters, formed a natural shelter around the trunk. Nearby was a small clearing where numerous small shrubs competed for the life-giving sunlight. The rest of the surrounding area was dense with trees and little or no underbrush. He ventured cautiously from among the branches, carefully observing the landmarks and taking compass readings. A short distance away, the ground sloped steeply until it touched the bed of a small creek, its clear water flowing gently across the pebbled floor. He splashed water on his face and filled his canteen with the sparkling cold water, then headed back to the tree which he decided would be his base of operation.

It was now light enough to read a map. His position was about five kilometers from the dock where the *Bremerhaven* would soon be tied up. The sounds in the distance resumed and the world was waking up. Some of the buses would soon start running, he thought. He would make his way to the road and find the bus stop, but he must not attract any undue attention. He looked up through the opening in the forest. The sky was gray and the tops of the trees were beginning to sway in the breeze. The cold air from the north was probably moving in. He would need to dress for it. He removed the German made jacket and cap from his pack and put them on. He felt his face and realized that he had forgotten to shave, but he must appear as someone who had just emerged from one of the houses along the highway into town. He squeezed some shaving gel from a tube and spread it over his face, hung a miniature magnifying mirror on the tree and shaved. A splash of cold water from his canteen brought the blood rushing to his face and he felt refreshed.

It was six-thirty. He would take the 7:10 bus at a stop one-half a kilometer down the road from where he had entered the forest. After consulting the map one more time, he placed all his gear in the pack and carried it up into the tree. He returned and did the same with the case containing the radio set. He climbed up a short distance up the tree and tied these firmly against the trunk and branches, brushed himself off and headed for the road. Rabbits and birds darted across the footpath he had traversed the previous night. When he reached the road there was a stiff breeze coming from the northwest and the sky was heavily laden with fast moving dark clouds.

There was no one at the small bus shelter when he arrived. He read the schedule on the wall and the government posters exhorting the youth to join the Arbeitsfront or volunteer for armed services. Another poster showed a smiling Adolf Hitler mixing with a crowd of German workers. The poster announced a Strength Through Joy beer garden the following Sunday night. A near empty bus squeaked to a stop and honked its horn. Walter boarded and dropped the exact fare required into the fare box. The bus driver greeted him with a 'Good Morning' and 'Heil Hitler.' Walter returned the greeting.

"Are you new around here?" asked the driver.

"No. I usually take the later bus, but today I wanted to get to town earlier," replied Walter in German.

"Where do you work?" The driver appeared only casually interested.

"At the docks," responded Walter.

"Oh, then I think I know why you wanted to get there so early today," said the driver. "I suppose it is because the *Bremerhaven* is docking this morning."

"That is right," said Walter as he started for one of the empty seats in the middle of the bus. "I will be very busy when she arrives." He was mildly amused by his unintended prophesy and smiled to himself.

~~~

The center of the small city was awake and stirring like a disturbed ant hill. Factory workers jostled with one another and with office clerks, businessmen and sailors at bus stops and traffic lights. On the street, cars and trucks honked their horns impatiently at the slow moving lumber carriers and log transports moving to the city's sawmills clustered around the docks. There were no brown shirts or black uniforms visible and Walter prepared to disembark at the next stop.

"This is not the transfer point for the dockside bus," the driver reminded him as he stepped in front of the door.

"Yes, I know," said Walter, cursing himself for overlooking this detail in his preparation. He recovered quickly. "I need to pick up some rolls and coffee for lunch," he added. "I'll walk the rest of the way."

The bus driver eyed him curiously and wished him a good day.

Following the moving crowd along the city's main street he felt inconspicuous enough to walk into a restaurant for breakfast. He ordered sausage and eggs, brown bread and coffee. Glancing casually around, he observed that the other patrons were ignoring him and talking about their jobs, social events and the latest news from Berlin. He relaxed and the hot food felt good in his stomach after the night outdoors. This assignment is turning out to be a pleasant push-over, he thought.

Outside on the sidewalks only a sprinkling of pedestrians remained as the others entered their places of employment. These were mostly older people out for their morning groceries and children on their way to school. Walter walked confidently toward the dock. The bay was now in plain view and in the distance a freighter was moving slowly toward the wharf. He sat down on a park bench and watched until the ship maneuvered itself expertly into its berth. He continued down the descending street, counting the blocks and observing his position in relation to the wooded highland in the distance, several kilometers behind the city.

By mid morning the *Bremerhaven's* drawbridge came down, but no one left the ship. On the dock Walter mingled with the dockworkers and sightseers and observed the activity on the freighter's deck where the crew was readying the vessel for unloading. At fifteen minutes to noon, the captain and his officers walked down the gangplank and boarded a taxi. Several crew members disembarked and headed for a restaurant across the street. They carried no baggage and Walter concluded that they would return to the ship. He followed them into the restaurant and chose a table near where the sailors sat. He knew that, because they were still on duty and duty disciplined, there would probably be little loose talk around the table to which he could listen.

His conclusion was correct. The sailors spoke ambiguously about nocturnal exploits in New York and about the ships next stop at its home port of Hamburg. Walter observed what the other dockworkers were eating and ordered the same – soup and slices of smoked ham on dark brown bread. The sailors ordered corned beef and cabbage and steins of beer; drank toasts to the Fuehrer and to their next voyage. They drained their steins and ordered one more.

"All right mates. Just this one and no more," cautioned the boatswain. We still have work to do. You will all have enough of this tonight."

"Yes, all of us except poor old Heindrick and Kurt," said one of the sailors. "The poor bastards are really going to pay tonight for missing the curfew on that last night in New York."

"Knowing them, they will probably make their own party on board," said his mate.

"They had better not, or it's the work camp for them," said the boatswain sternly.

Except for the main street and one or two other thoroughfares, most of the city's major commercial arteries ran parallel to the docks. In the afternoon, Walter followed the near deserted sidewalk on one of these avenues until it turned into a footpath which disappeared into a small cul-de-sac bordered by a cluster of small warehouses. Behind the warehouses a small creek wound its way from the wooded hills above the city into the bay. On each side were thick stands of bulrushes, willow and other small bushes. What appeared to be a thoroughfare skirted the street and disappeared over the hill. Walter followed it for a few blocks. The wind which had blown steadily all day from the northeast was getting colder as the afternoon sun descended toward the horizon. He pulled his collar around his ears and stopped to talk to an old man out walking his dachshund.

"You had better go home and dress better than that," he admonished Walter. "Did you not hear that there might be snow tonight?"

Walter admitted that he had not heard the weather forecast and promised that he would remedy the clothing deficiency as soon as he got home. The old man shuffled off, murmuring to himself. The wind carried his short epilogue to Walter. "These young bucks have no feelings," he pronounced solemnly.

The dark clouds milled about angrily overhead, cutting off the late afternoon sun and causing an early dusk to descend. The street lights were turned on when Walter returned to his target late in the afternoon. The *Bremerhaven* was still where he had last seen it, its drawbridge down and several lights illuminating its deck. As the darkness enclosed the area and the dockworkers left for home, he positioned himself in a small space between the walls of two warehouses and observed the freighter. Sensing a long night ahead, he left his observation point and entered the restaurant where he had eaten earlier in the day. This time he indulged in the same meal enjoyed by the sailors at noon. At seven o'clock he returned to his spot between the two warehouses and watched groups of boisterous sailors beginning to emerge from the ship and heading for waiting taxis. The exodus from the ship had begun.

The massive hulk of the *Bremerhaven* lay tethered to the dock like a docile black sheep. She was the largest vessel in the port that night and loomed over the smaller craft like a slumbering giant. A lone sailor walked the deck for an hour and then disappeared below. On the dock the harbor police made their rounds every half hour, flashing their powerful lanterns on the vessels as they walked by. Flakes of snow fell intermittently from the low hanging clouds. The cold numbed his fingers and ears. He would have to strike before the snow covered the ground. According to his calculation the harbor police would make their next round at ten thirty. He would board the ship at ten thirty-three and leave it at ten fifty-five, five minutes before the harbor police made their rounds.

There were no pedestrians or traffic. Across the street the warehouses huddled against each other with only their fronts illuminated by the street lights. At ten-thirty the pair of harbor police walked by the freighter on schedule, flashing their lanterns on the drawbridge and the deck's edge. They walked along the dock and disappeared into the wall of falling snow.

Walter walked across the street into the dark shadows of the warehouses and remained in their protection until he was directly in front of the drawbridge. Between him and the ship was a lighted area which he could not avoid. He had to take a chance. His eyes scanned the area in all directions. There was no sign of anyone near by. He walked confidently toward the drawbridge and mounted the ramp. He did not look back. There was no turning back now.

Except for the several lights shining on the dock side, the ship's deck was dark. He headed for the dark side and listened. There were no sounds or footsteps. His own steps were noiseless against the steel floor because of the rubber heels and soles on his shoes. He found the companionway at the stern end of the vessel and followed it down to the hold on the lower deck. He listened. The engines and generators droned steadily in the bowels of the vessel. There were no other sounds. The darkness of the cargo area was punctuated by the light of a few widely spaced low wattage bulbs hanging over the aisle that ran between the stacks of wooden crates. He peered toward the bow end of the ship. As far as he could see there were rows of identical crates. He crept under one of the overhead lights and looked inside the containers. The crates were all stenciled with the words New York. Inside of each of them was an airplane engine. In the dull light he found the name of the manufacturer on the side of the engine. It was Grand Union Airplane Company. Tacked to the end of each shipping crate was the shipping tag. The destination was Frankfurt.

Removing the camera from a cigarette box inside his sleeve, he took pictures of the crates, their markings, and the shipping tags. His job was completed except for counting the number of engines in the hold. He returned to the shadows behind the crates and cautiously made his way toward the bow end of the ship and back on the other side. He estimated that there were about six hundred engines in the ship's hold. It was now seven minutes to eleven. His time on board the *Bremerhaven* was up. In the shadows of the starboard side, he made his way cautiously up the companionway onto the deck. The lights shone dimly in the wheelhouse, but there was no sign of anyone around the area.

Snowflakes were now drifting lazily in the still night air, melting as they fell on the steel floor of the ship's deck. Moving silently in the shadow of the wheelhouse and chimneys, Walter peeked around the corner across the lighted side of the deck. It was deserted. He walked to the railing and surveyed the dock area. No one was in sight. Sliding his hand along the railing, he descended briskly down the steps. He turned toward the street. A beam of light suddenly came on, swung around quickly and rested on him.

"Halt. Stay where you are. Harbor Police. Don't move!"

The beam of light hit him in the eyes and temporarily blinded him. He guessed that the light was about a hundred meters away. About twice that distance in the opposite direction, the shadows created by the warehouse beckoned him. He made a dash for the buildings, the wobbly shaft of light following him, cutting through the lightly falling snow.

"Halt, or we'll shoot," the policeman shouted.

Walter veered right into the temporary safety of the shadows cast by the row of warehouses. A shot rang out in the still night air and the bullet hit the wooden side of the building with a dull thud.

"Stop thief!" the policeman screamed. "We have you covered."

"To hell you have," mumbled Walter under his breath.

With memories of that afternoon's observations of the dock area still fresh in his mind, he headed for the row of building which ran to the edge of the wooded area. He was now out of range of the wavering beam of light which followed him. Suddenly the illuminated face of the lantern disappeared, but the shaft of light swung erratically from one side of the street to the other. He looked out from his position between the two warehouses and saw the policemen entering the restaurant. They went to call for help, thought Walter. This would give him a few extra minutes to run toward the wooded ravine.

The snow was now descending in dense flurries, the large flakes cooling his face and quickly covering his tracks. But would the snow cover his tracks fast enough so that they would be hard to follow? If the snow continued to fall and the reinforcements arrived quickly, they would track him like a cornered animal. There would be no escape, not even in the shelter of the trees and rushes along the creek.

He ran hard through the shadows, the falling snow now making him invisible from the street. The ravine should now be only about half a kilometer or so away. He stopped and listened. The muffled sounds of the city wafted through the floating snowflakes. With his hand cupped over his ear he turned in the direction of the creek. Sounds of singing and laughter rose above the sounds of the city in the background. The street lights were now widely spaced with long stretches of darkness in between them. At the end of the row of warehouses he cut over to the footpath running parallel to the street and dashed through the darkness toward the next street light. There he veered right into the darkness and listened. The sounds of singing and laughter were now closer. His eyes peered in the direction of the sounds. Through the falling snow he saw the glow of lights and the dark outline of a building. Staying in the shadows, he strode quickly toward the source of merriment ahead of him. As it came into view the noise got louder and he knew that he had stumbled across a dockside tavern.

Through the snow screen he caught glimpses of several automobiles, motorcycles and bicycles alongside the building. He crept closer and observed the scene. The bicycles looked inviting and would probably allow him to stay ahead of the pursuers at least for a while longer. Through the window, a muddled scene of activity could be discerned. Most of the patrons appeared to be at the opposite end of the building, probably where the bar was located. The automobiles cut off the view of the bicycles and motorcycles from the window.

Screened by the automobiles and his eyes focused on one of the bicycles, he crept toward the front of the building. Suddenly, the still air was shattered by the roar of engines and two headlight flared through the snow. He fell to the ground and rolled under one of the automobiles several meters from where the two riders stopped their machines, only a short distance from his emergency sanctuary. They stepped off their machines and swept the snow off their jackets, voicing obscenities at the elements and the condition of the streets.   Agreeing that it was a good night for imbibing, they left their motorcycles and walked into the tavern.   A wave of singing and laughter crashed through the air when the door of the tavern was opened.

In the distance the sound of wailing sirens told him that the chase was about to begin. The bicycle idea now seemed less attractive. The noise inside the tavern grew louder.   He crept out from beneath the automobile and glanced at the motorcycles. His heart pounded loudly when his eyes caught sight of a key chain fob reflecting the light from the window.   He edged closer to the vehicle and saw the key in the ignition switch. The wailing sirens were getting closer. They would soon be fanning out from the dock area and it was just a matter of time before one of them discovered his trail. His time was running out.   He sat on the motorcycle seat and found the crank.

Turning on the ignition key, he brought the crank down sharply with his right foot.   The machine, still warm, started immediately and the motor purred softly as he turned the throttle handle. He pushed the machine off its stand by shoving forward with his feet, then engaged the clutch and put the machine in gear.   The rear wheel slid sideways before it grasped the hard surface beneath the snow and the rider and vehicle lurched forward.   He drove it into the street and headed for the road which he knew would take him to the edge of the forest.

A dark wall of trees and shrubs to his right told him that he had reached the creek.   The street turned and joined the road which followed the waterway.   A blanket of snow now covered the surface of the road.   Behind him, the tire track formed a neat trail in the snow.   Snowflakes stung his face and clung to his eye lashes.   With squinting eyes, he leaned forward and accelerated the motor.   In the beam of the headlight, the road was rising steadily.   At the top of the incline, Walter stopped the machine and turned off the ignition.   His ears continued to ring from the sound of the motor.   There were no other sounds.   Down below, streams of light were moving in every direction.   One was headed for the base of the road leading to the forest.   He jumped on the motorcycle and kicked the crank.

The road was now sloping downward.   Soon it would join the highway that had taken him into the city earlier that day, and he would be between the forest and the bay.   A north wind was now blowing the snow across the road. Ahead of him, in the beam of the headlight, everything was white.   The ditch was filling in and snow was building up on the road surface.   He calculated where the center of the road should be and kept the machine on course.

The long expected moment arrived with a blast.   Suddenly the outline of the forest wall loomed through the falling snow flakes. He recollected the geography that he had committed to memory on the *Barrow* a few days earlier.   Another kilometer more and the sea would be only a short distance from the road.   The machine roared arduously, cutting through the deepening layer and occasional humps of drifted snow.

Beads of ice formed on his eye lashes, freezing them shut. He struggled to maintain the motorcycle on course with one hand on the handle bar and using the other to wipe the ice off his eye lashes.   Laboriously, the formidable kilometer was conquered and he stopped the machine. Without the roar of the motor the silence was deafening. The snow flakes continued to crash against his face and clothing indignantly, as though angrily objecting to his presence, or perhaps, his defiance of nature's determination to envelop the whole world in white. In the distance came the unmistakable muffled sounds of waves splashing on the beach.

Walter cast a quick glance behind him. A small, white halo of light told him that his track had been discovered. For the third time that evening he found himself faced with the urgency of executing an emergency move. Unless he disposed of the motorcycle and covered his tracks somehow, they would soon catch up to him with their faster four-wheeled vehicles. The map of the area popped into his mind again. He recalled a small craft dock almost in line with the edge of the forest. It should be near by. He started the motorcycle and ploughed forward. A sudden break in the forest and a white ribbon cutting through it told him that he had discovered the road to the dock. He turned left and accelerated.

With the motorcycle spinning and weaving over the last several hundred meters, the road suddenly began to slope over a bank. In front of him loomed the black expanse of water and the dock jutting out of it. At the base of the dock he turned down the throttle and studied the situation. The wind had blown the snow off the wooden surface of the dock, so he knew that there would be no tracks formed by the wheels. He started the machine, turned down the throttle and engaged the low gear. He followed it to near the edge of the dock, hanging on to the handle bars.

Near the end of the dock he turned off the headlight, turned up the throttle and watched as the machine lurched over the edge of the dock and sank into the water. The splash was followed by a gurgling fizzle and the inky water closed over it. In the distance the haze from the approaching headlights moved up and down and from side to side following the curves and contours of the road which Walter had just left. With a quick tug on the shoe laces, he quickly removed his boots and pulled off his trousers. He hung them around his neck and slid into the water at a point near the end of the dock.

In comparison to the cold air, the water at the mouth of the creek felt warm when he stepped into it. A line of white froth cutting across the beach laid the course and he followed it around the peninsula which he knew would lead him to the spot where he landed the previous night. His pursuers would soon lose his tracks and have to come up with a new strategy. He stopped and cupped his hand to his ear to drown out the sound of the waves. Angry voices rose and fell as they drifted across the slim peninsula. Beams of light moved across the snow laden sky like giant white clubs. A minute later the voices disappeared and the roar of the automobile engines announced their movement. Walter headed quickly toward the head of the bay. The moving haze in the sky told him that his pursuers had the same idea.

A large rock loomed eerily out of the shallow water and he leaned on its windward side and listened. The automobiles had now stopped at the very spot where he crossed the highway the previous night and the flashlight beams focused on the water's edge. The voices were closer and clearer now.

One voice barked out orders and from it he now realized that the pursuit had been taken over by the SS or SA, or both.

"Check the beach for tracks, and some of you follow that footpath into the trees," a loud voice commanded.

Two flashlight beams moved in his direction, pointing at the sand. They were looking for tracks, he thought. He pressed hard against the rock and waited. The torch bearers moved relentlessly through the falling snow. Walter prepared to remove his heavy jacket in case he had to swim out into the deep water. Because of the falling snow, the rock was still outside the range of the flashlight beams, but in a moment he would have to hide behind it and swim out into the bay. Suddenly the searchers stopped and flashed the beams of light across the water.

"Shit, Ludwig, there is no sign of the bastard here," said a voice. "The poor son of a bitch probably drowned. No one can last long out there in this weather, not even a miserable thief."

"Yah," agreed the second voice. "He will have to come out sooner or later or die out there in the water like a god dammed rat. Let's go back and tell the captain that we will come and pick up the body tomorrow."

They laughed and turned back toward the head of the bay. Walter returned to the windward side of the rock and listened. Lights flickered around the vehicles parked on the road, like a swarm of fireflies, and distorted voices floated across the bay. After several minutes, the lights were extinguished, motors roared and the vehicles turned around and disappeared toward the city. They had abandoned the chase for now.

CHAPTER 40

His feet now numb with cold and lack of movement, Walter stumbled toward the beach and sat on a piece of driftwood. He dried his feet on his pant legs and pulled on his dry socks and boots. They felt comfortable against his toes and feet, wrinkled by the long exposure in water. The snow continued to descend with a vengeance. If it persisted for another hour or so his tracks would be covered and he would be safe for a while. He headed in the direction of his footpath and his tree.

If there was any evidence of his pursuers' tracks in the snow, it was too dark to see them and his feet were too numb to feel it. He broke into a trot, stamping his feet to speed up the circulation to his soles and toes. Warmth from his body flowed through his clothing and dried his pant legs and cuffs. The path stretched through the dark forest like a weaving chalk line on a blackboard. The snow, which was now turning into ice pellets, stung his face. He pulled his cap down over his face and looking only at his feet he ran along the narrow path.

The forest looked strangely different in the snowstorm. He brought up his head and watched for the first turn in the path. It did not appear. Did he miss it, he wondered. But how could he? It was the only turn in the path between his tree and the road. It had to be only a short distance away. He slowed down to a fast walk. The path dipped and then rose. Strange, he thought, I don't remember that old creek bed. As he was about to retrace his steps back to the road, the path turned to the right and a small opening among the trees appeared in front of him. He passed through the opening and counted his paces. Suddenly a large tree loomed in front of him. He crawled into the shelter of its large branches and sat down on the snow-free mat of dry needles. Leaning gratefully against the ancient tree trunk he sighed and closed his eyes. This was his tree and he felt warm and secure inside its branches. He wondered if this is the feeling that chicks had when they gathered beneath the mother hen, then he dozed off.

He awoke with a start and checked his watch. The florescent hands showed almost three o'clock in the morning. Blackness was still all around him and his body shook from the cold. He stood up and straightened out his rigid body, pushing his head up through the branches. Outside it had stopped snowing and the wind had died down. He moved out to the edge of the tree branches and leaned over to see his tracks. They were covered with new fallen snow. No one would find him here now. Tomorrow he would radio Simpson and when night fell, he would make a dash for the bay and the *Barrow*. Meanwhile, there was enough darkness left for him to try to get two or three hours of sleep, but first he would retrieve his backpack and the radio.

Walter climbed up through the branches to where he had left the pack and the radio on the previous night. He raised himself up to the level where he thought he had left them and his hand reached out to feel the familiar rough canvas. There was nothing there but the tree trunk and the branches.

It was the same at the junction of the next row of branches and the next. He clung to the trunk and buried his face in his sleeve. It was all too apparent now. The pack and radio had either been discovered or he had the wrong tree.

His mind bounced wildly between despair and hope as he cautiously felt his way down the scaly trunk, considering the options now open to him. Should he set out to search for his real tree at dawn? What if he did not find it in time to get his radio message before the searchers returned, which they were sure to do? Even if he did find the radio set and sent his message to the *Barrow*, where would he hide until the boat arrived in the bay? He concluded that the only safe course was not to step out into the snow until the pursuers had abandoned the search or until the snow melted. That had to be it. As long as there were no tracks in the snow, no one would know he was hiding under the tree. The rabbits back home knew this, and so did the weasels and the foxes.

His first priority now was to stay awake and keep from freezing. He recalled his survival lessons, which when learned in a heated London classroom did not seem to have the same urgency as his situation did now. Keep moving. Keep your blood circulating. Help your body to generate its own heat. In a tight spot, exercise, do push-ups. All these rules popped back into his mind, one after the other. He found a level area of ground under the protective branches, straightened out his body and pushed himself up on his arms.

"One, two, three, four, five," he counted. "Ten. Twenty. Thirty. Forty. Fifty." The warmth collected inside his clothing. "Must not sweat," he reminded himself.

Feeling around his protected area, he found layers of spruce needles, which had been deposited over decades of time, lying soft and dry around the tree. Not far from the trunk he dug a hole in the mat of needles large enough to sit in. Needles taken out of the hole were piled on each side to build a low wall. He crawled into the nest. The soil, still warm from the summer heat, shared its radiant heat generously. He settled in for the wait.

The dark shadows of night grudgingly gave way to the dawn. Irregular billows of cheerless gray clouds dashed through the otherwise clear blue sky as he peered through the branches. The unfamiliar, daunting shapes of the night revealed themselves gradually, no longer alien and mysterious, but unthreatening parts of the landscape. Small avalanches of snow slid down the branches of nearby trees, breaking the silence of the forest. At last the long night was over. He took off his gloves and cupped his hands over his nose and mouth. The warm breath felt good on his icy skin. He climbed out of his nest and stretched from a thick branch which hung at just the right distance above his head.

A series of vigorous push-ups and his shivering body again radiated warmth inside his clothes. It was light enough now for him to study his surroundings more closely. He peeked out under the branches. The snow lay in a fluffy white mat, undisturbed and indifferent to his predicament. To step out into it would disclose his location and result in certain capture. He had to remain where he was. There were no other alternatives. He was a prisoner under a tree.

It was a large spruce tree with thick overhanging branches covering a circular area about eight or ten meters in diameter. This large dry circle around the trunk of the tree was now his sole domain. He felt the need to urinate and knew that a part of his snow-free area would have to be used for that purpose. He realized that his first priority now was to plan the best use of this limited space. Safety and a lookout position were his first priorities. The lookout point would have to be on the side where the path was located, he reasoned. If anyone approached, all that he would have to do is climb up into the branches. A new nest to sit in and sleep during the night would have to be located close to the lookout point where he could quickly cover it up if necessary. The exercise areas could be on either side. The toilet would be on the opposite far side near the edge of the circle. It was the first of the newly allocated areas to be used. Puffs of steam rose from the hot urine as it struck the ground and disappeared into the dry soil.

A small opening at eye level between the broad fan-like branches provided the desired observation point. He peered out at the still and silent forest. The snow laden trees hugged each other and only one stood alone – his tree. A glance to the right, where the tiny clearing should be, revealed only a few low bushes and smaller trees. Now he was convinced that this was not his first tree, the one with his sleeping bag and radio stored in its branches.

Today would be Sunday, he thought, so there should not be much activity on the road and in the city several kilometers away. Perhaps his followers would also take the day off. His thoughts again turned to survival and he lifted up mats made of layers of spruce needles and piled them up to form a soft sitting and resting area. Unless the weather changed very quickly and the snow melted, he could be here another night or even longer. He could not take a chance on stepping outside and looking for the tree with the radio in it until the snow melted or he was satisfied that the hunt for him was over. Would Simpson and Duke know about the freak snowstorm, he wondered. It probably snowed out there on the water also, but it depended upon how localized the storm system was. If not, then they surely must have heard about it on the radio. Simpson spent a lot of time in the radio room. He would know. Outside, the air, though clear, was still oppressively cold. Shafts of sunlight pierced through the small openings among the branches, but were not enough to warm up the early morning air.

"The human body, if well protected, is the best generator of heat," they told him during survival training. His body again felt rigid and cold. "But one must exercise the body to induce the heat producing process," the lecturer had advised. With the side of his boot, Walter swept the cones and other loose material from an area big enough to stretch out his body. He placed his gloved hands on the cleared area and stretched out his legs. One, two, three, four, five……ten…twenty…His breath became deeper and he felt the blood cruising rapidly through his arms and legs. Soothing heat returned to his body and small beads of sweat formed on his forehead. He stood up and swung from a low hanging branch.

Outside, the air, the trees and the snow, and the whole world, were still and silent as if frozen in time. It was nearly eight o'clock. He sat down in his nest and listened. Soon he detected a dull roar in the distance. The sound penetrated the silence of moments earlier. He tuned his ear to it and his breath became shallow and quiet. The sound was becoming louder. It became a purr and he knew that his pursuers had resumed their search. As the sound became louder and closer, he knew that they were headed in his direction. Shouts arose above the roar of the engines and the dull, thumping sound of wheels plowing through the snow. They were trucks or personnel carriers, he surmised, but he could not distinguish how many there were. The engines stopped and the shouting increased. It came from the bay area and continued for almost an hour. They are probably removing the motorcycle from the water, thought Walter.

The roar of the engines resumed, first one, then another and another. There were three vehicles, he concluded. The sounds became louder and moved closer, and then they stopped. One voice barked out indistinguishable orders and other voices dispersed in several directions. A small group of men appeared to be moving into the woods toward his hideout. He quickly leveled out the blanket of spruce needles and spread out the pine cones over the area to give it an undisturbed look. After climbing up a short distance into the tree, he cupped his hand to his ear. The voices were coming closer and becoming more distinguishable, but he could not see the searchers. There was laughter and levity among the group. They were now on the footpath and moving closer. Walter climbed up higher and listened.

"What does the Herr Captain think that he will find in this God forsaken place?" asked a voice.

"Even the rabbits have not come out of their burrows today," added another voice.

"How do you know that?" asked the first voice.

"Because there is no rabbit shit on the snow," answered the other. A roar of laughter rose through the trees.

These cannot be the SS, thought Walter. They are too easygoing. He smiled at the jocularity. He liked his pursuers. They reminded him of him and his friends when they went out hunting in the woods back home.

The voices were now almost in front of his tree. He hung tightly to the trunk and listened.

"Shit," declared one voice, "we are just getting our feet wet for nothing."

"You should aim a little higher when you are pissing and that wouldn't happen," advised another voice.

"Look. At least I have something to aim with," was the answer. More laughter.

"You know, Gunther, I think you are right," a third voice announced. "If anyone ended up here after coming out of the water, he would have screwed off a long time ago or else he would be frozen hard as dog shit. But if he is still here, God help him if he tries to get out now. There are more SAs at the edge of these woods than pricks in a whore house. I say that we go back and figure out another strategy."

"I hope he comes out real soon," said voice number one. "If he doesn't, old Herr Captain will keep us going around this bush until spring."

"One week at the most. The poor bastard cannot last without food much longer than that." The voices began to fade into the distance from where they had come earlier. Several minutes later the engines started and the vehicles followed the road skirting the forest. Walter was now convinced that they were members of the local police.

~~~

Food. He had been too occupied to think about food. But now that he had been reminded of it by his pursuers, his stomach made demanding sounds inside of him. He checked his pockets. He found his three-bladed knife, a metal tube with matches, his identification papers and a small camera, but nothing edible. A pair of boot laces, some German Marks and a handkerchief rounded out his possessions. He listened again. Stillness had returned to the forest.

The air inside the area covered by the tree branches was becoming warmer and more hospitable. It must be getting warmer outside, he concluded. He sat down on the newly assembled pile of needles, pulled the cap over his eyes and smiled. Somehow, after listening to his pursuers, the whole situation seemed less ominous and maybe even a bit humorous. From this point on it would be a battle of wits between the hunters and the hunted, with the craftiest side coming out the winner.

He recalled some of his hunting experiences at home. He had never shot a fox in all his life. Why? Because they were too crafty, that's why. And what would a fox do in a situation like this? He would hide and watch the hunters as they scurried around. The fox would probably be amused by the whole spectacle. Then what? Then when everything was clear, he would go about his business. Yes, but what about his tracks? You know, in all my years of hunting, I have never seen fox tracks, recalled Walter.

It was time to sit down and figure out a strategy, he told himself. He made himself comfortable inside his nest and scraped off an area of ground for a map. With a sharp stick he drew an X to show his position. A curved line stood for the footpath and a straight line for the road. In the distance, a horseshoe shape was the bay. The only thing missing was the original tree now harboring his radio and backpack. He closed his eyes and concentrated on the memory of his movements into the woods on each of the past two nights.

The first night had been dark. Pitch black. He had followed the path by feeling its hard surface with the soles of his shoes. At one point it veered slightly to the right and he kept on going into the woods until he found the large tree. On the second night it was snowing hard and as he followed the white ribbon through the trees the snow beat into his face and eyes. He kept his head down and saw only a short distance in front of the toes of his boots.

He could have taken a turn in the path without realizing it. If he did, he probably passed the first tree and walked into the woods and found another similar looking tree. He scratched out the first curved line and drew another line with two waves in it, like a gull in flight. The map showed that he was now near the joint of the second wing, and his other tree with the radio and pack was probably at the joint of the first wing, about a hundred steps or so back along the path from where he was now and another hundred steps inside the woods. He drew another X at that point, propped his stick against the tree and studied the improvised map.

Outside the twilight was drifting into darkness. The boughs and branches around him, which last night had looked so phantom-like and alien, now seemed more familiar and somehow friendlier, even in the gray twilight. But the cold, dark air was once again pushing in through the branches from the outside, attacking his toes and fingers and licking at his exposed ears and nose.

He got down and exercised until his toes burned inside his boots. When he stood up his mouth was hot and dry. He reached through a branch and brought in a handful of clean snow which he licked, letting it melt on his tongue and then swallowing it. It reminded him of the times he had done this in the woods at home. Some people said that eating snow made you even more thirsty, but the lecturer in London assured them that it was the best source of water outdoors in the winter when nothing else was available.

It was now more than twenty-four hours since he had eaten. He tried to dismiss the thought of food, but visions of roast chicken, steaming mashed potatoes and green beans flashed on the screen of his mind. What did the survival instructor say about food? "Pick it. Dig it. Catch it," he had said. The world is full of edible plants and animals. A good piece of advice, thought Walter, but about as practical in this situation as digging a hole in the desert in search of water.

Nearby, an owl announced his arrival with a haunting hoo-hoo sound. On his watch, Walter counted the number of hoots per minute and measured the intervals between them. He calculated the number of hoos the owl would call out in one night. At eight-thirty the owl flew toward the other side of the forest and Walter's attention again returned to his austere surroundings. After urinating and performing his warm-up exercises, he settled into his spruce needle nest, covered his legs with spruce needle mats and dozed off.

In the deepest crevices of his mind a familiar voice cried out: "Never fall asleep for longer than five minutes when the temperature is below freezing and you are not dressed for it. Don't give in to the temptation. Keep moving!" He recognized it as the voice of his survival instructor.

"Wake up Walter. Wake up right now," the voice commanded. That man must really have penetrated his mind, thought Walter.

He closed his eyes and opened one and then the other. It made no difference. The intense darkness now enveloped him from all sides. Feeling was the only way by which he could communicate with his surroundings. The voice in his head departed, leaving a mute silence which amplified each sound a thousand times. He ran his hand down the front of his legs. A ticklish tingle, almost like a small electric shock, followed his hands. He stood up and shook his body violently, then stretched out in the exercise area.

The strength was leaving his joints and muscles and he concentrated hard on raising himself to the push-up position. He held it briefly and then commenced his exercises, slowly at first, then faster. Warmth gradually returned; first to his torso, then to his arms and legs and gradually to his extremities. Except for his nose. It felt like an icicle stuck in his face. He cupped his hands and brought them over his mouth and face, then blew his hot breath into them. Gradually, his nose became a part of his face, warm, tingly and sore.

That was close, he told himself. He would not allow himself to fall asleep again even if it meant standing up for the rest of the night. He checked his watch. It was ten-thirty. A twinkle of light struck his eye as his gaze moved past the small openings between the branches. He brought his head to the right position to peek out through the opening into the sky. The star was there, shining bright. The clouds had moved out. A new weather system was moving in, he told himself. If it brings a warm south wind, the snow will melt and he will make his escape – if it melted fast enough. He looked through the branches and identified the shapes of the few remaining clouds drifting by. Flying geese, a cat's face, a horse's head, a woman in a babushka, a loaf of bread...his stomach jumped into action, coveting, churning, demanding. His eyes returned to the flying geese.

~~~

The seemingly eternal night was finally over. Slowly the light pushed in. A rosy hue rose over the tree tops like a flame. The sun had risen. He exercised, licked snow, redrew his map and rested briefly in between in his nest of matted spruce needles. Hunger was curtailing his energy and fogging his mind. The day wore slowly. On the road, the motor vehicle noises and voices returned. They are out there checking for tracks, he told himself. They will have to wait a long time before they find his. After a while, the vehicles and voices left. The day wore on and the November sun struggled to warm up the layer of snow. Water dripped off the tips of the boughs, but outside there was no change in the snow covered ground. As the afternoon sun skimmed the tree tops it bathed the western sky in a brilliant orange. It will be windy and warm tomorrow. He had learned this from his grandfather Axel Berglund.

His stomach grumbled angrily and demanded food. He ate more snow and urinated. As he was doing this he saw three rabbits feeding on saplings at the edge of the tree branches. They sensed the movement inside the tree and hopped away. In the distance several other rabbits were frolicking and feeding. Walter returned to his planning board on the ground.

Ingenious plans for acquiring food flowed through his head until late that night. One of them called for a bow and arrow made from a stick and his spare shoe laces. But how could he retrieve the rabbit if he should hit it with the improvised arrow, without making tracks in the snow? The same problem faced his stoning plan. There were several small stones around the base of the tree, but even if he could hit the animal and stun it, he could not bring it in without making tracks in the snow. A shoe lace snare seemed to be the best solution. He would set two tomorrow at day break, near the outside tips of the branches of his tree.

A rustling sound outside broke the stony silence. He peeked out through the opening and observed movement in the tree tops. The wind was coming up just as his grandfather's weather lore had predicted. Now if it was only strong enough and from the south, he would be out of the woods in twenty-four hours.

As if on cue, the air grew warmer throughout the night. It was not often that the temperature rose during the night. That was a sure sign that it was south wind. It grew stronger. The tree tops waved frantically and rubbed against each other creating strange noises. Time itself seemed to be spurred by the tempo of the wind and the first signs of morning seemed to appear faster than before. His excitement grew and his hunger pangs seemed less severe. Assisted by the warm wind and clear sky, the morning sun shone brilliantly and warm. Water laden snow slid off the tree branches, hitting the ground with gentle splashes. Drops of water fell through the branches. He did not hear the trucks and voices today. But he knew that they were out there looking for his tracks frantically before the snow melted.

By early afternoon, patches of brown soil and moss pushed up through the melting snow. The oppressive fingers of the cold lightless air which had tormented him for two days and nights retreated, replaced by the now soothing warm breezes. He entered his nest, leaned against the tree and fell asleep.

The owl returned to its perch on the nearby tree and resumed its hooting which it had interrupted the previous evening. Its call awoke the sleeping occupant of the great spruce. Walter awoke without stirring. His eyes caught a movement beside his right hand. He focused on the movement without moving his head. The object almost blended in with the reddish brown spruce needles, except for a hazy white outline around it body. It was a rabbit. Probably a young one, still innocent enough to trust unfamiliar forms. With a quick flip of his right hand, Walter grabbed its neck and lifted up the struggling animal. He put his thumb behind the rabbit's skull and pushed. A small crack sounded and the animal went limp.

He dropped the motionless animal on top of this map and stood up. Through the peep hole in the branches he saw the lengthening evening shadows and the owl in the neighboring tree. Gusts of warm wind swept through the forest carrying the moisture from the melting snow to the sea. He carefully surveyed the surrounding ground. Only a few patches of snow remained but the water-logged ground looked soft. It would not be wise to walk around trying to locate the radio tonight, he reasoned. If he did not find it before darkness set in, he may leave tracks on the forest floor which would be easily discovered by his pursuers next day. He picked up some wet snow from a nearby mound and sucked the water out of it.

Lifting the motionless rabbit off the ground, he held it between his knees and reached into his pocket for the jack knife. He ran the blade under the skin, making a slit from the back of one foot, around the anal opening and out toward the other foot. He cut around the orifice and peeled the skin away from the legs, then pulled it down to the animal's neck. The knife pressed against the neck bone and the head and skin dropped off leaving the naked legs and torso. The flesh was still warm. He cut around the hip and removed it from the joint. The carcass was then placed between a branch and the tree trunk for storage. He brought the dark red flesh to his mouth and hesitated. His stomach heaved and he vomited out the snow water that he just drank. Slowly he placed the severed hip on a branch and sat down with his back against the tree trunk. His hunger had left him.

It is possible to make a near-smokeless fire, they told him in the survival training classes. Complete combustion is smokeless. Twigs, if completely dry and without bark on them, will burn with a minimum of smoke. He picked some dry twigs from inside the tree's canopy and peeled the bark off them with the jack knife and his thumb nail. Darkness crept into his shelter again, but he continued to peel the twigs by feeling the bark. Tomorrow he would light a small fire and cook the hip, then head out in search of his first tree. As though discouraged by the sight of the raw meat, his stomach now seemed less demanding and the pangs of hunger subsided. He sat down and rehearsed his plan for next day. In the neighboring tree, the owl hooted inquisitively for a while and then flew away.

~~~

The twinkling stars paled as the faint light of dawn rose up above the trees. He sprang up and shook the brown needles off his jacket and trousers. This would be his fateful day. Outside the ground was bare except for small snow islands in dark secluded areas sheltered from the sun and wind by the trees. It was light enough to see the ground clearly and the openings between the groves of trees. He strained his ears, using his head as a direction finder, to catch any sounds from each direction. The wind had died down during the night leaving the cleanly swept air moist and full of forest smells.

He crept out of the canopy of the tree, stepping outside of its benevolent shelter for the first time in three days. His boots left no marks on the ground. Now was the time to go and look for the tree with the radio in it. Recalling the direction from which he had entered the forest, he set out to find the footpath. It was where he had imagined it would be. He followed it in the direction of the road, avoiding its muddy surface by walking on its grassy edge. When the path made a rapid turn to the left he continued ahead and walked into the woods. About a hundred steps ahead, a large tree stood out from all the rest and in front of it was a small clearing. His heart leapt with excitement as he carefully worked his way through the dense overhanging branches. Using its branches and trunk as a ladder he climbed partway up the tree watching for the familiar canvas backpack. Then he saw it. The backpack and radio stood there exactly as he had left them, huddled innocently between the branches and the trunk. Excited and elated, he carried them down. After listening carefully for sounds outside, he retraced his steps back toward the security of his tree.

There was no wind to sway the tree tops and they stood still like green pillars waiting for the warming rays of the rising sun. Summer's counteroffensive had triumphed temporarily and the late autumn sun was anxious to reign at least for one more day. Having at first tested the young man in the tree, nature was now making up to him by revealing its more gentle side. In the still air the radio signal would travel straight and strong.

He could wait no longer. He flicked the switch and a strong red light indicated clearly that the battery was still fully energized. With nervous fingers he pulled out the antenna and began to tap the keys. He pulled the headset over his ears and waited for an acknowledgement. It did not come. Again the message was tapped out. Still no response.

He stepped back and recalled the number of days since he had left the *Barrow*. Simpson said that they would wait three, maybe four days if the weather was bad. Perhaps, it did not snow out at sea and they had returned to London, giving him up for lost. He checked his watch. It was only ten to seven. Maybe Simpson and Duke were still asleep or having their breakfast in the galley, he reasoned. The antenna was telescoped back into the case and the cover came down over the radio set.

Breakfast. He wondered what Simpson and Duke were having for breakfast. His stomach convulsed inside of him and his eyes rested yearningly on the leg of rabbit sitting on the crotch. The bundle of twigs that he prepared the night before stood near the trunk of the tree. He felt for his pocket knife, opened it and dug a small pit in the bare ground. The twigs were carefully criss-crossed in the pit topped by the rabbit leg. Before striking the match, he stood still and listened. From the direction of the road came the now familiar roar of vehicle engines, and then stopped.

Voices rose up from the vicinity of the junction of the footpath with the road. He picked up the radio set and backpack and carried them carefully up into the tree. With the side of his foot he scattered the matted needles around and spread the cones randomly over them. He picked up the small piles of peeled twigs and placed them high in the tree branches and then climbed back into the branches and listened. Following a spirited discussion the searchers walked back toward the road. An engine started and roared away into the distance, following the edge of the forest. He climbed down warily, carrying the radio set. If his pursuers had not given up, he wondered how long it would be before the dogs would come.

He returned to the pit covered with dry needles and kicked them away to expose the excavation. The spruce needles stuck to the rabbit leg like burrs when he brought it down from the branch. The peeled twigs had stayed dry and he placed them into the small pit. He could wait no longer. Most of the smell and smoke of burning wood comes from the bark and leaves, they told him during survival training.

He replaced the clean sticks in the pit and after flicking the needles still clinging to it, he placed the rabbit leg and hip on top of the sticks. The waterproof tube had protected his matches well and he took one out and struck it. The flames burned cleanly with only small wisps of smoke when he held the match to the sticks. The raw flesh sizzled when the yellow flame licked around it. Slowly it turned from red to pink, then brown. His mouth watered as the seductive aroma of cooking meat filed his nostrils. Inside of him, his stomach spewed digestive juices in anticipation. The flames consumed the twigs, leaving a small bed of glowing embers. He turned the leg around and placed it over the embers.

Walter knew that what he was doing was risky, but unless he had something to eat he may not be able to run should he have to leave his shelter. The embers turned to ashes and he lifted the steaming leg from the pit. He broke a small piece of the sizzling meat and blew hard on it to cool it. His first impulse was to swallow it whole to appease his gnawing stomach, but decided that a few seconds devoted to chewing would allow the food to more quickly release the energy that he needed so desperately. When the meat cooled down, he bit into it ravenously, relishing each swallow. His stomach demanded more. He licked the bone clean then dug a hole for it with his knife. Outside a small mound of snow provided him with a handful of water filled crystals from which he sucked the water. The specks which had floated before his eyes earlier slowly disappeared and he returned to the shelter of his tree and covered over the ashen pit.

It was almost eight o'clock and the orange sun floated lazily above the tree tops. His grandfather had told him that an orange sun was a sign that the weather was about to change, but he could not remember the exact nature of the impending change. The thought of another snow storm prompted him to leap to his feet and scramble for the radio set.

"This is Willy's Boat Service. Come in Barrow," he tapped. Almost immediately the *Barrow* replied.

"Come in Willy."

"Will you be coming in for refueling today?" he asked.

"Same time," came the reply.

"I will be at the station."

"Good. Over and out." Simpson was all business as usual. But the message was clear. The *Barrow* will be in the bay at the same time that it had left him there four nights ago. He replaced the head set in the box and returned the radio to its hiding place in the tree.

Twelve more hours and he would be on his way to rendezvous with the *Barrow*. But should his pursuers return, he realized that he had not considered an alternative plan. Now that the *Barrow* crew knew that he was still there, they would probably wait even if he did not succeed in getting to her as planned. He sat down again to review his situation. Most of all he needed energy. Without it he was helpless, and that might just be the strategy that his pursuers were using. The one hipped rabbit hung limply from the branch where he tied it the evening before. Displaying great respect for the bounty, he took it down and removed the other hip and leg with his knife. The old tree provided an abundance of dried twigs which he peeled carefully and placed in the pit. The fire burned cleanly and the flesh sizzled, and then turned brown. Again he devoured it voraciously and then sipped water from the wet snow. Warm air seeped in under the branches from the outside. He leaned against the trunk and closed his eyes.

The light inside his shelter was a dusky gray when he awoke with a start. A glimpse of the sky through the branches revealed that, while he dozed, the hazy blue sky had been replaced by a low ceiling of dark cloud. He listened for sounds outside, and then emerged slowly from inside the canopy. The leading edge of the weather front had just passed through. To the east the sky was still a misty blue but to the west and almost above him now a bank of dark, ominous clouds churned. A drop of light rain fell on his face when he looked up, and then another and another. Back in the shelter of his tree, he could hear the raindrops falling on the branches. The rain was now falling steadily and it was only one o'clock. He had seven more hours of waiting inside the protective canopy of his tree, without a fire and with nothing to do except wait.

As the rain increased in intensity, he found comfort in knowing that his pursuers would not disturb him for a while. Monotony and boredom was the price that he would have to pay for safety. Thoughts of food reminded him again that he was hungry. There was still some good flesh left on the rabbit carcass. After removing the front legs and shoulders, he cut strips of muscle running down the animal's back. He then dug a hole with his knife and buried the limbless torso. Peeling twigs for the fire took almost an hour, but night still seemed like an eternity away. With the rain beating down outside, the branches of the tree seemed to close in around him. He longed for someone to talk to or even for some sound or motion. The owl was not likely to be back tonight. He lit the fire in the pit and watched the flames lick around the rabbit flesh. The fire offered a reprieve from the dull surroundings. It consumed the twigs and charred the rabbit flesh and demonstrated that, even in his narrow confinement, nature could be benevolent.

~~~

As much as he had dreaded the wretchedness of night over the past three days, tonight he was elated when darkness finally arrived. The rain continued to fall in small drops, barely more than a fog. Beside him the radio case and backpack were ready to go. All that remained between him and the safety and warmth of the *Barrow* was time and the dash to the sea shore. He propped the backpack against the tree and sat on it in deep thought.

His memory brought back scenes of other November nights at home. Stanley would be coming in from the barn, his kerosene lantern casting its orange light on the snow and creating long shadows against the out-buildings. A crackling fire in the kitchen stove and the smells of food cooking met him at the door. Stanley had much to tell, even when he went no further than the haystack in the meadow, Walter recalled. There is a new pair of coyotes in the aspen grove in the hollow, he would announce. A flock of partridges were feeding at the straw pile. The neighbor's cattle had broken through the fence and heading for the hay stack. To him these events were newsworthy. They were part of the ever changing scene.

Stanley did not care about politics, or cities, or wars. He had seen and heard enough of those things and they were not for him. The joys of work and home were all he wanted, and these he had in abundance. So why trouble your head with all those things he would say. His wife and children were always waiting for him around the well-laden supper table. He was abundantly blessed. This was his kingdom. He and his father, and their wives and children, had carved it out of the wilderness and knew every inch of the land, and it knew them. There was a quiet partnership between them and the land.

Would Stanley believe that he had spent four days and nights under a tree? Walter wondered. It would make good conversation while sitting around the hot stove on those long winter nights, maybe even more interesting than talking about partridges and the neighbor's cattle. The he remembered that these things were not to be discussed, not even with family. He swore to it even before he had come to London. The soft, steady patter of rain drops beat a peaceful rhythm in the branches above him and he dozed off.

Large drops of cold water formed in the branches above him and fell on his head and outstretched legs, then dribbled onto his face and ankles and awakened him. His watch showed almost eight-thirty. Between him and the *Barrow* were a half hour of time and an eternity of skulking through the dark trying to find the spot where he was dropped off four nights earlier. Those would be his most dismal moments, he said to himself. He put the watch to his ear to ensure that this, his one active contact with the outside world, was still working. In the stillness of his confined space, the ticking of the small instrument beat like a hammer on an anvil. It was time to leave. In the inky darkness, he felt his way out from among the rain soaked branches and listened. There were no sounds, other than the constant patter of raindrops falling on the forest floor.

He returned to the tree and adjusted the backpack on his shoulders. The driest area inside the canopy of the tree was located near the trunk and he stayed in its shelter to avoid the drops, now falling steadily from above. In final preparation, he reviewed the map in his mind, which he had earlier drawn on the ground in his shelter, the route that would take him to his destination. There was no moon. The sky was covered with thick cloud and the space between them and the ground was filled with falling rain. Like a blind man, all his movements would be directed through feeling and knowledge of the terrain and surroundings. His only reference point would be the map in his head. He closed his eyes and reviewed the route he would soon follow.

It was eight thirty-five and the long awaited moment arrived like a clap of thunder. Before feeling his way cautiously out through the branches, he kissed the trunk of the tree and thanked it for its hospitality. The gesture brought a smile to his face as he struck out for the footpath with a light heart and a new determination.

With his mind fastened on the imaginary map, he concentrated on staying in a straight line and steady course. To deviate from it would mean a night of aimless wandering through the rain soaked woods and almost certain capture later. Counting his steps and placing each foot directly in front of the other, he suddenly found himself in an open area. This had to be the small clearing in the woods that he found shortly after leaving the footpath four nights ago. With the toe of his boot, he felt around for the hard surface of the path. When he found it he turned right and followed its slippery surface toward where the road should be. Mud clung to his boots with every step and covered his knees after every fall.

The distance over which he had run in several short minutes now took an eternity to cover. He pushed ahead and suddenly the path fell out from under his feet and he slid down a steep decline. When he stood up again he felt the rain sweeping at him from the left instead of falling straight down as it had done in the woods. He knew immediately that he had reached the road which skirted the bay.

In the distance the soft swishing sounds told him that he had emerged safely from the underbrush and the forest and was now near the water. The gravely surface of the road crunched under his feet when he stepped onto its raised surface. The map in his head told him that not far to the right and a short distance ahead was the old wooden fence which he had only felt in the dark and never seen. Beyond that all that he would have to do is follow the sound of the waves to the beach.

About one hundred and fifty paces farther he appeared to have found the crest of the road and his memory told him that this was where he had emerged from the bay shore four nights ago. He turned right into the ditch and suddenly bumped into the wooden fence rails. In the distance the sound of the waves grew louder. He followed the sound, stepping blindly into depressions and protrusions and falling over clumps of bushes and rocks. Struggling forward toward the sound of the waves, he stumbled onto the smooth sandy surface of the beach. He straightened his hunched frame and checked his watch. It was five minutes to nine. With a sharp flip of his shoulders he pushed the backpack forward onto the back of his neck. This would make it easier for him to maneuver in the water in case he had to swim to the *Barrow*.

The rain continued to beat relentlessly and mercilessly against his face and dripping garments. Water sloshed round in his sodden boots. He cupped his hand around his ear and listened. Only the sound of the waves breaking on the beach filled the air. He strained his ears, filtering out the constant and familiar sea sounds and searching for sounds of the *Barrow* and its crew. There were no sounds other than the sea.

I must try to contact them by radio, he thought. Desperately he sought for a spot in the dark surroundings on which to set his radio case. He stumbled across a rock with a fairly flat surface and opened the case. He pulled out the antenna and turned on the switch. The red light cast a beautiful glare in the pitch black surroundings. He reached for the key and prepared to tap out the message when a familiar purr came from inside the bay. He closed the radio case and ran into the water. Soft sounds of oars in the water announced an approaching row boat. He reached into the waterproof container and brought out a match and lit it, protecting it from the breeze and rain inside his cupped hands.

"Willy?" It was the familiar voice of Simpson.

"Yes. Over here," replied Walter.

"Light another match," said Simpson softly.

Walter fumbled inside his rain-soaked jacket and brought out the match tube. The lighted match cast its weak glow in the surface of the water.

"Okay. Stay where you are," advised Simpson.

The boat slid silently to where he was standing in the water. "You appear to be awful anxious to get out of here," observed Simpson.

Walter placed his radio set inside the boat and fell into the bobbing vessel. "Another five minutes and I would have started to swim back to London," he said.

"There were times during the past day or so when we thought that you already had," laughed Simpson as he turned the boat toward the purring sound in the distance.

~~~

By midnight the *Barrow* was in the open Baltic, heading west. Below deck Walter sat at a food-laden table in the galley, his clothes clean and dry and his face washed and shaven. Simpson watched with amusement as Walter consumed enormous quantities of hot meat, potatoes and vegetables.

"If you don't slow down, you might sink this ship," warned Simpson in jest.

"Don't laugh," responded Walter between bites of roast beef. "Do you know what I have had to eat in the last four days? A small rabbit, that's what. And I was lucky to have that."

"Stewed or roasted?" Simpson was frivolous, trying to get Walter in a lighter mood.

"Raw, or damned near raw," growled Walter.

"So was all this worth it?" asked Simpson.

"It might be for somebody, but not for me," responded Walter. "Nothing is worth the ordeal that I went through, as far as I am concerned. Nothing."

"Why do you say that?" asked Simpson.

"Because there I was, risking my life and running away from people taking pot shots at me and then nearly starving and freezing to death. And what for? In order to keep watch on what our so-called enemy is doing. You know, at times during this whole thing, I asked myself who my enemy really was."

"You are obviously very distressed after your experience," said Simpson. "But you must always remember that this is a risky job and not a very rewarding one. Remember how anxious you were to get at the enemy of your parents when you went to see Major Bradley about this job? Now you are doing that by bringing out information that will help to stop some of those things happening in the future." He paused and observed Walter. "Anyway, what did you find on that ship?" he asked.

"A hold full of aircraft engines."

"What kind?" asked Simpson.

"I don't know one aircraft engine from another, but I did manage to get some pictures. I hope that the film stayed dry."

"I am sure it did. So what other things did you notice about what were going on there?" asked Simpson patiently.

"They are American engines, on their way to the Bauer Motor Works from Grand Union Aircraft Company," said Walter as he stood up to leave.

"That was a good piece of work, old chap," Simpson did not disguise his exuberance. "You'll feel a lot better after you have had a good rest and we will talk some more about it." He stood up and headed for the radio room and Walter stumbled into his cabin and fell into his berth. The *Barrow* rocked gently as it made its way across the inky Baltic.

CHAPTER 41

Winter descended gradually on London, replete with its mantle of gray skies and dense fog. Inside the creaky old classrooms of the spy school, a new emphasis emerged – the German language. Whole mornings were devoted to language training. The security wall around Germany was becoming more difficult to breach, explained the instructors. Anyone not speaking good German would be suspect and this could hinder or prevent intelligence from being collected. Also, the safety of the agents would be at stake. Intensive linguistic training filled the morning period. Lectures and demonstrations on the establishment of networks, and the collection and transmission of information, occupied the trainees during the early afternoon sessions. Survival, forging of documents and assuming new identities and personalities rounded out the training day. An atmosphere of foreboding change permeated the school.

Throughout the winter, headlines in the London newspapers dwelled on the emerging European enigma – Germany and its National Socialist Party. Favorable reports of the country's miraculous economic recovery were countered by others denouncing the oppression and annihilation of political enemies, of the church and of Jews. The alleged buildup of military might was debated vigorously, some feeling that Germany was not to be trusted, while others believed that the country had been badly served by the Treaty of Versailles and should be allowed more than just a token military force. They proclaimed that Germany had learned its lesson in the Great War and would never again succumb to the military ambitions of some of its leaders as it had done in the past.

"We all know what is going on there and how fast they are moving toward military confrontation. We know because we have seen it, but there are those who hide their heads in the sand." Simpson seemed almost discouraged as he confided this to Walter and Victor on an evening in late January. "For us, our jobs will be much different as Germany moves closer and closer to the point where she feels strong enough to thumb her nose at the rest of Europe. It is now only a matter of time. Next spring our methods will have to change and when war comes it will be different again. They are becoming less and less tolerant of anything that is not German. That is why we have to be so concerned about improving our use of their language. To do otherwise would expose us to suspicion and increased danger. When we go back there we may need to live and work among Germans. It is no longer possible for foreign nationals to move freely about the country. Von Nicolai has taken care of that."

"I am working hard to get rid of my American accented German," announced Victor proudly.

"And I already love sausages and sauerkraut," added Walter.

"You farm boys will eat anything," said Simpson.

"Except half cooked rabbit," declared Walter. "Never again."

"I can see that you two young bucks are not in the mood to talk serious business, so why don't we go down to the Cock and Lion for a couple." They agreed.

Several weeks later, on the evening of March 7, 1936, the two young men heard about the first installment of Simpson's prophesy being fulfilled. Throughout the day, BBC Radio interrupted the regular programming to announce to a stunned audience that, on Hitler's orders, German troops violated international agreements and occupied the Rhineland. By moving troops into this demilitarized zone, Germany now had guns and soldiers only steps away from the French border.

"Wow," declared a surprised Victor. "Do you realize that these guys are only a few hundred miles from where we are sitting right now?"

"At least they moving west instead of east," commented Walter. "Sliworski will be relieved to hear that."

"Don't worry. They will get around to the Poles and the Czechs later," said Victor. "And you know what? I'll bet no one steps in to stop them."

"Well, I sure as hell will," snapped Walter. "I wish they would teach us something about sabotage. I would dearly love to blow up a couple of those ships that are bringing in arms and machinery to help Hitler take over those countries."

"Shit. What can one person do?" said Victor. "Look at that man Churchill. He's trying to warn the people here about what Germany is up to, and what do they do? They ignore him. And even worse, they label him a raving lunatic bent on scaring the hell out of the peace loving public. I tell you what. It's a hell of a lot better that they should have the pants scared off them now than to have to crap in them later."

Walter listened to Victor's censure of humanity with amusement. "You know, Victor," he said, "one thing that this job has done for you is improve your language. I have never heard you express yourself quite so colorfully before."

"Ah, shut up," said Victor facetiously. "You are just as bad as the rest of them."

"To hell I am," laughed Walter. "I have been shot at twice and it's pretty hard to be complacent when bullets are whizzing past your ass."

"Speaking of language, I must say that yours is becoming pretty urbane too," said Victor. "When I first met you the only vocabulary you had was about horses, coyotes, square dances and grandmother. Now you are beginning to sound like a man of the world."

"I still miss all those things, and furthermore I don't even know what urbane means," countered Walter.

A muted knock rattled the heavy wooden door. Simpson walked in and plopped his lanky frame into the stuffed chair. His sharp blue eyes darted about the room then focused on the two young man who were already poised for the announcement which they sensed was coming."

"We have our orders," said Simpson.

They did not respond, but waited for Simpson to continue.

"HQ has spoken. As soon as conditions are right, Walter, you and I are going to the Dresden area to keep an eye on troop movements and set up a ring of agents. Victor, you will be doing somewhat the same thing with someone else, to whom you will be introduced soon, only it will be in and around the big cabbage, Berlin."

He waited for a reaction. Victor spoke. "How come Walter gets the plum job and I get the hornet's nest?"

"That is not quite so," corrected Simpson. "The hornet's nest is really where Walter and I are going. Or it will be as soon as Hitler decides to move in and take what he has always said rightfully belongs to Germany – the Sudetenland. Must say though that the country there is quite beautiful. Hills, trees, lakes and all that."

"So when do we ship out?" asked Walter.

"Not for a while yet. You will both need a few weeks to familiarize yourselves with the new duties and the places to which you are being assigned."

"But will you be there to show me around?" protested Walter. "Why should I have to go through all that again?"

"Let's just say that I will indeed be around, but only from time to time," explained Simpson. "But for most of the time you will be working by yourself."

~~~

Seen from the north side of the river, the three church spires reached majestically heavenward, their bases seemingly firmly planted in the River Elbe. Passengers on the evening train from Prague peered out of the windows at Dresden's imposing skyline. On the river, barges and small craft plied leisurely over the glasslike water, their sides burnished by the light of the setting sun.

Walter looked over at Simpson. "Peaceful place," said Simpson in German.

Walter shook his head to indicate agreement. The peaceful scene was somehow not quite what he had expected. Some passengers began to gather their belongings in preparation for disembarking. Less than an hour earlier they all had been interrogated by customs and immigration officers at the Czech-German border. Walter, traveling as Karl Buettner produced his faked passport, appropriately signed. He was returning from a trip to Prague on behalf of his employer Neisse Photography and Camera Shop. Simpson identified himself as Rhienhart Holtz, a fine paper salesman from Prague. The border officials stamped their passports routinely.

At the station the two separated, having agreed that they would meet at a designated commercial hotel in the city center where reservations had been made for them. Inside the train depot only city and railroad police observed and assisted the arrivals. The SS and SA whom Walter had expected to see were nowhere in sight. Relaxed and now more at ease, he joined the other business travelers and hailed a cab. A pleasant male hotel clerk at the desk checked him into the hotel room and wished him an enjoyable stay. He slumped into the stuffed chair near the partly open window and breathed in the cool spring air. It smelled of lilac blossoms and automobile exhaust. The street noises outside reminded him of his arrival in Washington more than three years ago, and of Susan. He wondered what she would be doing and whether she remembered their pledge to meet again. He had not been real close to a girl since that time. There were many girls in London, but most of his time was devoted to training and little time was left for socializing. The organization did not encourage fraternizing with strange women and did not create conditions for this to occur. This looked like a quiet easy going place. Perhaps he would have an opportunity to meet another girl with whom he could be friends, just like he and Susan had been. Yes, he would make a point of it.

A knock sounded on the door and he opened it, expecting Simpson to be there. Instead he stood face to face with a lean, blond haired man with glasses and a short moustache. He was dressed in a business suit and felt hat.

"I am Adam Kunec, manager of the Neisse Photography and Camera Shop," announced the visitor. "May I come in?"

Walter held the door open and Kunec walked in. His eyes swept the room, and then rested on Walter.

"Neal will be here any minute now. I have heard a lot about you. What is a young man like you doing in this business?"

"It's a long story, but I guess it goes back to my parents and what happened to them," said Walter.

"Yes. I have heard about that, too," said Kunec. "And you are doing well by them from what I hear. But I think that you will find the work here rather tame compared to some of your previous jobs." He peered inside the lamp shade and examined the pictures hanging on the wall.

"We will discuss your job in more detail when Neal gets here."

· Kunec answered the knock on the door. Simpson entered the room looking uncomfortable in a dark business suit and tie.

"I see that you two have met, so let us all go and have something to eat," suggested Simpson.

The soft glow from the ornamental street lamps complimented the flower boxes and blooming ornamental trees as they drove through the picturesque city in the warm spring air.

"There is the Hoftheater," said Kunec pointing at a Renaissance style structure on the right. "And the Opera House, built in 1878."

"Somehow this place does not look like some of the other German places that I have seen," said Walter. "Too peaceful. Where are all he SS and SA?"

"It is deliberate," explained Kunec. "They are going out of their way to present a prosperous and friendly face. The border with Czechoslovakia is easy to cross. It is all part of a scheme to win the hearts of the border people, at least of those who are not already Nazi, and eventually take over the

Sudetenland."

"Then you really are expecting another Rhineland?" asked Simpson.

"Later this year, maybe next year, but not much later," asserted Kunec.

"And after that?" asked Simpson.

"And after that, the rest of Czechoslovakia."

"So why are we here then?" asked Walter. "If everything is so certain and so neat and tidy, what can we do to change that?"

"For the same reason that we went to all the other places," said Simpson. "To tell the rest of the world back there what is happening here." He thought for a moment and added, "And also to find out what we can about the Heydrich Enigma."

"There are lots of rumors around here about that thing," said Kunec.

"And what the heck is the Heydrich Enigma?" asked Walter.

"It is a cipher machine that the Germans are developing and testing. It is a machine that sends coded messages and decodes it at the other end. If they start a war and have that thing on their side, we will be in for a lot of trouble," warned Simpson.

"So will our job be to go chasing after an enigma?" asked Walter almost sarcastically.

"Not right away, unless, of course, you stumble over it," answered Simpson. "There are many others looking for the thing. By all of us working together, the puzzle may one day be solved, that is, if the Poles have not already solved it. I hear that they are working hard at doing just that. Just keep your eyes and ears open."

"There is a factory somewhere near here that is apparently making rotors for the machine," said Kunec.

"Just give me a couple of weeks, I'll get into that place and bring out anything you want." boasted Walter.

"It is not that easy," explained Kunec. "The factory that we think is doing it is a virtual armed camp. Nobody can enter except the workers and no one can take anything in or out of the place."

"So one of your jobs here will be to gradually try to know someone who works there and gather information from them, or even put an agent right in the factory," said Simpson. "Of course, Mr. Kunec will be helping you in this. From here on he will be known to us as Pavel."

"This is all news to me," said Walter. "You said that the reason we are coming here is to watch for troop movements. Has everything changed now?"

"Troop movements will still be our number one priority, but that is the easy part" answered Simpson. "If what Pavel tells us is true, you may expect to see a lot of Reichswehr troops around here before too long. But we know how quickly you get bored, so we threw in that deal about Enigma."

"This still sounds like it is going to be a vacation after the other jobs I've had," said a confident Walter.

"Just do not get caught," warned Pavel. "They will not waste much time getting you up there to that decapitator near Berlin if they catch you."

"They are going to have to go some to catch me," bragged Walter. "And where will you be all this time, sir?" he asked Simpson.

"Across the border in Czechoslovakia where it is safe," laughed Simpson. "But we will have regular contact. Pavel will advise you."

Kunec stopped the car in front of a restaurant and they sat down for a late dinner.

~~~

From his apartment in the Friedrichstadt quarter of the city, Walter gazed upon the lofty octagonal tower of the Rathaus, standing vigilant above the city. A cool breeze from the river flowed gently through the window, driving out the oppressive stale air that had occupied the room during the day. It had been another uneventful week. He wondered how much longer Simpson would allow him to remain in Dresden observing recruits playing war games with cardboard-clad Volksvagons dressed to look like tanks and armored troop carriers, and field maneuvers with wooden barrel howitzers, carried out in soccer fields. To the young artillerymen, dressed in crisp new uniforms, jackboots and steel helmets, it was all very serious business. He wondered why the Wehrmacht did not send them some of the real machines that he had seen stored in the bunker near Stettin.

"Propaganda," explained Simpson on one of his visits, when asked the question. "On this side of the country they want to appear as the poor oppressed nation, suffering from the inequities of the Treaty of Versailles and striving to improve their defenses in the face of a sea of enemies." The citizens of Dresden loved it. They watched with pride as the confident and well disciplined recruits trained in the soccer fields and goose stepped through the streets in their weekly parades. Even to Walter it was a thrill to observe the Spartan dedication of these young soldiers to their tasks. Tourists from the Czechoslovakian side watched the show with tears in their eyes.

"Discipline. That's what these trainees have," he reported to Simpson several days earlier. His mentor agreed. "Too bad the Poles don't have more of that," he confided to Walter. "They are a people stifled by resistance to change, a bungling bureaucracy, and a military still drawing their field guns with horses. Some day soon they may have to pay for their folly. By then it may be too late. But then the Poles have been fortunate in that they have nearly always benefited from favorable treaties. This is not because of their prowess in winning military battles, but because of their strategic location in Europe." When Simpson left for the other side of the border, Walter thought about his mentor's assessment of the Polish situation and wondered if he was becoming discouraged. He was startled by a knock on the door. It was Pavel.

"I was day dreaming," he apologized. "Thinking about how little information I have provided so far on this assignment."

"Well then, rejoice," said Pavel. "We have found a most interesting project for you."

"Yes? Really?" said Walter. "What is this all about?"

"We have found a worker in the precision works department of the plant whom we think is a Polish sympathizer. I would like you to get to know her."

"Her?" asked the astonished young man.

"Yes, her," responded Pavel with a grin. "Here is a profile of her and her daily routine," he added, removing some papers from a brown envelope.

"Eva Moravic is the twenty-three year old daughter of a Czechoslovakian father and German mother. Blonde, slender and blue-eyed, she is fun loving and unattached. Her father was born in Silesia and fought in Franz Joseph's army in the World War. He moved to Dresden in the 1920s and married the daughter of a German factory worker. It is known that Moravic was a supporter of the young Czechoslovakian Republic and returned there often to visit. Eva is his oldest daughter. On Saturday afternoons she goes to the market and on her way back she often likes to stop in front of the ancient Prinzen Palais to watch the weekly parade of the SS and Wehrmacht soldiers and cadets. This is where you will find her next Saturday."

Crowds of on-looker stood six deep in front of the venerable stone building as the platoons of soldiers and cadets marched by, moving with precision to the stirring martial music. Pavel and Walter observed the crowd from the front of the Prinzen Palais.

"There she is," said Pavel after scanning the heads of the assembled crowd for several minutes. "She is the one with the blue kerchief on her head and carrying a basket."

Walter indicated that he saw the person whom Pavel was describing.

"Go and stand beside her," said Pavel. "Check to see if she is the one whom I described to you."

On the pretext of trying to get a better view of the marching soldiers, Walter pushed his way through the crowd and stood beside the girl with the kerchief knotted behind her head. He looked across at Pavel who nodded his head in the affirmative.

"You will find her there every Saturday during the summer," said Pavel when Walter rejoined him.

"She is such an innocent young thing," said a gleeful Walter. "Fresh as a mountain stream. I think I am going to enjoy this assignment."

~~~

Scrubbed, clean shaven and wearing freshly pressed pants and shirt, Walter paced impatiently in front of the Prinzen Palais. The Saturday morning crowd was gathered on the sidewalks waiting for the platoons of soldiers to march by. She appeared around the corner, now bareheaded and wearing a loose fitting skirt and short sleeved red and white blouse. She placed her woven basket in front of her and stood in tip-toe to see above the crowd. Walter moved in behind her and then squeezed over to stand in front of the crowd and off to one side.

In the distance, the sound of martial music announced the approaching band. The first platoon appeared around the bend in the street. He edged closer to her and cut off her view to the left. The sound of marching feet got louder, combined with the rousing strains of the brass wind instruments. Applause broke out as the precision drilled units of young infantry men marched by, their jackboots and freshly pressed tunic sleeves moving in unison. Walter stepped back and let the girl move into his spot. She smiled and thanked him softly. The last platoon filed off down the street.

The girl picked up her basket and turned to leave. She looked up at him and their eyes met.

"It was nice of you to let me have your spot," she said smiling.

"I am glad you enjoyed it," he answered trying hard to maintain his composure. "It was a wonderful sight, was it not?"

"Yes. I enjoy the music," she said. "We never had anything like that around here until this started."

"Is that right?" He tried to sound incredulous.

"No. Not until the new government took over," she answered. "You sound like you are not from around here."

"No, I am not. I have only been here for a few weeks."

"Really? And where did you come from?" she asked.

"I was born in Stettin." He picked the place with which he felt most familiar.

"Oh. That is a long way from here."

"Not really that far."

She started to walk away.

"Here, let me carry that," he said, taking the basket from her.

"Thank you. But were you going my way," she asked.

"I can go any way at all. I am not doing anything else right now."

They walked across the street and paused in front of a tea house. "Would you like to drop in here for some refreshments?" he asked shyly.

"Now wait a minute." She stopped abruptly. "I do not even know your name."

"Oh, I am sorry. I was enjoying myself so much, I forgot to tell you. It is Karl Buettner. And what is yours?"

"Eva Moravic," she replied.

"That is a nice name," he said in a sincere voice.

"Thank you. Now we can have some tea, but there is a nicer place than this one farther down the street."

She sipped her tea slowly and observed him over the rim of her cup. "If you are from Stettin, what are you doing here?" she asked.

"Oh, I came out to help my uncle who manages the Neisse Photography and Camera Shop."

"Many of the young men who used to be unemployed around here have joined the Wehrmacht. Some even joined the SS. The smarter ones," she said.

"I think that I will do the same one of these days," he said.

"You really should not. War is so disrupting and frightening. I like it nice and peaceful. Just the way it is now."

"But it may not be that way much longer now," he suggested.

"Maybe not. But let us not talk about it. It makes me nervous. And I must really be going home now or my mother will start to worry." She stood up to leave. "Thank you. This was nice."

"I am sorry to see you leave so soon," he said. "Will you be out here watching the parade again next week?" he asked.

"Oh, I probably will. I am usually on my way home from the market about that time."

"May I join you there, then?" he asked.

"If you wish," she answered casually.

They walked out of the restaurant and she turned into a side street and walked away slowly. His eyes followed her and, as if aware of this, she turned around and waved.

The hot, humid days of the week seemed to pass more slowly than usual. They moved at their own pace and seemed to be oblivious to the impatient excitement building up within him as he contemplated seeing the girl again. Kunic noted the reflective mood.

"How did you like the girl?" he asked.

"She seems to be a real nice person," answered Walter.

"Do not get too serious with her; only friendly enough to get what we are after," Kunic advised in a fatherly voice.

"No. I will not," he answered halfheartedly.

Saturday morning arrived, seemingly oblivious to his escalating excitement, but replete with a clear azure blue sky and a sun which he thought shone more brilliantly than in the preceding days. Vehicles and pedestrians, all intent on their own mission, crammed the main thoroughfares, filling them with a thousand sounds and smells. With a smile on his face and a light step, Walter moved along with the crowds on his way to the Prinzen Palais.

It was still too early for the parade and only a few people had arrived to select choice positions along the parade route. He sat in the shade of a walnut tree and watched the cheerful onlookers assemble. An official military vehicle cleared the route in advance of the parade. In the distance a young woman approached, carrying a wicker basket. Walter jumped to his feet and walked quickly toward her.

"Hello, Eva!" he called as she approached. She smiled.

"I have been her about an hour waiting for you," he said.

"I am sorry. Am I late?" she asked.

"I don't know," he answered, "but I thought that you would never arrive."

"Oh, Karl, you say the nicest things." She blushed as she observed his excitement at her arrival.

"Here. Give me that," he said, taking the basket containing the bread and vegetables which she had picked up at the market. "Let us find a good spot on the boulevard. The parade will soon be here."

Staccato drum beats in the distance became louder as the orderly line of white helmeted marchers appeared around the bend in the street. The brass instruments joined in and the band picked up its beat. A platoon of goose-stepping SS recruits marched past the crowd, followed by several platoons of Reichwehr troops. The crowds clapped and cheered as the parade disappeared down the street.

"Are they not beautiful?" she whispered, holding back her emotions.

Walter nodded in agreement. The crowd dispersed and they were left standing alone.

"Shall we go back to the same place?" he asked.

"I would love to," she responded. They retraced their steps of a week earlier and chose he same table.

"Well, what have you been doing all week?" she asked.

"Waiting for today," he answered innocently.

She lifted her eyes away from her cup and studied him discretely, then shook her head in disbelief. "I do not know what to think of you," she said.

"Why don't we do something together today?" he blurted.

"What would you like to do?" she asked.

"Anything that you like to do."

"Do you like cycling? I love to cycle around the parks on nice days like this," she offered. "Do you have a bicycle?"

"No, I do not, but I can borrow my uncle's." He remembered seeing an old bicycle at the back of the camera shop. "We can go this afternoon, if that is fine with you."

"All right. I will take the food back to mama and meet you in front of Georgenschloss. Do you know where that is?"

"Yes," he lied. But he knew that he would find it.

"Good. We can ride around the grounds for a while. There are a few interesting things to see there."

Almost everyone he asked knew where the old royal palace was located and Walter had no problem finding it after appropriating the bicycle from Pavel's shop. He arrived in front of the Georgenschloss and sat on a stone retainer wall. She pedaled toward him several minutes later, her face pink from the exercise, and her eyes beaming.

"This is going to be fun," she said. "Let us take a ride around the grounds."

She headed down a narrow lane with him in pursuit. He followed behind her, captivated by her soft blonde hair billowing in the breeze and the undulating motion of her hips as she pedaled along in front of him. She looked back and laughed. "Come on, slow turtle, and I will show you where King Frederick Augustus used to ride his horse."

She turned into a narrow path and stopped. "They say that when the castle was new, this area here was still out in the country, even though it is not all that far from the castle. So the king had enough space in which to exercise his steed. Let us sit down and rest for a while."

They leaned their bicycles against a tree and sat down on the grass. She pulled her legs under her and smoothed out her skirt.

"You know. I have just figured you out," she announced. "In spite of your bravado when we first met, you are really quite shy. So that is why I do most of the talking."

"You go right ahead," he said. "I could listen to you all day."

"Except that when you talk, you do say the nicest things," she countered. "But let us talk about you for a change."

"Oh, no," he insisted. "I want to know more abut you."

"There is not much to know," she said, appearing modest. "I come from a family of five. My father is Silesian and my mother German. Their loyalties differ, but they get along quite well. I work in a factory where we produce precision parts, like special types of gears, sprockets, bushings, bearings and things like that. I work with rotors for some kind of a communication device which is assembled somewhere else. Some of the things that we make are classified, so there is tight security all around the place and we cannot talk too much about what goes on there. And that is about it. And what do you do?"

"Oh, there is nothing special about my work," he explained. "I help my uncle in the darkroom to develop and print photographs. I sell a few cameras and photography equipment and now I am learning to repair cameras. My family is all in Stettin. My mother is Polish and my father German."

"Is that why you speak German with an accent?" she asked.

He felt his face turning red. This was the first time that this had been brought to his attention. "It could be," he answered. "You see, I learned Polish at the same time as I was learning German, so that could have done it."

"It really does not matter," she said. "I think that some older people make much of these things, but I don't care." She stood up and brushed the grass off her skirt. "Well, where should we go now?"

"Why don't we go for some tea or coffee and some sweets, and then ride around to where I live and I will show you my apartment."

She gazed into his eyes and laughed. "I will ride by to see the outside of the building, but I cannot go in. Maybe some other time."

"As you wish," he said, obviously disappointed.

~~~

Except for short reprieves brought about by occasional rainstorms and showers, the oppressive heat of mid-summer hung heavily over the city. The earlier cool breezes off the river changed to wafts of hot humid air, laden with smells of fish and algae. The joy of pedaling through the city and countryside waned after several weeks and Walter and Eva were now spending most of their Saturday afternoons in his apartment.

On the first Saturday in August, the day began with oppressive heat and a hazy sky which hung shroud-like over the city. By early afternoon the clouds moved in and rain began to fall. It beat rhythmically against the bedroom window of his apartment.

"I really must go now. My parents will wonder where I am in this rain and you know how they worry about me."

"But you cannot go out in the rain. You will get all wet. Just come back here for a few more minutes and the rain may slow down or go away," he coaxed.

She fell back into his outstretched arms and he rolled over her.

"You know, you are going to wear me out if you don't watch it," she sighed contentedly.

"Do you not enjoy it?" he asked.

"Of course. You are the best," she answered.

"You mean that there have been others?"

"Nothing serious. I had a few short whirls with a couple of those cocky SS recruits, but it was nothing like this."

His eyes shifted away and he gazed at the rain splattered window.

"Really, Karl. It was nothing," she insisted.

"Is that why you go to watch the parade every Saturday? Do you still see them?" he asked.

"They call on me once in a while. But I am yours. Honest. I would do anything for you."

He did not answer.

"I mean that, Karl. You just name it and I will do it."

"No. That is all right, Eva. Just as long as I can see you from time to time, I will be happy."

She planted a kiss on his cheek. "You are a nice boy, Karl. Well, I see that it has stopped raining, so I must leave. Are you going to see me next Saturday?"

"Of course," he replied. "It will be a long week as usual."

She tucked her sweater around her shoulders. "Now you just sit here right here and rest. I will find my way out."

Kunic paced restlessly around the shop, picking up cameras and lens, brushing them off, and then replacing them. His eyes had a far-away look. Walter observed him with apparent curiosity.

"Is something wrong?" he asked.

"I do not like it, Walter," he exclaimed. "Things are looking bad. Troop concentrations are building up along the border. There are rumors that the Nazis are experimenting with new weapons and with new methods of communication. And nearly everyone keeps saying, do not worry, they will not do anything drastic. But I say, just watch them. That is what they said about the Rhineland. Now they say that the Rhineland really belonged to Germany, so let them have it. But the Nazi say that the Sudetenland also rightfully belongs to them. Also Austria and the Polish Corridor, and for that matter, Poland herself."

"But what can we do that we are not already doing?" asked Walter.

"We must speed up our gathering of information so that England and France will realize what is happening here, before it is too late."

"I think that I should be able to ask for the information on the rotors very soon, maybe even this Saturday," said Walter.

"Try harder, Willy. Neal is getting impatient."

In preparation for the annual Nuremberg National Socialist Party Festival in September the local regiments staged a rehearsal of the march-past which would soon take place in front of the Fuehrer. A swastika festooned reviewing stand, occupied by several colonels and their staffs was located near the Prinzen Palais. The bands blared their rousing martial strains as the companies of SS, Wehrmacht, Luftwaffe and SA marched past the reviewing stand in perfect unison, their banners fluttering in the wind.

On the sidewalks and boulevards the onlookers cheered and sang along with the music. Eva wiped the tears from her eyes as the SS recruits goose stepped smartly in front of them, their colorful ensigns trembling in the breeze.

"This is more beautiful than a ballet," she said softly, holding back her emotions.

They walked silently along the tree lined street toward Walter's apartment, each lost in their own thoughts.

"Have you thought any more about joining any of the services?" she asked.

"Not really'" he answered. "But before long I will receive the call."

"That is good," she said happily. "I would not want you to go away right now. Unless, of course, there is a war, and then you will have no choice. You would go then, wouldn't you?"

"I probably will." He hesitated for a moment. "But I would like to finish what I am doing first."

She stopped and looked at him inquisitively. He tried to appear unnerved.

"I am sorry. I let it slip out by mistake. It is really nothing," he said.

"What is it that you want to finish?" she asked. "Are you keeping something from me?"

"There is not much to tell," he said. "You see, my uncle and I are working on the development of a system which will transmit typed and written messages through wires. This will do away with the system that is now being used by railroads whereby codes are tapped out and audible sounds are received at the other end. What my uncle is developing is a system that would silently transmit messages which will be transcribed on paper at the other end."

"Really? And you say it is nothing important," she exclaimed. "And how is it coming along?"

"It was going very well until recently. Right now we seem to have encountered what looks like a major difficulty, one that may cause my uncle to abandon the project. Too bad, because it would have been a good thing for the railroads and for people who want to send long distance messages fast."

"Send written messages by wire," she exclaimed. "Just think of what value that would be to the military. What kind of problem did you run into?"

They arrived at the door of his apartment building. "Would you come in for a minute and I will tell you the sad story?"

"Of course I will. Don't I always?"

"I thought that maybe today, after seeing your old friends in the parade you would be of a different mind."

"No Walter. They are in love with their uniforms, discipline and ideals. I need somebody warm and human like you. So tell me about your problems."

Inside the apartment he sat down in his chair and sighed. "Yes, we are so close and yet so far in our search for a new way of sending messages. All that we have to solve is one problem and then I think we will have it finished. That problem has to do with the design of a cylinder which will set off electrical impulses as the typed message spins around with it. If we can design that part, I think that we will have the answer."

He gazed at the floor and ran his fingers through his hair. She watched him in silent thought. "You know, I think that we make something nearly like that where I work. They call them rotors. I understand that they too are to be used for sending signals."

"It must be something entirely different," said Walter, trying to appear disinterested. "No one anywhere, as far as we know, has made anything like we have in mind."

"You never know," she said. "Maybe you can get some idea from it. I wish I could show you one of those things, but I would never be able to get past the inspection point with it."

"I would not want you to try that," he said. "I would certainly not want you to put yourself in danger for us. My uncle will probably be able to figure it out in time, but by that time someone else may have beat him to it." With a faraway look in his eyes, he fidgeted with the button on his shirt. "But if you really want to help, even a drawing of the thing may help to show us if there are any ideas that we can use from it, which I doubt." he added.

"Oh, drawings? I have seen them around the plant. Yes, I could probably get you a drawing of that item. You know, the kind that shows all sorts of wires and switches, figures and arrows, and things like that. I could stick it inside my blouse where no one would ever look and sneak it out that way."

"Would you really want to do something like that?" he asked.

"Only for you," she said.

He took her hand and they entered the bedroom and closed the door behind them.

Next day, an intense Pavel listened as Walter explained the arrangements he had made with Eva.

"And what precautions did you take?" he asked

"What precautions do I need with Eva? She is so innocent and unsuspecting, and furthermore she is in love with me."

"In this business you trust no one, especially your lover," counseled Pavel.

"I asked her to meet me Saturday before the parade at a spot on the grounds of the Prinzen Palais, rather than at my place. So I did change the routine a bit," explained Walter.

"You learned well," said Pavel. "I will take care of the rest of the security."

~~~

Pavel was absent from the shop for much of the week, leaving Walter and another clerk to look after the customers. He returned shortly before noon Friday and took Walter inside his office. His face was drawn and his forehead furrowed. He eyes peered out at Walter from deep inside their sockets. Walter had never seen him this distressed.

"I do not like it, Willy," he confessed. "There is something peculiar going on. We may have to make a contingency plan involving Neal because if the original plan fails, you and I will be in great danger. So before you go anywhere tomorrow, call in here on the pretense that you are picking up the bicycle, and we will have your orders."

"But this is my project," protested Walter. "Eva and I have it all arranged. What do you mean it does not look good?"

"I will tell you tomorrow. Come by here anyway," said Pavel. "If everything is as simple as you say, then fine, you can pick up the bicycle and go. If not, then we will want to make other arrangements. That is an order from Neal."

"You and Neal just do not trust anyone, do you?" complained Walter.

"Only the trustworthy," replied Pavel.

Saturday morning arrived with dark clouds speeding ominously across the sky, blotting out the sun and filling the streets with gray shadows. A cool breeze from the northeast made the day more reminiscent of November than late September. Walter walked down the nearly vacant street to the camera shop, his spirits dampened by the bleak day as well as by Pavel's fear of danger and by the thought of having to exploit his dear friend in order to obtain the information the organization needed. He hesitated momentarily on the sidewalk in front of the shop, and then walked in.

There were no customers in the shop. Pavel was standing behind the counter, his hands gripping its edge and his eyes gazing blankly out the window.

Without looking at Walter, he said, "You cannot go. It is too dangerous."

"What do you mean, it is too dangerous?" asked Walter. "What can a young girl like Eva do to make it so dangerous?"

"We have our orders," said Pavel with finality.

"I must go," pleaded Walter. "I cannot let her down."

"You do not seem to understand," said Pavel impatiently. "In this business, when someone says you do not go, you do not go. It is as simple as that. That is, unless you want to go on a one-way trip."

"So what do I do now?" asked Walter, accepting the finality of the order.

"You work here, making yourself as conspicuous as possible until eleven thirty. At that time you will leave this place and walk to your apartment, making yourself as visible as possible. Stay in your apartment until your orders arrive."

The morning finally ticked away to eleven thirty and Walter left for his apartment. Meanwhile, in the park near the Prinzen Palais, the breeze rustled the leaves and blew dust into his face as Neal sat on the small wooden bench where Walter was to meet up with Eva. He was alone. The cool weather did not invite strollers along the walk. From time to time he glanced discreetly over his left shoulder, looking down the path. From behind the clump of shrubbery came the crunching sound of tires on coarse sand. He looked up and the girl on the bicycle stopped before she reached him and glanced around. She looked concerned, and then moved toward Neal slowly.

"Excuse me, sir. Did you see a young man here?"

"Is his name Karl," asked Neal in German.

"Yes. That is right. How did you know?"

"I am his uncle. He could not come because he was not feeling well. So he sent me to tell you and that he was sorry."

"Oh, that is too bad. Give him my regrets. Tell him I will meet him here next Saturday." She started to turn her bicycle around to leave.

"Karl said you would have something for him and he asked me to get it from you," said Simpson.

She hesitated, her face pale and her mouth slightly open.

"That is all right," said Simpson. "Karl told me all about your arrangement. And I am his partner in this anyway. He said that he really had to have it today, and he would be very disappointed if I came back empty-handed. I must have something to take back to him, or he will not know what happened, and that I actually saw you."

She reached slowly inside her blouse and produced a folded brown envelope. He stood up and walked to the front of her bicycle. She handed him the envelope cautiously and turned the front wheel of her bicycle to leave. Simpson caught the wheel between his legs and held it while he opened the envelope. Inside it was three sheets of plain white paper. He reached into his inside pocket and produced a small metal tube. He brought it close to her face and pressed a button. She gasped and fell across the handlebars. Simpson caught her limp body and carried her into the shrubbery. After propping the bicycle against a tree, he disappeared behind the hedge.

~~~

Small groups of onlookers were already selecting their spots along the parade route as Walter walked back to his apartment. He stopped at the tea house for tea and a small cake, and chatted with the waitress about the weather and the parade. The waitress asked where his friend was.

It was the first Saturday in several weeks on which he had walked back to his apartment alone. This, plus the gloomy weather, put him in a melancholy mood. He walked slowly through the hallway and unlocked the apartment door. Slumped in the old armchair, with his hands clasped in front of him was Simpson. He observed Walter with a blank stare. Walter hesitated in front of the closed door, surprised at his mentor's unexpected presence.

"Oh, hello there, sir. I didn't expect to see you here today."

"It was a last minute decision," said Simpson dryly.

"I hear that I botched my assignment," said Walter.

"Not completely," said Simpson. "I kept your rendezvous for you."

"Oh, that is great," said Walter, relieved. "Did you see Eva and did she bring the drawings?"

"Yes, on both counts," replied Simpson, "except that the drawings were blank."

"What do you mean the drawings were blank?" asked Walter caustically.

"That is exactly what I mean. Blank paper in an envelope," said Simpson. He reached into his pocket and brought out the brown envelope. Walter's face paled and his lips pursed as he looked at the blank pages.

"Why would she do that?" he pondered.

"Because you, my innocent friend, were set up," said Simpson.

"So what happened? What did she say? Did she tell anyone about our arrangement?"

"We will find out in a few minutes because we are going by there to see what is happening. In fact we should leave right now."

They left the building and Simpson drove past the grounds of the Prinzen Palais. An ambulance drove out of the back entrance, followed by an official SS car. City police and black uniformed troopers milled about the grounds behind the building. Out on the street the parade was arriving on schedule.

"Who are they looking for?" asked Walter innocently.

"You," responded Simpson.

"Me? Then let's get out of here," insisted Walter.

"You are right. Normally we would be getting our respective asses out of the country and heading across the border, but we do not want to compromise Pavel, so you will hang around for a while. Pavel is too valuable to the organization and we do not want to lose him, so you will stay around for a while and make it appear like things are normal."

Simpson drove around the block and they returned to the apartment. Walter remained silent until they were inside.

"How did you know that this was going to happen?" he asked.

"Our informant told us that your friend was fraternizing with the black shirts during the week, so we could not take any chances."

"Eva would never do that. She's my good friend," said Walter, looking despondent.

"She was your good friend," said Simpson.

"What do you mean she was my good friend?" asked Walter.

"I had to eliminate her. She knew too much and was too dangerous," said Simpson.

"You had to eliminate her?" gasped Walter. "You mean you killed her?"

"That is exactly what I mean," he answered, with no hint of compassion.

"How?"

"With a small blast from my cyanide gun," explained Simpson.

His lips pursed and his fists clenched, Walter stood up and glared at Simpson. "Why you heartless son-of-a-bitch, how could you do that to an innocent, loving person like her?" he screamed.

"She was not the innocent loving person that you took her for," said Simpson calmly. "And if I had not come along when I did, do you realize where you would be now? You would be at Gestapo headquarters. So please do not create a commotion or we will both soon be in trouble."

"I don't give a damn about you, you blood thirsty bastard," he shouted. "You have no respect for people or love. The only thing that you are interested in is this goddamned organization."

Simpson reached inside his jacket and drew a small pistol from his pocket. He pointed it at Walter. "You are right about what you say about the organization, and we expect that from you too as long as you are in its service. So you make one more sound, my hayseed friend, and you will join your friend in kingdom come so fast that you will not know what hit you. This is a silent weapon, so no one will hear it. The police and SS will be pleased because the case of the dead girl will be solved and the SS will arrest Pavel and lead him to the chopping block in Berlin. Is that what you want?"

Walter slumped down into his chair and covered his eyes with his hand. Simpson put the gun back in his pocket.

"Oh, how I hate this business," Walter moaned. "Please take me out of here."

"That is better. I am glad that we have not completely wasted our time training you," said Simpson. "But you cannot leave now. If you do, then you will be suspected of the killing. As it is, several people know that you were nowhere near the place when it happened. So if you stick around for a while till the stink blows over, you can leave knowing that Pavel will not be implicated, by association. At this point we are assuming that they would think that the girl believed that you made up the story about your uncle and that, in fact, Pavel did not know anything about it. I am going back across the border now. You will continue to carry on as though nothing has happened, except that you have lost a very dear friend. If you should get into trouble meanwhile, do not panic, we will not be too far away." Simpson left without saying good-bye. Walter leaned forward in his chair staring at the floor. The door opened and closed, and his mentor was gone.

CHAPTER 42

"I am sorry that the plan did not work out," Pavel lamented late Monday morning. "But it was worth the try." It was the first time he had mentioned the incident.

"It was the first assignment in which I failed," said Walter.

"You do not need to apologize," said Pavel. "We underestimated their alertness and you let emotions get in the way of business, and you very nearly paid for it. But it looks like the whole thing will blow over. This is the third day now since the incident, so maybe nothing will happen. But I would still be very careful. They will probably be watching us, especially you. And do not worry about me. Neal has arranged for my quick exit should it become necessary."

For the next two days, Walter moved in a normal routine between the shop and his apartment. The life of the city continued as before, and he was sure that no one was following or watching him. He missed Eva and the evenings in the apartment seemed torturously long with the prospect of meeting her now gone forever. He listened to the radio and read books on photography to keep his mind off her. The days went by slowly. He hoped that Simpson would call him away.

It was now almost a week since the incident. Next morning the parade would go by the Prinzen Palais and neither he nor Eva would be there to watch it. He wondered how Eva's family was reacting to the tragedy. He felt guilty and ashamed, and wished that they would contact him so he could share his sorrow with them.

The sound of loud footsteps in the hallway was followed by a knock on his door. He answered it quickly, expecting to see Simpson. Instead he stood face to face with a policeman.

"Are you Karl Buettner?" the policeman asked.

"Yes."

"You are to come with me to the police station," instructed the policeman.

"For what reason?" asked Walter.

"For questioning in connection with an incident on the grounds of the Prinzen Palais last Saturday morning."

"I was nowhere near the Prinzen Palais last Saturday morning," said Walter firmly. "I was working at the camera shop."

"You can tell that to the investigating officer'" said the policeman. "My orders are to bring you in for questioning."

"I'll get my cap and jacket," said Walter. He took his jacket and removed the brown envelope from its pocket and slid it onto the top shelf of the closet. The policeman waited inside the doorway.

The police station was vibrant with sounds of telephones ringing and police officers conversing with each other and the detainees. He was taken to the interrogation room. A sergeant and an officer entered the room, the latter carrying a file. They sat across the table from him.

"Your name, please," requested the sergeant.

"Karl Buettner."

"Address?"

"574 Kulmbach Street. Apartment 3."

"Where do you work?"

"At Neisse Photography and Camera Shop."

The constable recorded the questions and Walter's answers.

"Where were you last Saturday between ten o'clock in the morning and twelve thirty?"

"At work until twelve and then I came down-town for a few minutes before continuing on to my apartment," answered Walter.

"Did anyone beside your employer see you between these hours?"

"Yes. There were several people in the shop during the morning. At noon I stopped at the restaurant on my way home and talked to the waitress."

"Did you know a person by the name of Eva Moravic."

"Yes."

"Did you see her last Saturday?"

"No."

"Had you planned to see her Saturday afternoon?"

"Yes, but I could not go to meet her because I was needed at the shop."

"Did you let her know that you would not meet her?"

"No. I did not realize that I could not go until it was too late to advise her."

"Did you send someone else to meet her?"

"No."

The sergeant leaned back in is chair, his eyes focused on Walter. "Had you intended to receive anything from the Moravic girl?' he asked.

"I do not know how to answer that," explained Walter. "You see, she often brought me a bun or pieces of cheese from the market."

Walter sat still during a long pause while the sergeant examined the file.

"Retain Herr Buettner as a material witness," he ordered.

The constable led Walter to a small cell beneath the main floor of the police station. Along the wall was a cot with a thin straw mattress and covered with a gray blanket. A toilet bowl and a water tap and basin made up the balance of the cell's contents, except for a tin mug which stood on a concrete ledge beside the bed.

"I would like to have my personal papers out of my jacket pocket," requested Walter.

"We will hold them for you," said the constable as he locked the cell door.

There were no windows or fans in the area and musty air hung still and heavy in the small cell. It smelled of mould, stale cigarette smoke and disinfectant. All was quite, except for the occasional loud tramping noise of the guards' boots on concrete, which echoed through the hallway. Walter took off his shirt and pants and crawled under the gray blanket. He dozed off and awoke sometime later, shivering under the thin blanket. He put his head under the blanket and breathed deeply. After exhaling deeply several times, the warm breath replaced the chilly air and he fell asleep.

He awoke to the sound of clanging doors down the hall from his cell. After splashing water from the tap on his face, he dressed. A guard brought his breakfast of porridge with skim milk and a cup of black coffee. He ate off the tray while sitting on the edge of the cot. The guard watched him from the hallway through the iron bars. When he had eaten the porridge and drank the coffee, the guard returned and took the tray away without saying a word.

It must be early morning, he thought. There was movement in the hallway and sounds from some of the other cells. He sat up in his cot and leaned against the cold concrete wall, reading the graffiti of the cell's former occupants by the dim light of the single bulb hanging from the ceiling.

What seemed like two pairs of footsteps in the hall became louder and a police constable stopped before his door and unlocked it. He was carrying Walter's cap and jacket on his arm and some papers in his hand.

"Here are your belongings, Buettner," said the constable. "Get dressed and be ready to leave in ten minutes."

"Where are we going?" asked Walter.

"You will find out when you get there," said the constable as he locked the iron door.

A few minutes later he returned with another policeman who put handcuffs on Walter. For the first time he felt like a prisoner. They led him out of the cell through a back door into a waiting car. The car sped through the busy street and crossed the bridge toward the Albertstadt quarter. The clock in the tower showed fifteen minutes to eight.

The car pulled up in front a plain three-storey brick building with stone steps leading up to the double-door entrance. The constable led him up the steps to the door and then up another set of stairs to a large empty office on the main floor. He sat down on a varnished wooden bench between two policemen. The office door opened and a stalwart man in a well fitting black uniform entered. The peak of his cap came down over half of his forehead and on the black band above it was attached a badge showing a skull and two crossed bones. His countenance was accentuated by his piercing blue eyes and narrow lips.

Both policemen jumped to their feet and saluted. "Heil Hitler!"

"Heil Hitler. Is this the witness?"

"It is Herr Captain," answered one of the constables.

"I will take over now. You may leave and wait outside," said the SS officer. He returned their salutes and sat down behind a heavy wooden desk. After removing his cap, he placed it carefully in front of him, and opened a file which was sitting on the desk.

"What is your name?"

"Karl Buettner."

The questions were a repeat of the ones he had answered on the previous night. The captain closed the file and fixed his eyes on Walter.

"Who is your accomplice?"

"Accomplice, sir? I do not understand," said Walter.

"Who was the man who met the Moravic girl in your place?"

"I did not know that someone else had met her," lied Walter. He felt his face turning red. The officer observed his every move.

"You say that you are from Stettin?"

"Yes sir," replied Walter. "You will find that information in my personal papers should you wish to do so."

"May I, please," said the Captain. After examining the documents he placed them in the file folder.

"What was your relationship with the Moravic girl?" he asked mechanically.

"We were very good casual friends. I was very fond of her."

"Did her parents know about your relationship with the Moravic girl?"

"They knew that she was seeing someone every Saturday at the parade, but she never talked much about them and I never did see them," explained Walter.

"Did she mention having any other male friends," asked the captain.

"Yes. She mentioned being friendly with two members of the SS."

"I see," said the captain. "Why did you come to Dresden?"

"To help my uncle. He offered to teach me the business."

"And then what?"

"Then I hope to go back to Stettin and join up for military service. And after that I will have a trade to fall back on."

"You have an odd accent," observed the captain.

"My mother was Polish and I was raised in the Polish sector of the city."

"Did you learn to speak Polish?"

"Yes. At the same time as I was learning German."

"The SS captain picked up his cap and carefully placed it on is head. He lifted up the phone.

"All right, I am finished," he said into the phone. He stood up and looked down at Walter.

"We will have to hold you here until we check out a few things. Then if everything is as you say it is, you will be free to leave."

Two young SS troopers entered the room, saluted and stood at attention.

"You will detain Herr Buettner while the investigation continues," directed the captain. He returned to the desk and reopened the file. Walter was shown out of the office and escorted up the stairs to the top floor of the building. There he was taken to a small room with a small iron-barred window near the ceiling. A small bed and a wooden table and chair made up the furnishings. In a tiny cubicle, with a sliding curtain were a toilet and a basin. The two young troopers locked the door and left without speaking.

Shaken by the cold efficiency of the latest incident, Walter lay on the small bed and gazed at the smoke-stained white plaster ceiling. He wondered if Pavel knew of his arrest. No doubt Pavel would realize that something was wrong because he had not been at work for more than two days now. What about Simpson? He said he would not be far away if trouble should strike. Maybe it didn't matter anyway, because, like the captain said, if everything was like he said it was, he would soon be free.

Two days passed and no one came inside the room except the security guard who delivered his food three times a day and stayed to watch while Walter shaved with a razor which the guard brought and then took away with him. He began to feel like an unwelcome guest, tolerated by his hosts because he may be of some use in the future. He wished he was back home, or in London, or anywhere except where he was.

~~~

On the third day of his confinement Walter felt abandoned as he sat on the cot gazing at the barred widow. When the routinely regular footsteps sounded in the hallway, he expected that his breakfast was about to be delivered. Instead the door flew open and three SS troopers stepped in.

"All right, Buettner, gather up your things and come with us," one of them ordered.

He picked his jacket up off the back of the chair and walked to the door. The three troopers led him down the stairway into the basement level of the building and entered a long narrow room at the end of the hallway. In it were a chair with straps on each arm rest and a flat stand resembling a billiard table with two leather straps at each end. In one corner was a cupboard with two doors. A concrete compartment with a water pipe and a faucet stood in another corner of the room.

One of the SS men took his jacket away from him and pushed him into one of the chairs. He threw the jacket into a corner.

"All right Buettner, if that is your name, we have to get a few things straight here before we let you out. So we will begin now," said the SS corporal.

"What is your name?"

"Karl Buettner."

"Where do you work?"

"At the Neisse Photography and Camera Shop."

"Did you know Eva Moravic?"

"Yes."

"Did you meet her last Saturday?"

"No."

"Who did?" the corporal demanded.

"I do not know."

"Who was you accomplice?"

"I had no accomplice. I did not need one."

"Just answer the questions. Where were you born?"

"In Stettin."

"What is your father's name?"

"Heinrich Buettner."

The corporal walked around the chair, tapping a rubber truncheon on the palm of his hand.

"You know, Buettner, we checked your story in Stettin and we found that there is no record of you having been born there."

"There must be some mistake," said Walter. Surely headquarters would not give him an identity that did not stand up, he reasoned in his mind.

"So who are you and what is your business in Dresden?" asked the corporal impatiently.

"I am Karl Buettner and I work in the Neisse Photography and Camera Shop."

"We will see," said the corporal. He motioned to the two troopers standing by. They took Walter's arms and strapped them to the chair. Before backing away, one of them landed his fist on Walter's jaw. His head flew back violently.

"Who are you?" asked the corporal.

"Karl Buettner."

The other trooper landed a punch on his mouth.

"Who was you accomplice?"

"No one. I have no need for an accomplice," Walter blurted out through his bleeding mouth.

He received a blow to the nose. Blood ran down his lips and dripped off his chin.

"Who are you?"

"Karl Buettner."

A blow to his ear set off a siren in his head.

"All right. Set him up on the table," ordered the corporal.

The two SS troopers lifted him roughly out of the chair and pushed him down onto the table. They pulled off his shirt and pants and fastened down his wrists with the leather straps. One assistant unlocked the cupboard and returned with a thin metal rod. After the corporal dealt several blows to his back with the rubber truncheon, the rod bearer whipped his buttocks with the metal rod. Blood continued to flow from his nose and his face lay in it on the table.

"Who are you? What did you want from the woman?"

"Karl Buettner. I wanted nothing from her."

The interrogation and beating continued intermittently for several hours. His skin and flesh became tender and raw and each blow became more painful. He was hungry and thirsty and wanted to urinate. Dried blood caked around his nose and mouth and matted his hair. The hissing sound of the rod as it whipped through the air continued.

After what seemed like an eternity, a knock on the door interrupted the interrogation. A guard brought three trays of food and coffee. The beatings stopped while the three SS men ate sausages, potatoes and green cabbage served on the trays. He remembered that he had not eaten since the previous evening, but he was no longer hungry. When his three tormenters had finished eating, they burped and lit their cigarettes. They blew the smoke in his face.

"So you are not going to cooperate," said the corporal. "Turn him over."

The two assistants released the straps and turned him face up. Blows from the truncheon and metal rods landed on his chest and stomach. They worked their way down to his testicles. Tears came to his eyes. He winced and ground his teeth. The blows were now on his shins and ankles and were a welcome relief from those on his wounded upper body.

"All right, men. Give him a drink."

They unfastened the straps and led him to the water tap. The tap was turned on and the cold water filled the shallow trough on the floor. The metal rod handler pushed Walter's head into the water and held it down.

"What is your name?" the corporal barked.

Walter sputtered and gulped mouthfuls of water. He held his breath and kicked to get free. The truncheon came down hard on his calves.

"Who was your accomplice?"

The voice now seemed to come from a distance, from a source suspended in space. It sounded remote and hollow. He could not answer. A numbing blackness filled his head and when he awoke sometime later he found himself on a hard wooden cot in a small cell. His flesh ached and he felt welts all over his body. Except for a cut from a blow on his mouth, his skin was not broken. His torturers were obviously experts at their job. A single electric bulb hung from the ceiling, casting a cold white light around the room. Since there were no windows, he had no way of knowing whether it was night or day. His flesh felt cold and he gathered the single worn blanket around him, which was all that covered the small cot.

A pitted porcelain pitcher with water stood beside the toilet bowl. He put it to his mouth and sipped some of the warm stale water and spit it out together with the dark clots of blood from his mouth. He then took a few long draughts and replaced the pitcher carefully for further use. He felt the urge for solid food as he walked around the cell to get the stiffness out of his body, then laid down on half of the blood-stained blanket. He covered himself up with the other half and dozed off. He was awakened by the door opening. The two junior SS adjutants entered.

"All right, terrorist pig," one of them shouted. "The captain wants to see you right now."

His companion lifted Walter up by the hair and dragged him toward the door. He stumbled into the hallway and straightened out his aching body.

"Here, put on your pants," roared one of the assistants, throwing Walter's shirt and pants into his face. "Do you think the captain wants to see your miserable body?" They pushed and dragged him through the hall and up the stairs.

The SS captain sat behind his desk with only a file folder before him. He motioned to the two adjutants to seat Walter in the chair at the front of his desk.

"I am sorry that my men have had to treat you so harshly, but you are a prisoner and you must cooperate," said the captain. "You must be hungry so I have arranged for some food for you."

He rang a bell. The door to an adjoining room opened and a young recruit pushed in a cart with a tray of food and drink on it. Upon the captain's signal, he positioned it in front of another chair and the two SS men led Walter to the seat.

"Eat," said the captain.

His mouth was swollen tight and his teeth ached, but Walter eagerly devoured small pieces of the sausages, mashed potatoes and boiled carrots. The hot tea warmed his stomach and he felt rejuvenated. The captain leafed through the file while Walter ate, observing his indulgence from time to time.

"There, is that not better than putting up all that mindless resistance?" he said in a kinder tone when Walter had finished eating. "Would you not rather be treated with respect, than trying to be a hero in order to protect someone? You know that they would never do that for you. The fact that they allowed you to be taken is an example of their disregard for you. By tonight you could be a free man, to do as you please, if you just answer our questions."

"I am not protecting anyone," said Walter.

"Just tell us who met the girl and you are a free man," said the captain.

"I was nowhere near when it happened. How am I to know?" asked Walter.

The captain closed the file and put on his cap. He glared at Walter, who glared back defiantly.

"Take him away," he shouted.

In the hallway, the two assistants punched him in the face as he stumbled from side to side between them. Blood was pouring from his nose and mouth when they returned him to the narrow room with the billiard-sized table and the strapped chair. They pushed him onto the table and after strapping him down, repeated the beating of the previous day. After what felt like several hours, he was thrown head first into the water. He was too weak and sore to kick or even move his limbs. He felt no more pain and his mind became fuzzy, and then went blank.

When Walter awoke he lay shivering on the thin blanket covering the cot in his cell. He peered through his swollen eyelids at the ceiling. Tears came into his eyes and blurred his vision. Red and blue welts crisscrossed his body and his testicles had swollen to the size of lemons. He pulled the skimpy blanket over his shoulders and placed his bare feet on the cold concrete floor. He walked around slowly, each agonizing step filling him with excruciating pain. After several torturous steps around his small cell, his body began to feel looser and he went to the pitcher and washed out his mouth.

Walter waited for his tormenters to return. This time they did not return as soon as they had on the previous day and when they did, they took him directly to the narrow room. After several blows to his head, he was strapped to the table and received another beating. This was followed by a trip to the trough and another period of unconsciousness.

He awoke as before, shivering, and his face and hair covered with dry, caked blood. His fingers were swollen and he could barely see out of his swollen eyelids. Slowly he lifted one and then the other foot over the side of the cot, and pushed up the rest of his body. This time he could not straighten himself out and he crouched over as walked slowly around the cell.

How much longer would they continue to torture him, he wondered. And why was not anyone coming to help? But then, how could they? Even if they knew where he was, the building was probably well guarded. But there was one way out of this intolerable predicament. He remembered the pill sewn into a seam of his pants and he searched for it frantically. He found that the seam had been cut and he realized that his captors had cheated him out of this means of escape.

A careful check of the door and walls revealed no possible way out of the cell. He pushed the old wooden chair under the ventilator and stretched his aching body up to where he could reach it. It was bolted on with four hexagonal nuts which would require a special wrench to dislodge. He stepped down off the chair and sat on the cot. He realized that at the moment there was no way to escape the torture except to tell what he knew. But he would not do that, at least not yet. His young body was resilient and he could take a few more beatings. Perhaps, something would happen meanwhile. He covered his aching shoulders with the flimsy blanket and fell into a fitful sleep.

~~~

The door flew open and two SS officers entered. He awoke abruptly and watched the two tormenters approach him. One of them put his face close to Walter's and spit in his eye.

"Verfluchte Polen," he screamed. "Dirty Poles. They try to stand up to our superior intelligence. And look who they send to murder our innocent Aryan women – a stupid Polish pig who says he knows nothing about it."

He landed a fist to the side of Walter's head that sent him reeling to the floor. His partner picked up the limp body and held him while the first tormenter kicked Walter in the testicles. They carried his wilted body between them through the hall and up the stairs to the captain's office.

The captain had a complacent look on his face. He waved the two adjutants away after they had deposited Walter's limp body on the chair in front of his desk.

"Well, well, well," he said smugly, "you are even better than we imagined. That fellow Sliworski must think that we are pretty stupid to send someone as wet behind the ears as you are to match wits with us. So you are their stooge? Those Verfluchte Polen will stop at nothing. Imagine them sending someone like you – an amateur – to obtain secrets on our unique and superior Enigma machine. If they knew their business they would have discovered that the most important parts for it are not even made here, but in another town along the Silesian border.

"I can tell you that now because soon you will have no head to remember it. You know Buettner, or whatever your name is, if you had talked, I would probably be dismissing you right now. Instead, you allowed your accomplice, that so-called manager of the camera store to escape to Czechoslovakia. So now I will be sending you to Berlin to stand trial in the People's Court where you will be sentenced to pay for your crimes at Ploetzensee. What have you got to say now?"

Walter remained silent. He recalled the posters on billboards in Stettin declaring that the names listed on them had been decapitated at Ploetzensee after trial in People's Court. He wondered under which alias his name would appear.

"Take him away and clean him up. I want him to be healed and on the train in one week from tonight." He turned to Walter and sneered. "Too bad that you Poles do not learn your lesson and accept that you are an inferior race."

The two SS men led him to the door. "Take it easy on him. We want the world to know that we treat our prisoners with more respect than they deserve."

They snapped to attention and said "Heil Hitler," then led their prisoner to a room on the second floor of the building.

"Take it easy on the poor fellow. We want his head to be all nice and healed up for when they chop it off," they joked as they entered the room. A small bed with a mattress and pillow stood in one corner and a table and chair in another. In a cubicle, a clean washroom with a toilet and basin presented a welcome sight. There were no windows and the bulb in the ceiling flooded every corner of the room with its sterile white light.

Shortly after the SS men left, an orderly came in and took him to a shower in an adjoining room, after which he rubbed ointment on the welts which covered Walter's tender torso. He began to feel like a human again. Food was delivered three times a day and he soon began to recover his strength.

Recalling the numerous lectures that they had received during training on the art of escape, Walter made a mental list of the alternatives that may present themselves. On the odd occasion he dared to envisage what awaited him if he did not manage to escape. With his captors now almost completely aware of his true identity, he could probably not count on help from the organization, so he was on his own. He checked the room. It was escape proof. If he had any chance at all of escape, it would have to be while awaiting transfer from one location to another, or on the train.

With regular meals, showers and a good bed, his body healed quickly. By the sixth day there were few visible bruises, and except for the cut in his lip, his face was almost back to normal. He was becoming excited about the prospect of freedom and when doubts about his planned escape entered his mind he dismissed any thoughts of execution by beheading. A new suit of clothes, shirt, socks and shoes were delivered to the room on the seventh day. It seemed ironic that a person on his way to the guillotine should be so properly attired. He knew that on that evening he would be on the train to Berlin.

Early in the afternoon the SS corporal came in and announced that he would be accompanying the prisoner. The train would leave at eight that evening and he would be picked up at seven. The corporal spoke in a respectful manner, without any signs of the cruel animosity that he had exhibited toward Walter in their earlier encounters. Was it because they knew that he would no longer be a threat once he was deposited in the Ploetzensee prison, Walter wondered.

At six, the guard brought a tray of hot food and some wine. This was followed by cakes and coffee. Compared to his earlier treatment in their hands, he now felt like a celebrity. Was this the same as the custom of serving the condemned person a good last meal before execution, or were they buttering him up in the hope of obtaining valuable information from him, he wondered. He was all ready when the corporal arrived at seven, resplendent in his black uniform, complete with a skull badge on his cap. The corporal announced that his colleague will be meeting them at the station so that he would not be lonely on his last train trip. Walter had no delusions about the purpose of the trip and did not respond.

A soft, mild evening greeted Walter as he stepped out of the building where he had been a prisoner for over a week. The sounds of voices and the roar of traffic lifted his spirits and he smiled at the driver as he and the corporal entered the car. But a sense of uneasiness and sadness came over him when he realized that he was no longer a part of all this activity, but rather a distant observer. He watched sadly out of the car window as the streets, which had by now become familiar to him, sped by.

The fast train to Berlin stood motionless at the station platform, hissing defiantly, as Walter and his two uniformed companions clamored aboard with the other departing passengers. Inside the coach, the two escorts sat together facing Walter near the front of the car. On his way into the coach, Walter made quick mental notes of the location of the train's layout – the entrances, platforms, smoking room, washroom and emergency tool compartments. They had no sooner seated themselves when the scream of the whistle and the grinding sound of turning wheels announced the train's departure, on time. Germany's trains always ran on time.

As the train started to move, a tall, lanky man with a reddish brown moustache and wire-rimmed spectacles entered the coach. He wore a business suit and a felt hat and carried a small overnight case which he hoisted slowly into the overhead rack behind Walter's seat, while surveying the coach and its passengers. He hesitated for a moment and caught Walter's eye, then winked, smiled and sat down. Walter thought he recognized the man's face from somewhere and his actions were unmistakably those of someone he knew. The realization hit him like a bolt of lightning. It was Simpson! That son-of-a-gun had somehow learned about Walter's transfer to Berlin and came aboard disguised as a traveling salesman. His situation felt less ominous now, but spells of hot and cold sweat followed each other throughout his body as he contemplated what it might be that Simpson expected of him.

~~~

Flecks of light streaked by the windows as the train glided past the lampposts and lighted windows of the city. The passengers settled down in their seats to while away the time that it would take to get to their destinations. The faces of the two escorts remained stony and silent as they sat staring at nothing in particular. A peculiar silence followed as the train thundered out from the confines of the city and roared into the black night.

His captors had not returned his watch and he wondered what time it was and how long they had been traveling. It seemed like perhaps an hour, but was probably less because time seemed to move slowly when one had nothing to do except worry. Suddenly he saw a movement in the seat in front of him. Part of Simpson's head appeared above the back of the seat and when he caught Walter's eye he stepped out into the aisle. With a sight nod of his head he invited Walter to follow him to the back of the coach.

He knew that his two escorts would not let him go to the back of the coach alone and Simpson probably did also. When he caught the corporal's eye, Walter shifted about nervously, crossing his legs first one way and then another. He held his forearm across his abdomen and leaned forward.

"I have to go to the toilet," he said.

"Shut up and behave yourself!" ordered the corporal, trying to avoid attracting attention.

"I have a real bad pain in my gut. I cannot hold it any longer," pleaded Walter.

"Shut up, I say."

Walter winced and then squirmed in excruciating pain.

"I don't think I can hold it," he whispered.

"Ah, let the poor bastard go before he shits his pants and stinks up the place," said the adjutant.

"Well, fine. We will both go with him. You stay a short distance behind." The corporal stood up and motioned to Walter to follow. "Stand up and let's go. These goddamned Poles cannot even discipline their guts. They eat like pigs and shit like pigeons," the corporal grumbled as he turned toward the back of the coach with Walter and the adjutant following.

With his forearm on his stomach and shoulders slightly hunched over, Walter walked along the narrow passageway following the corporal. The adjutant was several steps behind. The door of the toilet was locked and when the corporal rattled it, the slurred voice of a drunk man came from inside. The corporal rattled the door again.

"Come out you drunken pig and let other people use the facility," he roared.

"All right, all right. Don't get excited," croaked Simpson.

"I will give you fifteen seconds," roared the corporal as he pounded on the door. Suddenly the door opened to the inside and the corporal was pulled in. There were some shuffling sounds inside the washroom then the door flew open. As the corporal fell forward a lightning swift blow to the head knocked him out and he lay face down on the floor of the washroom. Before the adjutant realized what had happened, Walter pushed him over his colleague and Simpson delivered a heavy blow to his head with a short metal rod. It landed with a dull, sickening thud.

"Quick." ordered Simpson in a hushed voice, "Let's get them out of here before somebody shows up."

With the washroom situated near the rear of the coach and the outer door only a few steps away, Simpson and Walter quickly dragged the two bodies to the platform and heaved them over the railing. They peeked through the back door to ensure that no one had become aware of the incident. The passengers were all in their seats.

"Get in the washroom and lock the door. Stay there until the train stops," said Simpson. "When it does, I will be waiting for you. We will get off at the station and head back." He straightened out his tie and returned to his seat.

Walter sat on top of the toilet cover with his head in his hands. The whole incident had taken less than five minutes. His brain reeled as his body swung from side to side with the motion of the train. Just to think that his life had probably been saved by the same person whom he had called a blood-thirsty bastard only several days ago was too much for him. The grinding sound of steel on steel announced that the brakes were being applied gradually and that soon the train would be at the station in the next town. Simpson had timed the operation to the minute.

~~~

Simpson retrieved his overnight case and casually descended from the train, then stepped off onto the platform. Walter followed. A car stood in front of the station in the small town when they emerged from the depot. The driver started the engine as soon as they entered.

"Everything is good and on schedule," announced Simpson in German as the car turned into the street and then headed out into open country toward Dresden. Walter sat quietly in the back seat.

"Well, that was a close one, old chap, was it not?" said Simpson as they entered the main road.

"You know," said Walter, "I was planning to pull off a similar stunt even before I saw you, except that I was going to make a run for it and jump off the train while it was in motion."

"It is a good thing that you did not have to do that, otherwise you would be the one all crumpled up in the ditch instead of your two friends."

"Friends, hell. Those two thugs damned near killed me several times. And they couldn't wait to see my head lopped off when we got to Berlin," said Walter. "That is why it was such a relief to see you come in wearing that crazy moustache and those silly glasses. But how did you know that I would be on that train?"

"Know? Hell, I did not know anything. I just showed up for every train to Berlin this week, knowing that sooner or later they would be taking you there. When I saw you arrive tonight, I just bought a ticket and followed you in. But not before I arranged for a friendly taxi to take us back to the border."

"And how do we get across when we get there?" asked Walter.

"Very simple. In this bag I have two sets of peasant's clothing and two sets of identification papers. Tonight we get off at a farm house on the border and tomorrow after we change, we walk across, complete with two day's growth of whiskers."

"And after that?"

"Then it is back to London," said Simpson. "Things are a bit too hot for you here now."

"I believe that," sighed Walter, "especially now that they have found out who I am."

"Did you tell them who you are?"

"Hell, no. But they told me that they know that I am a spy working for Sliworski."

"If you did not tell them, they will never know for sure. It is all a part of their bluff," said Simpson.

CHAPTER 43

Nobody spoke about the faces that were missing among the trainees when classes resumed in October. Outside of the classrooms, muted discussions were heard among the trainees about the indifference with which the information they had provided was being met in Great Britain and among the nations of Europe and in America.

In only four years Adolf Hitler had crumpled the Treaty of Versailles, rebuilt Germany's army and air force, marched across the Hohenzollern Bridge into the Rhineland, decimated his political foes, dismembered the Catholic Church and arranged for the murder of Austria's chancellor. Those who bothered to read the *Mein Kampf* wondered if Hitler was already well on his way to making Germany "the Lord of the earth." But in spite of all these developments, skepticism appeared to greet the information being acquired at great risk about the massive changes taking place in that country. In the corridors of power only Winston Churchill warned that "Germany was a country fertile in military surprises." Those who had been there and seen for themselves knew what these surprises were and that the fuse was lit and burning fast, but they were nearly alone.

Inside the classrooms the focus of the training was changing in anticipation of the armed aggression which they knew would soon erupt in Europe. Small arms and bayonet practice, radio communication, infiltration, disguise and survival were high on the curriculum. But this year a new subject – sabotage – would receive much more attention and respect.

Politics in Great Britain and Europe were far from normal. On the dreary evening of January 20, 1936 the venerable old monarch, King George V of Great Britain was dead. He was one of the few in royalty who warned that "without a strong and healthy body-politic in the area which lies between Germany and Russia there can be no peace or security in Europe." While the world mourned, he was succeeded by his independent-minded son Edward, whose political mind was a mystery.

The next day classes were dismissed and Walter and Victor walked through the ghostly fog back to the apartment. The world had somehow lost some of its neatness and order and even nature seemed to be conspiring to blot out the way ahead.

"What do you think of all this?" asked Victor as he collapsed into the cushioned arm chair in the apartment.

Walter stared at the ceiling in deep thought. He spoke slowly and quietly. "Back home I would often watch colonies of ants at work in and around their ant hills. They had no concern about what was going on in other ant hills, or even outside of the immediate area of their own ant hills, except to use it as a source of food and building materials for the colony. Whenever anyone stepped on the ant hill or kicked it, they panicked for a moment and then almost immediately began to rebuild it. Next day you could hardly tell than anything had happened to that ant hill. I can't help but notice the similarity between those ant hills and what is happening in all these countries of Europe who share the continent with each other. They are too concerned about their own little ant hill to worry about what is going on in the next ant hill."

"Say, that is quite an interesting similarity," said Victor. He paused for a moment to contemplate the analogy. "But did you ever notice what happens to a strange ant, or any other insect, when it ventures inside the vicinity of the ant hill?" he asked.

"Yes. It is immediately attacked by the warrior ants and dragged inside the ant hill."

"And you never see it again?" asked Victor.

"Never," answered Walter. "Now do you see how we fit into that scene?"

Victor observed Walter with a puzzled look and then turned on the radio. They recognized the voice of the late king.

"The path indicated by political wisdom and political necessities is clear. We have to tread this path without hesitation; we have to move forward to create a new world." After a moment of silence the solemn voice of the radio announcer said," Ladies and gentlemen, we have brought you excerpts from some of the speeches made by out late and beloved monarch, King George V."

After several more weeks of intensive training in combat theory, the trainees were transferred to a secluded camp in the highlands of Scotland for physical conditioning. Walter and Victor were again teamed up for the demanding twenty mile cross country marches and for the more interesting exercises in the use of explosives for sabotaging railways, ships, industrial machinery and buildings. The foggy dampness of the rugged Scottish wilderness provided the seclusion needed for the private practice of these antics and the two young men looked forward with anticipation to the day when their training could be put to practical use.

By the middle of April they were back in England for more training in the art of avoiding capture, planning escape, creating and using false documents, using information drops, setting up and using radio sets and even becoming familiar with German eating habits and dress codes. Near the end of May, Simpson announced their new assignments. Victor would go to the Czechoslovakian border region and Walter to the coastal area of Pomerania.

"You will have two main tasks," Simpson explained to Walter. "One will be to observe the shipping along the coast and determine what are their cargos and destination. The other will be to work with our Polish colleagues out of the port of Gdynia in the distribution and concealment of arms caches and explosives along the coastal area."

"Victor, you will pick up where Walter left off last fall," added Simpson. "It would not be safe to send Walter back there now that they know him."

"Stay away from those sweet young Dresden girls if you value your head," warned Walter.

"Now is that not an interesting switch in attitude on the part of a certain young chap whose emotional level on that same subject reached such a high pitch that my own life and limb were placed in jeopardy," chided Simpson.

"Your cool and efficient approach to the problem helped me to see the error of my ways, especially after you persuaded me in no uncertain terms," laughed Walter, recalling Simpson's threat to pull the trigger if he did not go along with the proposed plan.

"It may seem funny now, but at that time it was very serious business. I am sorry that I had to threaten you," explained Simpson. "Let us look upon that as valuable experience for both of us and a demonstration of how experience is so valuable in this business. And speaking of experience, I do not want you two getting reckless with any of the explosives with which you will be entrusted. I hear that you two clowns damned near blew up all of Scotland during your training."

They looked at each other and grinned sheepishly. "That was the most fun that we have had since we've come over here," explained Victor.

"Good. When things get really hot over there, I will know where to get a couple of happy demolition experts," promised Simpson.

~~~

Once more the *Barrow's* bow pointed to the east and headed across the channel into the North Sea and up the Kiel Canal. A new skipper guided the craft confidently along the same route that Duke had taken many times before with his perpetual smile visible through the windows surrounding the wheel house. Simpson called the new captain Laird, but Walter knew that, as in the case of Duke, the skipper's real identity was a mystery which no one cared to reveal.

The water sparkled with shades of red and amber in the persistent May sun, and when Walter was not below deck being briefed by Simpson, he sat on the deck absorbing its soothing rays. The craft plied its way through the glassy sea, from time to time passing close to the tips of peninsulas where the land and trees stood like purple cliffs at the edge of the endless water. This was the same body of land from which on three occasions he had fled in terror. Now it stood there placid and almost inviting.

Simpson strolled leisurely onto the deck and stopped beside Walter. "I see that you are surveying your target area," he observed.

"I was really thinking more about how peaceful it looks from here," admitted Walter.

"That is because, from a distance, one gets a different perspective. No doubt, if a person was able to look upon the earth from the moon, it would be the most peaceful looking object that one has ever seen. But once you set foot on it, all that changes and it may not be as friendly as you expected."

"Oh, I don't know about that," said Walter. "It is very peaceful where I come from."

"That is because no one covets the place as yet. But things can change very quickly. I imagine that way back in history, this place was peaceful, too."

"That must have been before man came around," said Walter.

"You do have a point," conceded Simpson.

The port in Gdynia was bustling with fishing boats and freighters moving in and out of the harbor. Laird guided the Barrow to the dock where the smaller fishing vessels were tied up and Simpson and Walter disembarked. They walked slowly along the old wooden wharf. A rustic boat measuring about twenty meters bobbed lazily amid a slew of other fishing vessels. Its wooden hull was scoured by the years of plying the waves in the Baltic fishing grounds and its weather-beaten deck was worn and undulating. On its port side the name *Wrona* was painted in peeling black paint.

"There she is," announced Simpson. "This will be your luxury liner for the next few weeks."

They were greeted by an old fisherman called Janusz. A long gray moustache straddled his linear mouth and his head was mounted to his bony shoulders by a short slender neck. His pants were held up by a pair of worn and oily suspenders. He slowly straightened his arched back and shook Walter's hand. His hand was rough and calloused, but warm and firm.

"Do you know how to fish?" he asked Walter.

"No. I am afraid I don't."

"Then I will teach you," said the old man.

"Janusz knows every inch of the coast line," explained Simpson. "He will keep you well informed as well as occupied. He also knows almost everyone along the coast."

"These days you have to be careful about whom you trust," injected Janusz. "But when they see me in this old boat, they do not bother me. She used to belong to the provincial government in Warsaw, even before Poland became independent again," he explained proudly. "And she is sound. Will stand up in any storm better than any of those new cardboard baskets they make nowadays. Come along, let me show you below deck."

A small cabin was crowded into the bow of the ancient vessel, behind a larger area which may have once been a galley. In the stern of the boat was the cargo area and tanks for the day's catch. The smells of fish, tar and diesel fuel filled the air inside the vessel. Janusz took them back to the galley and slid one of the walls over to reveal a storage compartment.

"This is where we will carry our supplies," he said as he winked at Simpson. "I will get them loaded tonight, and then Wladimar and I can start working tomorrow morning."

"That is very good, Captain Janusz," commented Simpson. "I will brief Walter tonight aboard our boat and bring him back here tomorrow."

On a map spread out on the table in Walter's cabin, Simpson marked the target areas where the caches were to be taken. They were scattered along the coastline between the Polish corridor and Swinemunde.

"There are many Polish families along the coastal area. Captain Janusz will arrange the contacts for you and each of them will have their instructions. You will ensure that the caches are delivered and taken to the proper target area. The locals will show you their hiding places. And stay out of sight of the Gestapo, because if they really know who you are, they will not let you get away this time. But this is a relatively safe area. That is why you have been assigned here until the heat is off and they have forgotten about the event in Dresden. I will send further instructions through Captain Janusz."

The blazing June sun cut through the cool offshore breezes as Walter walked briskly along the dock, dressed in the manner of local fishermen and carrying a soiled and beaten haversack. Captain Janusz welcomed him on board the *Wrona* as an official member of the crew, his eyes beaming with excitement. He led Walter to the galley and slid the wall over to expose a stack of wooden boxes with rope handles.

"These are our charges," he beamed." Enough to blow up a small city. If only someone had given us some of this during the Great War we could have finished it a lot sooner. This time we will be prepared, thanks to Colonel Sliworski and our friend Pan Neal."

They walked through to the cabin where a bunk was made up with a flannel sheet, a white pillow and a gray woolen blanket.

"This will be yours," said the captain. "I will sleep in the galley or on the bridge. Do you know how to cook? I will show you how to cook fish like you never tasted before. We will get going very soon. Today we will try out our wings. Tomorrow we will soar like a hawk and dive down on our target. Let us go to the bridge and see if we can get this old tub started."

The engine chugged away contentedly in the bowels of the boat as Captain Junusz guided her proudly out of the harbor and out into the Gulf of Danzig. By mid morning the tip of a narrow peninsula came into view. Janusz swung the boat to the left and followed the coastline to the west. Around eleven o'clock he disengaged the propeller shaft and came out on the deck.

"Let us catch some dinner," he called to Walter. "Here is you first lesson in fishing. I will show you how to cast a net."

He unfolded the end of the net and flung it over the side of the boat in one coordinated movement of his arms and body.

"Tomorrow you will show me how well you can do it. Now I will start the boat moving again while you see that the rest of the net is unfolded and drops into the water evenly. If it gets too full, wave your arms and I will stop the boat," he chuckled.

The *Wrona* chugged along slowly, pulling the net behind it, the wooden floats marking the area covered by the net. They bobbed up and down with the waves and several disappeared into the water. Janusz pointed from the bridge and laughed. When the sun reached the noon-day point in the sky, he steered the boat into a sheltered cove and dropped anchor. Together they pulled the net in and removed the vaulting fish from the entangled net. Janusz picked out two of the smaller fish with silvery scales and pointed noses and they carried the others to the holding tanks below deck.

"I will cook these two for us. They are the best," said Janusz. "You like fish, Wladimar? I will teach you how to make fish taste like smoked ham, only better."

He put the fish on a cutting board and, holding the tail with his left hand, he removed the scales with several swipes of his knife. With one blow each, he whacked the heads ad tails off the fish and then removed the offal and threw it overboard. He dropped a beaten up metal pail over the side of the boat and brought up some water with which he washed the fish. Then he motioned to Walter to follow him into the galley where he lit an old oil stove.

"Pork lard from smoked pork. That is the secret," he confided to Walter as he placed the fish in a smoke stained pan. "My wife likes to boil fish, but I say to her, 'Why throw out all that flavor with the water?' This way you keep all the good taste in the fish and add a bit more from the fat."

The tantalizing aroma of the frying fish displaced the smells of tar and diesel fuel and Walter's mouth watered in anticipation of savoring the crumbly white flesh of the fresh catch. In another pot, Janusz boiled four potatoes. He took a loaf of bread out of a wooden box and sliced half of it into thick slices. From another box he brought out two enameled metal plates, two cups and knives, forks and spoons. He placed one whole fish and two boiled potatoes on each plate and took them to the old wooden table.

"Eat, Wladimar, and tell me if you have ever tasted better."

"No, Janusz. I have never tasted better fish," confessed Walter.

"You are a good boy, Wladimar," said Janusz proudly, "and it is good to have a capable helper like you. I think we will do some good business along the coast tomorrow. This afternoon I will teach you how to pilot the *Wrona*."

"I would be honored to do that," said Walter, "but tell me, why do you call your boat a crow? Back home we had crows all over the place and they never seemed to be too fond of water."

"True, Wladimar, but if you watch a crow carefully you would see that they are intelligent, hardy, observant, responsible, sneaky, not very beautiful and practically indestructible. How many times have you seen a dead crow? People say that they live as long as fifty years. That is how long I want my *Wrona* to live."

Janusz shaded his eyes with his hand and gazed at the descending sun. An orange hue covered the fiery ball, announcing the approaching end of the day and another nice day on the morrow. They pulled in the net and headed for a small port near the Polish-German border. Other fishing vessels in the area had already docked when they arrived and the buyers were on the dock, examining the day's catch and haggling over the prices. Janusz sold his catch and walked into the village to buy some fresh bread while Walter went below to boil potatoes, fry sausages and make the tea. His first day as a fisherman had been a pleasant one and that night he slept soundly in his new bed as the boat rocked gently on the waves.

~~~

The aging, slow-moving fishing vessel plodded along the coast, its nets plucking up the dissenting fish from their rich feeding grounds and the captain ferrying them to the small fishing ports along the way. Janusz did not talk much during the day. While Walter guided the boat along the edges of the reefs and out into the water, the captain sat on an old wooden chair and gazed out across the sea. From time to time he would get up and check the floaters to see if the net was still in position. In the evenings before retiring he talked about his youth, the regiment in which he had served during the Great War and his love for Poland.

For much of his life Janusz had lived as a citizen of an occupied country. "A man must have a country to live for," he would say. "But a man must also have a cause and in those days we did. Today, the young people have already forgotten about the struggles that were needed to hold our country together, even though it was divided. That is why the country is straining under the yoke of a floundering government and a fat bureaucracy. That is why we are not preparing for the bad times that are coming. One day soon we will pay for it and receive yet another lesson on how important it is to always put the good of the country before the interests of one's self. One of these days the Lord might say, 'All right Poland. You have had your chances, many of them, and you have not learned from them. This is a national sin and the price of sin is death.' Only then shall we realize that we have exchanged our pride and love of freedom for indifference and false security, and Poland will join all the other great kingdoms that once were but no longer are."

His voice trailed and his eyes stared blankly into the distance. The silence was overpowering. Walter appeared restless as he crossed his legs and coughed.

"Maybe things are not so bad," he said, trying to console the old man. "You still have men like Sliworski and Bashinski who are concerned about the future of Poland. And then there are Poland's friends – Britain and America. They will surely send help when you need it."

"Poor old Bashinski," sighed Janusz. "He means well, but he still thinks that the way to defend the country is with horses and lancers. You and I know that the next war will be fought with steel vehicles, air planes, cannons, bombs and ships. Sliworski knows that, but the other generals do not know or do not want to believe it. As for the British and Americans, they will only come to help us when it is to their benefit to do so. And I would not blame them. Why should they sacrifice their own young men because we are too stupid to defend ourselves? But we must have hope. And anyway, there are you and I and many others like us who have a job to do. And we shall begin tomorrow."

He sprang to his feet, his eyes blazing with enthusiasm. "Tomorrow we make our first delivery north of Stolpe for use when our garrisons at Gdynia and Westerlund are threatened. We will be ready for them this time even if we have to fight with sickles and pitch forks."

Walter watched the old captain with some amusement. He had never seen him so impassioned before and he wondered what prompted it. It reminded him about something that Simpson had said about the Poles.

"Neal once told me that the reason that the Polish people have always survived is because of their will to fight. He said that when the last bullet is spent and the men are all killed, their women will continue to fight by clawing the enemy's eyes out with their finger nails."

"Your friend Neal has us figured out well," he said approvingly. "And he should know because he fought with us for a while the last time."

Janusz climbed up on a stool and removed a loose board from the ceiling of the galley, then reached in and brought out a plain envelope. They sat down and the captain took a map out of the envelope and spread it on the table. He studied it for several moments.

"Ah, yes," he said, pointing at a spot on the map. "This is where we are now and this is where we will be tomorrow, the Lord willing." His finger followed the coast line to a small cove. "Right here, Pan Bremner will meet us and pick up the first shipment. You will go back with him about three kilometers inland to make sure that the shipment reaches its destination and is placed in storage. I will return here for you near sundown and we will head out and drop anchor before it gets dark. Now let us get some sleep."

~~~

The *Wrona* chugged contentedly as she followed the coastline westward, one end of the fish net secured to the stern of the boat. On the eastern horizon the sun climbed higher into the clear sky as it moved inland from where it rose out of the sea. Janusz looked at the sun and shook his head in the affirmative.

"Yes. It will be a good day for haying, Wladimar," he said.

Walter shrugged his shoulders. Janusz observed his confusion and let out a hearty laugh. "You will see what I mean later," he shouted over the noise of the boat's engine.

Near high noon they reached the cove. The small bay was sheltered and the water was still. A small sandy beach ran into the lowland, the edges of which were covered with tall grass. Farther out, some of the grass had been cut and piled into small haycocks. Beyond the meadow, the forest rose like a wall of dark cliffs. As they drew closer they noticed a wagon, drawn by two horses, standing beside a small hay stack.

Captain Janusz steered the boat closer to shore and shut off the engine. Walter dropped the anchor and the old vessel bobbed gently in the almost still water. They stepped out on deck and Janusz waved to the man standing beside the wagon. The man waved back three times.

"We can put the boat down and load it," said Janusz.

The old wooden life boat was let down over the side with ropes and tied up to the *Wrona*. They went down below deck and Janusz slid open the wooden panel, exposing the caches.

"We will give old Bremner three on this trip," he said. "We do not want to sink the lifeboat."

They carried the heavy wooden boxes up to the deck and Janusz eased them down to Walter in the life boat. The heavily loaded craft was slowly rowed to shore. On shore, the boxes were removed from the boat, then carried into the meadow and placed on the wagon. Bremner covered them quickly with several forkfuls of hay. The whole operation took only several minutes. Bremner stuck his fork into the ground and he and Janusz laughed.

"This is Wladimar," said Janusz. "He is my first mate, deck hand and cook." Bremner's calloused hand got a firm lock on Walter's hand. "Welcome to the land of your ancestors," he said in Polish. "Well, let us have something to eat,"

Bremner picked up a white cloth bag from beside the haystack and brought out a loaf of brown bread, some sausages, ham slices, cheese, a bottle of schnapps and a shot glass. He filled the glass and passed it to Janusz. The old man downed it in one gulp and wiped his mouth with the end of his shirt sleeve. He passed the bottle and glass to Walter who poured out half a glass and downed it slowly. They watched him with amusement.

"His gullet is not used to it yet. He is too young. Ours is tough as leather," said Janusz. He drank to their health and the success of their preparatory project.

Bremner filled his glass again and brought it to his lips. "To peace and brotherhood," he toasted and threw his head back to swallow the drink.

The farmer removed the bits from the horses' mouths and dropped an armful of hay before them, and the three men sat down on the shady side of the hay stack to eat. They talked about the fine haying weather and the good fishing and how the weather was changing for the best. When they had finished eating, Bremner put the bottle and leftovers into the bag and carried it to the wagon. He forked several smaller haycocks into the hayrack and hitched the horses to the wagon.

"Wladimar is going with you," said Janusz. "I will just fish around this bay until he returns."

"I will see that he gets back on time," promised Bremner.

The wagon creaked and groaned under the weight of the hay and the wooden boxes as it rolled across the hard-packed trail. Bremner and Walter sat at the front of the bouncing hayrack.

"You have probably never had a ride like this before," said the farmer.

"Oh yes, I have. Many times," said Walter. "Back home on the farm it was my job to haul the hay out of the meadows to the barn."

"So you did some work around the farm," said Bremner casting approving glances at Walter. "Janusz did not tell me that. I thought you might be one of those city fellows who have never had the pleasure of riding on a deep cushion of hay."

"I am happy to have the opportunity to enjoy it again. It has been quite a while since the last time I did it. Did Captain Janusz tell you where I come from?" asked Walter.

"Yes. He told me that this summer he would have an American of Polish descent with him on his trip," said Bremner.

"Canadian," corrected Walter.

"It is the same thing to us," said Bremner. "You all speak the same language and dress the same. It is only in Europe where everyone is different. That is the curse of God on Babylon, when he said he would cause each tribe to speak a different language so that they could not communicate with each other. In Europe that gives us an excuse to go on killing each other to prove that one of us is better than the other."

"That is too bad," said Walter. "This is such a beautiful place otherwise."

"Yes," said Bremner. "God had blessed us with everything except tolerance and love for each other."

It was still early afternoon they arrived at the gate of the farmyard. A squat stone cottage faced the road and, behind it, a wooden barn and other outbuildings backed onto a grove of evergreen and deciduous trees. The farmer maneuvered the hayrack close to the barn and they pitched the hay into the loft. The exposed boxes were hauled to the front of a small stone building and placed beside the door.

"This is my root cellar," explained Bremner. He drove the wagon near the barn and unhitched the horses. Inside the barn another team of horses stood in their stall.

"We will drive these two back," explained Bremner. "Give the others a chance to rest."

They walked back across the yard to the root cellar and carried the boxes down into a dark corner of the small underground bunker.

"This is where they will stay until needed," said Bremner as they made their way up the stairs and out into the bright sunlight.

Bremner led the second team of horses out of the barn and took them to the water trough. While the horses drank, he pumped water into a tin cup and gave it to Walter, and then refilled it for himself. The horses were hitched to the wagon and they headed back to the cove. In the west the blazing sun was touching the tops of the trees when they arrived at the bay. The *Wrona* was anchored at almost the same spot where they had left it and Janusz was on the deck waving at the arrivals. He stepped into the small boat and rowed to shore. Walter loaded another small stack of hay into the hayrack while Bremner and Janusz toasted each other with the remainder of the schnapps. They shook hands with Bremner and returned to the *Wrona* as the farmer drove his wagon out of the meadow. The boat headed for the nearest port where Janusz sold his day's catch.

~~~

That day's exercise was repeated many times during the summer and early fall. The participants were not always farmers. Sometimes they were fishermen, sometimes merchants, but they were all dedicated to laying up a store of ammunition and explosives between the Polish Corridor and Kohlberg and Westerlund for that fateful day which they all believed was coming. This was the most tender spot of Poland's anatomy, they would explain. So they had to be ready.

The space between the sliding panel and the hull was mysteriously filled with more boxes every time they docked the boat in Gdynia between fishing trips. Walter was charged with the responsibility of seeing the boxes to their destination and providing Janusz with a log of the deliveries and drawings of the location of each container. This would make it easier to find them during an emergency, explained the captain. During these relatively relaxed weeks, Walter and Janusz gained much respect for each other. Because they worked so well as a team, the captain's fishing business did not suffer, and even though Janusz did not mention it, his countenance revealed it.

"Why are they doing this?" asked Walter one evening.

"Who?" asked Janusz innocently. "You mean Pan Bremner and all those others? Well, they each have their reasons. Bremner is angry because they Germanized his name four generations ago. The others have relatives in Poland or are tired of Germany's belligerence robbing them of their sons. But most of all, they have not forgotten their roots and that this territory once belonged to Poland."

"One thing that I can say about Poland is that it certainly never loses the loyalty of its people, even though it may lose everything else from time to time," observed Walter.

"How about you, Wladimar?" asked the old man. "Have you ever asked yourself why you are here doing this?"

Walter was taken aback. "Why yes, of course," he answered. "I needed a job and ended up in England doing this."

"But is that really why you are here?" said Janusz. "There are other jobs. Why did you choose this one?"

Walter thought for a moment. "I suppose that I was really driven by a desire to avenge my parents' deaths," he confessed.

"And what was it that killed your parents, Wladimar?" asked Janusz. "Was it not also the age-old hostility between Poland and Germany?"

"No one knows that for sure," answered Walter, "except my grandmother who has never forgotten it. There is no doubt in her mind."

"Yes. I hear that she loved her country very much until the day she left," said Janusz.

"And still does," said Walter. "But how do you know so much about my family?"

Janusz paused and gazed at the floor as if contemplating an answer. "Because I knew them once," he answered. "In fact I was on the boat when your parents were taken down the Vistula and out to Bornholm Island. On the day that they escaped, I was the deckhand and cook and some other things on this very boat that we are on now."

"This boat?" asked Walter incredulously.

"Yes. But she was much younger then and her name was the *Mazovia*." A broad smile covered Janusz's face.

"Why did you not tell me about this sooner?" asked Walter.

"I thought that we should not talk about these things until after our work was finished. I did not know how it might affect you," explained Janusz. "I know that in your work there is little room for sentiment and things of the heart, but now that we are finished, it should not matter." He observed Walter's reaction and seemed relieved. "I have been wanting to tell you the story since I first met you. You should have seen your father coming out of that compartment behind the panel where he and Litvak were hiding while the harbor police checked the boat at Danzig. It was the most joyous scene that I had ever seen. To this day I am proud of having been a part of it, even though it turned out to be such a tragedy for your parents in the end. After we drop anchor tonight I will show you where everything took place that fateful day."

Walter left the bridge and walked slowly and silently below deck. He entered the galley and sat down at the table imagining the scene that must have taken place at that very spot almost thirty years ago when the *Mazovia* headed into the Baltic.

~~~

The *Barrow* was tied up at the dock in Gdynia when Janusz maneuvered the *Wrona* into its berth, two days after their return schedule began. The clean white lines of the boat stood out starkly against the weathered hulks of the fishing vessels on either side. Janusz and Walter tied the *Wrona* to the moorings and followed the wooden pier toward the *Barrow*. Simpson was standing on the deck and welcomed them back enthusiastically. His sun-tanned face was shaded by the peak of a sailor's hat. He wore a clean, white long-sleeved sweat shirt and blue trousers.

"Was it a good summer?' he asked Janusz in Polish.

"One of the best we have ever had," answered Janusz. "We completed our task and also caught a lot of fish."

"And Walter?"

"The best vacation I have had since coming here," said Walter.

"And did Janusz tell you the story about the *Wrona*?"

"Not until two days ago," answered Walter.

"And?"

"I am glad that he did not tell me about it sooner. I don't think I would have enjoyed the summer as much if I had known," said Walter.

"And how do you feel about it now?" asked Simpson.

"It feels kind of odd, as though time has come around in a full circle and I will soon wake up and find out that it is all a dream'" replied Walter. "But there are lots of things about this whole business that I still do not understand. For example, how come you are here casually docked and waiting just as we arrive?"

"Oh, that one is easy," responded Simpson. "It is because this is the day that Janusz said he would return. At four o'clock, in fact."

Walter looked at his watch. It was four thirty.

"Let us all go down below and see if we can find something to drink," suggested Simpson. "We must celebrate your successful mission."

They consumed several bottles of English beer which Simpson had earlier placed in a large wooden ice-bucket to cool. Janusz smacked his lips and proclaimed that the English should learn something about beer-making from the Dutch. Not the Germans, he cautioned, because they themselves were trying to copy the Dutch master brewers. Simpson disagreed. It was the Danes who perfected beer-making, he declared. Therefore, it was the Danes whom the British should copy. Walter terminated the discussion by declaring that all beer tasted the same to him and that the best beer in the world was probably being brewed at that very moment by a peasant somewhere on the Polish plains.

The steward-deckhand stuck his head inside the doorway and announced that the roast duck dinner was ready. Simpson declared that an impasse in the debate had obviously been reached which could only be resolved by forgetting about the whole thing and concentrating on something different. Wine was more worthy of their attention at the moment, he said, and opened a bottle to support his decision. They drank to peace and war, to the new British king and to the president of Poland. The moon was high above the horizon when Janusz stepped off the *Barrow* and weaved his way down the deck toward the *Wrona*, in full song.

"Tomorrow I will check with HQ to see if they have anything for us to finish off here," said Simpson when they returned below deck. "But tonight we sleep off the effects of a cardinal gastronomic sin; that of mixing beer and wine. May God have mercy on our heads. Good night, old chap."

Walter found his bunk and tumbled into it.

Simpson walked down the clean wooden deck drawing hard on the cool morning air. The rising sun emerged from the ocean in a blazing red ball, proclaiming another clear day in the offing. Simpson turned around to find that the sound of footsteps behind him were Walter's. They agreed that the best antidote for morning-after tremors was a walk in the fresh air, followed by a good breakfast. They sensed that the steward-deckhand was alert to their needs when the smell of bacon and coffee greeted them as they came down the companionway.

"Before we leave I will go to the radio room and try to reach London," said Simpson when they had finished eating their breakfast. "This will give you a chance to wash up and shave, something that I am sure you missed doing last night."

"A person can wash and shave anytime," said Walter, "but there are not too many occasions for fellowship like we enjoyed last night."

"Must say that we were all in the right mood for it," agreed Simpson as he stepped out of the galley. "I will be back as soon as I can."

Walter lay back on his bunk trying to remember the first time he had been introduced to the vessel. That was three years ago, he calculated. Duke was the skipper then and had taken him and Victor to Torun where his father and mother had once lived. It was a small world, but a long way from where he started.

Simpson looked pleased when he returned from the radio room. "Well, it is not so bad, old chap. In fact, quite simple," he announced.

"We will be going back to London and preparing for a totally new training program this winter."

CHAPTER 44

The news that Germany was developing a decipher machine called *Enigma* rocked the intelligence community in Great Britain, Poland and the U.S. It was described as a system of multiple electric rotors that produced ciphers and codes of greater complexity and combination of letters and numbers than the human mind could manipulate on its own. To make it even more unsolvable, the machine's opposite number had to be perfectly set to unscramble the incoming messages. With a potential enemy using this system, the defending powers would be helpless to read the operation orders of the enemy forces. The side using the system would have a great military and strategic advantage over its opponents.

When training resumed at the spy school in London, a select group of operatives was chosen specifically for the task of trying to obtain the secrets of the *Enigma* machine, if not the machine itself. While Victor was among those chosen because of his experience the previous summer, Walter was not to be in that special contingent of agents. When Victor returned from the Silesian region, he brought back reports that the SS had a net out for Walter, whose picture was displayed on billboards in Dresden. The notices branded him as responsible for the slaying of a young Dresden girl and that he should be apprehended on sight. To be caught in the Dresden area would probably result in his immediate transfer to the Ploetzensee prison in Berlin.

This development notwithstanding, Walter was included in most of the decipher training, coding and decoding, and the operation of short wave transmitters and receivers. The intelligence coming out of Germany verified that the next military conflict in Europe would be conducted with tanks, armored cars, air planes and ships. Wireless communication would be of extreme importance and whoever had the most secure system would have an enormous military advantage.

With the increased vigilance now evident in all of Germany, the operatives would have to be almost invisible and above suspicion. To facilitate sending information out of Germany, the training also concentrated on the use of secret inks, making microfilms and the use of rice paper which could be safely chewed and swallowed if necessary. As the school director announced on opening day, "We are no longer playing spy games. This is the real thing."

Events in Europe now pointed to the almost certain and imminent outbreak of war, a fact still wishfully dismissed by the British Parliament and its counterparts in France and the United States and most European countries. Meanwhile, Adolf Hitler was developing a close friendship with Benito Mussolini of Italy, for whom he admitted a veiled admiration. Mussolini's first trip outside of his own country in 14 years was made to Germany. As the Italian leader's train approached the railway station in Munich, it was joined by the train carrying Hitler on another track. As the separate trains neared the city, a demonstration of German locomotion precision occurred in which the two trains approached in precise alignment and at exactly the same speed. Hitler succeeded in demonstrating to his visitor a symbolism which was described as 'the parallelisms of the two revolutions' then taking place in Germany and Italy. To impress Mussolini even further, he was greeted by a double line of busts of Roman emperors arranged in perfect order at the Munich railway station. This impressive display was meant to imply that Mussolini was restoring Italy to the former glory it enjoyed during Roman times.

The Nazi were meeting with popular success in other places also. On March 12, 1937, German troops crossing the border into Austria were greeted by large crowds of people showering them with flowers and waving Nazi flags. Hitler arrived later in the day to a thundering ovation in Vienna and an emotional welcome in his hometown of Linz. Austrian Chancellor Schuschnigg was soon dispatched to a concentration camp in Germany and Austria officially became part of the Third Reich. Hopes of a lasting peace were starting to fade even in the most sanguine political minds in Great Britain and France.

New recruits arrived almost weekly at the spy school in London. The first group who had arrived three or four years earlier was now considered seasoned veterans, with many interesting experiences to share. Trainees were segregated into specialty groups, with the highest priority given to the communications and sabotage units. With Victor assigned to the communications unit, he and Walter only saw each other in the apartment which they continued to share.

"So what do you think of all that is happening at the school these days?" asked Walter one evening.

"I think that the time has come to separate the men from the boys and I am not sure in which category I belong," responded Victor. "This job is no longer the vacation that it was at the beginning. It is getting downright dirty and I am not sure that it is what I expected when I joined."

"Believe me," said his grim-faced friend, "I found that out the hard way when I was being interrogated in Dresden last fall. This is serious stuff and we either have to start playing dirty ourselves or pack up and go home."

"You are assuming that we have that choice," said Victor. "I am not so sure that we do, considering what we know. But I can take another summer like the last one. Thanks to you, things were stirred up so badly in Dresden that they didn't dare send me into the city. That is why I hung around the Silesian towns along the border. And you know what? That little bit of information that the SS fellow gave you regarding the Enigma machine was correct. I guessed that he told you that because he thought you would not live long enough to tell anybody."

"Yeah. I guess he thought that I would not be able to talk much without a head. But I must say that whatever happens this summer, I am a bit nervous about showing my face anywhere in Germany again, at least until they forget about me," said Walter. "I guess I will have to forget about why I came here in the first place and just continue playing the game."

~~~

As the budding leaves and blossoms ushered in the spring, the spy school trainees were pumped up and ready to disperse around the continent. Many felt that 1938 would be the last year during which they would have an opportunity to operate in an environment of peace. This may have been the reason why HQ stepped up its activity and the assignments came earlier than usual. Victor returned to Silesia, now a province ripe for takeover by the Nazi regime. After the closing sessions, Simpson invited Walter into his office.

"So, Walter. We have our orders for your next assignment."

Walter waited submissively for the verdict.

"Because of the dangerous atmosphere currently existing for you in Germany, we would like you to remain low key until the thing blows over," explained Simpson. "So you will be doing something totally different, outside of Germany this time."

"You mean that I will be working along the border, something like Victor did last summer, or like I did with Janusz?"

"Not really. You will still be collecting information, but not from Germany this time, but from Poland," explained Simpson.

"Are you saying that I will be spying on Poland? How can that be? Are we not working together with Sliworski in this thing?" fretted Walter.

"Yes. In the broader scheme of things we are," said Simpson. "But we usually get only one side of the story from Sliworski and his colleagues, and sometimes it may be a bit embellished. We feel that we need to know more and you are the right person to get that information for us."

"Why me? What makes you think that I am the right person to do it?" asked Walter.

"Because you already have been doing something like that from time to time," explained Simpson. "On several occasions I have heard you comment on Poland's shortcomings and how, in some ways, they can learn from the Germans. You have a good eye for these things and we would like you to use this talent to gather some information while we are waiting for things to cool off for you in Germany."

"And what kind of information will I be looking for and where?" asked Walter.

"Several different types, but mainly about what the ordinary citizen in the country is thinking these days. Are they expecting a war and, if so, do they think they are ready for one? What do they think of their army, navy and air force? Are they confident that these services can protect their country in case of a German or Russian invasion? If not, what changes do they think are needed?

"The second part of your assignment will involve the military itself. You will be required to get some true numbers from lower level military personnel on exactly what the country has in the way of armaments, such as tanks, armored cars, cannon, air planes, mortars and so on. Granted,

Sliworski provides us with these figures, but we would like to hear them from other sources as well.

"And thirdly, we would like to know how the Polish people feel about the country's economy and politics. Do they feel that the country is well governed and that their economy is good, or are they dissatisfied with how things are going on in these two areas? How do they feel about the future?" Simpson waited for Walter's reaction.

"I know little, or nothing about the army and things like that," said Walter. "And there must be other people who know more about economics than I do. As you know, I only have a Grade 11 education."

"True enough," agreed Simpson. "But this is not about being a military expert or an economist. It is about listening to ordinary people and putting down on paper what they say and think. You have already shown that you can do that, and that you are good at it. With respect to things of a military nature, you will receive instruction before you leave on the different types of armaments, their sizes, uses and so on. You will learn the difference between an anti-tank gun and a cannon, for example."

"And will Sliworski know that I am sneaking around in his backyard?"

"I cannot tell you that right now. We have arranged with Sliworski to use you for a special task in another area. I will say though, that you will not mention to anyone that you know Sliworski. In fact, we will give you a Polish alias and arrange for your employment and lodgings at each of your destinations, the same as we did in Germany. You will start out slowly by spending a few weeks with Captain Janusz as your contact man. Later as you move farther out, you will work with others, such as Litvak around Torun and Lubicz. Your third and final location will be Warsaw, where you will try to get as much of the military information as you can."

"And what happens to me if Sliworski finds out that I am working on his turf without his permission?" asked Walter uneasily.

"In some ways we are doing this for him also. But do not worry about that aspect of this exercise. Just maintain your detached manner and pretend that you are just an ordinary Pole going about making a living. If he does find out about it, we have many ways of explaining it to him to his satisfaction, I am sure," confided Simpson.

~~~

His head crammed with the names and sizes of mortars, field guns, anti-tank guns, howitzers and assorted rifles and machine guns, Walter was once more on board the *Barrow* with Simpson and Laird. The trip no longer induced the excitement and wonder of his previous journeys through the Kiel Canal, the Baltic coast and the stops at Gydna and Torun. Spring had already awakened the dormant vegetation along the coast and the emerging leaves on the trees created an emerald green background to the white and pink blossoms of the wild fruit trees and bushes. The beauty of the scene belied the tension that was building up in the towns and cities on the mainland.

In Gdyna, Captain Janusz welcomed them casually, as if there had never been any doubt in his mind that they would return. He had arranged for an apartment for Walter in Gdyna, but they would use the coast and the Vistula River as the main access to their target destinations. Walter, with his new identity of Jan Smygalski, would be the deckhand on the *Wrona* when he was not engaged in collecting information for the organization. With the details of the arrangement agreed to by Simpson and Janusz aboard the *Barrow*, Walter transferred his belongings to the more sparse surroundings of the *Wrona*. His first assignment would be in the Gdyna-Westerplatte area at the mouth of the Vistula, explained Simpson before the *Barrow* left for other destinations along the coast.

It was an easy adjustment for him, as he and Janusz combed the fishing grounds and returned to the towns and cities along the coast at the end of the day to sell their catch. The routine was the same as on the previous summer, except that most of the return trips would have Gydna and Danzig as their destination, from where Walter could venture out to gather information. Gdyna was a new port built to compensate for Poland's diminishing access to the free port of Danzig, known to the poles as Gdansk. Westerplatte nearby was designed to protect the entry to the Vistula River. In it an undisclosed number of Polish soldiers kept their vigil over the traffic moving into the port and up the river.

Sailors and a smaller number of soldiers were a common sight in each of these three places and Walter's first task was to find the spots where the fishermen and the military mixed. With the help of Janusz he discovered a popular bar near the docks, called the Pritzwalk. Here the military mixed with dockworkers and fishermen in friendly camaraderie in late afternoons and evenings. Walter's guise as a deckhand played out well and he soon became a recognized regular named Jan. The barroom revelry was at times interspersed with serious introspections in which Walter also became involved, and bits of information flowed out in an unpredictable pattern. The mood of the military contingent members varied from bravado to concern for the future.   One mustached sergeant-major was especially vocal after consuming several beers.

"The soldiers on Westerplatte are the cream of the regiment and each one of them would lay down his life for the country and his mates'" he boasted. "But we cannot help but wonder what will happen to us when the hostilities start. We are at the head of Poland. Through here flows all the country's overseas trade, both imports and exports.

"So when things get hot, do you know where the shooting will start? Right here, that is where, the life-line of the country. We are ready to do our duty, but what about the politicians? They have agreed to a ridiculous arrangement with the League of Nations which allows us only one company of soldiers. But tell me, what can we do with a hundred and fifty or so soldiers and a few guns. How long can this handful of men stand up to a shipload of attackers?"

"We should not talk so freely, Stefan," admonished a young lieutenant. "One never knows who is listening."

"We are all honorable Poles here," his colleague assured him. "There are no strangers among us. Look around the table. We are all soldiers except for

Jan who is a fisherman and not interested in military things. Is that not right, Jan?"

"I know nothing about things like that," Walter assured them. "But I can see why the sergeant-major would be concerned. We go past Westerplatte often and it does seem to be quite exposed. It seems to me that a place like that would have to be heavily fortified to stand up to any attack."

"See? He agrees with me," proclaimed the sergeant-major jubilantly as the waiter brought another tray of beer and their conversation turned to another subject.

As the days turned into weeks, Walter's military friends became more fond of his company. They thought he would make a good soldier. Before the month was up, he not only learned the number of military personnel in the garrison but also that it had forty-one machine guns, four mortars, two anti-tank guns and one infantry gun. Their commander was a seasoned veteran who had the loyalty and affection of al the soldiers.

"We know that we are here all alone and maybe forgotten, isolated on a narrow neck of old Poland and hemmed in by the Germans on two sides, but we are ready," explained one of the soldiers. "We will fight to the last man if we need to. No, we do not expect Warsaw to put a whole regiment here. They would not be allowed to do so even if they wanted to do it. Our orders are to defend our positions for at least 12 hours as a diversion tactic and that is what we plan to do."

Walter forwarded the last report with a footnote. "Please send some beer money. These soldiers drink it like water." Simpson's written response came back through Janusz. "Good work Willy 22. Slow down your regular activity and concentrate on fishing for a few days while we make final arrangements in Torun. Tell your friends in Gdyna that you and Janusz are going to fish on the river for a while and that you will see them later. Stay focused. Janusz will have the beer money for you."

~~~

When the train stopped in Torun he was met by Litvak and a stocky, somber-faced man with wire-rimmed glasses and wearing a vest and suit jacket. Litvak recognized Walter immediately.

"The world has gone around a full circle in twenty-five years," he said excitedly. "This is where I first met your father, and here you are, almost a perfect image of him, as I told you the first time we met in Lubicz. This is your new employer, Leon Novosad."

They stopped in front of a shop in the busy business section of the city.

"Brother Novosad here will be your contact with Neal and I will be around if you need me," explained Litvak as they disembarked from Novosad's automobile in front of the shop. "This is his place of business. You should be able to meet a lot of people here, and from what I hear from Neal, you will have no trouble making friends. That is good, because friends share a lot of secrets and feelings and that will make your work easier. After you are settled in your apartment, Pan Novosad and I will explain some of the things that we see are happening here."

The shop which they entered stocked everything from tea, sugar, salt and flour, to work clothes, boots, nails' small hand tools and implements. Novosad explained that the customers ranged from factory workers to farmers, to teachers and office workers. Walter would spend the next few days working alongside the merchant learning the business and later he would get to serve the customers by himself. Most of the customers spoke Polish, but Walter's knowledge of German would also come in handy at times. Litvak advised him that his name would continue to be Jan Smygalski and that his home was in Gdyna. Novosad unlocked a cupboard in the cramped office at the back of the shop and brought out a plain envelope.

"These are your personal papers. They were sent here by Neal from London. It is not likely that you will be asked for them here, but you should study your identity just the same now that you are away from Gdyna. From this moment we will always refer to you as Jan Smygalski."

The two men drove Walter to an old brick house a few blocks away from the shop. They were met by a smiling, middle-aged woman, trimly dressed in a flowered frock and hair tied up with a kerchief.

"This is your new tenant, Pana Kowalska. His name is Jan Smygalski. He will be working at my shop for a few weeks," explained Novosad.

"Welcome to my humble dwelling. I hope that you will be comfortable here," said Kowalska. She took him up to his room where a clean bed, table, chair and chest of drawers were neatly arranged. A bouquet of flowers rested on the table. "Dinner will be served at six-thirty and breakfast at seven," she advised.

Life in Torun appeared to move at a leisurely pace in spite of the country's depressed economy and fragile political situation. Peasant strikes had been common in 1936 and 1937, but most of them took place in Galicia and Volkynia where the ethnic Ukrainians felt that they were being unfairly exploited. However, even they were becoming less demanding than they had been in the past. Since 1929 when Josef Stalin began his drive to collectivize Soviet agriculture, it was the rich and middle class peasants who were deported to exile and death.

Compared with this, the life of the peasant in Poland seemed more secure, if not more prosperous, and the demands for separation gradually became more muted. But as the depression grew more severe and the Polish commanders and officials became more arrogant, unrest was rearing its ugly head again as the 1930s wore on, this time among other workers as well as the peasants. This was not as evident in Torun where some industries and business were beginning to prosper. Here the most visible socio-economic problem appeared to involve the Jews.

It did not take Walter long to recognize that, being Jewish merchants, both Litvak and Novosad conducted themselves warily. They sat in the back office and discussed the situation in hushed tones. One day Novosad looked out the door and noticing that there were no customers in the shop, motioned to Walter to come in.

"Brother Litvak and I have been discussing what has been happening to our people and thought that you should know something about it also," he said.

"Yes," added Litvak. "Some ugly things are beginning to get uglier. Some of our Polish friends seem to think that we have been responsible for the depression. There has always been that ancient prejudice against Jews based on religion, but now it is becoming more political and we are getting worried."

"We knew that things were getting serious when they started to bar Jewish students from training in the legal and medical professions," added Novosad. "They said that Jews already occupy about half of these positions and that is enough. But we know that this imbalance, as they call it, occurred during a time when unofficial restrictions had been in place for many years. Maybe that is because Polish students are just not interested in these professions. But now they have made it official and will not allow more Jews than Poles into the classes. When times are tough, people like to look for someone to blame for their hardships and we are easy targets. Now that the Jewish population has grown by a million since 1919, some people seem to think that we are trying to take over the country."

"You may wonder how all this affects your work here," said Litvak to Walter. "Brother Novosad and I think that the people in Britain and America should hear about what is happening here, and coming through you to Pan Simpson, they may be more likely to believe it. But you do not need to take our word for what is happening here. I am sure that you will soon see for yourself, if you have not already done so"

It did not take long for this prediction to materialize. One morning Walter was alone in the building. A middle-aged man and a woman walked into the shop. As they were paying for their purchase, the man cast his gaze upon Walter.

"You do not look Jewish," he said.

"No. I am Polish," said Walter.

"So what are you doing working for a Jew?" asked the man.

"I needed work and Pan Novosad gave me a job," explained Walter.

"Exactly," said the woman. "They have all the money and are the only ones who can afford to hire our people, now that they own most of the businesses in Poland."

"Pan Novosad has been good to me," said Walter.

"Sure, he is good to you because you can make him some money. As for the rest of us, he skins us every time we buy something," proclaimed the angry woman.

"They should all be thrown into the Bereza Kartuska camp instead of those poor Ukrainians and communists," pronounced the man indignantly. "This country will be better off for it."

Taken aback, Walter said nothing as the couple stomped out of the shop. He wondered if anyone back home felt the same about the Jewish merchants in Ralston.

In spite of his many contacts with the local people at the shop, Walter found that one of the best places to gauge the mood of the people was in the parks, especially among the older population. Here, elderly men sat and played cards or engaged in discussions and debates. These were the people who remembered the days of the Partition, the Great War and several other military events since then. They were there to celebrate the joy of liberation after more than a hundred years of suppression. But now the depression seemed to be robbing them of their national spirit and eternal hope. Their voices were voices of disillusionment and cynicism. Their former national pride and combative reflexes were gone. Resigned to their fate, they sat around and played cards, smoked their pipes and on occasion talked politics.

"How many prime ministers have we had since the war?" one of them asked. "Eight, nine, ten? I am not sure. And what did they do for Poland? Nothing. They were too busy fighting among themselves."

"There were some good ones among all of those," injected another.

"Oh, yes? Just name me one," challenged the first one.

"Pilsudski was quite good for Poland," he answered, "when he was the president."

"I remember those days. That man had no clear idea of what he wanted to do, except show off his authority," said Number One.

"He also believed that Poland should have a stronger form of government and allow the army to develop without political interference. That was good," said Number Two.

A third participant entered the discussion. "Do you know who our best president was? Emperor Franz Joseph, that is who. While the Austrians were in charge of their slice of Poland, everything was in order and working well. We had our schools, our language and there were jobs for whoever wanted to work."

"So why did you fight against them, Dombrowski?" asked the other.

"Because I did not know any better then and I did not know what was coming after that. If I had known, I may have stayed at home."

"I suppose you think that this fellow Hitler is good, too," said Number Two.

"Maybe that is what it takes to straighten out some of these countries. Look at Austria. They welcomed him with cheers and flowers," he answered.

"May God have mercy on this poor country," said Number Two.

~~~

There was little military presence in Torun except when a naval training vessel tied up for a day or two while the crew took shore leave. One of these arrived in port about three weeks after Walter's arrival in Torun. That evening he made his way to the bar where Novosad said that the crew congregated. The sailors sat at separate tables in one end of the room and the civilians at the other. As the evening wore on, the patrons became livelier and more festive. The sailors mixed with the civilians and the earlier barriers disappeared. Since he was not familiar with Polish songs, Walter avoided the more musically inclined groups and he and another civilian sat with a small party of garrulous sailors in one corner of the room. There the spirited conversation dwelled on the sailor's exploits at various ports of call and the imbibing capacity of the celebrants.

"What the hell. We may as well celebrate now because who knows where we will be a year or two from now," philosophized one of the sailors.

"Yes. When the Germans come after us with those ships that they are building, loaded with all kinds of fancy guns and cannon, our leaky Polish tubs will go down like pebbles in the water," said another.

"I understand that Germany is not allowed to build up a navy," said Walter, looking innocent.

"Do not let anyone tell you that. We see shiploads of parts for naval vessels and submarines coming into German ports almost every day from Finland, Spain and other places. They are not fooling anyone except the Polish government," said the sailor.

"And, of course, our glorious allies, Great Britain and France," corrected the other. "Yes, they will have one mighty navy in a year or two. It will make our four destroyers and five submarines look like a set of toys."

"You have forgotten that we also have one huge mine layer," boasted the first sailor sarcastically

"What do you expect when Pilsudski convinced everyone that Russia is the enemy we need to worry about. 'Keep your eyes on the east,' he warned, 'because Russia, not Germany, is our historic enemy.' So what good is a navy when our enemy is on dry land?" intoned another.

"Do not worry," an older sailor advised his younger crew mates. "We will have our ships when the time comes. And even if we do not, we can still kick the asses of any Germans who enter our ports and waterways. We are Poles and we do not run away from anyone. That is why Poland is still here."

"Well spoken, comrade," chimed in the others as they raised their glasses to the future. As the sailors began to leave the bar in twos and threes, Walter also wound his way back to his apartment to record his observation.

Business at Novosad's shop declined daily as fewer and fewer customers walked through the door. In the countryside, the emergence of cooperatives enabled the peasants and rural population to by-pass the Jewish shops in the city. Townspeople, now enjoying a slowly improving economy, chose more sophisticated shops over the usually drab general stores. This increased the economic pressure on Jewish merchants and generated friction between them and the Poles as the business rivalries intensified. The competition spread to other areas of activity, including education. In the university, Jewish students were obliged to sit at the back of the classroom and their entrance into schools of higher learning was restricted. At the elementary level, the subsidies provided to Polish schools were not available to Jewish institutions. As Zionism caught the imagination of younger Jews, they organized their own form of education, sports and self-help groups. Splits between the two societies which had lived together in relative harmony for generations began to appear.

One day in mid-summer Novosad invited Walter into his office. His somber face was taut and his brow furrowed. "I do not think that it is a good idea for you to stay here any longer," he said. "People can see that there is not enough business to occupy the both of us, and if you stay, they may begin to get suspicious. So I am going to ask Neal to move you to your next job."

"That will be fine," said Walter. "I have seen and heard about as much as I can expect around here. It is time for me to move along."

CHAPTER 45

The orders from HQ came down quickly. Simpson would not be accompanying Walter on this trip, they said, but all the arrangements would be ready in a few days. He would retain his current identity of Jan Smygalski and a job was waiting for him at the other end. Several days later Litvak arrived at the shop in a melancholy mood.

"I had wanted to take you to Lubicz again, but it is not wise to do that in these times," he said. "The people in the village are difficult to trust anymore. In the old days when your parents and grandparents were here, you knew who your friends were, but no more. Maybe when times get better, you can come back and see once again where your family once lived. But I think I can still do something for you. Your father once told me that he and your mother became friends on the banks of the Vistula. It might be nice for you to go and see this place before you leave. It is not far from the end of the trolley line. Here, I will draw a map for you."

Litvak brought a pencil and piece of paper and drew a rough map of the area, showing the end of the trolley line and the Vistula River.

"If you go on a week day, there will not be many people around and you will be able to enjoy the memory of your parents in peace," he suggested.

"Neal wants you to take the train to Warsaw next Thursday," said Novosad, handing Walter a plain envelope. "Your ticket and the name and address of your employer are there. You will be working for Zenon Wasyk, who operates a beer hall in Warsaw. He will meet you at the station and give you further instructions. You can use the next two days to get ready and you may even want to take Brother Litvak's suggestion and go down to the Vistula."

"Yes. I think I will do that," said Walter. "I have heard some of that story, but it would be interesting to see where it all happened."

Picking up the lunch which Mrs. Kowalska had packed for him, Walter boarded the trolley car. He stayed on it to the end of he line then followed Litvak's map to the bank of the river. Litvak was right. There was no one there except a young couple who frolicked among the trees. Walter wondered if that is what his parents did when they first met there. He sat under a tree and leaned against its trunk. He watched the river flow lazily to the north just as it had done more than thirty years earlier and for eons before that. He closed his eyes and imagined what his parents may have looked like in those days, then dozed off. He was awakened by voices and when he opened his eyes the young couple was standing a short distance away.

"We came up to see if you are fine," said the young man.

"Yes, I am fine. I guess I dozed off for a while. This place is so quiet and peaceful," said Walter. "Do you come here often?"

"Oh yes. Magda and I met here a year ago and we try to come back as often as we can. Today we decided that we would get married and you are the first one to hear about it," said the excited young man.

"That is wonderful," said Walter. "I hope that you will be happy and prosperous."

"If only there will be peace in the land," said the young man. They thanked him and walked toward the trolley stop, hand in hand.

Mrs. Kowalska was quiet as she served the evening meal. "So you are leaving us so soon," she said.

"Yes," responded Walter. "Business has not been good and Pan Novosad cannot afford to keep me any longer, so I have to go to Warsaw to look for work."

The landlady wiped her hands on her apron and paused as if to contemplate the wisdom of revealing her thoughts.

"Is it not shameful what our people are doing to the Jews?" she asked. "Poland used to be the one place where they could lead a peaceful life among us. We did not bother them and they did not bother us. We all tried to get along with each other the best we could. In other eastern European countries they were harassed and made to suffer, but Poland tolerated them and tried to live peacefully together. I do not know what is happening to our people these days."

"Maybe hard time bring out the worst in people," said Walter.

"Hard time and the thirst for power, too," she added. "Everyone tries to think that they are better than the other person. Look at what is happening in the Rhineland. I have a sister who is married to a man in Saar. In her letters she tells me what is going on there now, especially to the children, since the Germans took over. They have to listen to Hitler's speeches at school as part of their learning, and when the boys are ten years old they have to join the Hitler Youth program. Parents are not allowed to give their children what the Germans call foreign names. They fly the swastika flag at the school and even in front of the Catholic cathedral. They are even changing the street names and are pulling down statues and burning books. But one of the worst things for the children is that they are teaching them prejudice and intolerance. Would you believe that in their art classes they have to draw pictures of a Jew, and not very complimentary ones at that, but only demeaning ones. The more uncomplimentary the drawing, the better mark they get. God help us all if they should come here also."

"Maybe Germany has taken what she believes belonged to her and now we can all go about living our lives without worrying," said Walter. She did not appear convinced.

"I would like to believe you," said Kowalska, "but our leaders here seem to be asleep at the table while the soup is getting cold. They think that the Russians will come to our aid when the Germans come. When has this ever happened?"

~~~

As the train sped through the Polish countryside, Walter made notes of his conversation with Kowalska. He felt secure in the knowledge that he would not be crossing any borders on this trip and that no one would ask him for his identification papers. The danger and excitement seemed to have gone out of his work since his experience in Dresden. He wondered what Warsaw would be like and whether his work there would be more interesting.

"Warsaw next," announced the conductor as he swayed from side through the coach. The passengers shuffled around, got their belongings together and looked out of the train windows. A buzz of activity and muffled voices filled the air as the grinding sound of braking wheels announced the train's approach to the station. The train stopped and the passengers spilled out onto the platform and down into the ancient railway station. At the bottom of the stairs a middle-aged man, wearing a felt hat, gray jacket and white shirt and tie held a sign with JAN S. printed on it in wax pencil.

"I am Jan Smygalski," said Walter as he approached the man.

"And I am Zenon Wasyk," said the man. "Welcome to Warsaw. We will drop your belongings off at your apartment and then I will take you to where you will be working. I know Neal and I know who you are, so you do not need to be careful around me. But to everyone else you will be Jan Smygalski from Gdyna, working for me at the beer hall."

The outside of Wasyk's beer hall displayed a plain wooden sign with stylized lettering declaring that Beer and Food was served there. There was no other name on the front of the building. Its plain exterior belied its more aesthetic interior with its cloth covered wooden tables, comfortable chairs and subdued lighting.

"We get a lot of business people, politicians, government officials and military officers here," explained Wasyk. "They like it here because it is not too common or too high brow. They can relax here. After you learn the business of serving these customers you will get to know them better and they will get to trust you. There are a lot of interesting conversations carried on here."

The art of filling beer glasses with just the desired amount of foam and of transporting trays of glasses from the bar to the tables was quickly mastered by the new waiter at Zenon Wasyk's beer emporium. Taking the customers' orders and executing the financial transactions also became routine. Walter heeded Wasyk's advice and only became involved in brief conversations when the patrons engaged him. As Jan Smygalski from Gydna, he soon earned the respect and trust of the customers, most of whom were regular clientele. They usually arrived singly or in pairs and chose to sit with others whom they appeared to know. Each small group spoke freely and usually picked up their discussions from where they left off on the previous visit.

Walter noted a pattern in the patrons' interactions. Businessmen tended to sit with politicians, military persons with government officials and professors and students with their own kind or by themselves. Over-indulgence was rare, as was unruly behavior. Discussions were serious and restrained, but open to debate. "This group recognizes the gathering international storm and the threat that it could soon bring to their country," explained Wasyk. "They feel like prisoners of an ineffective government and ego-driven traditionalist generals." Walter noted that while some spoke longingly about the Pilsudski era, other felt that his influence had left the country's military in a sorry state of non-preparedness.

The size of the armed forces was kept at a high level under Pilsudski's "loving eccentric" stewardship, but the country could live to regret his failure to modernize its army. Proud of Poland's historical dependence on its cavalry units, the old general continued to believe that horses could be depended upon to provide the required military mobility. He had resisted moves to change to a motorized cavalry, even while intelligence coming out of Germany indicated that armored cars and tanks were totally replacing horses in that country. Upon his death in May 1935, the Polish military found itself without any anti-aircraft guns or organized armored units, and its air force was practically non-existent. Efforts to change this inadequacy were met with strong opposition from the old generals who still wielded power and whose cavalry units had distinguished themselves in the Great War.

A six-year plan to build up the Polish armament industry was adopted in July 1936. "What is needed is a radical rationalization," agreed the military table at Wasyk's beer hall. "Here it is 1938 and we are still pretending that it is 1918. Someone has to recognize that our military equipment is still in short supply and of poor quality. What would happen if someone should decide to attack us now? We would not last a week. "On paper we have thirty infantry divisions, eleven cavalry brigades and ten armored battalions, but we know that these are just figures and figures cannot fight a war," declared one of the officers. "The bravery for which Polish soldiers are renowned and the love of one's country can only go so far," they agreed. On the pretence of figuring out the tab for the latest round of beer, Walter noted the figures that he had just heard.

Each passing day it seemed that the discussions about the country's defense strategy became more intense. "Can we continue to think that we are the counterbalance between Germany and Russia?" asked the academic table. "Pilsudski believed strongly that Russia is our historic and mortal enemy. He refused to consider any anti-German pact with the Soviet Union because this could result in Soviet military divisions moving west into the Polish territory which the Russians had always claimed belonged to them. So what guarantee do we have that they would later move out again, he asked? His protege Josef Beck also felt that the irreconcilable antagonism between Nazism and Bolshevism favored Poland because any German expansion would take a south-easterly direction through Austria and Czechoslovakia. The capitulation of Austria favors this thesis. Are we worried too much about Germany when we might have a friend in Moscow? Is that not why we signed the Non-Aggression Pact with the Soviets in 1932?"

Their answer came two weeks later when Josef Stalin invited the Polish communist leaders to Moscow, then arrested and murdered most of them. When he had dissolved the Polish Communist Party, he explained cynically that he was forced to do this because it was polluted with nationalism.

A subdued group of patrons occupied the tables over the next few days. "All is not lost," declared the economist at the academic table. "Kwiatowski's expansionist policies have already resulted in the index of industrial output going up by forty-two points, while the indexed output of goods produced increased even faster by about fifty points. At least we will have the money with which to improve our military."

"How can you say that our economy is good when we have one of the highest rates of unemployment in Europe?" asked one of the students.

"And that in itself is not all bad," explained the professor. "You see, it provides the country with a dependable pool of manpower for the military."

"But most of these unemployed are poor illiterate peasants in the rural areas," argued the student.

"My point exactly," retorted the professor. "Eastern Europe has always used its peasantry as incubators for the army, especially for the infantry and cavalry. These young men have traditionally been looked upon as an expendable commodity – cannon fodder – and most useful for the advance units."

"Is that why there has been so little attempt made to improve the economic position of our peasants?" asked the student.

"That is a good observation," responded the professor.

"No wonder that this continent is so cursed," concluded the student.

~~~

Walter yearned for action. While he was comfortable in his situation in Warsaw, he sometimes felt that he was still being punished for having failed his assignment in Dresden. In his reports to Simpson, he sometimes admitted that he was out of his element when listening to the academics and military officers. "For example," he noted in his last report, "what does the index of industrial output mean? And how about 'the indexed output of goods produced'?"

The response from Simpson seemed to reveal the amusement with which he must have interpreted Walter's confusion. After explaining the meaning of the indices, his advice assumed a more serious tone. "Hang in there, Willy. Do not underestimate the value of what you are doing." Walter submissively returned to his waiter's job at the beer hall.

As the political tensions in Europe intensified, the military tables at the beer hall became more vocal. This nervousness seemed to peak in early October when Sudetenland was ceded to Germany without a shot being fired and after the leaders of Britain and France signed an agreement with Hitler allowing him to annex the region. Shortly after, Poland invaded the Ciezyn district of Czechoslovakia with its large Polish population. As the tables at Wasyk's beer emporium rejoiced, Hitler confronted Poland with his first demand for the return of Gdansk to Nazi Germany and for territorial rights to the Polish Corridor. Much to Hitler's consternation, Poland's President Sigley-Rydz rejected the idea. The simmering Central European political caldron was beginning to boil.

The debates returned to Poland's readiness, should it be invaded. "We have forty or so French R-35 tanks," confided one of the army officers. "But how effective would they be? A soldier walking at a fast pace can pass one of these tanks moving at top speed. All that he has to do is throw a grenade or place a mine in front of it and, BOOM! No more R-35."

"Let us not surrender and lose the war before it even starts," cautioned another officer. "You know that we have more than those R-35s. For example, there are about a hundred R-17s and around 135 Polish 7TP light tanks, and 38 Vickers light tanks, not to mention the more than 500 TKs, TKSs and TFKs, and about a hundred armored cars. We are not totally unprepared."

"The question is not so much about how many we have, but how many the enemy has," said the first officer. "And beside that, the R-17s are all obsolete."

Walter struggled to hold back sharing his knowledge of the inventory of shiny, new equipment stored in the German bunker. Did Sliworski know about these and if so, did he share that information with the Polish politicians and generals? The work which he and the other agents were doing began to have some relevance to the situation in this country, but he wondered if anyone was listening. Was this why HQ and Simpson were so intent on knowing exactly what was happening in Poland? He decided that in the short time that he had left before departing from Warsaw, he would try to gather as much military intelligence as he could.

This did not prove to be a difficult task. The patrons of the beer hall, apparently secure in the knowledge that their discussions were private, made no effort to conceal what they knew about the country's military strength. Perhaps, this was is why Wasyk was so insistent that Walter first gained the trust of the patrons after he arrived at the beer hall. After all, who would suspect that a young waiter from Gydna would be interested in their discussions, or even know anything about the topics being discussed?

The debate about the adequacy of the armored motorized brigades heated up and revealed that, in spite of the traditionalists who still held power, the army had managed to acquire about a hundred Wz model armored cars which were made in Poland. They also took pride in the ten armored trains which the army hoped to have ready for action by the following year. The discussions revealed that the army's fire power consisted of a motorized unit of twenty-one heavy 220 mm mortars, more than a thousand French model 1897 75 mm guns and more than 400 Russian model 1902 guns. They also had nearly 900 pieces of 100 mm Skoda howitzers, which were being produced in Poland and more than 250 105 mm French guns and 43 larger 120 mm guns. The pride of the infantry and cavalry were the more than a thousand Bofors 40 mm guns which were excellent anti-tank weapons produced at home, under license.

"This all sounds very good," explained a senior officer, "but we only have about 150 or so 75 mm guns, so our anti-aircraft fire power is very low."

"But do not forget that we still have our 800 P-11c fighters which can intercept enemy aircraft before they get to their targets, so the shortage of anti-craft fire power may not be as serious as it seems."

"That sounds very impressive when you talk in numbers. But remember that all those fighters are obsolete and in the process of being replaced," countered his fellow officer.

"They could still have a nuisance value as interceptors while our 100 or so P-7s come at the enemy. We should soon have many more of these as new ones are delivered. Some of them can support our P-37 bombers, and if the worst should happen, we can always put machine guns on our Czapla and R-13 reconnaissance planes. I think we have about eighty of them. You must also remember that our P-37 Los bomber is a first class aircraft which took first prize at this year's international air show," explained a captain.

The backs of fake checks were soon crowded with numbers as Walter made frequent forays between tables and the bar. With this stream of information flowing to HQ, Walter felt that his work in Warsaw would soon be over and he would be called back to London. In any event, it was near the end of October and the training at the spy school will probably soon resume. As he pondered these scenarios he walked past a shop on a main avenue and was shocked to see a newly painted sign stuck on its window. It read "Don't Buy From Jews". At another shop a block farther down the street he saw another sign reading, "A Poland Free From Jews Is A Free Poland." He had seen things like this in Germany, but in Poland?

That evening he walked into the university district to see if this anti-semitic fever was visible there. He was met by groups of students walking arm in arm singing patriotic songs, but no signs. Maybe what he saw earlier was just an isolated case, the work of a disgruntled individual. He wished that he had someone with whom to discuss this situation, but without Victor or Janusz there, he kept his thoughts to himself. Perhaps he could engage the usually introspective Wasyk in a discussion over the next few days to see if he knew about these things. This all became unnecessary when several days later Wasyk advised Walter that Neal would meet him in Torun in three days.

CHAPTER 46

Radical changes were taking place at the spy school when training resumed in November. This year the trainees were divided into two groups, a larger section of new recruits and a smaller contingent of experienced operatives. Walter was part of the latter group. Victor, who had gone back to the United States for his father's funeral did not return. Others seemed to be missing also, but no one asked what happened to them and no one offered this information. In Victor's absence, Walter was assigned a smaller flat on the upper level of Mrs. Jenkin's boarding house.

The winter months dragged slowly and Walter immersed himself in his training, especially in the art of sabotage. He was fascinated by the possibilities for disrupting vital rail movements and sinking ships with a strategically placed small explosive, and by the confusion that a severed telephone or telegraph wire could cause. The enormous power and portability of small plastic bombs and how a whole army's fuel supply could be blown up in a few seconds fascinated him. This was the kind of action for which he yearned.

Over the winter Stanley's letters had announced that times were slowly improving at home. The dry years appeared to be over and farm prices were better. Maybe it was time that Walter should come home and settle down, he suggested. Major Bradley often inquired about him and, when told that there were no letters for months at a time, he said he understood. With Victor back in the U.S. and with the movement of the operatives restricted, Walter often wondered if he should not follow in Victor's footsteps and leave.

"The situation on the continent is becoming critical for us," said Simpson when Walter broached the subject. "We need every person that we can get. We have spent a lot of time and money training you. It takes time and money to train new operatives and because the governments still do not yet appreciate the value of the work that we are doing, our resources are very limited. You are a good operative, Walter, and that is why I did not send you to Germany during the past few months. I did not want to take a chance on losing you like we did several of the others. It would help me personally if you could persevere another summer. I will try to make your work more interesting and exciting."

Buoyed by Simpson's vote of confidence in him, Walter settled in to make the best of a lonely and dreary winter. He spent more time at the gym and at the indoor shooting range. On occasion he and Simpson would take an evening out to visit the pubs in central London or to see a movie.

"They look at me strangely as soon as I open my mouth," complained Walter as they sat in a crowded bar.

"That is OK. They think that you are an American graduate student and I am your professor," laughed Simpson.

"Why not?" said Walter. "I have been everything else."

On the continent Poland was buoyed by the decision of Great Britain and France to proclaim the guarantee of Polish independence and the inviolability of Poland's borders.   This rejoicing was doused in April when Germany terminated its non-aggression treaty with Poland and again demanded the annexation of Gdansk, plus German controlled highways and railroads through Poland and East Prussia.   Poland again promptly rejected these demands.

Spring came early in 1939. With it came increasing pressures from the Soviet Union on Poland to guarantee passage of troops through the country. Poland continued to reject the request claiming it to be a threat to her sovereignty, but internally confessing the distrust of her neighbor whom the Poles knew would be difficult to dislodge once a Soviet presence was established in eastern Poland.   The stakes in the international poker game were rising and the players' hands were carefully shielded.

The training at the spy school was winding down and the assignments were handed out.   Walter continued to frequent the rifle range and gymnasium.   One day in the middle of May, Simpson invited him into his office.

"We have been asked to do a special project and I think that you are the guy to do it," he explained to Walter.

"I do hope that it involves some action," said Walter. "But right about now, I am willing to do anything."

"You will be glad to know that it is a relatively simple exercise, yet it could involve a small degree of danger. Our informants tell us that a small Finnish freighter will be docking at Elbing, a small port on the Vistula River, in several days. HQ would like us to take a peek at her cargo. She is on her way to a German port and we are very interested in knowing what she is carrying."

"Sounds like a piece of cake." said Walter confidently. "A small ship from a small country, docking at a small out-of-the-way port. It will take one day, maybe two to complete. What then?"

"The we return to London for reassignment."

"So what's the story?" asked Walter. "What do they think is on this ship?"

"No one is sure what the cargo is. It comes in wooden crates which are whisked to some small shipyards in Germany. The origin of the shipment is Finland. Your task will be to find out what is in those crates and this is the way we will do it. Because it will not do for the *Barrow* to be prowling around the area too openly, you will go down there with Janusz. He will drop you off somewhere on the coast and you will walk the rest of the way. Our local informants tell us that early evening is the best time to get into the ship. The crew goes out to eat around five-thirty, leaving a lone watch on duty for about an hour and a half. During this period you will go on board and get the information. After you leave the ship you will make your way along the coast to the point where Janusz dropped you off earlier and, because it will now be dark, I will be there to pick you up in a small row boat and take you to the *Barrow* which will be waiting for us."

Simpson spread a map out on the desk and pointed to a coastal area enclosed by a curved finger of land stretching out toward Konigsberg.

"It's about five miles from the Elbing wharf to where the *Barrow* will be waiting, right here." Simpson placed an X on the map. "So we will have to get our timing just right. I will be waiting for you at the appointed time at this spot – about four miles from Elbing. We will get across Frisches Hoff to a narrow point on the peninsula, then walk across to the other side where the *Barrow* will be waiting for us about a quarter of a mile out in the water. The whole operation should take no more than four hours, so we should be on our way back to London by midnight. Study the map carefully and memorize all the landmarks and features."

~~~

The old fisherman shaded his squinting eyes as he steered the ancient vessel northeast, skirting the narrow protuberance of land which dissected the bay. His rough hands grasped the helm tightly as the *Wrona* tossed gently across the pulsating waves. Walter stood beside him observing the coastline through his binoculars.

"That is a very unusual piece of geography," he said.

"They say that God put that land there many years ago to protect the Tuetonic Knights from the Swedes," explained Janusz with a twinkle in his eyes.

"The Prussians must have made up that story," suggested Walter.

Janusz remained quiet for the rest of the trip. He steered an erratic course in order to avoid the attention of the East Prussian vessels and to stay clear of the larger ships in deep water. A cool breeze blew stiffly from the north and clumps of dark clouds raced across the sky.

"Rain tonight," predicted Janusz, looking at the sun struggling out from behind a cloud.

"After midnight it can rain it wants to," said Walter. "I will be back aboard the *Barrow*, nice and dry."

The dark green mass on their right faded into the bright sun and they knew that they had reached the tip of the slender peninsula. Janusz turned the wheel sharply and the *Wrona* shuddered as it turned slowly to the right. Inside the lagoon the water was smoother and the vessel picked up speed.

"We are less than a half hour from our destination," said Janusz. "Perhaps you should go down and have something to eat. Stas will have some nice fresh bread and some cheese and sausage for you in the galley. He will have something for you to take with you also. I will stay here and watch out for snoops."

Muffled sounds of the thumping engine filled the dusky cramped chamber below the deck. Stas, the deckhand, moved about quietly, tidying up the small table and placing food on separate pieces of brown wrapping paper. He observed Walter with sad eyes as he set the food in front of him, and then he left the galley without asking any questions.

After eating a large slice of brown bread and some sausages and cheese, Walter wrapped a smaller portion in paper and placed it in his backpack along with his maps and binoculars. He sat down and glanced around the small room, imagining the scene which must have occurred there twenty-seven years earlier. He ran his fingers around the edge of the old wooden table and wondered if his parents had touched that very spot on that fateful day. Janusz had described the scene so well. It was a happy and emotional day, full of hope for a better future for all those who were leaving. But it was not to be that way. For the two young people who would be his parents, this was nothing more than a prelude to further tragedy, one which they would not survive. He closed his eyes and pictured his father, young and robust, but serious in demeanor, and his mother with a slight smile on her face. He saw Sliworski, tall and straight and much younger than now, congratulating them all on their success and thanking Litvak for all that he had done for the family. Now he was here alone. The world was no better than it had been then, and he was gathering information for a cause about which no one seemed to care.

He opened his eyes and got up slowly. He walked to the panel and slid it open. A wooden box of explosives was still there. With a flat iron bar, he pried the cover open and chose two charges with timers, then replaced the cover. He placed them on the table and wrapped brown paper around them and slipped them inside his backpack. The chugging of the engine slowed down. Stas entered the galley and said that they were entering the small bay where he would disembark. Walter placed the bag over his shoulder and climbed up the narrow companionway. Stas was lowering the small boat over the side. Janusz waved to Walter to come to the bridge. He grasped Walter's hand and hugged him.

"Good luck, my son," he said, with a look of concern in his face. "Please be careful. It has been a blessing to be with you these past few days and last summer. I hope that we will meet again. Now you must go. We cannot stay in this place too long without causing suspicion."

Walter walked quickly to the edge of the deck and let himself down into the row boat. Stas rowed silently toward the beach and pulled the boat onto the sand. Walter jumped out and waved to Janusz, then disappeared into a thick stand of shrubs and trees.

The sound of the *Wrona's* engine faded into the distance as Walter sat down and examined the map and his surroundings. He folded the map carefully and placed it inside his bag, then followed the edge of the forest to the southwest staying just inside the thick stand of vegetation. Inside the grove of trees the air was still. In the distance, faint sounds of the city and the occasional blasts of ships' horns could be heard. A little used farm trail skirted the forest and continued through the fields and pastures. The solid dense growth soon changed to clumps of shrubbery and isolated trees. The trail became a lane and then a road. The road entered a street and Walter followed it toward the city.

Just as Simpson had explained, a small freighter stood moored at a single isolated dock at the end of the wharf. To avoid attracting attention, Walter placed his backpack inside a culvert and walked toward the wharf. When he was close enough to see, he noted that the ship's name was *Turku* and she was flying the Finnish flag just as Simpson said she would. The gangplank was not yet down and on her deck several sailors milled about in preparation for unloading the vessel. It was almost five o'clock and the unloading would probably not begin until next day.

Joining some other curious onlookers, he walked by the dock slowly, observing the proximity of the other vessels, warehouses and natural cover. The area around the dock was strangely silent. There were no watchmen or police to be seen, only a few sailors and dock workers going about their business. Simpson had chosen a good one. This was going to be easy, thought Walter as he studied the scene from an old bench against an abandoned warehouse. If Simpson was right about the ship's schedule, the crew should be disembarking in about an hour and a half. Walter went back to the culvert and retrieved his backpack. He sat down behind a clump of bushes and ate the food that Stas had prepared for him.

He returned to the old warehouse with the backpack tucked under his arm. A narrow gangplank now connected the *Turku* to the dock. On deck several sailors stood around in small groups with their haversacks at their feet. A bus turned off the street and descended cautiously down the incline to the dock. It stopped near the end of the gangplank and the crew of the *Turku* filed down and stepped inside the vehicle. When the bus drove out toward the city, a taxi arrived and picked up the captain and his officers. The dock was deserted. Walter checked the time. It was six-thirty.

On the western horizon the sun sank slowly into a fiery haze. Overhead it was clear, but in the distance a bank of dark clouds moved in slowly from the sea. He knew that in two or three hours the rain which Janusz forecast would arrive.

Not wanting to attract attention, Walter walked casually down the dock and up the gangplank of the *Turku*. The deck was deserted. He found the companionway and climbed down quietly, pausing occasionally to listen. There were no sounds around him except those of the generator engine purring deep down in the bowels of the vessel. He descended cautiously into the cargo area.

Except for the engine room, the hold extended the full length of the ship and was illuminated only by a single light near the stairway and several others widely spaced along the passageway. The hold was filled with stacks of large wooden crates, with one walkway in the middle and two on each side. He peered through the wooden slats at the contents. Each crate contained a heavy steel panel welded onto a steel frame and reinforced with U-shaped bars. The panels were slightly curved and had rivet holes along the edges. It was obvious that the panels were designed to be connected together to produce something, but what?

Walter moved silently among he crates searching for documents or some other clues. Some of the panels had slightly different shapes and curvatures and each crate was numbered. He noticed that he was standing beside crate number fifty-five. In front of him the numbers were smaller, while behind him they were larger. Between the widely spaced lights it was nearly dark. He moved from crate to crate looking for diagrams or other documents.

There was none; only numbers on the crates which got smaller as he moved down the aisle.

How would Simpson know what these things were if he did not find some clues, he wondered. Perhaps, he could sketch one of them. He was near the end of the stack and there were only a few crates left. At the end of the stack he peered intently into crate number one to make a mental picture of its contents. As he moved around the crate his eyes caught sight of a heavy brown paper pouch tacked to the inside of the crate. He pulled it off and opened it. It was a drawing describing the plan for positioning and connecting the panels together to make up a part of the hull of a submarine. He folded the drawing and stuck it into his backpack, then turned toward the stairs to leave.

Walter was relieved. Now Simpson would know, as would HQ, whoever that was, and they would do something about it. But would they? Twenty-seven years ago his father had the same faith in people and look at what happened to him. Now it was within his power to do something about it.

He stopped beside crate number thirty-six. Tomorrow or the day after, or the following week, this will be part of a submarine or whatever they made with them, and what good would it be knowing that number thirty-six arrived in Elbing and was unloaded, then moved somewhere for assembling? No! Telling someone about it was not enough. Reaching into his backpack he took out one of the charges and set it inside number thirty-six and set it to go off in twenty-two minutes. His heart thumped inside his chest. He had not felt excitement like this since the time he shot his first coyote. Moving silently in the shadows, he found crate number seventy-two, the closest to the engine room, and placed the other explosive inside of it. He checked his watch and set this one for twenty minutes, then stole quietly up the ramp.

The dock area was still deserted. He followed a footpath along the water's edge. When he was sure that no one could see him, he broke into a run. The explosives would go off in a few minutes and would, no doubt, alert the patrols and police. He might be safer out on the water, he reasoned, if only he could find a boat.

The path ran into a narrow sandy beach and as he broke into the open he saw a portly old man with a large white moustache putting a long cane fishing pole into a row boat. As the old man leaned over the boat, Walter came up behind and pinned his arms behind him with one hand and put a headlock on him with his other arm. The old man's eyes bulged with fear.

"Do not kill me," he gasped. "I have no money."

"Don't worry, grandpa," said Walter in German. "All I want to do is borrow your boat."

"Take it. Take it," pleaded the old man.

"But first I will have to tie you up so you do not go running to the police. If you shout, I will choke you," warned Walter.

Walter ripped the straps off his backpack and tied the old man's hands together.

"Come with me quietly," he ordered.

He led the old man toward a clump of bushes, sat him down and tied his feet with the man's own belt. He took the man's handkerchief and tied it around his mouth, then got into the boat and rowed hard toward the channel.

The dark clouds were moving in overhead and an early dusk was falling. In about an hour Simpson would be waiting for him and in about ten minutes the charges would go off. He could still see the *Turku*, her rusty hull sitting placidly in the still water of the harbor. Soon her innards would belch loudly and burst through the deck. This he had to see.

He slowed down his rowing in order not to attract attention of the other boaters in the water, with his back facing the bow so that he could watch the *Turku*. His watch told him that in two minutes the charges would go off and the excitement would begin. He rowed steadily toward the northeast for his rendezvous with Simpson, his eyes set on the *Turku*.

A cloud of black smoke puffed out of the bow end of the freighter, followed by another near the stern. The sound of the explosions reached him a second or so later. The old vessel bobbed frantically, and then settled slowly into the water. He continued rowing. The adrenalin pulsed through his system and he felt exhilarated.

In a few minutes the sirens wailed ominously and frantic activity became evident on the docks. In the distance flashing red lights converged toward the remnants of the freighter from several directions. He paused and listened. Mixed sounds of wailing sirens, men shouting and barking dogs wafted across the water. The dark clouds were moving in and the early dusk obscured the visibility. As he steered around the bend in the channel he observed the streams of water from the firemen's hoses falling into the burning ship.

The channel was getting wider and he knew that he was at least halfway to the appointed meeting place with Simpson. A cloud of black smoke was all that was visible behind him now. The sirens had stopped. Soon the search for the saboteur would begin.

He paused again and listened. The sound of a power boat drifted across the water and he heard the sound of a hull cutting through the water. The white shape of a launch appeared in the distance behind him. As it drew nearer he saw its black uniformed occupants sitting rigidly inside the boat, with their weapons in front of them. Several others scanned the water with their binoculars. Walter picked up the old man's fishing rod and dropped the line into the water. As the launch went by, it slowed down momentarily, and then resumed its speed upon the orders of one of the officers with binoculars. When the launch disappeared around a bend, he put down the fishing rod and rowed frantically down the channel.

The forest along which he had walked earlier in the day was on his right, dark against the evening sky. He reasoned that he could move more quickly on foot, so he rowed toward the shore and abandoned the boat. The roar of the motor launch floated across the water as he picked up his bag and ran toward the forest. At the edge of the tree line he stopped again and listened.

The sound of the motor had stopped and now loud voices were coming from where he had left the row boat. The searchers appeared to be spreading out in various directions. He leaped forward and ran hard down the path. A few minutes later he burst into the open area of the small bay where Janusz had left him earlier that day. There was no sign of Simpson. He checked his watch. He was seven minutes early.

Walter returned quickly to the shelter of the trees and listened. From a distance, the soft purr of a motor drifted across the water. He leaned against a tree trunk to rest and his heart leaped with excitement. The sound of the motor became louder. As he listened he thought he heard the crunch of twigs breaking beside the path, but darkness was descending and obscured his vision. The sound of the motor had stopped. Soon Simpson would be coming ashore. Walter paused a moment and listened. There were no more sounds. He picked up his bag and started down the path to the beach. As he walked past a thick growth of shrubbery a black uniform jumped out with a rifle and bayonet pointed at Walter.

"Verfluchte Polen," shouted the SS trooper. "You did not think that you would get away from us, did you?" He pointed the rifle at Walter. "No. I am not going to shoot you. That would be too easy. I am going to cut your guts out and leave you to die like a pig."

He lunged forward and Walter felt the cold point of the bayonet in his belly. The thrust of the weapon pushed him backward and he fell on his back with the bayonet still stuck in his abdomen. The trooper swore as he placed his foot on Walter's stomach to pull out the bayonet.

"Speak, Polish pig," he shouted. He pointed the rifle at Walter's chest. "Tell me who you are or you die."   ˎ

Walter tried to speak but the words would not come. The trees began to whirl around him and from the whirling circle Simpson jumped out swinging a short wooden club. The club landed on the trooper's head with a dull thud and white and red matter splattered over Walter. He tried to stand up and fell back.

"Don't move, old chap," said Simpson. "I'll get you to the boat, but first I have to get rid of your friend here."

Simpson dragged the dead trooper behind the bushes and kicked sand over the blood on the ground. He returned and opened Walter's pants and gazed at the wound.

"Why, you lucky bastard," he said. "The goddamned bayonet went straight into your belt buckle. It's a good thing for you or we would be picking your guts up off the ground. I'll stuff my handkerchief in it to stop the bleeding till we get to the *Barrow*. Then we had better get our asses out of here or we will be joining your friend behind those bushes."

He picked up Walter and swung him over his shoulder and held him there with one arm. With his other hand he reached into his jacket and brought out a pistol. On the beach he listened carefully for sounds then placed Walter in the bow of the boat. He pushed the boat into the water and rowed silently for a distance. When they were about a quarter of a mile out on the water Simpson started the motor and set it at low throttle. As the boat bumped heavily over the waves, Walter lost consciousness. When he awoke, the rain was beating down on his face and the sky was black. As the surface of the water became smoother Walter knew that they were approaching the other side of the bay. Simpson beached the boat and felt Walter's head with his hand.

"Are you awake, old chap?" he asked.

"Yes," groaned Walter. "I just came to several minutes ago."

"Can you stand up?" asked Simpson.

"I'll try," Walter answered.

He held on to the edge of the boat and pulled himself up. His pants were soaked and blood trickled down his legs. He tried to straighten up but the pain was too excruciating and he moved slowly toward Simpson in a hunched position.

"I will try to walk by myself as long as I can," he said.

"It's more than two miles to the other side," said Simpson. "We will take our time. I don't think they can find us in this darkness. So you take it nice and easy. I will carry you when you feel faint."

They walked across the broad beach and onto the gravelly knolls, Walter pressing on his abdomen with his arm. The sky was now coal black and Simpson flicked on his battery lantern from time to time to read the terrain. A misty rain came down in sheets and the ground and rocks became slippery. Walter pushed forward for a while then fell down in a heap. Simpson slung him over his shoulder and carried him over the rough terrain in the middle of the peninsula. About an hour later they reached the wide beach on the Baltic side and Simpson eased Walter to his feet. He walked unsteadily across the hard surface to the water's edge. Simpson flashed a signal with his lantern and the *Barrow* returned the signal.

"Thank God she is still here," he said. "Now we will have to swim for it. I'll help you along, but you will need to take off your boots and pants or we will both sink."

"The plans. They are in my pants pocket," gasped Walter.

"I'll put them in my waterproof pouch," said Simpson.

He removed Walter's belt and pulled off his pants and boots, then shone the lantern on the wound.

"It is still bleeding a bit, but a dip in the salt water will disinfect it a bit if nothing else," he said grimly. "Hang in there, fellow. We will soon have you in the hospital at Gydna."

They walked out into the water and swam toward where the signal from the *Barrow* had come. Salt water seeped into the wound and Walter felt it penetrating the broken flesh like a red-hot poker. The stinging and burning sensation mixed with the painful spasms in his abdomen and a swirling black mass filled his head. The will to stand upright surrendered and his arms and legs went limp. As he sank into the water, Simpson caught him and locked his elbow around Walter's head. With powerful strokes of his one free arm, he dragged Walter's limp body toward the *Barrow*.

God, how far a quarter of a mile seems when the only strength available in the whole universe is your own, thought Simpson. Rain was beating down relentlessly into the inky water from the ebony black sky as he swam into the wall of darkness. Except for the lame body of his wounded companion beside him, there was no other point of reference in sight. He paused and shouted at the top of his voice.

"Skipper. Where the hell are you?"

The white haze of a single light appeared about five hundred yards ahead on his left. Simpson shifted his direction and swam strongly toward the light. The luminous glow gradually became a clear point of light and the ghostly outline of the boat emerged slowly in the darkness.

"Get the sling ready," shouted Simpson. "We have a casualty."

Another light went on and the skipper and the deckhand moved quickly about the dimly illuminated deck. With waves beating against the slippery hull, Simpson positioned Walter's limp body on the canvas and rope conveyance swinging over the side of the boat.

"Careful now. Lift up, slowly," he shouted.

He watched as Walter's near-naked body moved up toward the railing, his limbs hanging loosely over the canvas sides. Simpson scrambled up the rope ladder and jumped onto the deck.

"Skipper," he ordered, "full steam ahead to Gdyna. This man is badly hurt. Steward, you and I will clean his wound and make him as comfortable as we can. Let's carry him down to the galley. I'll radio Gdyna later to have an ambulance waiting at the dock."

The skipper ran to the bridge and engaged the propeller. The engine roared angrily as the boat lunged forward on its course to Gdyna. Below deck, Walter was placed on a blanket on the floor of the galley. Simpson felt his pulse and put his head against Walter's chest to listen for a heart beat. Relieved and satisfied that Walter was still alive, he commenced his first aid procedures.

"Get some heavy bandages and warm water," he ordered the steward, "and the bottle of alcohol from the first aid cabinet."

The steward stood back, pale-faced and speechless, pointing at Walter's abdomen.

"Get going. Don't just stand there. This man needs help," screamed Simpson.

"Look," said the distressed steward. "Look what's hanging on to his wound."

Simpson moved his eyes quickly from Walter's face to the wounded abdomen. He recoiled in horror.

"What the hell is that?" he asked.

"I don't know sir," answered the steward. "It looks like it might be a leech of some kind."

The creature's anterior was embedded in the raw flesh and its long pinkish-gray wormlike body squirmed against Walter's thigh. Simpson instinctively reached down to pull it off the wound.

"Don't do that, sir," cautioned the steward. "You will tear the flesh off, too. They say if you apply some strong solution to the creature's body, it will let go."

"Pass me that bottle of alcohol," said Simpson.

He opened the bottle and poured some of the liquid along the flat slimy body of the leech. It wriggled its body and slowly formed into a coil, and then went limp. Simpson pulled it off the wound carefully and threw the slimy mass against the floor.

"Throw it overboard," he ordered. Then looking at the motionless creature on the floor, he added, "No. Don't do that. The doctors in Gdyna may want to see it. Put it in a container of sea water."

He leaned over Walter's prostrate body and removed the bloody handkerchief from inside the wound. After washing the gash and applying alcohol, he applied absorbent cotton and bandaged the area with heavy gauze. The two men carried Walter to the cabin and placed him on the bunk.

~~~

His eyes opened slowly and surveyed the sterile whiteness of the room. Pangs of pain cut across his abdomen when he moved his legs or torso. His mouth was dry and his forehead burned with fever. Beside his bed were a doctor in a white lab coat and two uniformed nurses. He moved his head slowly and glanced around the room.

"Where am I?" he whispered.

"In hospital, in Gdyna. I am Doctor Brezinski. Just take it easy. Do not try to move for a while. You were badly hurt, but it could have been much worse."

"Am I going to be all right?" asked Walter.

"Yes. You will eventually," said the doctor. "We operated on you early this morning. There is no serious damage to your organs, only some bad bruises and damaged tissue, but the abdominal cavity has not been badly damaged. You lost a lot of blood and we will have to build that up again before you can go anywhere."

"Where is my friend?" asked Walter, not knowing under which name Simpson would have identified himself.

"Mister Neal will be here as soon as we contact him," answered the doctor.

Simpson entered the ward an hour later, a hint of a smile on his drawn face. "Well, you gave us quite a scare," he said.

"The last thing that I remembered was trying to swim toward the *Barrow* with that cold rain beating in my face," said Walter.

"You were out so cold that I had no trouble pulling you along with me to the boat. But it was the trip here that both impressed and frightened me. I never saw the old bark move as fast as it did last night, but I still had visions of not getting here on time. We must have made it in record time. The ambulance was waiting and so were the doctors in the operating room, so the rest of the exercise was quite routine."

"Thank you for saving my life," whispered Walter. "I am sorry that I fumbled the project so badly."

"On the contrary," said Simpson. "I examined the plans that you brought out with you and they provide us with some of the best strategic information that we have. HQ is delighted."

"How about the explosions?" asked Walter.

"That is another matter," said Simpson. "We will talk about that later."

"Do you think that I will be able to stay with the organization?" he asked.

"We will see how things go when we get back to London. Now, do as the doctor says and get yourself all patched up. I'll come back from time to time to see how you are doing."

~~~

There was no movement of air in or out of the open window. Outside there was no breeze and the heat wave continued relentlessly. Inside it was hot and stifling. Walter looked out of the open window of the flat. On the street below the sweaty pedestrians moved slowly, stopping frequently in the shade of the trees lining the sidewalks. For London the heat was unusual and it added to Walter's desire to escape the confinement of his apartment.

Since his return from the hospital in Gdyna he had been waiting patiently for word on his next assignment. He had disguised his pain and loss of appetite, hoping that Simpson would believe that he was ready for action. He wished that Victor was there so they could discuss his latest adventure and the concerns that were bothering him. The doctors had prescribed that his convalescence should be as free as possible from demanding physical or mental effort and even venturing away from the flat into town was considered as undesirable. He had walked around the block and sat in a nearby park, but after a month, severe boredom was challenging him both mentally and physically. Simpson had not come around often and they had yet to talk about the incident at Elbing.

He leaned back in the spongy stuffed chair and dozed off. His mind closed out the sounds from the street and replaced them with scenes from his past. He sat on a horse which looked like May and they were beside a lake. It was the lake in which he had learned to swim. It looked cool and inviting in the bright summer sun. He slid off the horse and walked into the water. It was now still and warm and teeming with leeches. They clung to his legs and abdomen and as he ran out of the water, they fell off. He looked across the water to the island where his cousin Jan was waving and calling for him to swim across.

He opened his eyes and saw Simpson standing before him. "When I knocked and you did not answer, I tried the door and it was open. I thought something may be wrong, so I walked in to check."

"I guess I dozed off," said Walter. "This heat is so close. It is hard to stay awake."

"Well, you will soon be able to escape it," said Simpson. "I have news for you."

"Does that mean that I have a new assignment?" asked Walter.

"No," answered Simpson gravely, "not quite that. But it may be even better than an assignment."

"You mean that I am out; finished with the organization?" asked Walter.

"I am afraid that is it, at least for the time being," answered Simpson.

"Is it because of my accident or the explosions?"

"Probably a bit of both, but mainly because of your wound," answered Simpson. "As you know, one has to be in tip-top condition for this type of work. But to be honest with you, HQ was somewhat upset about the explosions. They reminded me that we are not in a sabotage mode of operation and engaging in it might hinder our other objectives."

"Objectives, shit!" protested Walter. "What the hell is the good of objectives if no one does anything about them?

"It is not for us to question those things," explained Simpson. "Our job is to produce the information. The politicians are the ones who make the decisions on its use."

"In that case I am glad to be getting out of this racket," hissed Walter. "I am not about to have my guts cut out and my ass shot at again while the politicians decide what is in it for them."

"You were a good agent. Walter," said Simpson, "but this is a thankless job. If we get caught, no one admits to knowing us and in wartime we do not have the same immunity that the regular military has. When we are finished, our names and our achievements disappear forever, except in the records of HQ and its affiliates. After our job is done, there are no plaudits, no honor, only memories. You and I have some good memories, Walter, but only we ourselves can relish them. They are not for others to share. You are still young. You can go back to your old life and forget all about this and what is going on here and on the continent. There is a fairly nice bundle of cash in your holding account, so you should have something to work with. As for me, I will have to carry on because this is my whole life. I know nothing better."

"You have been like a father and brother to me, neither of whom I now have, and I appreciate all that you have done for me," said Walter. "I am sorry if my actions in Elbing may have embarrassed you. I am afraid that I got carried away and took things into my own hands."

"Don't worry, old chap. We all got a good chuckle out of it, but that didn't make it anymore legal, of course," said Simpson.

"So what is the plan?" asked Walter.

"You will sail for Montreal next week."

CHAPTER 47

The hot dry air settled in during late summer and pressed relentlessly down on the inhabitants of the cities, towns and villages of the counties in western Poland. They sought refuge from it in their cottages, under trees and in the water. It will soon rain, they proclaimed hopefully, but it was nearly September and the heat continued; dank, stifling and foreboding. The shriveled crops were gathered from the sun burnt fields and the dirt roads, baked hard by the hot sun, were swept clean by the dry winds.

Across the border in Germany, clouds of dust could be observed by the inhabitants of the nearby villages, and the polished helmets of the tank crews flashed in the sun. The Fourth Army amassed its troop and tank units west of Bydgoszcz and Zahn, while the massive Tenth Army settled in west of Lodz. It was now only a matter of time. That fateful minute was known only to one man, the now great and powerful Fuehrer Adolf Hitler.

In Poland, the time for hoping was past. The generals mobilized their cavalry with its thousands of poorly trained peasant lancers riding recently acquisitioned horses and supported by vintage tanks and field guns mostly salvaged from the Great War. They passed through the villages and towns, stopping for food and water. The villagers cheered and tossed flowers at them. They said that the Polish army would soon be on its way to Berlin; as soon as Poland's great allies, Great Britain and France came to the assistance of their age-old friend to fight their common enemy.

All day they poured through Lubicz, men on horseback and on foot, the sound of their boots striking the hard ground marking time with the rousing Polish patriotic songs. Streams of sweat trickled down from beneath their military headgear with the shiny Polish eagle on the front. They laughed and waved at the cheering and weeping villagers.

"To Berlin. To Berlin," they shouted.

The colonel in one of the armored cars raised his hand in a sign for the officers to stop their units for a rest, and ordered the driver to take him to a small warehouse at the edge of the village. Litvak was sitting at a rough wooden table in his small office, gazing blankly out of the window when Sliworski's car arrived. He stood up slowly and opened the door. When they had shaken hands, Colonel Sliworski asked to go inside and they sat down.

"Well, my friend. This is it. It is just a matter of time now."

"Nobody believed that this would happen again. And so soon," said Litvak sadly. "For me it is nothing. I have lived my life. But look at all those innocent young boys going to their slaughter – to fight with horses against steel. Where was everyone when Hitler was planning all this?"

"They were in their houses of parliament, in their homes and offices, on their farms and in their factories hoping desperately that man, through the centuries, may have learned his lesson. So people believed only what they wanted to believe and here we are about to repeat our old mistakes again. But we cannot condemn the past. We must do the best we can with the present. That is why I have come here to see you. You have always been a good friend of Poland and I would like to express our appreciation by arranging for your transportation to the safety of Warsaw. If you and your wife could be ready tomorrow, I will send a driver to pick you up."

Litvak fixed his dark eyes on the colonel and shook his head. "No, my friend. Poland has already rewarded me amply with a good life for me and my wife. I cannot run away from here now. This is my home. Thank you for your kindness. Your people have already repaid me a thousand-fold."

The colonel walked slowly to the door. He held out his hand. "In that case, I must leave you as time is now most precious. If we do not see each other again, Shalom, and God be with you."

"Shalom, my dear friend," replied Litvak. "May we live to meet again soon."

~~~

In the groves and thickets, the tanks and armored troop carriers lay silent, their noses and guns pointed toward the east. As dusk descended their drivers and passengers moved about confidently in their blue and gray uniforms and shiny black boots. They smoked and talked quietly about the heat of the previous day and the performance of their new vehicles and equipment. In the grass, great choruses of crickets chirped in unison, stopped and listened, then started again.

At midnight the message from Berlin cracked through the still air and the *Enigma* machines printed out the message. "The attack on Poland is to be carried out in accordance with the preparation for Case White. Date of attack: September 1, 1939: Time of attack: 4:04 a.m.: Adolf Hitler." Three hours later, the sound of engines rose out of the groves. The iron monsters moved out into the open and settled into formation to wait for the appointed minute to head across the border.

In the east, the raven sky gradually gave way to a transparent dark blue and then an eerie pink. The moment had arrived and the massed Panzer divisions of the German Wehrmacht struck quickly across the Polish frontier like moving walls of steel. Overhead a vast aerial formation of Luftwaffe bombers and fighters blackened the early morning sky, paving the way for the iron armada with its mission of death and destruction.

Across the border in the surprised Polish camps, regiments of soldiers rode out to meet the steel invaders and the shooting began. Horses and men fell before them like grain before a scythe. The whining sounds of shells and thunderous explosions filled the morning air. Neighing and screaming horses reared as their riders fell, and then they too tumbled headless on top of the dead and wounded. And the steel armored front continued unrelentingly eastward.

Ahead of the front, the towns and villages emptied quickly as men, women and children packed roads leading to the east. They rode, walked, pushed and carried, and were carried, in a great ribbon of humanity, stretching as far as the eye could see. Behind them, Stuka bombers dove downwards, and strafed the column of human flesh with machine gun fire. The victims fell and the others carried on, not knowing where they were going, but determined to seek out a haven of safety in the east.

In the great battlefields of Wielkopolska and around the cities of Czestochowa, Poznan, Chognice and Koronowo the outnumbered and under equipped Polish army fought hard, hitting the invaders in their soft underbelly behind the tanks. Regiments regrouped in the forests and on the banks of the great rivers for the expected enemy assaults. But it was all in vain. In three days the Panzers crossed the Vistula, overran Torun and swept through the villages along the Vistula and the Drewca. Farther north, the garrison of Westerplatte and Gdansk lasted the prescribed twelve hours.

The dismembered army retreated and there was no more resistance at Lubicz when the armored cars and troop carriers drove pompously into the village. Wehrmacht troops rode at rigid attention in their shiny vehicles, their uniforms clean and pressed and steel helmets gleaming in the sun. The vehicles stopped and the soldiers strutted about with mechanical precision, returning later to the small market square behind the remaining silent and frightened villagers. An armored car filled with SS officers drove into the square and a major got out and walked to the center of the crowd.

"All right now, citizens of Lubicz," he addressed them in Polish. "Yesterday a new age dawned over Europe. If you go along with the new system you will benefit from the new order, but if you do not, you will be considered enemies of the state and dealt with accordingly. Before we introduce our new system, we must ensure that there are no resisters or Jews among you. For this reason, I must now ask for your help. Do you know of any resisters among you here now?"

The villagers remained silent, gazing blankly across the square. Some moved restlessly from one foot to another.

"All right then," shouted the major, "If you do not cooperate with us, we cannot cooperate with you. Today the Wehrmacht soldiers will remove all the food and live animals in your village and no food will be brought in until you help us."

The crowd remained silent and the SS major sat down in his car to wait. In a few minutes a frightened red-faced man leaped out of the crowd.

"Herr Major," he said in German, "There are spotters in the church spire."

"Thank you, Herr Citizen," said the major. "Now the rest of you look at what this brave man has done for your village. If he had not told us that, we would have had to destroy your beautiful old church. He has also saved you from losing your farm animals and food and starving to death. Now, has anyone got any more information?"

Several villagers moved over to the informer and spat on him. The major's face turned red and he signaled for his captain to move in beside him. "I am instructing Captain Kraus to arrange for an immediate assault on the spotters in the church steeple. Now, has anyone thought of any more information that I may need?"

The hush continued as the major returned to the center of the square. The SS troopers walked through the crowd and the major stood at ease and waited, his hands clasped behind his back. The crowd remained silent for several minutes, and several children began to cry. A panic-stricken woman near the back of the crowd screamed: "Litvak is a Jew. He has been stealing our cheese, eggs, chickens and garden crops for many years and look at how poor we are. Now go and leave us alone."

"Which one of you is Litvak?" asked the major.

The villagers remained silent and the major turned to the woman. "All right sister, you have done only one half of your job. Now you will show me which one is the Jew."

"He is the one over there. The dark one with the short beard," she said pointing at Litvak.

The SS major walked to Litvak and stood before him. "You have been betrayed," he sneered. "Did you think that you could trust these Poles? You should have known better. Now will you admit that you are a Jew?"

Litvak gazed silently at the villagers across from him.

"I will ask you again. Are you a Jew?"

Litvak remained silent.

"We have ways of finding out, you know," said the major angrily. "Sergeant, bring the troopers over here."

Two SS troopers marched briskly and came to attention beside the major.

"See if he is a Jew," said the major, pointing at Litvak.

One of the troopers walked over to Litvak and pulled down his pants. The other opened up his underwear. Litvak remained erect, gazing blankly straight ahead. The second trooper put his bayonet under Litvak's penis and lifted it up.

"That is enough," order the major. "Take the Jew to the transport vehicle. You may now all go to your homes. Heil Hitler!"

The major, the captain and the troopers climbed into the armored car and drove eastward out of the village. A platoon of Wehrmacht soldiers remained in the village square. Shots were heard from inside the church.

On September 17 the Soviet Union launched an attack on Poland's eastern border, using sixty of its best divisions. Meanwhile, Germany continued its drive to the east and on September 27, Warsaw capitulated. Three days later, Poland with its cities reduced to rubble, collapsed and surrendered as its friends stood by and watched. More than 66,300 of its troops had been killed and 133,700 wounded. When it was all over, 507,000 Polish troops had been captured by the Germans and 200,000 by the Soviets. For the first time in the history of warfare, civilian casualties outnumbered those of the military as unknown thousands of men, women and children were killed and murdered as the armies advanced and occupied the nation. Only about 100,000 military personnel escaped to Romania, Hungary and the Baltic Republics.

CHAPTER 48

It was a different September in rural mid-western Canada. An air of excitement pervaded among the young men in the communities. With the war raging in Europe, it was just a matter of time before their own country would be directly involved and there would jobs and adventures for everyone. The older generation who had arrived from Europe and still had memories of other wars spoke in hushed tones as they gathered on the street corners of towns and villages. In their homes and farms they huddled around their battery radios and listened intently to the sonorous voice of Lorne Greene as he read the news and special bulletins from war departments around the world, over the CBC.

In the fields, the golden shocks of grain, which the locals called stooks, squatted like flocks of sheep in the stubble, stretching out over dips and knolls and reaching out to the edges of the aspen groves. The drought years were over and timely showers throughout the summer had helped the heads of standing wheat and barley to fill out and they waved, plump and golden brown, waiting for the harvest. All day, the clattering grain binder drawn by four horses, with Stanley at the controls, had cut the grain and formed the straw into sheaves and Walter, following behind, piled the sheaves into stooks to dry.

The orange rays of the late afternoon sun reflected off the stubble, turning the field into a sea of gold. In the next field, where Stanley was now working, he halted the four-horse team drawing the binder and waved at Walter to follow him home. Walter removed his gray raw-leather gloves, now moist with perspiration, picked up the empty water jug and headed for the farmstead.

It had been a perfect day for the harvest and Walter was tired, but happy. His muscles ached and the soles of his feet tingled as he walked across the soft soil in the field, whistling happily. In the barnyard, the animals stood around motionless, absorbing the last rays of the sinking sun. Inside the barn he helped Stanley remove the harness from the horses and filled their mangers with hay while Stanley led them to the water trough. Europe and its problems seemed so far away and Walter felt contented.

Smells of roast chicken and newly baked bread drifted through the screen door of the farm kitchen. Inside, Anna was filling bowls with steaming hot food and setting them on the table.

"What's new on the radio?" asked Stanley as he passed through the kitchen.

"The Germans broke through the Polish defenses along the Vistula, and Westerplatte has fallen. They say it will be over in a few weeks if Britain and France do not jump in," said Anna.

"Did they say anything about the area around Torun and Lubicz?" asked Stanley.

"It sounded like the Germans passed through there yesterday."

"Poor old Litvak. I wonder what will happen to him, if he is still there," pondered Stanley.

"Oh, he will survive. He always has," Anna assured him. "But I almost forget. There is going to be a special newscast from the BBC this evening at a quarter after seven. Our stations are expecting an important announcement."

"Let's catch it after supper," suggested Stanley.

At seven fifteen the mellow tones of the BBC announcer were picked up by the CBC network.

"This is the BBC in London. Ladies and gentlemen, the Right Honorable Neville Chamberlain."

After a short pause and several bursts of static, the quiet voice of an obviously shaken man came through the speaker.

"I am speaking to you from the Cabinet Room at Number 10 Downing Street. This morning the British ambassador in Berlin handed the German government a final note stating that unless we heard from them by eleven o'clock that they were prepared to withdraw their troops from Poland, a state of war would exist between us. I have to tell you now that no such undertaking has been received and that, consequently, this country is at war with Germany.

"We have a clear conscience. We have done all that any country could do to establish peace. Now may God bless you all, may He defend the right. It is the evil things that we shall be fighting against – brute force, bad faith, injustice, oppression and persecution – and against them I am certain that the right will prevail."

This grave announcement was followed by the news from the front in Poland where the Germans had made further advances and were headed to Warsaw. Thousands more soldiers and civilians had been killed, towns and villages strafed and cities bombed. Stanley turned off the radio.

"They will get theirs now," he said gleefully. "Just wait till the British get there. They'll chase the Germans out and put everything straight."

"I wouldn't count on it," said Walter.

"What do you mean?" asked Stanley incredulously. "Why would they declare war if they don't mean it?"

"You mark my word," said Walter. "In a few days Poland will be thoroughly beaten and not one British soldier will have set foot in the country."

Stanley observed him curiously. "How can you be so sure?" he asked.

"I just know," said Walter. "And in a few days you will too."

~~~

Canada declared war on Germany several days after Great Britain and the face of the country immediately began to change. Proud young men in well-pressed khaki and blue uniforms became a common sight on the street of the cities, towns and villages. The talk around the supper tables was about who was the latest one in the neighborhood to "sign up." Farmers were asked to increase their production of pork, butter, eggs and other produce for shipment to Great Britain. Jobs were opening up in the cities as industry geared up for the production of war equipment and air planes.

After harvest Walter called on Major Bradley who was now the local recruitment officer and offered himself for military service. Following his rejection for health reasons, Walter spent the winter in his grandmother's house and helped Stanley on the farm. His wound flared up from time to time during the winter and early spring and he kept to himself most of the time.

In the third week of May, Walter received news of the annual spring dance at the local school and he decided to break his self-imposed seclusion. Fiddle and guitar music, intermingled with voices and laughter, drifted out of the open windows and across the clearing in the school yard as he and his cousins approached it from the lane. Outside, groups of young men drank beer and poked fun at each other and at the occasional pair of adventurous and giggly girls who ventured out to one of the cars parked beside the building.

The rutted farm lane along which Walter walked had not changed much since he attended the annual harvest dance at to one-room schoolhouse eight years earlier. But he knew that many other things would be different, especially the faces. Although he had been back home for several months now, he had not ventured out much or met many of the people in the community.

The ones who were children when he left would surely have changed, and several of the young men of his age had since gone off to war. He approached the group of young men cautiously. They saw him approaching and the talk and laughter subsided. Their eyes peered at him through the dusk. Walter walked through the shaft of white light coming out of the open door.

"Well, I'll be gone to hell," one of them announced. "Look who's here. If it isn't old Wally Berglund. It's about time you came out of hiding. What the hell have you been up to, trying to get rich?"

"Shit no," intoned one of the others, "He is just staying home to count all that money he made while he was away."

"Hello boys," said Walter. "Nice to see you all again. Let's see. You're Jim and there's John, and Sandy and Bill."

They shook hands. "To tell you the truth," said Walter, "I've been meaning to get out a bit more, but that's not easy to do in the winter time if you don't have a car."

"Here, have a beer," said Jim. "Sandy, open one for good old Wally here."

"Should we be drinking here like this?" asked Walter innocently. "What if the cops should drive up?"

"Piss on the goddamned cops. They had better not come here if they know what is good for them. This is our territory," proclaimed Jim.

Their laughter echoed back from the thick grove of trees. John reached into the beer carton sitting on the ground and brought up four more bottles of beer.

"Say, Wally, remember those great square dances that you used to call. Nobody around here can call square dances worth a shit anymore," said Jim.

"Yeah. Why don't you finish your beer and come inside. Maybe we can get them to play a square dance and you can call it," suggested Sandy. "I'm sure you haven't forgotten how. We'll get a circle and lift up some of those sweet young girls."

"Sure," said Walter. "But I would like to just stand around for a while and get used to the place again."

"You'll probably have your chance," said Sandy. "That fiddler there; he likes to scrape away at those fucking waltzes for half the night anyway."

They finished their beer and threw their empty bottles into the grass. The empties hit the ground with a tinkling thud. When the four friends entered the schoolhouse the music had stopped and groups of men gathered on one side of the floor and women on the other. Several soldiers in khaki uniforms, with caps stuck through their shoulder lapels, were sprinkled among the crowd. The eyes of the older people followed the four when they walked into the room from the outside. Some of those who had known him came up and shook Walter's hand.

The three musicians returned to the platform at the front of the room and the dance resumed. The bravest of the men walked across the room and asked the girls to dance. Those with the prettiest faces and slimmest bodies went first and the good dancers followed. The several whom were left cast envious glances at the popular ones on the floor while engaging in intermittent small talk.

At the end of the set, Sandy jumped up on the small platform and spoke to the fiddler. He made some persuasive movements and pointed at Walter. The musician nodded affirmatively and Sandy called for silence above the din of the crowd.

"Ladies and gentlemen," he announced. "It has been a long time since we have had a real good square dance in this place. Maybe seven or eight years, as far as I am concerned. We had a good caller in those days, and then he went away. Tonight he is back and he has agreed to call a square dance for us. Walter Berglund, please come up to the front."

Scattered applause and several shouts of approval followed Walter to the front of the dance floor. The fiddler drew his bow across the strings.

"I hope I can remember how it goes," Walter apologized.

The three musicians broke into a familiar square dance tune and the couples assembled in the middle of the room.

"Join your hands and circle four," Walter called. "Swing your partner. Allemande left."

With beads of sweat shining on their foreheads, the men swung their smaller female partners, lifting them up off the floor and eliciting gleeful screams. On the sidelines, the bystanders cheered and clapped in time to the music.

"Bow to your lady and see her home," concluded Walter, and the music stopped.

"Intermission time," shouted the fiddler, and the dancers moved out toward the open door.

"That was great fun, Walter," said Jim. "Let's go outside and finish that beer."

They returned to the Model A Ford where the beer was hidden and leaned against the car with beer bottles in hand. Other revelers with similar ideas streamed out of the building and wandered out into the darkness. Two young men in uniform came out toward where Walter and his friends were standing.

"Nice square dance you called there, Berglund," said one of the soldiers.

"Thank you'" said Walter.

"I suppose you spend a lot of time practicing."

"No. In fact I have not called one for several years. Why would you think that?" asked Walter.

"Because a person who comes out here to keep out of the army must have lots of time on his hands," said the soldier.

"I really am not here to hide from the army," explained Walter. "I just happen to not be physically fit for military service, so I am trying to do my share by raising food."

"Yes. That is the excuse that all the chicken shit draft dodgers use. They want somebody else to fight the war for them while they find excuses to stay at home and look after the women."

"Now look here you guys," said Jim. "This guy is no draft dodger. So don't go making any trouble here. We are having a nice dance and everyone is enjoying themselves. We don't want any trouble."

"Who's talking to you," said the second soldier. "Or are you one of them, too?"

"One of what?" asked Jim.

"One of those god damned zombies," said the soldier.

"No one is going to call me a zombie," roared Jim as he slipped off his jacket and started moving aggressively toward the two soldiers.

"Let's not have any trouble, Jim," said Walter, grasping his arm. "There is enough of that over there in Europe. Maybe these fellows have reason to feel disappointed in us. We live here free to do as we wish while they may soon have to be on the firing line."

"We feed the bastards," hissed Jim.

"I am sorry this happened," said Walter when the tempers cooled down.

"I think I will go home now. Thanks for everything fellows. See you all again."

"Yes. That's just like a firkin' zombie," shouted the soldier. "Running away and letting someone else fight his battles."

Walter walked out of the school yard into the field and followed the rutted country lane toward the farm. The sound of the music and laughter faded into the night. He felt sad and disillusioned.

~~~

The old woman sat on a wooden box cleaning the onion bulbs in preparation for spring planting, oblivious to everything around her. The onions which she had planted earlier were already pushing up through the soil, as were the peas and radishes. The black soil was soft and moist reflecting Stanley's attention to proper land use and preparation. The vegetable beds stood staked and orderly waiting for the seeds. Her hands worked mechanically and her eyes reflected her distant thoughts. She did not see Walter approaching. The melancholy look on her face turned to a faint smile when she saw him.

"Good morning, grandma," said Walter. "I hope I did not frighten you,"

"No, my son, my mind was far away, but I did see you coming."

"Those are nice sets," he observed.

"Yes, the Lord was good to us last summer and they came well through the winter," said Mrs. Berglund. "But I can tell that you look concerned about something. Is there something wrong?"

"No. Nothing, really. I went to the spring dance last night," said Walter.

"That is good, Wladimar," she said kindly. "You should get out among people more often. You have been back here for a few months and never seem to go anywhere."

"Yes. I have been thinking about that, grandmother." He picked an onion bulb out of the basket and examined it mindlessly. "But it is not the same as it was before. Sometime I don't even know who I really am anymore and the people have changed. I can't seem to get interested in becoming a part of the community again. Maybe if I joined the army I would find myself."

"You know that you have already tried that. But you haven't talked like this before, Wladimar. Did something happen last night?"

"No. Nothing serious," he said. "But there were some soldiers there and a couple of them got after me. They wondered why I wasn't in the army. They accused me of hiding here to avoid being drafted."

"Wladimar, Wladimar," she pleaded. "You have already done much; maybe even more than any soldier can do. And even if you wanted to join, they would not take you with that wound in your belly."

"Yes. You are right in some ways, but these guys do not know that. Although they may still take me in the air force. I understand that they are not as fussy on the physical fitness thing as the army is," said Walter. He paused. "I worry a lot about what is happening in the world these days. Look at how fast Poland disappeared. Now they have Norway, Denmark, Holland, Belgium, Luxembourg, and even France. Is it Britain's turn next? How can a small, unprepared island like Britain hold off an enemy that is so powerful? And I know just how powerful they are. I know that I should not talk about this, but I need to say it. I saw it with my own eyes. But, of course, no one paid any attention to what we were saying. No one believed us, except Mr. Churchill and that good old King George. They laughed at Churchill and called him a war monger. Now they throw him the torch after it has burned down to their fingers and expect him to carry it as if he has that responsibility to the world, for being so prophetic."

"The lord is good. He will help Mr. Churchill," she assured him.

"Grandmother," said Walter, "If the lord is so good, why does he let a lunatic like Hitler take over a quarter of the world?"

"It must all come to pass as it is written," she explained. "You said yourself that Churchill was a prophet, so you must believe in prophesy. It is not Hitler who thrust himself upon man. It is man who sought and found someone to fulfill the prophesy and his name just happened to be Hitler. But if Hitler had not come, someone else would have come. Maybe not now, but surely later."

"I have never heard you talk like this before. Where did you see this in the Bible?" asked Walter. "I have not read much of the Bible, but even so, I don't remember reading anything like that."

"In many places, but nowhere as clear as in John's Book of Revelation. 'And I looked, and behold a pale horse; and his name who sat upon him was Death and Hell followed him. And power was given unto them over the fourth part of the earth, to kill with sword and with hunger, and with death, and with the beasts of the earth.' And you just said that Germany has already conquered one-quarter of the world."

"How could something like that have anything to do with what is happening now?" he asked. "It talks about swords and beasts. Nowadays, it's tanks, airplanes and anti-aircraft guns. He surely must have been writing about something that happened long ago."

"Those are all symbols," she explained. "John did not know anything about the types of machines that they would have now and he was explaining it in terms of what he knew in his time, using words that people of those days would understand. He was explaining God's power to cleanse the world. 'For the great day of his wrath is come, and who shall be able to stand?' he wrote. Is that not what is happening today?"

"If God wants this to happen then what's the use of trying to fight it?" asked Walter. "It sounds like He's fixed it so that evil will overcome good."

"The Bible also promises those who are righteous that God will lead them into living fountains of water, and he shall wipe all tears from their eyes. This too shall come to pass," she said reverently.

"Sure. Especially after most of them are dead," said Walter cynically.

"OK. So then what? Will there be peace forever like they said there would be after the first Great War?"

"I see that I have not convinced you very well. But that is not surprising. Even I did not understand these things for many years. I attended church and went through the motions, but deep in my heart I hated someone or something. I hated the Germans and the Russians, and even the Turks, for things that they did to us a long time ago, but I forgot about some of the things that we had done to others. And the church did not teach me how to love and forgive, only how to hate everyone who was different. And millions of others carried hate in their hearts for things that happened in the past and that cannot be changed. Soon these feeling burst out into violence and we ended up creating more reasons why we think we should hate each other."

"So it sounds to me like there is no hope for anything better in this world," said Walter.

"There is hope, Wladimar," she said, smiling. "John also wrote, 'The second woe is past and the third cometh quickly.' The third day still has to come before all is fulfilled, but if we do not heed its warning we shall be plunged into darkness for another ten thousand years. So the all-powerful Spirit has given us this warning, but He has also given us free choice. Man has always had the privilege of choosing his own path. This time if we chose to go along as we have been, the end is clear. We will face our Armageddon and enter into another period of darkness."

"The way you explain it, there really is no hope for us," said Walter.

"There is hope. We can still win the Battle of Armageddon, after which we are promised one thousand years of peace. I told you that we have free choice. If each one of us chooses to fight our own Armageddon in our hearts, we will not need to fight it on a battlefield. The light is free and the Spirit inside of us is shouting at us to embrace it. But the battle will need to be fought in one place or the other. We each have to fight our own darkness and when enough of us win that battle, we will experience the New Jerusalem. That has been prophesied. But I will not be here to see it, and you may not be here either."

"So what can a person like me do then?" asked Walter.

"Start with yourself, Wladimar. Forget about the past. Find the peace and love that resides within you and share it with everyone you meet. The Spirit resides within you. Listen to its gentle voice and follow its advice. If everyone in the world does this, then there will be no more conflict and suffering, the Battle of Armageddon will have been won in our hearts and we will have found the land of living waters, which the Bible promises. The battle of the third day will no longer need to take place on the battlefield of Europe, the Middle East or anywhere else, because we would have fought and won it in our own hearts."

"Your knowledge of these things surprises me, grandmother," said Walter. "Maybe you could advise me what I should do with my life right now."

"You have had your adventures. Wladimar. Now find yourself a good woman and settle down on a piece of land and work it well like your uncle has done. It is the most noble of all vocations. It will help you to find the peace that you seek."

He turned to walk toward the garden gate, then stopped and turned around. "Grandmother," he said, "you are the wisest person that I have ever known. Since you cannot be a priest, I think you should have been a queen."

"Maybe in the next life," she said, smiling.

EPILOGUE

Cold gusts of wind swept between the rows of tall, gray office buildings in the mid-western city, blowing dust and papers around the man's feet. He walked slowly, holding his arm tightly against his abdomen. Pain and desperation were reflected in his face as he examined a small slip of paper in his hand. His eyes looked at the number above the door of the building and he entered. Inside, the directory indicated that the Department of Veterans Affairs was on the third floor.

The woman behind the desk was engaged in a telephone conversation, discussing her son's birthday party.

"Yes sir, what can we do for you?" she asked after several minutes.

"I would like to talk to someone privately," he said timidly.

"Are you a veteran?" she asked.

He hesitated for a moment while the woman cast suspicious glances.

"Yes," he replied.

"Sit down there, please, and I will ask Mr. Edwards to see you."

The man in the drab office sat behind a heavy wooden desk, topped by a large piece of green blotter paper on a thick cardboard backing with imitation leather corners. Several brown file folders with columns of dates and signatures were scattered on top of the desk. He introduced himself as Don Edwards and motioned to a heavy wooden chair. He sat own behind the desk, his soft paunch leaning against its edge, straining the buttons on his shirt and exposing a part of his flab.

"Yes sir. What is the nature of your business here today?" he asked in an indifferent tone.

"My name is Walter Berglund," he answered. "Many years ago I received this wound in the service of my country and now the pain has come back and it is getting so bad that I can't stand it any longer."

"So what do you want us to do?" asked Edwards.

"I would like to go to a veterans' hospital for an examination and operation, if necessary, and after that I would like to receive a pension to live on. You see, I can no longer work because of this condition."

"Do we have a file on you, Mr. Berglund?"

"I don't think so," he replied.

"And you say that you are a veteran" he commented.

"Yes."

"In what outfit did you serve in World War II?"

"You see, sir, I did not serve in World War II," explained Walter.

"Well then, was it in the Korean War? It surely could not have been

World War I. You do not appear to be old enough to have done that."

"No. Neither of those. I served before the war."

"Before the war?" the bureaucrat looked aghast. "Where?"

"In Europe."

"With what outfit?"

"The Seven Twenty-Twos," said Walter.

The man reached for a manual and flipped through it, then laid it down with a look of desperation.

"Mr. Berglund. Is this some kind of a game you are playing?" he sneered. "If it is, then I must advise you that I have no time for games. We are all very busy people here."

"All that I can tell you, Mr. Edwards, is that I served the Seven-Twenty Twos from 1934 to 1939 in Poland, Germany and England. I am not allowed to tell you anything else."

"OK. So you served with this outfit. What was your service number?"

"We did not have service numbers in that organization. It was not like the army," explained Walter.

"Look, Mr. Berglund. You are wasting my time and you really must leave now," said Edwards. "There is nothing I can do for you if you have no number or record of service."

"Oh, I have a record of service all right," said Walter.

"Good," said the man, somewhat relieved. "Where is it?"

"Either in Leningrad or London,"

"In either Leningrad or London? And how did it get there?"

"It used to be in Warsaw, but when the Russians liberated the city, they moved all our records to Leningrad."

Edwards lifted himself out of his chair and walked partially around his desk, looking at the floor.

"Mr. Berglund, you really must leave now. There is nothing that we can do for you."

"I really need help badly, Mr. Edwards. I have nowhere else to go."

Walter pushed his hand against his abdomen and looked pleadingly at the bureaucrat.

"Just wait a minute and I will go and talk to my supervisor," said Edwards.

Edwards entered the office next door and closed the door. He leaned over and put his head close to the man at the desk.

"Just when you think you've seen and heard them all, someone comes along with something better," he whispered.

"What have you got this time?" asked the supervisor.

"I have this nut in my office who wants to go to a veterans' hospital and says he needs a pension. He says that he served all over Europe from 1934 to 1939 with an outfit called the Seven Twenty-Twos, whatever that was. And to top it all off, he claims that his records are in Leningrad."

The supervisor was amused by the story and he and Edwards broke out in a hearty laugh. In the next office, Walter hearing the hilarity got up to leave.

"Send him to the welfare office," suggested the supervisor after he had stopped laughing.

"Susan, give Mr. Berglund the address and telephone number of the welfare office," Edwards called to the receptionist.

Grimacing with pain and with disappointment in his eyes, Walter walked through the crowded street, staring vacantly into the distance. He entered an ancient downtown apartment block and picked up the newspaper from beside his door. Above a picture of a cenotaph loaded with wreaths, the headline read:

25 YEARS AFTER WORLD WAR
COUNTRY HONORS THOSE WHO SERVED

Walter felt faint. There was a bench beside the door, and he sat down and buried his face in his hands.

The author wishes to acknowledge the assistance and support of members of his family: son Mark for page layout and critique of style; son Don for designing the book jacket; son Jeff for moral support and wife Ollie for her encouragement. Their suggestions for the title were also invaluable.

ISBN 142517300-4